The Best American Mystery Stories 1999

The Best American Mystery Stories 1999

Edited and with an Introduction
by Ed McBain

Otto Penzler, *Series Editor*

Sig Edelman

HOUGHTON MIFFLIN COMPANY
BOSTON · NEW YORK

HOUGHTON MIFFLIN COMPANY
BOSTON · NEW YORK

ISSN 1094-8384
ISBN 0-395-93916-x
ISBN 0-395-93915-1 (pbk.)

Printed in the United States of America

QUM 10 9 8 7 6 5 4 3 2

Contents

Foreword

NOW THAT *Best American Mystery Stories* has its third annual volume, two elements have accrued that were impossible when we were just starting up. Like so many sets of circumstances, they are undeniably linked yet totally disparate.

The first is that the books have enjoyed delightful success (for which I, my publisher, and the contributors sincerely thank you). Weeks on local best-seller lists and on the national best-seller compilations of Ingram, America's largest book wholesaler, bring a flush of gratitude and excitement that is unlike most other human experience. If anything of a similar nature has occurred in your life, you know precisely what I mean. If it hasn't (and I truly hope it does), trust me, it brightens your life.

"Did we make the list?"

"Yes, we're number five."

"YESSS!"

Indelibly connected with such euphoric moments, and patently a vital part of them, is the review attention from magazines and newspapers. When someone calls and says, "Did you see the review in whatever-publication-that-I-haven't-ever-read-before-in-my-life-but that-is-now-my-absolute-favorite-publication-in-all-the-land?" I say, "No-but-would-you-read-it-to-me-please-but-first-tell-me-is-it-good-or-bad?" in about a tenth of a second, each syllable running into the next so utterly that I'm certain the entire sentence is incomprehensible gibberish (of which I have been accused even when enunciating impeccably, I'll concede, but that's not really the point).

While these moments do not occur often enough (three times a day, every day for, say, six months would be about right), what they lack in frequency is made up in the pure toe-curling elation of having good words in the air, filling the room as if with the "Hallelujah" Chorus.

Perhaps wrongly, I have a very proprietary feeling for this series of books. I live with each book for a full year, reading hundreds of stories and skimming hundreds of others. It's easy with the mystery anthologies and magazines, and the stories personally submitted by authors, editors, publishers, and good souls who just want to make sure something worthwhile isn't missed. Then, I'm pretty sure there's a mystery story in my hands. But many small literary magazines don't send subscriptions or tearsheets, and neither do many of the larger consumer magazines, so all the stories between their covers need to be scanned to see if they are appropriate for consideration for this book.

Full disclosure. I have a friend and colleague, Michele Slung, the world's fastest and smartest reader, whose help in the above process is invaluable. She can spend several ten- or twelve-hour days going through an entire year's worth of *The New Yorker, Harper's,* women's magazines that carry fiction, and stacks of literary magazines and come back with five photocopied stories. "Here," she'll say, "these might qualify. Forget the rest." What she can speed-read in one day would take me two weeks, which helps me to be confident that just about every mystery and crime story published in the United States or Canada is read during the course of the year. If a story doesn't make it into this book, it is unlikely that it was overlooked.

Which brings me back to that proprietary sense. Knowing how thorough the process is for being considered for a place in one of the annual volumes in this series, I regard it as a serious honor to be short-listed, as it were. To make the cut onto the list of the top fifty stories of the year is not easy, and it may be even more difficult for the guest editor to select the top twenty from that group, all of which are good. It may be much like the feeling a good teacher has when she sends her class off after graduation and later learns that some of them have had great success in life. I *care* about these stories and their creators, and I want them to have success, so it is a joyful moment when it comes to them, whether as part of a good review or as a surprisingly active seller. That both these delightful events have come to pass fills me with gratifying avuncular pride.

In the first paragraph, I suggested that two entirely disparate sets of circumstances have come to pass as this series has been published. The second is a bit, shall we say, less fulfilling than the first. It is the relentless, if sometimes well-meaning, second-guessing of readers, critics, authors, and just about anyone who may pass in the street. "Why didn't you pick X story? Why did you think this story by Y author was better than the other one? You call *that* a mystery story? Why did you have to pick such a dirty story? Such language! My favorite writer in the whole world is Z, and he wrote a dozen mysteries last year. Couldn't you pick even one of them?"

None of these is an unfair question. The process of filling a book with what those of us who work on it regard as the best mystery fiction of the year is not an exact science. Informed reading remains somewhat subjective, no matter how hard one tries to be fair.

To pick a couple of authors who deserve to be named, Lawrence Block and Joyce Carol Oates each wrote three stories that could easily have been included in this volume. It wasn't an easy choice to zero in on the ones that were selected. It wasn't a whimsical decision. It wasn't throwing darts at a board. These just appealed to me more, and clearly to the guest editor as well.

What *I* call a mystery story is not what everyone else would call a mystery story. This will be the third year in a row in which I define my terms, and I will probably continue to do so forever, because it is important. My definition of a mystery is a fictional work in which a crime, or the threat of a crime, is central to the plot or theme of the story. *The Great Gatsby*, in which a murder occurs, is not a mystery, as the entire story has unfolded before that event takes place. *Crime and Punishment* is a mystery because, without the crime, there is no book. All the stories in this book are mysteries by that definition. Detective stories, which many people use as their narrow definition of a mystery, are merely one subgenre of this literary form.

Many readers are offended by gutter language, descriptive sex, extreme violence, and other elements of some mystery stories in this and in the previous volumes of this series. It just can't be helped. As an old-fashioned guy, I am often shocked, sometimes offended, by what I see on prime-time television, not to mention what appears in movies and in some literature. This is what is. It does not enter the equation when selecting stories. If you are a little nervous about such things, you can relax. Nothing in this book is any more graphic than the media accounts of President Clinton's clandestine activities.

Being a popular writer does not necessarily make one a fine writer. Sometimes being a fine writer helps make one a popular writer. The single criterion for selecting the stories for this book, indeed for this series, is that they be well written. Detective story, crime story, suspense story. Makes no difference. By a huge best-selling author or by a first-time author in a small literary magazine. Makes no difference. Clean or dirty, long or short. Makes no difference. Good. That makes the difference.

Writers, editors, and publishers (or the people who love them) who would like to have their work considered for this series, please do feel encouraged to submit stories to me. Any fictional work published in the United States or Canada by an American or Canadian author is eligible. Provide a legible copy of the manuscript, tear sheets, or the entire publication. If the works appears in one of the standard mystery magazines, save the postage, as they are all read carefully. Nothing will be returned, even if you include a self-addressed stamped envelope. No critical remarks will be offered, so please don't ask. No submissions via electronic mail will be considered. I do not own a computer (though there are several on the premises of my bookshop, I do not consider them mine) and do not know how to turn one on. My assistant is far too busy to print out stories for me. Please screen your submissions. You may, of course, submit as many as you like, but I get nervous when a dozen stories or more appear in an envelope. Gee, I wonder, do you suppose the author really believes they are *all* that good? Unpublished material is not eligible. Absolute final date for submissions is December 31. You can only imagine the warmth I feel for those who send their stories that were published in April to me during the week before Christmas. Submissions should be sent to Otto Penzler, The Mysterious Bookshop, 129 West 56th Street, New York, New York 10019.

I have been remiss in the past about failing to thank the guest editors in print. Robert B. Parker, Sue Grafton, and now Evan Hunter (Ed McBain) have taken a great deal of time from their very full lives to read a lot of stories, write thoughtful introductions, and even to help promote the books. Clearly, the series would have been diminished without their involvement. I am blessed to have them as colleagues, and even more to have them as friends.

O.P.

Introduction

THERE USED TO BE a time when a person could make a decent living writing crime stories. Back then, a hardworking individual could earn two cents a word for a short story. *Three* cents, if he was exceptionally good. It beat polishing spittoons. Besides, it was fun.

Back then, starting a crime story was like reaching into a box of chocolates and being surprised by either the soft center or the caramel or the nuts. There were plenty of nuts in crime fiction, but you never knew what kind of story would come out of the machine until it started taking shape on the page. Like a jazz piano player, a good writer of short crime fiction didn't think he knew his job unless he could improvise in all twelve keys. Ringing variations on the theme was what made it such fun. Getting paid two or three cents a word was also fun.

For me, Private Eye stories were the easiest of the lot. All you had to do was talk out of the side of your mouth and get in trouble with the cops. In the PI stories back then, the cops were always heavies. If it weren't for the cops, the PI could have solved a murder — *any* murder — in ten seconds flat. The cops were always dragging the PI into the cop shop to accuse him of having murdered somebody just because he happened to be at the scene of the crime before anybody else got there. Sheesh! I always started a PI story with a blonde wearing a tight shiny dress who, when she crossed her legs, you saw rib-topped silk stockings and garters taut against milky white flesh. Boy. Usually, she wanted to find her missing husband or somebody. Usually, the PI fell in love with her by the end of the story, but he had to be careful because you couldn't trust girls who crossed their legs to show their garters. A Private Eye was Superman wearing a fedora.

The Amateur Detective was a private eye without a license. The people who came to the Am Eye were usually friends or relatives who never dreamed of going to the *police* with a criminal problem, but who couldn't afford to pay a private detective for professional help. So, naturally, they went to an amateur. They called upon a rabbi or a priest or the lady who was president of the garden club, or somebody who owned cats, or a guy who drove a locomotive on the Delaware Lackawanna, and they explained that somebody was missing or dead, and could these busy amateurs please lend a helping hand? Naturally, the garage mechanic, or the magician, or the elevator operator dropped everything to go help his friend or his maiden aunt. The Am Eye was smarter than either the PI or the cops because solving crimes wasn't his usual line of work, you see, but boy, was he good at it! It was fun writing Am Eye stories because you didn't have to know anything about criminal investigation. You just had to know all the station stops on the Delaware Lackawanna.

Even more fun was writing an Innocent Bystander story. You didn't have to know anything at *all* to write one of those. An Innocent Bystander story could be about any man or woman who witnessed a crime he or she should not have witnessed. Usually, this was a murder, but it could also be a kidnapping or an armed robbery or even spitting on the sidewalk, which is not a high crime, but which is probably a misdemeanor. Go look it up. When you were writing an Innocent Bystander story, you didn't have to go look anything up. You just witnessed a crime and went from there. My good friend Otto Penzler, who edits this series, insists that if any book, movie, play, or poem has in it *any* sort of crime central to the plot, it is perforce a crime story. This would make *Hamlet* a crime story. *Macbeth,* too. In fact, this would make William Shakespeare the greatest crime writer of all time. But if Penzler's supposition is true, then spitting on the sidewalk would be a crime worthy of witness by an Innocent Bystander.

Okay, the Innocent Bystander witnesses a heavyset gentleman clearing his throat and spitting on the sidewalk. He mutters something like "Disgusting!" at which point a dozen men in black overcoats, all of them speaking in Middle European tongues, start chasing him, trying to murder or maim him or worse. At some point in the story, depending on how short it will be, the police could enter as well, accusing the Innocent Bystander of having been the one who'd spat on the sidewalk in the first place. It all turns out all right when a blonde wearing a shiny dress and flaunting rib-topped gartered silk stockings clears her throat and fluently explains everything in eight different foreign languages, thereby clearing up all the confusion as wedding bells chime.

It was better to be an Innocent Bystander than either a Man on the Run or a Woman in Jeopardy, even though these three types of crime fiction were kissing cousins. The similarity they shared was that the lead character in each of them was usually an innocent boob. The Innocent Bystander *is*, of course, innocent. Otherwise he would be a Guilty Bystander. But the Woman in Jeopardy is usually innocent as well. Her problem is that somebody is trying to do dire harm to her, we don't know why. Or if we *do* know why, we also know this is all a terrible mistake, because she's *innocent,* can't you see she's *innocent?* If only we could tell this to the homicidal maniac who is chasing her day and night, trying to hurt her so badly.

Well, okay, in some of the stories she wasn't all *that* innocent. In some of the stories, she once did something sinful but not too terribly awful, which she's sorry for now but which this lunatic has blown up out of all proportion and is turning into a federal case, shooting at her and trying to strangle her and everything. It was best, however, to make her a truly innocent little thing who didn't know why this deranged person was trying so hard to kill her. It was also good to give her any color hair but blond. There *were* no innocent blondes in crime fiction.

A Man on the Run was innocent, too, but the police (*those* guys again) didn't think so. In fact, they thought he'd done something very bad, and so they were chasing him. What they wanted to do was put him in the electric chair or send him away for life. And so, naturally, he was running. The thing *we* didn't know was whether or not he really *was* guilty. We certainly *hoped* he wasn't, because he seemed like a personable enough fellow, although a bit sweaty from running all the time. But maybe he *was* guilty, who knew? Maybe the cops — *those* rotten individuals — were right for a change. All we knew for sure was that this man was *running*. Very fast. So fast that we hardly had time to wonder was he guilty, was he innocent, was he in the marathon? The only important thing a writer had to remember was that before the man could *stop* running, he had to catch the guy who really *did* what the reader was hoping he *didn't* do, but which the police were sure he *did* do. At three cents a word, the longer he ran, the better off the writer was.

Cops.

When I first started writing the Cop Story, I knew only one thing about policemen: they were inhuman beasts. The problem was how to turn them into likable, sympathetic human beings. The answer was simple. Give them head colds. And first names. And keep their dialogue homey and conversational. Natural-sounding people with runny noses and first names had to be at least as human as you and I were. Keeping all this firmly in mind, writing a sympathetic Cop Story became a simple matter.

"Good morning, Mrs. Flaherty, is this here your husband's body with the ice pick sticking out of his ear here?"

"Yes, that is my dearest George."

"Excuse me, ma'am, I have to blow my nose."

"Go right ahead, Detective."

"When did you catch that cold, Harry?"

"I've had it for a week now, Dave."

"Lots of it going around."

"My husband George here had a bad cold, too, was why he stuck the ice pick in his own ear."

"What have you been taking for it, Harry?"

"The wife made me some chicken soup, Dave."

"Yeah, chicken soup's always good for a cold."

"Oh dear, just look at all that blood."

"Sure is a sight, ma'am."

"Didn't know a person could bleed that much from the ear, did you?"

"No, ma'am, I surely did not."

"Mind your foot, ma'am. You're stepping in it."

"Oh dear."

"Hot milk and butter's supposed to be good, too."

"Medical Examiner should be here any minute, Harry. Maybe he can give you something for it."

"I miss him so much."

Once you humanized cops, everyone could understand exactly how good of heart and decent they were, and the rest was easy.

The hardest story to write was what was called Biter Bit. As the name suggests, this is a story in which the perpetrator unwittingly becomes the victim. For example, I make an elaborate plan to shoot you, but when I open the door to your bedroom, you're standing there with a pistol in your hand, and *you* shoot *me*. Biter Bit. I once had a wonderful idea for a Biter Bit story. This writer keeps submitting stories to the same editor who hates his work and who keeps rejecting them with a little slip saying "Needs work." So the writer writes a story titled "Needs Work," and he puts it in a manila envelope rigged with a letter bomb, which he mails to the despised editor, hoping to read in the next day's newspaper that the man has been blow to smithereens. Instead, there's a letter from the editor in the writer's mailbox, and when he opens the envelope, it explodes.

I know.

It needs work.

I promise you that the stories in this collection do not need work. You will shortly discover that today's crime story has come a long way from the prototypes of long ago. Show me an advertising man picking up a smoking gun beside the body of a gorgeous blonde exposing gartered silk stockings, and I will show you a man writing copy for the Model-T Ford. Show me a man kneeling on the fire escape outside the window of an unaware girl doing her nails, and I will show you a barber shop quartet singing "If I Could Shimmy Like My Sister Kate."

But show me invention . . .

Show me wit . . .

Show me discovery . . .

Show me freshness . . .

And I will show you . . .

These.

Enjoy.

ED McBAIN

The Best American
Mystery Stories 1999

LAWRENCE BLOCK

Keller's Last Refuge

FROM *Playboy*

KELLER, REACHING for a red carnation, paused to finger one of the green ones. Kelly green it was, and vivid. Maybe it was an autumnal phenomenon, he thought. The leaves turned red and gold, the flowers turned green.

"It's dyed," said the florist, reading his mind. "They started dyeing them for St. Patrick's Day, and that's when I sell the most of them, but they caught on in a small way year-round. Would you like to wear one?"

Would he? Keller found himself weighing the move, then reminded himself it wasn't an option. "No," he said. "It has to be red."

"I quite agree," the little man said, selecting one of the blood-red blooms. "I'm a traditionalist myself. Green flowers. Why, how could the bees tell the blooms from the foliage?"

Keller said it was a good question.

"And here's another. Shall we lay it *across* the buttonhole and pin it to the lapel, or shall we insert it *into* the buttonhole?"

It was a poser, all right. Keller asked the man for his recommendation.

"It's controversial," the florist said. "But I look at it this way. Why *have* a buttonhole if you're not going to *use* it?"

Keller, suit pressed and shoes shined and a red carnation in his lapel, boarded the Metroliner at Penn Station. He'd picked up a copy of *GQ* at a newsstand in the station, and he made it last all the way to Washington. Now and then his eyes strayed from the page to his boutonniere.

It would have been nice to know where the magazine stood on

the buttonhole issue, but they had nothing to say on the subject. According to the florist, who admittedly had a small stake in the matter, Keller had nothing to worry about.

"Not every man can wear a flower," the man had told him. "On one it will look frivolous, on another foppish. But with you —"

"It looks okay?"

"More than okay," the man said. "You wear it with a certain flair. Or dare I say panache?"

Panache, Keller thought.

Panache had not been the object. Keller was just following directions. Wear a particular flower, board a particular train, stand in front of the B. Dalton bookstore in Union Station with a particular magazine until the client — a particular man himself, from the sound of it — took the opportunity to make contact.

It struck Keller as a pretty Mickey Mouse way to do things, and in the old days the old man would have shot it down. But the old man wasn't himself these days, and something like this, with props and recognition signals, was the least of it.

"Wear the flower," Dot had told him in the kitchen of the big old house in White Plains. "Wear the flower, carry the magazine —"

"Tote the barge, lift the bale . . ."

"— and do the job, Keller. At least he's not turning everything down. What's wrong with a flower, anyway? Don't tell me you've got Thoreau on the brain."

"Thoreau?"

"He said to beware of enterprises that require new clothes. He never said a thing about carnations."

At ten past noon Keller was at his post, wearing the flower, brandishing the magazine. He stood there like a tin soldier for half an hour, then left his post to find a men's room. He returned feeling like a deserter, but took a minute to scan the area, looking for someone who was looking for him. He didn't find anybody, so he planted himself where he'd been standing earlier and just went on standing there.

At a quarter after one he went to a fast-food counter for a hamburger. At ten minutes of two he found a phone and called White Plains. Dot answered, and before he could get out a full sentence she told him to come home.

"Job's been canceled," she said. "The guy phoned up and called it off. But you must have been halfway to D.C. by then."

"I've been standing around since noon," Keller said. "I hate just standing around."

"Everybody does, Keller. At least you'll make a couple of dollars. It should have been half in advance —"

"*Should* have been?"

"He wanted to meet you first and find out if you thought the job was doable. *Then* he'd pay the first half, with the balance due and payable upon execution."

Execution was the word for it. He said, "But he aborted before he met me. Doesn't he like panache?"

"Panache?"

"The flower. Maybe he didn't like the way I was wearing it."

"Keller," she said, "he never even saw you. He called here around ten-thirty. You were still on the train. Anyway, how many ways are there to wear a flower?"

"Don't get me started," he said. "If he didn't pay anything in advance —"

"He paid. But not half."

"What did he pay?"

"It's not a fortune. He sent us a thousand dollars. Your end of that's nothing to retire on, but all you had to do besides stand around was sit around, and there are people in this world who work harder and get less for it."

"And I'll bet it makes them happy," he said, "to hear how much better off they are than the poor bastards starving in Somalia."

"Poor Keller. What are you going to do now?"

"Get on a train and come home."

"Keller," she said, "you're in our nation's capital. Go to the Smithsonian. Take a citizen's tour of the White House. Slow down and smell the flowers."

He rang off and caught the next train.

He went home and hung up his suit, but not before discarding the touch of panache from his lapel. He'd already gotten rid of the magazine.

That was on a Wednesday. Monday morning he was in a booth at one of his usual breakfast places, a Greek coffee shop on Second Avenue. He was reading the *Times* and eating a plate of salami and eggs when a fellow said, "Mind if I join you?" He didn't wait for an answer, either, but slid unbidden into the seat across from Keller.

Keller eyed him. The guy was around forty, wearing a dark suit and an unassertive tie. He was clean-shaven and his hair was combed. He didn't look like a nut.

"You ought to wear a boutonniere," the man said. "It adds, I don't know, a certain something."

"Panache," Keller suggested.

"You know," the man said, "that's just what I was going for. It was on the tip of my tongue. Panache."

Keller didn't say anything.

"You're probably wondering what this is all about."

Keller shook his head.

"You're not?"

"I figure more will be revealed."

That drew a smile. "A cool customer," the fellow said. "Well, I'm not surprised." His hand dipped into the front of his suit jacket, and Keller braced himself with both hands on the edge of the table, waiting to see the hand come out with a gun.

Instead it emerged clutching a flat leather wallet, which the man flipped open to disclose an ID. The photo matched the face across the table from Keller, and the accompanying card identified the face as that of one Roger Keith Bascomb, an operative of something called the National Security Resource.

Keller handed the ID back to its owner.

"Thanks," Bascomb said. "You were all set to flip the table on me, weren't you?"

"Why would I do that?"

"Never mind. You're alert, which is all to the good. And I'm not surprised. I know who you are, and I know *what* you are."

"Just a man trying to eat his breakfast," Keller said.

"And a man who's evidently not put off by all that scary stuff about cholesterol. Salami and eggs! I have to say I admire you, Keller. I bet that's real coffee, too, isn't it?"

"It's not great," Keller said, "but it's the genuine article."

"My breakfast's an oat-bran muffin," Bascomb said, "and I wash it down with decaf. But I didn't come here to put in a bid for sympathy."

Just as well, Keller thought.

"I don't want to make this overly dramatic," Bascomb said, "but it's hard to avoid. Mr. Keller, your country has need of your services."

"My country?"

"The United States of America. *That* country."

"My services?"

"The very sort of services you rode down to Washington prepared to perform. I think we both know what sort of services I'm talking about."

"I could argue the point," Keller said.

"You could."

"But I'll let it go."

"Good," Bascomb said, "and I in turn will apologize for the wild goose chase. We needed to get a line on you and find out a few things about you."

"So you picked me up in Union Station and tagged me back to New York."

"I'm afraid we did, yes."

"And learned who I was, and checked me out."

"Like a book from a library," Bascomb said. "Just what we did. You see, Keller, your uncle would prefer to cut out the cutout man."

"My uncle?"

"Sam. We don't want to run everything through What's-his-name in White Plains. This is strictly need-to-know, and he doesn't."

"So you want to be able to work directly with me."

"Right."

"And you want me to . . ."

"To do what you do best, Keller."

Keller ate some salami, ate some eggs, drank some coffee.

"I don't think so," he said.

"I beg your pardon?"

"I'm not interested," Keller said. "If I ever did what you're implying, well, I don't do it anymore."

"You've retired."

"That's right. And even if I hadn't, I wouldn't go behind the old man's back, not to work for someone who sent me off on a fool's errand with a flower in my lapel."

"You wore that flower," Bascomb said, "with the air of a man who never left home without one. I've got to tell you, Keller, you were born to wear a red carnation."

"That's good to know," Keller said, "but it doesn't change anything."

"Well, the same thing goes for your reluctance."

"How's that?"

"It's good to know how you feel," Bascomb said. "Good to get it all out in the open. But it doesn't change anything. We need you, and you're in."

He smiled, waiting for Keller to voice an objection. Keller let him wait.

"Think it through," Bascomb suggested. "Think U.S. Attorney's Office. Think Internal Revenue Service. Think of all the resources of a powerful — some say too powerful — federal government, lined up against one essentially defenseless citizen."

Keller, in spite of himself, found himself thinking it through.

"And now forget all that," said Bascomb, waving it all away like smoke. "And think of the opportunity you have to serve your nation. I don't know if you've ever thought of yourself as a patriot, Keller, but if you look deep within yourself, I suspect you'll find wellsprings of patriotism you never knew existed. You're an American, Keller, and here you are with a chance to do something for America and save your own ass in the process."

Keller's words surprised him. "My father was a soldier," he said.

> Breathes there the man, with soul so dead,
> Who never to himself hath said,
> This is my own, my native land!

Keller closed the book and set it aside. The lines of Sir Walter Scott were quoted in a short story Keller had read in high school. The titular man without a country was Philip Nolan, doomed to wander the world all his life because he'd passed up his own chance to be a patriot.

Keller didn't have the story on hand, but he'd found the poetry in *Bartlett's Familiar Quotations,* and now he looked up "patriotism" in the index. The best thing he found was Dr. Samuel Johnson's word on the subject. "Patriotism," Dr. Johnson declared, "is the last refuge of a scoundrel."

The sentence had a nice ring to it, but he wasn't sure he knew what Johnson was getting at. Wasn't a scoundrel the furthest thing from a patriot? In simplest terms, a patriot would seem unequivocally to be one of the good guys. At the very least he devoted himself to serving his nation and his fellow citizens, and often enough he wound up giving the last full measure of devotion, sacrificing himself, dying so that others might live in freedom.

Nathan Hale, say, regretting that he had but one life to give for his country. John Paul Jones, declaring that he had not yet begun to fight. David Farragut, damning the torpedoes, urging full speed ahead.

Good guys, Keller thought.

Whereas a scoundrel had to be a bad guy by definition. So how could he be a patriot, or take refuge in patriotism?

Keller thought about it, and decided the scoundrel might take refuge in the *appearance* of patriotism, wrapping selfish acts in the cloak of selflessness. A sort of false patriotism, to cloak his base motives.

But a true scoundrel couldn't be a genuine patriot. Or could he?

If you looked at it objectively, he had to admit, then he was probably a scoundrel himself. He didn't much feel like a scoundrel. He felt like your basic New York single guy, living alone, eating out or bringing home takeout, schlepping his wash to the laundromat, doing the *Times* crossword with his morning coffee. Working out at the gym, starting doomed relationships with women, going to the movies by himself. There were eight million stories in the naked city, most of them not very interesting, and his was one of them.

Except that every once in a while he got a phone call from a man in White Plains. And packed a bag and caught a plane and killed somebody.

Hard to argue the point. Man behaves like that, he's a scoundrel. Case closed.

Now he had a chance to be a patriot.

Not to seem like one, because no one would know about this, not even Dot and the old man. Bascomb had made himself very clear on the point. "Not a word to anyone, and if anything goes wrong, it's the same system as *Mission: Impossible*. We never heard of you. You're on your own, and if you try to tell anybody you're working for the government, they'll just laugh in your face. If you give them my name, they'll say they never heard of me. Because they never did."

"Because it's not your name."

"And you might have trouble finding the National Security Resource in the phone book. Or anywhere else, like the *Congressional*

Record, say. We keep a pretty low profile. You ever heard of us before? Well, neither did anybody else."

There'd be no glory in it for Keller, and plenty of risk. That was how it worked when he did the old man's bidding, but for those efforts he was well compensated. All he'd get working for NSR was an allowance for expenses, and not a very generous one at that.

So he wasn't doing it for the glory, or for the cash. Bascomb had implied that he had no choice, but you always had a choice, and he'd chosen to go along. For what?

For his country, he thought.

"It's peacetime," Bascomb had said, "and the old Soviet threat dried up and blew away, but don't let that fool you, Keller. Your country exists in a permanent state of war. She has enemies within and without her borders. And sometimes we have to do it to them before they can do it to us."

Keller, knotting his necktie, buttoning his suit jacket, didn't figure he looked much like a soldier. But he felt like one. A soldier in his own idiosyncratic uniform, off to serve his country.

Howard Ramsgate was a big man, broad-shouldered, with a ready smile on his guileless, square-jawed face. He was wearing a white shirt and a striped tie, and the pleated trousers of a gray sharkskin suit. The jacket hung on a clothes tree in the corner of the office.

He looked up at Keller's entrance. "Afternoon," he said. "Gorgeous day, isn't it? I'm Howard Ramsgate."

Keller supplied a name, not his own. Not that Ramsgate would be around to repeat it, but suppose he had a tape recorder running? He wouldn't be the first man in Washington to bug his own office.

"Good to meet you," Ramsgate said, and stood up to shake hands. He was wearing suspenders, and Keller noticed that they had cats on them, different breeds of cats.

When you pictured a traitor, he thought, you pictured a furtive little man in a soiled raincoat, skulking around a basement or lurking in a shabby café. The last thing you expected to run into was a pair of suspenders with cats on them.

"Well, now," Ramsgate was saying. "Did we have an appointment? I don't see it on my calendar."

"I just took a chance and dropped by."

"Fair enough. How'd you manage to get past Janeane?"

The secretary. Keller had timed her break, slipping in when she ducked out for a quick cigarette.

"I don't know," he said. "I didn't notice anybody out there."

"Well, you're here," Ramsgate said. "That's what counts, right?"

"Right."

"So," he said. "Let's see your mousetrap."

Keller stared at him. Once, during a brief spate of psychotherapy, he had had a particularly vivid dream about mice. He could still remember it. But what on earth did this spy, this traitor —.

"That's more or less a generic term for me," Ramsgate said. "That old saw — create a better mousetrap and the world will beat a path to your door. Emerson, wasn't it?"

Keller had no idea. "Emerson," he agreed.

"With that sort of line," Ramsgate said, "it was almost always Emerson, except when it was Benjamin Franklin. Solid American common sense, that's what you could count on from both of them."

"Right."

"As it happens," Ramsgate said, "Americans have registered more patents for mousetraps than for any other device. You wouldn't believe the variety of schemes men have come up with for snaring and slaughtering the little rodents. Of course" — he plucked his suspenders — "the best mousetrap of all's not patentable. It's got four legs and it says meow."

Keller managed a chuckle.

"I've seen my share of mousetraps," Ramsgate went on. "Like every other patent attorney. And every single day I see something new. A lot of the inventions brought to this office aren't any more patentable than a cat is. Some have already been invented by somebody else. Not all of them do what they're supposed to do, and not all of the things they're supposed to do are worth doing. But some of them work, and some of them are useful, and every now and then one of them comes along and adds to the quality of life in this wonderful country of ours."

Solid American common sense, Keller thought. This great country of ours. The man was a traitor and he had the gall to sound like a politician on the stump.

"So I get stirred up every time somebody walks in here," Ramsgate said. "What have you brought for me?"

"Well, let me just show you," Keller said, and came around the desk. He opened his briefcase and placed a yellow legal pad on the desktop.

"'Please forgive me,'" Ramsgate read aloud. "Forgive you for what?"

Keller answered him with a choke hold, maintaining it long enough to guarantee unconsciousness. Then he let go and tore the top sheet from the legal pad, crumpled it into a ball, dropped it into the wastebasket. The sheet beneath it, the new top sheet, already held a similar message: "I'm sorry. Please forgive me."

It wouldn't stand up to a detailed forensic investigation, but Keller figured it would make it easy for them to call it suicide if they wanted to.

He went to the window, opened it. He rolled Ramsgate's desk chair over to the window, took hold of the man under the arms, hauled him to his feet, then heaved him out the window.

He put the chair back, tore the second sheet off the pad, crumpled it, tossed it at the basket. That was better, he decided — no note, just a pad on the desk, and then, when they look in the basket, they can come up with two drafts of a note Ramsgate decided not to leave after all.

Nice touch. They'd pay more attention to a note if they had to hunt for it.

Janeane was back at her desk when he left, chatting on the phone. She didn't even look up.

Keller, back in New York, started each of the next five days with a copy of the *Washington Post* from a newsstand across the street from the UN building. There was nothing in it the first morning, but the next day he found a story on the obituary page about an established Washington patent attorney, an apparent suicide. Keller learned where Howard Ramsgate had gone to college and law school and read about a couple of inventions he had helped steer through the patent process. The names of his survivors were given as well — a wife, two children, a brother in Lake Forest, Illinois.

What it didn't say was that he was a spy, a traitor. Didn't say he'd had help getting out the window. Keller, perched on a stool in a coffee shop, wondered how much more they knew than they were letting on.

The next three days he didn't find another word about Ramsgate. This wasn't suspicious in and of itself — how often was there a follow-up to the suicide of a not-too-prominent attorney? — but Keller found himself trying to read between the lines of other stories, trying to find some subtle connection to Ramsgate's death. This lobbyist charged with illegal campaign contributions, that Japanese tourist caught in the crossfire of a drug-related shootout, a key vote on a close bill in Congress — any such item might some-how link up to the defenestration of Howard Ramsgate. And he, the man who'd made it happen, would never know.

On the fifth morning, as he found himself frowning over a minor scandal in the mayor's office, it occurred to Keller to wonder if he was being watched. Had anyone observed him in the days since Ramsgate's death? Had it been noted that he was starting each day not around the corner from his apartment with the *New York Times* but five blocks away with the *Washington Post?*

He thought it over and decided he was being silly. But then was he being any less silly buying the *Post* each morning? He'd tossed a pebble into a pond days ago, and now he kept returning, trying to detect a subtle ripple on the pond's smooth surface.

He got out of there and left the paper behind. Later, thinking about it, he realized what had him acting this way.

He was looking for closure, for some sense of completion. When-ever he did a job for the old man, he made a phone call, got a pat on the back, bantered a bit with Dot, and, in the ordinary course of things, collected his money. That last was the most important, of course, but the acknowledgment was important, too, along with the mutual recognition that the job was done and done satisfactorily.

With Ramsgate he got none of that. There was no report to make, nobody to banter with, no one to tell him how well he'd done. Tight-lipped men in Washington offices might be talking about him, but he didn't get to hear what they were saying. Bas-comb might be pleased with what he'd done, but he wasn't getting in touch, wasn't dispensing any pats on the back.

Well, Keller decided, that was okay.

Because, when all was said and done, wasn't that the soldier's lot? There would be no drums and bugles for him, no parades, no medals. He would get along without feedback or acknowledgment, and he would probably never know the real results of his actions, let alone the reason he'd drawn a particular assignment in the first place.

He could live with that. He could even take a special satisfaction in it. He didn't need drums or bugles, parades or medals. He had been leading the life of a scoundrel, and his country had called on him. And he had served her.

No one had given him a pat on the back. No one had called to say well done. No one would, and that was fine. The deed he had done, the service he had performed, was its own reward.

He was a soldier.

Time passed, and Keller got used to the idea that he would never hear from Bascomb again. Then one afternoon he was standing in line at the half-price-tickets booth in Times Square when someone tapped him on the shoulder. "Excuse me," a fellow said, handing him an envelope. "Think you dropped this."

Keller started to say he hadn't, then stopped when he recognized the man. Bascomb! Before he could say anything the man was gone, disappearing into the crowd.

Just a plain white envelope, the flap glued down and taped shut. Nothing written on it. From the heft of it, you'd put two stamps on it before putting it in the mail. But there were no stamps, and Bascomb had not entrusted it to the mails.

Keller put it in his pocket. When he got to the front of the line he bought a ticket to that night's performance of a fifties musical. He thought of buying two tickets and hiding one in a hollowed-out pumpkin. Then, when the curtain went up at eight o'clock, Bascomb would be in the seat beside him.

He went home and opened the envelope. There was a name, along with an address in Pompano Beach, Florida. There were two Polaroid shots, one of a man and woman, the other of the same man, alone this time, sitting down. There were nine hundred-dollar bills, used and out of sequence, and two fifties.

Keller looked at the photos. They'd evidently been taken several years apart. The fellow looked older in the photo that showed him unaccompanied, and was that a wheelchair he was sitting in? Keller thought it might be.

Poor bastard, Keller started to think, and then caught himself. The guy had no pity coming. The son of a bitch was a traitor.

The thousand in cash fell a ways short of covering Keller's expenses. He had to pay full coach fare on the flight to West Palm Beach, had to rent a car, had to stay three nights in a hotel room before he could get the job done and another night afterward, before he could catch a morning flight home. The $500 he'd received as expenses for the Howard Ramsgate incident had paid for the Metroliner and his room and a good dinner, with a couple of dollars left over. But he had to dip into his own pocket to get the job done in Pompano Beach.

Not that it really mattered. What did he care about a few dollars one way or the other?

He might have cut corners by getting in and out faster, but the operation turned out to be a tricky one. The traitor — his name was Drucker, Louis Drucker, but it was simpler for Keller to think of him as "the traitor" — lived in a beachfront condo on Briny Avenue, right in the middle of Pompano Beach. The residents, predictably enough, had a median age well into the golden years, and the traitor was by no means the only one there with wheels on his chair. There were others who got around with aluminum walkers, while the more athletic codgers strutted around with canes.

This was the first time Keller's work had taken him to such a venue, so he didn't know if security was as much of a priority at every senior citizens' residence, but this one was harder to sneak into than the Pentagon. There was an attendant posted in the lobby at all hours, and there was closed-circuit surveillance of the elevators and stairwells.

The traitor left the building twice a day, morning and evening, for a turn along the beach. He was always accompanied by a woman half his age who pushed his chair on the hard-packed sand, then read a Spanish-language magazine and smoked a cigarette or two while he took the sun.

Keller considered and rejected elaborate schemes for getting into the building. They'd work, but then what? The woman lived in the traitor's apartment, so he'd have to take her out, too. He had no compunction about this, recognizing that civilian casualties were inevitable in modern warfare, and who was to say she was an entirely unwitting pawn? No, if the only way to nullify the traitor led through her, Keller would take her out without a second thought.

But a double homicide made for a high-profile incident, and why draw unnecessary attention? With an aged and infirm quarry, it was so much simpler to make it look like natural causes.

Could he lure the woman off the premises? Could he gain access during her absence? And could he get out unobtrusively, his work completed, before she got back?

He was working it out, fumbling with a plan, when Fate dropped it all in his lap. It was midmorning, with the sun climbing the eastern sky, and he'd dutifully dogged their footsteps (well, *her* footsteps, since the traitor's feet never touched the ground) a mile or so up the beach. Now the traitor sat in his chair facing the ocean, his head back, his eyes closed, his leathery skin soaking up the rays. A few yards away the woman lay on her side on a beach towel, smoking a cigarette, reading a magazine.

She put out the cigarette, burying it in the sand. And, moments later, the magazine slipped from her fingers as she dozed off.

Keller gave her a minute. He looked left, then right. There was nobody close by, and he was willing to take his chances with those who were fifty yards or more from the scene. Even if they were looking right at him, they'd never realize what was happening right before their eyes. Especially given the ages of most of those eyes.

He came up behind the traitor, clapped a hand over his treacherous mouth, used the thumb and forefinger of his other hand to pinch the man's nostrils closed, and kept his air shut off while he counted, slowly, to a number that seemed high enough.

When he let go, the traitor's hand fell to one side. Keller propped it up and left him looking as though asleep, baking like a lizard in the warm embrace of the sun.

"Where have you been, Keller? I've been calling you for days."

"I was out of town," he said.

"Out of town?"

"Florida, actually."

"Florida? Disney World, by any chance? Do I get to shake the hand that shook the hand of Mickey Mouse?"

"I just wanted a little sun and sand," he said. "I went to the Gulf Coast. Sanibel Island."

"Did you bring me a seashell, Keller?"

"A seashell?"

"The shelling is supposed to be spectacular there," Dot said. "The island sticks out into the Gulf instead of stretching out parallel to the land, the way they're supposed to."

"'The way they're supposed to'?"

"Well, the way they usually do. So the tides bring in shells by the carload and people come from all over the world to walk the beach and pick them up. But why am I telling you all this? You're the one who just got back from the damn place. You didn't bring me a shell, did you?"

"You have to get up early in the morning for the serious shelling," Keller said, wondering if it was true. "The shellers are out there at the crack of dawn, like locusts on a field of barley."

"Barley, huh?"

"Amber waves of grain," he said. "Anyway, what do I care about shells? I just wanted a break."

"You missed some work."

"Oh," he said.

"It couldn't wait, and who knew where you were or when you'd be back? You should really call in when you leave town."

"I didn't think of it."

"Well, why would you? You never leave town. When's the last time you had a vacation?"

"I'm on vacation most of my life," he said. "Right here in New York."

"Then I guess it was about time you went away for something besides work. I suppose you had company."

"Well . . ."

"Good for you, Keller. It's just as well I couldn't reach you. But next time . . ."

"Next time I'll keep you posted," he said. "Better than that, I'll bring home a seashell."

This time he didn't try to track the story in the papers. Even if Pompano Beach had a newspaper of its own, you couldn't expect to find it at the UN newsstand. They'd have the *Miami Herald* there, but somehow he didn't figure the *Herald* ran a story every time an old fellow drifted off in the sunshine. If they did, there'd be no room left in the paper for hurricanes and carjackings.

Besides, why did he want to read about it? He had carried out his mission and the traitor was dead. That was all he had to know.

It was almost two months before Bascomb got in touch again. This time there was no face-to-face contact, however fleeting.

Instead, Keller got a phone call. The voice was presumably Bas-comb's, but he couldn't have sworn to it. The call was brief, and the voice never rose much above a low murmur.

"Stay home tomorrow," the voice said. "There'll be something delivered to you."

And in fact the FedEx guy came around the following morning, bringing a flat cardboard envelope that held a photograph, an index card with a name and address printed on it, and a sheaf of used hundreds.

There were ten of the bills, a thousand dollars again, although the address this time was in Aurora, Colorado, which involved quite a few more air miles than Pompano Beach. That rankled at first, but when he thought about it he decided there was something to be said for the low payment. If you lost money every time you did this sort of thing, it underscored your commitment to your role as a patriot. You never had to question your motives, because it was clear you weren't in it for the money.

He squared up the bills and put them in his wallet, then took a good long look at the photo of the latest traitor.

And the phone rang.

Dot said, "Keller, I'm lonesome and there's nothing on TV but Sally Jessy Raphaël. Come on out here and keep me company."

Keller took a train to White Plains and another one back to New York. He packed a bag, called an airline, and took a cab to JFK. That night his plane landed in Seattle, where he was met by a lean young man in a double-breasted brown suit. The fellow wore a hat, too, a fedora that gave him a sort of retro look.

The young man — Jason, his name was — dropped Keller at a hotel. In the morning they met in the lobby, and Jason drove him around and pointed out various points of interest, including the Kingdome and the Space Needle and the home and office of the man Keller was supposed to kill. And, barely visible in the distance, the snow-capped peak of Mount Rainier.

They ate lunch at a good downtown restaurant, and Jason put away an astonishing amount of food. Keller wondered where he put it. There wasn't a spare ounce on him.

The waitress was refilling the coffee when Jason said, "Well, I was starting to wonder if we missed him today. Just coming through the door? Gray suit, blue tie? Big red face on him? That's Cully Wilcox."

He looked just like his photo. It never hurt, though, to have somebody ID the guy in the flesh.

"He's a big man in this town," Jason said, his lips barely moving. "Harder they fall, right?"

"I beg your pardon?"

"Isn't that the expression? 'The bigger they are, the harder they fall'?"

"Oh, right," Keller said.

"I guess you don't feel like talking right now," Jason said. "I guess you got things to think about and details to work out."

"I guess so," Keller said.

"This may take a while," he told Dot. "The subject is locally prominent."

"Locally prominent, is he?"

"So they tell me. That means more security on the way in and more heat on the way out."

"Always the way when it's somebody big."

"On the other hand, the bigger they are, the harder they fall."

"Whatever that means," she said. "Well, take your time, Keller. Smell the flowers. Just don't let the grass grow under your feet."

Hell of a thing, Keller thought.

He muted the TV just in time to stop a cute young couple from advising him that Certs was two, two, two mints in one. He closed his eyes and adapted the dialogue to his own circumstances. *"Keller is a contract killer." "No, Keller is a traitor killer." "He's two, two, two killers in one."*

It was tough enough, he thought, to lead one life at a time. It was a lot trickier when they overlapped. He couldn't stall the old man, couldn't put off the trip to Seattle while he did his Uncle Sam's business in Colorado. But how long could he delay the mission? How urgent was it? He couldn't call Bascomb to ask him. So he had to assume a high degree of urgency.

Which meant he had to find a way to do two, two, two jobs in one.

Just what he needed.

It was a Saturday morning, a week and a half after he'd flown to Seattle, when Keller flew home. This time he had to change planes in Chicago, and it was late by the time he got to his apartment. He'd already called White Plains the night before to tell them the job was done. He unpacked his bag, shucked his clothes, took a hot shower, and fell into bed.

The following afternoon the phone rang.

"No names, no pack drill," said Bascomb. "I just wanted to say, Well done."

"Oh," Keller said.

"Not our usual thing," Bascomb went on, "but even a seasoned professional can use the occasional pat on the back. You've done fine work, and you ought to know it's appreciated."

"That's nice to hear," Keller admitted.

"And I'm not just speaking for myself. Your efforts are appreciated on a much higher level."

"Really?"

"On the highest level, actually."

"The highest level?"

"No names, no pack drill," Bascomb said again, "but let's just say you've earned the profound gratitude of a man who never inhaled."

He called White Plains and told Dot he was bushed. "I'll come out tomorrow around lunchtime," he said. "How's that?"

"Oh, goody," she said. "I'll make sandwiches, Keller. We'll have a picnic."

He got off the phone and couldn't think what to do with himself. On a whim he took the subway to the Bronx and spent a few hours at the zoo. He hadn't been to a zoo in years, long enough for him to have forgotten that they always made him sad.

It still worked that way, and he couldn't say why. It's not that it bothered him to see animals caged. From what he understood, they led a better life in captivity than they did in the wild. They lived longer and stayed healthier. They didn't have to spend half their time trying to get enough food and the other half trying to keep from being food for somebody else. It was tempting to look at them and conclude that they were bored, but he didn't believe it. They didn't look bored to him.

He left unaccountably sad as always and returned to Manhattan. He ate at a new Afghan restaurant and went to a movie. It was a western, but not the sort of Hollywood classic he would have preferred. Even after the movie was over, you couldn't really tell which ones were the good guys.

Next day Keller caught an early train to White Plains and spent forty minutes upstairs with the old man. When he came downstairs Dot told him there was fresh coffee made, or iced tea.

He went for the coffee. She already had a tall glass of iced tea poured for herself. They sat at the kitchen table and she asked him how it had gone in Seattle. He said it went okay.

"And how'd you like Seattle, Keller? From what I hear it's everybody's city du jour these days. Used to be San Francisco and now it's Seattle."

"It was fine," he said.

"Get the urge to move there?"

He had found himself wondering what it might be like, living in one of those converted industrial buildings around Pioneer Square, say, and shopping for groceries at Pike Market, and judging the quality of the weather by the relative visibility of Mount Rainier. But he never went anywhere without having thoughts along those lines. That didn't mean he was ready to pull up stakes and move.

"Not really," he said.

"I understand it's a great place for a cup of coffee."

"They're serious about their coffee," he allowed. "Maybe too serious. Wine snobs are bad enough, but when all it is is coffee . . ."

"How's that coffee by the way?"

"It's fine."

I bet it can't hold a candle to the stuff in Seattle," she said. "But the weather's lousy there. Rains all the time, the way I hear it."

"There's a lot of rain," he said. "But it's gentle. It doesn't bowl you over."

"It rains but it never pours?"

"Something like that."

"I guess the rain got to you, huh?"

"How's that?"

"Rain, day after day. And all that coffee snobbery. You couldn't stand it."

Huh? "It didn't bother me," he said.

"No?"

"Not really. Why?"

"Well, I was wondering," she said, looking at him over the rim of her glass. "I was wondering what the hell you were doing in Denver."

The TV was on with the sound off, tuned to one of the home-shopping channels. A woman with unconvincing red hair was modeling a dress. Keller thought it looked dowdy, but the number in the lower right corner kept advancing, indicating that viewers were calling in a steady stream to order the item.

"Of course, I could probably *guess* what you were doing in Denver," Dot was saying, "and I could probably come up with the name of the person you were doing it to. I got somebody to send me a couple of issues of the *Denver Post,* and what did I find but a story about a woman in someplace called Aurora who came to a bad end, and I swear the whole thing had your fingerprints all over it. Don't look so alarmed, Keller. Not your actual fingerprints. I was speaking figuratively."

"Figuratively," he said.

"It did look like your work," she said, "and the timing was right. I'd say it might have lacked a little of your usual subtlety, but I figure that's because you were in a big hurry to get back to Seattle."

He pointed at the television set. He said, "Do you believe how many of those dresses they've sold?"

"Tons."

"Would you buy a dress like that?"

"Not in a million years. I'd look like a sack of potatoes in something cut like that."

"I mean any dress. Over the phone, without trying it on."

"I buy from catalogs all the time, Keller. It amounts to the same thing. If it doesn't look right, you can always send it back."

"Do you ever do that? Send stuff back?"

"Sure."

"He doesn't know, does he, Dot? About Denver?"

"No."

He nodded, hesitated, then leaned forward. "Dot," he said, "can you keep a secret?"

She listened while he told her the whole thing, from Bascomb's first appearance in the coffee shop to the most recent phone call, relaying the good wishes of the man who never inhaled. When he was done he got up and poured himself more coffee. He came back and sat down and Dot said, "You know what gets me? 'Dot, can you keep a secret?' Can *I* keep a secret?"

"Well, I —"

"If I can't," she said, "then we're all in big trouble. Keller, I've been keeping *your* secrets just about as long as you've had secrets to keep. And you're asking me —"

"I wasn't exactly asking you. What do they call it when you don't really expect an answer?"

"Prayer," she said.

"Rhetorical," he said. "It was a rhetorical question. For God's sake, I know you can keep a secret."

"That's why you kept this one from me," she said, "for lo these many months."

"Well, I figured this was different."

"Because it was a state secret."

"That's right."

"Hush-hush, your eyes only, need-to-know. Matters of national security."

"Uh-huh."

"And what if I turned out to be a Commie rat?"

"Dot —"

"So how come I all of a sudden got a top-secret clearance? Or is it need-to-know? In other words, if I hadn't brought up Denver . . ."

"No," he said. "I was planning to tell you anyway."

"Sooner or later, you mean."

"Sooner. When I called yesterday and said I wanted to wait until today to come up, I was buying a little time to think it over."

"And?"

"And I decided I wanted to run the whole thing by you, and see what you think."

"What I think."

"Right."

"Well, you know what that tells me, Keller? It tells me what *you* think."

"And?"

"And I think it's about the same thing I think."

"Spell it out, okay?"

"C-O-N," she said, "J-O-B. Total B-U-L-L-S-H — Am I getting through?"

"Loud and clear."

"He must be pretty slick," she said, "to have a guy like you jumping through hoops. But I can see how it would work. First place, you want to believe it. 'Young man, your country has need of you.' Next thing you know, you're knocking off strangers for chump change."

"Expense money. It never covered the expenses, except the first time."

"The patent lawyer, caught in his own mousetrap. What do you figure he did to piss Bascomb off?"

"No idea."

"And the old fart in the wheelchair. It's a good thing you iced the son of a bitch, Keller, or our children and our children's children would grow up speaking Russian."

"Don't rub it in."

"I'm just making you pay for that rhetorical question. All said and done, do you think there's a chance in a million Bascomb's on the level?"

Keller made himself think it over, but the answer wasn't going to change. "No," he said.

"What was the tip-off? The approval from on high?"

"I guess so. You know, I got a hell of a rush."

"I can imagine."

"I mean, the man at the top. The big guy."

"Chomping doughnuts and thinking of you."

"But then you think about it afterward, and there's just no way. Even if he said something like that, would Bascomb pass it on? And then, when I started to look at the whole picture . . ."

"Tilt."

"Uh-huh."

"Well," she said, "what kind of a line do we have on Bascomb? We don't know his name or address or how to get hold of him. What does that leave us?"

"Damn little."

"Oh, I don't know. We don't need a hell of a lot, Keller. And we do know something."

"What?"

"We know three people he wanted killed," she said. "That's a start."

Keller, dressed in a suit and tie and sporting a red carnation in his buttonhole, sat in what he supposed you would call the den of a

sprawling ranch house in Glen Burnie, Maryland. He had the TV
on with the sound off, and he was beginning to think that was the
best way to watch it. The silence lent a welcome air of mystery to
everything, even the commercials.

He perked up at the sound of a car in the driveway, and as soon
as he heard a key in the lock, he triggered the remote to shut off
the TV altogether. Then he sat and waited patiently while Paul
Ernest Farrar hung his topcoat in the hall closet, carried a sack of
groceries to the kitchen, and moved through the rooms of his
house.

When he finally got to the den, Keller said, "Well, hello, Bascomb. Nice place you got here."

Keller, leading a scoundrel's life, had ended the lives of others in
a great variety of ways. As far as he knew, though, he had never
actually frightened anyone to death. For a moment, however, it
looked as though Bascomb (né Farrar) might be the first. The man
turned white as Wonder bread, took an involuntary step backward,
and clasped a hand to his chest. Keller hoped he wasn't going to
need CPR.

"Easy," he said. "Grab a seat, why don't you? Sorry to startle you,
but it seemed the best way. No names, no pack drill, right?"

"What do you think you're doing in my house?"

"The crossword puzzle, originally. Then when the light failed I
had the TV on, and it's a lot better when you don't know what
they're saying. Makes it more of an exercise for the imagination."
He leaned back in his chair. "I'd have joined you for breakfast," he
said, "but who knows if you even go out for it? Who's to say you
don't have your oat-bran muffin and decaf at the pine table in the
kitchen. So I figured I'd come here."

"You're not supposed to get in touch with me at all," Farrar said
sternly. "Under any circumstances."

"Give it up," Keller said. "It's not working."

Farrar didn't seem to hear him. "Since you're here," he said, "of
course we'll talk. And there happens to be something I need to talk
to you about, as a matter of fact. Just let me get my notes."

He slipped past Keller and was reaching into one of the desk
drawers when Keller took him by the shoulders and turned him
around. "Sit down," he said, "before you embarrass yourself. I already found the gun and took the bullets out. Wouldn't you feel
silly, pulling the trigger and all it does is go *click*?"

"I wasn't reaching for a gun."

"Maybe you wanted this, then," Keller said, dipping into his breast pocket. "A passport in the name of Roger Keith Bascomb, issued by the authority of the government of British Honduras. You know something? I looked on the map, and I couldn't *find* British Honduras."

"It's Belize now."

"But they kept the old name for the passports?" He whistled soundlessly. "I found the firm's literature in the same drawer with the passport. An outfit in the Caymans, and they offer what they call fantasy passports. To protect yourself, in case you're abducted by terrorists who don't like Americans. Would you believe it — the same folks offer other kinds of fake ID as well. Send them a check and a photo and they'll set you up as an agent of the National Security Resource. Wouldn't that be handy?"

"I don't know what you're talking about."

Keller sighed. "All right," he said. "Then I'll tell you. Your name isn't Roger Bascomb, it's Paul Farrar. You're not a government agent, you're some kind of paper pusher in the Social Security Administration."

"That's just a cover."

"You used to be married," Keller went on, "until your wife left you for another man. His name was Howard Ramsgate."

"Well," Farrar said.

"That was six years ago. So much for the heat of the moment."

"I wanted to find the right way to do it."

"You found me," Keller said, "and got me to do it for you. And it worked, and if you'd left it like that you'd have been in the clear. But instead you sent me to Florida to kill an old man in a wheelchair."

"Louis Drucker," Farrar said.

"Your uncle, your mother's brother. He didn't have any children of his own, and who do you think he left his money to?"

"What kind of a life did Uncle Lou have? Crippled, immobile, living on painkillers . . ."

"I guess we did him a favor," Keller said. "The woman in Colorado used to live two doors down the street from you. I don't know what she did to get on your list. Maybe she jilted you or insulted you, or maybe her dog pooped on your lawn. But what's the difference? The point is, you used me. You got me to chase around the country killing people."

"Isn't that what you do?"

"Right," Keller said, "and that's the part I don't understand. I don't know how you knew to call a certain number in White Plains, but you did, and that got me on the train with a flower in my lapel. Why the charade? Why not just pay the money and let out the contract?"

"I couldn't afford it."

Keller nodded. "I thought that might be it. Theft of services, that's what we're looking at here. You had me do all this for nickels and dimes."

"Look," Farrar said, "I want to apologize."

"You do?"

"I do, I honestly do. The first time, with that bastard Ramsgate, well, it was the only way to do it. The other two times I could have afforded to pay you a suitable sum, but we'd already established a relationship. You were working, you know, out of patriotism, and it seemed safer and simpler to leave it at that."

"Safer."

"And simpler."

"And cheaper," Keller said. "At the time, but where are you in the long run?"

"What do you mean?"

"Well," Keller said, "what do you figure happens now?"

"You're not going to kill me."

"What makes you so sure?"

"You'd have done it," Farrar said. "We wouldn't be having this conversation. You want something, and I think I know what it is."

"A pat on the back," Keller said, "from the man who never inhaled."

"Money," Farrar said. "You want what's rightfully yours, the money you would have been paid if I hadn't misrepresented myself. That's it, isn't it?"

"It's close."

"Close?"

"What I want," Keller said, "is that and a little more. If I were the IRS, I would call the difference penalties and interest."

"How much?"

Keller named a figure, one large enough to make Farrar blink. He said it seemed high, and they kicked it around, and Keller found himself reducing the sum by a third.

"I can raise most of that," Farrar told him. "Not overnight. I'll have to sell some securities. I can have some cash by the end of the week, or the beginning of next week at the latest."

"That's good," Keller said.

"And I'll have some more work for you."

"More work?"

"That woman in Colorado," Farrar said. "You wondered what I had against her. There was something, a remark she made once, but that's not the point. I found a way to make myself a secondary beneficiary on an individual's government insurance policy. It's too complicated to explain, but it ought to work like a charm."

"That's pretty slick," Keller said, getting to his feet. "I'll tell you, Farrar, I'm prepared to wait a week or so for the money, especially with the prospect of future work. But I'd like some cash tonight as a binder. You must have some money around the house."

"Let me see what I've got in the safe," Farrar said.

"Twenty-two thousand dollars," Keller said, slipping a rubber band around the bills and tucking them away. "That's what, fifty-five hundred dollars a pop?"

"You'll get the balance next week," Farrar assured him. "Or a substantial portion of it, at the very least."

"Great."

"Anyway, where do you get fifty-five hundred? There were three of them, and three into twenty-two is seven and a third. That makes it" — he frowned, calculating — "seven thousand, three hundred thirty-three dollars a head."

"Is that right?"

"And thirty-three cents," Farrar said.

Keller scratched his head. "Am I counting wrong? I make it four people."

"Who's the fourth?"

"You are," Keller told him.

"If I'd wanted to wait," he told Dot the next day, "I think he probably would have handed over a decent chunk of cash. But there was no way I was going to let him see the sun come up."

"Because who knows what the little shit was going to do next."

"That's it," Keller said. "He's an amateur and a nut case, and he already fooled me once."

"And once is enough."

"Once is plenty," Keller agreed. "He had it all worked out, you know. He'd manipulate Social Security records and get me to kill total strangers so that he could collect their benefits. Total strangers!"

"You generally kill total strangers, Keller."

"They're strangers to me," he said, "but not to the client. Anyway, I decided to take a bird in the hand, and the bird comes to twenty-two thousand. I guess that's better than nothing."

"It was," Dot said, "last time I checked. And none of it was work, anyway. You did it for love."

"Love?"

"Love of country. You're a patriot, Keller. After all, it's the thought that counts."

"If you say so."

"I say so. And I like the flower, Keller. I wouldn't think you'd be the type to wear one, but I have to say you can carry it off. It looks good. Adds a certain something."

"Panache," he said. "What else?"

GARY A. BRAUNBECK

Safe

FROM *Robert Bloch's Psychos*

1

VIOLENCE NEVER REALLY ENDS, no more than a symphony ceases to exist once the orchestra has stopped playing; bloodstains and bullet holes, fragments of shattered glass, knife wounds that never heal properly, nightmarish memories that thrash the heart . . . all fasten themselves like a leech to a person's core and suck away the spirit bit by bit until there's nothing left but a shell that looks like it might once have been a human being.

My God, what do you suppose happened to that person?

I heard it was something awful. I guess they never got over it — hell, you can just look at 'em and know that.

Drop a pebble in a pool of water, and the vibrations ripple outward in concentric circles. Some physicists claim that the ripples continue even after they can no longer be seen.

Ripples continue.

A symphony does not cease.

And violence never really ends.

It took half my life to learn that.

2

Three days ago, a man named Bruce Dyson walked into an ice cream parlor in the town of Utica, Ohio, and opened fire with a semiautomatic rifle, killing nine people and wounding seven others before shooting himself in the head.

Some cry, others rage, many turn away, and life will go on until the next Bruce Dyson walks into the next ice cream parlor, or bank, or fast-food restaurant; then we'll shake our heads, wring our hands once again, and wonder aloud how something so terrible could happen.

Newscasts were quick to mention Cedar Hill and draw tenuous parallels between what took place there and what happened in Utica. When one of my students asked me if I was "around" for the Cedar Hill murders, I laughed — not raucously, mind you, but enough to solicit some worried glances.

"Yes, I was around. Excuse my laughing, it's just that no one has ever asked me that before."

At a special teachers' meeting held the previous evening, a psychologist had suggested that we try to get our students to talk about the killings; four of the dead and three of the wounded had attended this school.

"Do any of you want to discuss what happened in Utica?"

Listen to their silence after I asked this.

"Look, I don't want to make anyone feel uncomfortable, but odds are someone in this room knew at least one of the victims. I know from experience it's not a good idea to keep something like this to yourself. You have to let someone know what's going on inside you."

Still nothing — a nervous shrug, perhaps, a lot of downcast stares, even a quiet tear from someone in the last row of desks, but no one spoke.

I rubbed my eyes and looked toward the back wall where the ghosts of the Cedar Hill dead were assembling.

Go on, they whispered. *Remember us to them.*

"Sixteen people were shot. You have to feel something about that."

A girl in one of the middle rows slowly raised her hand. "How did you . . . how'd you deal with what happened in Cedar Hill?"

"In many ways I still *am* dealing with it. I went back there a while ago to find some of the survivors and talk with them. I needed to put certain things to rest and — wait a second."

The ghosts of the four dead students joined those from Cedar Hill. All of them smiled at one another like old friends.

I wished I could have known them.

Tell them everything.

Go on.

I nodded my head, then said to the class: "Let's make a deal. I'll tell you about Cedar Hill only if you agree to talk about Utica. Maybe getting things out in the open will make it easier to live with. How's that sound?"

Another student raised a hand and asked, "Why do you suppose somebody'd do something like that?"

Tell the tale, demanded the ghosts.

Remember us to them . . .

3

I've gotten a little ahead of myself.

My name is Geoff Conover. I am thirty-six years old and have been a high school history teacher for the last seven years. I am married to a wonderful woman named Yvonne who is about to give birth to our first child, a boy. She has a six-year-old girl from her previous marriage. Her name is Patricia and I love her very much and she loves me, and we both love her mother and are looking forward to having a new member added to our family.

This story is not about me, though I am in it briefly under a different name. It's about a family that no longer exists, a house that no longer stands, and a way of life once called Small Town America that bled to death long before I explained to my students how violence never really ends.

I did go back to Cedar Hill in hopes of answering some questions about the night of the killings. I interviewed witnesses and survivors over the telephone, at their jobs, in their houses, over lunches, and in nursing homes; I dug through dusty files buried in moldy boxes in the basements of various historical society offices; there were decades-old police reports to be found, then sorted through and deciphered: I tracked down more than two hundred hours' worth of videotape, then subjected my family to the foul moods that resulted from my watching them; dozens of old statements had to be located and copied; and on one occasion I had to bribe my way into a storage facility in order to examine several boxes of aged evidence. There were graves to visit, names to learn, individual histories lost among bureaucratic paper trails that I had to assemble, only to find they yielded nothing of use — and I would be lying if I said that I did not feel a palpable guilt in deciding that so-and-so's life didn't merit so much as a footnote.

I do not purport to have sorted everything out. In some instances the gaps between facts were too wide and I had to fill them with conjectures and suppositions that, to the best of my knowledge and abilities, provided a *rightness* to the story that nothing else could. Yvonne says I did it to forgive myself for having survived, to be free of the shame, anger, guilt, and confusion that have for so long threatened to diminish me. She may be right. No one asked me to do it; nonetheless, certain ghosts demanded it of me — and I say this as a man who'd never thought of himself as being particularly superstitious.

I cleared my throat, smiled at the ghosts in the back of the room, and said to my students, "In order for you to understand . . ."

4

. . . what took place in Cedar Hill, you first have to understand the place itself, for it shares some measure of responsibility.

If it is possible to characterize this place by melting down all of its inhabitants and pouring them into a mold so as to produce one definitive citizen, then you will see a person who is, more likely than not, a laborer who never made it past the eleventh grade but who has managed through hard work and good solid horse sense to build the foundation of a decent middle-class existence; who works to keep a roof over his family's head and sets aside a little extra money each month to fix up the house, maybe repair that old back-door screen or add a workroom; who has one or two children who aren't exactly gifted but do well enough in school that their parents don't go to bed at night worrying that they've sired morons.

Perhaps this person drinks a few beers on the weekend — not as much as some of his rowdier friends but enough to be social. He's got his eye on some property out past the county line. He hopes to buy a new color television set. He usually goes to church on Sundays, not because he wants to but because, well, you never know, do you?

This is the person you would be facing.

This is the person who would smile at you, shake your hand, and behave in a neighborly fashion.

But never ask him about anything that lies beyond the next paycheck. Take care not to discuss anything more than work or favorite television shows or an article from this morning's paper. Complain about the cost of living, yes; inquire about his family, by all means; ask if he's got time to grab a quick sandwich, sure; but never delve too far beneath the surface, for if you do, the smile will fade, that handshake will loosen, and his friendliness will become tinged with caution.

Because this is a person who feels inadequate and does not want you to know it, who for a good long while now has suspected that his life will never be anything more than mediocre. He feels alone, abandoned, insufficient, foolish, and inept, and the only thing that keeps him going sometimes is a thought that makes him both smile and cringe: that maybe one of *his* children will decide, *Hey, Dad's life isn't so bad, this burg isn't such a hole in the ground, so, yeah, maybe I'll just stick around here and see what I can make of things.*

And what if they do? How long until they start to walk with a workman's stoop, until they're buying beer by the case and watching their skin turn into one big nicotine stain? How long until they start using the same excuses he's used on himself to justify a mediocre life?

Bills, you know. Not as young as I used to be. Too damn tired all the time. Work'll by God take it out of you.

Ah, well . . . at least there's that property out past the county line for him to keep his eye on, and there's still that new color television set he might just up and buy . . .

Then he'll blink, apologize for taking up so much of your time, wish you a good day, and head on home because the family will be waiting supper.

It was nice talking to you.

Meet Cedar Hill, Ohio.

Let us imagine that it is evening here, a little after ten P.M. on the seventh of July, and that a pair of vivid headlight beams have just drilled into the darkness on Merchant Street. The magnesium-bright strands make one silent, metronome-like sweep, then coalesce into a single lucent beacon that pulls at the vehicle trailing behind.

Imagine that although the houses along Merchant are dark, no one inside them is asleep.

The van, its white finish long faded to a dingy gray, glides toward its destination. It passes under the diffuse glow coming down from the sole streetlight, and the words "Davies' Janitorial Service" painted on its side can be easily read.

The gleam from the dashboard's gauges reveals the driver to be a tense, sinewy man whose age appears to fall somewhere between a raggedy-ass forty-five and a gee-you-don't-look-it sixty. In his deeply lined face are both resignation and dread.

He was running late, and he was not alone.

A phantom, its face obscured by alternating knife slashes of light and shadow, sat on the passenger side.

Three others rode in the back.

None of them could summon enough nerve to look beyond the night at the end of his nose.

The van came to a stop, the lights were extinguished, and with the click of a turned key, Merchant Street was again swallowed by the baleful graveyard silence that had recently taken up residence there.

The driver reached down next to his seat and grabbed a large flashlight. He turned and looked at the phantoms, who saw his eyes and understood the wordless command.

The driver climbed out as the phantoms threw open the rear double doors and began unloading the items needed for this job.

Merchant Street began to flicker as neighbors turned on their lights and lifted small corners of their curtains to peek at what was going on, even though no one really wanted to look at the Leonard house, much less live on the same street.

The driver walked up onto the front porch of the Leonard house. His name was Jackson Davies, and he owned the small janitorial company that had been hired to scour away the aftermath of four nights earlier, when this more or less peaceful industrial community of forty-two thousand had been dragged — kicking, screaming, and bleeding — into the national spotlight.

Davies turned on his flashlight, gliding its beam over the shards of broken glass that littered the front porch. As the shards caught the beam, each glared at him defiantly: *Come on, tough guy, big macho Vietnam vet with your bucket and Windex, let's see you take us on.*

He moved the beam toward a bay window on the right. Like all the first-floor windows of the house, this one was covered by a large sheet of particle board crisscrossed by two strips of yellow tape. A long, ugly stain covered most of the outside sill, dribbling over the edge in a few places down onto the porch in thin, jagged streaks. Tipping the beam, Davies followed the streaks to another stain, darker than the mess on the sill and wider by a good fifty percent. Just outside this stain was a series of receding smears that stretched across the length of the porch and disappeared in front of the railing next to the glider.

Footprints.

Davies shook his head in disgust. Someone had tried to pry loose the board and get inside the house. Judging by the prints, they'd left in one hell of a hurry, running across the porch and vaulting the rail — scared away, no doubt, by neighbors or a passing police cruiser. Probably a reporter eager to score a hefty bonus by snapping a few graphic photos of the scene.

Davies swallowed once, loud and hard, then swung the light over to the front door. Spiderwebbing the frame from every conceivable angle were more strips of yellow tape emblazoned with large, bold, black letters: "Keep Out by Order of the Cedar Hill Police Department." An intimidating, hand-sized padlock held the door securely closed.

As he looked at the padlock, a snippet of Rilke flashed across his mind: *Who dies now anywhere in the world, without cause dies in the world, looks at me —*

And Jackson Davies, dropout English Lit major, recent ex-husband, former Vietnam vet, packer of body bags into the cargo holds of planes at Tan Son Nhut, onetime cleaner-upper of the massacre at My Lai 4, hamlet of Son My, Quang Ngai Province, a man who thought there was no physical remnant of violent death he didn't have the stomach to handle, began muttering. "Goddamn, god*damn, goddamn,*" and felt a lump dislodge from his groin and bounce up into his throat and was damned if he knew why, but suddenly the thought of going into the Leonard house scared the living shit out of him.

Unseen by Davies, the ghosts of Irv and Miriam Leonard sat on the glider a few yards away from him. Irv had his arm around his wife and was good-naturedly scolding her for slipping that bit of poetry into Davies's head.

I can't help it, Miriam said. *And even if I could, I wouldn't. Jackson read that poem when he was in Vietnam. It was in a little paperback collection his wife gave to him. He lost that book somewhere over there, you know. He's been trying to remember that poem all these years. Besides, he's lonely for his wife, and maybe that poem'll make it seem like part of her's still with him.*

Could've just gone to a library, said Irv.

He did, but he couldn't remember Rilke's name.

Think he'll remember it now?

I sure do hope so. Look at him, poor guy. He's so lonely, God love 'im.

Seems antsy, don't he?

Wouldn't you be? asked Miriam.

That was really nice of you, hon, giving that poem back to him. You always were one for taking care of your friends.

Charmer.

What can I say? Seems my disposition's improved considerably since I died.

Oh, now, don't go bringing that up. There's not much we can do about it.

How come that doesn't make me feel any better?

Maybe this'll do the trick, said Miriam. *"Who laughs now anywhere in the night, without cause laughs in the night, laughs at me."*

Don't tell me, tell the sensitive poetry soldier over there.

I just did.

They watched Davies for a few more seconds: he rubbed his face, then lit a cigarette and leaned against the porch railing and looked out into the street.

It's not right, said Irv to his wife. *What happened to us wasn't fair.*

Nothing is, dear. But we're through with all of that, remember?

If you say so.

Worrier.

Yeah, but at least I'm a charming worrier.

Shhh. Did you hear that?

Hear what?

The children are playing in the backyard. Let's go watch.

A moment later, the wind came up, and the glider swung back, then forward, once and once only, with a thin-edged screech.

Jackson Davies dropped his cigarette and decided, screw this, he was going to go wait down by the van.

He turned and ran into a phantom, then recoiled. The phantom stepped from the scar of shadow and into the flashlight's beam, becoming Pete Cooper, one of Davies's crew managers.

Davies, through clenched teeth, said, "It's not a real good idea to sneak up on me like that. I have a tendency to hurt people when that happens."

"Shakin' in my shoes," said Cooper. "You gettin' the jungle jitters again? Smell that napalm in the air?"

"Yeah, right. Whacked-out Nam vet doing the flashback boogie, that's me. Was there a reason you came up here, or did you just miss my splendid company?"

"I just . . ." Cooper looked over at the van. "Why'd you bring the Brennert kid along?"

"Because he said yes."

"C'mon, fer chrissakes! He was *here,* you know? When it happened?"

Davies sighed and fished a fresh cigarette from his shirt pocket. "First of all, he wasn't here when it happened, he was here *before* it happened. Second, of my forty-eight loyal employees, not counting you, only three said they were willing to come out here tonight, and Russ was one of them. Do you find any of this confusing so far? I could start again and talk slower."

"What're you gonna do if he gets in there and sees . . . well . . . everything and freezes up or freaks or something?"

"I talked to him about that already. He says he won't lose it, and I believe him. Besides, the plant's going to be laying his dad off in a couple of weeks and his family could use the money."

"Fine. I'll keep the other guys in line, but Brennert is *your* problem."

"Anything else? The suspense is killing me."

"Just that this seems like an odd hour to be starting."

Davies pointed at the street. "Look around. Tell me what you don't see."

"I'm too tired for your goddamn riddles."

"You never were any fun. What you don't see are any *reporters* or any trace of their nauseating three-ring circus that blew into this miserable burg a few nights back. The county is paying us, and the county decided that our chances of being accosted by reporters would be practically nil if we came out late in the evening. So here we are, and I'm no happier about it than you are. Despite what people say, I do have a life. Admittedly, it isn't much of one since my wife decided that we get along better living in separate states, but it's a life nonetheless. I just thank God she left me the cats and the Mitch Miller sing-along records, or I'd be a sorry specimen right about now. To top it all off, I seem to have developed a retroactive case of the willies."

A police cruiser pulled up behind the van.

"Ah," said Davies. "That would be the keys to the kingdom of the dead."

"You plan to keep up the joking?"

Davies's face turned into a slab of granite. "Bet your ass I do. And I'm going to keep on joking until we're finished with this job and loading things up to go home. The sicker and more tasteless I can make them, the better. Don't worry if I make jokes; worry when I stop."

They went to meet the police officers, unaware that as they came down from the porch and started across the lawn they walked right through the ghost of Andy Leonard, who stood looking at the house where he'd spent his entire, sad, brief, and ultimately tragic life.

5

On July fourth of that year, Irv Leonard and his wife were hosting a family reunion at their home at 182 Merchant Street. All fifteen members of their immediate family were present, and several neighbors stopped by to visit, watch some football, enjoy a hearty lunch from the ample buffet Miriam had prepared, and see Irv's newly acquired pearl-handled antique Colt Army .45 revolvers.

Irv, a retired steelworker and lifelong gun enthusiast, had been collecting firearms since his early twenties and was purported to have one of the five most valuable collections in the state.

Neighbors later remarked that the atmosphere in the house was as pleasant as you could hope for, though a few did notice that Andy — the youngest of the four Leonard children and the only one still living at home — seemed a bit "distracted."

Around 8:45 that evening, Russell Brennert, a friend of Andy's from Cedar Hill High School, came by after getting off work from his part-time job. Witnesses described Andy as being "abrupt" with Russell, as if he didn't want him to be there. Some speculated that the two might have had an argument recently that Andy was still sore about. In any case, Andy excused himself and went upstairs to "check on something."

Russell started to leave, but Miriam insisted he fix himself a sandwich first. A few minutes later, Andy — apparently no longer upset — reappeared and asked if Russell would mind driving Mary

Alice Hubert, Miriam's mother and Andy's grandmother, back to her house. The seventy-three-year-old Mrs. Hubert, a widow of ten years, was still recovering from a mild heart attack in December and had forgotten to bring her medication. Brennert offered to take Mary Alice's house key and drive over by himself for the medicine, but Andy insisted Mrs. Hubert go along.

"I thought it seemed kind of odd," said Bill Gardner, a neighbor who was present at the time, "Andy being so bound and determined to get the two of them out of there before the fireworks started. Poor Miriam didn't know what to make of it all. I mean, I didn't think it was any of my business, but somebody should've said something about it. Andy started getting outright rude. If he'd been my kid, I'd've snatched him bald-headed, acting that way. And after his mom'd gone to all that fuss to make everything so nice."

Mrs. Hubert prevented things from getting out of hand by saying it would be best if she went with Russell; after all, she was an "old broad," set in her ways, and everything in an old broad's house had to be *just so* . . . besides, there were so many medicine containers in her cabinet, Russell might just "bust his brain right open" trying to figure out which was the right one.

As the two were on their way out, Andy stopped them at the door to give Mrs. Hubert a hug.

According to her, Andy seemed "really sorry about something. He's a strong boy, an athlete, and I don't care what anyone says, he should've got that scholarship. Okay, maybe he wasn't as bright as some kids, but he was a fine athlete, and them college people should've let that count for something. It was terrible, listening to him talk about how he was maybe gonna have to go to work at the factory to earn his college money . . . everybody knows where that leads. I'm sorry, I got off the track, didn't I? You asked about him hugging me when we left that night . . . well, he was always real careful when he hugged me never to squeeze too hard — these old bones can't take it . . . but when he hugged me then, I thought he was going to break my ribs. I just figured it was on account he felt bad about the argument. I didn't mean to create such a bother, I thought I had the medicine with me, but I . . . forget things sometimes.

"He kissed me on the cheek and said 'Bye, Grandma. I love you.' It wasn't so much the words, he always said that same thing to me every time I left . . . it was the way he said them. I remember thinking he was going to cry, that's how those words sounded, so I said, 'Don't worry about it. Your mom knows you didn't mean to be so surly.' I told him that when I got back, we'd watch the rest of the fireworks and then make some popcorn and maybe see a movie on the TV. He used to like doing that with me when he was littler.

"He smiled and touched my cheek with two of his fingers — he'd never done that before — and he looked at Russ like maybe he wanted to give him a hug, too, but boys that age don't hug each other, they think it makes them look like queers or something, but I could see it in Andy's eyes that he *wanted* to hug Russ.

"Then he said the strangest thing. He looked at Russ and kind of . . . *slapped* the side of Russ's shoulder — friendly, you know, like men'll do with each other when they feel too silly to hug? Anyway, he, uh, did that shoulder thing, then looked at Russ and said, 'The end is courage.' I figured it was a line from some movie they'd seen together. They love their movies, those two, always quoting lines to each other like some kind of secret code — like in *Citizen Kane* with 'Rosebud.' That kind of thing.

"It wasn't until we were almost to my house that Russ asked me if I knew what the heck Andy meant when he said that.

"I knew right then that something was wrong, terribly wrong. Oh Lord, when I think of it now . . . the . . . the *pain* a soul would have to be in to do something . . . like that . . ."

Russell Brennert and Mary Alice Hubert left the Leonard house at 9:05. As soon as he saw Brennert's car turn the corner at the end of the street, Andy immediately went back upstairs and did not come down until the locally sponsored Kiwanis Club fireworks display began at 9:15.

Several factors contributed to the neighbors' initial failure to react to what happened. First, there was the thunderous noise of the fireworks themselves. Since White's Field, the site of the fireworks display, was less than one mile away, the resounding boom of the cannons was, as one person described, "damn near loud enough to rupture your eardrums."

Second, music from a pair of concert hall speakers that Bill Gardner had set up in his front yard compounded the glass-rattling noise and vibrations of the cannons. "Every Fourth of July," said Gardner, "WLCB [a local low-wattage FM radio station] plays music to go along with the fireworks. You know, 'America the Beautiful,' 'Stars and Stripes Forever,' Charlie Daniels's 'In America,' stuff like that, and every year I tune 'em in and set my speakers out and let fly. Folks on this street want me to do it, they all like it.

"How the fuck was I supposed to know Andy was gonna flip out?"

Third and last, there were innumerable firecrackers being set off by neighborhood children. This not only added to the general racket but also accounted for the neighbors' ignoring certain visual clues once Andy moved outside. "You have to understand," said one detective, "that everywhere around these people, up and down the street, kids were setting off all different kinds of things: firecrackers, sparklers, bottle rockets, M-80s, for God's sake! Is it any wonder it took them so long to tell the difference between an exploding firecracker and the muzzle flash from a gun?

"Andy Leonard had to've been planning this for a long time. He knew there'd be noise and explosions and lights and a hundred other things to distract everyone from what he was doing."

At exactly 9:15 P.M., Andy Leonard walked calmly downstairs carrying three semiautomatic pistols — a Walther P.38 9mm Perabellum, a Mauser Luger 7.65mm, and a Coonan .357 Magnum — as well as an HK53 5.56mm assault rifle, all of which he'd taken from his father's massive oak gun cabinet upstairs.

Of the thirteen other family members present at that time, five — including Irv Leonard, sixty-two, and his oldest son, Chet, twenty-five — were outside watching the fireworks. Andy's two older sisters, Jessica, twenty-nine, and Elizabeth, thirty-four (both of whose husbands were also outside), were in the kitchen hurriedly helping their mother put away the buffet leftovers so they could join the men on the front lawn.

Jessica's three children — Randy, age seven; Theresa, four; and Joseph, nine and a half months — were in the living room. Randy and his sister had just finished changing their baby brother's diaper and were strapping him into his safety seat so they could hurry up and get outside. Joseph thought they were playing with him and so thrashed and giggled a lot.

They didn't notice their uncle.

Elizabeth's two children — Ian, twelve, and Lori, nine — were thought to be already outside but were upstairs in the "toy room," which contained, among other items, a pool table and a twenty-seven-inch color television for use with Andy's extensive video game collection.

By the time Andy walked downstairs at 9:15, Ian and Lori were already dead, their skulls crushed by repeated blows with, first, a gun butt, then a pool cue, and, at the last, billiard balls that were crammed into their mouths after their jaws were wrenched loose.

Laying the HK53 across the top of the dinner table, Andy stuffed the Mauser and blood-spattered Walther into the waist of his jeans, then walked into the kitchen, raised the .357, and shot his sister Jessica through the back of her head. She was standing with her back to him, in the process of putting some food into the refrigerator. The hollow-point bullet blew out most of her brain and sheared away half of her face. When she dropped, she pulled two refrigerator shelves and their contents down with her.

Andy then shot Elizabeth — once in the stomach, once in the center of her chest — then turned the gun on his mother, shooting at point-blank range through her right eye.

After that, things happened very quickly. Andy left the kitchen and collided with his niece who was running toward the front door. He caught her by the hair and swung her face-first into a fifty-inch-high cast-iron statue that sat against a wall in the foyer. The statue was a detailed reproduction of the famous photograph of the American flag being raised on Mt. Suribachi at Iwo Jima.

Theresa slammed against it with such force that her nose shattered, sending bone fragments shooting backward down her throat. Still gripping her long strawberry-blond hair in his fist, Andy lifted her off her feet and impaled her by the throat on the tip of the flagstaff. (The blood patterns on the wall behind the statue indicated an erratic arterial spray, leading the on-scene medical examiner to speculate she must have struggled to get free at some point; this, along with the increase in serotonin and free histamine levels in the wound, indicated Theresa had lived at least three minutes after being impaled.)

Seven-year-old Randy saw his uncle impale Theresa on the statue, then grabbed the carrying handle of Joseph's safety seat and ran toward the kitchen. Andy shot him in the back of his right leg. Randy went down, losing his grip on Joseph's safety seat, which skittered across the blood-sopped tile floor and came to a stop inches from Jessica's body. Little Joseph, frightened and helpless in the seat, began to cry.

Randy tried to stand, but his leg was useless, so he began moving toward Joseph by kicking out with his left leg and using his elbows and hands to pull himself forward.

Nine feet away, Andy stood in the kitchen entrance watching his nephew's valiant attempt to save the baby.

Then he shot Randy between the shoulders.

And the kid kept moving.

As Andy took aim to fire again, the front door swung open, and Keith Shannon, Elizabeth's husband, stuck his head in and shouted for everyone to hurry up and come on.

Keith saw Theresa's body dangling from the statue and screamed over his shoulder at the other men out on the lawn, then ran inside, calling out the names of his wife and children.

He never stopped to see if Theresa was still alive.

Andy stormed across the kitchen and through the second, smaller archway that led into the rooms on the front left side of the house. As a result of taking this shortcut, he beat Keith to the living room by a few seconds, enabling him to take his brother-in-law by surprise. Andy emptied the rest of the Magnum's rounds into Keith's head and chest. One shot went wild and shattered the large front bay window.

Andy tossed the Magnum aside and pulled both the Mauser and the Walther from his jeans, holding one pistol in each hand. He bolted from the living room, through the dining room, and rounded the corner into the foyer just as Irv hit the top step of the porch.

Andy kicked open the front door. For the next fifteen seconds, while the sky ignited and Lee Greenwood sang how God should bless this country he loved, God bless the U.S.A., the front porch of the Leonard house became a shooting gallery as each of the four remaining adult males — at least two of whom were drunk — came up onto the porch one by one and was summarily executed.

Andy fired both pistols simultaneously, killing his father, his uncle Martin, his older brother Chet, and Tom Hamilton, Jessica's husband.

A neighbor across the street, Bess Paymer, saw Irv's pulped body wallop backward onto the lawn and yelled for her husband, Francis. Francis took one look out the window and said, "Someone's gone crazy." Bess was already dialing the police.

Andy went back into the house and grabbed the rifle off the dining-room table, picked up the Magnum as he passed back through the living room, then headed for the kitchen, where Randy, still alive, was attempting to drag Joseph through the back door. When he heard his uncle come into the kitchen, Randy

reached out and grabbed a carving knife from the scattered contents of the cutlery drawer, which Miriam had wrenched free on
her way down, then threw himself over his infant brother.

"That was one brave kid," an investigator said later. "Here he was,
in the middle of all these bodies, he had two bullets in him so we
know he was in a lot of pain, and the only thing that mattered to
him was protecting his baby brother. An amazing kid. If there's one
bright spot in all this, it's knowing that he loved his brother enough
to . . . to . . . ah, hell. I can't talk about it right now."

For some reason, Andy did not shoot his nephew a third time. He
came across the kitchen floor and raised the butt of the rifle to
bludgeon Randy's skull, and that's when Randy, in his last moments, pushed himself forward and jammed the knife in his uncle's
calf. Then he died.

Andy dropped to the floor, screaming through clenched teeth,
and pulled the knife from his leg. He grabbed his nephew's lifeless
body and heaved it over onto its back, then beat its face in with his
fists. After that, he loaded fresh clips into the pistols, grabbed
Joseph, stumbled out the back door to the garage, and drove away
in Irv's brand-new pickup.

At 9:21 P.M., the night duty dispatcher at the Cedar Hill Police
Department received Bess Paymer's call. As was standard operating
procedure, the dispatcher, while believing Bess had heard gunfire,
asked if she were certain that someone had been shot. This dispatcher later defended this action by saying, "Every year we get
yahoos all over this city who decide that the Kiwanis fireworks
display is the perfect time to go out in their backyard and fire their
guns off into the air — well, the Fourth and New Year's Eve, we get
a lot of that. We had every unit out that night, just like every
holiday, and there were drunks to deal with, bar fights, illegal fireworks being set off — M-80s and such, traffic accidents . . . holidays
tend to be a bit of a mess for us around here. Seems that's when
everybody and their brother decides to act like a royal horse's ass.

"The point is, if we get a report of alleged gunfire during the
fireworks, we're required to ask the caller if anyone's been hurt. If
not, then we get to it as soon as we can. If we had to send a cruiser
to check out every report of gunfire that comes in on the Fourth,
we'd never get anything else done. I didn't do anything wrong. It's
not my fault."

It took Bess Paymer and her husband the better part of two

minutes to convince the dispatcher that someone had gone crazy over at the Leonard house and shot everyone.

Francis, furious by this point, grabbed the phone from his wife and informed the dispatcher in no uncertain terms that they'd better make it fast because he was grabbing his hunting rifle and going over there himself.

A cruiser was dispatched at 9:24 P.M.

At 9:27, a call came in from the Leonard house; by noon the next day, the phone call had been replayed on every newscast in the country:

"This is Francis Paymer. My wife and I called you a couple of minutes ago. I'm standing in the . . . the kitchen of the Leonard house . . . that's One-eighty-two Merchant Street . . . and I've got somebody's brains stuck to the bottom of my shoe.

"There's been a shooting here. A little girl's hanging in the hall-way, and there's blood all over the walls and the floors and I can't tell where one person's body ends and the next one begins because everybody's dead. I can still smell the gunpowder and smoke.

"Is that good enough for you to do something? C-could you maybe please if it's not too much trouble send someone out here NOW? It might be a good idea, because the crazy BASTARD WHO DID THIS ISN'T HERE —

"— and I think he might've took a baby with him."

By 9:30 P.M., Merchant Street was clogged with police cruisers.

And Andy Leonard was halfway to Moundbuilder's Park, where the Second Presbyterian Church was sponsoring Parish Family Night. More than one hundred people had been gathered at the park since five in the afternoon, picnicking, tossing Frisbees, play-ing checkers, or flying kites. A little before nine, the president of the Parish Council had arrived with a truckload of folding chairs that were set up in a clearing at the south end of the park.

By the time Francis Paymer made his famous phone call, one hundred seven parish members were seated in twelve neat little rows watching the fireworks display.

Between leaving his Merchant Street house and arriving at Moundbuilder's Park, Andy Leonard shot and killed six more peo-ple as he drove past them. Two were in a car; the other four had been sitting out on their lawns watching the fireworks. In every case, Andy simply kept one hand on the steering wheel while shoot-ing with the other through an open window.

At 9:40 P.M., just as the fireworks kicked into high gear for the grand finale, Andy drove his father's pickup truck at eighty miles per hour through the wooden gate at the northeast side of the park, barreled across the picnic grounds, over the grassy mound that marked the south border, and went straight down into the middle of the spectators.

Three people were killed and eight others injured as the truck plowed into the back row of chairs. Then Andy threw open the door, leaped from the truck, and opened fire with the HK53. The parishioners scrambled in panic, many of them falling over chairs. Of the dead and wounded at the park, none was able to get farther than ten yards away before being shot.

Andy stopped only long enough to yank the pistols from the truck. The first barrage with the rifle was to disable; the second, with the pistols, was to finish off anyone who might still be alive.

At 9:45 P.M., Andy Leonard crawled up onto the roof of his father's pickup truck and watched the fireworks' grand finale. The truck's radio was tuned in to WLCB. The bombastic finish of *The 1812 Overture* erupted along with the fiery colors in the dark heaven above.

The music and the fireworks ended.

Whirling police lights could be seen approaching the park. The howl of sirens hung in the air like a protracted musical chord.

Andy Leonard shoved the barrel of the rifle into his mouth and blew most of his head off. His nearly decapitated body slammed backward onto the roof, then slid slowly down to the hood, smearing a long trail of gore over the center of the windshield.

Twenty minutes later, just as Russell Brennert and Mary Alice Hubert turned onto Merchant Street to find it blocked by police cars and ambulances, one of the officers on the scene at the park heard what he thought was the sound of a baby crying. Moments later, he discovered Joseph Hamilton, still alive and still in his safety seat, on the passenger-side floor of the pickup. The infant was clutching a bottle of formula that had been taken from his mother's baby bag.

6

I stopped at this point and took a deep breath, surprised to find that my hands were shaking. I looked to the ghosts, and they whispered, *Courage.*

I swallowed once, nodded my head, then said to my students, "That baby was me.

"I have no idea why Andy didn't kill me. I was taken away and placed in the care of Cedar Hill Children's Services." I opened my briefcase and removed a file filled with photocopies of old newspaper articles and began passing them around the room. I'd brought some of my research along in case I'd needed it to prompt discussion. "The details of how I came to be adopted by the Conover family of Waynesboro, Virginia, are written in these articles. Suffice it to say that I was perhaps the most famous baby in the country for the next several weeks."

One student held up a copy of an article and said, "It says here that the Conovers took you back to Cedar Hill six months after the killings. Says you were treated like a celebrity."

I looked at the photo accompanying the article and shook my head. "I have no memory of that at all. At home, in a box I keep in my filing cabinet, are hundreds of cards I received from people who lived in Cedar Hill at that time. Most of them are now either dead or have moved away. When I went back I could only find a few of them.

"It's odd to think that, somewhere out there, there are dozens, maybe even hundreds, of people who prayed for me when I was a baby, people I never knew and never will know. For a while I was at the center of their thoughts. I like to believe these people still think of me from time to time. I like to believe it's those thoughts and prayers that keep me safe from harm.

"But as I said in the beginning, this story isn't really about me. If there's any great truth here, I'm not the one to say what it might be. The moment that officer found that squalling baby on the floor of that truck, I ceased to be a part of the story. But it's never stopped being a part of me."

7

Details were too sketchy for the 11:00 P.M. news to offer anything concrete about the massacre, but by the time the local network affiliates broadcast their news-at-sunrise programs, the tally was in.

Counting himself, Andy Leonard had murdered thirty-two people and wounded thirty-six others, making his spree the largest single mass shooting to date. (Some argued that since the shootings took place in two different locations they should be treated as two separate incidents, while others insisted that since Andy had continuously fired his weapons up until the moment of his death, including the trail of shootings between his house and the park, it was all one single incident. What could not be argued was the body count, which made the rest of it more than a bit superfluous.)

Those victims were what the specter of my uncle was thinking about as Jackson Davies and Pete Cooper walked through him.

Andy's ghost hung its head and sighed, then took one half-step to the right and vanished back into the ages where it would relive its murderous rampage in perpetuity, always coming back to the moment it stood outside the house and watched as two men passed through it on their way toward a police officer.

8

Russell Brennert looked at the two other janitors who'd come along tonight and knew without asking that neither one of them wanted him to be here. Of course not, *he* had known the crazy fucker, *he* had been Andy Leonard's best friend, *his* presence made it all just a bit more real than they wanted it to be. Did they think that some part of what had driven Andy to kill all of those people had rubbed off on him as well? Probably — at least that would explain why they hadn't told him their names.

Hell with it, he thought. Call them Mutt and Jeff, and leave it at that.

He checked to make sure each plastic barrel had plenty of extra trash bags. Then Mutt came over and, fighting the smirk trying to sneak onto his face, asked, "Hey, Brennert — that's your name, right?"

"Yeah."

"We were just wonderin' if, well, it's true, y'know?"

"If *what's* true?"

Mutt gave a quick look to Jeff, who turned away and oh-so-subtly covered his mouth with his hand.

Russell dug his fingernails into his palms to keep from getting angry; these guys were going to pull something, or say something, he just knew it.

Mutt sniffed dryly as he turned back to Russell. He'd given up trying to fight back the smirk on his face.

Russell bit his lower lip. *Stay cool, you can do it, you need the money . . .*

"We'd just been wonderin'," said Mutt, "if it's true that you and Leonard used to . . . go to the movies together."

Jeff snorted a laugh and tried to cover it up by coughing.

Russell held his breath. "Sometimes, yeah."

"Just the two of you, or you guys ever take dates?"

You're doing fine, just fine, he's a mutant, just keep that in mind . . .

"Sometimes it was just him and me. Sometimes he'd bring Barb along."

"Yeah, yeah . . ." Mutt leaned in, lowering his voice to a mock-conspiratorial whisper. "The thing is, we heard that the two of you went to the drive-in together a couple of days before he shot everybody."

Fine and dandy, yessir. "That's right. Barb was going to come along, but she had to baby-sit her sister at the last minute."

Mutt chewed on his lower lip to bite back a giggle. Russell caught a peripheral glimpse of Davies and Cooper heading back up to the porch with one of the cops.

"How come you and your buddy went to the drive-in all by yourselves?"

"We wanted to see the movie." *Jesus, Jackson, get down here, will you?*

Russell didn't hear all of the next question because the pulsing of his blood sounded like a jackhammer in his ears.

". . . thigh?"

Russell blinked, exhaled, and dug his nails in a little deeper. "I'm sorry, could you run that by me again?"

"I said, last week after gym when we was all in the showers, I noticed you had a sucker bite on your thigh."

"Birthmark."

"You sure about that? Seemed to me it looked like a big ol' hickey."

"Stare at my thighs a lot, do you?"

Mutt's face went blank. Jeff jumped to his feet and snarled, "Hey, watch it, motherfucker."

"Watch what?" snapped Russell. "Why don't you feebs just leave me alone? I've got better things to do than be grilled by a couple of redneck homophobes."

"Ha! *Homo,* huh?" said Mutt. "I always figured the two of you musta been butt buddies."

"Fag bags," said Jeff, then the two flaming wits high-fived each other.

Russell suddenly realized that one of his hands had reached over and gripped a mop handle. *Don't do it, Russ, don't you dare, they're not worth it.* "Think whatever you want. I don't care." He turned away from them in time to see a bright blue van pull up behind the police cruiser. A small satellite dish squatted like a gargoyle on top of the van, and Russell could see through the windshield that Ms. Tanya Claymore, Channel 9's red-hot news babe, was inside.

"Oh shit," he whispered.

One of the reasons he'd agreed to help out tonight — the money aside — was so he wouldn't have to stay at home and hear the phone ring every ten minutes and answer it to find some reporter on the other end asking for Mr. Russell Brennert, oh this is him? I'm Whats'isname from the In-Your-Face Channel, Central Ohio's News Authority, and I wanted to ask you a few questions about Andy Leonard blah-blah-blah.

It had been like that for the last three days. He'd hoped that coming out here tonight would give him a reprieve from everyone's constant questions, but it seemed —

— put the ego in park, Russ. Yeah, maybe they called the house and Mom or Dad told them you'd be out here, but it's just possible they came out in hopes of getting inside the house for a few minutes' worth of video for tomorrow's news.

Mutt smacked the back of his shoulder much harder than was needed just to get his attention. "Hey, yo! Brennert, I'm talking to you."

"Please leave me alone? Please?"

All along the murky death membrane that was Merchant Street, porch lights snapped on and ghostly forms shuffled out in bathrobes and housecoats, some with curlers in their hair or shoddy slippers on their feet.

Mutt and Jeff both laughed, but not too loudly.

"What's it like to cornhole a psycho, huh?"

"I —" Russell swallowed the rest of the sentence and started toward the house, but Mutt grabbed his arm, wrenching him backward and spinning him around.

One of the tattered specters grabbed her husband's arm and pointed from their porch to the three young men by the van. Did it look like there was some trouble?

The ghosts of Irv and Miriam Leonard, accompanied by their grandchildren Ian, Theresa, and Lori, stood off to the side of the house and watched as well. Irv shook his head in disgust, and Miriam wiped at her eyes and thought she felt her heart aching for Russell, such a nice boy, he was.

On the porch of the Leonard house, an impatient Jackson Davies waited while the officer ripped down the yellow tape and inserted the key into the lock.

"Jackson?" said Pete Cooper.

"What?"

Cooper cleared his throat and lowered his voice. "Do you remember what you said about no reporters being around?"

"Yeah, so wha —" Then he saw the Channel 9 news van. "Ah, fuck me with a fiddlestick! They plant a homing device on that poor kid or something?" He watched Tanya Claymore slide open the side door and lower one of her too-perfect legs toward the ground like some Hollywood starlet exiting a limo at a movie premiere.

"Dammit, I *told* you bringing Brennert along would be a mistake."

"Thank you, Mr. Hindsight. Let *me* worry about it?"

Cooper gestured toward the news van and said, "Aren't you gonna do something?"

"I don't know if I can." Davies directed this remark to the police officer unlocking the door. The officer looked over his shoulder and shrugged, then said, "If she interferes with your crew performing the job you pay them for, you've got every right to tell her to go away."

"Just make sure you get her phone number first," said Cooper.

Davies turned his back to them and stared at Tanya Claymore. If she even so much as *looked* at Russell, he'd drop on her like a curse from heaven.

Down by the trash barrels and buckets, Mutt was standing less than an inch from Russell's face and saying, "All right, bad-ass, let's get to it. People're sayin' that you maybe knew what Andy was gonna do and didn't say anything."

"I didn't," whispered Russell. "I didn't know."

Some part of him realized that Tanya's cameraman had turned on his light and was taping them, but he was backed too far into a corner to care right now.

"Yeah," said Mutt contemptuously. "I'll just bet you didn't."

"I *didn't* know, all right? He never said . . . a thing to me."

"According to the news, he was in an awful hurry to get you out before he went gonzo."

For a moment, Russell found himself back in the car with Mary Alice, turning the corner and being almost blinded by visibar lights, then that cop came over and pounded on the window and said, "This area's restricted for the moment, kid, so you're gonna have to —" and Mary Alice shouted, "Is that the Leonard house? Did something happen to my family?" And then the cop shone his flashlight in and asked, "You a relative, ma'am?" and Mary Alice was already in tears, and Russell felt something boiling up from his stomach because he saw one of the bodies being covered by a sheet, and then Mary Alice screamed and fell against him and a sick cloud of pain descended on their skulls —

"*I had no idea,* okay?" The words fell to the ground in a heap. Russell thought he could almost see them groan before the darkness put them out of their misery. "Do I have to keep on saying that, or should I just write it in braille and shove it up —"

"— you knew, you *had* to know!" The mean-spirited mockery of earlier was gone from Mutt's voice, replaced by anger with some genuine hurt wrapped around it. "He was your best friend!"

You need the money, Russell.

"Two of 'em was always together," said Jeff, just loud enough for the microphone to get every word. "Everybody figured that Brennert here was gay and was in love with Andy."

Three hundred dollars, Russell. Grocery money for a month or so. Mom and Dad will appreciate it.

It seemed that both of his hands were gripping the mop handle, and somehow that mop was no longer in the bucket.

He heard a chirpy voice go into its popular singsong mode: "This is Tanya Claymore. I'm standing outside the house of Irving and Miriam Leonard at One-eighty-two Merchant Street, where —"

"You wanna do something about it?" said Mutt, pushing Russell's shoulder. "Think you're man enough to mess with me?"

Russell was only vaguely aware of Davies coming down from the porch and shouting something at the news crew; he was only vaguely aware of the second police officer climbing from the cruiser and making a beeline to Ms. News Babe; and he was only vaguely aware of Mutt saying, "How come you came along to help with the cleanup tonight? Idea of seeing all that blood and brains get you hard, does it? You a sick fuck just like Andy?" But the one thing of which he was fully, almost gleefully aware was that the mop had become a javelin in his hands and he was going to go for the gold and hurl the thing right into Mutt's great big ugly target of a mouth —

Three hundred dollars should just about cover the emergency room bill —

Then a hand clamped down so hard on Mutt's shoulder that Russell thought he heard bones crack.

Jackson Davies's smiling face swooped in and hovered between them. "If you're finished with this nerve-tingling display of machismo, we have a house to clean, remember?" Still clutching Mutt's shoulder in a Vulcan death-grip, Davies hauled the boy around and pushed him toward one of the barrels. "Why can't you use your powers for good?"

"Hey, we were just —"

"I know what you were *just,* thank you very much. I'd appreciate it" — he gestured toward Jeff — "if you and the Boy Wonder here would get off your asses and start carrying supplies inside." Russell reached for a couple of buckets, but Davies stopped him. "Not you, Ygor. You stay here with me for a second." Mutt and Jeff stood staring as Ms. News Babe came jiggling up to Russell in all of her journalistic glory.

Davies glowered at the two boys and said, "Yes, her bazooba-wobblies are very big, and no, you can't touch them. Now get moving before I become unpleasant."

They became a blur of legs and mop buckets.

Russell said, "Mr. Davies, I'm sorry, but —"

"Hold that thought."

Tanya and her cameraman were almost on top of them; a microphone came toward their faces like a projectile.

"Russell?" said Tanya. "Russell, hi. I'm Tanya Claymore, and —"

"A friend of mine once stepped on a Claymore," said Davies. "Made his sphincter switch places with his eardrums. I was scraping his spleen off my face for a week. Please don't bother any member of my crew, Ms. Claymore."

The reporter's startling green eyes widened. She made a small, quick gesture with her free hand, and her cameraman swung around to get Davies into the frame.

"We'd like to talk to *both* of you, Mr. Davies —"

"Go away." Davies looked at Russell, and the two of them grabbed the remaining buckets and barrels and started toward the house.

Tanya Claymore sneered at Davies's back, then turned around and waved to the driver of the news van. He looked over, and she mimed talking into a telephone receiver. The driver nodded his head and picked up the cellular phone. Tanya gave her mike to the cameraman and took off after Davies.

"Mr. Davies, please, could you — dammit, I'm in heels! Would you wait a second?"

"She wants me," whispered Davies to Russell. Despite everything, Russell gave a little smile. He liked Jackson Davies a lot and was glad this man was his boss.

Tanya stumbled up the incline of the lawn and held out one of her hands for Davies to take hold of and help her.

"Are those fingernails real or press-ons?" asked Davies, not making a move.

Russell put down his supplies and gave her the help she needed. As soon as she reached level ground, she offered a sincere smile and squeezed his hand in thanks.

Davies said, "What's it going to take to make you leave us alone?"

Her eyes hardened, but the smile remained. "All I want is to talk to the both of you about what you're going to do."

"It's a little obvious, isn't it?"

"Central Ohio would like to know."

"Oh," said Davies. "I see. You're in constant touch with central Ohio? Champion of the common folk in your fake nails and designer dress and tinted contacts?"

"Does all that just come to you or do you write down ahead of time and memorize it?"

"You're not being very nice."

"Neither are you."

They both fell silent and stood staring at each other.

Finally, Davies sighed and said, "Could we at least get our stuff inside and get started first? I could come out in a half hour and talk to you then."

"What about Russell?"

Russell half raised his hand. "*Russell* is right here. Please don't talk about me in the third person."

"Sorry," said Tanya with a grin. "You haven't talked to *any* reporters, Russell. I don't know if you remember, but you've hung up on me twice."

"I know. I was gonna send you a card to apologize. We always watch you at my house. My mom thinks you look like a nice girl, and my dad's always had a thing for redheads."

Tanya leaned a little closer to him and said, "What about you? Why do you like watching me?"

Russell was glad that it was so dark out, because he could feel himself blushing. "I, uh . . . I — look, Ms. Claymore, I don't know what I could say to you about what happened that you don't already know."

The radio in the police cruiser squawked loudly, and the officer down by the vans leaned through the window to grab the mike.

"All right," said Tanya, looking from Davies to Russell, then back to Davies again. "I won't lie to either of you. The news director would really, really prefer that I come back tonight with some tape either of Russell or the inside of the house. I almost had to beg him to let me do this tonight. Don't take this the wrong way — especially you, Russell — but I'm sick to death of being a talking head. Don't ever repeat that to anyone. If —"

"Oh, allow me," said Davies. "If you don't come back tonight with a really boffo piece, you'll be stuck reading Teleprompters and covering new mall openings for the rest of your career, right?"

Tanya said nothing.

Russell looked over at his boss. "Uh, look, Mr. Davies, if this is gonna be a problem, I can —"

"She's lying, Russ. Her news director is all hot to trot for some shots of the inside of the house, and he'll do anything for the exclusive pictures, won't he? Up to and including having his most popular female anchor lay a sob story on us that sounds like it came out of some overbaked nineteen-forties melodrama. Nice try, though. Goddammit — it wouldn't surprise me if you and your crew were the ones who tried to break in."

Tanya looked startled. "What? Someone tried to break into the house?"

"Wrong reading, sister. Don't call us, we'll call you."

The hardness in Tanya's eyes now bled down into the rest of her face. "Fine, Mr. Davies. Have it your way."

The officer in the cruiser walked up to his partner on the porch, and the two of them whispered for a moment, then came down toward Davies and Tanya.

"Mr. Davies," said the officer who'd unlocked the door, "we just received orders that Ms. Claymore and her cameraman are to be allowed to photograph the inside of the house."

Behind her back, Tanya gave a thumbs-up to the driver of the news van.

"What'd you do," asked Davies, "have your boss call in a few favors, or did you just promise to fuck the mayor?"

"*Mr. Davies,*" said one of the officers. The warning in his voice was quite clear. "Ms. Claymore can photograph only the foyer and one other room. You'll all go in at the same time. I will personally escort Ms. Claymore and her cameraman into, through, and out of the house. She can only be inside for ten minutes, no more." He turned toward Tanya. "I'm sorry, Ms. Claymore, those're our orders. If you're inside longer than ten minutes, we're to consider it to be trespassing and are to act accordingly."

"Well," she said, straightening her jacket and brushing a thick strand of hair from her eye, "it's nice to see that the First Amendment's alive and well and being slowly choked to death in Cedar Hill."

"You should attend one of our cross burnings sometime," said Davies.

"You're a jerk."

"How would you know? You never come to the meetings."

"That's enough, boys and girls," said Officer Lock and Key. "Could we move this along, please?"

"One thing," said Tanya. "Would it be all right if we got some shots of the outside of the house first?"

"You'd better make it fast," said Davies. "I feel a record-time cleaning streak coming on."

"Or I could get them later."

Russell had already walked away from the group and was setting his supplies on the porch. The front door was open and the overhead light in the foyer had been turned on, and he caught sight of a giant red-black spider clinging to the right-side wall —

He turned quickly away and took a breath, pressing one of his hands against his stomach.

Mutt and Jeff laughed at him as they walked into the house.

Pete Cooper shook his head and dismissed Russell with a wave of his hand.

The ghosts of the Leonard family surrounded Russell on the porch, Irv placing a reassuring hand on the boy's shoulder while Miriam stroked his hair and the children looked on in silence.

Tanya Claymore's cameraman caught Russell's expression on tape.

It wasn't until Jackson Davies came up and took hold of his hand that Russell snapped out of his fugue and, without saying a word, got to the job.

And all along Merchant Street, shadowy forms in their house-coats and slippers watched from the safety of front porches.

9

Even more famous than Francis Paymer's phone call is Tanya Claymore's videotape of that night. It ran four and a half minutes and was the featured story on Channel 9's six o'clock news broadcast the following evening. Viewer response was so overwhelming that the tape was broadcast again at 7:00 and 11:00 P.M., then at 6:00 A.M. and noon the next day, then again, reedited to two minutes, forty-five seconds, at 7:00 and 11:00 P.M.

It is an extraordinary piece of work, and I showed it to my students that day. I eventually received an official reprimand from the school board for doing it — several of the students had night-mares about it, compounding those about the Utica killings — but I thought they needed to see and hear other people, strangers, express what they themselves were feeling.

The ghosts wanted to see it again, as well.

As did I — and why not? In a way, it is not so much about the aftermath of a tragedy as it is a chronicle of my birth, a point of reference on the map of my life: *This is where I really began.*

10

The tape opens with a shot of the Leonard house, bathed in shadow. Dim figures can be seen moving around its front porch. Sounds of footsteps. A muffled voice. A door being opened. A light coming on. Then another. And another.

Silhouettes appear in an upstairs window. Unmoving.

The camera pulls back slightly. Seen from the street, the lights from the house form a pattern of sorts as they slip out from the cracks in the particleboard over the downstairs windows.

It takes a moment, but suddenly the house looks like it's smiling. And it is not a pleasant smile.

All of this takes perhaps five seconds. Then Tanya Claymore's voice chimes softly in as she introduces herself and says, "I'm standing outside the house of Irving and Miriam Leonard at One-eighty-two Merchant Street, where, as you know, four nights ago their son Andy began a rampage that would leave over thirty people dead and over thirty more wounded."

At that very moment, someone inside the house kicks against the sheet of particleboard over the front bay window and wrenches it loose while a figure on the porch uses the claw end of a hammer to pull it free. The board comes away, and a massive beam of light explodes outward, momentarily filling the screen.

The camera smoothly shifts its angle to deflect the light. As it does so, Tanya Claymore resolves into focus like a ghost on the right side of the screen. Whether it was purposefully done this way or not, the effect is an eerie one.

She says, "Just a few moments ago, accompanied by two members of the Cedar Hill Police Department, a team of janitors entered the Leonard house to begin what will most certainly be one of the grimmest and most painful cleanups in recent memory."

She begins walking up toward the front porch, and the camera follows her. "Experts tell us that violence never really ends, no more than a symphony ceases to exist once the orchestra has stopped playing."

As she gets closer to the front door, the camera moves left while she moves to the right and says, "And like the musical resonances that linger in the mind after a symphony, the ugliness of violence remains."

By now she has stepped out of camera range, and the dark, massive bloodstain on the foyer wall can be clearly seen.

At the opposite end of the foyer, a mop head drenched in foamy soap suds can be seen slapping against the floor. It makes a wet, sickening sound. The camera slowly zooms in on the mop and focuses on the blood that is mixed in with the suds.

The picture cuts to a well-framed shot of Tanya's head and shoulders. It's clear she's in a different room, but which room it might be is hard to tell. When she speaks, her voice sounds slightly hollow and her words echo.

"This is the only time that a news camera will be allowed to photograph the interior of the Leonard house. You're about to see the kitchen where Miriam Leonard and her two daughters, Jessica Hamilton and Elizabeth Shannon, spent the last few seconds of their lives, and where seven-year-old Randy Hamilton, with two bullets in his small body, fought to save the life of his infant brother, Joseph.

"The janitors have not been in here yet, so you will be seeing the kitchen just as it was when investigators finished with it."

For a moment, it looks as if she might say something else, then she lowers her gaze and steps to the left as the camera moves slightly to the right and the kitchen is revealed.

The sight is numbing.

The kitchen is a slaughterhouse. The contrast between the blood and the off-white walls lunges out at the viewer like a snarling beast escaping from its cage.

The camera pans down to the floor and follows a single splash pattern that quickly grows denser and wider. Smeary heel- and footprints can be seen. The camera moves upward: part of a hand-print in the center of a lower counter door. The camera moves farther up: the mark of four bloody fingers on the edge of the sink. The camera moves over the top of the sink in a smooth, sweeping motion and stares at a thick, crusty black whirlpool twisting down into the garbage disposal drain.

The camera suddenly jerks up and whips around, blurring everything for a moment, a dizzying effect, then comes to an abrupt halt. Tanya is standing in the doorway of the kitchen with her right arm thrust forward. In her hand is a plastic pistol.

"This is a rough approximation of the last thing Elizabeth Shannon saw before her youngest brother shot her to death."

She remains still for a moment. Viewers cannot help but put themselves in Elizabeth's place.

Tanya slowly lowers the pistol and says, "The question for which there seems to be no answer, is, naturally, 'Why did he do it?'

"We put that question to several of the Leonards' neighbors this evening. Here's what some of them had to say about seventeen-year-old Andy, a young man who now holds the hideous distinction of having murdered more people in a single sweep than any killer in this nation's history."

Jump-cut to a quick, complicated series of shots.

Shot 1: An overweight man with obviously dyed hair saying, "I hear they found a tumor in his brain."

Insert shot: Merchant Street as it looked right after the shootings, clogged with police cruisers and ambulances and barricades to keep the growing crowd at bay.

Shot 2: A middle-aged woman with curlers in her hair saying, "I'll bet you anything it was his father's fault, him bein' a gun lover and all. I heard he beat on Andy a lot."

Insert shot: Lights from a police car rhythmically moving over a sheet-covered body on the front lawn.

Shot 3: An elderly gentleman in a worn and faded smoking jacket saying, "I read there were all these filthy porno magazines and videotapes stashed under his mattress, movies of women having relations with animals and pictures of babies in these leather sex getups . . ."

Insert shot: Two emergency medical technicians carrying a small black body bag down the front porch steps.

Shot 4: A thirtyish woman in an aerobics leotard saying, "I felt that he was always a little *too* nice, you know? He never got . . . angry about anything."

Insert shot: A black-and-white photograph of Andy taken from a high school yearbook. He's smiling, and his hair is neatly combed. He's wearing a tie. The voice of the woman in shot 4 can still be heard over this photo, saying, "He was always so calm. He never laughed much, but there was this . . . *smile* on his face all the time . . ."

Shot 5: A little girl of six, most of her hidden behind a parent's leg, saying, "I heard the house was haunted and that ghosts told him to do it . . ."

Insert shot: A recent color photograph of Andy and Russell Brennert at a Halloween party, both of them in costume. Russell is Frankenstein's monster, and Andy, his face painted to resemble a smiling skeleton, wears the black hooded cloak of the Grim Reaper. He's holding a plastic scythe whose tip is resting on top of Russell's head. The camera moves in on Russell's face until it fills the screen, then abruptly cuts to a shot of Russell in the foyer of the Leonard house. He's on his knees in front of the massive bloodstain on the wall. He's wearing rubber gloves and is pulling a large sponge from a bucket of soapy water. A caption at the bottom of the screen reads: "Russell Brennert, friend of the Leonard family."

He squeezes the excess water from the sponge and lifts it toward the stain, then freezes just before the sponge touches the wall.

He is trembling but trying very hard not to.

Tanya's shadow can be seen in the lower right-hand corner of the frame. She asks, "How do you feel right now?"

Russell doesn't answer her, only continues to stare at the stain.

Tanya says, "Russell?"

He blinks, shudders slightly, then turns his head and says, "Wh-what? I'm sorry."

"What were you thinking just then?"

He stares in her direction, then gives a quick glance to the camera. "Does he have to point that damn thing at me like that?"

"You have to talk to a reporter eventually. You might as well do it now."

He bites his lower lip for a second, then exhales and looks back at the stain.

"What're you thinking about, Russell?"

"I remember when Jessie first brought Theresa home from the hospital. Everyone came over here to see the new baby. You should've seen Andy's face."

Brennert's voice begins to quaver. The camera slowly moves in closer to his face. He is oblivious to it.

"He was so . . . *proud* of her. You'd have thought she was *his* daughter."

He reaches out with the hand not holding the sponge and presses it against the stain. "She was so tiny. But she couldn't stop giggling. I remember that she grabbed one of my fingers and started . . . chewing on it, you know, like babies will do? And Andy and I looked at each other and smiled and yelled, 'Uncle attack!' and he s-started . . . he started kissing her chubby little face, and I bent down and put my mouth against her tummy and started blowing real hard, you know, making belly-farts, and it tickled her so much because she started giggling and laughing and squealing and k-kicking her legs . . ."

The cords in his neck are straining. Tears well in his eyes, and he grits his teeth in an effort to hold them back.

"The rest of the family was enjoying the hell out of it, and Theresa kept squealing . . . that delicate little-baby laugh. Jesus Christ . . . he *loved* her. He loved her *so much,* and I thought she was the most precious thing . . . she always called me 'Uncleruss' — like it was all one word."

The tears are streaming down his cheeks now, but he doesn't seem aware of it.

"I held her against my chest. I helped give her baths in the sink. I changed her diapers — and I was a helluva lot better at it than Andy ever was . . . and now I gotta . . . I gotta scrub this off the wall."

He pulls back his hand, then touches the stain with only his index finger, tracing indiscernible patterns in the dried blood.

"This was her. This is all that's . . . that's left of the little girl she was, the baby she was . . . the woman she might have grown up to be. He loved her." His voice cracks, and he begins sobbing. "He loved all of them. And he never said anything to me. I didn't know, I swear to *Christ* I didn't know. This was her. I — oh, *goddammit!*"

He drops down onto his ass and folds his arms across his knees and lowers his head and weeps.

A few moments later, Jackson Davies comes in and sees him and kneels down and takes Russell in his arms and rocks gently back and forth, whispering, "It's all right now, it's okay, it's over, you're safe, hear me? Safe. Just . . . give it to me, kid . . . you're safe . . . that's it . . . give it to me . . ."

Davies looks up into the camera, and the expression on his face needs no explaining: *Turn that fucking thing off.*

Cut to: Tanya, outside the house again, standing next to the porch steps. On the porch, two men are removing the broken bay window. A few jagged shards of glass fall out and shatter on the porch. Another man begins sweeping up the shards and dumping them into a plastic trash barrel.

Tanya says, "Experts tell us that violence never really ends, that the healing process may never be completed, that some of the survivors will carry their pain for the rest of their lives."

A montage begins at this point, with Tanya's closing comments heard in voice-over.

The image, in slow motion, of police officers and EMTs moving sheet-covered and black-bagged bodies.

"People around here will say that the important thing is to remove as many physical traces of the violence as possible. Mop up the blood, gather the broken glass fragments into a bag and toss it in the trash, cover the scrapes, cuts, and stitches with bandages, then put your best face forward because it will make the unseen hurt easier to deal with."

The image of the sheet-covered bodies cross-fades into film of a memorial service held at Randy Hamilton's grade school. A small choir of children is gathered in front of a picture of Randy and begins to sing. Underneath Tanya's voice can now be heard a few dozen tiny voices softly singing "Let There Be Peace on Earth."

"But what of that 'unseen hurt'? A bruise will fade, a cut will get better, a scar can be taken off with surgery. Cedar Hill must now concern itself with finding a way to heal the scars that aren't so obvious."

The image of the children's choir dissolves into film of Mary Alice Hubert standing in the middle of the chaos outside the Leonard house on the night of the shootings. She is bathed in swirling lights and holds both of her hands pressed against her mouth. Her eyes seem unnaturally wide and are shimmering with tears. Police and EMTs scurry around her, but none stops to offer help. As the choir sings, "To take each moment and live each moment in peace e-ter-nal-ly," she drops slowly to her knees and lowers her head as if in prayer.

Tanya's voice-over continues: "Maybe tears will help. Maybe grieving in the open will somehow lessen the grip that the pain has on this community. Though we may never know what drove Andy Leonard to commit his horrible crime, the resonances of his slaughter remain."

Mary Alice dissolves into the image of Russell Brennert kneeling before the stain on the foyer wall. He is touching the dried blood with the index finger of his left hand.

The children's choir is building to the end of the song as Tanya says, "Perhaps Cedar Hill can find some brief comfort in these lines from a poem by German lyric poet Rainer Maria Rilke: 'Who weeps now anywhere in the world, without cause weeps in the world, weeps over me.'"

The screen fills with the image of Jackson Davies embracing Russell as sobs rack his body. Davies glares up at the camera, then closes his eyes and lowers his face, kissing the top of Russell's head. This image freezes as the children finish singing their hymn.

Tanya's voice once more, soft and low, no singsong mode this time, no inflection whatsoever: "For tonight, who weeps anywhere in the world, weeps for Cedar Hill and its wounds that may never heal.

"Tanya Claymore, Channel 9 News."

11

After the tape had finished playing and the lights in the classroom were turned back on, a student near the back of the room — so near, in fact, that Irv Leonard's ghost could have touched the boy's head, if he'd chosen to — raised his hand and asked, "What happened to all those people?"

"Tanya Claymore was offered a network job as a result of that tape. She eventually became a famous news anchor, had several public affairs with various coworkers, contracted AIDS, became a drug addict, and drove her car off a bridge one night. Jackson Davies remarried his ex-wife, and they live in Florida now. He'll turn seventy-one this year. Mary Alice Hubert died of a massive coronary six months after the killings. Most of Cedar Hill turned out for her funeral. Russell Brennert stayed in Cedar Hill and eventually bought into Jackson Davies's janitorial service. When Davies retired, Russell bought him out and now owns and operates the company. He'll turn fifty-two this year, and he looks seventy. He never married. He drinks too much and has the worst smoker's hack I've heard. He lives in a small four-room apartment with only one window — and that looks out on a parking lot. He told me he doesn't sleep well most of the time, but he has pills he can take for that. It still doesn't stop the dreams, though. He doesn't have many friends. It seems most people still believe he must have known what Andy was going to do. They've never forgiven him for that." I looked at the ghosts and smiled.

"He was so happy when I told him who I was. He hugged me like I was his long-lost son. He even wept. I invited him to come and visit me and my family this Christmas. I hope he comes. I don't think he will, but I can hope."

The room was silent for a moment, then a girl near the front, without raising her hand, said, "I knew Ted Gibson — he was the first person that Dyson shot. He . . . he always wanted me to go to Utica with him to try their ice cream. I was supposed to go with him that day. I couldn't . . . and I don't even remember why. Isn't that terrible?" Her lower lip quivered, and a tear slipped down her cheek. "Ted got killed, and all I could think of when I heard was I wonder what kind of ice cream he was eating."

That ended my story, and began theirs.

One by one, some more hesitant than others, some angrier, some more confused, my students began talking about their dead and wounded friends, and how they missed them, and how frightened they were that something so terrible could happen to someone they knew, maybe even themselves, had the circumstances been different.

The ghosts of Cedar Hill listened, and cried for my students' pain, and understood.

12

Before they left that day, someone asked me why I thought Andy had done it. I stopped myself from giving the real answer — what I perceive to be the real answer — and told them, "I think losing out on the scholarship did something to him. I think he looked at his future and saw himself being stuck in a factory job for the rest of his life and he became angry — at himself, at his family, at the town where he lived. If he had no future, then why should anyone else?"

"Then why didn't he kill his grandmother and Russell, too? Why didn't he kill you?"

Listen to my silence after he asked this.

Finally, I said, "I wish I knew."

I should have gone with my first answer.

I think it runs much deeper than mere anger. I think when loneliness and fear drive a person too deep inside himself, faith shrivels into hopelessness; I think when tenderness diminishes and bitterness intensifies, rancor becomes a very sacred thing; and I think when the need for some form of meaningful human contact becomes an affliction, a soul can be tainted with madness and allow violence to rage forth as the only means of genuine relief, a final, grotesque expression of alienation that evokes *feeling something* in the most immediate and brutal form.

The ghosts of my birth seem to agree with that.

You read the account of the Utica killings in the paper and then move quickly on to news about a train wreck in Iran or a flood in Brazil or riots in India or the NASDAQ figures for the week, and unless you are from the town of Utica or in some way knew one of the victims or the man who killed them, you forget all about it because you can't understand how a person, a *normal enough* person, a person like you and me, could do such a horrible thing. But he did, and others like him will, and all you can hope for is not to be one of the victims. You pray you will be safe. It is easier by far to understand the complicated financial maneuverings of Wall Street kingpins than an isolated burst of homicidal rage in a small Midwestern city.

They are out there, these psychos, and always will be. Another Andy Leonard could be bagging your groceries; the next Bruce Dyson might be that fellow who checks your gas meter every month. You just don't know — and there's the rub.

You *won't* know until it's too late.

I wish you well, and I wish you peace. My penance, if indeed that's what it is, must nearly be paid by now. The ghosts don't come around as much as they used to. The last time I saw them was the night my son was born; they came to the hospital to look at him, and to tell me that I was right, that those prayers spoken by strangers for the baby I once was are still protecting me, and will keep myself and my family safe from harm.

I'll pray, as well. I'll pray that the next Andy Leonard or Bruce Dyson doesn't get that last little push that topples him over the line: I'll pray that these psychos go on bagging groceries or checking gas meters or delivering pizzas and never raise a hand to kill, that the police in some other small town will be quick to stop them from getting to you if they ever do cross the line; I'll pray that no one ever picks up a paper and reads your name among the list of victims.

Because that kind of violence never really ends.

I hold my son. I kiss my wife and daughter.

The story is over.

Except for those who survived.

We continue.

Safe from harm, I pray.

Safe . . .

THOMAS H. COOK

Fatherhood

FROM *Murder for Revenge*

WATCHING THEM from a distance, the way she rocked backward and forward in her grief, her arms gathered around his lifeless body, I could feel nothing but a sense of icy satisfaction, relishing the fact that both of them had finally gotten what they deserved. Death for him. For her, perpetual mourning.

She'd worn a somber gown for the occasion, her face sunk deep inside a cavernous black hood. She stared down at him and ran her fingers through his blood-soaked hair, her features so hideously distorted by her misery it seemed impossible that she'd ever been young and beautiful, or ever felt delight in anything.

By then the years had so divided us and embittered me that I could no longer think of her as someone I'd once loved. But I *had* loved her, and there were times when, despite everything, I could still recall the single moment of intense happiness I'd had with her.

She'd been only a girl when we first met, the town beauty. Practically the only beautiful thing in the town at all, for it was a small, drab place set down in the middle of a desert waste. To find something beautiful in such a place was nearly miracle enough.

She was already being pursued by the local boys, of course. They were dazzled by her black hair and dark oval eyes, skin that gave off a striking olive glow. I yearned for her no less ardently than they, but I kept my distance.

Looking out my shop window, I would often see her as she swept down the street, heading toward the market, a large basket on her arm. Coming back, the basket now filled with fruit and vegetables, she'd sometimes stop to wipe a line of sweat from her forehead, her eyes glancing briefly toward the very window where I stood, watching her, and from which I always quickly retreated.

The fact is, she frightened me. I was afraid of the look that might come into her eyes if she saw me staring at her, their pity, perhaps even contempt, for a portly, middle-aged bachelor who worked in a dusty shop, lived alone in a single musty room, had no prospects for the future, and who had nothing to offer a vibrant young woman like herself.

And so I never expected to speak to her or approach her in any way. To the extent that she would ever know me, it seemed certain it would be as the anonymous figure she sometimes noticed as she made her way to the market, a person of no consequence or distinction, as flat and featureless in her mind as the old stones she trod upon. My fate would be to watch her silently forever, see her life unfold from behind my shop window, first as a young woman hastening to the market, then as a bride strolling arm-in-arm with her new husband, finally as a mother with children following behind her, her beauty deepening with the years, becoming fuller and richer while I kept my post at the window, growing old and sickly, a ghostly, gray-haired figure whose life had finally added up to nothing more than a long and fruitless longing.

Then it happened. One of those accidents that make a perpetual mystery of life, that bless the unworthy and doom the deserving, and which give to all of nature the aspect of a flighty, cruel, and unloving queen.

One of my customers had tethered a horse to the post outside my shop. It was sleek and beautiful, and coming back from the market, the girl of my dreams stopped to admire it. First she patted its haunches. Then she moved up the twitching flanks to stroke its moist black muzzle. Finally, she fed it an ear of corn from the overflowing basket she'd placed at her feet.

"It is yours?" she asked me as I came out the door, my arms filled with the wood I used in my trade.

I stopped, astonished to see her staring at me, unable to believe that she'd actually addressed her question to me.

"No," I said. "It belongs to one of my customers."

She returned her attention to the horse, drawing her fingers down the side of its neck, twining her fingers in its long brown mane. "He must be very rich to have a horse like this." She looked at the wood still gathered in my arms. "What do you do for him?"

"Build things. Tables. Chairs. Whatever he wants."

She offered a quick smile, patted the horse a final time, then retrieved her basket from the street and sauntered slowly away, her brown arms swinging girlishly in the afternoon light, her whole manner so casual and lighthearted that only a sudden burst of air from my mouth made me realize that during the time I'd watched her stroll away from me, I had not released a breath.

I didn't talk to her again for almost three months, though I saw her in the street no less often than before. A young man sometimes joined her now, as beautifully tanned as she was, with curly black hair. He was tall and slender, and his step was firm, assured, the walk of a boy who had never wanted for anything, who'd inherited good looks and would inherit lots of money, the sort whose bright future is entirely assured. He would marry her, I knew, for he seemed to have the beauty and advantage that would inevitably attract her. For days I watched as they came and went from the market together, holding hands as young lovers do, while I stood alone, shrunken and insubstantial, a husk the smallest breeze could send skittering down the dusty street.

Then, just as suddenly, the boy disappeared, and she was alone again. There were other changes, too. Her walk struck me as less lively than it had been before, her head lowered slightly, as I had never seen it, her eyes cast toward the paving stones.

That anyone, even a spoiled, wealthy youth, might cast off such a girl as she seemed inconceivable to me. Instead, I imagined that he'd died or been sent away for some reason, that she had fallen under the veil of his loss, and might well be doomed to dwell within its shadows forever, a fate in one so young and beautiful that struck me as inestimably forlorn.

And so I acted, stationing myself on the little wooden bench outside my shop, waiting for her hour after hour, day after day, until she finally appeared again, her hair draped over her shoulders like shimmering black wings.

"Hello," I said.

She stopped and turned toward me. "Hello."

"I have something for you."

She looked at me quizzically, but did not draw back as I approached her.

"I made this for you," I said as I handed it to her.

It was a horse I'd carved from an olive branch.

"It's beautiful," she said, smiling quietly. "Thank you."

"You're welcome," I said and, like one who truly loves, asked nothing in return.

We met often after that. She sometimes came into my shop, and over time I taught her to build and mend, feel the textures and qualities of wood. She worked well with her hands, and I enjoyed my new role of craftsman and teacher. The real payment was in her presence, however — the tenderness in her voice, the light in her eyes, the smell of her hair — how it lingered long after she'd returned to her home on the other side of town.

Soon, we began to walk the streets together, then along the outskirts of the village. For a time she seemed happy, and it struck me that I had succeeded in lifting her out of the melancholy I had found her in.

Then, rather suddenly, it fell upon her once again. Her mood darkened and she grew more silent and inward. I could see that some old trouble had descended upon her, or some new one that I had not anticipated and which she felt it necessary to conceal. Finally, late one afternoon when we found ourselves on a hill outside the village, I put it to her bluntly.

"What's the matter?" I asked.

She shook her head, and gave no answer.

"You seem very worried," I added. "You're too young to have so much care."

She glanced away from me, let her eyes settle upon the far fields. The evening shade was falling. Soon it would be night.

"Some people are singled out to bear a certain burden," she said.

"All people feel singled out for the burdens they bear."

"But people who feel chosen. For some special suffering, I mean. Do you think they ever wonder why it was them, why it wasn't someone else?"

"They all do, I'm sure."

"What do you think your burden is?"

Never to be loved by you, I thought, then said, "I don't think I have one burden in particular." I shrugged. "Just to live. That's all."

She said nothing more on the subject. For a time, she was silent, but her eyes moved about restlessly. It was clear that much was going on in her mind.

At last she seemed to come to a conclusion, turned to me, and said, "Do you want to marry me?"

I felt the whole vast world close around my throat, so that I only stared at her silently until, at last, the word broke from me. "Yes." I should have stopped, but instead I began to stammer. "But I know that you could not possibly . . . that I'm not the one who can . . . that you must be . . ."

She pressed a single finger against my lips.

"Stop," she said. Then she let her body drift backward, pressing herself against the earth, her arms lifting toward me, open and outstretched and welcoming.

Any other man would have leapt at such an opportunity, but fear seized me and I couldn't move.

"What is it?" she asked.

"I'm afraid."

"Of what?"

"That I wouldn't be able to . . ."

I could see that she understood me, recognized the source of my disabling panic. There seemed no point in not stating it directly. "I'm a virgin," I told her.

She reached out and drew me down to her. "So am I," she said.

I didn't know how it was supposed to feel, but after a time she grew so warm and moist, my pleasure in her rising and deepening with each offer and acceptance, that I finally felt my whole body release itself to her, quaking and shivering as she gathered me more tightly into her arms. I had never known such happiness, nor ever would again, since to make love to the one you love is the greatest joy there is.

For a moment we lay together, she beneath me, breathing quietly, the side of her face pressed against mine.

"I love you," I told her, then lifted myself from her so that I could see her face.

She was not looking at me, nor even in my direction. Instead, her eyes were fixed on the sky that hung above us, the bright coin of the moon, the scattered stars, glistening with tears as she peered upward to where I knew her thoughts had flown. Away from me. Away. Away. Toward the one she truly loved and still longed for, the boy whose beauty was equal to her own, and for whom I could serve as nothing more than a base and unworthy substitute.

*

And yet I loved her, married her, then watched in growing astonishment as her belly grew day by day until our son was born.

Our son. So the townspeople called him. So she called him and I called him. But I knew that he was not mine. His skin had a different shade, his hair a different texture. He was tall and narrow at the waist, I was short and stocky. There could be no doubt that he was the fruit of other loins than mine. Not my child, at all, but rather the son of that handsome young boy she'd strolled the town streets with, and whose disappearance, whether by death or desertion, had left her so bereft and downcast that I'd tried to cheer her with a carved horse, walked the streets and byways with her, soothed and consoled her, sat with her on the far hillside, even made love to her there, and later married her, and in consequence of all that now found myself the parent and support of a child who was clearly not my own.

He was born barely six months after our night of love. Born weighty and full bodied and with a great mass of black hair, so that it could not be doubted that he had lived out the full term of his nurture.

From the first moment, she adored him, coddled him, made him the apple of her eye. She read to him and sang to him, and wiped his soiled face and feet and hindquarters. He was her "dear one," her "beloved," her "treasure."

But he was none of these things to me. Each time I saw him, I also saw his father, that lank and irresponsible youth who'd stolen my wife's love at so early an age that it could never be recaptured by her or reinvested in me. He had taken the love she might have better spent elsewhere, and in doing that, he had left both of us impoverished. I hated him, and I yearned for vengeance. But he had fled to parts unknown, and so I had no throat to squeeze, no flesh to cut. In his stead, I had only his son. And thus, I took out my revenge on a boy who, as the years passed, looked more and more like his youthful father, who had the same limber gait and airy disposition, a boy who had little use for my craft, took no interest in my business, preferring to linger in the town square, talking idly to the old men who gathered there, or while away the hours by reading books on the very hillside where I'd made love to his mother, and who, even as I'd released myself to her, had slept in the warm depths of her flesh.

I often thought of that. The fact that my "son" had been inside her that night, that my own seed had labored to reach a womb already hardened against them. Sometimes, lost in such dreadful speculations I would strike out at him, using my tongue like a knife, hurling glances toward him like balls of flame.

"Why do you hate him so?" my wife asked me time after time during those early years. "He wants to love you, but you won't let him."

My response was always the same, an icy silence, followed by a shrug.

And so the years passed, my mood growing colder and more sullen as I continued to live as a stranger in my own household. In the evening, I would sit by the fire and watch as a wife who had deceived me and a son who was not my son played games or read together, laughed at private jokes, and discussed subjects in which I had no interest and from whose content and significance I felt purposely excluded. Everything they did served only to heighten my solitary rage. The sound of their laughter was like a blade thrust into my ear, and when they huddled in conversation at the far corner of the room, their whispers came to me like the hissing of serpents.

During this time my wife and I had terrible rows. Once, as I tried to leave the room, she grabbed my arm and whirled me back around. "You're driving him from the house," she said. "He'll end up on the street if you don't stop it. Is that what you want?"

For once, I answered with the truth. "Yes, I do. I don't want him to live here anymore."

She looked at me, utterly shocked not only by what I'd said, but the spitefulness with which I'd said it. "Where do you expect him to live?"

I refused to retreat. "I don't care where he lives," I answered. "He's old enough to be on his own." There was a pause before I released the words I'd managed to choke back for years. "And if he can't take care of himself, then let his *real* father take care of him for a while."

With that, I watched as tears welled up in her eyes before she turned and fled the room.

But even after that, she didn't leave. Nor did her son. And so, in the end, I had to stay in the same house with them, live a life of silent, inner smoldering.

A year later he turned fifteen. He was nearly a foot taller than I was by then. He'd also gained something of a reputation as a scholar, a fact that pleased his mother as much as it disgusted me. For what was the use of all his learning if the central truth of his life remained unrevealed? What good all his command of philosophy and theology if he would never know who his father was, never know where he'd gotten his curly black hair and lean physique, nor even that keenness of mind which, given the fact that he thought me his natural father, must have struck him as the most inexplicable thing of all?

But for all our vast differences of mind and appearance, he never seemed to doubt that I truly was his father. He never asked about other relatives, nor about any matter pertaining to his origins or birth. When I called him to his chores, he answered, "Yes, Father," and when he asked my permission, it was always, "May I, Father?" do this or that. Indeed, he appeared to relish using the word. So much so, that I finally decided it was his way of mocking me, calling me "Father" at every opportunity for no other reason than to emphasize the point either that he knew I was not his father, or that he wished that I were not.

For fifteen years I had endured the insult he represented to me, my wife's deviousness, her false claim of virginity, the fact that I'd had to maintain a charade from the moment of his birth, claiming a paternity that neither I nor any of my neighbors for one moment believed to be genuine. It had not been easy, but I had borne it all. But with his final attempt to humiliate me by means of this exaggerated show of filial obedience and devotion, this incessant repetition of "Father, this" and "Father, that," he had finally broken the back of my self-control.

And so I told him to get out, that he was no longer welcome in my house, that no more meals would be provided, nor any bed for him to sleep in, nor a fire to warm him, nor clothes for his back.

We stood together in the backyard, he watching me silently while I told him all this. He'd grown a beard during the preceding few weeks, his hair had fallen to his shoulders, and he'd taken to going barefoot. "Yes, Father" was all he said when I finished. Then he turned, walked back into the house, gathered a few personal items in a plain cloth knapsack, and headed down the street, leaving only a brief note for his mother, its sneeringly ironic message clearly intended to render me one final injury, "Tell Father that I love him, and that I always will."

*

I didn't see him again for eighteen years, though I knew that my wife maintained contact, sometimes even making long treks to visit whatever town he was passing through. She would return quite exhausted, especially in the later years, when her hair was gray and her once radiant skin had become so easily bruised that the gentlest pressure left marks upon it.

I never asked about her trips, never asked a single question about how her son was doing. Nor did I miss him in the least. And yet, his absence never gave me the relief I'd expected. For it didn't seem enough, my simply throwing him out of the house. I had thought it might satisfy my need to get even with his father and my wife for blighting my life, forcing me to live a transparent and humiliating lie. But it hadn't.

Vengeance turned out to be a hungrier animal than I'd supposed. Nothing seemed to satisfy it. The more I thought of my "son," the more I got news of his various travels and accomplishments, heard tales of the easy life he had, merely wandering about, living off the bounty of others, the more I wanted to strike at him again, this time more brutally.

He had become quite well known by then, at least in the surrounding area. He'd organized a kind of traveling magic show, people said, and had invented an interesting patter to go along with his tricks. But when they went on to describe the things he said, it seemed to me that the "message" he offered was typical of the time. He was no different from the countless others who believed that they'd found the secret to fulfillment, and that their mission was to reveal that secret to the pathetic multitude.

I knew better, of course. I knew that the only happiness that is possible comes by accepting how little life has to offer. But knowing something and being able to live according to that knowledge are two different things. I knew that I'd been wronged, and that I had to accept it. But I could never put it behind me, never get over the feeling that someone had to pay for the lie my wife had told me, the false son whose very existence kept that lie whirling madly in my brain. I suppose that's why I went after him again. Just the fact that I couldn't live without revenge, couldn't live without exacting another, graver penalty.

It took me three years to bring him down, but in the end it was worth it.

*

She never knew that I was behind it. That for the preceding three years I'd silently waged my campaign against him, writing anonymous letters, warning various officials that he had to be watched, investigated, that he said violent things, urged people to violence, that he was the leader of a secret society pledged to destroy everything the rest of us held dear. By using bits of information gathered from my wife, I kept them informed about his every move so that agents could be sent to look and listen. He was arrogant and smug, and he had his real father's confidence that he could get away with anything. I knew it was just a matter of time before he'd say or do something for which he could be arrested.

I did all of that, but she never knew, never had the slightest hint that I was orchestrating his destruction. I realized just how fully I had deceived her only a few minutes after they'd finally peeled her away from his dead body and took it away to prepare it for burial. We were walking down the hill together, away from the place where they'd hung him, my wife muttering about how terrible it was, about how brutally the mob had taunted and reviled him. Such people could always be stirred up against someone like our son, she said, a "true visionary," as she called him, who'd never had a chance against them.

I answered her sharply. "He was a fraud," I said. "He didn't have the answer to anything."

She shook her head, stopped, and turned back toward the hill. It was not only the place where they'd executed him, but also the place where we'd first made love, an irony I'd found delicious as they'd led him to the execution site, his eyes wandering and disoriented, as if he'd never expected anything so terrible to happen to him, as if he were like his real father, wealthy and irresponsible, beyond the fate of ordinary men.

A wave of malicious bitterness swept over me. "He got what he deserved," I blurted out.

She seemed hardly to hear me, her eyes still fixed on the hill, as if the secret of his fate were written on its rocky slope. "No one told me it would be like this," she said. "That I would lose him in this way."

I grasped her arm and tugged her on down the hill. "A mother is never prepared for what happens to her child," I said. "You just have to accept it, that's all."

She nodded slowly, perhaps accepting it, then walked on down the hill with me. Once at home, she lay down on her bed. From the adjoining room, I could hear her weeping softly, but I had no more words for her, so I simply left her to her grief.

Night had begun to fall, but the storm that had swept through earlier that day had passed, leaving a clear blue twilight in its wake. I walked to the window and looked out. Far away, I could see the hill where he'd been brought low at last. It struck me that even in the last moments of his life, he'd tried to get at me just one more time. In my mind I could see him glaring down at me, goading me in exactly the way he had before I'd kicked him out of the house, emphasizing the word *Father* when he'd finally spoken to me. He'd known very well that this was the last time he'd ever talk to me. That's why he'd made such a production of it, staring right into my eyes, lifting his voice over the noise of the mob so that everybody would be sure to hear him. He'd been determined to demonstrate his defiance, his bitterness, the depth of his loathing for me. Even so, he'd been clever enough to pretend that it was the mob he cared about. But I knew that his whole purpose had been to humiliate me one last time by addressing me directly. "Father," he'd said in that hateful tone of his, "Father, forgive them, for they know not what they do."

JEFFERY DEAVER

Wrong Time, Wrong Place

FROM *The Best of the Best*

HE SAW THE CAR five miles down the road, lights swinging left
and right as the driver went through the Harrier Pass switchbacks.

Pretty fast for this road, he thought. And found his damp right
hand resting on the butt of his revolver.

"Mobile One." The woman's voice clattered from the loud-
speaker on top of the Dodge. "Hey, Hal. You there, Hal?"

He reached inside the squad car and snagged the microphone
from the dash.

"Go ahead, Hazel."

"Cold out there?"

It was only mid-September but the weather in the Green Mountains could claim lives as early as October, and the wet air tonight
was raw as torn metal.

"'Course it's cold. Where's Billy?"

"On Seventeen. 'Bout, lessee, five miles from the interstate.
Stopped a drunk and's got him in the car 'cause what else is he
gonna do with him? Right? But no sign of the perps."

She said the last word as if she'd been waiting a long time to
drop it into a sentence and Runyer guessed this might've been
the case. Pequot County had plenty of drunks and disorderlies, a
few sickos, and, because of the school, cut-ups galore. But real
honest-to-God *perpetrators* . . . well, Hal Runyer hadn't had many
of them.

"Anything more on the job?" he asked.

"What job?"

"The heist," he said, irritated. "The stickup. The robb-er-y?"

"Oh, yeah. S'why I called. We got a call from *Captain* Jarrett. At

Troop G. Known him ten years and he *still* calls himself Cap-tain Jarrett. Anyway, he says the FBI's taking over. Should we be feeling bad about that?"

"No, Hazel. We should be feeling good about that." Runyer watched the lights grow closer. The car was moving damn fast. On the shoulder a time or two but not drunk careless. More *urgent* careless. He reached inside and flicked on the light bar. "Listen. Where's Rudy? He at Irvine, like I told him?"

"Gaithersberg Road and Fifteen. That where you told him?"

"Close enough. When're the feds coming up?"

"Dunno. I can —"

"S'okay. I gotta go, Hazel. Here's a car needs checking."

"Roger, Sheriff." And added a snappy "Over and out." Which Hazel always looked forward to ending transmissions with.

"Yeah, yeah, out."

The wind blew hard and Runyer shivered. Around him were empty shacks and rusting cultivators and the black spikes of a billion trees. This was still supposedly leaf season but the weather'd been mean the past two weeks, and instead of going to vibrant reds and golds the leaves had suddenly turned sick yellow and leapt off the trees. They now lay on the ground like a ragged sou'wester covering the body of a drowned fisherman.

He watched the car lights growing closer through the dank mist, his hand kneading his revolver.

It'd been the biggest robbery in the history of Pequot County.

That evening, just before closing, a Secure Courier truck had pulled up to the back door of the Minuteman Bank & Trust in downtown Andover.

Witnesses said the whole thing couldn't have taken more than ten seconds. The driver and his first assistant opened the truck's door, and the robbers "were just *there,*" Frank Metger, the bank's security guard, said. "I dunno where they were hiding."

He'd gone for his Smith & Wesson but a third robber stepped out of the shadows on the concrete retaining wall behind the strip mall and let loose one shot with his pistol, one of those huge ones with a telescopic sight on it, like the boys were always admiring down at Baxter's Guns but never buying. "Ka-poweee! Hit 'bout an inch from my head," Frank said. "And I went down fast. I'm not the least ashamed to say it. Not that I couldn'ta taken him, I had the old Smittie out and cocked."

The perps jumped into two cars and sped off in opposite directions, taking with them three-quarters of a million dollars.

Not long after which the phone rang in Hal Runyer's split-level. Lisa Lee handed him the cordless, interrupting some important business with his son. Runyer listened to his deputy and realized that the radio-controlled Piper Cub, laid out like a surgical patient in front of them, would have to remain wingless for the rest of the evening, at least.

Now lights like dying suns appeared behind the trees and the approaching car sped through the last curve before the roadblock. The surprised driver skidded the silver Lexus, exhaust simmering, to a stop ten feet from the cruiser.

Two men inside, their eyes following Runyer's with curiosity. The driver seemed amused. They were young. Lean. Buzz cuts under worn baseball caps. Runyer got a faint whiff of beer and thought: Students.

"Hey, Officer," the driver said cheerfully. "Roadblock, huh? Just like the movies."

"That's right. How you fellas doing tonight?"

"Well, truth is we're not finding as many young lovelies as we'd hoped but 'side from that we're doing fine."

"Good, Runyer said and glanced across the seat. "You doing fine, too?"

"Yessir," the passenger said. "Top-notch. You bet."

"What exactly's the problem, Officer?"

They seemed like good boys, fun-loving, here in Andover on jock scholarships, armed with Dad's fine car and plenty of pocket money. But one of Runyer's first lessons from his predecessor had been that, even in sleepy Andover, the friendliest-seeming folk often aren't and you've got to be most cautious of the ones leaning hard to be on your side.

The driver kept both his hands on the wheel. His buddy's right hand was just coming up from the crack beside the right-hand door. Putting it away at least — whatever *it* was — instead of picking it up. The bottle probably. But they weren't impaired and Runyer decided to let a DUI check go.

"Where you headed?"

The driver grinned. "Just, you know, out for a drive."

The flashlight strayed into the backseat. No ski masks or black pullovers. No canvas bags chocked with enough money to live on for a hundred years, in Pequot County at least. But what about the trunk?

"There's some bar we heard about," the passenger said. "I don't know. Some action."

"Action?"

The young man swallowed. "Well, we were looking for some action. That's what I meant. You know."

Runyer noticed that with every word his friend said, the driver was getting madder and madder. And he thought: Problem. We got ourselves a problem here. How do I handle it? He didn't know. The bulk of arrests in Andover involved liquor, pot, or cars. Runyer couldn't remember the last time he'd actually handcuffed somebody. He wondered if he could still do it without embarrassing himself or tearing flesh.

"I wonder if I could see your license and registration."

"Well, you know, it's funny," the driver said, the words clipped. Like his mind was somewhere in front of his voice. "Ninety-nine times out of a hundred you got your license with you. That one time you don't, you get stopped."

"You don't." Runyer offered a grin of his own. "How 'bout the vehicle's registration?"

"Sure, Officer."

He searched the glove compartment and door pocket, then found it in the sun visor. The driver glanced at the small card as he passed it out the window.

Runyer read it and looked up. "That's you? Thomas Gibson?"

"Yessir."

The sheriff stared at the slip of DMV cardboard, afraid to take his eyes off it. Reading the name over and over, as if it was a fax about a deceased loved one.

Thomas Gibson . . .

Of 3674 Muller Lane, Portsmouth, Vermont.

The best-known OB-GYN in Pequot County. Who'd delivered Runyer's sister's first not long ago.

Who'd called Hazel exactly thirty minutes before the Minuteman robbery to report his car stolen.

"Fine," Runyer said earnestly. "Good." Wondering why on earth he had.

Pistol out. Stepping back, pointing it from one of the disgusted, sneering faces to the other. Their smiles were gone.

"I'm gonna say some things and you better listen. I want to see all four of those hands at all times. If one of them disappears, I'm shooting whoever it belongs to. If you reach for the gearshift lever, I'm shooting you. I'm going to ask you to get out of the car in a minute and if either of you runs, I'm shooting you. We clear on that?"

"Officer, come *on*," the passenger whined.

"Shut up, Earl," the driver barked.

Something flickered in the distance. A flash of light. The driver glanced in his rearview mirror and gave a slight smile. Another car was coming down the road and Hal Runyer knew in his heart it was their partner.

"Driver, hands on the wheel. And you, put 'em on the dash."

"You —"

"Do it!"

"Oh-*kay*," the driver snapped. This was all a huge inconvenience to him.

Earl's shrill voice: "Gare, what're we gonna do?"

"You're going to be quiet is what *you're* going to do," Gare muttered, flexing his long fingers.

The second car had whipped through the switchbacks and was bottoming out of Harrier Pass. The lights vanished as the car went behind a hill. It'd be at the roadblock in three minutes.

"Driver, leave your left hand on the wheel and with your right reach out and open the door." Was this how he should do it? He thought so. But he wished he knew for sure.

Gare sighed and did what he was told. He climbed slowly from the car, keeping his hands extended.

Earl was looking like a spooked bird, eyes flicking sideways in jerky little movements.

Runyer pitched his only pair of cuffs to Gare. "Get those on. Bet you know how."

Light glowed on the near horizon of the highway. Runyer could hear the urgent shush of the tires on the damp asphalt.

Gare glanced toward the light and grinned slightly. He clicked the cuff on one hand.

"Come on, man," Earl said to Runyer. "Can't we work something out? We got plenty of money."

"Oh, shut *up*," Gare barked.

"So. We're adding bribery to all this."

Another flicker of light. The car was growing closer.

Gare tensed and Runyer's pistol lifted slightly. "I want that second cuff on *now!*"

"How 'bout my boy Earl? No bracelets for 'm?"

The approaching car wasn't more than a hundred feet away. "*I* have to put those on, I'll ratchet 'em good and tight and leave 'em that way. You'll wish you'd done it yourself."

Earl opened the passenger door. Something fell to the ground at his feet. No bottle. It was metal.

"Freeze right there."

Earl ducked a little but Runyer brought him up to standing again with the muzzle.

"Look, Officer —" Gare began. The gun swung back his way.

The car rounded the curve.

What do I do? With three of 'em here, what do I *do?* I should call in for help. Should've done that right up front. Hell. And the squad car's thirty feet away.

"Now. I'm not telling you again."

Click, click. The cuffs were on. Runyer led Gare to the front fender. Keeping his pistol aimed at Earl, he eased Gare facedown onto the hood, bent at the waist. His body made a wingless angel in the dew on the glittery silver paint.

"Now you," Runyer said to Earl. "Come here."

The car came around the curve fast and skidded to a stop. The man behind the wheel opened the door and it took Runyer no more than a second to glance at his face and realize he wasn't the partner. But a second was all Gare needed. Fast as falling rock he snapped upright. His cuffed hands slammed into Runyer's head, tearing his ear with the links. He grabbed the sheriff's gun hand.

Earl bent fast at the knees and came up with the gun that had fallen out of the car when he'd opened the door.

Runyer held onto Gare like a college wrestler. The men rolled on the ground, through wet grass, mulchy leaves, oil, deer piss. Struggling to get Gare down and losing — the small man was strong as roots and Runyer had to keep away from the teeth especially.

"Don't *move,*" Earl screamed, waving his gun in their direction.

"Officer!" the other driver called.

"Get outa here," Runyer shouted.

The man hesitated only for a moment, then turned to leap back into his car.

Earl ran toward him. "You, stay there! Stay there!"

The gunshot was a short, sharp crack, swallowed by the misty dampness. The man flew backward.

Oh, Lord . . .

Then Gare elbowed the sheriff hard in the gut and won the pistol. He pressed the muzzle against Runyer's throat, cocked the gun.

"No," Runyer whispered.

"Maybe," Gare answered smartly, grinning. He rubbed the muzzle over the sheriff's skin.

"Look what I done, Gare," Earl whispered. "He's dead. His whole head . . . look."

"Oh, Jesus Christ, quit whining! Put that sack o' shit in the car and get rid of it. Do it!"

Earl gazed down at the limp body of the man he'd just killed. The eyes were open; they caught white moonlight and glowed eerily. Earl looked uneasily at his partner, wiping his palm on his unclean jeans. "Oh, man." Finally he grabbed the body, muscled it into the car.

"Where — ?"

"The *bushes!* Drive it into the bushes! Where d'you think?"

As Earl hid the car, Gare turned back to Runyer. He fished the cuff key from his uniform pocket and unlocked them. "Now," he mocked, "we've got some rules. One is, get on your belly." He shoved Runyer onto the cold asphalt.

"Rule two is you give me any crap and you get shot."

"Gare —"

"What? *What?*"

"Tell him it wasn't my fault. I mean, shooting that guy."

"Of *course* it wasn't. It was *his* fault, Earl." He nodded at Runyer. "He shouldn't've stopped us."

"Look, mister," Runyer said, "so far it's just manslaughter. If you —"

Gare sighed, lifted the revolver, and pulled the trigger.

The powder granules hurt most of all, stinging Runyer's face and his right hand, which he'd lifted defensively. He hardly felt the bullet, other than the punch in the stomach and the snap of his rib.

"Oh." Runyer sank down on his elbow. "My." He felt loose inside, unattached.

"I *told* you rule number two. Weren't you listening?"

"Lisa Lee," Runyer whispered. He held his belly. But not too tight. He was afraid to touch the bullet hole.

The cold autumn wind was powerful in the Green Mountains. It carried sounds a long way despite the hilly terrain. They could hear the sirens real clear.

The men looked up at the spiky horizon and saw a carnival of flashing lights.

"Two of 'em," Gare said. "Shit."

"Mebbe three. Could be three."

Gare ran to the squad car, got inside. He shut off the light bar, then started the car over the cliff, stepping out just before it nosed over. It fell with the sound of crushing foliage.

Through a peppery haze Runyer saw Gare lift his head and look up into the hills. There were two faint yellow lights one hundred yards away. Porch lights. They flickered through the branches.

"Up there. Let's go." He nodded at the twin glow through the mist.

Runyer moaned as a wash of pain flowed through him.

Their eyes turned to him. The men looked at each other, then walked toward him.

He wasn't going to plead, he told himself, hearing the skittery boots on the asphalt.

Gare and Earl stood over him, looking down.

"Please," Runyer whispered.

"Get him in the car," Gare said to Earl. "Move."

He drove up the hill real slow, no lights, and that was how he surprised the couple in the cabin.

While Earl hid the Lexus out back, Gare kicked the door in, fast, pushing Runyer in front of him, poking the gun toward the man and woman, who sat on the couch, drinking wine. She barked a fast scream and the trim, white-haired man turned fast toward the shotgun over the mantel.

Through the haze of his pain Runyer was thinking: No, no. Don't do it.

But Gare cocked the pistol and the man stopped in his tracks at the sound, turned back, hands up high, like in a movie. He was so surprised by the break-in that for a minute he didn't even know he was supposed to be afraid. He squinted at Gare and the sheriff, then glanced at his wife. And you could see his face just cave, like loose shale. "Please," he said, the word rattling from his throat. "Please don't hurt us."

"Just shut up and do like you're told. Nobody'll get hurt."

Runyer lay on the floor, eyes darting around the place. Typical of a lot of the rental cabins around here. A big living room, wood-paneled, filled with mismatched furniture. Two small bedrooms downstairs, a loft upstairs. The walls and floors polyurethaned yellow pine. Glassy-eyed hunting trophies.

Then he found what he was looking for: the phone, on the wall in the kitchen.

But Gare'd been doing his own surveying. Runyer should've guessed that a seasoned perp wasn't going to miss a telephone. He stepped into the kitchen and ripped the unit down.

"Any other phones?" he snapped.

"I . . . no."

"Any *cell* phones?"

A pause. The husband looked mortified.

"Well?" Gare shouted.

"In my pocket," the husband said quickly. "I forgot. My jacket."

"You forgot. Right." Gare smashed the phone under his boot. Then he called, "Get those curtains closed."

The man's wife — *her* white hair was in a French braid, the way Lisa Lee wore it for PTA meetings and church potlucks — hesitated for a moment. She looked at her husband.

"Now!" Gare barked, and she hurried off to draw the thick drapes covering the windows.

"Anybody else in the house?"

"I —" the man began. "We didn't do anything —"

"Is there anybody else . . . in . . . the . . . house?" Gare demanded. Pointing his gun at the husband's sun-wrinkled face.

"No. I swear."

Earl stepped inside. "Hey. They got 'emselves a Lincoln out there. Let's take it and —"

Gare snapped, "We're not going anywhere yet. Keep 'em covered." He stepped to the door, shut off the porch lights. Gazed down the hill. Runyer could see the flashing lights streak past on the highway. The cars — there were two — didn't even slow up. Runyer'd never told Hazel where exactly on the road he'd set up the roadblock. Route 58 was thirty-seven miles long.

Gare closed the door, turned to the couple. The husband had sat down, he was breathing heavily.

"Too much excitement for you, old man?" Gare laughed.

"He has a bad heart," the wife whispered. "Couldn't you just —"

"And *he's* got a bad gut," Gare said, nodding toward Runyer. "So whyn't you shut up, lady, 'fore you catch something, too?"

"Listen . . . Gare," Runyer said. "There're troopers out looking for you. We —"

"For *us?*" Earl blurted, panic in his round, peach-fuzzed face.

"Relax," Gare said to him. "He doesn't mean 'us.' Nobody can ID us." He waved the gun at Runyer. "And you, quiet."

The wife sat down next to Runyer and glanced at his wound. "I'm a nurse," she said to Gare. "Let me take a look at him."

"Go on. But don't do anything stupid, lady."

"I just want to help him."

"Hold up there." Gare found some clothesline and tied the husband's hands. His wife's, too.

"I can't work on him this way," she protested weakly.

"Then you can't work on him," Gare responded as he rummaged through the breakfront drawers.

In the light, Runyer could see he'd been wrong about them being college kids. He saw bad teeth, scars, callused hands. Their pedigree was all over them: day labor, taverns, construction jobs till they were thrown off the site drunk or thieving, maybe a teenage wife at home — a girl who cringed automatically whenever a man shouted.

"When d'you get shot?" she asked, struggling to open her nurse's kit.

"Twenty minutes ago."

She took his blood pressure, awkwardly with her bound hands. "Not too bad. And" — she examined the entrance wound — "from where you got hit, I'd say the bullet missed the major veins and arteries." She taped a pad over the puncture in his gut.

"But I better get to a hospital pretty soon," Runyer said.

She leveled her blue-gray eyes at him. "That's right."

"How much time do I have?"

The lie died in her throat, and she decided to tell him the truth. "Two hours, three," shooting a prickly injection into his arm. In a few murky seconds the pain was floating out the window, along with the horror of what she'd just told him. He expected the dope would make him groggy and it did a little, but mostly with the pain gone he found he could think straighter.

And what he thought was, once again: What'm I gonna do here? I'm willing, I've still got some strength left. But I don't have a clue. Ten years of law enforcing in Andover doesn't prepare you for this sort of thing.

He looked over the couple as they gazed miserably across the room at their captors. Runyer'd seen plenty of sorrow on his job, pain, too. Most of it as a result of car wrecks and domestic violence. But he didn't think he'd ever seen two more sorrowful people than these two. On the table, by the wineglasses, were a few unopened gift packages and a cake. Written on it: "Happy Birthday, Martin." They'd come up here from Boston or Hartford for the celebration and to spend the weekend looking at leaves and hiking. And now this had happened.

"How much of that dope you have left?" he asked, whispering.

She looked his way. "The painkiller? Isn't it working?"

"I don't mean that," he said. "Any chance we could stick him with one of those needles?"

"But he's got a gun," the husband said quickly. "They both do." He reminded Runyer of the young professors from UV, whose gift of smarts didn't quite make up for their paltry self-confidence.

She shook her head and said to Runyer, "Not much. A couple more shots like the one I just gave you. Not enough to knock anybody out."

"Please," the husband gasped suddenly, lifting his tied hands.

"Please what?" Gare whirled around, snapping.

"Just, can't you just take our car and let us be?"

"'Let us be'?" he growled. "Listen, mister, I didn't *want* to come here. This isn't my fault. If that asshole hadn't stopped us, we'd be long gone by now. And that fellow on the highway'd still be alive."

"*What?*" the husband whispered.

Runyer answered, "They shot a man who stopped when I was trying to arrest them."

The husband fell silent and stared at the floor. His wife muttered, "My God, my God."

Runyer was looking at her. He saw a long, handsome face whose attractiveness was partly that she didn't pretend to be young. The skin was matte, free of makeup except for a sheen of pink on her lips. She wore a white cashmere sweater and black slacks.

She wiped the sweat from Runyer's forehead with her sleeve and he didn't think he'd ever felt anything so soft as that fuzzy cloth. It reminded him of Pete's baby comforter, a shabby blue thing the boy had carried with him everywhere till the age of five — when balsa wood suddenly took the place of wool and satin as his youthful obsession.

Gare glanced at the birthday cake and presents. "Lookit."

Earl called, "Hey, we're crashing a party, looks like."

"That you, Martin?"

The husband nodded.

Gare asked, "So, Marty, how old?"

"I . . . uh." His voice faded as he grew flustered, staring at the black barrel of the gun.

Gare laughed. "It's not that tough a question."

"I'm fifty," the man finally answered.

"Whoa, that old?" Gare mused. "And you, what's your name?"

"Jude," the wife answered.

"Come on, Jude. We're going to sing 'Happy Birthday' to Marty. Hey, Earl, this'll be a kick."

"Stop it!" she gasped. "Please."

"You better sing, too, Sheriff. That's one of the rules."

"You can go straight to hell." Runyer said this before thinking and he fully expected Gare to shoot him again. But the young man was enjoying his game too much to pay the sheriff much mind. He sat down in between the couple and made a show of arranging the cake in front of Martin, who sat with his hands in front of him, nearly paralyzed. He put his arms around the couple. Rubbing the gun over the poor man's cheek, Gare started singing in an eerie, off-pitch voice. "Happy birthday to you . . . Come on, Earl, let's hear you!"

Earl kept a smile on his face but beneath it the fear and distaste were clear. "Gare . . ."

"Sing!" Gare raged. "You, too, goddamn it," he barked at Jude. "Sing! Happy birthday to you . . . happy birthday to you . . ."

Their ragged voices grunted, or whispered, the words to the song. Martin's eyes were closed and Jude's hands quivered in her terror. Runyer watched the piteous spectacle: the gun caressing

Martin's face, Jude's glazed expression, Gare's mad smile as he boomed the lyrics, then called for everyone to take it from the top. The sheriff would've traded his house and land to have his pistol back in his hand for ten seconds.

The singing faded, replaced by another sound — sirens again.

Gare was suddenly all business. "Check it out," he commanded Earl, who scurried over to the front window. Gare rose and stepped into the shadows near the door, the gun ready.

Runyer saw clearly that these two weren't really partners at all. Gare was smart — he'd've been the mastermind behind the robbery — and in the end he wouldn't have a lot of patience for people like Earl. And as for *that* boy . . . he kept looking at his friend every half minute, like a puppy. Earl, Runyer decided, was their key to freedom.

"Who are they?" Martin whispered.

"They robbed a bank downtown today. Nearly killed a guard. There's another one, too."

"Another one?"

"A partner. He took off in a different car. They do that sometimes. To fool us — 'cause we'd be looking for three men together." Runyer didn't add that he knew "they" did this because he saw it on a *Barnaby Jones* rerun, with his son sitting on his lap and popcorn stuttering madly in the microwave.

Runyer closed his eyes and swallowed hard. Man, I'm sweating. Why'm I sweating so much?

Jude wiped his forehead again. She didn't seem like a nurse, not a hospital nurse anyway. With her dangling Indian earrings and her thin figure — from yoga or dancing, he guessed — she reminded him of Lisa Lee's sister. A charmer but the family wacko, into herbs and crystals.

Thinking of his wife, he gave a distant laugh. Jude looked at him with a smile of curiosity.

"I was remembering something. . . . Last week Lisa Lee and I were at this Autumnfest? In Andover?"

"That's your wife? Lisa Lee?"

Runyer nodded. "We were leaving and I couldn't find our truck. I thought, hell, I hope nobody stole it — we've had a bunch of car thefts up here lately. Turned out it wasn't, I just forgot where I parked. But I remember saying to Lisa Lee, 'You know, stealing cars is about the worst we get here in Andover. Makes me feel like

I'm just playing at my job. Like I'm not a real cop. Sometimes I wouldn't mind a little more action.'"

Jude laughed softly. Martin didn't. He seemed to be counting his own heartbeats.

"Boy, mis-take!" Runyer concluded. "Never ever ask for something you might get. I'd make that a rule of life."

He looked at Jude's hand. She wore a gold ring with a blue stone in it. "That's pretty." He reached up to touch it. Then he realized his finger was bloody and he pulled back. "S'the color of Lisa Lee's eyes. What kind of stone is it?"

"Topaz."

"Thought they were yellow."

"They come in blue, too."

The glitchy pain spread a little farther. He gasped. "Oh . . . oh . . ."

Martin looked at him now, wide-eyed. "Please," he called. "This man . . ."

Gare looked up from the cabinet he was ransacking.

"He's hurt bad."

"Of course he's hurt bad. I put a .38 slug through his belly." He grinned. "So, Marty, tell me . . . who're you expecting?"

Martin and Jude looked at each other.

Gare bent from the waist and caressed Martin's face with the muzzle of his gun. "Who . . . are you . . . expecting?"

"Nobody."

"Somebody named Cara, maybe?"

"How —?" Jude began then stopped herself. Gare held up a birthday present. A card said, *Love, Cara.*

Martin couldn't think of anything fast enough. "She's —"

"She's our daughter," Jude said.

"She coming to this party?" Earl asked, jumping playfully over the back of a tartan plaid couch and landing on the cushion.

"No," Martin blurted. "She isn't."

"What's she look like?" Earl asked.

"Just forget her," Martin whined. "Look, what do you want? You want money? I can get you money. Whatever you want, I'll get it for you. I'm well off. . . ."

"Yeah? What do you do, Marty?"

"I have a wholesale business. It makes a lot of money. I can get you —"

"What, write me a check? Let you all take a little drive into town and hit the ATM while Earl and I wait here?"

Edgy, Jude said, "How 'bout if I get you men something to eat?"

"Now, why'd you wanna do a nice Samaritan thing like that?" He was examining the knicknacks on the mantelpiece — a collection of ceramic birds. A spread-wing eagle caught his eye, and he rubbed the detail of the feathers with a finger.

"Because if you're feeling fat and sassy you might be more inclined to let us go." She tried to laugh. The sound fell flat.

Gare shrugged. "I could use some food. Earl, go with her."

Runyer, thinking: The two of them alone in the kitchen. She could talk to Earl, tell him Runyer would testify that the killing was accidental. Tell him to give up Gare before he ended up dead himself or socked away in prison for two lifetimes.

He rolled over so that he was looking into her face. Gare couldn't see him.

"Jude," he whispered. "Listen . . ."

Her eyes flicked down.

"You've got to talk to him. To Earl. Tell him that I'll —"

Gare's hand clamped down hard on Runyer's shoulder and jerked him over onto his back. The pain jabbed him like a dentist's drill.

"What're you saying, Sheriff?"

Sweat dripping into his eyes, Runyer stared at the smooth, round face inches from his.

"You asking her to bring you back a nice little knife or something?" He turned to Jude and set one of her gold earrings swinging with the muzzle of Runyer's own service pistol. "What was he asking you?"

Horrified, Martin opened his mouth but whatever he was going to say was choked off by the sight of a pistol against his wife's head.

"Because," Gare continued, "that'd be breaking rule number two. And we know what happens then." He swung the gun toward Runyer's belly, caressed the bloody front of his uniform.

"I wanted some water is all. Just some water."

"I'll decide what you get and when you get it." Standing up, Gare said to Earl: "Go on. Just be sure and frisk her when you come back." His slick face cracked another of its horrid grins. "Take your time, if you want."

"No!" Martin snapped. "You son of a bitch!"

"What'd you say?" Gare spun around, slipped the gun into his belt. Doing that — putting it away, not pointing it — sickened Runyer. It meant violence, not a threat, was coming. "What?" he whispered.

"Don't you dare touch her." At last there was some steel in Martin's voice.

But all this did was notch up Gare's anger.

Circling again, slow, he stared Martin down like a scolded dog.

"Just let me make them some food," she pleaded. "What would you boys like? I'm a good cook. Tell them I'm a good cook, Martin. Tell them."

Gare jerked Martin to his feet. "Now say it. . . . What don't you want me to do?"

"Hurt her."

"Thought you said 'touch her.'"

"I . . . that's what I mean."

"But she might like getting touched." He looked Jude over, her slim figure under the fuzzy white sweater, the close-fitting slacks. "You're an old man, Martin. Bet nothing works quite like it used to, right? I'll bet you've been neglecting her. And she's just coming into her prime. That's what you hear on the talk shows."

"No, just . . . leave her alone."

"Say please."

"Please."

"You say it, but you don't mean it. Maybe if you were on your knees. Get on your knees. Go ahead. Do it."

"Gare," Earl said uneasily.

Martin swallowed and looked from his wife to Runyer. "You go to hell," he shrieked. And lunged for the robber, grabbing him by the collar.

"Whoa, here," Gare said, laughing. He slugged Martin hard in the belly and sent him careening into the wall. He reached out to catch himself, but with his hands tied, he could grip only the drapes. They didn't hold and he fell hard to the floor, knocking the wind out of his lungs. He curled up like a hedgehog as Gare started beating him.

"No!" Jude cried. "His heart . . . please, don't!"

But Gare lost interest after a half dozen blows. He stood up, flexed his hand. "Now, go make some food like I asked. I want a burger. Or something hot."

She started toward her husband.

"Don't worry about him. I said *food*."

When Earl came over to take Jude to the kitchen Runyer caught his eye. The young man returned the look, curious for a moment, then lifted Jude to her feet and led her to the kitchen.

Gare glanced at the sheriff but ignored him. He was just a mote — an expression of Runyer's father-in-law, meaning somebody floating around in the background, inconsequential. No, it was Martin who fascinated him. He pulled a knife out of his pocket and enjoyed watching the man go wide-eyed. Then he chuckled and cut the rope, retying his hands behind his back. "Just so you don't do anything stupid again." Surveying the knots, he said, "So, you're fifty, huh? How 'bout the witch in there?"

"The same. We're the same age."

"That's about how old my mother is. My dad, too, he's still alive. I don't remember his birthday. That's funny, isn't it? You'd think I'd remember. You remind me of him sort of. He was kind of a wuss, too. No balls."

"Look, son, please . . . I've gotta get to the john. I mean really."

"*Grand*son's more like it," Gare said, grabbing Martin by the hair again, examining the evasive eyes. "Well, grandpa, you really gotta go?"

"I do, yes. See, I'm hyperglycemic borderline diabetic. And —"

"Yadda, yadda, yadda. You wanna piss, just say you wanna piss. Don't explain so damn much. Geez."

Gare dragged him to the bathroom and humiliated Martin further by leaving the door open and staring at the poor man while he did his business.

When they returned he pushed Martin down onto the floor beside Runyer. He smelled the air, the cooking beef. "How's that food coming?" Gare shouted.

"Almost ready," Jude called. The thought of eating nauseated Runyer.

Gare sat down in front of Martin, cross-legged, studied him again, like a bug in a bottle. Finally he mused, "You think a person can live too long?"

"What do you mean?"

"Don't you think there comes a point you're not alive anymore? You're not really living. Just getting by. You might as well just pack it in. Haven't you ever felt that?"

"No."

"You really want to live?" Gare asked, as if he was truly surprised.

"Of course I do," the man answered earnestly. "You think 'cause you're younger and stronger the world's yours. My family and I have a right to live, too."

"But live what kind of life?" Gare shot back. "Look at us — a month ago Earl and I did a job near Poughkeepsie and getting away we were driving down the Taconic at a hundred fifteen miles an hour. See, *that* was being totally alive. You ever done that? 'Course not. You're just a goddamn salesman —"

"I'm not a salesman. I own a big —"

Gare wrinkled his face up. "You ever do *anything* crazy? Skydive? Ski?"

"No, but —"

"*No, but,*" he mocked. "How 'bout when you were young? You do anything ballsy then?"

"I guess." He looked at the kitchen as if Jude would testify on his behalf. "I had a souped-up car. I —"

"But then," Gare continued, "you got old, right? You got scared."

"I had a family to support!" Martin snapped back. "I had my business. Employees to take care of. I couldn't afford to screw around like you."

"Pitiful," Gare whispered, shaking his head. "Pitiful."

Runyer lay on his side, bloody, a bullet deep in his body. But it seemed to him that Martin was wounded a lot deeper — by this cold taunting.

"You don't understand," Martin blurted.

"Oh, yeah, I do. I understand perfectly."

Jude and Earl brought the burgers in and she put the dishes on the table. Even across the room Runyer could see her shaking hands.

"Soup's on," she said with fake cheer.

Gare stared at Martin for a moment longer, then went to the table and sat down.

Runyer caught Jude's eye and glanced at Earl, then pantomimed drinking a glass of water. Jude seemed to understand and turned toward the kitchen.

"Where you going, grandma?" Gare snapped.

"To get some water for the sheriff."

"Earl, you do it."

"But —"

"Do it!"

Thank you, Runyer thought. Yes!

Earl fetched the water. As he bent down to set it on the floor, his pistol pointed at Runyer's head, the sheriff whispered quickly, "Let's work out something, Earl. You give him up, and I'll testify for you at trial. About the shooting. That it was an accident. You got my word."

Earl froze, looked at him for a moment. He just about dropped the glass when Gare called, "Earl!"

The young man swiveled around.

"S'getting cold," Gare said. "Come on and eat."

Earl stared at Runyer for a moment, set the glass down, and returned to the table without a word.

Gare put his napkin in his lap carefully, then picked up his utensils with precise gestures. Runyer was surprised at his behavior until he realized he'd seen this before — Gare had learned his manners in reform school.

He and Earl began conversing in whispers.

"Your daughter?" Runyer asked the couple. "She *is* coming here tonight, isn't she?"

Martin's eyes met Jude's. She nodded. And Runyer now understood why Martin was so upset.

"She drove up from Boston this afternoon. She went shopping and was going to meet us tonight for a little party. Stay the weekend."

"When's she due?"

An elaborately carved clock — with a weird grinning face, like the old man in the moon — showed the time. 7:10.

"Ten minutes ago."

The pain stretched luxuriously through Hal Runyer and dripped into his bowels. He gasped and thought of Lisa Lee's aunt, dying of cancer. When they'd talked about the woman — friends, family, and doctors — nobody ever talked about the cancer itself, or about her coming death. They'd talked about pain.

He gasped and closed his eyes. Then risked a look at his belly. The blood had spread in a huge slick. He knew he didn't have much time left. Runyer looked over at the table and once again caught Earl's eye. The man looked away fast, continued to poke at his burger. He nodded as Gare said something to him and went right on nodding.

"What're they talking about?" Martin asked in his nervous lilt.

"Whether or not to kill us," Runyer answered.

Martin lowered his head to his wife's and they huddled, an armless embrace.

Runyer floated away somewhere momentarily — because of the drugs, or the pain, or the despair — and he gazed at the couple as if he were looking down at them from above, saw them with startling clarity. And if maybe they were a little too L. L. Bean for Runyer's taste, if they were spooked as deer at the moment, if they didn't have the inclination, or backbone, to approach life the way Gare thought was important, still they were good people — and brave in their own way. Martin was somebody who'd provided for his family and for the people who worked for him. Jude had raised a child and nursed patients. Which is what real courage was, Runyer reckoned. Not driving fast or sticking up banks. So where their captors felt contempt for these folks, Runyer couldn't. He felt only an overwhelming desire to save them, to salvage what he could of their lives.

The sheriff had pinned his hopes on Earl but it was obvious that wasn't going to work out. So he now eased close to Jude. "Listen. I've been thinking. Your daughter's due here any minute, right?"

Martin nodded.

"Your legs're free. What if you two were to go through that window there? Run down the driveway and hide in the pine trees for her? When she shows up, you all hightail it outa here. You'll probably get a little cut and bruised but that'll be the worst of it."

"How?" Jude asked. "They'd come after us."

"I'll hold 'em off. With that scattergun on the mantel."

"It's not loaded," Martin whispered. "I checked when we got here."

Runyer'd figured. Vermont wasn't NRA territory but people knew guns and nobody'd ever mount a loaded double-barrel within a child's reach.

"But they don't know that."

"Don't!" Martin rasped. "Let's just do what they want."

Jude added, "If you don't shoot them outright they'll figure out the gun's empty."

"Don't think they'd want to take that kind of chance with a ten-gauge goose gun. Besides, they'd figure with me being a cop it'd make sense to give 'em a chance to surrender. 'Put your hands up.' That kind of thing."

Then Jude was smiling kindly. "I know what you're trying to do," she said. "I appreciate it, Sheriff. But . . . how old're you?"

"Thirty." It had been his birthday, too — just last week. He didn't mention this.

"And you're a married man and probably've got kids."

"This's my job," he continued. "I get paid —"

"You don't get paid to sacrifice your life for a couple of stodgy old tourists like us. That's what you'd be doing. And you know it."

"I'm thinking of your daughter, too," he said. "'Sides, if there's any way *I'm* surviving this it's if somebody brings some help. Soon."

Martin said, "You're wrong, Sheriff. I don't think they really want to hurt us. Let's just wait."

"We can't!" Runyer whispered urgently. "Gare's going to kill us."

"How can you be so sure?"

"Because of blame. Weren't you listening to him? He's got this talent for pitching blame like horseshoes. Everything that happens is somebody else's fault. That lets him do whatever he wants. Murder included."

Martin looked at the window Runyer wanted them to leap through. He gazed at it the way a man accustomed to losing foot races looks at a cinder track.

The sheriff said to Jude, "I think it's the only way. I want you to knock that lamp over there. I'll make a run for the shotgun and you two go through the window. It can't be more'n four feet to the ground."

Martin whispered urgently, "But if it doesn't work they'll kill us all, Cara, too. If we promise we won't tell anybody, if we *swear* it, they'll probably let us go. I have a feeling."

Jude was Runyer's only hope and he kept his eyes in hers. Finally, she said, "I'll do whatever my husband wants."

Martin asked, "You really think we can make it?"

"That depends," Runyer answered. "How bad do you *want* to make it?"

For an instant Runyer could see Martin was right on the border-line. His eyes grew sharp as he judged the angles, the distance to the window. But then he shook his head slightly.

And so there was nothing to do but go ahead by himself and hope that Jude would rally her husband to make the plunge to safety.

He waited until Gare and Earl were looking at their food, then gripped Martin's shoulder and pulled himself to his feet. "I'm going," he whispered. "Get the hell out that window!"

Ignoring the electric pain that stabbed through him, Runyer moved as quietly as he could toward the gun over the mantel.

Martin's voice seared the hell out of him. "No, don't!" He lurched forward and slammed into the sheriff, who tumbled over on his side in a jolt of agony.

The captors leapt up from the table.

"He was going for the shotgun," Martin cried. "It wasn't us! We told him not to!"

"Martin," Jude spat out in disgust.

"It was *his* idea. . . ." Martin wailed. "We didn't do anything."

And for a moment Runyer found himself agreeing with Gare: the man was truly pitiful.

You've got to be most cautious of the ones leaning hard to be on your side. . . .

Earl dragged them both back into the corner and delivered a kick to Runyer's belly that no amount of morphine would dull. He gasped and rolled up tight.

"Look what you did," Jude cried to her husband.

He just killed us all, the sheriff thought. *That's* what he did.

"I don't want anybody to get hurt."

"Good man, Marty." Gare pulled the scattergun off the wall and broke it open. "Wouldn'ta done you a lotta good. Stupid of you. Stupid. Tie their feet, Earl."

As the young man cinched their ankles, Gare walked toward the huddling trio and snapped the gun closed. That damn grin of his blossomed again and he drew back the butt of the gun like a baseball bat. Runyer lowered his head, waiting for the crushing blow.

A loud rap sounded on the door and they heard, "Mom, Dad? Hey, some welcome! What's with the porch lights?"

A tall, attractive woman, mid-twenties, wearing an expensive shearling coat, stepped inside.

"Cara!" Jude cried. "Run!"

But Earl put his hand on her back and shoved her toward them. She barked a panicked scream and flung her arms around her father, buried her head in his chest, sobbing. The girl glanced at Runyer's bloody wound and began to cry harder. "What's going on?"

Her mother edged closer and they pressed together.

Gare stepped outside. He returned a moment later. "Nobody else around. She's alone."

"Who are you?" Cara asked.

Gare said nothing. But his eyes told Runyer the whole story: What's coming's our fault. We screwed up their getaway from the bank and a man got killed. Martin reminded Gare of his father and that, too, set off his anger like a fast-burning fuse. He's innocent; *we've* caused this grief, and that gives him the okay to kill us all.

And damn if he probably isn't going to blame us for him feeling guilty after he does.

"Earl," Gare said. "Come on over here. Stand by me."

"We gonna take her car?"

"No, we're going to take their Lincoln. But there's something we have to do first."

"What?"

"You know."

Earl wiped his hand on his jeans, looked from his buddy back to the people on the floor. He seemed to sense what was coming and glanced at Gare uneasily.

What was he thinking about? What Runyer had told him?

Would he stand up to Gare at the last minute?

"You can do it, Earl," Gare whispered.

Runyer stared into the young man's black eyes. Thinking: Remember what I said, Earl, remember it, remember, remember, *remember*. . . . It's the only way you can save yourself.

"Go on," Gare said.

"I can't," Earl muttered.

His friend's low voice growled, "Listen, Earl, the job tonight went just like we'd planned, right? Piece of cake. And we were heading home, no harm for anybody. It wasn't our fault this happened. We didn't *want* to come here, did we?"

"No."

"They know our names," Gare continued. "They know what we look like."

"Don't do it, Earl," Runyer said. "Don't ruin your life."

"Oh, listen to *him*," Gare spat out. "*He's* the one tried to shoot us. Marty, too — he went for that scattergun. Remember? When we walked in? And don't think that old lady wouldn't shoot us down, too, she had the chance."

"Earl!" Runyer called.

The young man's eyes swayed from his friend to Runyer and back again. The gun lowered.

Come on, Runyer thought, come on. . . . *Remember.*

"And know what else he did?" Earl said suddenly, an icy glint in his eyes. "That sheriff there? He said if I turned you in, he'd go easy on me."

"He did that?" Gare, sounding shocked, frowned.

"Whispered it to me when I brought him the water."

"He thought you were a snitch, huh?" Gare said. "That's what he thinks of you — that you'd turn on your buddy."

Earl turned to the sheriff. "You son of a bitch. You thought I'd snitch?"

"Earl, don't —"

"You're first. I do him first, Gare?"

"That's fine by me."

Martin and Jude were silent. Runyer lowered his head.

"No," Cara whispered. "God, no."

Runyer fixed his wife and son in his mind and dropped his head to his chest. Earl stepped closer. Ten feet away. He couldn't miss.

Lisa Lee . . .

Hal Runyer knew he wasn't going to the heaven he promised Petey was "up there," somewhere beyond where the boy's fragile planes flew. No, he was going to black sleep. His breath hissed in and out and he squinted as the tears came.

Picturing his wife, his son, losing himself in the sad euphoria of the final daydream . . .

Then he heard something odd. Like the punch of unexpected thunder. A voice. Martin's, but different. Matter of fact. Calm. It said one word. "Down."

The women dropped to the floor. Cara hit the pine floorboards and hooked Runyer's collar, yanking him prone, too. Martin's hands — somehow free — swung around from behind his back, holding a huge pistol. His feet were still tied so he stood tall as he began firing, not even trying to duck. He fired the first shot at Gare but the boy's instincts were honed and he dove to the floor behind a couch in a half-second.

Earl was crouching, staring at his friend.

Martin said to the terrified young man, "Drop it."

But Earl went wide-eyed and lifted the gun, pulling the trigger madly. The slug missed by a yard and before he could fire again Martin squeezed off another round and a tiny dot appeared in the center of Earl's chest. He stumbled backward with a choked "Gare, oh, look, look." Then collapsed on his side.

With the knife she was holding, Cara sliced through the rope binding Martin's feet and he dropped down behind a table. Runyer realized this was how she'd cut the ropes tying his arms — reaching around his back to hug him. She now cut Jude's hands free, too, pulled a second pistol from her waistband, and passed it to the older woman.

Fast as snakes, Gare popped up behind the couch and fired. Three, four times. But they were panicked shots and all of them missed. Gare emptied Runyer's pistol and snagged Earl's from his bloody, twitching hand. While Gare peppered the wall with bullets Martin took his time and squeezed off rounds carefully, forcing the captor back into the corner behind a cedar chest.

"Go right," Martin called. Jude rolled toward the kitchen, an elegant maneuver, and made her way around Gare's flank.

"Think you're hot shit?" Gare screamed, scared as a baby.

Martin ignored him, jumped over the low table, and ducked as the spray of bullets from Gare's gun slapped the walls. He rolled behind the large armoire.

"Position," he called to Jude.

"You son of a bitch," Gare snarled. "You're dead! You're both dead."

"Position," Jude càlled.

Martin sized up the room and said, "All right, son. It's over."

"Like hell." Three more shots. A window broke, raining glass onto Cara and Runyer.

"Shoot?" Jude asked.

"Wait." Then he called, "We've got you in a cross-fire, Gare. And we have more ammo than you do. You can't win. But you can save your life. If you want to."

They heard hard breathing. Gare coughed once and spat.

"Shit. I'm bleeding. My shoulder!"

"You don't want us to come get you, son."

Slowly Gare stood.

"Gun down," Jude barked. "Now. I won't tell you a second time."

The pistol hit the couch. Cara snagged it before it bounced twice and had it unloaded in an instant. She pulled some plastic hogties from her shearling coat pocket and handed them to Martin, who bound Gare's hands.

"How did . . ."

"Just lie down there." Martin and Cara helped him down on his belly. They tied his ankles.

"You're going to kill me," he blubbered. "Just do it! Get it over with! I dissed you, I said all those things. And now you're going to kill me."

Runyer was gazing at the gun in Martin's hand. It was a big pistol, a Colt Python with an eight-inch barrel. With a telescopic sight mounted on the top vents.

Martin went through Gare's pockets, pulled out a box cutter, some papers, a wad of bills. He tossed them on a table. Then he nodded at Jude, and together the couple dragged him into the bedroom. They rested him facedown on the floor, where he cried and moaned.

They returned to the living room and sat down in front of the sheriff. Martin pulled on gloves and began wiping the big Colt.

"You were good," Runyer said to him. "Really good." Deciding that it was a lot harder for a brave man to act like a coward than the other way around. Since they so rarely need to.

"Had to get their guard down," Martin said, meticulous as he removed the fingerprints.

"Had *me* fooled, too," Runyer admitted.

"Wished we *could've* kept you fooled, too. But . . . well, didn't work out that way."

"No. I guess not. She's not your daughter, is she? Cara?"

"Nope," Martin answered, distracted by his task. "She's our partner. Backup mostly."

"How?" Runyer asked her. "How'd you know?"

"Oh, we have codes," Jude said as if it was obvious.

Martin continued, "When we meet at a safehouse after a job, if there's anyone in the place who shouldn't be there, we leave a sign.

Tonight if both the bathroom and kitchen lights were on at the time Cara'd know something was wrong. She was supposed to pretend she was our daughter. Buy us some time and maybe get a weapon to us. I staged that fight to pull the shade down so she could look in and get an idea about what was going on."

Taking a breath a little deeper than he should've, Runyer gasped at the pain.

Cara said, "I got here ten minutes ago. I saw those two. I could've taken them out then but I didn't know if there was anybody upstairs or in the basement."

"But you're a nurse," Runyer said to Jude. Trying to disprove these facts encircling him.

"I just know some first aid. Helpful in this line of work."

"But your birthday . . . ?" Runyer began, looking at Martin.

"Oh," he answered, "that's true. It's today. And I *am* fifty."

"You picked a funny way to celebrate."

The man shrugged. "Big cash delivery at a low-security bank. Didn't have much choice. We go where the work is."

The friendliest-seeming folk often aren't . . .

Jude looked over Martin with a cryptic gaze, then said to Cara, "Let's get the car packed up."

The women vanished.

. . . and you've got to be most cautious of the ones leaning hard to be on your side.

When they were alone Martin said, "What you were going to do . . . with the ten-gauge . . . appreciate it. But it wouldn't've worked. They'd've killed us on the spot."

Runyer nodded at Earl's body. "Stealing the Lexus . . . *that's* what they meant by the job tonight. Not the bank."

"I guess so." Martin turned toward the sheriff, who was gazing at the pistol in his hand. Man, it looked big. Bigger than any weapon Runyer'd ever seen. "So," he said.

"So," Runyer echoed. "Say, one thing I noticed."

"What's that?"

"You've been pretty free telling me who you are and what you did and all. Just wondering, d'I just jump outa a frying pan?"

"That depends," said Martin.

Jack Applebee, president of Minuteman Savings, had wanted to give the hero a nice watch, bestowed at an official ceremony. Juice and cake and Ritz crackers. Paper streamers. Folks in Andover just love their official get-togethers.

But Runyer wasn't in the mood. Besides, Sheriff's Department regulations won't let officers accept rewards. So Applebee settled for a handshake at Runyer's hospital bedside, surrounded by Lisa Lee, Pete, a half dozen friends and family, and a Pequot County *Democrat* reporter.

The banker talked about gratitude and courage, and also managed to work in a few words about the new Minuteman branch at Elm and Seventeenth and, naturally, the grand opening home-equity loan special. The old guy was in a great mood, and why not? Of the $687,000 stolen, nearly half was recovered. More than he'd ever expected to see again. Gare and Earl's partner made off with the rest of it. The federal agents and Vermont troopers couldn't figure out how he slipped through the roadblocks — they were plentiful and well manned. But clearly the robbers were pros and would've had escape routes worked out ahead of time.

Defendant Garrett Allen Penbothe adamantly denied that they'd even stuck up the bank in the first place, and so he wasn't about to offer any information about the elusive third partner. He and Earl, he claimed, had bused up to Andover that afternoon to steal a car, which they'd done a half dozen other times over the past month. And he came up with a version of the robbery so far-fetched that even the *Democrat,* which'll print anything shy of alien visitations, decided not to include it in their articles about the trial.

The prosecution witnesses — a businessman and his family whose rental cabin Gare and Earl tried to hide in — confirmed Runyer's story about the shootout and offered generous words about the sheriff's courage, and marksmanship, in a tense situation.

Gare's defense lawyer tried to argue that the young man was the real victim of these events. "My client and his friend just happened to be in the wrong place at the wrong time."

But prosecutor Harv Witlock latched on to the phrase for his own and used it liberally during his summation, saying excuse me but wasn't it Sheriff Runyer and the murdered passerby who'd had the bad luck here? A question that took the jury all of thirty-two minutes to answer. Gare is presently a long-term guest at a piney resort near the Canadian border known as the Tohana Men's Colony.

Hal Runyer elected to take sick leave for the first time in his decade of wearing the sheriff's badge. And after that fortnight he took another batch of time: vacation, which he'd also earned plenty of. Not that he had much choice about going back to work. Mentally, he was a mess. He couldn't sleep for more than an hour without waking in a torrid sweat. And he was plenty skittish when he was awake, too. Noises especially would send him bouncing off the walls. His wound took forever to heal and he could barely move on damp days.

So he spent his time puttering around the house, learning to cook, helping Lisa Lee with her realtor paperwork, shaving wing struts with a razor knife and painting fuselages. Petey had the classiest RC model plane in the county that fall.

A month after the robbery Runyer woke up early one frosty Tuesday and called the mayor at home. He quit the force. No explanations given or asked for. And when he hung up the phone he felt great. That night he took his family out to dinner and while they ate Houlihan's prime rib special he told them the news. He tried to gauge his wife's reaction and didn't have a clue.

It was a week later that a small package, no return address, was delivered to the house. Runyer started to open it, then noticed it was addressed only to Lisa Lee and he passed it over to her. She opened it with mixed suspicion and anticipation and gave a brief gasp. The black velvet box held a gold ring set with a big blue topaz. No name of a store, nothing other than a card that said, "For Lisa Lee."

Runyer was a generous man but his gifts leaned more toward the practical or, at best, decorative. A luxury like this was quite a jolt for her. She threw her lengthy arms around his neck. "But we can't afford it, honey."

Gazing at the anonymous note, piecing things together, he said, "No, it's okay. It's a thank-you present."

"From who?"

"Those people in the cabin."

"The ones you saved after the bank robbery? The couple and their daughter?"

"The wife . . . she had one of these rings and I told her it reminded me of your eyes. I guess she remembered that."

"It must've cost a fortune," Lisa Lee said, dazzled by the stone.

"He runs some kind of business. Bet he got it wholesale."

"We'll have to send them a nice note."

"I'll take care of that," he said. If he sounded evasive, she didn't seem to notice.

Life's a funny thing, Runyer found himself thinking as he stood in that hot kitchen with his wife in his arms. Sometimes every soul in the world but you seems to know what's what and is more than happy to tell you so. And most of the time you go along with them. But if you live long enough — maybe thirty years, maybe fifty — you get to the point when you're just not willing to hand off certain choices anymore. The important ones anyway. You do what you think's best and go on about your business.

"Which finger should I wear it on?" Lisa Lee asked.

"Well, let's see where it looks right." Runyer took his wife's hand and gratefully endured the hug despite the loving pain she inflicted on his torn belly.

The next day Hal Runyer climbed the stairs to the Sheriff's Department office, moving a little slower than he had before the shooting.

"Well, look who it is," Hazel said, eyeing his starched khakis. "You didn't *call*. We heard you were quitting."

"Naw, just a mix-up. I straightened it out with the mayor last night."

He snagged the report log from the desk in her cubicle and asked, "What's going on 'round town?"

"Not too much. Pretty quiet morning."

Runyer lifted aside a stack of files from his chair and sat at his desk. He started to read.

BRENDAN DUBOIS

Netmail

FROM *Playboy*

BY THE TIME my guns were cleaned and the dinner dishes were put away, it was night. I went upstairs to the spare bedroom that I've turned into an office, carrying a glass of wine. The office is lined on all sides with bookshelves, and between the two windows is a metal desk I picked up at a yard sale last summer. I flipped on the computer and dialed into the Mycroft-Online computer service.

E-mail waited for me.

I sat back in the chair, wineglass in my hand. With my other hand I reached for the mouse. Something was wrong. I shouldn't be getting e-mail. My phone number was unlisted, I picked up the mail — usually addressed to Occupant — at the post office once a week and no one at all had my e-mail address. But there was a little blinking icon in the center of the menu screen, showing a chubby mailman waving a letter at me.

I looked out the windows at the darkening fields and woods. Relax, I thought. It was undoubtedly spam, electronic junk mail sent to everyone who subscribes to my online service. I sipped from my glass and clicked on the icon, and after a confusing jumble of letters and numbers came this message:

TO: Sopwith12
FROM: Anon666

Sopwith12, you've been a bad boy. We have the evidence we need and if you don't do exactly as we say, we will go public. This is no joke. Reply within one day or you'll regret it.

A tingly feeling raced up my arms. Sopwith12 was my online ID. This wasn't an anonymous spam. I put the glass down and thought for a moment, then clicked on an icon shaped like a New England town hall, complete with white pillars. A message came up that said MEMBER DIRECTORY and I typed in ANON666. Within a second or two, the answer came back: No such member is listed on Mycroft.

I logged off, shut down the computer, and stared out the dark windows for a while.

It was spring in Pinette, Maine, and the next morning I was outside, working. I had chainsawed down a dead oak a few weeks back and had cut logs in two-foot lengths. I was now splitting each log for firewood. It was satisfying work, and I soon stripped off my sweatshirt and T-shirt, keeping on only my work boots, jeans, and the nine-millimeter Smith & Wesson, which was strapped to my side.

With each fall of the ax, I thought about my brief electronic message. I had been in Pinette for a while, and had gotten used to my new life. There was always work to be done on the dozen or so acres I owned, and I had the television and the public library and mail-order books. Still, I sometimes woke up at two or three in the morning, imagining I could hear the far-off sounds of Boston or New York or London or Tokyo.

It was the computer that saved me from turning into an unshaven recluse who cut paper dolls in his off-hours. Sitting in my tiny upstairs room with the computer linked to the Internet, I was wired to the whole globe. It wasn't the real thing, but with me exiled to this little Maine town and forbidden from traveling, it was the next best thing. I explored colleges, universities, museums, and scientific laboratories. I saw the view from cameras set up in Bombay, Antarctica, and at the top of Mauna Loa in Hawaii. I visited the home pages of college students, X-rated film stars, and bagpipe players. It was intoxicating, traveling down those little bundles of fiber. But I had one hard-and-fast rule: Thou shalt lurk — thou shalt not contact.

There are chat rooms, discussion areas, and mail server lists along the tangled wires of the Internet, and while I poked my head into these areas every now and then, I never said hello. I've read enough amusing stories of frat boys pretending to be sex-crazed housewives on the Net to know that I should never trust anyone on the other end of a computer terminal.

So, no messages, no mail.

But now someone was contacting me, with a message that made me want to load every weapon in the house.

Later that day I went into town and picked up my mail at the post office, a counter in the Pinette General Store. The store is in a big rambling building that was built in 1825 and has wide floorboards, worn down in the middle by generations of Mainers. Everything from battery cables to soup mixes to motor oil is stocked on the sagging shelves. It's owned by Miriam Woods, a woman with dark brown hair and even darker eyes lightly framed by wrinkles. She was widowed five years ago when Mr. Woods was downing a pine tree and misjudged the tree's fall. Besides being the store's owner, the postmaster (or postmistress, I can't keep track of what's what nowadays), and one of the town's three selectmen (or selectwomen), Miriam is also my unofficial intelligence source for what's going on in town.

She had on jeans and a University of Maine sweatshirt, both of which fit her nicely. The store was nearly empty of customers when she reached under the counter and handed over my thin collection of mail. After the usual chitchat of small-town happenings, I said, "I was wondering if I could borrow your son for a while."

"Eric?" she asked.

"Well, yes, unless you have a couple of stealth sons living in your basement, that's the one I'm talking about."

She took a rubber band, snapped it in my direction, and asked, "How about tonight?"

"Tonight sounds good."

"How does dinner sound?"

"Sounds better," I said. "And dessert?"

Another snapped rubber band, this one striking my shoulder. "Hardly. This is a school night for Eric. He'll be in."

"Fine, then. Rain check?"

A wink. "Always."

The mail took about a minute to flip through and dispose of, and I went home to shower and change. I had time to kill before heading over to Miriam's, so I turned on the computer and logged onto Mycroft-Online. The chubby, cheery mailman waved his hand at me.

You Have Mail.

I double-clicked on the icon and up popped another message:

TO: Sopwith12
FROM: Anon666
  We know you've read the message, so stop ignoring us. You've been a
bad boy and we have the evidence. Unless you pay up, we'll let the world
know about it. Reply now.

Some possible replies flitted through my mind, most of them
containing words that the Catholic nuns had once said would tar-
nish my soul. So with thanks to the Sisters of Mercy, I sent a quick
answer back:

TO: Anon666
FROM: Sopwith12
  Tell me more.

I left it at that. I spent the next hour exploring the computers of
the Jet Propulsion Laboratory in Pasadena and downloading photographs of Jupiter.

Before dinner I was in Eric's room as his mom hurled herself
around the kitchen downstairs. Like most relationships, mine and
Miriam's is based on trust, friendship, and treaties. One treaty
revolves around the kitchen. I stay out of it while she prepares
dinner, and when I'm cleaning up she's on the couch with a magazine or newspaper.
  Another treaty — unknown to her but one I set up a while ago —
dictates that I treat her fourteen-year-old son, Eric, as a real person,
not as an impediment to my "getting lucky," as some men tactlessly
put it. In return, he speaks to me in whole sentences and doesn't
ask embarrassing questions about my future plans with his mother.
He's tall, almost as tall as I am, and slightly gangly, with his mother's
brown hair and eyes. His room is tiny and cluttered, the walls
bedecked with posters of sports stars and space shuttles. But there's
a tidy place around the computer, which he bought a couple of
years ago after working long hours at the local lumberyard.
  He's had far more experience exploring cyberspace than I have.
I got right to the point when I sat down on his bed.
  "I have a little computer problem, one I don't want your mother
to know about," I said.

"Oh?" he said, smiling at being taken into my confidence. "With hardware or software?"

"Mailware, if there's such a word," I said. I pulled out two folded pieces of paper from my pocket, which were the first and second e-mails from Anon666, with the body of the messages cut away. I passed the papers to him.

"I got these messages this week, and I want to know where they're from," I said. "I don't know anybody called Anon666."

"Uh-huh," he said, looking over the papers. "What online service are you using?"

"Mycroft."

He looked at me, smirking. "Come on, Owen. Get out of the Steam Age. Upgrade yourself, why don't you?"

"One of these days, but not now. What does this tell you?"

He looked over the papers and said "Hmm" a few times and then passed them back to me. "Black and deep."

"Excuse me?"

"Look at the header."

"The what?"

Eric, God bless him, was patient with his elders. "Just above where it says To and From. The header information, all those letters and numbers. That tells you how the message got from the sender's computer to your computer. There are a number of systems and computers it passes through to get to your little computer, hooked up to your girlie-man online service. The header tells you how it got there."

I looked back at the numbers and letters.

"And what does it tell you?"

"Third line down. Phrase there says 'anon.service.se.' That tells me that whoever sent this message sent it through a mail-forwarding computer system in Sweden. Message goes there and all other forwarding info gets stripped out, so when it pops up in your mailbox, you don't know who sent it. Could be someone in Siberia, could be someone in Portland. Perfect way to send anonymous messages."

"Any way of finding out more?"

He laughed and leaned back in his chair. "That's what I mean by black and deep. This is serious spookland stuff. Even if you sniffed around in Sweden you wouldn't find them. Maybe you could get the sender's real ID from the National Security Agency folks down in Fort Meade — man, they've got computers you wouldn't believe."

A friendly voice from downstairs. "Hey, guys, come on down! It's getting cold!"

"In a sec, Ma," Eric said. He looked at me and said, "What's the matter, Owen? Someone sending you death threats?"

I shrugged. "Just junk mail."

After dinner Miriam walked me out to my truck. It was a cool night, but there was a warm smell of things growing and coming back to life that promised a long summer. We walked hand in hand and she turned to me as we reached my truck's door.

"Thanks for a good night," I said.

She squeezed my hand. "My pleasure, sir. And did you get what you needed from Eric?"

"Sure did," I said. "I had a little bug with my computer and he fixed it for me." Which was mostly true.

"And how long did it take him?"

"About thirty seconds."

She laughed. "That's my Eric." And as quick as her laugh, her mood turned somber. "Computers will take him far, if I can ever afford to get him into college."

"There are scholarships, you know, and grants."

"You must not read the papers anymore, Owen," she said bitterly. "We're in an era of self-sufficiency. Every man, woman, and fatherless son for himself."

"Don't fret," I said. "I'm sure something will come up."

I moved closer and she whispered, "Just a quick kiss, all right? I don't want my son seeing a man's hands up my shirt."

A soft kiss to her lips. She squeezed my hand again and whispered, "Next week he's off visiting his uncle and aunt in Vermont. Come back for dinner then."

I kissed her again. "I'm getting hungry already."

I took a detour home, driving up Phelan's Hill, the highest peak in town. On top is a fire tower, manned in the summertime. Two other cars were up there, so I parked on the far side of the dirt lot. Young love hates to be disturbed.

From the windshield I could make out the sparse lights of Pinette. I settled back into the seat of the truck. Off to the right, by the fire tower, was a collection of barbecue stands and wooden picnic tables. Two years ago, there had been nothing here except a gravel parking lot, and some townspeople asked the selectmen to purchase the picnic tables and barbecue stands to turn the fire tower into a picnic area. The board had refused. But a month or so later, an anonymous donor had given the necessary funds to the town, and the picnic area was built.

Below the hill, in town, was a new Little League field. Outstanding mortgages for three or four elderly residents had been discreetly paid. There was a well-stocked food bank at the Congregational church. All taken care of anonymously.

And in a couple of years, a certain young mother would find in her mailbox a hefty check made out to her son, from something called the Northern Maine Woods Scholarship Organization. In the cover letter, it would state that these scholarships were reserved for the sons and daughters of lumber workers killed in the woods, kids who had expressed a desire to study computers.

The thought made me smile. Maybe it should be called an association instead of an organization. That sounded better. From one of the cars I heard soft cries, and the honk of a horn as an arm or leg pressed against the steering wheel. Another smile.

Not a bad place to be. I had adjusted to exile in Pinette and liked being anonymous, especially anonymous with a fat bank account. That account helped with a lot of things, including odd guilt pangs from old times.

But now I had an e-mail buddy on the other end of the telephone wire. That would have to be taken care of, and soon. I started the truck and headed back home.

The next day I received a reply from my anonymous correspondent:

TO: Sopwith12
FROM: Anon666
Here's the deal. Fifty thousand dollars cash and we don't turn you in. If you don't reply, the evidence we have will be made public. You have 24 hours to respond.

I looked at the screen, thinking of the complexity of computer systems and the men and women who have sweated to wire the world. The people who had placed me in this little town had made a number of promises; chief among them was the assurance that I would never be charged with anything, ever again.

But someone out there knew something. How?

I moved my fingers to the keyboard and sighed. I sent my reply.

TO: Anon666
FROM: Sopwith12

Before anybody gets paid anything, I want to know what evidence you're talking about.

Then I switched off the computer and went through the house, gathering my collection of pistols, rifles, and shotguns. In my backyard I set up targets and shot away all afternoon until my ears rang, even through ear protection, and the forefinger on my right hand developed a blister.

I ate grilled-cheese-and-tuna sandwiches over the kitchen sink and spent the evening in front of the fire, cleaning my guns. Usually the scent of gun oil and the precision of the cleaning process calm me down and bring everything into soft focus, but not tonight.

The next day I chopped more wood, set up a new bird feeder at the edge of the woods, and changed the wiper blades on my truck. But all day I kept glancing up at the office window on the second floor of the house, as if I half-expected to see a mailman there, waving at me.

After washing my hands for the fourth time, I trudged upstairs and flipped on the computer, smiling wryly. Surfing the Net was usually my reward for a hard day of work, something to look forward to. My not-so-friendly correspondent had changed that.

The icon popped up. Just for once, couldn't the programmers at Mycroft make that mailman a mailwoman? Just for a change? I double-clicked.

My mailbox contained two pieces of mail. I called up the first, from Anon666. This one had a name, EVIDENCE, and it indicated that four files were attached to it. These were graphic files, with easy-to-understand instructions on how to view them, which I followed. The images scanned themselves into place on my computer screen. Each was a picture of young boys or girls, or both, involved in activities that would make the picture takers instantly eligible for ten to fifteen years in jail. I closed the files and trashed them, and then went out and washed my hands again. When I came back, I opened up the second message:

TO: Sopwith12
FROM: Anon666
    Now that you have viewed the evidence, here's the deal. Fifty thousand dollars or we let the information out that you're a collector and trader. You have 24 hours to respond.

I was smiling as I typed my reply:

TO: Anon666
FROM: Sopwith12
    Sorry, stupid. I have many faults, but activity involving children isn't one of them. Peddle your wares elsewhere, and while you're at it, piss off.

I whistled as I went downstairs. The idiot on the other end had undoubtedly screwed up the address. Sopwith21 or Sopwith11 would be getting blackmail notes next. If so, he would get what he deserved.

I decided to call Miriam.

The postmistress and first selectwoman of Pinette lay in bed with me, one foot idly tracing my leg. Her head was on my shoulder and the room smelled musky and warm, and she was gently interrogating me.

"We've known each other for a while, now, haven't we," she murmured.

"Uh-huh," I said, staring up at the dark ceiling, my eyelids fluttering open and shut.

"And all I know about you is that you're retired, you made some good investments at a younger age, and you're living off that."

"You've got a good memory."

I winced as she turned her foot and started scraping my leg with an untrimmed toenail. "I want to know more."

"What?" I said in mock anger. "And take the mystery and romance out of our relationship?"

She paused for a moment, then giggled and said, "I'm beginning to feel like one of those threatened women in dopey made-for-TV movies. You know, lonely woman falls in love with dashing stranger, and by the fourth commercial she's being found in pieces in shallow graves in New Jersey."

"Do you feel threatened?"

"Hmmm," she said, burrowing into my shoulder. "Not yet. But I would like to know more about you."

I stifled a sigh. Conversations like this inevitably end up losers. "Okay. Tonight and for one night only. Ask three questions and you get three answers. All right?"

"Really?"

"Yep, and to show you how fair I am, I won't count that as a question. Go ahead."

I could feel her body tense as she thought, and then she said, "Where are you from?"

"Valparaiso, Indiana." True.

"Where did you work before you came to Maine?"

"A company called Seylon Systems. It's now defunct." Which was true, if the fact that its other founding members were now dead or in jail equaled defunction.

"And what did you do there, for Seylon Systems?"

"I solved problems." Okay, that one was a stretch, but true enough.

"What kind of problems?"

I pulled the blanket over my chest. "Sorry, that's question four."

"Bastard," she said, grabbing my nose and yanking it back and forth. We wrestled under the covers until we were both out of breath. I was resting on top of her when she said, "You know, I might go to Kyle Brewer one of these days."

"And why would you be bothering the chief of police?"

She slapped my ribs. "Maybe I'll have him do a trace on you and get the real skinny."

I kissed her on the nose and said as gently as I could, "Miriam, please don't do that."

Instant defensiveness. "Why not?" Her voice lowered. "Are you in trouble?"

"Not at all," I said. "And I want to keep it that way." I wondered how this was going to go and what she was going to say, and she surprised me by holding me tight.

"Then I'll stay quiet," she said.

*

A few days later I started digging up ground to plant some corn, a rough and dirty job. After another over-the-sink meal and a long shower, I went up to the computer.

You Have Mail.

Tap-tap went my fingers on the keyboard. Up popped a new message:

TO: Sopwith12
FROM: Anon666
Insults get you nowhere. Results count. And here's one result: We don't care what you say or claim. We get the money or this information goes public. This means you: Owen P. Taylor, Rural Route 4, Pinette, Maine. You have 24 hours, or copies of this information go to the local police, the state police, and the newspapers. Feel like explaining this to them?

The walls of the room seemed to close in about my shoulders, making me feel like I couldn't move, couldn't breathe. If Anon666 went through with his threat, I could expect a search warrant or two to be executed at my little house. Then questions would be asked, and re-asked, and after that . . . well, I wouldn't have to worry about my freshly planted corn crop. The raccoons or woodchucks would get it. Not me.

I typed my reply:

TO: Anon666
FROM: Sopwith12
Deal.

Then I shut off my computer and proceeded to get drunk.

The next day I went down to the cellar, clicking on humming fluorescent lights. The workbench filled with tools and odd bits of junk stood in one corner next to a pile of cardboard boxes and a pegboard holding hammers, screwdrivers, and an awl. I inserted the awl into two of the peg holes and moved the board on well-oiled hinges to uncover a safe in the concrete wall. I unlocked it and reached inside, past souvenirs and odds and ends. I pulled out bands of money, fifties and hundreds. Mad money, so to speak.

I counted and separated the bills, put them back, and went up-stairs. My computer sentinel was cheerful as ever. Today's message was:

TO: Sopwith12
FROM: Anon666

Glad to see you come to your senses. The deal is $50,000 and no more messages from us. Wire the money to the Grand Breeze Bank of the Cayman Islands, to account number 448–2036. Get it there within 48 hours or the mailing begins.

I rubbed at my jaw and sent the reply with a slap to the keyboard:

TO: Anon666
FROM: Sopwith12

No deal. Payment will be in cash. Wire transfers leave records. And I want a face-to-face handoff, in public. I'm not leaving $50,000 on a park bench or in a bus terminal locker. That's my offer, and it's not negotiable.

I stayed online for a while, digging around in the computers of the Department of the Interior, and was surprised when a chime went off.

You Have Mail.

Damn. Anon666 must have been sitting at his computer, waiting for a reply. What an eager fellow.

TO: Sopwith12
FROM: Anon666

Do you think we're your local bank, that you can negotiate with us? The original deal stands. A wire transfer within 48 hours or we go public.

My reply was just as quick:

TO: Anon666
FROM: Sopwith12

Nope. It's my deal or you don't get your $50,000. If you go ahead with your threat, you don't get your money, and I show people copies of the e-mail messages you've been sending and explain how I've been set up. Inconvenient but bearable. And I'll be $50,000 richer. My deal, or publish and be damned.

I went into town to have lunch with the postmistress. I dropped off a few envelopes, which included money orders to the local Girl Scout and Boy Scout troops, as well as to a convent of nuns up the road who were having problems with a leaky roof. The money orders were signed Mark Twain.

When I got back that night, I had an answer.

TO: Sopwith12
FROM: Anon666

Deal. Be at the park bench near the subway entrance at Harvard Square in Cambridge at 9:00 A.M. this Saturday. Have the money in a red toolbox, a small one that looks like a tackle box. And no tricks! My associates will be watching, and if something goes wrong, the pictures go out.

My reply was quick and to the point: See you there.
Then I went downstairs and got to work.

Saturday morning about 4:00 A.M., I swung out of bed and got dressed in the dark, shivering from the cold. The next several hours were going to be challenging, but not so challenging as they would be were Anon666 farther away. If he were in New York City or Dallas or Los Angeles, the risk would have been greater.

In my cold, dark kitchen I picked up the toolbox and went out to the rear porch. I waited in the night, listening to the crickets. A half-moon illuminated the backyard. My truck was parked off to the side by the barn. I wondered if my watchers were still, invisibly, on the job, and hoped I wouldn't find out. Near the porch door I picked up a knapsack and slung it over my back. Something inside gurgled as I adjusted the straps. I went outside through the porch door and right past the truck, keeping the barn between me and the front yard, and then I was into the dark of the woods.

I started to jog along a path I had carefully cut through these woods. Though it was dark, I had placed at eye level little glowing dots that marked the trail. The knapsack bounced on my back and I heard a flurry of wings as I disturbed something in my path. After about twenty minutes I emerged onto a swampy bit of land that opened up to a well-lit parking lot and row upon row of cars — Powell's Motors, in Fyfield, the next town over from Pinette. I knelt down and undid my pack. From the pack I took out a car battery, a small can of gasoline, a set of Maine license plates, and a hot-wiring kit. In another fifteen minutes I was on the road, heading south, the rising sun at my left shoulder.

Harvard Square, Cambridge. Noisy, with lots of cars. Downtown Pinette doesn't even have a traffic light. I sat on a park bench near

the entrance to the subway (they call it the T) and waited, the
toolbox in my lap. I had on a Red Sox baseball cap, jeans, and a
bright red windbreaker. Colorful. A trio of musicians was playing
for spare change near the T entrance — trumpet, violin, and guitar
doing something awful to Mozart. I looked at faces, wondering
which belonged to the man — could it be a woman? — who had
been torturing my life.

Then I knew. A man came up to me, grinning widely. He wore
khaki slacks, heavy boots, and an Army jacket. His beard was about
three steps beyond stubble and his hair was long. He looked like
the kind of guy who puts his hair in a ponytail on dates. He sat down
next to me and said, "Well," in a cheerful voice.

"Excuse me?"

He looked straight ahead, still smiling. "Glad to see you're on
time. I take it the money's in the toolbox?"

"It is."

"So, why don't you hand it over and we can both be on our ways?"

I rubbed along the metal edges of the toolbox. "You'll get it, but
I want some questions answered."

"Huh," he said. "Not part of the deal."

"No, but it's the deal that's here. Some questions and answers,
and then you'll get the box."

He shrugged. "Why the hell not. Fire away."

"I take it you're Anon666."

He smiled again. "The same. But why don't you call me . . . Tom,
for now."

"All right, Tom it is." I shifted so I could look at him better. "This
was all a scam, right? You probably sent out hundreds, maybe thousands, of those messages by electronic mail, trying to get a nibble.
Right?"

He winked. "That would be giving up trade secrets, now,
wouldn't it?"

"But that's what happened, right? You're skilled in computers
and you saw an opportunity. Send out untraceable threats to thousands of addresses and hope that someone who is feeling guilty or
who likes privacy will pay up. Right?"

No answer, just a smirk. I went on. "So, why did you do it? Running low on funds?"

He laughed and put his hands in his jacket. "I did it because I
could, that's why. There are kids out there, two or three years out of

college, who work at companies designing software. When the companies go public, the kids are millionaires before they're thirty. Can you believe that? Ready to retire."

He was still smiling but there was an edge to his voice. "I've worked eighty to ninety hours a week, in three start-up companies, and all three have gone bust. I've got enough stock options to paper a room with. So I saw a way of using my skills to make some extra income. New skills are taking over society, and I'm pleased to be able to use them. Now, that's enough chitchat. Open that box, just a crack, so I can see the money."

I lifted the lid and angled the toolbox around so that the bundles of $100 bills were visible, and his grin got even wider. "Nice, very nice," he said. "How about handing it over?"

I closed the lid, snapped it shut, and said, "One more question and it's all yours."

The smile started to fade. "Make it quick."

"You married, Tom? You got kids, maybe live with a girlfriend?"

He held out a hand. "I'm all by my lonesome, but that will probably change next week. Say, at Club Med?"

Another laugh and I passed him the toolbox. I said, "It's all yours."

He grabbed it and headed to the subway entrance without looking back.

I waited a few seconds, ditched the cap and windbreaker, and followed.

He lived one stop away, near Porter Square. Shadowing him was almost too easy. He was focused on the toolbox with that delighted smirk on his face. I kept him in view from an adjoining car and trailed him when he got off in a residential area with big Victorian houses that had been divided into apartments. I winked at a couple of kids scurrying by on bicycles.

He bounded up the front steps of a large white house and let himself in with a key. I waited up the street a bit, leaning against an oak tree. Cars were parked up and down both sides of the roadway. I stood there, hands tucked into my pants pockets, thinking of Tom and that little phrase he had used.

What was it? Something about new skills taking over society and his being pleased to have them. Yeah.

*

Even though I was expecting it, the explosion on the upper floor of the old Victorian made me jump.

Both windows blew out to the street with a rocketing blast that echoed a few times. Even a part of the roof, black shingles flying, was peeled away by the force. A ball of flame and smoke roared up through the roof, car alarms started blaring, and there were screams from people running on the sidewalk as pieces of wood and glass fell to the street and bounced off car roofs.

I smiled and walked away. There's something to be said for old skills, too.

That night, safely back in Pinette, I was in Miriam's arms when she said, "What is it with you? You've been grinning ever since you got here."

"I'm a happy guy, that's what."

"Happy about what?" she asked, rubbing slow circles on my back.

"Happy that I took care of a job today, one that's been bothering me for a while."

Her hands pressed deeper. "And what was the job?"

"Hmmm," I murmured, burrowing underneath the blankets. "It's a secret."

"What?" she said, with mock dismay. "And you can't tell me?"

"Well, I could . . ." I said, letting my voice trail off.

"And why not?"

I tickled her ribs and she jumped. "Because if I told you, then I'd have to kill you."

She giggled and gently tapped my face. "Some joke."

I kissed her. Some joke.

Three days later FBI agents knocked on my door. I had just finished washing the kitchen floor when I heard their strong *rap-rap* on the screen door to the porch. I went out, wiping my hands on a towel, and there were two of them, in dark blue business suits, holding up their badges.

"Federal Bureau of Investigation, Mr. Taylor," the older one said. "I'm Special Agent Cameron, and this is Special Agent Pierce. Mind if we come in?"

"Not at all," I said, and they walked in with me. "Sorry about the floor, guys. I just washed it."

Agent Cameron's hair was thinning on the sides and graying, and the younger one, Agent Pierce, wore his black hair in a crewcut. I understand they're coming back into fashion.

"Can I get you guys anything to drink? Water? Soda?"

They both shook their heads and the older agent said, "Do you mind if I get to work, Mr. Taylor?"

"Not at all," I said, sitting down at the kitchen table with that day's *Portland Press Herald*. Agent Cameron left the kitchen and I heard him go upstairs as the younger agent sat across from me. I spread open the newspaper and said, "How do you think the Red Sox will do this year?"

No reply. I looked up to see him staring at me with disgust.

"Have I said something that offended you, Agent Pierce?"

"You and what you've done are offensive, Taylor," he said. His hands were placed on the table in front of him, and his fingers were thick and stubby.

"All done in the service of my country, or so I was told," I said as I turned a page.

"Don't tell me you still believe that," Agent Pierce said, nearly spitting out the words.

"Why not?" I asked.

Agent Cameron came back into the kitchen. "Upstairs is all in order. You still have the agreed-upon number of firearms?"

"I do."

"If you don't mind, I'll go down to the cellar."

"Be my guest."

Agent Pierce and I glared at each other, then I went back to my newspaper. Agent Cameron came back twice, to announce searches of the barn and my pickup. A few minutes after that he and Agent Pierce stood in my kitchen, and the older agent said, "Everything appears to be in order. No violations. No evidence that you've left town. And how is life in this little town treating you, Taylor?"

There were a lot of possible answers to that question, and I chose one that seemed pretty neutral. "I'm getting used to it."

For the first time, I saw Agent Cameron smile. "Just be glad we didn't place you in upper Alaska or the Texas panhandle. At least the weather here is relatively moderate."

I smiled back. "Ain't it the truth."

As they turned to leave Agent Cameron stopped and said some-

thing that made my knees lock: "Oh, if you have a moment, there is
a matter we'd like to discuss with you. It concerns a bombing death
in Cambridge."

"Oh?"

The younger agent said, "Have you heard about it?"

"Something in the paper yesterday. Some computer worker.
Right?"

"Very right," Agent Cameron said. "A powerful blast. It was fortunate that the other two apartments in the building were empty at
the time. The explosion made identifying the body . . . extremely
challenging. We'd like to talk to you about it."

I clasped my hands behind my back, ensuring that they wouldn't
shake. "Go right ahead."

Agent Pierce frowned. "Not here, Taylor. Down in Cambridge."

"Excuse me?"

Agent Cameron said, "We'd like your expertise. Look over the
scene, check out the few fragments we found. Maybe you could
offer us a few leads."

The kitchen floor seemed to sag beneath my feet. "Do I have to?"

Agent Cameron shrugged. "Consider it a favor."

I made a show of looking around my house. "Well, gentlemen, I
did a favor for you folks some years ago that ended up with me
being exiled to a town that doesn't even have a bookstore. I'm
afraid my favor quotient is used up."

Agent Pierce glared some more and Agent Cameron merely
shrugged. They left and drove away, and though I felt like dancing
around the house with glee, I kept still.

You never knew who might be watching. Or for that matter, who
might be getting a message.

LOREN D. ESTLEMAN

Redneck

FROM *Mary Higgins Clark Mystery Magazine*

"DON'T TAKE no pictures. I ain't looking for evidence for no divorce court. I just want to know is she cheating."

As he spoke, Billy Fred McCorkingdale polished off another rib and laid the bone across the ends of the other three in the latest layer. He had a respectable log cabin going.

The place was called Dem Bones and occupied a sheet-metal barn on Michigan Avenue in Ypsilanti — or Ypsitucky, as it's sometimes called, for the legions of skilled and unskilled workers who swarmed up Old 23 from Kentucky and points south after Pearl Harbor. They came to Detroit to build tanks and bombers and stayed on after Hiroshima. Billy Fred was a tinsmith at the General Motors Powertrain plant nearby, and his raw hands and big forearms were just what you'd expect of someone who worked with tin snips all day. He had a gourd-shaped head, narrow at the top, small eyes set close, and a nose like a rivet punched way too far above his wide, expressive mouth. He shaved his hair around his ears, which stuck out enough without help.

"That's good," I said, "about the pictures. Because I'm not taking the job. I can recommend a couple of good divorce men."

"I got your name from a divorce man. He said you were the best shadow in Detroit. I want to know where she goes when I'm at work and if she meets anyone. I don't need to know who he is. I can't work things out with her till I know what it is I'm dealing with."

For a second-generation native, he had a redneck accent as broad as the Ohio River.

"That's all?" I emptied my coffee cup and signaled for a refill. I'd been about to leave.

"I ain't been a good husband for a long time, Mr. Walker. I caught overtime fever: sixteen-hour days, holidays and weekends. I told myself the extra money was for her, but that don't cover the bar time I spent after work. It ain't her fault if she had to go looking for company. But I got to know."

The waitress refilled my cup. I sipped, studying Billy Fred's puppy-dog look. "My fee's five hundred a day," I said. "First three days up front."

He plucked a roll of bills from inside his coat, pulled off the rubber band, and counted fifteen hundred dollars in fifties and hundreds onto the table in front of me. My poker face must have slipped, because he said, "Overtime fever, remember? It ain't worth nothing without Lynne."

I put the bills in my wallet, wrote him out a receipt, and opened my notebook. "Tell me about Lynne."

Lynne McCorkingdale clerked in a Perry Drugs in Romulus, next door to Detroit Metropolitan Airport. All the shelves were equipped with horizontal bars like a boat's, to keep merchandise from falling off when 737s roared overhead. I bought a bottle of aspirin to get a look at her. She was several years younger than her husband, fine-boned and blond, with a short, breezy haircut and gray eyes — pretty in a fussed-over kind of way. She'd have looked better in less makeup, but I'm old-fashioned about such matters. She rang me up with barely a glance.

She drove a blue Chevy Cavalier, two years old, parked in a municipal lot a block from the store. I found a slot farther down the row and pulled the Cutlass into it. The store closed in twenty minutes. I watched a couple of seagulls fighting over half a Hostess cupcake; then Lynne came around the corner and got into the Cavalier and backed out. I gave her till the end of the row, then followed. The gulls took off.

I didn't expect anything the first night; nothing is what I got, not counting a necktie I bought from one of the floating stalls at Fairlane, Dearborn's largest shopping mall, while waiting for Lynne to come out of the Gap. She bought a blouse in Hudson's, a Clint Black CD in Recordtown, looked at a bra in Victoria's Secret without buying it, drank a Coke at Arby's, and went home, where nobody came or left until Billy Fred's Jimmy thundered into the garage at half-past ten. Thirty minutes later the lights went out. I hung around another hour just for the hell of it, but Lynne didn't shinny down the drainpipe. I clocked out.

The next day was Saturday, a half-day at the drugstore. She left at noon, drove to Detroit, and spent the afternoon in the library downtown, where she researched a paper for the night course she attended Tuesdays and Thursdays at Wayne State University. I interested myself in the out-of-town newspapers and tried not to feel guilty about spending Billy Fred's overtime dollars reading the box scores in the *Cleveland Plain Dealer.*

After the library closed, we had supper in a diner on Woodward. I sat at the end of the counter with the combined Saturday edition of the *News and Free Press;* she read a Danielle Steel paperback from her purse. So far she fit the profile of an errant wife as well as I qualified for a seat on the next space shuttle.

At eight o'clock she looked at her watch, put the book back into her purse, and paid for her meal at the cash register. I laid a ten-spot on the counter to cover my Reuben and the tip and went out behind her.

She took Woodward down to Jefferson and turned left. I closed in to avoid losing her in the homeward traffic from Belle Isle Park and the marinas on Lake St. Clair — too close to follow her when she swung left into a parking lot without signaling, unless I wanted to draw attention to myself. I continued for another eighth of a mile, then turned around in the driveway of an apartment complex and backtracked.

The parking lot belonged to the Alamo Motel: cable in every room and room service around the clock. Only they'd chopped up and sold the cable for the copper years ago, and the restaurant had closed at the request of the health department.

I thought at first she'd given me the slip — turned around and gone back the way she'd come while I was playing catch-up. Then I spotted her Cavalier in a slot behind the motel, next to the Dumpster. I drove back around to the front, got out, and went into the lobby.

It was clean enough. The linoleum had a fresh coat of wax, and the air smelled of Lysol and Raid. The clerk was a slender black in his early twenties, with thick glasses and his hair shaved down to stubble. He used a finger to mark his place in a textbook on abnormal psychology and asked me if I wanted a room.

I showed him the badge from the Wayne County Sheriff's Department. "Blond woman, about twenty-five. Five four, hundred and ten, short hair, gray eyes, pink sweater. What room's she in?"

"Can I see some ID?"

"Amos Walker." I gave him one of my cards. "The badge is a gag. I use it to serve papers."

"Then I guess I don't have to tell you anything."

I pointed at his textbook. "Wayne State?"

"U of D, third year."

"I hear tuition's stiff." I fished a twenty out of my wallet.

"I'm on scholarship."

"Basketball?"

"Academic. Four point O, all four years at Mumford."

I pulled back the twenty and laid one of Billy Fred's fifties on the desk. He chewed the inside of his cheek. Then he took his finger out of the book, replaced it with the bill, found a registration card in the box on the desk, and slapped it down in front of me.

"Mr. and Mrs. Robert Brown," I read. "Bob showed up yet?"

"I wouldn't know. Nobody goes in through the lobby."

Room 112. I skidded the card back his way. "I guess *Smith* is out of style."

"I never ask." He opened his book again.

There were four outside entrances to the motel. Room 112 was at the opposite end of the hall from a door with a large number "1" flaking off the glass. A cigarette machine stood just inside. After a quick reconnoiter I went back to the Cutlass and smoked a cigarette. I smoked another, then turned on the radio and listened to the ball game. In the bottom of the seventh a black Ford Taurus came down the row and backed into a space three cars down from Lynne's Cavalier. A tall, fair-haired party in a sport shirt and slacks got out and went through Door Number One carrying a gym bag.

I trotted in behind him and busied myself with the cigarette machine while he walked down the hall and knocked at 112. The door opened, and Lynne McCorkingdale drew him into the room with her arms around his neck.

Back in the car I listened to the Tigers lose and then a couple of experts tell us why. I heard a call-in talk show and the same details of the same drive-by shootings, child abductions, and congressional investigations on three different news programs. By then it was after midnight, and neither Lynne nor her fair-haired companion had emerged. I went home.

Billy Fred and the customer's chair in my office were a snug fit. He sat hunched over, licking his big thumb and turning the pages of my typewritten report without comment, his lips moving. When he finished, he read it again. Then he carefully laid it on my desk, with an expression on his gourd-shaped face I can still see when I close my eyes.

"I wrote down the license number of the Taurus," I said. "I could have someone run it, if you're interested."

"I already told you I don't want to know his name."

I opened the safe that came with the office, took out five hundred dollars in cash, and put it on top of the report. "It only took two days. I'm returning the rest of your advance."

"I don't want it."

"You won't say that after the divorce."

"Who said I want a divorce?"

"Put it toward a reconciliation then," I said. "Dinner at the Whitney, flowers, a night in a hotel. Not the Alamo."

After a long time he got up and put the bills into a pocket of his coat. "You done your job."

I could have left it there. Nothing that happened from then on was my business. "It's not the worst thing that can happen in a marriage," I said.

"You married?"

"I was."

"She cheat?"

"Not how you think."

He shook his head. "I love Lynne. Nothing don't make sense without her."

Any way I dissected that sentence didn't please me. I clapped him on the shoulder, and he left.

Two nights later I got home from a tail job that ended in Toledo, slapped a slice of ham between two slices of bread, poured a glass of milk, and turned on the news. An EMS team appeared, pushing a pair of figures covered in sheets on stretchers into the back of a van. A sign in the background identified the Alamo Motel.

*

"Twelve-gauge shotgun, double-O buck, two rounds per customer, fired at close range. You don't get any surer than that." The ugly words were coming out of an attractive face. Mary Ann Thaler, detective lieutenant, closed the file on the autopsy report on her desk at Felony Homicide and folded her slender hands on top of it. She was wearing her light-brown hair short these days and had a white silk scarf around her throat.

"Recover the weapon?" I asked.

"We think. McCorkingdale had a twelve-gauge Ithaca pump in his bedroom and a box of double-O shells. Of course, you can't trace shotgun pellets like you can bullets. But the gun had been cleaned very recently. No dust inside the barrel."

"Everybody in Ypsilanti owns a shotgun. They won't sell you a house there if you don't."

"Excuse me, but wasn't it you who came in here two minutes ago and dropped this on my desk?" She slid a copy of the report I'd typed for Billy Fred from under the autopsy file.

"Just playing devil's advocate. It isn't every day I provide someone with a motive for double murder."

"I'm not here to dispel your guilt complex. I've got a philandering wife and her lover, both shot to pieces. I've got the gun. And I've got the redneck cuckolded husband in an interrogation room, with nothing to account for his whereabouts at the time of the shoot. If they were all this easy, I'd be an inspector by now."

"Any ID yet on the guy?"

She consulted her notebook. "Kenneth Brindle, thirty-three, single, apartment in Madison Heights. Pharmacist. Apparently he and Lynne met a couple of months ago when he filled in at the drugstore in Romulus."

I got out my own notepad and read her the license number I'd gotten off the Taurus. She found the proper page in hers and nodded. "Shame," she said. "He had only two payments to go."

"I deliberately waited till the next day to tell Billy Fred. Didn't they know it was bad luck to go to the same place twice?"

"They probably got a hint at the end." She tapped her coral nails on the desk. "It wasn't your fault. He was bound to find out sooner or later and do what he did."

"I'm supposed to know a thing or two about people. I didn't figure him for that. I still don't."

Her telephone whirred. She picked up, said yes three times, and cradled the receiver. "That's a big ten four. McCorkingdale just confessed."

I felt my face sag. I pushed back my chair and stood. "Thanks, Lieutenant. Let me know when you need a statement. I'll be in the unemployment line."

"People get killed every day," she said, "especially in this town. Somebody plugged 'Joey Bats' Battaglia this morning in front of the Michigan Central Depot. He's gasping out what's left of his life at Detroit Receiving."

"Wasn't me. Fingering lonely wives is more my speed."

Billy Fred got three inches of type in the *Free Press* city section Tuesday morning, bumped to page three by the front-page spread on Joseph "Joey Bats" Battaglia, who was said to have been cutting a deal with the Justice Department on a labor-racketeering charge when his union brothers hung a price tag on him. He'd hoped to throw them off by taking a train to Miami instead of flying, but he was in the ICU at Detroit Receiving Hospital with his kidneys punctured and his ticket intact. His mistress, a local waitress and part-time professional singer, had been waiting inside the depot when Battaglia stepped out for a smoke. Cigarettes kill.

Joey led off the noon and evening news reports. Billy Fred got the pickup spot after the sports and weather and was forgotten by Thursday.

Not entirely, though.

The employee-break room at the Powertrain plant was painted sunset orange and electric blue, probably as a respite from the grays and beiges in Assembly. I found Merle Ketch sitting at one of the trestle tables, reading a magazine and drinking from a can of Pepsi.

My badge impressed him more than it had the clerk at the Alamo. He laid down the magazine and sat up straight. "I put in my two hundred hours," he said. "I got the judge's signature on the papers at home." His redneck accent was even stronger than my former client's.

I sat down across from him. "Relax, Mr. Ketch. Personnel told me you work Billy Fred McCorkingdale's shift. I understand you're friends."

"We bowl and go see the Tigers. You can't get much friendlier than that. This about Lynne?"

"What did he tell you about Lynne?"

"I don't want to get him in trouble."

I dug out the good-old-boy grin. "He was arraigned yesterday in Recorder's Court on a charge of open murder. How much more trouble could he get in?"

Ketch went sullen. "They ought to pay him a bounty. If my Judy was ever to step out on me, I'd wring her neck."

"Not very nineties."

"Some things don't change."

"Did he tell you his wife was seeing anyone?"

"Like I said, we're friends. He hired some detective to follow her around. I told him just what I told you. All the boys on the shift are behind him. One or two of our granddaddies done the same thing down home. They none of 'em never saw the inside of a prison."

"You said all that?"

"Hell, yes. Man can only take so much."

"Did it occur to you that you might be putting ideas in his head?"

"What if I did? Billy Fred's a hero. Just like them boys that take just so much crap from their supervisors, then come in blasting with a big old AK-47. That's how this here country got started."

"I don't think there were any assault rifles at Valley Forge." I drew a doodle of a clown in my notebook. "Mind if I ask where you were Monday night?"

He drained the last of his Pepsi, then crushed the can. "Break's over."

"I thought you got fifteen minutes."

"I do. You just used up your last minute."

I left but didn't want to. I liked Merle. I hadn't liked anyone so much since the Ayatollah.

The young man behind the desk at the Alamo was still reading about abnormal psychology. I asked him if he was cramming for a final.

"Aced it yesterday. You'd be surprised how much of this applies to my job." His eyes were alert behind the thick spectacles. "I told the police you were asking about Mr. and Mrs. Brown before it happened. My statement's on the record."

"You're safe. I'm not a suspect. Lieutenant Thaler says you told her no one came in asking about them the night of the shooting. Anybody else come in that night?"

"Just Mrs. Brown, to pay for the room. Mondays are slow. I never did see Mr. Brown. Not that Mr. Brown."

"Get a lot of Browns, do you?"

"Like you said, *Smith*'s out of style."

"What I can't figure out is how McCorkingdale knew what room they were in if he didn't come in and ask."

"I'm no detective."

"You're a psych student. Pretend it's a pop quiz."

He smiled for the first time. He'd inherited the smile from every night clerk who had ever stood in the lobby of a hotel where the guests paid in cash. I laid a fifty-dollar bookmark on the desk. This one went into his shirt pocket.

"She asked for the same room she had Saturday night. It was vacant, so I gave it to her. Maybe her husband guessed she'd do that and went straight there without stopping here to inquire."

"One night's pretty much like all the rest in this place. You're sure you didn't forget?" I handed him the photograph of Merle Ketch I'd gotten from the personnel manager at Powertrain.

The kid glanced at it, then handed it back. "I saw McCorkingdale on the news. This isn't him."

"I didn't say it was."

"Well, I didn't see him either."

"Or maybe he paid you up through next semester to forget you did."

He adjusted his glasses. "Education's expensive. Look, just because I have to do a little grifting doesn't mean I'd cover up for a killer."

I put away the photograph. "Okay."

"Okay?" His forehead wrinkled.

I pointed at the book. "I read the same text in college. They ought to update them every twenty years or so. Anyway, you passed."

I went out to my car, but I didn't drive away. I'd parked it at a discreet angle so I could see through the glass doors into the lobby.

I was prepared for a very long wait. The clerk's kidneys were much younger than mine, and for all I knew he'd taken a break just before I arrived. But I had the whole night to see this through. And an empty coffee can for emergencies.

Luck smiled after twenty minutes. The clerk slid off his high stool, laid down the textbook, stretched, and went through a door behind the desk. I was out of the car in less than five seconds. The file box was on the shelf under the desk where he'd had it Saturday.

When he came back from the bathroom, he found me standing there scratching my chin with the corner of a registration card from Monday night.

I caught Mary Ann Thaler in the squad room, dunking a tea bag into a cup of hot water. It was the 8:00 P.M. to 4:00 A.M. shift, and we had the place all to ourselves. The lieutenant looked as fresh as the morning in a royal-blue silk blouse and a black skirt.

"I got the message you left this afternoon," she said. "We checked out Merle Ketch. He was drinking beer with some buddies in the Sidecar Tavern when the thing went down at the Alamo. That good a friend he wasn't. Sorry."

"I'm not interested in him anymore. I need a pass to see Billy Fred."

"Now? What've you got?"

"I'll tell you after I talk to him."

"Withholding evidence, are we?"

"A hunch isn't evidence. What about it?"

"I don't guess it would hurt. I've got my hands full enough with Joey Bats without worrying about McCorkingdale."

"Any change?"

"His vitals have stabilized, whatever that means, but the news isn't good. These pro jobs don't leave much to go on."

"Talk to his mistress?"

She nodded. "She didn't see anything. She was inside the station, reading a paperback."

"Ask her where she was Saturday night."

"Not without knowing why, I won't."

"I'll fill you in while you write out that pass."

The visitors' room I was shown into at the Wayne County Jail was drywalled and painted a not unpleasant shade of ivory, but it had no decorations or outside windows or features of any kind except the two doors that led into it and a table and two folding chairs. I was seated there thirty seconds when Billy Fred McCorkingdale came in, accompanied by a turnkey in a deputy's uniform who took a glance around, then departed, locking the door behind him. His slab face remained in the steel-gridded window.

Billy Fred sat down facing me. His eyes were sunken. I saw no recognition in them.

"Amos Walker," I reminded him. "You hired me last week."

"I know." His voice grated, as if he hadn't used it in days. He hadn't said a word at his arraignment.

"I talked to Merle Ketch," I said. "You got lousy taste in friends."

He shrugged and said, "Merle's company."

"You'd do better with a parakeet. I suppose he told you his grand-daddy wrung his wife's neck for straying, and the jury let him off."

"Cut her throat, he said."

"Things have changed since then. People don't walk on their knuckles. They don't hang their long johns in the backyard and they almost never acquit wife murderers. Even when the wives are unfaithful."

He said nothing.

"Life in Jackson's ten times as long as life on the outside," I went on. "Those rednecks you work with will have plenty of time to forget all about what a hero you are, and you'll be in for another thirty years. Take back the confession."

He squeezed his eyes shut. Tears came out of the cracks. He raised his hands to his face. "I killed her," Billy Fred said. "I murdered Lynne."

"No, you didn't."

"It's my fault she's dead."

"Better, but still not accurate. It may be your fault she went looking for attention, but that's between you and a therapist. I know one, if you don't mind waiting for him to graduate. Lynne's dead, and so is that poor slob Kenneth Brindle because some bottom feeder who didn't know either of them from Rembrandt kicked down the door of their room and blew them into kibble. And he's out there walking around while you're in here blubbering and being admired by that dirtbag Merle Ketch."

His face went blank but only for a moment. He was listening now.

"I sneaked a peek at the Alamo registration cards," I said. "I did it the same way the killer did Monday night — waited for the clerk to go to the bathroom and went in and rifled the box. Your wife and Brindle weren't the only couple who registered as Mr. and Mrs. Brown that night. There was one other."

His fingers made deep indentations in the table's padded vinyl top, but he kept quiet.

"The clerk at the Alamo scores tuition money for college the same way employees in ratty hotels the world over draw cash. He registered a party he recognized from TV and the newspapers and accepted a bribe to forget he ever saw him. *That* was the phony Brown the killer was looking for."

"Who?"

"I don't know the killer's name. I only know why he did it. He was hired to kill a man registered as Brown and the woman he had with him, to eliminate her as a witness. He was in a hurry. As soon as he found a card with that signature and a room number, he stopped looking. Once that door flew open, he didn't have time for a positive ID. He saw a man and a woman in bed, shot them both twice, and took off. I doubt he knew he'd killed the wrong Browns until he saw the news later."

"Who?" he asked again, but it wasn't the same question.

"The other Browns? 'Joey Bats' Battaglia and his girlfriend. They hauled out of there after the big noise and before the cops arrived. That's why Joey was in such a hurry to leave town the next day. He wasn't so lucky that time. That time the shooter made up for his mistake."

"Like hell he did." He had his face in his hands again.

"All this is speculation so far," I said, "although the desk clerk's ready to talk. The cops figured they had their man — you — so they never bothered to check the registration cards. They're talking to Battaglia's mistress now. If she confirms that she and Joey were at the Alamo Monday night, you'll have a defense. But you have to retract that confession."

"Sure." He was staring down at his hands: big hands, callused all over, with decades of dirt and steel shavings ground deep into the knuckles. "Poor Lynne."

I got up and signaled to the turnkey, who let himself in. Billy Fred rose. At the door to the cells he looked back over his shoulder. "I'm hiring you again. Trust me on the advance?"

"Hiring me for what?"

"You're the detective."

The guard followed him out and drew the door shut with a click.

It looked as if I had underestimated Joey Bats's luck. On Thursday the head of surgery at Detroit Receiving Hospital announced at a press conference that his team had managed to save one of the patient's kidneys. Arrangements had been made to transfer him to Hutzel Hospital for recovery as early as the weekend.

When the appointed day arrived, a crew consisting of a nurse and a pair of interns, with a uniformed police officer looking on, strapped their charge to a gurney and ferried him for security's sake through an exit normally reserved for mortuary cases. An intern held open the door to the ambulance while his partner and the nurse prepared to slide the patient inside.

Just as they lifted the stretcher, an ambulance bearing the logo of another company rolled around the corner, squished to a stop, and two men in ski masks piled out of the back. One of them covered the uniformed cop with an automatic pistol. His companion sprinted up to the gurney and swung up a shotgun with the stock and barrel sawed off. Before he could squeeze the trigger, the patient sat up and shot him in the chest with a .38 revolver. This startled the man with the pistol just long enough for the "nurse" to produce a nine-millimeter Beretta from the folds of her uniform. "Police!" Mary Ann Thaler shouted. "Drop the weapon!"

He dropped the weapon. At this point the driver of the second ambulance floored the accelerator. Tires spun, and the vehicle took off. The uniformed officer drew his sidearm, crouched, and fired a single shot through the open door at the back of the ambulance. The vehicle veered sharply, jumped the curb, and slammed into a steel post holding up a sign calling for silence. The horn sounded in a long, irritating blast. It didn't stop until one of the "interns," a detective with Felony Homicide, grabbed the driver by his collar and pulled his dead body away from the steering wheel.

By the time I got free of the gurney, the uniform had Ski Mask Number One facedown on the ground with his wrists in cuffs. The second "intern," another plainclothesman, bent over Ski Mask Number Two with the shotgun in hand. "This one's still breathing, Lieutenant," he said.

Thaler knelt and stripped off the man's mask. He had one of those faces you couldn't have picked out of a lineup if you were married to him — young and unlined without a single distinguishing feature. I holstered my revolver under the paper gown I had on over my clothes and got down on one knee beside the lieutenant.

I said, "Joke's on you, fella. Joey died Thursday morning. The whole thing was a gag to bring you back for a third try."

"I just figured that out," he said. "Bonehead play. That's two this week," he said. "Stupid." Pink bubbles rippled between his lips.

I was tingling now, but I didn't have time to savor it. "What was the first?"

"The Alamo." He coughed and gurgled, or maybe it was an attempt to laugh. "Remember the Alamo — get it?"

"Got it," I said. And he was gone.

Lieutenant Thaler and I stood. "Deathbed confession," she said and put away her Beretta. "Looks like your client's off the hook."

"Yeah," I said. "Too bad it's not the one that counts."

GREGORY FALLIS

And Maybe the Horse Will Learn to Sing

FROM *Alfred Hitchcock Mystery Magazine*

"IT'S MY HUSBAND," Chloe Stenning said. "He's . . . I think he's been cheating on me."

Now that's a sad thing for a person to say out loud to a total stranger. Even if the stranger is a private detective.

And me . . . was I the least bit sympathetic? Did I feel even a lick of empathy? No, I wasn't, and no, I didn't. What I was thinking was this: I *hate* this work. I was thinking: I really hate Kevin Sweeney.

"Why do you think he's cheating on you?" I asked.

"Well, Mr. Wheeler . . ."

"Call me Joop," I said. No need to be formal. I mean, the woman was fessing up her deepest, darkest suspicions about her husband. I could let her call me by my name.

"Joop?" she asked. "Is that Dutch? I notice you have an accent."

I come from South Carolina. Which is separated from the Netherlands by a big chunk of the Atlantic Ocean. "Tell me about your husband," I said.

And she told me. It was, sad to say, a common story. Her husband Eddie had been working late for the last six weeks or so. Not terribly late . . . just a couple of hours. And not every night . . . just once or twice a week.

"But you don't think he's really working late," I said. "Is that right?"

She nodded.

"I've tried calling him at his office when it happens," she said. "His co-workers always tell me he's gone."

"Maybe the co-workers made a mistake," I said. Though it didn't seem likely.

Chloe Stenning didn't seem to think much of the idea either. She shook her head. "No, he's cheating on me. I know it."

"How do you know it?"

"I just know it."

Well, it's hard to argue with that logic. "Have you asked him?"

She shook her head.

"Don't you think you should?"

"No," she said. "I don't want him to think I'm suspicious."

"I see," I said. Which was as big a lie as I've told in recent history.

I looked at my notepad and silently cursed Kevin Sweeney. And as long as I was silently cursing, I put in a word or two for Sweeney's wife Mary Margaret. And a few more for Professor Warren Lister. I gave my own fool self a few choice words as well.

Sweeney and I have a small private investigative agency in one of those quaint little Massachusetts seacoast villages north of Boston. Mostly what we do is criminal defense work. A little arson, a little murder, a little drug dealing in the night. It may not be nice, but it feels cleaner than most domestic work. There is something about an imploding relationship that makes a simple robbery-homicide seem almost tidy.

But sometimes, when the cash flow gets a tad tight, Sweeney and I have to take on domestic cases. And our cash flow had become a cash trickle. Which was why I was sitting in our conference room with Chloe Stenning and Warren Lister.

Professor Warren Lister. He was the reason I was silently cursing Sweeney and his normally charming wife. Mary Margaret had decided to go back to school and finish her degree. Which is a fine thing in itself. But she took a sociology course that happened to be taught by our boy Warren. And when he learned Mary Margaret's husband was a licensed private investigator, he went quivery all over and asked her to arrange a meeting with him. Which she did. Who wants to irritate their professor?

Sweeney, to give him credit — which I sorely hate to do — wasn't at all happy about meeting Warren. Sweeney's a former police officer, and he's got a cop's disdain for and suspicion of academics. Still, he dearly loves his wife and would do just about anything for her.

So Sweeney agreed to meet Warren for lunch one day. And he persuaded me to tag along as well. I thought it could be a hoot. And

I figured I'd get myself a free lunch. And besides, I'd do just about anything for Mary Margaret Sweeney my ownself.

We met in one of those trendy restaurants. Lots of wood and brass, high fern content, omelettes with goat's cheese, a microbrewery. After we ordered, Warren told us he wanted to study us. Not us in particular but private investigators. He wanted to follow us around over the summer break, he said, and look at what we did and how we did it. He said he wanted to explore our "occupational milieu" and our "work culture."

Sweeney was reluctant. "I don't know," he said. "I'm not even sure we have an occupational milieu."

It was clear Sweeney didn't want his wife's sociology professor hanging out with us over the summer. You could almost see his flesh crawl at the idea. He looked to me for support.

"Sure we do," I said. "We've got bags full of occupational milieu. We've got enough occupational milieu to choke a donkey." I dearly love making Sweeney uncomfortable. It's wrong, I know, and I ought to be terribly ashamed of myself.

Warren looked at me when I spoke up. I knew that look. A lot of folks up north, the moment they hear a Southern accent they think two things. Dumb and racist. They seem to think all Southern white folks spend their time picking their teeth and trying to find some way to keep black folks down. I'm used to it. Mostly. Besides, in this biz it sometimes helps to have folks think you're dumber than you really are.

"I don't know," Sweeney said again. "Dr. Lister, we do . . ."

"Call me Warren," Lister said. He was trying for that just-us-boys thing. But it wasn't working.

"Warren, we do private investigations," Sweeney said. "The operative word there is 'private.' I don't think our clients would like it if we brought along observers."

Warren was ready for that one. He told us about the "rigorous human subject policies" of the university and offered to show us the confidentiality restrictions covered in his research proposal.

I don't know about other folks, but I'd rather shove a fondue fork in my eye than read a research proposal.

"Oh, I don't think we need to see the proposal right now," I said. "You can mail a copy of it to Sweeney."

Sweeney didn't seem amused. I pointed with my fork. "You going to eat those fries, Warren?"

Warren pushed his french fries in my direction. Then he proceeded to swear enough oaths to secrecy and confidentiality and discretion to please the CIA, MI5, and a computer software company.

Sweeney tried a few more discouraging words, but old Warren said he was ready to do whatever it took. And me, I egged the poor sap on.

Which is where I made my big mistake. Most of the misery I've suffered in my semi-long and somewhat wicked life has been self-inflicted. I'd forgotten that when the semester ended Sweeney and Mary Margaret were heading to Ireland for two weeks. Which meant I was the only person with an available occupational milieu for Warren to study. So in trying to tweak Sweeney's nose all I'd managed to do was to step on my own dick. There's a lesson there, I suspect.

So that's how I found myself sitting in the conference room with a Yankee sociology professor and a woman who'd decided her husband was cheating on her.

"Mrs. Stenning, do you love your husband?" I asked.

She nodded. "Yes, I do."

"Talk to him," I said. "Ask him what's going on. There might be a simple explanation for his behavior."

"I can't do that," she said. "I can't confront him until I know."

"You don't need to confront him, Mrs. Stenning," I said. "But if you love your husband, you should trust him enough to . . ."

"But I don't trust him," she said. "Why are you trying to talk me out of this? Don't you want my case?"

Well, no, I didn't want her case. But I did want her money. "I'm sorry," I said. "I just don't want you to rush into this. This is an important decision."

She gave me a cold look. And got out her checkbook.

Before I let Chloe Stenning leave the office, I asked her a lot of really nosy questions and suggested some rude behavior she should try. A lot of detective work involves really nosy questions and rude behavior. I asked about her sex life with her husband — folks having affairs often show either an increase or a decrease in their sexual appetite. It turned out she and Eddie hadn't done it at all in the last couple of months. I asked if her Eddie had showed any radical mood swings, any bursts of anger or tears — having and hiding an affair plays hell with a person's nerves. Chloe said Eddie had seemed sort of quiet and depressed ever since he started coming home late.

Warren sat quietly through all the questions, trying not to look uncomfortable. It's not pleasant, listening to folks bare their souls. But you get used to it.

I suggested that Chloe start searching her husband's clothes, looking for anything that might indicate he was trashing around. Motel receipts, the scent of perfume or smoke on his clothes, someone else's hair. What Sweeney would call trace evidence. And I suggested she go through all of Eddie's old credit card receipts. And that she listen in on his phone calls if she could. And that she start keeping track of the odometer on Eddie's car so we could tell how far he was driving.

I suggested all sorts of despicable stuff, stuff you should never ever do to a person you love.

Chloe seemed eager to help.

Warren sat there taking it all in. Soaking up that occupational milieu. I think he was trying for a hard-boiled look, but he was only managing to look professorial and confused.

So there we were the next day, Warren and I, sitting in my car parked outside the gate to the Creighton Shipyard. We were waiting for Eddie Stenning to come cruising through the gate in his company car. A white Saturn.

I'm a Southern boy. I belong to a culture well grounded in conversation. I found it impossible to sit there with another person in the car and not talk. So I heard myself putting voice to the thought that had been wasping around in my brain ever since we took the case.

"I hate marital work," I said.

"Why?" he asked. He opened his little notebook. To record my thoughts, I suppose. I must have been letting a little work culture peek out. But that's what he was there for, so I gave it to him.

"I hate it on account of it's ugly," I said. "Two folks who are supposed to love each other. Who probably *used* to love each other. And now one of them is paying us good money to follow the other. It's just ugly. And besides, it probably won't matter what we learn."

"Why not?"

Cars were beginning to leave the shipyard gate. The day shift was over.

"It never does any good," I said. "Once a person is suspicious enough to hire a PI to follow their spouse around, the relationship is headed for disaster. If we confirm the client's suspicions, the relationship usually goes down in flames. If we don't confirm the client's suspicions, the client usually stays suspicious. Which means the relationship will probably go down in flames."

"If it doesn't do any good, why do you do it?"

I grinned. "A man's got to buy beans and tortillas," I said. "Besides, I keep hoping that if I can give a suspicious spouse some good news maybe they'll keep things together long enough to work out their problems. Maybe the horse will learn to sing."

Warren looked at me like I'd taken leave of my senses. I've seen that look before. Sweeney looks at me that way all the time. "What's that about a horse?" he asked. "I don't understand."

"There he is," I said. I pointed to a white Saturn in the middle of the slow stream of cars leaving the shipyard.

I started the engine, shifted into first, and then just sat there.

Warren leaned forward as the Saturn drove off. "Let's go," he said. "He's getting away."

I shook my head. "Maybe not," I said, and pointed out the window. "'Cause there he is again."

A second white Saturn was leaving the gate. Then a third. And a fourth.

Over the next fifteen minutes we counted fourteen white Saturns. It seemed every mid-level executive in the Creighton Shipyard was issued a white Saturn.

"Now what do we do?" Warren asked.

"Do you watch the television news at eleven?" I asked.

Warren looked confused, but he nodded.

"Good," I said. "I'll come pick you up at your house when the news is over. We'll take care of it then."

Warren was sitting on his porch waiting for me when I drove up. He was in my car almost before it stopped. Grinning like he'd just won the pumpkin judging contest.

"What is it we're going to do?" he asked. He was dressed all in black. Black jeans, black turtleneck, black sneakers. The sneakers had that right-out-of-the-box look. I suppose I was lucky he wasn't wearing a ninja mask and toting those little throwing stars.

"We're going to make it a little easier to follow Eddie Stenning from work tomorrow," I said.

Warren's eyes were all glittery bright. It affects some folks that way. Being out late at night when all the decent people are at home in bed. Out on some secret mission, preparing to do something a little shady. Some folks get caught up in it. They think it's sexy.

And it is, sort of. It's a sick thing, maybe, but it's fun. Not that I'd have admitted it to Warren.

"I see," Warren said. "We're going to plant a tracking device on his car."

"Well, we're going to do something a tad less James Bond than that," I said. "I'm a low-tech sort of guy."

Warren was grinning like a coke fiend. That boy was like to wet his pants with excitement.

It didn't take long to get to the Stennings' house — a two-story Tudor-looking unit with a bay window and some sort of creeping ivy that was slowly destroying the neighbors' privacy fence. Stenning didn't live all that far from Warren. The upper middle class tends to congregate in convenient clumps.

I mentioned that to Warren, thinking he might like a bit of PI wisdom.

"Propinquity," he said.

"Pardon?"

"Propinquity," he said again. "The tendency toward geographical proximity among social classes."

"Ah," I said. "Propinquity. Right."

I drove a block past the Stenning house and parked.

"Pass me over that flashlight, would you?" I keep a big five-cell Maglite in the car. Everybody should. You never know when you're going to need a flashlight.

Warren handed me the flashlight. "What do you want me to do?" he asked.

"I don't want you to do anything," I said, "except hush up. This is only going to take a second, but you need to be quiet. Take some notes or something."

The lights were off in the house. The Saturn was parked in the drive.

Warren was hovering around me like a moth. "Won't the flashlight attract attention when you turn it on?" he whispered.

"Why on earth would I turn it on?" I asked.

I walked up to the Saturn and used the big Maglite to smash the right taillight. Didn't hardly make a sound at all.

Tuesday afternoon only one white Saturn with a busted taillight drove out the shipyard gate.

Eddie Stenning was a delight to tail. He drove like a Mormon. He used his turn signals, he came to a full stop at stop signs, he slowed up and prepared to stop at yellow lights. My grammy could have tailed Eddie. And my grammy drinks a bit.

Eddie drove straight home.

He did the same thing Wednesday afternoon.

That's the nature of surveillance work. There's a lot of waiting. You just have to learn patience. It's a zen thing — sitting quietly and waiting, being aware without anticipation or expectation. Taking the world exactly as it comes.

I'm used to it. I even sort of enjoy it. But old Warren, he didn't have a good grasp on the tao of surveillance. He had no tolerance at all for sitting and watching. Not many Yankees do. I blame it on the fact that there aren't enough porches up north. Folks never acquire the knack of sitting quietly and watching the world move by.

Warren fidgeted like a drunk with the DT's. And the man could not keep quiet. Once he got over his Yankee reserve, he began to ask questions. Asked me about PI work, about growing up in the segregated South, about the lack of depth in the Red Sox bull pen, about the Mars lander.

By Thursday afternoon I was giving some serious thought to tying Warren up and chunking him in the trunk.

That was the afternoon Eddie Stenning turned off his usual route home.

"Where's he going?" Warren asked.

"How should I know?"

Warren's eyes got big and lit up. He was jazzed. "This is it, isn't it. He's going . . . to wherever it is he's going."

And this guy is a college professor. "There's no need to get ourselves in a sweat just yet," I said. "He might just be heading for the drive-thru window at Colonel Sanders. Or maybe he's got to pick up the dry cleaning."

"My God, this is fun," Warren said.

I wasn't sure why Warren was so worked up. It wasn't like we were in a high-speed pursuit. Eddie was still driving with all the reckless daring of Ward Cleaver on tranquilizers.

Then Eddie turned into one of the arched entrances of the Steadwell Gardens Cemetery.

I was stunned. "Well, I'll be damned and go to hell," I said.

Warren goggled at me. "What? What's the matter?"

I drove past the entrance and pulled the car over to the curb.

"Aren't we going to follow him in?" Warren asked.

But I was already halfway out the door by that time, and jogging back to the entrance. I heard Warren open his door and follow along after.

By the time I got to the entrance Eddie and his Saturn were nowhere to be seen.

I couldn't help but grin. "That dog," I said.

"What's going on?"

"We just got scraped off," I said.

"What? What? Scraped off? I don't understand."

"Scraped off," I said. "It's what you do when you don't want to be followed. The followee scrapes off the follower."

But it was clear Warren was still confused. So I explained.

Steadwell Gardens is the oldest and largest cemetery in town. It takes up three or four suburban blocks and looks like a private golf course. Lots of tall trees, softly rolling hills, narrow curving roads. The trees are planted in such a way as to give grieving families lots of privacy, so Steadwell Gardens feels more like a whole bunch of little cemeteries instead of one really big one. And surrounding the whole thing is a lovely green privacy hedge about six feet tall and thick as brick.

Steadwell Gardens is a great place to be dead. It's also a great place to spot and lose a tail. First off, it's just plain tough to tail somebody in a cemetery. Any cemetery. At any time. There isn't a lot of traffic in cemeteries, and folks tend to drive real slow. So it's easy to spot somebody following you. Stevie Wonder could probably spot a tail in a cemetery.

Second, Steadwell Gardens has six different entrances on four different streets. Which means you can enter on Willow Street and exit on Pine, or on Mission Avenue, or on Dugdale Street. Or you can leave by another exit farther down on Willow. That means a single PI can't cover all the exits. Which basically means you lose the subject. Scraped off."

"And you think he drove in there deliberately?"

"Well, yeah," I said. "Nobody drives into a cemetery by accident. The question is, did he drive in there deliberately to scrape us off."

"Couldn't he just be visiting a grave?"

"Sure he could," I said. "That's the most innocent and most likely explanation. But here's a true thing about PI work. The most innocent and most likely explanation isn't necessarily what happens."

Warren actually wrote that down. "What do we do now?"

"We get back in the car, and we drive around the block for a while looking for Eddie," I said. "And later on, unless we get real lucky, we'll call Chloe Stenning and tell her we lost her husband."

And that's just what we did. Drove around the block four times without seeing any white Saturns. Drove through the cemetery twice, but that's a big chunk of land and it would have been really easy to miss Eddie. Drove to a nearby convenience store and stopped at the pay phone.

"Mrs. Stenning?" I said into the telephone. "Your husband took a different route out of the shipyard this afternoon. But I'm afraid we lost him."

"Lost him?"

"Yes, ma'am." I did what most folks do when forced to admit failure. I fell back on jargon in an effort to sound competent. "The subject — your husband — left the shipyard west gate at 5:11 P.M. My associate and I maintained mobile surveillance until we reached Willow Street, at which time —"

"Willow?" she asked. "What was he doing over there?"

"I'm afraid I don't know, ma'am," I said. "We lost him at 5:26 P.M. We attempted to reacquire the subject — your husband — for approximately twenty minutes without success."

I hurried on before she could comment on that. "Would you please note the exact time he arrives at home this evening? And check his odometer. That will help us to determine the radius of his possible movements."

It was all nonsense, of course. It probably wouldn't tell us anything useful at all. But it had the sound of military precision about it, and clients eat that military-sounding stuff up with a spoon. If you can't give them good service, you can at least give them the illusion of it.

Warren and I got back in the car. "Now what?" he asked.

"Now we go home," I said. "We'll try again tomorrow."

"That's it?" he said. "We just go home? That's not very satisfying. In fact, it's damned frustrating."

"Welcome to the exciting world of private investigation," I said.

The next morning Warren and I discussed a plan in case Eddie tried to scrape us off at the cemetery again. "Are you a good runner?" I asked him.

"I do three miles every morning."

I looked at him. Three miles. In the morning. I have never understood the attraction of running for fun. The whole concept is foreign to me. I declare, it must be a form of madness. But it's not a form I'm familiar with. Madness in South Carolina takes a less strenuous form. My Uncle Peawood is loonier than a peach orchard boar, but he knows enough not to get up in the morning and go *running*.

"Good," I said. I handed him one of our Handi-Coms, a little two-way radio, and showed him how to use it.

"If it looks like we're going to the cemetery again," I said, "I'll pass Eddie and drop you at the first entrance. You head in and try to follow him on foot. I'll keep circling the cemetery. If I see him pull out, I'll tail him. You'll have to grab a cab home. If I don't see him, I'll keep circling until you come out. Any questions?"

I'll say this for the professor — he was game to try just about anything. He thought the idea of jogging through a cemetery sounded like fun. He even went home to fetch a bright red jogging outfit before we headed for the shipyard to tail Eddie. Said he wanted to stay in character. Whatever that meant.

I admit I had high hopes for that afternoon. It was a Friday and a payday. Perfect time for old Eddie to be meeting his outside squeeze. If that was what he was doing.

Eddie, though, was a good boy; he drove straight home. He did the same thing for the first three days of the next week. The only excitement was on Tuesday when Eddie pulled into a gas station. I was able to scribble in my notepad that Eddie put seven dollars of unleaded in his Saturn. It was going to be hard to make that sound impressive in our report to Chloe.

It was a painful time. Warren decided we were meant to be friends and friends "share" things. He took to telling me all about his life. He talked about his academic career (he was unhappy with it), about the pressure he was under to publish in the most influential scholarly journals (he was unhappy with it), about his colleagues (he was unhappy with them), about his marriage (guess what).

Now, Southern folk talk a lot. At least, we do in my part of South Carolina. But we don't talk about ourselves. And certainly not about our feelings. Not with near strangers. But we're also raised to be polite, so I nodded and clucked and sympathized with poor Warren's terrible hardships. But I was never so happy as I was on that Thursday when Eddie turned off his usual route home.

When it looked like he was headed toward Steadwell Gardens again, I turned to Warren. "You ready?" I asked.

"Ready," he said. His eyes were sparkling, and he was grinning like he was the illegitimate child of Charles and Camilla. He began to do stretching exercises in the car.

I passed Eddie just before we turned onto Willow. And got caught behind a big funeral procession. Not mafiosi big, but big enough that it had traffic backed up a bit as they turned into the leafy archway of Steadwell Gardens. I kept an eye on Eddie in the rearview mirror just to make sure he made the turn and was behind us. I'd have looked like a pure born fool if our boy had kept going straight through the intersection.

I passed the funeral procession, made sure Warren had the Handi-Com turned on, pulled over to the side of the road, and dropped him off. He was jogging merrily through the arch as I drove away.

At the stop sign on the corner I held a long stop, waiting for Eddie to appear in the rearview mirror. The funeral procession had made it in the gate and the cars backed up behind it were just breaking free.

I watched Eddie Stenning turn under the arch.

"He's coming your way," I said into my Handi-Com.

"Roger that," Warren said, his voice flattened by the little speaker. "I have visual contact." Roger that? Visual contact? Give the man a walkie-talkie and he becomes General George Patton. Pretty soon he'd be calling in coordinates for an artillery strike.

I drove slowly around the corner.

"Subject is turning right," Warren said. "Proceeding at a moderate . . . uh . . . at a moderate . . ."

"Pace?" I suggested. I made a U-turn and drove back the way I'd come. "Speed?"

"The funeral," Warren said. "It's stopping right in front of us."

"So?" I said. "It's a cemetery. They have to stop to bury the bodies. No drive-by burials allowed."

"What do I do?"

"What do you mean?"

"All the mourners are getting out of their cars," Warren said. "I can't go jogging through them."

"Why not?"

"It's not done," Warren said.

"What's Eddie doing?"

"He's driving slowly," he said. "The mourners are letting him pass. But he's in a car. I'm in a red jogging suit."

"Warren, you said you wanted to study the private investigator's work culture," I said. "Well, our work culture includes jogging through funerals. Get after Eddie."

I drove slowly and cursed amateurs. Which wasn't fair. I know if I'd been wearing a bright red jogging outfit I'd have found it difficult to jog through a group of mourners. But that didn't stop me from cursing.

"What's going on?" I barked into the Handi-Com.

It took a moment for Warren to answer. "He . . . I, uh, I got . . . we got scraped off."

"We what?"

"I lost him," Warren said. And even through the tinny Handi-Com speaker I could hear the embarrassment and failure in his voice. "He went around a corner, and by the time I got there, he was gone. There's a Y intersection. One way goes over a hill, the other around a small grove of trees. I guess I chose the wrong branch."

Well, at least he'd stopped talking like GI Joe.

I sped up, hurrying over to the south side of the cemetery. No Eddie in a Saturn. I continued to circle the cemetery. Nothing.

"What should I do?" Warren asked.

"I'll pick you up outside the west gate," I said.

Another hesitation. "I don't know which gate is the west gate," he said.

"You went in the east gate," I said. "The west gate will be on the opposite side."

"I'm all turned around," he said sadly. "I don't even know where I am."

"Head toward the setting sun," I told him.

"I'm sorry," Warren said. "I messed up."

Roger that.

It was not fun to report to Chloe Stenning that we'd lost her husband again. And lost him in the very same neighborhood we'd lost him in the last time.

"Did he know you were following him?" she asked.

"I don't think so," I said. "He wasn't driving like he thought he was being tailed. But he's lost us twice now. Does he have any reason to think he might be being followed?"

"Maybe," she said. "If he's cheating on me, he might be expecting to be followed. It's happened before."

"You hired a detective agency before?" I asked.

"Not me," she said. "His ex-wife. When Eddie was having an affair with me. She had us followed."

"Oh," I said. What else was there to say?

"I should have known," she said. "You marry a man who cheats on his wife, you marry a man who cheats on his wife."

The next afternoon I took up station outside the shipyard gate alone. Entirely alone. Sans Warren. Warrenless. It was great.

I hadn't booted old Warren out of our occupational milieu. I'd just put him in his own car and stationed him inside the east entrance of Steadwell Gardens. As long as Eddie Stenning followed his usual pattern, we were fairly well prepared. My biggest fear was that Eddie would get that taillight fixed. Then I'd have to vandalize his car all over again.

Two nights later Eddie turned off his usual route, heading toward Steadwell Gardens. When we were in range, I alerted Warren.

"Red Dog One, this is Red Dog Leader," I said. "The Eagle is landing. I repeat, the Eagle is landing."

"What?" Warren asked.

"Eddie," I said. "He's about to turn onto Willow. So hop out of your car and start stretching."

"Ten-four."

This time when Eddie pulled into the arched cemetery entrance I hung back a moment, then followed him in.

"I see him," Warren reported. "He's turning right, just like before. I'm behind him but keeping apace."

A creature of habit, our Eddie. I turned right and dawdled along, out of sight of both Eddie and Warren.

"He's at the Y intersection and going up the rise," Warren said. "Just as I thought. I chose the wrong turn last time." He sounded pleased with himself, although a tad winded.

I could see Warren jogging over the rise as I came to the Y intersection. I slowed down just a bit.

Warren reported his position faithfully, if a bit breathlessly, as Eddie took a circuitous route through the cemetery. I was actually enjoying myself. The trees were pretty, the grass was summer green. And if I'd had the windows down and the air conditioning off, I suspect I'd've heard the birds singing. It was like driving slowly in a park. Well, a park full of buried dead folks.

"Whoa!" Warren called out. "He's stopping." He and Eddie were just a short ways in front, around a blind corner blocked by tall poplars.

"Stopping?" I pulled to a stop. "Did he spot you?"

"I don't think so. What should I do?"

"Keep jogging," I said. "Act like you're just jogging through the cemetery. Once you get past him, find a place to hide and wait. Report back when you're set."

A few moments later Warren buzzed back. "I'm set," he said. "I don't think he can see me."

"What's he doing?" I asked.

"He's still there."

"Still where?" I'm normally a calm man. But I declare, there were moments when I wanted to beat Warren Lister like a redheaded stepchild.

"He's at a grave."

A grave? I got out of the car and hurried to the poplars. I peeked through them. And sure enough, there was Eddie Stenning's Saturn. And a few yards away, near some pretty little juniper bushes, was Eddie Stenning his ownself. He was sort of crouched in front of a modest granite headstone. Tidying up a grave.

"I see him," I said to the Handi-Com.

"You see him? Where are you?"

I told him.

"What do we do now?" Warren asked.

"We have him surrounded," I said. "He's not going anywhere. Now we wait and we see what happens."

And we waited. Waited about forty-five minutes. During which Eddie fussed over the grave and talked. I suppose he was talking to whoever was dead under the headstone.

I went back to the car, got my camera, and took a few photographs. Just to document it.

Eddie stood up eventually. He put his hand on the headstone. It seemed a strangely intimate gesture. I've seen Sweeney reach out and touch his wife's shoulder like that when he's heading out the door. There was a sweetness to it.

It was almost too intimate to photograph. But I fired off a frame anyway.

"He's leaving," Warren informed me.

"I see that."

"Shall I follow him out?"

I told him not to bother. We knew where Eddie was spending his lost moments. We just didn't know who he was spending them with. After Eddie drove off, Warren and I slowly converged on the headstone. It said:

> IMELDA STENNING
> *All that live must die*
> *Passing through nature to*
> *eternity*

"His mother?" Warren asked.

I pointed out the dates. "Wasn't old enough to be his mother," I said.

"His sister, then."

I shook my head. "I don't think so."

"Then who?"

"His ex-wife."

Warren's eyes went wide. "My goodness," he said.

And suddenly I was grinning. I felt like I'd just won a roll of quarters at the slot machines.

"What?" Warren asked. "Why are you grinning?"

"We get to give good news to Chloe Stenning," I said. "Maybe the horse *will* learn to sing."

"That's the second time you've said that," Warren said. "What does it mean?"

"It's an old Persian folktale," I said. "There was a criminal, a thief, who was scheduled to be beheaded. As he was being led to the chopping block, he called out to the king, saying, 'If you spare my life, I'll teach your horse to sing hymns.' The king must have had a sense of humor on account of he spared the thief's life and gave him a year to teach the horse to sing. If he failed, at the end of the year he'd go back to the block. So the thief began to spend all his time with the king's horse, singing hymns to it. All the other criminals laughed. 'You'll never be able to teach that horse to sing,' they told him. And the thief just smiled. He said, 'I have a year. A lot can happen in a year. Maybe the horse will die. Maybe the king will die. Maybe I'll die. And who knows, maybe the horse will learn to sing.'"

Warren blinked at me a few times. "I don't understand," he said.

"We're giving Chloe Stenning good news," I said. "We're telling her that her husband isn't having an affair, which is what she's expecting to hear. Maybe this will give them the chance to work out their problems. What we're really doing is we're giving Chloe and Eddie time to teach the horse to sing."

"That bastard," Chloe Stenning said.

"Pardon?" I said.

After we left the cemetery, I called Chloe to tell her we'd discovered where her husband was spending his time. She said Eddie had just walked in the door and she couldn't talk. She asked us to come over the next day.

By the time we met the following day I'd done a bit more research. Imelda Stenning had in fact been Eddie's ex-wife. She'd died of uterine cancer a couple of months ago. About the time Eddie began coming home late.

Chloe invited us into the living room. We all sat on the edges of the furniture, like funeral-goers. I explained the situation, showed Chloe the photographs, and gave her a nicely jacketed copy of the final report. With a bill discreetly attached.

She flipped through the photos, pausing at the last one. The one with Eddie touching the headstone.

"I knew it," she said softly, with resignation. "I knew he was cheating on me."

"Cheating on you?" I asked.

She nodded. "I never thought it would be with his ex-wife."

"Uh, Mrs. Stenning . . . his ex-wife is dead," I said.

"I know," she said. She dropped the photographs on the coffee table. "I know she's dead. And he still loves her. How am I going to compete with her now?"

Warren and I left as soon as we politely could. "Goodness," he said when we were in the car. "It was like something had died inside her. Is it always like that?"

I shook my head. "Not always. Some folks get angry and throw things."

"Maybe you should have told her the story about the horse."

"It's a good story, isn't it," I said.

Warren nodded. "But it's just a story."

I shrugged. "Maybe."

TOM FRANKLIN

Poachers

FROM *Texas Review*

AT DAWN, on the first day of April, the three Gates brothers banked their ten-foot aluminum boat in a narrow slough of dark water. They tied their hounds, strapped on their rifles, and stepped out, ducking black magnolia branches heavy with rain and Spanish moss. The two thin younger brothers, denim overalls tucked into their boots, lugged between them a styrofoam cooler of iced fish and coons and possums. The oldest brother — bearded, heavyset, twenty years old — carried a Sunbeam Bread sack of eels in his coat pocket. Hooked over his left shoulder was the pink body of a fawn they'd shot and skinned, and, over the right, a stray dog to which they'd done the same. With the skins and heads gone and the dog's tail chopped off, they were difficult to tell apart.

The Gateses climbed the hill, clinging to vines and saplings, slipping in the red clay, their boots coated and enormous by the time they stepped out of the woods. For a moment they stood in the road, looking at the gray sky, the clouds piling up. The two younger ones, Scott and Wayne, set the cooler down. Kent, the oldest, removed his limp cap and squeezed the water from it. He nodded and his brothers picked up the cooler. They rounded a curve and crossed a one-lane bridge, stopping to piss over the rail into creek water high from all the rain, then went on, passing houses on either side: dark warped boards with knotholes big enough to look through and cement blocks for steps. Black men appeared in doors and windows to watch them go by — to most of these people they were something not seen often, something nocturnal and danger-ous. Along this stretch of the Alabama River, everyone knew that the brothers' father, Boo Gates, had married a girl named Anna when he was thirty and she was seventeen, and that the boys had been born in quick succession, with less than a year between them.

But few outside the family knew that a fourth child — a daughter, unnamed — had been stillborn, and that Boo had buried her in an unmarked grave in a clearing in the woods behind their house. Anna died the next day and the three boys, dirty and naked, watched their father's stoop-shouldered descent into the earth as he dug her grave. By the time he'd finished it was dark and the moon had come up out of the trees and the boys lay asleep upon each other in the dirt like wolf pups.

The name of this community, if it could be called that, was Lower Peachtree, though as far as anybody knew there'd never been an Upper Peachtree. Scattered along the leafy banks of the river were ragged houses, leaning and drafty, many empty, caving in, so close to the water they'd been built on stilts. Each April floods came and the crumbling land along the riverbank would disappear and each May, when the flood waters receded, a house or two would be gone.

Upriver, near the lock and dam, stood an old store, a slanting building with a steep, rusty tin roof and a stovepipe in the back. Behind the store the mimosa trees sagged, waterlogged. In front, beside the gas pump, long green steps led up to the door, where a red sign said "Open." Inside to the right, like a bar, a polished maple counter covered the entire wall. Behind the counter hung a rack with wire pegs for tools, hardware, fishing tackle. The condoms, bullets, and tobacco products, the rat poison and the Old Timer knife display were beneath the counter.

The store owner, Old Kirxy, had bad knees, and this weather settled around his joints like rot. For most of his life he'd been married and lived in a nice house on the highway. Two-story. Fireplaces in every bedroom. A china cabinet. But when his wife died two years ago, cancer, he found it easier to avoid the house, to keep the bills paid and the grass mowed but the door locked, to spend nights in the store, to sleep in the back room on the army cot and to warm his meals of corned beef and beef stew on a hot plate. He didn't mind that people had all but stopped coming to the store. As long as he served a few long-standing customers, he thought he'd stick around. He had his radio and one good station, WJDB of Thomasville, and money enough. He liked the area, knew his regulars weren't the kind to drive an hour to the nearest town. For those few people, Kirxy would go once a week to Grove Hill to shop for goods he'd resell, marking up the price just enough for a reasonable profit. He didn't need the money, it was just good business.

Liquor-wise, the county was dry, but that didn't stop Kirxy from selling booze. For his regulars, he would serve plastic cups of the cheap whiskey he bought in the next county or bottles of beer he kept locked in the old refrigerator in back. For these regulars, he would break packages of cigarettes and keep them in a cigar box and sell them for a dime apiece, a nickel stale. Aspirins were seven cents each, Tylenol tablets nine. He would open boxes of shotgun shells or cartridges and sell them for amounts that varied, according to caliber, and he'd been known to find specialty items — paperback novels, explosives, and, once, a rotary telephone.

At Euphrates Morrisette's place, the Gates brothers pounded on the back door. In his yard a cord of wood was stacked between two fenceposts and covered by a green tarp, brick halves holding the tarp down. A tire swing, turning slowly and full of rainwater, hung from a white oak. When Morrisette appeared — he was a large, bald black man — Kent held out the fawn and dog. Morrisette put on glasses and squinted at both. "Hang back," he said, and closed the door. Kent sat on the porch edge and his brothers on the steps.

The door opened and Morrisette came out with three pint jars of homemade whiskey. Each brother took a jar and unscrewed its lid, sniffed the clear liquid. Morrisette set his steaming coffee cup on the windowsill. He fastened his suspenders, looking at the carcasses hanging over the rail. The brothers were already drinking.

"Where's that girl?" Kent asked, his face twisted from the sour whiskey.

"My stepdaughter, you mean?" Morrisette's Adam's apple pumped in his throat. "She inside." Far away a rooster crowed.

"Get her out here," Kent said. He drank again, shuddered.

"She ain't but fifteen."

Kent scratched his beard. "Just gonna look at her."

When they left, the stepdaughter was standing on the porch in her white nightgown, barefoot, afraid, and rubbing the sleep from her eyes. The brothers backed away clanking with hardware and grinning at her, Morrisette's jaw clenched.

Sipping from their jars, they took the bag of eels down the road to the half-blind conjure woman who waited on her porch. Her house, with its dark drapes and empty parrot cages dangling from the eaves, seemed to be slipping off into the gully. She snatched the eels from Kent, squinting into the bag with her good eye. Grunting, she paid them from a dusty cloth sack on her apron and muttered to herself as they went up the dirt road. Wayne, the youngest, looked back, worried that she'd put a hex on them.

They peddled the rest of the things from their cooler, then left through the dump, stumbling down the ravine in the rain, following the water's edge to their boat. In the back, Kent wedged his jar between his thighs and ran the silent trolling motor with his foot. His brothers leaned against the walls of the boat, facing opposite banks, no sound but rain and the low hum of the motor. They drank silently, holding the burning whiskey in their mouths before gathering the will to swallow. Along the banks, fallen trees held thick strands of cottonmouth, black sparkling creatures dazed and slow from winter, barely able to move. If not for all the rain, they might still be hibernating, comatose in the banks of the river or beneath the soft yellow underbellies of rotten logs.

Rounding a bend, the brothers saw a small boat downriver, its engine clear, loud, and unfamiliar. Heading this way. The man in the boat lifted a hand in greeting. He wore a green poncho and a dark hat covered with plastic. Kent shifted his foot, turning the trolling motor, and steered them toward the bank, giving the stranger a wide berth. He felt for their outboard's crank rope while Scott and Wayne faced forward and sat on the boat seats. The man drawing closer didn't look much older than Kent. He cut his engine and coasted up beside them, smiling.

"Morning, fellows," he said, showing a badge. "New district game warden."

The brothers looked straight ahead, as if he wasn't there. The warden's engine was steaming, a flock of geese passed overhead. Wayne slipped his hands inside the soft leather collars of two dogs, who'd begun to growl.

"You fellows oughta know," the warden said, pointing his long chin to the rifle in Scott's hands, "that it's illegal to have those guns loaded on the river. I'm gonna have to check 'em. I'll need to see some licenses, too."

When he stood, the dogs jumped forward, toenails scraping aluminum. Wayne pulled them back, glancing at his brothers.

Kent spat into the brown water. He met the warden's eyes, and in an instant knew the man had seen the telephone in the floor of their boat.

"Pull to the bank!" the warden yelled, drawing a pistol. "Y'all are under arrest for poaching!"

The Gateses didn't move. One of the dogs began to claw the hull and the others joined him. A howl arose.

"Shut those dogs up!" The warden's face had grown blotchy and red.

The spotted hound broke free and sprang over the gunnel, slobber strung from its teeth, and the man most surprised by the game warden's shot was the game warden himself. His face drained of color as the noise echoed off the water and died in the bent black limbs and the cattails. The bullet had passed through the front dog's neck and smacked into the bank behind them, missing Wayne by inches. The dog collapsed, and there was an instant of silence before the others, now loose, clattered overboard into the water, red-eyed, tangled in their leashes, trying to swim.

"Pull to the goddamn bank!" the warden yelled. "Right now!"

Scowling, Kent leaned and spat. He laid his thirty-thirty aside. Using the shoulders of his brothers for balance, he made his way to the prow. Scott, flecked with dog blood, moved to the back to keep the boat level. At the front, Kent reached into the water and took the first dog by its collar, lifted the kicking form, and set it streaming and shivering behind him. His brothers turned their faces away as it shook off the water, rocking the whole boat. Kent grabbed the rope that led to the big three-legged hound and pulled it in hand over hand until he could work his fingers under its collar. He gave Wayne a sidelong look and together they hauled it in. Then Kent grabbed for the smaller bitch while Wayne got the black and tan.

The warden watched them, his hips swaying with the rise and fall of the current. Rain fell harder now, spattering against the aluminum boats. Kneeling among the dogs, Kent unsnapped the leash and tossed the spotted hound overboard. It sank, then resurfaced and floated on its side, trailing blood. Kent's lower lip twitched. Wayne whispered to the dogs and placed his hands on two of their heads to calm them — they were retching and trembling and rolling their eyes fearfully at the trees.

Scott stood up with his hands raised, as if to surrender. When the man looked at him, Kent jumped from his crouch into the other boat, his big fingers closing around the game warden's neck.

Later that morning, Kirxy had just unlocked the door and hung out the *Open* sign when he heard the familiar rattle of the Gates truck. He sipped his coffee and limped behind the counter, sat on his stool. The boys came several times a week, usually in the afternoon, before they started their evenings of hunting and fishing. Kirxy would give them the supplies they needed — bullets, fishing line, socks, a new cap to replace one lost in the river. They would fill their truck and cans with gas. Eighteen-year-old Wayne would get the car battery from the charger near the woodburning stove and replace it with the drained one from their boat's trolling motor. Kirxy would serve them coffee or Cokes — never liquor, not to minors — and they'd eat whatever they chose from the shelves, usually candy bars or potato chips, ignoring Kirxy's advice that they ought to eat healthier: Vienna sausages, Dinty Moore, or Chef Boyardee.

Today they came in looking a little spooked, Kirxy thought. Scott stayed near the door, peering out, the glass fogging by his face. Wayne went to the candy aisle and selected several Hershey bars. He left a trail of muddy boot prints behind him. Kirxy would mop later.

"Morning, boys," he said. "Coffee?"

Wayne nodded. Kirxy filled a styrofoam cup, then grinned as the boy loaded it with sugar.

"You take coffee with your sweet'ner?" he said.

Kent leaned on the counter, inspecting the hardware items on their pegs, a hacksaw, a set of Allen wrenches. A gizmo with several uses, knife, measuring tape, awl. Kirxy could smell the booze on the boys.

"Y'all need something?" he asked.

"That spotted one you give us?" Kent said. "Won't bark no more."

"She won't?"

"Naw. Tree 'em fine, but won't bark nary a time. Gonna have to shoot her, I expect."

His mouth full of chocolate, Wayne looked at Kirxy. By the door, Scott unfolded his arms. He kept looking outside.

"No," Kirxy said. "Ain't no need to shoot her, Kent. Do what that

conjure woman recommends. Go out in the woods, find you a
locust shell stuck to a tree. This is the time of year for 'em, if I'm not
mistaken."

"Locust shell?" Kent asked.

"Yeah. Bring it back home and crunch it up in the dog's scraps,
and that'll make her bark like she ought to."

Kent nodded to Kirxy and walked to the door. He went out, his
brothers following.

"See you," Kirxy called.

Wayne waved with a Hershey bar and closed the door.

Kirxy stared after them for a time. It had been a year since they'd
paid him anything, but he couldn't bring himself to ask for money;
he'd even stopped writing down what they owed.

He got his coffee and limped from behind the counter to the
easy chair by the stove. He shook his head at the muddy footprints
on the candy aisle. He sat slowly, tucked a blanket around his legs,
took out his bottle, and added a splash to his coffee. Sipping, he
picked up a novel — Louis L'Amour, *Sackett's Land* — and reached
in his apron pocket for his glasses.

Though she had been once, the woman named Esther wasn't much
of a regular in Kirxy's store these days. She lived two miles upriver
in a shambling white house with magnolia trees in the yard. The
house had a wraparound porch, and when it flooded you could fish
from the back, sitting in the tall white rocking chairs, though you
weren't likely to catch anything. A baby alligator maybe, or sometimes bullfrogs. Owls nested in the trees along her part of the river,
but in this weather they seemed quiet; she missed their hollow
calling.

Esther was fifty. She'd had two husbands and six children who
were gone and had ill feelings toward her. She'd had her female
parts removed in an operation. Now she lived alone and, most of
the time, drank alone. If the Gates boys hadn't passed out in their
truck somewhere in the woods, they might stop by after a night's
work. Esther would make them strong coffee and feed them salty
fried eggs and greasy link sausages, and some mornings, like today,
she would get a faraway look in her eyes and take Kent's shirt collar
in her fingers and lead him upstairs and watch him close the bathroom door and listen to the sounds of his bathing.

She smiled, knowing these were the only baths he ever took.

When he emerged, his long hair stringy, his chest flat and hard, she led him down the hall past the telephone nook to her bedroom. He crawled into bed and watched her take off her gown and step out of her underwear. Bending, she looked in the mirror to fluff her hair, then climbed in beside him. He was gentle at first, curious, then rougher, the way she liked him to be. She closed her eyes, the bed frame rattling and bumping, her father's old pocket watch slipping off the nightstand. Water gurgled in the pipework in the walls as the younger brothers took baths, too, hoping for a turn of their own, which had never happened. At least not yet.

"Slow, baby," Esther whispered in Kent's ear. "It's plenty of time. . . ."

On April third it was still raining. Kirxy put aside his crossword to answer the telephone.

"Can you come on down to the lock and dam?" Goodloe asked. "We got us a situation here."

Kirxy disliked smart-assed Goodloe, but something in the sheriff's voice told him it was serious. On the news, he'd heard that the new game warden had been missing for two days. The authorities had dragged the river all night and had three helicopters in the air. Kirxy sat forward in his chair, waiting for his back to loosen a bit. He added a shot of whiskey to his coffee and gulped it down as he shrugged into his denim jacket, zipping it up to his neck because he stayed cold when it rained. He put cotton balls in his ears and set his cap on his bald head, took his walking cane from beside the door.

In his truck, the four-wheel-drive engaged and the defroster on high, he sank and rose in the deep ruts, gobs of mud flying past his windows, the wipers swishing across his view. The radio announcer said it was sixty degrees, more rain on the way. Conway Twitty began to sing. A mile from the lock and dam Kirxy passed the Grove Hill ambulance, axle-deep in mud. A burly black paramedic wedged a piece of two-by-four beneath one of the rear tires while the bored-looking driver sat behind the wheel, smoking and racing the engine.

Kirxy slowed and rolled down his window. "Y'all going after a live one or a dead one?"

"Dead, Mr. Kirxy," the black man answered.

Kirxy nodded and speeded up. At the lock and dam, he could see a crowd of people and umbrellas and beyond them he saw the dead man, lying on the ground under a black raincoat. Some onlooker had begun to direct traffic. Goodloe and three deputies in yellow slickers stood near the body with their hands in their pockets.

Kirxy climbed out and people nodded somberly and parted to let him through. Goodloe, who'd been talking to his deputies, ceased as Kirxy approached and they stood looking at the raincoat.

"Morning, Sugarbaby," Kirxy said, using the childhood nickname Goodloe hated. "Is this who I think it is?"

"Yep," Goodloe muttered. "Rookie game warden of the year."

With his cane, Kirxy pulled back the raincoat to reveal the white face. "Young fellow," he said.

There was a puddle beneath the dead man. Twigs in his hair and a clove of moss in his breast pocket. With the rubber tip of his cane, Kirxy brushed a leech from the man's forehead. He bent and looked into the warden's left eye, which was partly open. He noticed his throat, the dark bruises there.

Goodloe unfolded a handkerchief and blew his nose, then wiped it. "Don't go abusing the evidence, Kirxy." He stuffed the handkerchief into his back pocket.

"Evidence? Now, Sugarbaby."

Goodloe exhaled and looked at the sky. "Don't shit me, Kirxy. You know good and well who done this. I expect they figure the law don't apply up here on this part of the river, the way things is been all these years. Them other wardens scared of 'em. But I reckon that's fixing to change." He paused. "I had to place me a call to the capitol this morning. To let 'em know we was all outa game wardens. And you won't believe who they patched me through to."

Kirxy adjusted the cotton in his right ear.

"Old Frank David himself," the sheriff said. "Ain't nothing ticks him off more than this kind of thing."

A dread stirred in Kirxy's belly. "Frank David. Was he a relation of this fellow?"

"Teacher," Goodloe said. "Said he's been giving lessons to young game wardens over at the forestry service. He asked me a whole bunch of questions. Regular interrogation. Said this here young fellow was the cream of the crop. Best new game warden there was."

"Wouldn't know it from this angle," Kirxy said.

Goodloe grunted.

A photographer from the paper was studying the corpse. He glanced at the sky as if gauging the light. When he snapped the first picture, Kirxy was in it, like a sportsman.

"What'd you want from me?" he asked Goodloe.

"You tell them boys I need to ask 'em some questions, and I ain't fixing to traipse all over the county. I'll drop by the store this evening."

"If they're there, they're there," Kirxy said. "I ain't their damn father."

Goodloe followed him to the truck. "You might think of getting 'em a lawyer," he said through the window.

Kirxy started the engine. "Shit, Sugarbaby. Them boys don't need a lawyer. They just need to stay in the woods, where they belong. Folks oughta know to let 'em alone by now."

Goodloe stepped back from the truck. He smacked his lips. "I don't reckon anybody got around to telling that to the deceased."

Driving, Kirxy turned off the radio. He remembered the Gates brothers when they were younger, before their father shot himself. He pictured the three blond heads in the front of Boo's boat as he motored upriver past the store, lifting a solemn hand to Kirxy where he stood with a broom on his little back porch. After Boo's wife and newborn daughter had died, he'd taught those boys all he knew about the woods, about fishing, tracking, hunting, killing. He kept them in his boat all night as he telephoned catfish and checked his trotlines and jugs and shot things on the bank. He'd given each of his sons a specific job to do, one dialing the rotary phone, another netting the stunned catfish, the third adjusting the chains which generated electricity from a car battery into the water. Boo would tie a piece of clothes line around each of his sons' waists and loop the other end to his own ankle in case one of the boys fell overboard. Downriver, Kent would pull in the trotlines while Wayne handed him a cricket or cockroach or catalpa worm for the hook. Scott took the bass, perch, or catfish Kent gave him and slit its soft cold belly with a fillet knife and ran two fingers up into the fish and drew out its palmful of guts and dumped them overboard. Sometimes on warm nights cottonmouths or young alligators would follow them, drawn by blood. A danger was catching a snake or snapping turtle on the trotline, and each night Boo whispered for Kent to be careful, to lift the line with a stick and see what he had there instead of using his bare hand.

During the morning they would leave the boat tied and the boys would follow their father through the trees from trap to trap, stepping when he stepped, not talking. Boo emptied the traps and rebaited them while behind him Kent put the carcass in his squirrel pouch. In the afternoons, they gutted and skinned what they'd brought home. What time was left before dark they spent sleeping in the feather bed in the cabin where their mother and sister had died.

After Boo's suicide, Kirxy had tried to look after the boys, their ages twelve, thirteen, and fourteen — just old enough, Boo must've thought, to raise themselves. For a while Kirxy let them stay with him and his wife, who'd never had a child. He tried to send them to school, but they were past learning to read and write and got expelled the first day for fighting, ganging up on a black kid. They were past the kind of life Kirxy's wife was used to living. They scared her, the way they watched her with eyes narrowed into black lines, the way they ate with their hands. The way they wouldn't talk. What she didn't know was that from those years of wordless nights on the river and silent days in the woods they had developed a kind of language of their own, a language of the eyes, of the fingers, of the way a shoulder moved, a nod of the head.

Because his wife's health wasn't good in those days, Kirxy had returned the boys to their cabin in the woods. He spent most Saturdays with them, trying to take up where Boo had left off, bringing them food and milk, clothes and new shoes, reading them books, teaching them things and telling stories. He'd worked out a deal with Esther, who took hot food to them in the evenings and washed and mended their clothes.

Slowing to let two buzzards hop away from a dead deer, Kirxy lit a cigarette and wiped his foggy windshield with the back of his hand. He thought of Frank David, Alabama's legendary game warden. There were dozens of stories about the man — Kirxy had heard and told them for years, had repeated them to the Gates boys, even made some up to scare them. Now the true ones and the fictions were confused in his mind. He remembered one: A dark, moonless night, and two poachers use a spotlight to freeze a buck in the darkness and shoot it. They take hold of its wide rack of horns and struggle to drag the big deer when suddenly they realize that now three men are pulling. The first poacher jumps and says, "Hey, it ain't supposed to be but two of us dragging this deer!"

And Frank David says, "Ain't supposed to be none of y'all dragging it."

The Gates boys came in the store just before closing, smelling like the river. Nodding to Kirxy, they went to the shelves and began selecting cans of things to eat. Kirxy poured himself a generous shot of whiskey. He'd stopped by their cabin earlier and, not finding them there, left a quarter on the steps. An old signal he hadn't used in years.

"Goodloe's coming by tonight," he said to Kent. "Wants to ask if y'all know anything about that dead game warden."

Kent shot the other boys a look.

"Now I don't know if y'all've ever even seen that fellow," Kirxy said, "and I'm not asking you to tell me." He paused, in case they wanted to. "But that's what old Sugarbaby's gonna want to know. If I was y'all, I just wouldn't tell him anything. Just say I was at home, that I don't know nothing about any dead game warden. Nothing at all."

Kent shrugged and walked down the aisle he was on and stared out the back window, though there wasn't anything to see except the trees, ghostly and bent, when the lightning came. His brothers took seats by the stove and began to eat. Kirxy watched them, remembering when he used to read to them, *Tarzan of the Apes* and *The Return of Tarzan*. The boys had wanted to hear the books over and over — they loved the jungle, the elephants, rhinos, gorillas, the anacondas thirty feet long. They would listen intently, their eyes bright in the light of the stove, Wayne holding in his small dirty hand the Slinky Kirxy had given him as a Christmas present, his lips moving along with Kirxy's voice, mouthing some of the words: *the great apes; Numa the lion; La, Queen of Opar, the Lost City.*

They had listened to his Frank David stories the same way: the game warden appearing beside a tree on a night when there wasn't a moon, a tracker so keen he could see in the dark, could follow a man through the deepest swamp by smelling the fear in his sweat, by the way the water swirled; a bent-over shadow slipping between the beaver lairs, the cypress trees, the tangle of limb and vine, parting the long wet bangs of Spanish moss with his rifle barrel, creeping toward the glowing windows of the poacher's cabin, the deer hides nailed to the wall. The gator pelts. The fish with their grim smiles hooked to a clothes line, turtle shells like army helmets drying on the windowsills. Any pit bull or mutt meant to guard the place lying with its throat slit behind him, Frank David slips out of the fog with fog still clinging to the brim of his hat. He circles the cabin, peers in each window, mounts the porch. Puts his shoulder through the front door. Stands with wood splinters landing on the floor at his feet. A hatted man of average height, clean-shaven: no threat until the big hands come up, curl into fists, the knuckles scarred, blue, sharp.

Kirxy finished his drink and poured another. It burned pleasantly in his belly. He looked at the boys, occupied by their bags of corn curls. A Merle Haggard song ended on the radio and Kirxy clicked it off, not wanting the boys to hear the evening news.

In the quiet, Kirxy heard Goodloe's truck. He glanced at Kent, who'd probably been hearing it for a while. Outside, Goodloe slammed his door. He hurried up the steps and tapped on the window. Kirxy exaggerated his limp and took his time letting him in.

"Evening," Goodloe said, shaking the water from his hands. He took off his hat and hung it on the nail by the door, then hung up his yellow slicker.

"Evening, Sugarbaby," Kirxy said.

"It's a wet one out there tonight," Goodloe said.

"Yep." Kirxy went behind the counter and refilled his glass. "You just caught the tail end of happy hour. That is, if you're off the wagon again. Can I sell you a tonic? Warm you up?"

"You know we're a dry county, Kirxy."

"Would that be a no?"

"It's a watch your ass." Goodloe looked at the brothers. "Just wanted to ask these boys some questions."

"Have at it, Sugarbaby."

Goodloe walked to the Lance rack and detached a package of Nip-Cheese crackers. He opened it, offered the pack to each of the boys. Only Wayne took one. Smiling, Goodloe bit a cracker in half and turned a chair around and sat with his elbows across its back. He looked over toward Kent, half-hidden by shadow. He chewed slowly. "Come on out here so I can see you, boy. I ain't gonna bite nothing but these stale-ass cheese crackers."

Kent moved a step closer.

Goodloe took out a note pad and addressed Kent. "Where was y'all between the hours of four and eight A.M. two days ago?"

Kent looked at Scott. "Asleep."

"Asleep," Scott said.

Goodloe snorted. "Now come on, boys. The whole dern county knows y'all ain't slept a night in your life. Y'all was out on the river, wasn't you? Making a few telephone calls?"

"You saying he's a liar?" Kirxy asked.

"I'm posing the questions here." Goodloe chewed another cracker. "Hell, everybody knows the other game wardens has been letting y'all get away with all kinds of shit. I reckon this new fellow had something to prove."

"Sounds like he oughta used a life jacket," Kirxy said, wiping the counter.

"It appears" — Goodloe studied Kent — "that he might've been strangled. You got a alibi, boy?"

Kent looked down.

Goodloe sighed. "I mean — Christ — is there anybody can back up what you're saying?"

The windows flickered.

"Yeah," Kirxy said. "I can."

Goodloe turned and faced the storekeeper. "You."

"That's right. They were here with me. Here in the store."

Goodloe looked amused. "They was, was they. Okay, Mr. Kirxy. How come you didn't mention that to me this morning? Saved us all a little time?"

Kirxy sought Kent's eyes but saw nothing there, no understanding, no appreciation. No fear. He went back to wiping the counter. "Well, I guess because they was passed out drunk, and I didn't want to say anything, being as I was, you know, giving alcohol to young-uns."

"But now that it's come down to murder, you figured you'd better just own up."

"Something like that."

Goodloe stared at Kirxy for a long time, neither would look away. Then the sheriff turned to the boys. "Y'all ever heard of Frank David?"

Wayne nodded.

"Well," Goodloe said. "Looks like he's aiming to be this district's game warden. I figure he pulled some strings, what he did."

Kirxy came from behind the counter. "That all your questions? It's past closing and these young'uns need to go home and get some sleep." He went to the door and opened it, stood waiting.

"All righty then," the sheriff said, standing. "I expect I oughta be getting back to the office anyhow." He winked at Kirxy. "See you or these boys don't leave the county for a few days. This ain't over yet." He put the crackers in his coat. "I expect y'all might be hearing from Frank David, too," he said, watching the boys' faces. But there was nothing to see.

Alone later, Kirxy put out the light and bolted the door. He went to adjust the stove and found himself staring out the window, looking into the dark where he knew the river was rising and swirling, tires and plastic garbage can lids and deadwood from upriver floating past. He struck a match and lit a cigarette, the glow of his ash reflected in the window, and he saw himself years ago, telling the boys those stories.

How Frank David would sit so still in the woods waiting for poachers that dragonflies would perch on his nose, gnats would walk over his eyeballs. Nobody knew where he came from, but Kirxy had heard that he'd been orphaned as a baby in a fire and found half-starved in the swamp by a Cajun woman. She'd raised him on the slick red clay banks of the Tombigbee River, among lean black poachers and white trash moonshiners. He didn't even know how old he was, people said. And they said he was the best poacher ever, the craftiest, the meanest. That he cut a drunk logger's throat in a juke joint knife-fight one night. That he fled south and, underage, joined the Marines in Mobile and wound up in Korea, the infantry, where because of his shooting ability and his stealth they made him a sniper. Before he left that country, he'd registered over a hundred kills, communists half a world away who never saw him coming.

Back home in Alabama, he disappeared for a few years, then showed up at the state game warden's office, demanding a job. Some people heard that in the intervening time he'd gotten religion.

"What makes you think I ought to hire you?" the head warden asked.

"Because I spent ten years of my life poaching right under your goddamn nose," Frank David said.

*

The Gates boys' pickup was the same old Ford their father had shot himself in several years earlier. The bullet hole in the roof had rusted out but was now covered with a strip of duct tape from Kirxy's store. Spots of the truck's floor were rusted away, too, so things in the road often flew up into their laps: rocks, cans, a kingsnake they were trying to run over. The truck was older than any of them, only one thin prong left of the steering wheel and the holes of missing knobs in the dash. It was a three-speed, a column shifter, the gear-stick covered with a buck's dried ball sack. The windows and windshield, busted or shot out years before, hadn't been replaced because most of their driving took them along back roads after dark or in fields, and the things they came upon were easier shots without glass.

Though he'd never had a license, Kent drove, he'd been doing this since he was eight. Scott rode shotgun. Tonight both were drinking, and in the back Wayne stood holding his rifle and trying to keep his balance. Below the soles of his boots the floor was soft, a tarry black from the blood of all the animals they'd killed. You could see spike antlers, forelegs, and hooves of deer. Teeth, feathers, and fur. The brittle beaks and beards of turkeys and the delicate, hinged leg bone of something molded in the sludge like a fossil.

Just beyond a *No Trespassing* sign, Kent swerved off the road and they bounced and slid through a field in the rain, shooting at rabbits. Then they split up, the younger boys checking traps — one on each side of the river — and Kent in the boat rebaiting their trotlines the way his father had shown him.

They met at the truck just before midnight, untied the dogs, and tromped down a steep logging path, Wayne on one end of four leashes and the lunging hounds on the other. When they got to the bottomland, he unclipped the leashes and loosed the dogs and the brothers followed the baying ahead in the dark, aiming their flashlights into the black mesh of trees where the eyes of coons and possums gleamed like rubies. The hounds bayed and frothed, clawed the trunks of trees and leaped into the air and landed and leaped again, their sides pumping, ribs showing, hounds that, given the chance, would never stop eating.

When the Gateses came to the giver two hours later, the dogs were lapping water and panting. Wayne bent and rubbed their ears and let them lick his cheeks. His brothers rested and drank, belching at the sky. After a time, they leashed the hounds and staggered downstream to the live oak where their boat was tied. They loaded the dogs and shoved off into the fog and trolled over the still water.

In the middle, Scott lowered the twin chains beside the boat and began dialing the old telephone. Wayne netted the stunned catfish — you couldn't touch them with your hand or they'd come to — and threw them into the cooler, where in a few seconds the waking fish would begin to thrash. In the rear, Kent fingered his rifle and watched the bank in case a coyote wandered down, hunting bull-frogs.

They climbed up out of the woods into a dirt road in the misty dawn, plying through the muddy yards and pissing by someone's front porch in plain sight of the black face inside. A few houses down, Morrisette didn't come to his door, and when Kent tried the handle it was locked. He looked at Scott, then put his elbow through the glass and reached in and unlocked it.

While his brothers searched for the liquor, Wayne ate the biscuits he found wrapped in tin foil on the stove. He found a box of Corn Flakes in a cabinet and ate most of them, too. He ate a plate of cold fried chicken liver. Scott was in a bedroom looking under the bed. In the closet. He was going through drawers, his dirty fingers among the white cloth. In the back of the house Kent found a door, locked from the inside. He jimmied it open with his knife, and when he came into the kitchen, he had a gallon jar of whiskey under his arm and Euphrates' stepdaughter by the wrist.

Wayne stopped chewing, crumbs falling from his mouth. He approached the girl and put his hand out to touch her, but Kent pushed him hard, into the wall. Wayne stayed there, a clock ticking beside his head, a string of spit linking his two opened lips, watching as his brother ran his rough hands up and down the girl's trembling body, over the nipples that showed through the thin cloth. Her eyes were closed, lips moving in prayer. Looking down, Kent saw the puddle spreading around her bare feet.

"Shit," he said, a hand cupping her breast. "Pissed herself."

He let her go and she shrank back against the wall, behind the door. She was still there, along with a bag of catfish on the table, when her stepfather came back half an hour later, ten gallons of whiskey under the tarp in his truck.

*

On that same Saturday Kirxy drove to the chicken fights, held in
Heflin Bradford's bulging barn, deep in woods cloudy with mosqui-
toes. He passed the hand-painted sign that'd been there forever, as
long as he could remember, nailed to a tree. It said *Jesus is not
coming.*

Kirxy climbed out of his truck and buttoned his collar, his ears
full of cotton. Heflin's wife worked beneath a rented awning, grill-
ing chicken and sausages, selling Cokes and beer. Gospel music
played from a portable tape player by her head. Heflin's grandson
Nolan took the price of admission at the barn door and stamped
the backs of white hands and the cracked pink palms of black ones.
Men in overalls and baseball caps that said *Cat Diesel Power* or *STP*
stood at the tailgates of their pickups, smoking cigarettes, stooping
to peer into the dark cages where roosters paced. The air was filled
with windy rain spits and the crowing of roosters, the ground littered with limp, dead birds.

A group of men discussed Frank David, and Kirxy paused to
listen.

"He's the one caught that bunch over in Warshington County,"
one man said. "Them alligator poachers."

"Sugarbaby said two of 'em wound up in the intensive care,"
another claimed. "Said they pulled a gun and old Frank David went
crazy with an axe handle."

Kirxy moved on and paid the five-dollar admission. In the barn,
there were bleachers along the walls and a big circular wooden
fence in the center, a dome of chicken wire over the top. Kirxy
found a seat at the bottom next to the back door, near a group of
mean old farts he'd known for forty years. People around them
called out bets and bets were accepted. Cans of beer lifted. Kirxy
produced a thermos of coffee and a dented tin cup. He poured the
coffee, then added whiskey from a bottle that went back into his
coat pocket. The tin cup warmed his fingers as he squinted through
his bifocals to see which bird to bet on.

In separate corners of the barn, two bird handlers doused their
roosters' heads and asses with rubbing alcohol to make them fight
harder. They tightened the long steel curved spurs. When the referee in the center of the ring indicated it was time, the handlers
entered the pen, each cradling his bird in his arms. They flashed
the roosters at one another until their feathers had ruffled with
bloodlust and rage, the roosters pedaling the air, stretching their

necks toward each other. The handlers kept them a breath apart for a second, then withdrew them to their corners, whispering in their ears. When the referee tapped the ground three times with his stick, the birds were unleashed on each other. They charged and rose in the center of the ring, gouging with spur and beak, the handlers circling the fight like crabs, blood on their forearms and faces, ready to seize their roosters at the referee's cry of "Handle!"

A clan of Louisiana Cajuns watched. They'd emerged red-eyed from a van in a marijuana cloud: skinny, shirtless men with oily ponytails and goatees and tattoos of symbols of black magic. Under their arms, they carried thick white hooded roosters to pit against the reds and blacks of the locals. Their women had stumbled out of the van behind them, high yellow like Gypsies, big-lipped, big-chested girls in halter tops tied at their bellies and mini-skirts and red heels.

In the ring the Cajuns kissed their birds on the beaks, and one tall, completely bald Cajun wearing gold earrings in both ears put his bird's whole head in his mouth. His girl, too, came barefoot into the ring, tattoo of a snake on her shoulder, and took the bird's head into her mouth.

"Bet on them white ones," a friend whispered to Kirxy. "These ones around here ain't ever seen a white rooster. They don't know what they're fighting."

That evening, checking traps in the woods north of the river, Wayne kept hearing things. Little noises. Leaves. Twigs.

Afraid, he forced himself to go on so his brothers wouldn't laugh at him. Near dark, in a wooden trap next to an old fence row, he was surprised to find the tiny white fox they'd once seen cross the road in front of their truck. He squatted before the trap and poked a stick through the wire at the thin snout, his hand steady despite the way the fox snapped at the stick and bit off the end. Would the witch woman want this alive? At the thought of her he looked around. It felt like she was watching him, as if she were hiding in a tree in the form of some animal, a possum, a swamp rat. He stood and dragged the trap through the mud and over the land while the fox jumped in circles, growling.

A mile upstream, Scott had lost a boot to the mud and was hopping back one-footed to retrieve it. It stood alone, buried to the ankle. He wrenched it free, then sat with his back against a sweet-

gum to scrape off the mud. He'd begun to lace the boot when he
saw a hollow tree stump, something moving inside. With his rifle
barrel, he rolled the thing out — it was most of the body of a dead
catfish, the movement from the maggots devouring it. When he
kicked it, they spilled from the fish like rice pellets and lay throbbing in the mud.

Downstream, as night came and the rain fell harder, Kent trolled
their boat across the river, flashlight in his mouth, using a stick to
pull up a trotline length by length and removing the fish or turtles
and rebaiting the hooks and dropping them back into the water.
Near the bank, approaching the last hook, he heard something. He
looked up with the flashlight in his teeth to see the thing untwirling
in the air. It wrapped around his neck like a rope, and for an instant
he thought he was being hanged. He grabbed the thing. It flexed
and tightened, then his neck burned and went numb and he felt
dizzy, his fingertips buzzing, legs weak, a tree on the bank distort-
ing, doubling, tripling into a whole line of fuzzy shapes, turning
sideways, floating.

Kent blinked. Felt his eyes bulging, his tongue swelling. His head
about to explode. Then a bright light.

His brothers found the boat at dawn, four miles downstream,
lodged on the far side in a fallen tree. They exchanged a glance,
then looked back across the river. A heavy gray fog hooded the
water and the boat appeared and dissolved in the ghostly limbs
around it. Scott sat on a log and took off his boots and left them
standing by the log. He removed his coat and laid it over the boots.
He handed his brother his rifle without looking at him, left him
watching as he climbed down the bank and, hands and elbows in
the air like a believer, waded into the water.

Wayne propped the second rifle against a tree and stood on the
bank holding his own gun, casting his frightened eyes up and down
the river. From far away a woodpecker drummed. Crows began to
collect in a pecan tree downstream. After a while Wayne squatted,
thinking of their dogs, tied to the bumper of their truck. They'd be
under the tailgate, probably, trying to keep dry.

Soon Scott had trolled the boat back across. Together they pulled
it out of the water and stood looking at their brother who lay across
the floor among the fish and turtles he'd caught. One greenish
terrapin, still alive, a hook in its neck, stared back. They both knew

what they were supposed to think — the blood and the sets of twin fang marks, the black bruises and shriveled skin, the neck swollen like mumps, the purple bulb of tongue between his lips. They were supposed to think *cottonmouth.* Kent's hands were squeezed into fists and they'd hardened that way, the skin wrinkled. His eyes half open. His rifle lay unfired in the boat, as if indeed a snake had done this.

But it wasn't the tracks of a snake they found when they went to get the white fox. The fox was gone, though, the trap empty, its catch sprung. Scott knelt and ran his knuckles along the rim of a boot print in the mud — not a very wide track, not very far from the next one. He put his finger in the black water that'd already begun to fill the track: not too deep. He looked up at Wayne. The print of an average-sized man. In no hurry. Scott rose and they began.

Above them, the sky cracked and flickered.

Silently, quickly — no time to get the dogs — they followed the trail back through the woods, losing it once, twice, backtracking, working against the rain that fell and fell harder, that puddled blackly and crept up their legs, until they stood in water to their calves, rain beading on the brims of their caps. They gazed at the ground, the sky, at the rain streaming down each other's muddy face.

At the truck, Wayne jumped in the driver's seat and reached for the keys. Scott appeared in the window, shaking his head. When Wayne didn't scoot over, the older boy hit him in the jaw, then slung open the door and pulled Wayne out, sent him rolling over the ground. Scott climbed in and had trouble getting the truck choked. By the time he had the hang of it, Wayne had gotten into the back and sat among the wet dogs, staring at his dead brother.

At their cabin, they carried Kent into the woods. They laid him on the ground and began digging near where their sister, mother, and father were buried in their unmarked graves. For three hours they worked, the dogs coming from under the porch and sniffing around Kent and watching the digging, finally slinking off and crawling back under the porch, out of the rain. An hour later the dogs came boiling out again and stood in a group at the edge of the yard, baying. The boys paused but saw or heard nothing. When the dogs kept making noise, Scott got his rifle and fired into the woods several times. He nodded to his brother and they went back to digging. By the time they'd finished, it was late afternoon and the hole was full of slimy water and they were black with mud. They each took off one of Kent's boots and Scott got the things from his pockets. They stripped off his shirt and pants and lowered him into the hole. When he bobbed to the top of the water, they got stones and weighted him down. Then shoveled mud into the grave.

They showed up at Esther's, black as tar.

"Where's Kent?" she asked, holding her robe closed at her throat.

"We buried him," Scott said, moving past her into the kitchen. She put a hand over her mouth, and as Scott told her what they'd found she slumped against the door, looking outside. An owl flew past in the floodlights. She thought of calling Kirxy but decided to wait until morning — the old bastard thought she was a slut and a corruption. For tonight she'd just keep them safe in her house.

Scott went to the den. He turned on the TV, the reception bad because of the weather. Wayne, a bruise on his left cheek, climbed the stairs. He went into one of the bedrooms and closed the door behind him. It was chilly in the room and he noticed pictures of people on the wall, children, and a tall man and a younger woman he took to be Esther. She'd been pretty then. He stood dripping on the floor, looking into her black and white face, searching for signs of the woman he knew now. Soon the door opened behind him and she came in. And though he still wore his filthy wet clothes, she steered him to the bed and guided him down onto it. She unbuckled his belt, removed his hunting knife, and stripped the belt off. She unbuttoned his shirt and rubbed her fingers across his chest, the hair just beginning to thicken there. She undid his pants and ran the zipper down its track. She worked them over his thighs, knees, and ankles and draped them across the back of a chair. She pulled off his boots and socks. Pried a finger beneath the elastic of his underwear, felt that he'd already come.

He looked at her face. His mouth opened. Esther touched his chin, the scratch of whiskers, his breath on her hand.

"Hush now," she said, and watched him fall asleep.

Downstairs, the TV went off.

*

When Goodloe knocked, Esther answered, a cold sliver of her face in the cracked door. "The hell you want?"

"Good evening to you, too. The Gateses here?"

"No."

Goodloe glanced behind him. "I believe that's their truck. It's kinda hard to mistake, especially for us trained lawmen."

She tried to close the door but Goodloe had his foot in it. He glanced at the three deputies who stood importantly by the Blazer. They dropped their cigarettes and crushed them out. They unsnapped their holsters and strode across the yard, standing behind Goodloe with their hands on their revolvers and their legs apart like TV deputies.

"Why don't y'all just let 'em alone?" Esther said. "Ain't they been through enough?"

"Tell 'em I'd like to see 'em," Goodloe said. "Tell 'em get their boots."

"You just walk straight to hell, mister."

Wayne appeared behind her, naked, lines from the bed linen on his face.

"Whoa, Nellie," Goodloe said. "Boy, you look plumb terrible. Why don't you let us carry you on down to the office for a little coffee? Little cake." He glanced back at one of the deputies. "We got any of that cinnamon roll left, Dave?"

"You got a warrant for their arrest?" Esther asked.

"No, I ain't got a warrant for their arrest. They ain't under arrest. They fixing to get questioned, is all. Strictly informal." Goodloe winked. "You reckon you could do without 'em for a couple of hours?"

"Fuck you, Sugarbaby."

The door slammed. Goodloe nodded down the side of the house and two deputies went to make sure nobody escaped from the back. But in a minute Wayne came out dressed, his hands in his pockets, and followed Goodloe down the stairs, the deputies watching him closely, and watching the house.

"Where's your brothers?" Goodloe asked.

He looked down.

Goodloe nodded to the house and two deputies went in, guns drawn. They came out a few minutes later, frowning.

"Must've heard us coming," Goodloe said. "Well, we got this one.

We'll find them other two tomorrow." They got into the Blazer and Goodloe looked at Wayne, sitting in the back.

"Put them cuffs on him," Goodloe said.

Holding his rifle, Scott came out of the woods when the Blazer was gone. He returned to the house.

"They got Wayne," Esther said. "Why didn't you come tell him they was out there?"

"He got to learn," Scott said. He went to the cabinet where she kept the whiskey and took the bottle. She watched him go to the sofa and sit down in front of the blank TV. Soon she joined him, bringing glasses. He filled both, and when they emptied them he filled them again.

They spent the night like that, and at dawn they were drunk. Wearing her robe, Esther began clipping her fingernails, a cigarette smoking in the ashtray beside her. She'd forgotten about calling Kirxy.

Scott was telling her about the biggest catfish they'd ever called up: a hundred pounds, he swore, a hundred fifty. "You could of put your whole head in that old cat's mouth," he said, sipping his whiskey. "Back fin long as your damn arm."

He stood. Walked to the front window. There were toads in the yard — with the river swelling they were everywhere. In the evenings there were rainfrogs. The yard had turned into a pond and each night the rainfrogs sang. It was like no other sound. Esther said it kept her up at night.

"That, and some other things," she said.

Scott heard a fingernail ring the ashtray. He rubbed his hand across his chin, felt the whiskers there. He watched the toads as they huddled in the yard, still as rocks, bloated and miserable-looking.

"That catfish was green," Scott said, sipping. "I swear to God. Green as grass."

"Them goddamn rainfrogs," she said. "I just lay there at night with my hands over my ears."

A clipping rang the ashtray.

He turned and went to her on the sofa. "They was moss growing on his nose," he said, putting his hand on her knee.

"Go find your brother," she said. She got up and walked unstead-

ily across the floor and went into the bathroom, closed the door.
When she came out, he and the bottle were gone.

Without Kent, Scott felt free to do what he wanted, which was to
drive very fast. He got the truck started and spun off, aiming for
every mud hole he could. He shot past a house with a washing
machine on the front porch, two thin black men skinning a hog
hanging from a tree. One of the men waved with a knife. Drinking, Scott drove through the mountains of trash at the dump and
turned the truck in circles, kicking up muddy roostertails. He
swerved past the Negro church and the graveyard where a group of
blacks huddled, four warbling poles over an open grave, the wind
tearing the preacher's hat out of his hands and a woman's umbrella
reversing suddenly.

When he tired of driving, he left the truck in their hiding place,
and using trees for balance, stumbled down the hill to their boat.
He carried Kent's rifle, which he'd always admired. On the river, he
fired up the outboard and accelerated, the boat prow lifting and
leveling out, the buzz of the motor rising in the trees. The water was
nearly orange from mud, the cypress knees nothing but knobs and
tips because of the floods. Nearing the old train trestle, he cut the
motor and coasted to a stop. He sat listening to the rain, to the
distant barking of a dog, half a mile away. Chasing something,
maybe a deer. As the dog charged through the woods, Scott closed
his eyes and imagined the terrain, marking where he thought the
dog was now, and where he thought it was now. Then the barking
stopped, suddenly, as if the dog had run smack into a tree.

Scott clicked on the trolling motor and moved the boat close to
the edge of the river, the rifle across his knees. He scanned the
banks, and when the rain started to fall harder he accelerated
toward the trestle. From beneath the cross ties, he smelled creosote
and watched the rain as it stirred the river. He looked into the gray
trees and thought he would drive into town later, see about getting
Wayne. Kent had never wanted to go to Grove Hill — their father
had warned them of the police, of jail.

Scott picked up one of the catfish from the night before. It was
stiff, as if carved out of wood. He stared at it, watching the green
blowflies hover above his fist, then threw it over into the cattails
along the bank.

The telephone rig lay under the seat. He lifted the chains quietly, considering what giant catfish might be passing beneath the boat this very second, a thing as large as a man's thigh with eyes the size of ripe plums and skin the color of mud. Catfish, their father had taught them, have long whiskers that make them the only fish you can "call." Kirxy had told Scott and his brothers that if a game warden caught you telephoning, all you needed to do was dump your rig overboard. But, Kirxy warned, Frank David would handcuff you and swim around the bottom of the river until he found your rig.

Scott spat a stream of tobacco into the brown water. Minnows appeared and began to investigate, nibbling at the dark yolk of spit as it elongated and dissolved. With his rifle's safety off, he lowered the chains into the water, a good distance apart. He checked the connections — the battery, the telephone. He lifted the phone and began to dial. "Hello?" he whispered, the thing his father had always said, grinning in the dark. The wind picked up a bit, he heard it rattling in the trees, and he dialed faster, had just seen the first silver body bob to the surface when something landed with a clatter in his boat. He glanced over.

A bundle of dynamite, sparks shooting off the end, fuse already gone. He looked above him, the trestle, but nobody was there. He moved to grab the dynamite, but his cheeks ballooned with hot red wind and his hands caught fire.

When the smoke cleared and the water stopped boiling, silver bodies began to bob to the surface — largemouth bass, bream, gar, suckers, white perch, polliwogs, catfish — some only stunned but others dead, in pieces, pink fruit-like things, the water blooming darkly with mud.

Kirxy's telephone rang for the second time in one day, a rarity that proved what his wife had always said: bad news came over the phone. The first call had been Esther, telling him of Kent's death, Wayne's arrest, Scott's disappearance. This time Kirxy heard Goodloe's voice telling him that somebody — or maybe a couple of somebodies — had been blown up out on the trestle.

"Scott," Kirxy said, sitting.

He arrived at the trestle, and with his cane hobbled over the uneven tracks. Goodloe's deputies and three ambulance drivers in rubber gloves and waders were scraping pieces off the cross ties

with spoons, dropping the parts in ziplock bags. The boat, two flattened shreds of aluminum, lay on the bank. In the water, minnows
darted about, nibbling.

"Christ," Kirxy said. He brought a handkerchief to his lips. Then
he went to where Goodloe stood on the bank, writing in his notebook.

"What do you aim to do about this?" Kirxy demanded.

"Try to figure out who it was, first."

"You know goddamn well who it was."

"I expect it's either Kent or Scott Gates."

"It's Scott," Kirxy said.

"How do you know that?"

Kirxy told him that Kent was dead.

"I ain't seen the body," Goodloe said.

Kirxy's blood pressure was going up. "Fuck, Sugarbaby. Are you
one bit aware what's going on here?"

"Fishing accident," Goodloe said. "His bait exploded."

From the bank, a deputy called that he'd found most of a boot.
"Foot's still in it," he said, holding it up by the lace.

"Tag it," Goodloe said, writing something down. "Keep looking."

Kirxy poked Goodloe in the shoulder with his cane. "You really
think Scott'd blow himself up?"

Goodloe looked at his shoulder, the muddy cane print, then at
the storekeeper. "Not on purpose, I don't." He paused. "Course,
suicide does run in their family."

"What about Kent?"

"What about him?"

"Christ, Sugarbaby —"

Goodloe held up his hand. "Just show me, Kirxy."

They left the ambulance drivers and the deputies and walked the
other way without talking. When they came to Goodloe's Blazer,
they got in and drove without talking. Soon they stopped in front of
the Gateses' cabin. Instantly hounds surrounded the truck, barking
viciously and jumping with muddy paws against the glass. Goodloe
blew the horn until the hounds slunk away, heads low, fangs bared.
The sheriff opened his window and fired several times in the air,
backing the dogs up. When he and Kirxy got out, Goodloe had
reloaded.

The hounds kept to the edge of the woods, watching.

His eye on them, Kirxy led Goodloe behind the decrepit cabin.

Rusty screens covered some windows, rags of drape others. Beneath the house, the dogs paced them. "Back here," Kirxy said, heading into the trees. Esther had said they'd buried Kent, and this was the logical place. He went slowly, careful not to bump a limb and cause a small downpour. Sure enough, there lay the grave. You could see where the dogs had been scratching around it.

Goodloe went over and toed the dirt. "You know the cause of death?"

"Yeah, I know the cause of death. His name's Frank fucking David."

"I meant how he was killed."

"The boys said snakebite. Three times in the neck. But I'd do an autopsy."

"You would." Goodloe exhaled. "Okay. I'll send Roy and Avery over here to dig him up. Maybe shoot these goddern dogs."

"I'll tell you what you'd better do first. You better keep Wayne locked up safe."

"I can't hold him much longer," Goodloe said. "Unless he confesses."

Kirxy pushed him from behind, and at the edge of the woods the dogs tensed. Goodloe backed away, raising his pistol, the grave between them.

"You crazy, Kirxy? You been locked in that store too long?"

"Goodloe," Kirxy gasped. The cotton in his left ear had come out and suddenly air was roaring through his head. "Even you can't be this stupid. You let that boy out and he's that cold-blooded fucker's next target —"

"Target, Kirxy? Shit. Ain't nothing to prove anybody killed them damn boys? This one snake-bit, you said so yourself. That other one blowing himself up. Them dern Gateses has fished with dynamite their whole life. You oughta know that — you the one gets it for 'em." He narrowed his eyes. "You're about neck deep in this thing, you know. And I don't mean just lying to protect them boys neither. I mean selling explosives illegally, to minors, Kirxy."

"I don't give a shit if I am!" Kirxy yelled. "Two dead boys in two days and you're worried about dynamite? You oughta be out there looking for Frank David."

"He ain't supposed to be here for another week or two," Goodloe said. "Paperwork —"

He fired his pistol then. Kirxy jumped, but the sheriff was looking past him, and when Kirxy followed his eyes he saw the dog that had been creeping in. It lay slumped in the mud, a hind leg kicking, blood coloring the water around it.

Goodloe backed away, smoke curling from the barrel of his pistol.

Around them the other dogs circled, heads low, moving sideways, the hair on their spines sticking up.

"Let's argue about this in the truck," Goodloe said.

At the store Kirxy put out the *Open* sign. He sat in his chair with his coffee and a cigarette. He'd read the same page three times when it occurred to him to phone Montgomery and get Frank David's office on the line. It took a few calls, but he soon got the number and dialed. The snippy young woman who answered told Kirxy that yes, Mr. David *was* supposed to take over the Lower Peachtree district, but that he wasn't starting until next week, she thought.

Where was he now? Kirxy wanted to know.

"Florida?" she said. "No, Louisiana. Fishing." No sir, he couldn't be reached. He preferred his vacations private.

Kirxy slammed down the phone. He lit another cigarette and tried to think.

It was just a matter, he decided, of keeping Wayne alive until Frank David took over the district. There were probably other game wardens who'd testify that Frank David *was* over in Louisiana fishing right now. But once the son-of-a-bitch officially moved here, he'd have motive and his alibi wouldn't be as strong. If Wayne turned up dead, Frank David would be the chief suspect.

Kirxy inhaled smoke deeply and tried to imagine how Frank David would think. How he would act. The noise he would make or not make as he went through the woods. What he would say if you happened upon him. Or he upon you. What he would do if he came into the store. Certainly he wasn't the creature Kirxy had created to scare the boys, not some wild ghostly thing. He was just a man who'd had a hard life and grown bitter and angry. Probably an alcoholic. A man who chose to uphold the law because breaking it was no challenge. A man with no obligation to any other men or a family. Just to himself and his job. To some goddamned game warden code. His job was to protect the wild things the law had deemed worthy: dove, duck, owls, hawks, turkeys, alligators, squirrels, coons, and deer. But how did the Gates boys fall into the category of trash animal — wildcats or possums or armadillos, snapping turtles, snakes? Things you could kill any time, run over in your truck and not even look at in your mirror to see dying behind you? Christ. Why couldn't Frank David see that he — more than a match for the boys — was of their breed?

Kirxy drove to the highway. The big thirty-ought-six he hadn't touched in years was on the seat next to him, and as he steered he pushed cartridges into the clip, then shoved the clip into the gun's underbelly. He pulled the lever that injected a cartridge into the chamber and took a long drink of whiskey to wash down three of the pills that helped dull the ache in his knees, and the one in his gut.

It was almost dark when he arrived at the edge of a large field. He parked facing the grass. This was a place a few hundred yards from a fairly well-traveled blacktop, a spot no sane poacher would dare use. There were already two or three deer creeping into the open from the woods across the field. They came to eat the tall grass, looking up only when a car passed, their ears swiveling, jaws frozen, sprigs of grass twitching in their lips like the legs of insects.

Kirxy sat watching. He sipped his whiskey and lit a cigarette with a trembling hand. Both truck doors were locked and he knew this was a very stupid thing he was doing. Several times he told himself to go home, let things unfold as they would. Then he saw the faces of the two dead boys. And the face of the live one.

When Boo had killed himself, the oldest two had barely been teenagers, but it was eleven-year-old Wayne who'd found him. That truck still had windows then, and the back windshield had been sprayed red with blood. Flies had gathered at the top of the truck in what Wayne discovered was a twenty-two caliber hole. Kirxy frowned, thinking of it. Boo's hat still on his head, a small hole through the hat, too. The back of the truck was full of wood Boo'd been cutting, and the three boys had unloaded the wood and stacked it neatly beside the road. Kirxy shifted in his seat, imagining the boys pushing that truck for two miles over dirt roads, somehow finding the leverage or whatever, the goddamn strength, to get it home. To pull their father from inside and bury him. To clean out the truck. Kirxy shuddered and thought of Frank David, then made himself think of his wife instead. He rubbed his biceps and watched the shadows creep across the field, the treeline dim and begin to disappear.

Soon it was full dark. He unscrewed the interior light bulb from the ceiling, pulled the door lock up quietly. Holding his breath, he opened the door. Outside, he propped the rifle on the side mirror, flicked the safety off. He reached through the window, felt along the dash for the headlight switch, pulled it.

The field blazed with the eyes of deer — red hovering dots staring back at him. Kirxy aimed and squeezed the trigger at the first pair of eyes. Not waiting to see if he'd hit the deer, he moved the gun to another pair. He'd gotten off five shots before the eyes began to disappear. When the last echo from the gun faded, at least three deer lay dead or wounded in the glow of his headlights. One doe bleated weakly and bleated again. Kirxy coughed and took the gun back into the truck, closed the door, and reloaded in the dark. Then he waited. The doe kept bleating and things in the woods took shape, detached, and whisked toward Kirxy over the grass like spooks. And the little noises. Things like footsteps. And the stories. Frank David appearing in the bed of somebody's *moving* truck and punching through the back glass, grabbing and breaking the driver's arm. Leaping from the truck and watching while it wrecked.

"Quit it," Kirxy croaked. "You damn schoolgirl."

Several more times that night he summoned his nerve and flicked on the headlights, firing at any eyes he saw or firing at nothing. When he finally fell asleep just after two A.M., his body numb with painkillers and whiskey, he dreamed of his wife on the day of her first miscarriage. The way the nurses couldn't find the vein in her arm, how they'd kept trying with the needle, the way she'd cried and held his fingers tightly, like a woman giving birth.

He started awake, terrified, as if he'd fallen asleep driving.

Caring less for silence, he stumbled from the truck and flicked on the lights and fired at the eyes, though now they were doubling up, floating in the air. He lowered the gun and for no good reason found himself thinking of a time when he'd tried fly fishing, standing in his yard with his wife watching from the porch, *Tarzan of the Apes* in her lap, him whipping the line in the air, showing off, and then the strange pulling you get when you catch a fish, Betty jump-

188 Poachers

ing to her feet, the book falling, and her yelling that he'd caught a bat, for heaven's sake, a *bat!*

He climbed back into the truck. His hands shook so hard he had trouble getting the door locked. He bowed his head, missing her so much that he cried, softly and for a long time.

Dawn found him staring at a field littered with dead does, yearlings, and fawns. One of the deer, only wounded, tried to crawl toward the safety of the trees. Kirxy got out of the truck and vomited colorless water, then stood looking around at the foggy morning. He lifted his rifle and limped into the grass in the drizzle and, a quick hip shot, put the deer out of its misery.

He was sitting on the open tailgate trying to light a cigarette when Goodloe and a deputy passed in their Blazer and stopped.

The sheriff stepped out, signaling for the deputy to stay put. He sat beside Kirxy on the tailgate, the truck dipping with his weight. His stomach was growling and he patted it absently.

"You old fool," Goodloe said, staring at Kirxy and then at the field. "You figured to make Frank David show himself?" He shook his head. "Good lord almighty, Kirxy. What'll it take to prove to you there ain't no damn game warden out there? Not yet, anyhow."

Kirxy didn't answer. Goodloe went to the Blazer and told the deputy to pick him up at Kirxy's store. Then he helped the old man into the passenger seat and went around and got in the driver's side. He took the rifle and unloaded it, put its clip in his pocket.

"We'll talk about them deer later," he said. "Now I'd better get you back."

They'd gone a silent mile when Kirxy said, "Would you mind running me by Esther's?"

Goodloe shrugged and turned that way. His stomach made a strangling noise. The rain and wind were picking up, rocking the truck. The sheriff took a bottle of whiskey from his pocket. "Medicinal," he said, handing the bottle to Kirxy. "It's just been two freak accidents, is all, Kirxy. I've seen some strange shit, a lot stranger than this. Them Gateses is just a unlucky bunch. Period. I ain't one to go believing in curses, but I swear to God if they ain't downright snake-bit."

Soon Goodloe had parked in front of Esther's and they sat waiting for the rain to slack. Kirxy rubbed his knees and looked out the windows where the trees were half-submerged in the rising floodwaters.

"They say old Esther has her a root cellar," Goodloe said, taking a sip. "Shit. I expect it's full of water this time of year. She's probably got cottonmouths wrapped around her plumbing." He shuddered and offered the bottle. Kirxy took it and sipped. He gave it back and Goodloe took it and drank, then drank again. "Lord if that don't hit the spot.

"When I was in the service," Goodloe went on, "over in Thailand? They had them little bitty snakes, them banded kraits. Poison as cobras, what they told us. Used to hide up under the commode lid. Every time you took you a shit, you had to lift up the lid, see was one there." He drank. "Yep. It was many a time I kicked one off in the water, flushed it down."

"Wait here," Kirxy said. He opened the door, his pants leg darkening as the rain poured in, cold as needles. He set his knee out deliberately, planted his cane in the mud and pulled himself up, stood in water to his ankles. He limped across the yard with his hand blocking the rain. There were two chickens on the front porch, their feathers fluffed out so that they looked strange, menacing. Kirxy climbed the porch steps with the pain so strong in his knees that stars popped near his face by the time he reached the top. He leaned against the house, breathing hard. Touched himself at the throat where a tie might've gone. Then he rapped gently with the hook of his cane. The door opened immediately. Dark inside. She stood there, looking at him.

"How come you don't ever stop by the store anymore?" he asked.

She folded her arms.

"Scott's dead," he said.

"I heard," Esther said. "And I'm leaving. Fuck this place and every one of you."

She closed the door and Kirxy would never see her again.

At the store, Goodloe nodded for the deputy to stay in the Blazer, then he took Kirxy by the elbow and helped him up the steps. He unlocked the door for him and held his hand as the old man sank in his chair.

"Want those boots off?" Goodloe asked, spreading a blanket over Kirxy's lap.

He bent and unlaced the left, then the right.

"Pick up your foot."

"Now the other one."

He set the wet boots by the stove.

"It's a little damp in here. I'll light this thing."

He found a box of kitchen matches on a shelf under the counter among the glass figurines Kirxy's wife had collected. The little deer. The figure skater. The unicorn. Goodloe got a fire going in the stove and stood warming the backs of his legs.

"I'll bring Wayne by a little later," he said, but Kirxy didn't seem to hear.

Goodloe sat in his office with his feet on the desk, rolling a cartridge between his fingers. Despite himself, he was beginning to think Kirxy might be right. Maybe Frank David *was* out there on the prowl. He stood, put on his pistol belt and walked to the back, pushed open the swinging door and had Roy buzz him through. So far he'd had zero luck getting anything out of Wayne. The boy just sat in his cell wrapped in a blanket, not talking to anybody. Goodloe had told him about his brother's death, and he'd seen no emotion cross the boy's face. Goodloe figured that it wasn't this youngest one who'd killed that game warden, it'd probably been the others. He knew that this boy wasn't carrying a full cylinder, the way he never talked, but he had most likely been a witness. He'd been considering calling in the state psychologist from the Searcy Mental Hospital to give the boy an evaluation.

"Come on," Goodloe said, stopping by Wayne's cell. "I'm fixing to put your talent to some good use."

He kept the boy cuffed as the deputy drove them toward the trestle.

"Turn your head, Dave," Goodloe said, handing Wayne a pint of Old Crow. The boy took it in both hands and unscrewed the lid, began to drink too fast.

"Slow down there, partner," Goodlow said, taking back the bottle. "You need to be alert."

Soon they stood near the trestle, gazing at the flat shapes of the boat on the bank. Wayne knelt and examined the ground. The deputy came up and started to say something, but Goodloe motioned for quiet.

"Just like a goddern bloodhound," he whispered. "Maybe I oughta give him your job."

"Reckon what he's after?" the deputy asked.

Wayne scrabbled up the trestle, and the two men followed. The boy walked slowly over the rails, examining the spaces between the cross ties. He stopped, bent down, and peered at something. Picked it up.

"What you got there, boy?" Goodloe called, going and squatting beside him. He took a sip of Old Crow.

When Wayne hit him, two-handed, the bottle flew one way and Goodloe the other. Both landed in the river, Goodloe with his hand clapped to his head to keep his hat on. He came up immediately, bobbing and sputtering. On the trestle, the deputy tackled Wayne and they went down fighting on the cross ties. Below, Goodloe dredged himself out of the water. He came ashore dripping and tugged his pistol from its holster. He held it up so that a thin trickle of orange water fell. He took off his hat and looked up to see the deputy disappear belly-first into the face of the river.

Wayne ran down the track, toward the swamp. The deputy came boiling ashore. He had his own pistol drawn and was looking around vengefully.

Goodloe climbed the trestle in time to see Wayne disappear into the woods. The sheriff chased him for a while, ducking limbs and vines, but stopped, breathing hard. The deputy passed him.

Wayne circled back through the woods and went quickly over the soft ground, half-crawling up the sides of hills and sliding down the other sides. Two hollows over, he heard the deputy heading the wrong direction. Wayne slowed a little and just trotted for a long time in the rain, the cuffs rubbing his wrists raw. He stopped once and looked at what he'd been carrying in one hand: a match, limp and black now with water, nearly dissolved. He stood looking at the trees around him, the hanging Spanish moss and the cypress knees rising from the stagnant creek to his left.

The hair on the back of his neck rose. He knelt, tilting his head, closing his eyes, and listened. He heard the rain, heard it hit leaves and wood and heard the puddles lapping at their tiny banks, but beyond those sounds there were other muffled noises. A mockingbird mocking a blue jay. A squirrel barking and another answering. The deputy falling, a quarter mile away. Then another sound, this one close. A match striking. Wayne began to run before opening his eyes and crashed into a tree. He rolled and ran again, tearing through limbs and briars. He leapt small creeks and slipped and got up and kept running. At every turn he expected Frank David, and

he was near tears when he finally stumbled into his family graveyard.

The first thing he saw was that Kent had been dug up. Wooden
stakes surrounded the hole and fenced it in with yellow tape that
had words on it. Wayne approached slowly, hugging himself. Something floated in the grave. With his heart pounding, he peered
inside. A dog.

Wary of the trees behind him, he crept toward their back yard,
stopping at the edge. He crouched and blew into his hands to warm
his cheeks. He gazed at the dark windows of their cabin, then
circled the house, keeping to the woods. He saw the pine tree with
the low limb they used for stringing up larger animals to clean, the
rusty chain hanging and the iron pipe they stuck through the back
legs of a deer or the rare wild pig. Kent and Scott had usually done
the cleaning while Wayne fed the guts to their dogs and tried to
keep the dogs from fighting.

And there, past the tree, lay the rest of the dogs. Shot dead.
Partially eaten. Buzzards standing in the mud, staring boldly at him
with their heads bloody and their beaks open.

It was dark when Kirxy woke in his chair; he'd heard the door
creak. Someone stood there, and the storekeeper was afraid until
he smelled the river.

"Hey, boy," he said.

Wayne ate two cans of potted meat with his fingers and a candy
bar and a box of saltines. Kirxy gave him a Coke from the red
cooler and he drank it and took another one while Kirxy got a
hacksaw from the rack of tools behind the counter. He slipped the
cardboard wrapping off and nodded for Wayne to sit. The storekeeper pulled up another chair and faced the boy and began saw-
ing the handcuff chain. The match dropped out of Wayne's hand
but neither saw it. Wayne sat with his head down and his palms up,
his wrists on his knees, breathing heavily, while Kirxy worked and
the silver shavings accumulated in a pile between their boots. The
boy didn't lift his head the entire time, and he'd been asleep for
quite a while when Kirxy finally sawed through. The old man rose,
flexing his sore hands, and got a blanket from a shelf. He unfolded
it, shook out the dust, and spread it over Wayne. He went to the
door and turned the dead bolt.

The phone rang later. It was Goodloe, asking about the boy.

"He's asleep," Kirxy said. "You been lost all this time, Sugarbaby?"

"That I have," Goodloe said, "and we still ain't found old Dave yet."

For a week they stayed there together. Kirxy could barely walk now, and the pain in his side was worse than ever, but he put the boy to work, sweeping, dusting, and scrubbing the shelves. He had Wayne pull a table next to his chair, and Kirxy did something he hadn't done in years: took inventory. With the boy's help, he counted and ledgered each item, marking them in his long green book. The back shelf contained canned soups, vegetables, sardines, and tins of meat. Many of the cans were so old that the labels flaked off in Kirxy's hand, so they were unmarked when Wayne replaced them in the rings they'd made not only in the dust but on the wood itself. In the back of that last shelf, Wayne discovered four tins of Underwood Deviled Ham, and as their labels fell away at Kirxy's touch, he remembered a time when he'd purposely unwrapped the paper from these cans because each label showed several red dancing devils, and some of his Negro customers had refused to buy anything that advertised the devil.

Kirxy now understood that his store was dead, that it no longer provided a service. His Negro customers had stopped coming years before. The same with Esther. For the past few years, except for the rare hunter, he'd been in business for the Gates boys alone. He looked across the room at Wayne, spraying the windows with Windex and wiping at them absently, gazing outside. The boy wore the last of the new denim overalls Kirxy had in stock. Once, when the store had thrived, he'd had many sizes, but for the longest time now the only ones he'd stocked were the boys'.

That night, beneath his standing lamp, Kirxy began again to read his wife's copy of *Tarzan of the Apes* to Wayne. He sipped his whiskey and spoke clearly, to be heard over the rain. When he paused to turn a page, he saw that the boy lay asleep across the row of chairs they'd arranged in the shape of a bed. Looking down through his bifocals, Kirxy flipped to the back of the book to the list of other Tarzan novels — twenty-four in all — and he decided to order them through the mail so Wayne would hear the complete adventures of Tarzan of the Apes.

In the morning, Goodloe called and said that Frank David had officially arrived — the sheriff himself had witnessed the swearing-in — and he was now this district's game warden.

"Pretty nice fellow," Goodloe said. "Kinda quiet. Polite. He asked me how the fishing was."

Then it's over, Kirxy thought.

A week later, Kirxy told Wayne he had to run some errands in Grove Hill. He'd spent the night before trying to decide whether to take the boy with him but had decided not to, that he couldn't watch him forever. Before he left he gave Wayne his thirty-ought-six and told him to stay put, not to leave for anything. For himself, Kirxy took an old twenty-two bolt action and placed it in the back window rack of his truck. He waved to Wayne and drove off.

He thought that if the boy wanted to run away, it was his own choice. Kirxy owed him the chance, at least.

At the doctor's office the young surgeon frowned and removed his glasses when he told Kirxy that the cancer was advancing, that he'd need to check into the hospital in Mobile immediately. It was way past time. "Just look at your color," the surgeon said. Kirxy stood, thanked the man, put on his hat, and limped outside. He went by the post office and placed his order for the Tarzan books. He shopped for supplies in the Dollar Store and the Piggly Wiggly, had the checkout boys put the boxes in the front seat beside him. Coming out of the drugstore, he remembered that it was Saturday, that there'd be chicken fights today. And possible news about Frank David.

At Heflin's, Kirxy paid his five-dollar admission and let Heflin help him to a seat in the bottom of the stands. He poured some whiskey in his coffee and sat studying the crowd. Nobody had mentioned Frank David, but a few old-timers had offered their sympathies on the deaths of Kent and Scott. Down in the pit the Cajuns were back, and during the eighth match — one of the Louisiana whites versus a local red, the tall bald Cajun stooping and circling the tangled birds and licking his lips as his rooster swarmed the other and hooked it, the barn smoky and dark, rain splattering the tin roof — the door swung open.

Instantly the crowd was hushed. Feathers settled to the ground. Even the Cajuns knew who he was. He stood at the door, unarmed, his hands on his hips. A wiry man. He lifted his chin and people tried to hide their drinks. His giant ears. The hooked nose. The eyes. Bird handlers reached over their shoulders, pulling at the numbered pieces of masking tape on their backs. The two handlers and the referee in the ring sidled out, leaving the roosters.

For a full minute Frank David stood staring. People stepped out the back door. Climbed out windows. Half-naked boys in the rafters were frozen like monkeys hypnotized by a snake.

Frank David's gaze didn't stop on Kirxy but settled instead on the roosters, the white one pecking out the red's eyes. Outside, trucks roared to life, backfiring like gunshots. Kirxy placed his hands on his knees. He rose, turned up his coat collar, and flung his coffee out. Frank David still hadn't looked at him. Kirxy planted his cane and made his way out the back door and through the mud.

Not a person in sight, just tailgates vanishing into the woods.

From inside his truck, Kirxy watched Frank David walk away from the barn and head toward the trees. Now he was just a bow-legged man with white hair. Kirxy felt behind him for the twenty-two rifle with one hand while rolling down the window with the other. He had a little trouble aiming the gun with his shaky hands. He pulled back the bolt and inserted a cartridge into the chamber. Flicked the safety off. The sight of the rifle wavered between Frank David's shoulders as he walked. As if an old man like Kirxy were nothing to fear. Kirxy ground his teeth: that was why the bastard hadn't come to his deer massacre — an old storekeeper wasn't worth it, wasn't dangerous.

Closing one eye, Kirxy pulled the trigger. He didn't hear the shot, though later he would notice his ears ringing.

Frank David's coat bloomed out to the side and he missed a step. He stopped and put his hand to his lower right side and looked over his shoulder at Kirxy, who was fumbling with the rifle's bolt action. Then Frank David was gone, just wasn't there, there were only the trees, bent in the rain, and shreds of fog in the air. For a moment, Kirxy wondered if he'd even seen a man at all, if he'd shot at something out of his own imagination, if the cancer that had started in his pancreas had inched up along his spine into his brain and was deceiving him, forming men out of the air and walking them across fields, giving them hands and eyes and the power to disappear.

From inside the barn, the rooster crowed. Kirxy remembered

Wayne. He hung the rifle in its rack and started his truck, gunned the engine. He banged over the field, flattening saplings and a fence, and though he couldn't feel his toes, he drove very fast.

Not until two days later, in the VA hospital in Mobile, would Kirxy finally begin to piece it all together. Parts of that afternoon were patchy and hard to remember: shooting Frank David, going back to the store and finding it empty, no sign of a struggle, the thirty-ought-six gone, as if Wayne had walked out on his own and taken the gun. Kirxy could remember getting back into his truck. He'd planned to drive to Grove Hill — the court house, the game warden's office — and find Frank David, but somewhere along the way he passed out behind the wheel and veered off the road into a ditch. He barely remembered the rescue workers. The sirens. Goodloe himself pulling Kirxy out.

Later that night two coon hunters had stumbled across Wayne, wandering along the river, his face and shirt covered in blood, the thirty-ought-six nowhere to be found.

When Goodloe had told the semiconscious Kirxy what happened, the storekeeper turned silently to the window, where he saw only the reflected face of an old, failed, dying man.

And later still, in the warm haze of morphine, Kirxy lowered his eyelids and let his imagination unravel and retwine the mystery of Frank David: it was as if Frank David himself appeared in the chair where Goodloe had sat, as if the game warden broke the seal on a bottle of Jim Beam and leaned forward on his elbows and touched the bottle to Kirxy's cracked lips and whispered to him a story about boots going over land and not making a sound, about rain washing the blood trail away even as the boots passed. About a tired old game warden taking his hand out of his coat and seeing the blood from Kirxy's bullet there, feeling it trickle down his side. About the boy in the back of his truck, handcuffed, gagged, blindfolded. About driving carefully through deep ruts in the road. Stopping behind Esther's empty house and carrying the kicking boy inside on his shoulder.

When the blindfold is removed, Wayne has trouble focusing but knows where he is because of her smell. Bacon and soap. Cigarettes, dust. Frank David holds what looks like a pillowcase. He comes across the room and puts the pillowcase down. He rubs his eyes and sits on the bed beside Wayne. He opens a book of matches and lights a cigarette. Holds the filtered end to Wayne's lips, but the boy doesn't inhale. Frank David puts the cigarette in his own lips, the embers glow. Then he drops it on the floor, crushes it out with his boot. Picks up the butt and slips it into his shirt pocket. He puts his hand over the boy's watery eyes, the skin of his palm dry and hard. Cool. Faint smell of blood. He moves his fingers over Wayne's nose, lips, chin. Stops at his throat and holds the boy tightly but not painfully. In a strange way Wayne can't understand, he finds it reassuring. His thudding heart slows. Something is struggling beside his shoulder and Frank David takes the thing from the bag. Now the smell in the room changes. Wayne begins to thrash and whip his head from side to side.

"Goddamn, Son," Frank David whispers, "I hate to civilize you."

Goodloe began going to the veterans' hospital in Mobile once a week. He brought Kirxy cigarettes from his store. There weren't any private rooms available, and the beds around the storekeeper were filled with dying ex-soldiers who never talked, but Kirxy was beside a window and Goodloe would raise the glass and prop it open with a novel. They smoked together and drank whiskey from paper cups, listening for nurses.

It was the tall mean one.

"One more time, goddamn it," she said, coming out of nowhere and plucking the cigarettes from their lips so quickly they were still puckered.

Sometimes Goodloe would wheel Kirxy down the hall in his chair, the IV rack attached by a stainless steel contraption with a black handle the shape of a flower. They would go to the elevator and ride down three floors to a covered area where people smoked and talked about the weather. There were nurses and black cafeteria workers in white uniforms and hair nets and people visiting other people and a few patients. Occasionally in the halls they'd see some mean old fart Kirxy knew and they'd talk about hospital food or chicken fighting. Or the fact that Frank David had surprised everyone and decided to retire after only a month of quiet duty, that the new game warden was from Texas. And a nigger to boot.

Then Goodloe would wheel Kirxy back along a long window, out of which you could see the tops of oak trees.

On one visit, Goodloe told Kirxy they'd taken Wayne out of intensive care. Three weeks later he said the boy'd been discharged.

"I give him a ride to the store," Goodloe said. This was in late May and Kirxy was a yellow skeleton with hands that shook.

"I'll stop by and check on him every evening," Goodloe went on. "He'll be okay, the doctor says. Just needs to keep them bandages changed. I can do that, I reckon."

They were quiet then, for a time, just the coughs of the dying men and the soft swishing of nurses' thighs and the hum of IV machines.

"Goodloe," Kirxy whispered, "I'd like you to help me with something."

Goodloe leaned in to hear, an unlit cigarette behind his ear like a pencil.

Kirxy's tongue was white and cracked, his breath awful. "I'd like to change my will," he said, "make the boy beneficiary."

"All right," Goodloe said.

"I'm obliged," whispered Kirxy. He closed his eyes.

Near the end he was delirious. He said he saw a little black creature at the foot of his bed. Said it had him by the toe. In surprising fits of strength, he would throw his water pitcher at it, or his box of tissues, or the *TV Guide*. Restraints were called for. His coma was a relief to everyone, and he died quietly in the night.

In Kirxy's chair in the store, Wayne didn't seem to hear Goodloe's questions. The sheriff had done some looking in the Grove Hill library — "research" was the modern word — and discovered that one species of cobra spat venom at its victim's eyes, but there weren't such snakes in southern Alabama. Anyway, the hospital lab had confirmed that it was the venom of a cottonmouth that had blinded Wayne. The question, of course, was who had put the venom in his eyes. Goodloe shuddered to think of it, how they'd found Wayne staggering about, howling in pain, bleeding from his tear ducts, the skin around his eye sockets dissolving, exposing the white ridges of his skull.

In the investigation, several local blacks including Euphrates Morrisette stated to Goodloe that the youngest Gates boy and his two dead brothers had molested Euphrates' stepdaughter in her own house. There was a rumor that several black men dressed in white sheets with pillowcases for hoods had caught and punished Wayne as he lurked along the river, peeping in folks' windows and doing unwholesome things to himself. Others suggested that the conjure woman had cast a spell on the Gateses, that she'd summoned a swamp demon to chase them to hell. And still others attributed the happenings to Frank David. There were a few occurrences of violence between some of the local whites and the blacks — some fires, a broken jaw — but soon it died down and Goodloe filed the deaths of Kent and Scott Gates as accidental.

But he listed Wayne's blinding as unsolved. The snake venom had bleached his pupils white, and the skin around his eye sockets had required grafts. The doctors had had to use skin from his buttocks, and because his buttocks were hairy, the skin around his eyes grew hair, too.

In the years to come, the loggers who clear-cut the land along the river would occasionally stop in the store, less from a need to buy something than from a curiosity to see the hermit with the milky, hairy eyes. The store smelled horrible, like the inside of a bear's mouth, and dust lay thick and soft on the shelves. Because they'd come in, the loggers would feel obligated to buy something, but every item was moldy or stale beyond belief, except for the things in cans, which were all unlabeled so they never knew what they'd get. Nothing was marked as to price either, and the blind man wouldn't talk. He just sat by the stove. So the loggers paid more than what they thought a can was worth, leaving the money on the counter by the telephone, which hadn't been connected in years. When plumper, grayer Goodloe came by on the occasional evening, he'd take the bills and coins and put them in Kirxy's cash drawer. He was no longer sheriff, having lost several elections back to one of his deputies, Roy or Dave. Now he drove a Lance truck, his routes including the hospitals in the county.

"Dern, boy," he cracked once. "This store's doing a better business now than it ever has. You sure you don't want a cracker rack?"

When Goodloe left, Wayne listened to the sound of the truck as it faded. "Sugarbaby," he whispered.

And many a night for years after, until his own death in his sleep, Wayne would rise from the chair and move across the floor, taking Kirxy's cane from where it stood by the coat rack. He would go outside, down the stairs like a man who could see, his beard nearly to his chest, and he would walk soundlessly the length of the building, knowing the woods even better now as he crept down the rain-rutted gullyside toward the river whose smell never left the caves of his nostrils and the roof of his mouth. At the riverbank, he would stop and sit with his back against a small pine, and lifting his white eyes to the sky, he would listen to the clicks and hum and thrattle of the woods, seeking out each noise at its source and imagining it: an acorn nodding, detaching, falling, its thin ricochet and the way it settles into the leaves. A bullfrog's bubbling throat and the things it says. The soft movement of the river over rocks and around the bases of cattails and cypress knees and through the wet hanging roots of trees. And then another sound, familiar. The soft, precise footsteps of Frank David. Downwind. Not coming closer, not going away. Circling. The striking of a match and the sizzle of ember and the fall of ash. The ascent of smoke. A strange and terrifying comfort for the rest of Wayne Gates's life.

VICTOR GISCHLER

Hitting Rufus

FROM *Lynx Eye*

SO I HAD a tidy sum in the Swiss account, and I figured one more job — any more jobs — and I'd really be pushing my luck, you know? Sooner or later the reflexes get slow, and the marks start shooting back. Who needed that shit? I'm good at what I do, but I didn't get no particular jollies out of it. I can spend the rest of my days sipping umbrella drinks in French Polynesia, and with the payoff I got from popping the little Arab at Disney, I can do it in style. It was easy. I got him with the high-powered scope and a Ruger .223 as he was coming down the big waterfall on Splash Mountain. You should see his souvenir photo.

But Stan, my broker, called and he asked as a favor to a friend of a friend of somebody who owes somebody else, would I go down to Mississippi and pop this moonshiner and as a matter of fact it's sorta like a charity case because the job only pays $14,762.

"Jesus, Stan. I never worked so cheap."

"I know, Charlie. I know," said Stan, and I could almost hear him shrugging his apology in his cheap tweed.

"What? $14,762? Are they taking taxes out for this now? What the hell kind of amount is that?"

"Well, it's kind of a funny deal," said Stan in a way I knew it wouldn't be. "It seems this moonshiner is kind of the boss of the town down there."

"Yeah?"

"Well, nobody likes him. He has a strong-arm on all the booze business. I don't know all the details, but the town pitched in to get him out of the way."

"Fourteen grand. Some town."

"I know, Charlie. I know," Stan whined. "But look. I owe a favor. I botched that business in Detroit last week, so I gotta make good. It's like you'd be doing it for me."

"Detroit. I heard about that. Who did you send?"

"I'm embarrassed to say."

"Was it Blade Sanchez, the knife man?"

Stan was silent for a while. "So sue me. I'm a softy. He needed the work."

"That's poor judgment, buddy."

"Be a pal. I'm in a fix here," Stan said.

"Okay. For you, I'll do it. Book the flight."

I took a big plane to a little plane to a bus to a truck full of chickens which let me off at some one-horse shithole called Grossburg, Mississippi. The town consisted of gray, wooden buildings which defied encroaching swamp and leaned in conspiratorially over the only paved road. I was conspicuous as hell since I was wearing a black double-breasted Brooks Brothers suit instead of denim overalls. Also, I didn't have a yellow-brown dribble of chewing tobacco running down my chin. Grossburg and its inhabitants looked like things not visually pleasing enough to be included in *Deliverance*.

I walked into a shack with a sign that read STORE. A toothless oldster sat hunched on a barrel behind an antique cash register. He spotted me and said, "Yassir?"

"I'm afraid I don't know exactly who I'm looking for. Who's in charge around here?"

"Of the store?"

I set my suitcase down and spread my arms. "Of this entire thriving metropolis."

"You're from up North, ain'tcha?"

"Yeah."

"You the one they call Charlie the Hook?"

I nodded slowly. "Uh-huh."

"We got a room for you upstairs." He jerked his thumb toward the back of the store and a bleak, dubiously constructed set of wooden stairs.

"Why?"

"You here to kill Rufus Lamonte, ain'tcha?"

"Is he the moonshiner you all pitched in to have rubbed out?"

"Yep."

"He's as good as dead."

"Okay by me," said the oldster. "That's a hundred thirty-three dollars of my VA check I was gonna use to put a new alternator in the Chevy. But we ain't got no motels nearabouts, and you can't kill old Rufus 'til tomorrow, so we got you a room upstairs."

"Let's say I was to have a nice lunch, see all of the tourist attractions in Grossburg, and then there was still daylight left. Is there any reason I couldn't kill old Rufus today?"

"He ain't here. Went down to Hattiesburg for the cock fights, and he won't be back 'til tomorrow. You know, I could tell you was from up North straightaway when you walked in. I can always tell."

"I see. Is the mayor or somebody here? Maybe I'd better talk to him."

"He's out of town."

"Where?"

"Hattiesburg."

"Cock fights?"

"Yep."

"I'll be upstairs."

I was coming out of the shower, drying my hair, when I saw the little flash of movement near the door. I latched onto her arm, twisted hard forcing her facedown onto the bed. She squealed in surprise and pain, and I put the snub-nose .38 against her temple and thumbed back the hammer.

"Okay. I'm sorry. I'm sorry." The words tumbled out of her quickly between winces of pain.

I said, "Who and why? And don't lie."

"I'm Annie Sue Lamonte. I heard Floyd tell Little Bill that the Yankee hired killer was here and in his room over the store, and I wanted to see if he was as handsome as everyone was saying."

I twisted harder.

"Ow! Quit it. Dammit, that hurts."

"I know what I look like," I said. "Look at me and tell me what I look like really." I twisted once more for emphasis.

"You have black hair and a receding hairline. You're a little jowly cheeked and I think you don't get enough sleep because you've got dark circles under your eyes. Also, maybe your nose has been broken a time or two. The eyes ain't so bad. Kinda gray."

"The truth shall set you free." I let go of her arm but kept the revolver trained on her.

"You know, for a naked man, you was able to come out with a pistol pretty quick. How'd you do that?"

I grabbed my pants from the back of a wooden chair and slipped them on. "Professional secret." I took a quick survey of Annie Sue Lamonte. She was a tan and pleasingly ample package crammed ambitiously and with some element of guile into denim cut-offs and a hot pink halter top. Her shoulder-length hair was vaguely blondish thanks to a bad, bad dye job. "I suppose you're some relation to Rufus Lamonte."

She raised herself to her knees and looked at me seriously. "Yes. He is in fact my stepdaddy, and that's what I came to talk to you about."

I stuck the revolver in my pocket and pulled a clean shirt out of my suitcase. "Go ahead."

"He knows you're here and why, and he's not coming into town tomorrow," she told me. "He's sending two of his boys, Clem and Joey, with shotguns to take care of you."

"How'd he find out about me?"

Her eyes grew big. "Why just simply the whole town knows you're here. You're the biggest thing to happen here since, well, forever."

I sat in the chair and pulled on my socks. "If you're Lamonte's stepdaughter, why are you telling me this?"

She straightened her back properly. "I have dreams and aspirations," she said formally. "I do not want to forever remain in this itty-bitty, good-for-nothing town."

"So leave."

She slumped heavily into the pillows. "I can't. I just can't. Daddy Rufus thinks that just because we ain't blood kin he can, well, take certain liberties, so he wants to keep me around."

I cleared my throat. "Well. Miss Lamonte, that's — hmmm — just frankly godawful, and I'm sorry that I had to hear that."

"But you see why I had to warn you," said Annie Sue. "You've got to live so you can kill Daddy Rufus absolutely dead, and I can get *out* of this place."

"Uh-huh. Just for the record, what do Clem and Joey look like?"

"Oh, you'll know 'em, all right," said Annie Sue. "They'll be the ones with the shotguns."

I tend to prowl. It's my nature, and when night falls, I like to have a little walk, just a little look around. But it's hard to prowl in a place like Grossburg, and what started as a prowl ended up as a parade. I was casually strolling down the sidewalk, and the townsfolk, eager to see the "Yankee hired killer," filed in behind me. A little, round tub of a man broke off from the crowd and approached me tentatively.

"Charlie the Hook?" he ran his hand nervously down the leg of his trousers before offering it to me. "I'm Mayor Cromwell. I heard you was asking about me?"

"Yeah. Listen, first of all I'm not exactly thrilled that everyone and his hog knows I'm in town to hit Rufus Lamonte. Usually, people in my line of work like to keep a low profile."

"Oh, sure, sure. I can imagine. I really can. When I heard you was coming I was just tickled pink, you know? On account of I'd like to see Rufus just as dead as can be, but by the time I heard, it was already all over town. I didn't spread the word. Honest. Word sort of spread itself."

"I don't care how many people you told personally, Cromwell. When you hire someone like me, it's your responsibility to keep it discreet."

"Hell, sure, I agree, but you got me all wrong, Mr. Hook," said Cromwell. "I mean, I am the elected mayor and all, but I don't make those kinds of decisions. Everyone knows who holds the real political power in Grossburg."

"And who's that?"

Cromwell pointed to one of the sagging gray buildings that housed a restaurant called Charlene's. "The women's circle. You'll find them in there at one of the tables in the back."

I nodded toward the restaurant. "In there?"

"Sure enough. It's quilting night."

"We are so very obliged you could make it on such short notice all the way down to Grossburg, Mississippi, Charlie. We are. We certainly are," said Charlene. Four old, old, old women sat in a circle at the very back of the restaurant. A heavy patchwork quilt covered their laps, and they sewed steadily as they conversed. Mayor Cromwell had introduced them as Charlene, Dorothea, Naomi, and May before bowing politely and leaving me with Grossburg's power brokers.

"Well, it's a favor for a friend," I explained vaguely.

"It certainly is a favor for us," said Charlene. "It certainly is."

All four women were equally shrunken, white-haired, and wrinkled. Naomi distinguished herself by being drunk. "Lester, dammit, git your black ass in here right now," she yelled into the back. A young black boy scrambled in with a jug and filled the Mason jar next to Naomi with white lightning. "What did I tell you about keeping that glass full, boy. Hell, you think I'm here for the quilting?"

"Sorry, Miss Naomi."

"All right. Now git."

Lester scurried away.

"We're so rude," said Charlene. "Can we offer you some refreshment?"

"Would you happen to have any Chivas?"

"What do you think?"

"Never mind."

"I'm curious, Charlie," said Dorothea. "How do you plan to undo old Rufus?"

"Yes, do tell us," broke in May. "Will you use something exotic and clever like a blow gun with poison darts?"

"No. I imagine I'll just pump some lead into his heart."

"I suppose simple is better," said May.

"Usually, I'd use a snub-nose," I explained. "It's small and becomes part of your fist." I took it out of the belt holster and showed them. "The trick is not to aim a gun like this. You get in close like you're going to punch him in the chest, then *bing bang,* you squeeze off two quick ones in the heart."

"My, that does sound simple," said May.

"Just as long as he's dead." Naomi took a generous swig from her Mason jar.

"Don't you get blood on you?" asked May.

"Sure."

"What's the trick?"

"Not minding that you get blood on you."

"I see."

From under the quilt, Dorothea produced a paper bag and handed it to Charlene.

"This is for you, Charlie." She handed the bag to me. "$14,762. I'm sorry it couldn't be more."

"That's okay," I said. "To tell the truth, I'm sort of enjoying myself. I never rubbed nobody out with the approval of a whole community before." I didn't bother telling her that I usually spent more than that on bullets in a year. "Just one thing. Why do you want Rufus out of the way so badly?"

"As you may have seen," began Charlene, "we ain't exactly strong on commerce and industry here in Grossburg."

"I noticed."

"Anyway, this town depends on what we make brewing our own corn liquor."

"Don't forget the marijuana," said May. "We're the biggest producers of grass in five counties."

"Exactly," said Charlene. "And Rufus comes in and takes over, monopolizing resources and manpower, and, well, this just ain't a big enough territory for two operations of any size. Naturally, we were so used to having things our way, we didn't know how to defend ourselves."

"He caught us with our panties down," clarified Naomi.

"He's troublesome," said May.

"He's a Goddamned son of a bitch is what he is," said Naomi. "He kicked my dog."

"Do kill him for us, won't you?" asked Charlene.

"I'll do my best."

I'd been sleeping for about an hour when Annie Sue entered my room quietly and slipped in next to me under the covers.

"Charlie," she whispered, "I've got to tell you about — hey! That's cold. What is that you're sticking in my ribs?"

I said, "You know what that is."

"Now I suppose you're going to shoot Annie Sue after what she's come to tell you?"

"So speak."

"Well, you just must have Daddy Rufus all worried to pieces because he's sending all four boys of his in the morning, not just Clem and Joey like I told you before. Also, I think one of his cousins is over from Plant City and he carries an automatic pistol and drives a car!"

"And you needed to be naked to tell me this?"

"I thought it would be less conspicuous."

"How old are you, Annie Sue?"

"I know you think I'm just a child, but I'm not. I'm nearly nineteen."

"Go home, Annie Sue."

"Don't you like girls, Charlie?"

"I like them just fine, but I need my sleep. I've got a lot of killing to do in the morning."

"Okay, but just remember. You had your chance."

I awoke with the dawn. This wasn't habit, but a chorus of roosters made sure the whole town was up. I splashed water in my face and dressed. I made sure the snub-nose was tucked tightly into the belt holster, and I opened my suitcase and fished out my extra guns, twin Smith and Wesson .357 magnums with six-inch barrels. Big, beautiful revolvers. I really should have had a pair of automatics for a job like this, but I was partial to the simple elegance of a spinning chamber. Maybe it's the cowboy in me. Anyway, I made up for the revolvers with a little 9mm Uzi. I slapped in a full clip, cocked one into the chamber, and thumbed off the safety. I shrugged into my shoulder holsters with the revolvers and put on my jacket.

Downstairs, I found the toothless oldster crouched behind a stack of flour bags. "Which way will they be coming from?"

He pointed out the window. "The Lamonte place is that way, so I reckon they'll be coming from the north."

"That's south."

"Right. South. That's what I meant."

I stepped onto the front porch of the store and settled myself into one of the weather-beaten rocking chairs. It was a nice day, actually. I liked the climate here, although I'm sure it had nothing on French Polynesia. Even the people seemed nice, if just a little backward. All in all it had been an interesting experience.

I didn't have to wait long. The pickup truck came from the south end of town at top speed in typical yahoo fashion. It was an old Ford with two rednecks in the front and two more standing in the bed waving shotguns and hollering. I kept the Uzi low until they got close. When one of the good old boys in the back tried to level his shotgun at me, I swung the Uzi around at the broad part of the truck and emptied a clip. The submachine gun sputtered-fire and bucked in my hands, puncturing the side of the pickup with metallic *tinks*. I caught one of the front tires and it blew, sending the pickup skidding into the post office and lurching to a halt with the crack of bent metal and the *clinkle* of broken headlights. The driver leaned dead against the steering wheel.

The other three boys leapt out and dove for cover on the other side of the truck. They popped up and let loose with a couple of shells from the shotguns that splintered the wood of the rocking chair, but I was already ducking back into the store.

"How's it going?" asked the oldster.

"So far, so good."

I dropped the machine gun and drew the magnums. The shotguns thundered and the store's front window exploded with buckshot, spraying glass over the interior of the store and the oldster behind the flour bags.

"You got insurance?"

"State Farm."

"Good for you."

I gave the boys a second to get curious, then rose and fired four quick shots from the revolvers. I got one in the shoulder and he dropped his shotgun. I got another in the face just below the left eye and he spun away in a shower of blood. I ducked back again, avoiding a rain of buckshot.

"Back door?"

The oldster pointed. "Through there."

I hot-footed it out the back and came around the side of the building. The last uninjured redneck was dragging his brother out of harm's way. I squeezed off two shots into each of them, and they fell dead. I walked over to the truck with a smoking revolver in each hand, my eyes darting from building to building looking for my next target. I surveyed my destruction, but none of the corpses looked like Rufus himself. I heard a car door slam just ahead of the gunshot that split the morning and sprayed my own blood all over my shoulder and jacket. Shit. The cousin with the car and the automatic. I spun quickly and sent him for cover with three shots. I hauled ass into Charlene's and ducked below the big picture window.

"He got you, huh?"

I looked into the face of the kid that Naomi had called Lester. "Yeah. Just a little." I'd caught a nice .45-caliber slug in the upper, fleshy part of my arm. It was a ragged, bloody mess. "You got a towel or something?"

He brought me a hand towel, and I wrapped it around the wound the best I could. I was a little dizzy, and I had a good sweat going.

"You probably been shot before, right?" asked Lester. "This ain't probably nothin' to you."

"Who am I, Wile E. Coyote? I'm bleeding, for Christ's sake." I let the pistols clatter out of my hands onto the tile floor and drew a handful of shells out of my jacket pocket. "Can you reload those?" I nodded at the revolvers.

He took my guns and counted the bullets. "There's only six of 'em."

"Put three in each, and see what he's doing."

Lester peeked out the window. "He's lookin' over here."

"Okay. Give me the guns." I checked them, then cocked each one.

Lester stuck his head up and looked out the big window. Three loud shots shattered the glass and sent Lester spinning back with a bloody gash in his head.

"Son of a bitch." I stood and emptied both guns into the cousin with the car. The bullets danced up his chest to his throat, sprouting a little trail of red blossoms. He convulsed and fell in a heap of dead flesh.

I checked Lester. He was dead. After waiting another half hour, I gave up on seeing Rufus.

I pulled the snub-nose as I entered my room over the store. The door was ajar, so I could tell someone had been there. On the bed was a folded piece of sky-blue stationery. I unfolded it, and in Annie Sue's unsteady scrawl I read:

Charlie,

The funniest thing happened. You know, it's strange how things just work out for the best. I wanted to leave this little town, and Daddy Rufus wanted to steal all the moonshine money he made without giving his sons their fair share. So we decided that while you were gunning down Clem and Joey and Jake and Rufus Junior and Rufus's cousin with the car, we'd take off and maybe head for Mexico. Rufus is happy because he gets me. I'm happy because I get to leave Grossburg, and the town's happy because they get rid of Rufus. I took all your money in that brown paper bag. Don't be mad. You did have your chance. Remember?

Love,
Annie Sue

This was all, of course, my own fault, but it didn't mean I wasn't going to give Stan a swift kick in the ass before I went to French Polynesia.

ED GORMAN

Out There in the Darkness

FROM *Robert Bloch's Psychos*

1

THE NIGHT IT ALL STARTED, the whole strange spiral, we were having our usual midweek poker game — four fortyish men who work in the financial business getting together for beer and bawdy jokes and straight poker. No wild card games. We hate them.

This was summer, and vacation time, and so it happened that the game was held two weeks in a row at my house. Jan had taken the kids to see her Aunt Wendy and Uncle Verne at their fishing cabin, and so I offered to have the game at my house this week, too. With nobody there to supervise, the beer could be laced with a little bourbon, and the jokes could get even bawdier. With the wife and kids in the house, you're always at least a little bit intimidated.

Mike and Bob came together, bearing gifts, which in this case meant the kind of sexy magazines our wives did not want in the house in case the kids might stumble across them. At least that's what they say. I think they sense, and rightly, that the magazines might give their spouses bad ideas about taking the secretary out for a few after-work drinks, or stopping by a singles bar some night.

We got the chips and cards set up at the table, we got the first beers open (Mike chasing a shot of bourbon with his beer), and we started passing the dirty magazines around with tenth-grade glee. The magazines compensated, I suppose, for the balding head, the bloating belly, the stooping shoulders. Deep in the heart of every hundred-year-old man is a horny fourteen-year-old boy.

All this, by the way, took place up in the attic. The four of us got

to know one another when we all moved into what city planners
called a "transitional neighborhood." There were some grand old
houses that could be renovated with enough money and real care.
The city designated a ten-square-block area as one it wanted to
restore to shiny new luster. Jan and I chose a crumbling Victorian.
You wouldn't recognize it today. And that includes the attic, which
I've turned into a very nice den.

"Pisses me off," Mike O'Brien said. "He's always late."

And that was true. Neil Solomon *was* always late. Never by that
much but always late nonetheless.

"At least tonight he has a good excuse," Bob Genter said.

"He does?" Mike said. "He's probably swimming in his pool." Neil
recently got a bonus that made him the first owner of a full-size
outdoor pool in our neighborhood.

"No, he's got patrol. But he's stopping at nine. He's got somebody trading with him for next week."

"Oh, hell," Mike said, obviously sorry that he'd complained. "I
didn't know that."

Bob Genter's handsome black head nodded solemnly.

Patrol is something we all take very seriously in this newly restored "transitional neighborhood." Eight months ago, the burglaries started, and they've gotten pretty bad. My house has been
burglarized once and vandalized once. Bob and Mike have had
curb-sitting cars stolen. Neil's wife, Sarah, was surprised in her own
kitchen by a burglar. And then there was the killing four months
ago, man and wife who'd just moved into the neighborhood, sav-
agely stabbed to death in their own bed. The police caught the guy
a few days later trying to cash some of the traveler's checks he'd
stolen after killing his prey. He was typical of the kind of man
who infested this neighborhood after sundown: a twentyish junkie
stoned to the point of psychosis on various street drugs, and not at
all averse to murdering people he envied and despised. He also
knew a whole hell of a lot about fooling burglar alarms.

After the murders there was a neighborhood meeting, and that's
when we came up with the patrol, something somebody'd read
about being popular back east. People think that a nice middle-
sized Midwestern city like ours doesn't have major crime problems. I invite them to walk many of these streets after dark. They'll
quickly be disabused of that notion. Anyway, the patrol worked this
way: each night, two neighborhood people got in the family van

and patrolled the ten-block area that had been restored. If they saw anything suspicious, they used their cellular phones and called police. We jokingly called it the Baby-Boomer Brigade. The patrol had one strict rule: you were never to take direct action unless somebody's life was at stake. Always, always use the cellular phone and call the police.

Neil had patrol tonight. He'd be rolling in here in another half hour. The patrol had two shifts: early, eight to ten; late, ten to twelve.

Bob said, "You hear what Evans suggested?"

"About guns?" I said.

"Yeah."

"Makes me a little nervous," I said.

"Me, too," Bob said. For somebody who'd grown up in the worst area of the city, Bob Genter was a very polished guy. Whenever he joked that he was the token black, Neil always countered with the fact that he was the token Jew, just as Mike was the token Catholic and I was the token Methodist. We were friends of convenience, I suppose, but we all really did like one another, something that was demonstrated when Neil had a cancer scare a few years back. Bob, Mike, and I were in his hospital room twice a day, all eight days running.

"I think it's time," Mike said. "The bad guys have guns, so the good guys should have guns."

"The good guys are the cops," I said. "Not us."

"People start bringing guns on patrol," Bob said, "somebody innocent is going to get shot."

"So some night one of us here is on patrol and we see a bad guy and he sees us and before the cops get there, the bad guy shoots us? You don't think that's going to happen?"

"It *could* happen, Mike," I said, "but I just don't think that justifies carrying guns."

The argument gave us something to do while we waited for Neil.

"Sorry I'm late," Neil Solomon said after he followed me up to the attic and came inside.

"We already drank all the beer," Mike O'Brien said loudly.

Neil smiled. "That gut you're carrying lately, I can believe that *you* drank all the beer."

Mike always enjoyed being put down by Neil, possibly because most people were a bit intimidated by him — he had that angry Irish edge — and he seemed to enjoy Neil's skilled and fearless handling of him. He laughed with real pleasure.

Neil sat down, I got him a beer from the tiny fridge I keep up here, cards were dealt, seven-card stud was played.

Bob said, "How'd patrol go tonight?"

Neil shrugged. "No problems."

"I still say we should carry guns," Mike said.

"You're not going to believe this, but I agree with you," Neil said.

"Seriously?" Mike said.

"Oh, great," I said to Bob Genter. "Another beer commercial cowboy."

Bob smiled. "Where I come from, we didn't have cowboys, we had 'mothas.'" He laughed. "Mean mothas, let me tell you. And practically *all* of them carried guns."

"That mean you're siding with them?" I said.

Bob looked at his cards again, then shrugged. "Haven't decided yet, I guess."

I didn't think the anti-gun people were going to lose this round. But I worried about the round after it, a few months down the line, when the subject of carrying guns came up again. All the TV coverage violence gets in this city, people are more and more developing a siege mentality.

"Play cards," Mike said, "and leave the debate society crap till later."

Good idea.

We played cards.

In forty-five minutes, I lost $63.82. Mike and Neil always played as if their lives were at stake. All you had to do was watch their faces. Gunfighters couldn't have looked more serious or determined.

The first pit stop came just after ten o'clock, and Neil took it. There was a john on the second floor between the bedrooms, and another john on the first floor.

Neil said, "The good Dr. Gottesfeld had to give me a finger-wave this afternoon, gents, so this may take a while."

"You should trade that prostate of yours in for a new one," Mike said.

"Believe me, I'd like to."

While Neil was gone, the three of us started talking about the patrol again, and whether we should go armed.

We made the same old arguments. The passion was gone. We were just marking time waiting for Neil, and we knew it.

Finally, Mike said, "Let me see some of those magazines again."

"You got some identification?" I said.

"I'll show you some identification," Mike said.

"Spare me," I said. "I'll just give you the magazines."

"You mind if I use the john on the first floor?" Bob said.

"Yeah, it would really piss me off," I said.

"Really?"

That was one thing about Bob. He always fell for deadpan humor.

"No, not really," I said. "Why would I care if you used the john on the first floor?"

He grinned. "Thought maybe they were segregated facilities or something."

He left.

Mike said, "We're lucky, you know that?"

"You mean me and you?"

"Yeah."

"Lucky how?"

"Those two guys. They're great guys. I wish I had them at work." He shook his head. "Treacherous bastards. That's all I'm around all day long."

"No offense, but I'll bet you can be pretty treacherous yourself."

He smiled. "Look who's talking."

The first time I heard it, I thought it was some kind of animal noise from outside, a dog or a cat in some kind of discomfort maybe. Mike, who was dealing himself a hand of solitaire, didn't even look up from his cards.

But the second time I heard the sound, Mike and I both looked up. And then we heard the exploding sound of breaking glass.

"What the hell is that?" Mike said.

"Let's go find out."

Just about the time we reached the bottom of the attic steps, we saw Neil coming out of the second-floor john. "You hear that?"

"Sure as hell did," I said.

We reached the staircase leading to the first floor. Everything was dark. Mike reached for the light switch, but I brushed his hand away.

I put a *ssshing* finger to my lips and then showed him the Louisville Slugger I'd grabbed from Tim's room. He's my nine-year-old, and his most devout wish is to be a good baseball player. His mother has convinced him that just because I went to college on a baseball scholarship, I was a good player. I wasn't. I was a lucky player.

I led the way downstairs, keeping the bat ready at all times.

"You sonofabitch!"

The voice belonged to Bob.

More smashing glass.

I listened to the passage of the sound. Kitchen. Had to be the kitchen.

In the shadowy light from the street, I saw their faces, Mike's and Neil's. They looked scared.

I hefted the bat some more and then started moving fast to the kitchen.

Just as we passed through the dining room, I heard something heavy hit the kitchen floor. Something human and heavy.

I got the kitchen light on.

He was at the back door. White. Tall. Blond shoulder-length hair. Filthy tan T-shirt. Greasy jeans. He had grabbed one of Jan's carving knives from the huge iron rack that sits atop the butcher-block island. The one curious thing about him was the eyes: there was a malevolent iridescence to the blue pupils, an angry but somehow alien intelligence, a silver glow.

Bob was sprawled facedown on the tile floor. His arms were spread wide on either side of him. He didn't seem to be moving. Chunks and fragments of glass were strewn everywhere across the floor. My uninvited guest had smashed two or three of the colorful pitchers we'd bought the winter before in Mexico.

"Run!" the burglar cried to somebody on the back porch.

He turned, waving the butcher knife back and forth to keep us at bay.

Footsteps out the back door.

The burglar held us off a few more moments, but then I gave him a little bit of tempered Louisville Slugger wood right across the wrist. The knife went clattering.

By this time, Mike and Neil were pretty crazed. They jumped him, hurled him back against the door, and then started putting in punches wherever they'd fit.

"Hey!" I said, and tossed Neil the bat. "Just hold this. If he makes a move, open up his head. Otherwise leave him alone."

They really were crazed, like pit bulls who'd been pulled back just as a fight was starting to get good.

"Mike, call the cops and tell them to send a car."

I got Bob up and walking. I took him into the bathroom and sat him down on the toilet lid. I found a lump the size of an egg on the back of his head. I soaked a clean washcloth with cold water and pressed it against the lump. Bob took it from there.

"You want an ambulance?" I said.

"An ambulance? Are you kidding? You must think I'm a ballet dancer or something."

I shook my head. "No. I know better than that. I've got a male cousin who's a ballet dancer, and he's one tough sonofabitch, believe me. You —" I smiled. "You aren't that tough, Bob."

"I don't need an ambulance. I'm fine."

He winced and tamped the washcloth tighter against his head. "Just a little headache is all." He looked young suddenly, the aftershock of fear in his brown eyes. "Scared the hell out of me. Heard something when I was leaving the john. Went out to the kitchen to check it out. He jumped me."

"What'd he hit you with?"

"No idea."

"I'll go get you some whiskey. Just sit tight."

"I love sitting in bathrooms, man."

I laughed. "I don't blame you."

When I got back to the kitchen, they were gone. All three of them. Then I saw the basement door. It stood open a few inches. I could see dusty light in the space between door and frame. The basement was our wilderness. We hadn't had the time or money to really fix it up yet. We were counting on this year's Christmas bonus from the Windsor Financial Group to help us set it right.

I went down the stairs. The basement is one big, mostly unused room except for the washer and dryer in the corner. All the boxes and odds and ends that should have gone to the attic instead went down here. It smells damp most of the time. The idea is to turn it into a family room for when the boys are older. These days it's mostly inhabited by stray waterbugs.

When I reached the bottom step, I saw them. There are four metal support poles in the basement, near each corner. They had him lashed to a pole in the east quadrant, lashed his wrists behind him with rope found in the tool room. They also had him gagged with what looked like a pillowcase. His eyes were big and wide. He looked scared, and I didn't blame him. I was scared, too.

"What the hell are you guys doing?"

"Just calm down, Papa Bear," Mike said. That's his name for me whenever he wants to convey to people that I'm kind of this old fuddy-duddy. It so happens that Mike is two years older than I am, and it also happens that I'm not a fuddy-duddy. Jan has assured me of that, and she's completely impartial.

"Knock off the Papa Bear bullshit. Did you call the cops?"

"Not yet," Neil said. "Just calm down a little, all right?"

"You haven't called the cops. You've got some guy tied up and gagged in my basement. You haven't even asked how Bob is. And you want me to calm down."

Mike came up to me then. He still had that air of pit-bull craziness about him, frantic, uncontrollable, alien.

"We're going to do what the cops *can't* do, man," he said. "We're going to sweat this sonofabitch. We're going to make him tell us who he was with tonight, and then we're going to make him give us every single name of every single bad guy who works this neighborhood. And then we'll turn all the names over to the cops."

"It's just an extension of the patrol," Neil said. "Just keeping our neighborhood safe is all."

"You guys are nuts," I said, and turned back toward the steps. "I'm going up and call the cops."

That's when I realized just how crazed Mike was. "You aren't going anywhere, man. You're going to stay here and help us break this bastard down. You're going to do your goddamned neighborhood *duty*."

He'd grabbed my sleeve so hard that he'd torn it at the shoulder. We both discovered this at the same time.

I expected him to look sorry. He didn't. In fact, he was smirking at me. "Don't be such a wimp, Aaron," he said.

2

Mike led the charge getting the kitchen cleaned up. I think he was feeling guilty about calling me a wimp with such angry exuberance. Now I understood how lynch mobs got formed. One guy like Mike stirring people up by alternately insulting them and urging them on.

After the kitchen was put back in order, and after I'd taken inventory to find that nothing had been stolen, I went to the refrigerator and got beers for everybody. Bob had drifted back to the kitchen, too.

"All right," I said. "Now that we've all calmed down, I want to walk over to that yellow kitchen wall phone there and call the police. Any objections?"

"I think blue would look better in here than yellow," Neil said.

"Funny," I said.

They looked like themselves now, no feral madness on the faces of Mike and Neil, no winces on Bob's.

I started across the floor to the phone.

Neil grabbed my arm. Not with the same insulting force Mike had used on me. But enough to get the job done.

"I think Mike's right," Neil said. "I think we should grill that bastard a little bit."

I shook my head, politely removed his hand from my forearm, and proceeded to the phone.

"This isn't just your decision alone," Mike said.

He'd finally had his way. He'd succeeded in making me angry. I turned around and looked at him. "This is my house, Mike. If you don't like my decisions, then I'd suggest you leave."

We both took steps toward each other. Mike would no doubt win any battle we had, but I'd at least be able to inflict a little damage, and right now that's all I was thinking about.

Neil got between us.

"Hey," he said. "For God's sake, you two, c'mon. We're friends, remember?"

"This is my house," I said, my words childish in my ears.

"Yeah, but we live in the same neighborhood, Aaron," Mike said, "which makes this 'our' problem."

"He's right, Aaron," Bob said from the breakfast nook. There's a window there where I sometimes sit to watch all the animals on sunny days. I saw a mother raccoon and four baby raccoons one day, marching single-file across the grass. My grandparents were the last generation to live on the farm. My father came to town here and ultimately became a vice president of a ball-bearing company. Raccoons are a lot more pleasant to gaze upon than people.

"He's not right," I said to Bob. "He's wrong. We're not cops, we're not bounty hunters, we're not trackers. We're a bunch of goddamned guys who peddle stocks and bonds. Mike and Neil shouldn't have tied him up downstairs — that happens to be illegal, at least the way they went about it — and now I'm going to call the cops."

"Yes, that poor thing," Mike said. "Aren't we just picking on him, though? Tell you what, why don't we make him something to eat?"

"Just make sure we have the right wine to go with it," Neil said. "Properly chilled, of course."

"Maybe we could get him a chick," Bob said.

"With bombers out to here," Mike said, indicating with his hands where "here" was.

I couldn't help it. I smiled. They were all being ridiculous. A kind of fever had caught them.

"You really want to go down there and question him?" I said to Neil.

"Yes. We can ask him things the cops can't."

"Scare the bastard a little," Mike said. "So he'll tell us who was with him tonight, and who else works this neighborhood." He came over and put his hand out. "God, man, you're one of my best friends. I don't want you mad at me."

Then he hugged me, which is something I've never been comfortable with men doing, but to the extent I could, I hugged him back.

"Friends?" he said.

"Friends," I said. "But I still want to call the cops."

"And spoil our fun?" Neil said.

"And spoil your fun."

"I say we take it to a vote," Bob said.

"This isn't a democracy," I said. "It's my house and I'm the king. I don't want to have a vote."

"Can we ask him one question?" Bob said.

I sighed. They weren't going to let go. "One question?"

"The names of the guys he was with tonight."

"And that's it?"

"That's it. That way we get him and his pals off the street."

"And then I call the cops?"

"Then," Mike said, "you call the cops."

"One question," Neil said.

While we finished our beers, we argued a little more, but they

had a lot more spirit left than I did. I was tired now and missing Jan
and the kids and feeling lonely. These three guys had become
strangers to me tonight. Very old boys eager to play at boy games
once again.

"One question," I said. "Then I call the cops."

I led the way down, sneezing as I did so.

There's always enough dust floating around in the basement to
play hell with my sinuses.

The guy was his same sullen self, glaring at us as we descended
the stairs and then walked over to him. He smelled of heat and
sweat and city grime. The long bare arms sticking out of his filthy
T-shirt told tattoo tales of writhing snakes and leaping panthers.
The arms were joined in the back with rope. His jaw still flexed,
trying to accommodate the intrusion of the gag.

"Maybe we should castrate him," Mike said, walking up close to
the guy. "You like that, scumbag? If we castrated you?"

If the guy felt any fear, it wasn't evident in his eyes. All you could
see there was the usual contempt.

"I'll bet this is the jerk who broke into the Donaldsons' house a
couple weeks ago," Neil said.

Now he walked up to the guy. But he was more ambitious than
Mike had been. Neil spat in the guy's face.

"Hey," I said, "cool it."

Neil glared at me. "Yeah, I wouldn't hurt his feelings, would I?"

Then he suddenly turned back on the guy, raised his fist, and
started to swing. All I could do was shove him. That sent his punch
angling off to the right, missing our burglar by about half a foot.

"You asshole," Neil said, turning back on me now.

But Mike was there, between us.

"You know what we're doing? We're making this jerk happy. He's
gonna have some nice stories to tell all his criminal friends."

He was right. The burglar was one who got to look all cool and
composed. We looked like squabbling brats. As if to confirm this, a
hint of amusement played in the burglar's blue eyes.

"Oh, hell, Aaron, I'm sorry," Neil said, putting his hand out. This
was like a political convention, all the handshaking going on.

"So am I, Neil," I said. "That's why I want to call the cops and get
this over with."

And that's when he chose to make his move, the burglar. As soon as I mentioned the cops, he probably realized that this was going to be his last opportunity.

He waited until we were just finishing up with the handshake, when we were all focused on one another. Then he took off running. We could see that he'd slipped the rope. He went straight for the stairs, angling out around us like a running back seeing daylight. He even stuck his long, tattooed arm out as if he were trying to repel a tackle.

"Hey!" Bob shouted. "He's getting away."

He was at the stairs by the time we could gather ourselves enough to go after him. But when we moved, we moved fast, and in virtual unison.

By the time I got my hand on the cuff of his left jeans leg, he was close enough to the basement door to open it.

I yanked hard and ducked out of the way of his kicking foot. By now I was as crazy as Mike and Neil had been earlier. There was adrenaline, and great anger. He wasn't just a burglar, he was all burglars, intent not merely on stealing things from me but on hurting my family, too. He hadn't had time to take the gag from his mouth.

This time, I grabbed booted foot and leg and started hauling him back down the stairs. At first he was able to hold on to the door, but when I wrenched his foot rightward, he tried to scream behind the gag. He let go of the doorknob.

The next half minute is still unclear in my mind. I started running down the stairs, dragging him with me. All I wanted to do was get him on the basement floor again, turn him over to the others to watch, and then go call the cops.

But somewhere in those few seconds when I was hauling him back down the steps, I heard edge of stair meeting back of skull. The others heard it, too, because their shouts and curses died in their throats.

When I turned around, I saw the blood running fast and red from his nose. The blue eyes no longer held contempt. They were starting to roll up white in the back of his head.

"God," I said. "He's hurt."

"I think he's a lot more than hurt," Mike said.

"Help me carry him upstairs."

We got him on the kitchen floor. Mike and Neil rushed around

soaking paper towels. We tried to revive him. Bob, who kept wincing from his headache, tried the guy's wrist, ankle, and throat for a
pulse. None. His nose and mouth were bloody. Very bloody.

"No way you could die from hitting your head like that," Neil
said.

"Sure you could," Mike said. "You hit it just the right way."

"He can't be dead," Neil said. "I'm going to try his pulse again."

Bob, who obviously took Neil's second opinion personally,
frowned and rolled his eyes. "He's dead, man. He really is."

"Bullshit."

"You a doctor or something?" Bob said.

Neil smiled nervously. "No, but I play one on TV."

So Neil tried the pulse points. His reading was exactly what Bob's
reading had been.

"See," Bob said.

I guess none of us was destined to ever quite be an adult.

"Man," Neil said, looking down at the long, cold, unmoving form
of the burglar. "He's really dead."

"What the hell're we gonna do?" Mike said.

"We're going to call the police," I said, and started for the phone.

"The hell we are," Mike said. "The hell we are."

3

Maybe half an hour after we laid him on the kitchen floor, he
started to smell. We'd looked for identification and found none.
He was just the Burglar.

We sat at the kitchen table, sharing a fifth of Old Grand-Dad and
innumerable beers.

We'd taken two votes, and they'd come up ties. Two for calling the police, Bob and I; two for not calling the police, Mike and
Neil.

"All we have to tell them," I said, "is that we tied him up so he
wouldn't get away."

"And then they say," Mike said, "so why didn't you call us before
now?"

"We just lie about the time a little," I said. "Tell them we called
them within twenty minutes."

"Won't work," Neil said.

"Why not?" Bob said.

"Medical examiner can fix the time of death," Neil said.

"Not that close."

"Close enough so that the cops might question our story," Neil said. "By the time they get here, he'll have been dead at least an hour, hour and a half."

"And then we get our names in the paper for not reporting the burglary or the death right away," Mike said. "Brokerages just love publicity like that."

"I'm calling the cops right now," I said, and started up for the table.

"Think about Tomlinson a minute," Neil said.

Tomlinson was my boss at the brokerage. "What about him?"

"Remember how he canned Dennis Bryce when Bryce's ex-wife took out a restraining order on him?"

"This is different," I said.

"The hell it is," Mike said. "Neil's right, none of our bosses will like publicity like this. We'll all sound a little — crazy — you know, keeping him locked up in the basement. And then killing him when he tried to get away."

They all looked at me.

"You bastards," I said. "I was the one who wanted to call the police in the first place. And I sure as hell didn't try to kill him on purpose."

"Looking back on it," Neil said, "I guess you were right, Aaron. We should've called the cops right away."

"Now's a great time to realize that," I said.

"Maybe they've got a point," Bob said softly, glancing at me, then glancing nervously away.

"Oh, great. You, too?" I said.

"They just might kick my black ass out of there if I had any publicity that involved somebody getting killed," Bob said.

"He was a frigging burglar," I said.

"But he's dead," Neil said.

"And we killed him," Mike said.

"I appreciate you saying 'we,'" I said.

"I know a good place," Bob said.

I looked at him carefully, afraid of what he was going to say next.

"Forget it," I said.

"A good place for what?" Neil said.

"Dumping the body," Bob said.

"No way," I said.

This time, when I got up, nobody tried to stop me. I walked over to the yellow wall telephone.

I wondered if the cozy kitchen would ever feel the same to me now that a dead body had been laid upon its floor.

I had to step over him to reach the phone. The smell was even more sour now.

"You know how many bodies get dumped in the river that never wash up?" Bob said.

"No," I said, "and you don't either."

"Lots," he said.

"There's a scientific appraisal for you. 'Lots.'"

"Lots and lots, probably," Neil said, taking up Bob's argument.

Mike grinned. "Lots and lots and *lots*."

"Thank you, Professor," I said.

I lifted the receiver and dialed 0.

"Operator."

"The Police Department, please."

"Is this an emergency?" asked the young woman. Usually, I would have spent more time wondering if the sweetness of her voice was matched by the sweetness of her face and body. I'm still a face man. I suppose it's my romantic side. "Is this an emergency?" she repeated.

"No; no, it isn't."

"I'll connect you," she said.

"You think your kids'll be able to handle it?" Neil said.

"No mind games," I said.

"No mind games at all," he said. "I'm asking you a very realistic question. The police have some doubts about our story and then the press gets ahold of it, and bam. We're the lead story on all three channels. 'Did four middle-class men murder the burglar they captured?' The press even goes after the kids these days. 'Do *you* think your daddy murdered that burglar, son?'"

"Good evening. Police Department."

I started to speak, but I couldn't somehow. My voice wouldn't work. That's the only way I can explain it.

"The six o'clock news five nights running," Neil said softly behind me. "And the DA can't endorse any kind of vigilante activity, so he nails us on involuntary manslaughter."

"Hello? This is the Police Department," said the black female voice on the phone.

Neil was there then, reaching me as if by magic.

He took the receiver gently from my hand and hung it back up on the phone again.

"Let's go have another drink and see what Bob's got in mind, all right?"

He led me, as if I were a hospital patient, slowly and carefully back to the table, where Bob, over more whiskey, slowly and gently laid out his plan.

The next morning, three of us phoned in sick. Bob went to work because he had an important meeting.

Around noon — a sunny day when a softball game and a cold six-pack of beer sounded good — Neil and Mike came over. They looked as bad as I felt, and no doubt looked, myself.

We sat out on the patio eating the Hardee's lunch they'd bought. I'd need to play softball to work off some of the calories I was eating.

Birdsong and soft breezes and the smell of fresh-cut grass should have made our patio time enjoyable. But I had to wonder if we'd ever enjoy anything again. I just kept seeing the body momentarily arced above the roaring waters of the dam, and dropping into white, churning turbulence.

"You think we did the right thing?" Neil said.

"Now's a hell of a time to ask that," I said.

"Of course we did the right thing," Mike said. "What choice did we have? It was either that or get our asses arrested."

"So you don't have any regrets?" Neil said.

Mike sighed. "I didn't say that. I mean, I wish it hadn't happened in the first place."

"Maybe Aaron was right all along," Neil said.

"About what?"

"About going to the cops."

"Goddamn," Mike said, sitting up from his slouch. We all wore button-down shirts without ties and with the sleeves rolled up. Somehow there was something profane about wearing shorts and T-shirts on a workday. We even wore pretty good slacks. We were those kind of people. "Goddamn."

"Here he goes," Neil said.

"I can't believe you two," Mike said. "We should be happy that everything went so well last night — and what're we doing? Sitting around here pissing and moaning."

"That doesn't mean it's over," I said.

"Why the hell not?" Mike said.

"Because there's still one left."

"One what?"

"One burglar."

"So?"

"So you don't think he's going to get curious about what the hell happened to his partner?"

"What's he gonna do?" Mike said. "Go to the cops?"

"Maybe."

"Maybe? You're crazy. He goes to the cops, he'd be setting himself up for a robbery conviction."

"Not if he tells them we murdered his pal."

Neil said, "Aaron's got a point. What if this guy goes to the cops?"

"He's not going to the cops," Mike said. "No way he's going to the cops at all."

4

I was dozing on the couch, a Cubs game on the TV set, when the phone rang around nine that evening. I hadn't heard from Jan yet, so I expected it would be her. Whenever we're apart, we call each other at least once a day.

The phone machine picks up on the fourth ring, so I had to scramble to beat it.

"Hello?"

Nothing. But somebody was on the line. Listening.

"Hello?"

I never play games with silent callers. I just hang up. I did so now.

Two innings later, having talked to Jan, having made myself a tuna fish sandwich on rye, found a package of potato chips I thought we'd finished off at the poker game, and gotten myself a new can of beer, I sat down to watch the last inning. The Cubs had a chance of winning. I said a silent prayer to the god of baseball.

The phone rang.

I mouthed several curses around my mouthful of tuna sandwich and went to the phone.

"Hello?" I said, trying to swallow the last of the bite.

My silent friend again.

I slammed the phone.

The Cubs got two more singles. I started on the chips, and I had polished off the beer and was thinking of getting another one when the phone rang again.

I had a suspicion of who was calling and then saying nothing — but I didn't really want to think about it.

Then I decided there was an easy way to handle this situation. I'd just let the phone machine take it. If my anonymous friend wanted to talk to a phone machine, good for him.

Four rings. The phone machine took over, Jan's pleasant voice saying that we weren't home but would be happy to call you back if you'd just leave your number.

I waited to hear dead air and then a click.

Instead, a familiar female voice said, "Aaron, it's Louise. Bob —" Louise was Bob's wife. She was crying. I ran from the couch to the phone machine in the hall.

"Hello, Louise. It's Aaron."

"Oh, Aaron. It's terrible."

"What happened, Louise?"

"Bob —" More tears. "He electrocuted himself tonight out in the garage." She said that a plug had accidentally fallen into a bowl of water, according to the fire captain on the scene, and Bob hadn't noticed this and put the plug into the outlet and —

Bob had a woodcraft workshop in his garage, a large and sophisticated one. He knew what he was doing.

"He's dead, Aaron. He's dead."

"Oh, God, Louise. I'm sorry."

"He was so careful with electricity, too. It's just so hard to believe —"

Yes, I thought. Yes, it was hard to believe. I thought of last night. Of the burglars — one who'd died, one who'd gotten away.

"Why don't I come over?"

"Oh, thank you, Aaron, but I need to be alone with the children. But if you could call Neil and Mike —"

"Of course."

"Thanks for being such good friends, you and Jan."

"Don't be silly, Louise. The pleasure's ours."

"I'll talk to you tomorrow. When I'm — you know."

"Good night, Louise."

Mike and Neil were at my place within twenty minutes. We sat in the kitchen again, where we were last night.

I said, "Either of you get any weird phone calls tonight?"

"You mean just silence?" Neil said.

"Right."

"I did," Mike said. "Tracy was afraid it was that pervert who called all last winter."

"I did, too," Neil said. "Three of them."

"Then a little while ago, Bob dies out in his garage," I said. "Some coincidence."

"Hey, Aaron," Mike said. "Is that why you got us over here? Because you don't think it was an accident?"

"I'm sure it wasn't an accident," I said. "Bob knew what he was doing with his tools. He didn't notice a plug that had fallen into a bowl of water?"

"He's coming after us," Neil said.

"Oh, God," Mike said. "Not you, too."

"He calls us, gets us on edge," I said. "And then he kills Bob. Making it look like an accident."

"These are pretty bright people," Mike said sarcastically.

"You notice the burglar's eyes?" Neil said.

"I did," I said. "He looked very bright."

"And spooky," Neil said. "Never saw eyes like that before."

"I can shoot your theory right in the butt," Mike said.

"How?" I said.

He leaned forward, sipped his beer. I'd thought about putting out some munchies, but somehow that seemed wrong given poor Bob's death and the phone calls. The beers we had to have. The munchies were too festive.

"Here's how. There are two burglars, right? One gets caught, the other runs. And given the nature of burglars, keeps on running. He wouldn't even know who was in the house last night, except for Aaron, and that's only because he's the owner and his name would be in the phone book. But he wouldn't know anything about Bob or Neil or me. No way he'd have been able to track down Bob."

I shook my head. "You're overlooking the obvious."

"Like what?"

"Like he runs off last night, gets his car, and then parks in the alley to see what's going to happen."

"Right," Neil said. "Then he sees us bringing his friend out wrapped in a blanket. He follows us to the dam and watches us throw his friend in."

"And," I said, "everybody had his car here last night. Very easy for him to write down all the license numbers."

"So he kills Bob," Neil said. "And starts making the phone calls to shake us up."

"Why Bob?"

"Maybe he hates black people," I said.

Mike looked first at me and then at Neil. "You know what this is?"

"Here he goes," Neil said.

"No; no, I'm serious here. This is Catholic guilt."

"How can it be Catholic guilt when I'm Jewish?" Neil said.

"In a culture like ours, everybody is a little bit Jewish and a little bit Catholic, anyway," Mike said. "So you guys are in the throes of Catholic guilt. You feel bad about what we had to do last night — and we did have to do it, we really didn't have any choice — and the guilt starts to prey on your mind. So poor Bob electrocutes himself accidentally, and you immediately think it's the second burglar."

"He followed him," Neil said.

"What?" Mike said.

"That's what he did, I bet. The burglar. Followed Bob around all day trying to figure out what was the best way to kill him. You know, the best way that would look like an accident. So then he finds out about the workshop and decides it's perfect."

"That presumes," Mike said, "that one of us is going to be next."

"Hell, yes," Neil said. "That's why he's calling us. Shake us up. Sweat us out. Let us know that he's out there somewhere, just waiting. And that we're next."

"I'm going to follow you to work tomorrow, Neil," I said. "And Mike's going to be with me."

"You guys are having breakdowns. You really are," Mike said.

"We'll follow Neil tomorrow," I said. "And then on Saturday, you and Neil can follow me. If he's following *us* around, then we'll see it. And then we can start following him. We'll at least find out who he is."

"And then what?" Mike said. "Suppose we do find out where he lives? Then what the hell do we do?"

Neil said, "I guess we worry about that when we get there, don't we?"

In the morning, I picked Mike up early. We stopped off for doughnuts and coffee. He's like my brother, not a morning person. Crabby. Our conversation was at a minimum, though he did say, "I could've used the extra hour's sleep this morning. Instead of this crap, I mean."

As agreed, we parked half a block from Neil's house. Also as agreed, Neil emerged exactly at 7:35. Kids were already in the wide suburban streets on skateboards and rollerblades. No other car could be seen, except for a lone silver BMW in a driveway far down the block.

We followed him all the way to work. Nobody else followed him. Nobody.

When I dropped Mike off at his office, he said, "You owe me an hour's sleep."

"Two hours," I said.

"Huh?"

"Tomorrow, you and Neil follow me around."

"No way," he said.

There are times when only blunt anger will work with Mike. "It was your idea not to call the police, remember? I'm not up for any of your sulking, Mike. I'm really not."

He sighed. "I guess you're right."

I drove for two and a half hours Saturday morning. I hit a hardware store, a lumber yard, and a Kmart. At noon, I pulled into a McDonald's. The three of us had some lunch.

"You didn't see anybody even suspicious?"

"Not even suspicious, Aaron," Neil said. "I'm sorry."

"This is all bullshit. He's not going to follow us around."

"I want to give it one more chance," I said.

Mike made a face. "I'm not going to get up early, if that's what you've got in mind."

I got angry again. "Bob's dead, or have you forgotten?"

"Yeah, Aaron," Mike said. "Bob *is* dead. He got electrocuted. Accidentally."

I said, "You really think it was an accident?"

"Of course I do," Mike said. "When do you want to try it again?"

"Tonight. I'll do a little bowling."

"There's a fight on I want to watch," Mike said.

"Tape it," I said.

"'Tape it,'" he mocked. "Since when did you start giving us orders?"

"Oh, for God's sake, Mike, grow up," Neil said. "There's no way that Bob's electrocution was an accident or a coincidence. He's probably not going to stop with Bob either."

The bowling alley was mostly teenagers on Saturday night. There was a time when bowling was mostly a working-class sport. Now it's come to the suburbs and the white-collar people. Now the bowling lane is a good place for teenage boys to meet teenage girls.

I bowled two games, drank three beers, and walked back outside an hour later.

Summer night. Smell of dying heat, car exhaust, cigarette smoke, perfume. Sound of jukebox, distant loud mufflers, even more distant rushing train, lonely baying dogs.

Mike and Neil were gone.

I went home and opened myself a beer.

The phone rang. Once again, I was expecting Jan.

"Found the bastard," Neil said. "He followed you from your house to the bowling alley. Then he got tired of waiting and took off again. This time we followed *him*."

"Where?"

He gave me an address. It wasn't a good one.

"We're waiting for you to get here. Then we're going up to pay him a little visit."

"I need twenty minutes."

"Hurry."

Not even the silver touch of moonlight lent the blocks of crumbling stucco apartment houses any majesty or beauty. The rats didn't even bother to hide. They squatted red-eyed on the unmown lawns, amid beer cans, broken bottles, wrappers from Taco John's, and used condoms that looked like deflated mushrooms.

Mike stood behind a tree.

"I followed him around back," Mike said. "He went up the fire escape on the back. Then he jumped on this veranda. He's in the back apartment on the right side. Neil's in the backyard, watching for him."

Mike looked down at my ball bat. "That's a nice complement," he said. Then he showed me his handgun. "To this."

"Why the hell did you bring that?"

"Are you kidding? You're the one who said he killed Bob."

That I couldn't argue with.

"All right," I said, "but what happens when we catch him?"

"We tell him to lay off us," Mike said.

"We need to go to the cops."

"Oh, sure. Sure we do." He shook his head. He looked as if he were dealing with a child. A very slow one. "Aaron, going to the cops now won't bring Bob back. And it's only going to get us in trouble."

That's when we heard the shout. Neil; it sounded like Neil.

Maybe five feet of rust-colored grass separated the yard from the alley that ran along the west side of the apartment house.

We ran down the alley, having to hop over an ancient drooping picket fence to reach the backyard, where Neil lay sprawled, face-down, next to a twenty-year-old Chevrolet that was tireless and up on blocks. Through the windshield, you could see the huge gouges in the seats where the rats had eaten their fill.

The backyard smelled of dog shit and car oil.

Neil was moaning. At least we knew he was alive.

"The sonofabitch," he said when we got him to his feet. "I moved over to the other side, back of the car there, so he wouldn't see me if he tried to come down that fire escape. I didn't figure there was another fire escape on the side of the building. He must've come around there and snuck up on me. He tried to kill me, but I had this —"

In the moonlight, his wrist and the switchblade he held in his fingers were wet and dark with blood. "I got him a couple of times in the arm. Otherwise, I'd be dead."

"We're going up there," Mike said.

"How about checking Neil first?" I said.

"I'm fine," Neil said. "A little headache from where he caught me on the back of the neck." He waved his bloody blade. "Good thing I had this."

The landlord was on the first floor. He wore Bermuda shorts and no shirt. He looked eleven or twelve months pregnant, with little male titties and enough coarse black hair to knit a sweater with. He had a plastic-tipped cigarillo in the left corner of his mouth.

"Yeah?"

"Two-F," I said.

"What about it?"

"Who lives there?"

"Nobody."

"Nobody?"

"If you were the law, you'd show me a badge."

"I'll show you a badge," Mike said, making a fist.

"Hey," I said, playing good cop to bad cop. "You just let me speak to this gentleman."

The guy seemed to like my reference to him as a gentleman. It was probably the only name he'd never been called.

"Sir, we saw somebody go up there."

"Oh," he said. "The vampires."

"Vampires?"

He sucked down some cigarillo smoke. "That's what we call 'em, the missus and me. They're street people, winos and homeless and all like that. They know that sometimes some of these apartments ain't rented for a while, so they sneak up there and spend the night."

"You don't stop them?"

"You think I'm gonna get my head split open for something like that?"

"I guess that makes sense." Then: "So nobody's renting it now?"

"Nope, it ain't been rented for three months. This fat broad lived there then. Man, did she smell. You know how fat people can smell sometimes? *She* sure smelled." He wasn't svelte.

Back on the front lawn, trying to wend my way between the mounds of dog shit, I said, "'Vampires.' Good name for them."

"Yeah, it is," Neil said. "I just keep thinking of the one who died. His weird eyes."

"Here we go again," Mike said. "You two guys love to scare the shit out of each other, don't you? They're a couple of nickel-dime crooks, and that's *all* they are."

"All right if Mike and I stop and get some beer and then swing by your place?"

"Sure," I said. "Just as long as Mike buys Bud and none of that generic crap."

"Oh, I forgot." Neil laughed. "He does do that when it's his turn to buy, doesn't he?"

"Yeah," I said, "he certainly does."

I was never sure what time the call came. Darkness. The ringing phone seemed part of a dream from which I couldn't escape. Somehow I managed to lift the receiver before the phone machine kicked in.

Silence. That special *kind* of silence.

Him. I had no doubt about it. The vampire, as the landlord had called him. The one who'd killed Bob. I didn't say so much as hello. Just listened, angry, afraid, confused.

After a few minutes, he hung up.

Darkness again; deep darkness, the quarter moon in the sky a cold golden scimitar that could cleave a head from a neck.

5

About noon on Sunday, Jan called to tell me that she was staying a few days extra. The kids had discovered archery, and there was a course at the Y they were taking and wouldn't she please please *please* ask good old Dad if they could stay. I said sure.

I called Neil and Mike to remind them that at nine tonight we were going to pay a visit to that crumbling stucco apartment house again.

I spent an hour on the lawn. My neighbors shame me into it. Lawns aren't anything I get excited about. But they sort of shame you into it. About halfway through, Byrnes, the chunky advertising man who lives next door, came over and clapped me on the back. He was apparently pleased that I was a real human being and taking a real human being interest in my lawn. As usual, he wore an expensive T-shirt with one of his clients' products on it and a pair of Bermuda shorts. As usual, he tried hard to be the kind of winsome neighbor you always had in sitcoms of the fifties. But I knew somebody who knew him. Byrnes had fired his number two man so he wouldn't have to keep paying the man's insurance. The man was unfortunately dying of cancer. Byrnes was typical of all the ad people I'd met. Pretty treacherous people who spent most of their time cheating clients out of their money and putting on awards banquets so they could convince themselves that advertising was actually an endeavor that was of consequence.

Around four, *Hombre* was on one of the cable channels, so I had a few beers and watched Paul Newman doing the best acting of his career. At least that was my opinion.

I was just getting ready for the shower when the phone rang.

He didn't say hello. He didn't identify himself. "Tracy call you?"

It was Neil. Tracy was Mike's wife. "Why should she call me?"

"He's dead. Mike."

"What?"

"You remember how he was always bitching about that elevator at work?"

Mike worked in a very old building. He made jokes about the antiquated elevators. But you could always tell the joke simply hid his fears. He'd gotten stuck innumerable times, and it was always stopping several feet short of the upcoming floor.

"He opened the door and the car wasn't there. He fell eight floors."

"Oh, God."

"I don't have to tell you who did it, do I?"

"Maybe it's time —"

"I'm way ahead of you, Aaron. I'll pick you up in half an hour. Then we go to the police. You agree?"

"I agree."

Late Sunday afternoon, the second precinct parking lot is pretty empty. We'd missed the shift change. Nobody came or went.

"We ask for a detective," Neil said. He was dark-sportcoat, white-shirt, necktie earnest. I'd settled for an expensive blue sportshirt Jan had bought me for my last birthday.

"You know one thing we haven't considered?"

"You're not going to change my mind."

"I'm not *trying* to change your mind, Neil, I'm just saying that there's one thing we haven't considered."

He sat behind his steering wheel, his head resting on the back of his seat.

"A lawyer."

"What for?"

"Because we may go in there and say something that gets us in very deep shit."

"No lawyers," he said. "We'd just look like we were trying to hide something from the cops."

"You sure about that?"

"I'm sure."

"You ready?" I said.

"Ready."

The interior of the police station was quiet. A muscular bald man in a dark uniform sat behind a desk with a sign that read "Information."

He said, "Help you?"

"We'd like to see a detective," I said.

"Are you reporting a crime?"

"Uh, yes," I said.

"What sort of crime?" he said.

I started to speak but once again lost my voice. I thought about all the reporters, about how Jan and the kids would be affected by it all. How my job would be affected. Taking a guy down to the basement and tying him up and then accidentally killing him —

Neil said: "Vandalism."

"Vandalism?" the cop said. "You don't need a detective, then. I can just give you a form." Then he gave us a leery look, as if he sensed we'd just changed our minds about something.

"In that case, could I just take it home with me and fill it out there?" Neil said.

"Yeah, I guess." The cop still watched us carefully now.

"Great."

"You sure that's what you wanted to report? Vandalism?"

"Yeah; yeah, that's exactly what we wanted to report," Neil said. "Exactly."

"Vandalism?" I said when we were back in the car.

"I don't want to talk right now."

"Well, maybe *I* want to talk."

"I just couldn't do it."

"No kidding."

He looked over at me. "You could've told him the truth. Nobody was stopping you."

I looked out the window. "Yeah, I guess I could've."

"We're going over there tonight. To the vampire's place."

"And do what?"

"Ask him how much he wants."

"How much he wants for what?" I said.

"How much he wants to forget everything. He goes on with his life, we go on with ours."

I had to admit, I'd had a similar thought myself. Neil and I didn't know how to do any of this. But the vampire did. He was good at stalking, good at harassing, good at violence.

"We don't have a lot of money to throw around."

"Maybe he won't *want* a lot of money. I mean, these guys aren't exactly sophisticated."

"They're sophisticated enough to make two murders look like accidents."

"I guess that's a point."

"I'm just not sure we should pay him anything, Neil."

"You got any better ideas?"

I didn't, actually. I didn't have any better ideas at all.

6

I spent an hour on the phone with Jan that afternoon. The last few days I'd been pretty anxious, and she'd sensed it, and now she was making sure that everything was all right with me. In addition to being wife and lover, Jan's also my best friend. I can't kid her. She always knows when something's wrong. I'd put off telling her about Bob and Mike dying. I'd been afraid that I might accidentally say more than I should and make her suspicious. But now I had to tell her about their deaths. It was the only way I could explain my tense mood.

"That's awful," she said. "Their poor families."

"They're handling it better than you might think."

"Maybe I should bring the kids home early."

"No reason to, hon. I mean, realistically there isn't anything any of us can do."

"Two accidents in that short a time. It's pretty strange."

"Yeah, I guess it is. But that's how it happens sometimes."

"Are you going to be all right?"

"Just need to adjust is all," I sighed. "I guess we won't be having our poker games anymore."

Then I did something I hadn't intended. I started crying, and the tears caught in my throat.

"Oh, honey," Jan said. "I wish I was there so I could give you a big hug."

"I'll be okay."

"Two of your best friends."

"Yeah." The tears were starting to dry up now.

"Oh, did I tell you about Tommy?" Tommy was our six-year-old.

"No, what?"

"Remember how he used to be so afraid of horses?"

"Uh-huh."

"Well, we took him out to this horse ranch where you can rent horses?"

"Uh-huh."

"And they found him a little Shetland pony and let him ride it, and he loved it. He wasn't afraid at all." She laughed. "In fact, we could barely drag him home." She paused. "You're probably not in the mood for this, are you? I'm sorry, hon. Maybe you should do something to take your mind off things. Is there a good movie on?"

"I guess I could check."

"Something light, that's what you need."

"Sounds good," I said. "I'll go get the newspaper and see what's on."

"Love you."

"Love you, too, sweetheart," I said.

I spent the rest of the afternoon going through my various savings accounts and investments. I had no idea what the creep would want to leave us alone. We could always threaten him with going to the police, though he might rightly point out that if we really wanted to do that, we would already have done it.

I settled in the five-thousand-dollar range. That was the maximum cash I had to play with. And even then I'd have to borrow a little from one of the mutual funds we had earmarked for the kids and college.

Five thousand dollars. To me, it sounded like an enormous amount of money, probably because I knew how hard I'd had to work to get it.

But would it be enough for our friend the vampire?

*

Neil was there just at dark. He parked in the drive and came in. Meaning he wanted to talk.

We went in the kitchen. I made us a couple of highballs, and we sat there and discussed finances.

"I came up with six thousand," he said.

"I've got five."

"That's eleven grand," he said. "It's got to be more cash than this creep has ever seen."

"What if he takes it and comes back for more?"

"We make it absolutely clear," Neil said, "that there is no more. That this is it. Period."

"And if not?"

Neil nodded. "I've thought this through. You know the kind of lowlife we're dealing with? A, he's a burglar, which means, these days, that he's a junkie. B, if he's a junkie, then that means he's very susceptible to AIDS. So between being a burglar and shooting up, this guy is probably going to have a very short lifespan."

"I guess I'd agree."

"Even if he wants to make our life miserable, he probably won't live long enough to do it. So I think we'll be making just the one payment. We'll buy enough time to let nature take its course — his nature."

"What if he wants more than the eleven grand?"

"He won't. His eyes'll pop out when he sees this."

I looked at the kitchen clock. It was going on nine now.

"I guess we could drive over there."

"It may be a long night," Neil said.

"I know."

"But I guess we don't have a hell of a lot of choice, do we?"

As we'd done the last time we'd been here, we split up the duties. I took the backyard, Neil the apartment door. We'd waited until midnight. The rap music had died by now. Babies cried and mothers screamed; couples fought. TV screens flickered in dark windows.

I went up the fire escape slowly and carefully. We'd talked about bringing guns, then decided against it. We weren't exactly marksmen, and if a cop stopped us for some reason, we could be arrested for carrying unlicensed firearms. All I carried was a flashlight in my back pocket.

As I grabbed the rungs of the ladder, powdery rust dusted my hands. I was chilly with sweat. My bowels felt sick. I was scared. I just wanted it to be over with. I wanted him to say yes, he'd take the money, and then that would be the end of it.

The stucco veranda was filled with discarded toys — a tricycle, innumerable games, a space helmet, a wiffle bat and ball. The floor was crunchy with dried animal feces. At least, I hoped the feces belonged to animals and not human children.

The door between veranda and apartment was open. Fingers of moonlight revealed an overstuffed couch and chair and a floor covered with the debris of fast food, McDonald's sacks, Pizza Hut wrappers and cardboards, Arby's wrappers, and what seemed to be five or six dozen empty beer cans. Far toward the hall that led to the front door, I saw four red eyes watching me, a pair of curious rats.

I stood still and listened. Nothing. No sign of life. I went inside. Tiptoeing.

I went to the front door and let Neil in. There in the murky light of the hallway, he made a face. The smell *was* pretty bad.

Over the next ten minutes, we searched the apartment. And found nobody.

"We could wait here for him," I said.

"No way."

"The smell?"

"The smell, the rats. God. Don't you just feel unclean?"

"Yeah, guess I do."

"There's an empty garage about halfway down the alley. We'd have a good view of the back of this building."

"Sounds pretty good."

"Sounds better than this place, anyway."

This time, we both went out the front door and down the stairway. Now the smells were getting to me as they'd earlier gotten to Neil. Unclean. He was right.

We got in Neil's Buick, drove down the alley that ran along the west side of the apartment house, backed up to the dark garage, and whipped inside.

"There's a sack in back," Neil said. "It's on your side."

"A sack?"

"Brewskis. Quart for you, quart for me."

"That's how my old man used to drink them," I said. I was the only blue-collar member of the poker club. "Get off work at the plant and stop by and pick up two quart bottles of Hamms. Never missed."

"Sometimes I wish I would've been born into the working class," Neil said.

I was the blue-collar guy, and Neil was the dreamer, always inventing alternative realities for himself.

"No, you don't," I said, leaning over the seat and picking up the sack damp from the quart bottles. "You had a damned nice life in Boston."

"Yeah, but I didn't learn anything. You know I was eighteen before I learned about cunnilingus?"

"Talk about cultural deprivation," I said.

"Well, every girl I went out with probably looks back on me as a pretty lame lover. They went down on me, but I never went down on them. How old were you when you learned about cunnilingus?"

"Maybe thirteen."

"See?"

"I learned about it, but I didn't do anything about it."

"I was twenty years old before I lost my cherry," Neil said.

"I was seventeen."

"Bullshit."

"Bullshit what? I was seventeen."

"In sociology, they always taught us that blue-collar kids lost their virginity a lot earlier than white-collar kids."

"That's the trouble with sociology. It tries to particularize from generalities."

"Huh?" He grinned. "Yeah, I always thought sociology was full of shit, too, actually. But you were really seventeen?"

"I was really seventeen."

I wish I could tell you that I knew what it was right away, the missile that hit the windshield and shattered and starred it, and then kept right on tearing through the car until the back window was also shattered and starred.

But all I knew was that Neil was screaming and I was screaming and my quart bottle of Miller's was spilling all over my crotch as I tried to hunch down behind the dashboard. It was a tight fit because Neil was trying to hunch down behind the steering wheel.

The second time, I knew what was going on: somebody was shooting at us. Given the trajectory of the bullet, he had to be right in front of us, probably behind the two Dumpsters that sat on the other side of the alley.

"Can you keep down and drive this sonofabitch at the same time?"

"I can try," Neil said.

"If we sit here much longer, he's going to figure out we don't have guns. Then he's gonna come for us for sure."

Neil leaned over and turned on the ignition. "I'm going to turn left when we get out of here."

"Fine. Just get moving."

"Hold on."

What he did was kind of slump over the bottom half of the wheel, just enough so he could sneak a peek at where the car was headed.

There were no more shots.

All I could hear was the smooth-running Buick motor.

He eased out of the garage, ducking down all the time.

When he got a chance, he bore left.

He kept the lights off.

Through the bullet hole in the windshield, I could see an inch or so of starry sky.

It was a long alley, and we must have gone a quarter block before he said, "I'm going to sit up. I think we lost him."

"So do I."

"Look at the frigging windshield."

Not only was the windshield a mess, the car reeked of spilled beer.

"You think I should turn on the headlights?"

"Sure," I said. "We're safe now."

We were still crawling at maybe ten miles per hour when he pulled the headlights on.

That's when we saw him, silver of eye, dark of hair, crouching in the middle of the alley waiting for us. He was a good fifty yards ahead of us, but we were still within range.

There was no place we could turn around.

He fired.

This bullet shattered whatever had been left untouched of the windshield. Neil slammed on the brakes.

Then he fired a second time.

By now, both Neil and I were screaming and cursing again.

A third bullet.

"Run him over!" I yelled, ducking behind the dashboard.

"What?" Neil yelled back.

"Floor it!"

He floored it. He wasn't even sitting up straight. We might have gone careening into one of the garages or Dumpsters. But somehow the Buick stayed in the alley. And very soon it was traveling eighty-five miles per hour. I watched the speedometer peg it.

More shots, a lot of them now, side windows shattering, bullets ripping into fender and hood and top.

I didn't see us hit him, but I *felt* us hit him, the car traveling that fast, the creep so intent on killing us he hadn't bothered to get out of the way in time.

The front of the car picked him up and hurled him into a garage near the head of the alley.

We both sat up, watched as his entire body was broken against the edge of the garage, and he then fell smashed and unmoving to the grass.

"Kill the lights," I said.

"What?"

"Kill the lights, and let's go look at him."

Neil punched off the headlights.

We left the car and ran over to him.

A white rib stuck bloody and brazen from his side. Blood poured from his ears, nose, mouth. One leg had been crushed and also showed white bone. His arms had been broken, too.

I played my flashlight beam over him.

He was dead, all right.

"Looks like we can save our money," I said. "It's all over now."

"I want to get the hell out of here."

"Yeah," I said. "So do I."

We got the hell out of there.

7

A month later, just as you could smell autumn on the summer winds, Jan and I celebrated our twelfth wedding anniversary. We drove up to Lake Geneva, in Wisconsin, and stayed at a very nice hotel and rented a Chris-Craft for a couple of days. This was the first time I'd been able to relax since the thing with the burglar had started.

One night when Jan was asleep, I went up on the deck of the boat and just watched the stars. I used to read a lot of Edgar Rice Burroughs when I was a boy. I always remembered how John Carter felt — that the stars had a very special destiny for him and would someday summon him to that destiny. My destiny, I decided that night there on the deck, was to be a good family man, a good stockbroker, and a good neighbor. The bad things were all behind me now. I imagined Neil was feeling pretty much the same way. Hot bitter July seemed a long way behind us now. Fall was coming, bringing with it football and Thanksgiving and Christmas. July would recede even more with snow on the ground.

The funny thing was, I didn't see Neil much anymore. It was as if the sight of each other brought back a lot of bad memories. It was a mutual feeling, too. I didn't want to see him any more than he wanted to see me. Our wives thought this was pretty strange. They'd meet at the supermarket or shopping center and wonder why "the boys" didn't get together anymore. Neil's wife, Sarah, kept inviting us over to "sit around the pool and watch Neil pretend he knows how to swim." September was summer hot. The pool was still the centerpiece of their life.

Not that I made any new friends. The notion of a midweek poker game had lost all its appeal. There was work and my family and little else.

Then, one sunny Indian summer afternoon, Neil called and said, "Maybe we should get together again."

"Maybe."

"It's over, Aaron. It really is."

"I know."

"Will you at least think about it?"

I felt embarrassed. "Oh, hell, Neil. Is that swimming pool of yours open Saturday afternoon?"

"As a matter of fact, it is. And as a matter of fact, Sarah and the girls are going to be gone to a fashion show at the club."

"Perfect. We'll have a couple of beers."

"You know how to swim?"

"No," I said, laughing. "And from what Sarah says, you don't either."

I got there about three, pulled into the drive, walked to the back where the gate in the wooden fence led to the swimming pool.

It was eighty degrees, and even from here I could smell the chlorine.

I opened the gate and went inside and saw him right away. The funny thing was, I didn't have much of a reaction at all. I just watched him. He was floating. Facedown. He looked pale in his red trunks. This, like the others, would be judged an accidental death. Of that I had no doubt at all.

I used the cellular phone in my car to call 911.

I didn't want Sarah and the girls coming back to see an ambulance and police cars in the drive and them not knowing what was going on.

I called the club and had her paged.

I told her what I'd found. I let her cry. I didn't know what to say. I never do.

In the distance, I could hear the ambulance working its way toward the Neil Solomon residence.

I was just about to get out of the car when my cellular phone rang. I picked up. "Hello?"

"There were three of us that night at your house, Mr. Bellini. You killed two of us. I recovered from when your friend stabbed me, remember? Now I'm ready for action. I really am, Mr. Bellini."

Then the emergency people were there, and neighbors, too, and then wan, trembling Sarah. I just let her cry some more. Gave her whiskey and let her cry.

8

He knows how to do it, whoever he is.

He lets a long time go between late-night calls. He lets me start to think that maybe he changed his mind and left town. And then he calls.

Oh, yes, he knows just how to play this little game.

He never says anything. He doesn't need to. He just listens. And then hangs up.

I've considered going to the police, of course, but it's way too late for that. Way too late.

Or I could ask Jan and the kids to move away to a different city with me. But he knows who I am, and he'd find me again.

So all I can do is wait and hope that I get lucky, the way Neil and I got lucky the night we killed the second of them.

*

Tonight I can't sleep.

It's after midnight.

Jan and I wrapped presents until well after eleven. She asked me again if anything was wrong. We don't make love as much as we used to, she said; and then there are the nightmares. "Please tell me if something's wrong, Aaron. Please."

I stand at the window watching the snow come down. Soft and beautiful snow. In the morning, a Saturday, the kids will make a snowman and then go sledding and then have themselves a good old-fashioned snowball fight, which invariably means that one of them will come rushing in at some point and accuse the other of some terrible misdeed.

I see all this from the attic window.

Then I turn back and look around the poker table. Four empty chairs. Three of them belong to dead men.

I look at the empty chairs and think back to summer.

I look at the empty chairs and wait for the phone to ring.

I wait for the phone to ring.

JOSEPH HANSEN

Survival

FROM *Alfred Hitchcock Mystery Magazine*

IT WAS a long drive north, half of California, all of Oregon, most of Washington, and then inland to George Stubbs's sister's house in Norton's Mill, Idaho, thirty miles from the Canadian border. And all the way, Stubbs's trophy cups had rattled in their carton behind the seat. Bohannon had wrapped and cushioned them in newspaper, but somehow they'd managed to rattle anyway.

He hadn't known what to do with them exactly. They had stood on the mantel of the boulder-built fireplace in his ranch house for eighteen or twenty years Stubbs had worked for him, lived side by side with him, been an interwoven part of his days. Those rodeo trophies for roping and bulldogging, for bronco busting and bull riding, had belonged on that mantel.

And it sure as hell had looked strange and naked once he'd taken them down and packed them for the trip, along with Stubbs's body in its coffin, to where the old man had said he wanted to be buried. In the same graveyard as his mother (God knew where his father's body lay), his brothers (who'd still been boys when they died), and his sister when her time came.

Norton's Mill had proved no different from what Bohannon had pictured, a sleepy little town among towering white pines. More Midwestern than Western, its houses were mainly woodframe, and two storied, and getting on for a hundred years old. The house where Ada Tanner lived was one of these, white, four-square, with a wide, comfortable front porch but no fancy architectural furbelows. A wire mesh fence enclosed the yard and fruit trees in the yard and flowerbeds.

Ada Tanner looked like her brother, talked like him, was straightforward and homey. Bohannon hadn't known of her existence till Stubbs gave in to the idea that he was going to die. Then he told Bohannon about her and the man she had married. Stubbs and Luke Tanner could not agree on whether it was raining. That was why he'd stayed away from his boyhood town even at the height of his rodeo fame and money. When Luke died, he'd thought about a trip to see Ada, but there was always so much to do at Bohannon's stables he'd put it off. And then he had become too arthritic, "stove up" as he put it, to travel.

So he did his traveling this October week in a pine box in the steel bed of Bohannon's green pickup truck. His trip home. Bohannon stayed for the funeral, of course, and the burial in the cemetery with its tilted headstones and lawns going brown for the winter. Nobody much came. Stubbs's glory days had gained him renown in Norton's Mill, but those glory days were the 1930s and 1940s, and the graveyard had claimed most of the people who'd remembered George Stubbs as a boy, before he'd left for more exciting places.

Women outlive men, so it was mostly whitehaired neighbor ladies who came for lunch to Ada Tanner's house following the ceremonies. There was one man, a skinny old geezer, who cornered Bohannon and talked about lunatics living in the woods up here, survivalists, anti-taxers, anti-blacks (there weren't but one or two blacks in the whole county), trying to live on forage, starving their children, sometimes freezing in the winters.

At last an old woman led him away. When they'd all gone, Bohannon told Ada Tanner good-bye, and she handed him a Bible, with red page-edges and floppy covers, plastic meant to look like leather. Stocky, ruddy-cheeked, hair freshly set for the funeral, she smelled of lavender soap and starch.

"I want you to have this," she said. "I wish it was a fine one, but I live on Social Security, and it's what's inside that counts. It's been my guide and mainstay all my life, so it's the gift I want to give you for being so good to George all those long years when he was past being able to do the strong, wild, crazy things he was so proud of."

"He didn't owe me," Bohannon said. "I owed him. I'd never have been able to make it without him. I'm going to miss him."

"I guess you don't call yourself one," she said, "but you're a Christian. Never mind" — she patted his hands as they held the Bible — "you have that, and keep it near you. It won't replace an old friend. But there's comfort in it."

"Thank you." Bohannon put on his sweat-stained Stetson and stepped out the screen door, an old one with a long black spring to pull it closed. The spring twanged. The door swung loosely shut. He crossed the porch. "Take care of yourself, Miz Tanner."

"Don't grieve," she said through the screen. "He's in a happy place now."

"If they have rodeos there," Bohannon said, and crossed over to the driveway, where the green pickup waited.

Nothing was wrong with the motel room that wasn't wrong with all motel rooms, but he slept badly and was up and showered and dressed by four-thirty and on his way home. In the dark. He had good sense, and most of the time he used it. But Stubbs's death had shaken him. And he began fretting and making bad decisions. Leaving Deputy T. Hodges in charge of the stables was asking too much of her. He'd rung her up every day of this trip, and she'd always sounded cheerful and on top of things and teased him for worrying. There was a hired hand. She wasn't alone, and she was young and strong, but she wasn't very big, and accidents could happen. Horses were unpredictable. No harm must come to T. Hodges. Not now. He couldn't take it.

So instead of returning to the coast and following the route that had brought him here, he took a state highway heading straight south, telling himself it would save time. Maybe it would have, but he wasn't going to find out. The highway wasn't much, and it soon entered a stand of giant Douglas firs that promised no end to itself. It was quiet, dim, and cold on that road. A little bit eerie. Soundless. He would have welcomed the rattling of those rodeo trophies now. He tried the radio, but reception was fitful and anyway he'd never much liked country and even less did he like gospel and that was all the music there was. The trip grew stranger by the hour. Where was everybody? Not another car, not another truck. The world could have ended for all he knew.

Then he had to stop. That famous tree we've all heard about — the one that falls in a forest where there's no one to hear, and therefore can it be said for sure that it made a sound when it fell? — that tree had fallen across the road. A tremendous tree. As thick through as his truck. He couldn't drive around it. The ditches beside the road were too deep. He got stiffly out of the truck, stretched, lit a cigarette, studied the tree, finished the cigarette, dropped it, put it out carefully under his worn boot, climbed back in the truck, and after some backing and filling, pointed it north again. He'd seen a turnoff a few miles back. It had had no sign- board, but it would take hours to get back to Norton's Mill and start the trip over. He'd try the side road, see where it led.

It was narrow, went crookedly through the trees, which grew denser here and were even older and thicker and taller than any he'd so far seen. Maybe the road had been graveled once. His tires threw up gravel now and then that rattled under the fenders. But before mankind had taken it over, he figured animals had laid it out and used it from the ancient start, deer, bear, puma. And when they came along, the Indians had seen no call to improve on it, and the Europeans when they got here hadn't wasted much energy on it. Why they'd wasted even one load of gravel Bohannon couldn't see. He saw no signs of human settlement.

Then he came around a bend and sawhorses stood across the road and beyond them a parked van. He braked the green pickup and stared. The sawhorses were old, unpainted. Unlike his truck, with its horsehead logo on the door, the van had no markings. Oh, a sign had one time been lettered on its side but then painted over. Maybe it had been white once, but it was gray now, mud-stained below, rain-spotted and dusty above, and crusty on its roof with bird droppings and brown pine needles. Its sliding door opened, and two young men jumped out of it wearing army camouflage fatigues and floppy camouflage hats. Each had a gun. One was a .357 Magnum. The other was an AK-47.

Bohannon had not brought his Winchester. In California he was licensed to keep it on its rack over the back window of the truck. But for getting without hassle from state to state he figured he'd better leave it at home. He jammed the truck into reverse and began backing as fast as he could. But not fast enough. The man with the AK-47 fired shots. Not at him. Not at the truck. Over the truck roof. Warning shots.

Bohannon braked, one rear wheel in the ditch. They came jog- ging up the road. He put up his hands. "Just a mistake," he said. "I got lost."

"You shoulda picked someplace else." Both boys had beard stub- ble and blue eyes and hair too long for their hats to conceal. "Get out of there."

"He don't look like no FBI," the boy with the handgun said.

"He looks like a goddamn Indian," the other one said. "Get out."

Bohannon got out. "My folks were Irish, if that's any help."

"You say," the AK-47 boy said. "Turn around. Hands on the hood there. Spread your legs."

"Who are you? What gives you the right to —"

"You're in Ninth Amendment America now." The boy held on to the gun but patted Bohannon down with his free hand. "We don't go by Jew York D.C. laws here. We got Christian laws, God's laws. Question isn't who we are." He straightened up and looked through the wallet he had taken from Bohannon's hip pocket. "It's who you are and what you're doing here. Oh my!" He turned to his partner. "Lookee here, Hadley. This man is a private investigator."

He grabbed Bohannon's arm and swung him around. "Who sent you? Who you working for? FBI? Alcohol, Tobacco, and Firearms? Who tipped you off to find us here? Nobody knows. Nobody."

"Including me," said Bohannon. "I just stumbled in here. The state road is blocked. A fallen tree. I was looking for a way to keep going south without —"

"You're lying." The boy slapped him.

"Don't be nervous," Bohannon said, "I'm not going to hurt you."

The boy slapped him again, and Bohannon punched him in the face, and he fell on his butt on the road and the gun went off. A chatter of fire into the air. He scrambled up. "Hell, it don't really matter who you are or why you come." He wiped his bloody mouth with a hand, looked at the hand, glared at Bohannon. "I'm going to shoot you dead one way or the other. 'Cause I can't let you go back and tell where we are." He jerked the gun barrel. "Go on. Walk into the trees. I'll be right behind you."

Bohannon didn't move. He heard footsteps. Someone was coming through the trees opposite. The boy took hold of him again, yanked him, shoved him toward the ditch, and a man appeared on the other side of the road. A middle-aged man, camouflage pants and jacket, also with long hair with a camouflage cap on it. Only his hair was gray. He wore Desert Storm dark glasses and a big old .45 revolver in a holster.

"Ford?" he said. "Hadley? What's all the ruckus? Anybody could have heard that gunfire. The whole damned U.S. Army could be down on us."

"Niggers," Ford jeered. "Mud people. Who cares?"

The middle-aged man walked up to Bohannon. "Who are you?"

"Bohannon is my name." Close up he recognized the man. His picture was in the files at the sheriff's substation in Madrone. Bohannon checked those files out now and then. Cunningham? Yes, Chester Cunningham. U.S. Marine Corps, retired. Something about stockpiling firearms, altering firearms, transporting firearms across state borders. "What's yours?"

Cunningham ignored that. "What are you doing here?"

"He's an investigator licensed by the State of California," Ford said. "You think he's going to tell us what he's doing here?"

"I think you should remember who you're talking to," Cunningham said, "and correct your tone." And to Bohannon, "Where did you learn I was here?"

Bohannon told his story again.

"I guess not," the man said.

"Captain?" The Hadley boy had been rummaging in the truck. "He might not be lying."

Cunningham and Ford looked at him. Bohannon looked, too. Hadley came bringing Ada Tanner's Bible. He said, "This man's a Christian."

"That right?" Cunningham held out a hand for the book, and the boy gave it to him. He looked at it thoughtfully for a minute, lifting it a little, weighing it in his hand. He blinked at Bohannon. "That a fact?"

Bohannon didn't answer.

Cunningham opened the truck door, laid the Bible on the seat, and turned on the radio. Staticky music played. A lush orchestra backed a sincere-sounding baritone who crooned, "'I am satisfied with Je-sus, He has meant so much to me-e-e . . .'" The music ceased. Cunningham slammed the door of the truck and said to Bohannon, "Come with me," motioned with the revolver for Bohannon to go ahead of him across the road and into the trees. Bohannon went.

"Don't mean nothing," Ford called. "About all you can get on the radio up here."

Cunningham stopped. "What do you want, Ford — rock and roll? Rap? Hip-hop?"

"No, sir," Ford said quickly, turning red. "'Course not."

Cunningham grunted. "Bring that truck to the compound." Then he nodded Bohannon into the trees. The walk was a long one. Then there was a small settlement of rough shacks set at odd angles to one another, a large open space between. At a guess the planks and two-by-fours had been sawn here out of trees felled illegally. With gas-powered saws: there were no power lines. He glimpsed crude outhouses set back in the brush. That meant no running water, didn't it? What then: a well, or maybe a spring or stream near enough to walk to with buckets? The old geezer at Ada Tanner's had been right: life here was primitive. Vehicles stood around, a sad assortment of rusty pickup trucks, vans, RVs, a once-racy red sportscar layered with dead pine needles, its cloth top hanging in tatters.

Two buildings rose up bigger than the rest, one living quarters, the other for storage, a warehouse. Or was it a barn? The pine smell that dropped from the huge trees was strong in the growing warmth of the day, but still he detected a whiff of horse. Cunningham pushed open the plank door into the house and motioned Bohannon through, went in after him, and closed the door.

Inside, in a wash of greenish daylight through dirty window-panes, sagged sorry old furniture, not much of it, a sofa, a greasy overstuffed armchair, side chairs with threadbare seats. On the mantel a row of smoky kerosene lanterns. Over them a big American flag. A case to hold rifles, the pane of one glass door cracked. A round dining table from fifty years ago or more. Some rickety unmatched chairs. A battered library table on one wall was heaped with papers, magazines, typewritten stuff. Tacked to the wall above it was a map of the eleven western states with colored push-pins stuck in it. A marked-up street map of some town was held by one of them.

At the far end of the room a kitchen housed a cast-iron cook-stove, shelves holding mismatched china, battered pots and pans hanging up, sooty skillets. Stacked on the floor were supplies, sacks of flour and rice, restaurant-size cans of baked beans, vegetable soup, sliced peaches, applesauce. Boxes of crackers and cold cereals, dehydrated milk and mashed potatoes. Great big cans of coffee. COFFEE. No brand name. Stairs fashioned of half logs climbed to a loft that bracketed the room below. He glimpsed tousled bedding.

"Sit down," Cunningham said. "Care for some coffee?"

"I'd like to buy it at a diner in the next town," Bohannon said.

"We can't always have what we'd like," Cunningham said with a thin smile. "Sit down." He raised his voice. "Selina?" The kitchen door opened. A thin woman in her mid-thirties came in, shut the door, set down a bucket of coal. Blond hair combed out long and straight. No makeup, but good features, good bones. She wore glasses, jeans, an unbuttoned lumberjack shirt, under it a black T-shirt with 9TH AMENDMENT stenciled on it, old workboots. But something about her said breeding, education. "Coffee," Cunningham told her, and sat down himself. In the overstuffed chair.

"Who's that?" she said, staring.

"Name's Bohannon."

"Do we know him?" She tilted her head. Then she gave it a shake. "No. We don't know him. So what's he doing here?"

Bohannon took off his hat and nodded to her. "I strayed in by accident."

"Bad luck," she said as if she sympathized. "And bad timing."

"Will you just get the coffee?" Cunningham said.

Her expression of alertness changed to one of wooden obedience. "Yes, sir," she said and turned to the stove.

"Do you know who I am?" Cunningham asked Bohannon.

"Is that captain a real rank or honorary?"

"Real. Vietnam. Actually" — the thin smile came back — "I'm the general, field marshal, chief of staff."

"President," the woman said and set down the coffee mugs, one beside the captain's chair, one beside Bohannon's. "Of Ninth Amendment America."

"You know what that means?" Cunningham asked.

"I get the feeling you're going to tell me," Bohannon said.

"'The enumeration in the Constitution of certain rights shall not be construed to deny or disparage others retained by the people.'"

"What others?"

"Those are the words the Founding Fathers wrote. That is the whole sum and substance of the Ninth Amendment. Every word of it." He gave a patronizing smile. "Good question, though. Gets to the heart of it. Most of the laws the overlords have passed since it was written deny and disparage the rights of the people. Taxes, licenses, building regulations, zoning regulations, speed limits, fishing rights, grazing rights, hunting rights, compulsory insurance, can't do this, can't do that, can't do the other thing. . . . Those elected so-called representatives in D.C. say what Ninth Amendment? What unnamed rights? We're the ones who make the laws. Can't run a country without laws. Can't run a country without taxes. You paid yours?"

"I see." Bohannon had put his hat on the floor. He picked it up and got out of the chair. Cunningham with surprising quickness pulled the .45 from its holster and pointed it at him. He didn't say anything, he just looked mean. Bohannon asked, "What about my rights? I'd like to leave here. I have horses to look after, a business to run. I have to get back to California."

"Sit down." He waited, with the gun pointed, and Bohannon sat down again. "You don't know my face? You never heard of Chester Cunningham?"

"In what connection?" Bohannon looked out the window beside the fireplace. "Politics? Run for office on the Ninth Amendment ticket, did you?"

"Don't play games," Cunningham said. "TV, radio, the newspapers. You're not a monk. Of course you've heard of me."

Bohannon judged the man needed for him to say yes, to light up with excitement if possible — even better, to fall down and worship. "I stable horses up in a canyon where TV doesn't reach any better than it probably reaches here." He looked around pointedly. "I don't see any TV set here. As to the radio, I check the weather reports. In my line of work you get up before sunrise, work all day, and you're ready for bed directly after supper. No, I don't read newspapers. No time."

"Well said." Cunningham nodded, holstered the gun, stood up. "I guess they school you in your identity so you've got a background all ready to spill when you get questioned."

"You can check it out. Phone down there. The San Luis Obispo County Sheriff's substation in Madrone. They'll back it up."

"I don't have a phone, but I expect they would. They're standing by waiting for me to call. With all the answers." He watched out the window as Ford and Hadley brought the green pickup into the compound and parked it. He turned back and said almost pleadingly, "Look, if you hadn't carried that private investigator's license, I wouldn't keep you. I mean, Ford and Hadley aren't out there to take prisoners, just to keep strangers off, and without that darn license, I'd've let you go. But you're law enforcement. And law enforcement means only one thing to me: trouble, and worse than trouble." He glanced toward the map on the wall. "The end of all my plans for America." He wagged his head sorrowfully. "I can't take a chance with you."

"If I was here on government assignment, do you think I'd've carried that license? I left my gun at home. Why wouldn't I have left the license?"

"Don't know, but it would have been prudent."

"And would I have come alone?"

That got Cunningham's attention. He took off the dark glasses and narrowed his eyes. "Somebody out there, counting the minutes you're here, waiting to move in?"

Bohannon gave a small laugh. "Would I say so if there were?"

Cunningham sighed and pulled the gun again. He motioned with it, meaning Bohannon was supposed to go out the door. Bohannon went out the door. Cunningham followed him and closed the door and pointed with the gun at one of the small buildings. "Keep you there," he said, "until I can decide what to do with you. Move."

Bohannon moved. Another blond youngster in camouflage pants, jacket, and combat boots came out of the storage building. He stopped, saluted Cunningham, and stared at Bohannon. "Who the hell is that?"

"Don't curse, Elroy, remember?"

"Forgot, captain, sir." He frowned hard at Bohannon. "He from the bank? I thought you said no prisoners."

"I don't know what you're talking about," Cunningham said. "And neither do you. Shut up, Elroy. You finished that mimeographing yet?"

"Yes, sir," Elroy said, not looking away from Bohannon, plainly puzzled and worried by him. "But that f—— I mean, that lousy Addressograph. That's real old, sir. Them cardboard stencils — they jam all the time. Can't we get a new one?"

"Get a rifle," said Cunningham, "see that it's loaded, and stand guard over this man until you're relieved. K building." And to Bohannon, "Over there, in the corner. March."

Elroy saluted and went back into the storage building, and out of the woods and into the open hardpan between the shacks came a teenage girl riding a tall, elegant, sorrel mare. The girl had long straight blond hair, wore a camouflage coverall too big for her and a floppy-brimmed camouflage hat. The mare was pregnant. On sighting the girl, Cunningham holstered the gun again and looked at his watch.

"Liberty," he said, "you've been gone too long. That means too far. That means you could have been seen. You want me to ground you?"

"No, Daddy," she said, patting the horse's neck, "we didn't go far."

"I doubt you know where you went," he said. "All right, you sponge her down now, clean her hooves, give her some oats, be sure she has water. Having your own horse means responsibility, hard work."

"I love looking after her," she said, and tilted her head at Bohannon. "Who are you? Is that your truck? With the horsehead on it?"

Bohannon said it was. "I keep a dozen horses on my place. She's about ready to foal, you know. You don't want to go too far with her. She could need help when her time comes."

"Help?" Cunningham snorted. "She's an animal. Instinct will —"

"She's not a cayuse," Bohannon said. "She's a Thoroughbred. Centuries of breeding. They can't survive without human help."

The girl said, "I know what to do. My horse book has got a whole chapter about it."

"Just the same," Bohannon said, "I'd keep her in her stall from here on out. With plenty of fresh dry straw."

"I know what to do," the girl repeated sulkily, reached down from the saddle, swung open a wide door, and rode the mare into the storage building. Looking after her, Bohannon glimpsed fifty-pound sacks of fertilizer, a truckload of them. Not to grow food. Not around here. They were labeled AMMONIUM NITRATE. He got a cold feeling in the pit of his stomach. There must be a ton of it. What was Cunningham going to blow up? The entire state?

"How did you come by a horse like that?" he said.

"Liberty wanted a horse, wouldn't leave me alone about it. You know how they nag." Cunningham grunted. "I took her in payment for a debt. No bargain. She'd never won a race."

Bohannon shrugged. "Maybe her foal will be a winner."

Cunningham's laugh was brief. "Another mouth to feed," he said. "Move."

The K building held a cot with a rolled-up sleeping bag on it, a tubular patio chair whose webbing a sun in a different climate had long ago bleached to gray and whose metal time and weather had pitted.

A set of battered veneered bookshelves had new-looking books on them. *The Turner Diaries, The Anarchist Cookbook, Christian Identity, Edible Wild Plants of the West, The Improvised Munitions Handbook.* Multiple copies. And brown-wrapped parcels, probably of the same books. A kerosene lantern with a smoke-smudged chimney, a single window with a huge tree trunk right up against it. No way out. Bohannon stood studying the room. Cunningham, from the open doorway, studied him. "Think I ought to chain you up?" he said.

Bohannon smiled. "Save yourself the trouble. Let me go."

Cunningham ignored that. "No, I don't think, with Elroy outside with his Uzi, you'll try to make a break. Anyway, the woods are full of my troops. You wouldn't get far."

"All night?" Bohannon said.

"All night, all day. Don't give it another thought. Read." Cunningham nodded at the bookcase. "*The Turner Diaries.* It will open your mind." He backed down the two short steps that led up to the door, began to close the door, and then said, "Anyway, you won't be here long. Just till I see if you're useful. If not, you won't be here at all."

Bohannon's brows went up. "In what way useful?"

"As a bargaining chip," Cunningham said and closed the door. It had a heavy slide bolt; Bohannon heard him rattle it into place. Cunningham said through the door, "If nature calls, just ask Elroy to take you. Elroy?"

"Sir," Elroy said.

Lunch when Elroy brought it was a wiener sandwich and a glass of milk. He wasn't sure what the milk tasted like but not milk. Powdered milk. He remembered the boxes stacked on the kitchen floor. The meat tasted like a hot dog, any hot dog. Mustard. Ketchup. Sweet relish. And the bread itself was good, fresh-baked, still a little warm. A treat. And he was hungry and finished the sandwich off in gulps, and the chocolate bar that lay beside it on the plate. A half hour afterward, when the bolt slid and the door opened, it was Cunningham's woman, Selina, who came to collect the plate and glass.

"That was good." Bohannon stood to hand them to her.

"You'll get damn tired of hot dogs," she said.

"Don't you mean darn?" he said with a little smile.

"Yes, I mean darn," she said and smiled back.

"And what did you mean when you said bad timing?"

"I meant sometimes we're busy around here." She wasn't going to stay and chat. She opened the door. "Tomorrow will be one of those times."

"All the more reason to let me go my way," Bohannon said.

"A sane person would think so." She went out and bolted the door.

And Bohannon lay on his bunk and read *The Turner Diaries,* which made clear on page after sneering, blustering, bloodthirsty page what the woman had meant. No admirer of this book could possibly be sane. If she knew that, why did she stay?

Elroy knocked at five and woke him. While reading he had drifted into a troubled sleep filled with murder, mayhem, bombings, and by contrast the quiet of the compound under its enormous trees was almost welcome. The blond kid brought in a battered old cafeteria tray. On it was a plate with beans and franks, a ketchup bottle, two slices of buttered bread on a side plate, another glass of milk, and a bowl of red Jell-O. Bohannon sat up on the edge of the bed, and Elroy handed him the tray. He studied him.

"You all right?"

"Nightmares." Bohannon set the tray on his knees and ran his fingers through his hair. "You know what the psychology books say about nightmares?"

"No, sir," Elroy said.

"The only ones who have them are children and artists."

"That right? I never did hear that. Which one are you?"

Elroy was brighter than Bohannon had expected. "Neither one, so I guess that makes the psychology books wrong, doesn't it?" He was hungry again and tilted ketchup over the beans and franks and filled his mouth. "What's this mimeographing you're doing for the captain?"

"*Ninth Amendment Bulletin,*" Elroy said. "The captain writes it; Miz Cunningham, she types the stencils; and I make the copies."

"And address the envelopes?" Bohannon took a bite of the bread. It was good again. "You complained about the Addressograph."

"I address 'em and stuff 'em," Elroy said wearily. "Takes forever."

"Big mailing list, is it?" Bohannon took a swallow of milk.

"I guess I better not tell you that." The boy wandered to the open door and, rifle cradled in his arms, stood there gazing out at the dying daylight through the trees. "Even if they are going to kill you."

Bohannon blinked. "I thought they were going to trade me off."

"Trade you off?" Elroy turned around. "For what? For who?"

Bohannon shrugged. "A bargaining chip, that's what the captain called me. Where do you mail all these copies of your bulletin? Coeur d'Alene?"

"Hell, no. That would give away where we're at, here."

"I guess it might at that." Bohannon continued to down the beans and franks and bread. "So what do you do about that?"

"Pack 'em all in a carton and truck 'em to Tacoma, and they forward the carton to Omaha or maybe El Paso or Enid, Oklahoma, and they take the envelopes out of the carton and mail 'em from there. Except sometimes it's Columbus, Georgia. Or San Diego."

"Must make getting contributions a little chancy," Bohannon said.

"I don't know. The captain — he's the one worries about the mail. I just follow orders." He sat down in the doorway, the rifle across his knees. Bohannon wondered if he could take the necessary six or eight steps silently enough to catch Elroy's thin neck in the crook of his arm and render him unconscious but guessed that even if he could there might be someone in the compound, or looking out a window, who would see him and shoot him for his trouble. He finished off the Jell-O, the last inch of milk, set aside the tray, slid the spoon into his boot, and lit a cigarette.

Elroy turned. "Say, how did you get to keep those? The captain don't allow smoking. No tobacco, no beer, no swearing . . ."

Bohannon held out the pack. "You want one?"

"I'm dyin' for one." Elroy came and got a cigarette and leaned for Bohannon to light it with a plastic throw-away lighter. "Oh, good," the boy said, blowing smoke away with a deep, grateful sigh. "Oh, yes."

"Not even rock and roll," said Bohannon. "What does the Ninth Amendment Militia do for fun?"

"Fun?" Elroy stared at him with an odd half smile. "Oh, mister. We're gonna have our fun tomorrow." He went back to the doorway and stood leaning there, looking out, enjoying the cigarette and chuckling to himself. "Oh yeah. We're gonna have real fun tomorrow."

"You mentioned a bank."

"Bank?" The boy turned, scowling. "Oh, you are for sure gonna be killed. You know way too much."

Bohannon put out his cigarette on the floor. "You going to rob a bank? Is that your idea of fun?"

"You got it backward, like most everybody," Elroy said. "It's the banks that are the robbers." He threw away his cigarette and turned. "Anyways, we ain't about money. We're about takin' this country back from the Jews and lawyers and niggers and immigrant trash from Mexico and China and all them and givin' it back to the white people the way God meant in the first place. And we ain't a militia either. We're a family."

Bohannon smiled thinly. "That just happens to carry guns at all times."

"We're embattled," Elroy said. "We tell the people of this country how things really are, and the rich and powerful don't like it. They'll kill us if they can. Them and their bought-and-paid-for army and FBI and all. We got to defend ourself, we got to defend the truth." He reached out. "I'll take that tray now. You need to go to the outhouse?"

"I thought you'd never ask," Bohannon said.

He lit the lamp and read about wild plants you could eat without poisoning yourself. It was more cheerful reading than *The Turner Diaries,* and he thought it might be useful if he could get away from here and past Cunningham's circle of fire and make his way by shank's mare to civilization, if there was civilization anywhere. He wasn't going to be able to memorize all this stuff, so he guessed he would take the book along. It was not going to be that hard to get out of here after all. The floor planks were indifferently nailed down. Using the spoon with patience, persistence, and main strength, he could pry up one plank with difficulty and another without difficulty. There was two feet of crawlspace under the shack. From there under cover of darkness he could creep into the ferns and brush beneath the trees and, if he went carefully, get back to the main road. Then he —

The bolt on the door rattled, the door opened, Selina came in. She pointed a Browning 9mm pistol at him. In a worn and weary way, she was beautiful in the lamplight. "I'd like the spoon back," she said.

"Shucks," he said and reached into his boot for it. He stood up to hand it over to her. "A feller can't have any fun around here."

She took the spoon and put it into a pocket of her jeans. She assumed a Colonel Klink accent. "No vun escapes from Stalag Thirteen."

"No one ever got shot at Stalag Thirteen either," he said.

"Life is not television." She backed to the door. Hand on the knob, she asked, "You need anything? Other than a crowbar?"

"How is Liberty's mare?" he said. "Liberty your daughter?"

She gave a short laugh. "She was, when I carried her in my belly. Since then she has had only one parent. Strange but true. And he has had only one true love. If anything happened to me, I doubt he'd notice. If anything happened to Liberty — God help us all."

"And if anything happened to him?" Bohannon asked.

Alarm flickered across her face, but she said stoutly, "He's not the kind of man things happen to. He makes things happen."

"That can be dangerous. Especially if you can't think straight."

"You're not talking about Chet Cunningham," she said.

"He's crazy, and you know it," Bohannon said.

"He's the sanest man in America." She pulled open the door.

"That's not an answer, that's a slogan. You're too bright for that."

"It's the truth," she said.

"He plans to shoot me," Bohannon said. "You going to let him do that?"

"You're not afraid," she said scornfully. "You were never afraid in your life. I know your kind. I married one."

"So you are going to let him shoot me?"

She took one step down. "That's between the two of you."

"Only if we both have guns." Bohannon held out his hand for the 9mm.

She smiled faintly and shook her head. "You want him to shoot me, too? How would that help?"

Bohannon sat on the cot.

"What about the horse?"

"Still pregnant."

She took the second step down, pulled the door shut, and bolted it.

Clattering and banging woke him. Through the cracks in the siding of the K building he saw light. He smelled gasoline. Young male voices called to each other. A starter mechanism whinnied, an engine clattered to life, died out, started up again. Another. The tailgate of a pickup truck banged shut, its chains rattling. More engines started. Cunningham barked orders and admonitions. There was a chorus of "Yessirs," and there was also laughter. Everybody sounded keyed up. The large door of the storage building slammed shut. The cars, trucks, vans began driving out of the compound. Right past him.

He crawled out of the sleeping bag and, through the crack between door and frame, caught glimpses of jittering headlights, red taillights. He peered at his watch. Two-thirty A.M. That busy tomorrow he'd heard about from Elroy and Selina started early, didn't it? A car braked, its door opened, someone came to his door, rattled the bolt, pushed the door open.

"You're awake," Cunningham said.

"It's nice of you to invite me out," Bohannon said, "but I'll need time to choose a frock. What do you suggest?"

"I suggest you read this." Cunningham held out Ada Tanner's Bible. "And meditate on it. Try the Twenty-third Psalm. That's the one the padre usually reads to condemned men. That and the part about 'I am the resurrection and the life.'"

Bohannon took the book. "Thoughtful of you," he said. "Appreciate it." He peered past the captain. "You taking my truck?"

"Spoils of war," Cunningham said.

"As Mrs. Napoleon said before Waterloo, when will you be back?"

"Forget it," Cunningham said. "This won't be Waterloo."

"If you were sure of that, you'd shoot me now."

Cunningham drew a breath to answer and didn't answer. He pulled the door shut, bolted it, and Bohannon listened to his footsteps cross the hardpan, heard the springs of the truck squeak slightly as the man climbed into it, heard the door slam, the parking brake let go, heard the gears grind because Cunningham didn't know this vehicle, and heard it drive away.

After that the silence of the forest night came and settled on the place, and he felt the high mountain cold, laid the Bible on the bookcase, crawled back into the sleeping bag, and, when he had stopped shivering, went to sleep. In a dream George Stubbs sat at the round kitchen table in the ranch house with his big drawing pad. He drew well for a man with no training. But he rarely drew anything but horses, and Bohannon took his hobby for granted and wasn't watching.

"Here it is," Stubbs said. "This is what you want." And he held up the pad for Bohannon to see. A horse's head in silhouette. "Now, ain't that just the ticket?"

And then Bohannon was awake in K building of Cunningham's compound, hundreds of miles from that kitchen, wondering what woke him. "The ticket to what, George?" he said, and worked his way out of the sleeping bag again and went to the door. He stood by the door listening. It was unnaturally quiet. If a guard was out there, he wasn't breathing. "Elroy?" he said. No answer.

Then he realized what he had heard that woke him. The bolt. He turned the knob and very gently pulled the door. It came open. His heart began thumping. He peered out. No Elroy. No light showed in the house across the way. She'd come in the dark, hadn't she, and gone back in the dark, and if she was watching from over there, she was watching from the dark. He smiled to himself. He'd had her figured right, after all. She wasn't going to let Cunningham kill him. Now, with all the longhaired boys with guns and grenades gone off with the sanest man in America, she was letting Bohannon walk away.

He put on his boots, jacket, hat, returned to the door, opened it, and stood with it open for a wary moment in the darkness and the silence and the cold. Then he took a step down. And waited. And another step. And waited. He wished to hell his truck was still here. He wished for a compass. For a map. For a flashlight. He made his way to the rear of K building and into the brooding, ancient darkness of the giant trees. He wanted to run. There wasn't much in the way of undergrowth to impede that. Only ferns. But there was no safe way to go fast.

Hands held out in the hope of not running into low branches, he started off. Was he heading for the state highway? Did it matter? He was putting Cunningham's camp behind him. Bark and sharp twigs kept scraping his hands. They'd be bloody before the night was out. Then they met something else. Fabric, and under the fabric, flesh and bone.

"Who the hell?" a voice said. A gun barrel poked his belly. A flashlight beam glared in his eyes. "Jesus Christ," the voice said. "How did you get out?"

"Don't you mean Judas Priest?" Bohannon said. "The door was open. I figured that meant I'd overstayed my welcome."

"Turn around." The gun barrel jabbed him again. "Go back."

And he went back, and was pushed into K building so hard he lost his footing and fell. And the door slammed. And the boy bolted the door. Disgusted, Bohannon clambered to his feet. She'd miscounted, hadn't she? Hadley had been left behind, cut out of the fun. Poor Hadley'd have to hear about Armageddon secondhand over breakfast.

But no one was back for breakfast. At six in the morning, the camp remained vacant and still. He heard the hooves of Liberty's horse pass. Dimly from across the way he heard coal dumped into the old cookstove. Hadley was red-eyed when he came with an M-16 to escort Bohannon to the outhouse. "You should get some sleep," Bohannon told him.

"If I'd slept last night," Hadley said, "you'd be in Coeur d'Alene by now."

"I don't understand how the captain could have left my door unbolted."

"He had a lot on his mind," Hadley said.

Back at K building Bohannon said, "You can sleep now."

"Not me," Hadley said sourly. "Gotta watch you. You're tricky."

"Not if you remember the bolt," Bohannon said.

Hadley closed the door and rammed the bolt to. "I got nothing on my mind. Just you."

Selina brought his breakfast on another of those battered cafeteria trays. It was scrambled eggs and Spam, toast and jam, a mug of coffee.

"You tried to leave us last night," she said. "I thought you'd get tired of hot dogs. But not so soon." She held out the tray. "In contrition I've brought you something different. Not better, just different."

He took the tray from her. "Appreciate the thought."

"The eggs are powdered," she said. "How did you get out?"

He looked at her. "You don't know? Somebody forgot to bolt the door."

"Hadley had stepped into the trees to relieve himself," she said. "It's lucky you happened to meet up with him."

"Not for me." Bohannon sat on the bed with the tray on his lap and began eating. The eggs had no taste at all, but they were hot and there was a good heap of them. The Spam tasted like salt. The jelly tasted like no known fruit or berry, but the bread was good and so was the coffee. She was still standing there. The Browning was tucked into her belt. He wiped his mouth on a paper napkin. "I ought to have chosen a different way out, right?"

Her smile was bleak. "So it seems."

"Hadley the only man left in the camp?"

"That would be telling," she said. "Anyway, I saw you leave. I'm a very light sleeper when Chet's away."

"Meaning you're worried." Bohannon held out his pack of cigarettes and saw her eyes light up. "When's he due back?"

She took a cigarette. "First, I am not worried. Chet knows what he's doing and just how to do it. Second, he'll be back when he's done it."

"And did you take aim at me from your window?" Bohannon held out his lighter, hoping she would bend close to take the light and he could get the Browning away from her. She didn't bend. She took the lighter, backed off a couple steps, lit her cigarette, tossed the lighter back to him.

"Thank you. That's good. A luxury we can't afford. Among many." She blew smoke away gratefully, watched Bohannon light his cigarette, and said, "No. I scrambled down from the loft, got my gun" — she touched the butt of the gun now — "and opened the front door. I was furious that Hadley had left his post. I wanted to run after you but" — she laughed at herself grimly — "I'd forgotten my boots. And while I dithered about that, Hadley brought you back."

"To your enormous relief," Bohannon said, watching her steadily.

She nodded. "Of course," she said, but she flushed a little.

"I suggested to Liberty she keep the mare in her stall until she foals, but I heard her ride out earlier."

"Liberty takes suggestions only from her father," Selina said.

"I hope she's back before the colt decides to arrive." Bohannon stood up to pass the tray over.

Selina took it one-handed and backed off, her other hand on the butt of the Browning. "Why not the filly?"

"No reason." Bohannon smiled. "What's the dam's name?"

"Paprika. For her color. She raced as a Nonstop-shopper."

Bohannon grunted. "Racing people drink too much."

Selina shrugged. "She never did stop. She just didn't run very fast."

"Why should she?" Bohannon said. "Every horse is not a fool."

The compound was still empty at noon. "Bohannon," Selina called. "Sit on the cot and stay there." Her boots knocked the steps. She slid back the bolt and pushed open the door. She set the tray on the floor to one side. "Wait," she said, "until you hear me bolt the door before you come for that."

"Where's Hadley?" Bohannon asked.

She shut the door and bolted it. "Don't worry. You're under guard."

Bohannon went and picked up the tray. "You mean by you? Where did Hadley go? Why did Hadley go?"

Maybe she stood there in the pine-splintered sunlight, thinking about answering, but she didn't answer. In a moment he heard her boots crossing the compound away from him. "They are late, aren't they?" he shouted. "Something went wrong."

It didn't provoke her. Not to speech. And he sat on the cot and ate canned chili not quite heated through. No fresh home-baked bread this time. A few stale soda crackers, that was all. And the usual glass of watery milk. He didn't hear the door to the house. He heard the door to the warehouse cum stable. And then in the hush, the startup of an automobile engine. Muffled. He had noticed on his brief escape attempt last night that all the junkyard vans, pickups, RVs had gone off with Cunningham's expeditionary forces. Except for the red runabout, of course. That would never go anywhere again. So the car he was hearing had been stored out of sight, indoors, hadn't it? He knocked with the handle of the spoon hard on a knothole. The knot fell out. He knelt and put his eye to the hole. And saw the car roll out of the warehouse. It looked new. Then it was out of his line of vision.

But his ears told him it had come this way. Moving too fast. It braked hard, the tires squealing on the hardpan. They kicked up dust. He smelled the dust. The horn blared. "Liberty!" Selina shouted. "Liberty! Come home." The horn blared again. "Damn," she said, and, leaving the motor idling, got out of the car, and he knew from the sound of her steps she was running. Into the house, out again, opening and closing the doors of the van, throwing things into the van, stopping for a moment with each load to lean on the horn. It trumpeted into the somber forest and echoed back. She shouted each time, "Liberty! Come home." And her voice echoed also and sounded lonely.

He called, "Shall I go fetch her?"

"I can't trust you," she said. But she came and opened the door and looked at him. She was holding the Browning. "You're the enemy."

He shrugged. "Hostilities are over. Aren't they?"

"Never," she said. "I'll find her myself, thanks."

But it wasn't necessary. Liberty had heard. And Liberty had come. Not riding her beloved Paprika. Leading her. And Bohannon saw why. The foal had shifted inside her. She looked twice as pregnant as before. Her bag was swollen. "She's going to foal, Mama." Liberty was pale. "Any minute now."

Bohannon asked, "Is her stall cleaned out? No junk on the floor? How big is it? She'll need room to walk around. No cracks the baby can put his legs through? Plenty of fresh straw?" He stepped forward. "I'd better look it over."

"Stay where you are," Selina said. And to Liberty, "Take her inside. I'll be along in a minute." Jerking the pistol at him, she told Bohannon, "Back off. Way back. That's it." And she pulled the door shut and bolted it.

Through the planks he called: "How many foals have you delivered?"

She didn't answer. The engine of the van quit. The huge, primeval silence of the place was back. He stretched out on the cot. You never knew about brood mares. They could drop their young before you could catch your breath. Or they could keep you waiting for hours. He closed his eyes.

What woke him was so unexpected he didn't open his eyes. He lay and held his breath, straining to hear because the sound was far off. The beat of helicopter rotors. He opened his eyes, lunged at the bookcase, and pawed the load of books off the first shelf. As he had thought, the shelf lay on pegs. It fit tightly, though, and he had to bang it with a fist from underneath to get it loose. He rammed with the end of it hard at the siding planks in the corner. The builders hadn't spared nails. With all his strength he banged at them again.

The whole of K building shuddered. But the planks didn't give. He kept ramming at them with the bookshelf, in a sweat to get out where that chopper could see him.

"What are you doing?" He turned. Selina stood in the open doorway. With the Browning leveled at him. "Drop the board," she said.

He laid the board on the cot. "I was getting worried about the foal."

"The man who loves horses," she said with a thin smile, "better than he loves freedom."

"What's happening?" he said.

"Nothing, but Liberty's too stressed to be out there alone with her, and I have packing to do."

Bohannon sat down and put on his boots.

"I noticed. Once she's through delivery, you plan to leave the horse and colt?"

"Maybe before," Selina said. "There are bigger issues at stake here than one little girl and her pet racehorse."

"We won't tell Elizabeth Taylor," Bohannon said.

He stood with Liberty outside the box stall. He was relieved that it was roomy and clean and that good daylight came from overhead. At times like this you had to be able to see clearly. "She gets up," Liberty said, "then she walks around. Then she lies down again. Now look. See her shudder? Look. She never holds her tail straight out like that. Look, Bohannon. She's kicking at her belly." The girl was trembling. He gave her a quick hug.

"It's all right. It's perfectly natural."

With a heavy thump and a heavy sigh, the broody mother lay down again, then scrambled up, rolling her eyes, and there was a rush of amniotic fluid, gallons of it. From out in the compound Selina shouted, "What was that?"

"She broke her water," Bohannon called. "Now the serious stuff begins."

"I think I'm going to throw up," Liberty said. But instead she cried.

One of the captain's favorite accommodations, a wood and canvas collapsing cot, was in this cubby beside the horse's stall, and Bohannon picked the weeping girl up and laid her on it. Whimpering, she curled tight, her face to the board wall. He covered her with an army blanket. "Everything's going to be fine," he told her.

Everything *was* fine. Eight or ten minutes later the mare was on her feet again and a long, slim leg stuck out beneath her tail, the blunt head of the foal with it. He breathed easier. The newborn's hoof had pierced the amniotic sack. The rest of the sack would slip away with the mare's contractions as they came. Or should. If not, he'd have to step in there and pull it off the nostrils so it could begin to breathe. An instant later the mare contracted again, the foal's nostrils were free, and it began to struggle.

"Liberty, come on." Bohannon turned, threw the blanket off, shook the girl awake. "You don't want to miss this. It may be the only miracle you'll ever see." He got her to her feet. She was numb the way a child is, roughly roused from sleep. He steered her by the shoulders. "Here. Stand here. Look. Look."

The foal struggled. The mare slowly, a little stunned, bending her graceful neck, reached around to help. The foal wriggled mightily, then dropped with a thump into the straw, legs sprawling. It was always a shock, the unbelievable length of a newborn foal's legs. Those were what a horse was all about, and this was the moment when that showed itself to the veriest fool. A horse was born for one thing only. A horse was born to run. The mare turned and bent to lick her newborn dry.

"She did it all herself." Liberty looked up at Bohannon, wonder in her eyes. "Just like Daddy said."

"Whatever happened to Daddy?" Bohannon said.

Liberty didn't hear. "I have clean towels to help her clean him up and dry him off." She turned away.

"She's doing fine," Bohannon said. "Let her do it. Come back. Watch."

Cleanup over, the mare began nudging the gangly little horse to urge it to its feet. It put those sticklike legs out, this way, that way, and trembling, teetering, began to stand. The dam put her elegant nose under to help.

"Wonderful!" Liberty clapped in delight.

And the little creature collapsed. It took two more tries, then he was firmly footed and his mother was nudging his butt with its damp whisk of tail to point him along to where her milk was waiting for him.

"Excuse me." Bohannon stepped out the big door into the golden sunlight slanting through the pines and, away from the hazards of straw and ammonium nitrate manure, lit a cigarette. Selina was across the way, setting a heavy cardboard storage file in the van. "You lose," he shouted. "It's a colt."

"This is not a woman's world." Selina slammed the van doors, climbed behind the wheel, started the engine. "Come on, Liberty. Time to leave. Your father will be frantic." She brought the van around in a quick circle to where Bohannon stood. Panic edged her voice. "Liberty, we have to go."

Bohannon raised his eyes. The helicopter was back. From high up, its jittery shadow flickered across the compound. "Forget it," he told her.

"What are you talking about? Liberty! Come out here. Right now."

Liberty appeared in her floppy camouflage coverall and hat. "I'm not going. You go on without me. Mama — he's just born. He can hardly walk. Anything could happen. And Paprika? After what she's been through?" Liberty waved her arms. "I'm her friend. I can't leave her. She trusts me."

"There's feed, there's water." Selina jumped down and came for the girl. "They'll be all right till we can send for them. A day, two days. What can happen?" She grabbed Liberty's wrist. "Come on now. Before it's too late."

Bohannon touched her, jerked his chin up. "It's already too late."

"Let me go!" Then she saw, and the starch went out of her. "Oh no."

Bohannon opened his mouth to speak, and a pickup truck banged noisily into the compound and slurred to a halt on the hardpan, kicking up a cloud of dust. The green pickup with the horsehead on the door. Bohannon's pickup. Ford jumped out of it clutching his AK-47. He came running toward them, wild with excitement and fear. "Where's the captain?"

"That's dried blood," Selina said. "Are you hurt?"

"No, but a lot of other people are. Hell, they're dead. I killed a lot of people, Miz Cunningham." He began to cry. "I wasn't supposed to. Nobody was supposed to kill anybody, just like hold them real quiet." He shook his head in agony. "I didn't mean it. But this nigger, this big security guard, he wouldn't stand still like I said, and he ran at me and I shot him and the gun kept on running and everybody in the place fell down, and, oh —" He dropped to his knees in the dust, head bowed, sobbing. "God forgive me for what I done." Then he was on his feet again, half crouched and staring all around. "Where's the captain? Where's everybody?"

"Not here," Selina said. She was very pale, and she was hanging onto Liberty, frightened by this maniac, but her voice stayed calm, the voice of the captain's lady. "You know what the orders were. If anything went wrong, no one was to return here. What's the matter with you, Ford?"

"He said he'd protect me," Ford said, "wouldn't let nothin' happen to me. Always promised us that. He'd look after us, all of us. And now look." He waved upward wildly at the helicopter. "They're after me, and they're going to get me and where is he? Where's the captain?"

"You stupid boy," she cried, "don't you understand? You've finished the captain. You've finished us all."

He stared at her, slack-jawed. Then he saw Bohannon, and his eyes lit up. "Oh no. Not all. Not me." Bohannon saw it coming, but he wasn't quick enough. He was past fifty. He could no longer move with the speed of the boy, and the boy caught him. "They can't take me. Not with a hostage. Come on." And he yanked and booted and hoisted Bohannon toward the truck, the rifle barrel at Bohannon's ear. It was awkward. He probably couldn't fire it if he tried, but Bohannon remembered the other morning on that lost roadway. The gun had gone off on its own. He didn't resist.

The boy slammed him against the cab.

"Open the door. Get in there."

And Bohannon did these things, and the next moment the boy was on the seat beside him, still clutching the AK-47. The engine revved. He clashed the gears. The pickup backed and slewed, going too fast. It braked, and the dust rose around them, blocking off the anxious faces of the two women. Then the truck raced ahead, moving off through the great trees, heading along the crooked little access trail, back to that dismal road.

But not all the way. An official car came ambling along to meet them. It stopped with its bumper against the bumper of the green pickup, and Ford said, "Hell," and two men in starchy tan uniforms got out of the car. It was a highway patrol car. They wore dark glasses, had their hair cropped tight around the ears, and looked about fifteen years old. Service revolvers were holstered on their hips, but they didn't seem about to draw these. They came ambling forward looking as if they meant no harm.

One of them called, "Mr. Bohannon, is it? Mr. Hack Bohannon? Green pickup with the horsehead on it? We been looking for you. Your friends down in California. They haven't heard from you. They're worried about you. Sheriff's department?"

"He don't count." Ford put his head out the window. "He's just my hostage. Corporal Ford, Ninth Amendment Militia? I got a gun here." He stuck it out the window and waved it. "See that? That's what counts. Now, you get back in that gov'mint car and get it the hell out of my way."

The patrolmen stopped. One of them looked skyward. "Whatever you say, but they're watching all this from up there. You won't get far."

"This thing can blow them right out of the sky," Ford said, "after it blows you into the ground. I've already killed twenty people. What have I got to lose?"

The men put their hands up and backed submissively toward the patrol car. Hanging out the truck window, Ford watched them, grinning. "Way to go," he said. He had forgotten Bohannon. And Bohannon struck him with a chop across the nape of his thin boy's neck. There was a crack of vertebrae. The boy's head drooped, and his cap fell off, and the AK-47 dropped to the roadway. Bohannon got out of the truck on the passenger side. He knew his smile was a little anemic, but he smiled it anyway.

"Good to see you," he said.

DAVID K. HARFORD

A Death on the Ho Chi Minh Trail

FROM *Alfred Hitchcock Mystery Magazine*

A Death

YEARS LATER I would think about Vietnam and how, when I first arrived in-country, I imagined that every Vietnamese I encountered on the crowded streets of Pleiku, each one plodding along country roads, all those bent toiling in the swampy ricefields, and even those hired to labor in the hot sun around the base camp for the Sixth Infantry Division (I envisioned them all as VC) might at any moment try to take my head off. It never dawned on me that some might be friendly and some might even be neutral about the war being fought all around them.

I was tentative and uncertain the first few weeks, frightened by the unfamiliar ways and circumstances of the war, frightened of the sights and sounds and smells of the city and of the strange, impoverished lifestyle of the people whose country I had come to occupy. I seemed to have absolutely nothing in common with them but a common enemy, and they could easily be that enemy.

As I became acquainted with my surroundings, my fears abated, and I relaxed a bit, got bolder, was content doing my job, got to know the people better, and although the war was still the only common thread I felt I had with the Vietnamese, I could soon move among them with ease and confidence — not totally trusting, mind you, but more curious than afraid. At that point I even found myself really getting into my work, loving it when it took me far from the boring confines of base camp, sometimes out deep into the more hostile areas of the Central Highlands.

But then, like a giant bell curve, as my time to leave the country neared and I'd survived ten or eleven months, I reverted to being overly cautious and fearful. I had made it through my year. Unlike too many others I'd seen, I was alive, and I intended to go home that way. This kept me, in the last days of my tour, staying as close to base camp as I could, letting the other guy go out to those places where I'd once ventured.

Nonetheless, I was riding high halfway through my tour and feeling bold the day Mitch called me from LZ Victoria, the forward firebase for the 3rd Brigade of the Sixth Infantry. He had someone he wanted me to talk to, he said. The man had a curious tale, and Mitch wasn't sure how to proceed, or if in fact he should proceed with an investigation at all.

It was this incident that made me realize that a common thread did indeed unite all of us in Vietnam, Vietnamese and GIs alike.

The three of us sat at a small table in the provost marshal's tent at LZ Victoria; I studied Pfc. Willard as he spoke. He gestured only a little, and his words were even and measured but not forceful.

"At first it just seemed odd, Mr. Hatchett. Too coincidental," he said to me. "That's why I decided to tell you the whole story and let you decide if the CID wants to look into this."

He glanced down at a paper bag stuffed full of something. He'd brought the bag with him and kept it drawn in close to his body. I hadn't asked about its contents, preferring to let him tell his story first. But whatever was in that bag, I sensed, was part of his tale. He clutched it like it contained the crown jewels of England.

"I'd known Berkley all my life," Willard said tonelessly. "We were from the same small town in Kansas, went to the same high school. I dated his sister. We went to basic training together, and then we came down together on orders for over here. I'd taken advanced training at the Signal School at Fort Gordon after basic; Berkley took Advanced Infantry Training at Fort Polk. Over here he caught the second of the eleventh infantry, and I got headquarters company. We'd meet from time to time at the brigade mess hall over coffee and catch each other up on any hometown news. So when he told me last week he was worried that some of his own men might be after him and said that they could easily frag him out in the bush, I believed him. I mean, I knew him, Mr. Hatchett. He was scared, and not sure what to do about it. That night he's dead; KIA'd out in the bush, just like he worried about."

A Death on the Ho Chi Minh Trail

"Did he mention specifically who in his unit might be after him and why?" I asked.

Fraggings — GIs intentionally killing other GIs — weren't all that common, but when it happened, it was usually a hard-driving officer or noncom who got the dubious honor bestowed upon him, usually during the heat and confusion of a firefight so it would go unnoticed.

Willard folded his hands atop the bag. They were large hands, callused, the hands of a Kansas farmboy, I imagined. His hair was straw-colored, his face freckled. "He mentioned no names, but since it happened while he was out on patrol, it's got to be one of the guys he went out with. It was only a six-man short-range recon patrol."

"You know where the 2/11th is?" I asked Mitch.

"Oh yeah. I sure do. It's not a full company, only a small detachment. But man oh man, the trouble." I noted the disgust in Mitch's voice, and I knew we'd be discussing the 2/11th in fuller detail after Willard left.

"The only thing Berkley said," Willard continued, "about why they might be out to get him was that 'they were up to no good again, and it was getting worse,' he said, and he didn't like it. That's how he put it. But like I said, he didn't know which way to turn. He wasn't real hot on going to his CO, I guess."

Mitch muttered, "That's understandable."

"Okay," I said. "Berkley goes out on patrol with these guys, some of whom were up to no good, and he comes back dead. Can I assume they got into some kind of firefight, then?"

"They got into something. We were monitoring it up at Brigade Headquarters. I could hear them yelling in the radio that they'd been ambushed or something or made contact somehow and were falling back. They weren't supposed to make contact, but sometimes you can't help it. Someone yelled to give them support. They wanted mortars. They wanted flares. They wanted out of there. They already had one KIA, their point man, they said, and they were bringing him in. Cover them. Over the radio I could hear men yelling in the background and 16s going off. It sounded like a real frenzy. It didn't last long because they were already breaking contact and were only a few clicks, a few thousand yards, outside our perimeter. It was then I learned the patrol was from the 2/11th and that Berkley was the KIA point man."

"When was this?" I asked.

"About one in the morning last Tuesday."

"Besides what he told you, is there anything else that makes you think someone did him during that firefight?"

Willard squinted, considering the seriousness of the question, then said slowly, "I wouldn't have thought —" He fidgeted. "Let's say I would have been only suspicious, given what Berkley had said — I mean, killing one of your own is too much to comprehend — so it would have weighed out evenly in me; the weight of that monstrous act against the weight of my suspicions. You know what I mean? I would've probably left the country suspicious but wouldn't've done anything about it if I hadn't gone to Grave Registration. That tipped the scales — ah man, him dying is going to rip his mom apart." Pfc. Willard twisted the edges of the bag, rolled them and unrolled them.

"What happened at Grave Registration?"

He opened the brown bag. "I got permission to go see him the next day. I guess to say good-bye, maybe take something of his back with me, back to his family. I even thought about calling his mom from here. You know, let me tell her. It might ease things. But I couldn't bring myself to do that." Willard drew a stabilizing breath because his voice was beginning to quaver.

"I was going to ask for his Zippo. He'd shown it to me the day before — he had had it engraved with his name and unit — but I couldn't find it among his personal effects, which is kind of odd because he always carried it. He smoked like a chimney. I always told him his smoking was going to kill him." Willard snickered bitterly at the irony. "Anyway, I figured the lighter got lost when they were bringing him in, probably fell out of his pocket.

"They already had Berkley laid out, stripped to his shorts. I could see where he took a burst full across the chest, probably killing him instantly. One shot high in the shoulder broke his shoulder. But most of the shots were across his chest and stomach. They'd cleaned the blood off some. His fatigue shirt was lying on the floor in a heap. When I saw his name tag and knew it was his shirt, I picked it up.

"Suddenly I was crying, holding the bloody fatigue shirt he wore — crying for him, crying for me, crying for his mom, crying for all of us, I guess — and I must have been more dazed and in shock than I realized because when I left I was still carrying his shirt wadded up in my fists."

He reached into the bag, pulled out an army jungle fatigue shirt, and held it up by the shoulders. I could read BERKLEY on the name tag above the pocket. I could also see Berkley was an Sp/4. The shirt was badly soiled with dried blood.

Standing up and stepping back a bit, Willard held the shirt so I could view it better from a distance. "It wasn't until the next day that I noticed it," he said, never taking his eyes off me, watching me scrutinize the bloodstained shirt.

Mitch was watching me, too. Other than the large amount of blood caked down the front, I saw nothing particularly unusual about it. "You noticed what?" I asked.

Mitch pushed his chair back, rising.

"No bullet holes, Hatch," he said. "There isn't a bullet hole in that shirt. There's blood all down the front, but that's it."

Mitch steered the jeep down the dirt road inside LZ Victoria. Along the perimeter, inside the coils of razor wire and barbed wire, sandbagged bunkers had been erected, every fourth one a towering command bunker. We stopped in front of one of them.

"Each unit is responsible for manning a section of bunkers twenty-four hours a day," Mitch said, pushing his OD — olive drab — baseball cap back. "The 2/11th has Sector Blue, these five bunkers you see here. Cut through the rolls of wire right in front of Sector Blue's command bunker is a path and a gate allowing patrols to go in and out of the perimeter at night, hopefully unseen."

I noted the path and a gate of sorts. I could see trip flares tied along the path and at least two Claymores set up and pointed down the path to protect it.

"A while back I got tipped off that the 2/11th bunker guards, led by one Staff Sergeant Reynolds, were sneaking Vietnamese prostitutes in through that gate at night onto the LZ and into their bunkers, if you can believe that."

"That's nuts," I said, astounded not only by the audacity but by the carelessness and stupidity of the act as well.

"Well, I caught them with four whores. I turned the women over to the National Police, who probably took their turn at them before letting them go, and I wrote up Sergeant Reynolds and his cohorts. It's bad enough that some of them were drunk, some probably smoked up, and two were sleeping on guard duty, but to open those gates and let God-knows-who in — well."

"Were they court-martialed?"

"They were reprimanded. I think Reynolds lost some pay, a mere slap on the hand. But understand, their CO at the time, Lieutenant Macy, was a wimp. No backbone; scared to death of his own men even. I heard his fear got worse the closer he got to going home. I had it put to me that Sergeant Reynolds actually ran the outfit. Maybe that's an exaggeration, but it probably isn't too far off. All Macy wanted was to leave. He finally got his wish. He was sent home last week. They just got a new CO, so maybe there'll be some changes for the better."

He put the jeep in gear. "I've had nothing but trouble with that unit since they got here. We're forever catching them in off-limits bars and whorehouses in Phu Bien, in unauthorized uses of army vehicles, drunk and disorderly. And most probably some blackmarketing is going on. Drugs, almost certainly. It's a rogue unit, I'll tell you. It's like a big party to them."

"About Berkley's shirt," I said as we bounced along the dusty road, "any possibility he was out on point not wearing a shirt?"

"Not from what I've been told."

"Oh?"

"After Willard showed me the shirt, I went to see an infantry captain friend of mine. Like you, I was thinking maybe Berkley had his shirt off when he was hit, then someone put it on him before they took him to Grave Registration. So I asked the captain if he or any of his men ever went shirtless on patrol at night. He laughed. No way, he said. First, the insects would eat you alive. Also, it's usually dark out there. I mean, these guys aren't carrying flashlights or anything, so they're all the time getting slapped by branches and scraped by thorns. Lots of guys wear flak jackets over their shirts. That's when I decided to call you."

"But he must have had his shirt off when he was shot. Unless the VC have a new kind of bullet. Maybe it was unbuttoned under his flak jacket, if he wore one. That might explain it."

"It wouldn't explain the shoulder wound. A flak jacket is sleeveless, like a vest. I told you it was curious, a real puzzler. Here we are. Maybe these guys can clear it up."

We pulled into the 2/11th's detachment area. As I glanced

around at the infantry unit's tents, their sandbagged walls built four feet high up the sides for protection against incoming mortars and rockets, I saw three men busy painting the wooden latrine, four others washing and polishing the company's jeeps and three-quarter-ton trucks, and a long line of soldiers being marched through the area picking up litter and cigarette butts.

The sides of the mess tent had been lifted to let fresh air through. Inside, I could see a half dozen men in white aprons mopping the wood floors, washing and polishing things.

"This is a switch," Mitch said, smiling slightly. "I might get to like this new CO of theirs. Look at how they've cleaned the place up."

As we approached the CO's tent, we could hear someone inside getting chewed out.

"Sergeant Reynolds," a voice growled, "I don't care how Lieutenant Macy ran things. Things are going to be run a whole lot different around here from now on. According to the inventory *I've* taken, we're missing about fifty cases of Lerps; we're missing two radios; none of the vehicles have spare tires. I haven't even gotten into the armament yet. The men's sleeping quarters are a mess.

"There'll be an inspection tomorrow at 0900. And you'd better start hunting around for those starlight scopes. I want to see them on my desk tomorrow morning. Am I clear on that, sergeant?"

"Yes, *sir*, Captain Boggs. You are very clear. Shall I steal a couple of starlight scopes off another unit, sir?"

"That'll be enough, Reynolds. Just find them."

We pushed through the flaps and entered the command tent. "Who are you?" Boggs asked, glaring at us like a hungry animal looking for something else to chew on and we looked good. Then his expression eased. "Oh yes, the MPs. Someone called and said you were coming over. I'm Captain Boggs, the new CO here."

"I'm Mr. Hatchett with the CID, and this is Mr. Mitchley, the provost marshal investigator for the MPs here on Victoria."

Still in a rigid stance Reynolds swiveled his head slowly until his eyes fell directly on Mitch, then on me.

"Sergeant," Captain Boggs said, "these men want to talk to you." He brushed past me on his way out of the tent. "You can use this tent if you want, Mr. Hatchett. I'll get the others."

He glanced back at Reynolds. "Sergeant, who was with you on that patrol last week, the night, ah — what was his name, the one killed while you were out on recon?"

"Berkley, sir. Sp/4 Berkley."

Reynolds was staring straight ahead again, not looking at any of us. A bit of blush was leaving his cheeks.

"And the others would be Watson, Thiel, and Jefferson, sir. Collins, too, but he's on R&R at Cam Ranh Bay. He should be back in a few days. Want me to get them, sir?"

"I'll get them. You stay here. I just took over last Wednesday," Boggs explained to Mitch and me, "so I don't know a lot of my men yet."

I nodded.

When Boggs had gone, Staff Sergeant Reynolds immediately relaxed.

"Boy, am I glad to be getting out of here," he said. "What a monster he is."

"Where you going?" I said, hoping to keep it informal. "Home?"

"The next best thing to home. Fort Dix, New Jersey. I've got orders to become a drill instructor for basic trainees. I was born and raised only ten miles from Dix. Hot damn. Good hit. I can live right at home." He took a seat at Captain Boggs's desk. Very bold he was, unafraid, it seemed, of further reprimands.

He shuffled through some of Boggs's papers and finally held up the inventory list. "How the hell am I supposed to know who ate more Lerps than they were supposed to? If the mess hall put out better meals, the guys wouldn't be eating the Lerps. How am I supposed to know where those starlight scopes are?" He tossed the paper aside. "Man, two weeks and I'm out of here. It cannot get here fast enough."

Lerps — LRRP really, but pronounced Lerp — stood for Long Range Reconnaissance Patrol, but what it referred to was food, freeze-dried food to be exact, very tasty food infantry units took out with them when they went on patrols. The meal packages, the Lerps, weighed less than the old C-rations, and by merely heating water over a lighted hunk of C-4 explosive and pouring the hot water into the freeze-dried packages, hot meals could be made in the bush far more efficiently and quicker and better tasting than ever before. Lerps also had a great commercial value, so they often ended up on the black market.

Starlight scopes were night vision equipment, a telescopelike device that allowed you to see at night by drawing on the light of the stars or the moon. They didn't work very well on moonless nights or on heavily clouded ones, but they were handy pieces of equipment. It was hard to imagine how a unit could lose two.

Sergeant Reynolds turned his attention to Mitch and me. "What is it about the night Berkley was killed that you want to know?"

"I'd prefer to wait for the others," I said. "Were you in charge that night?"

He furrowed his brow. He seemed young for a staff sergeant. "I'm in charge every night, Mr., Mr. —"

"Hatchett," I said. A big boy, too. Probably played football in high school before joining the army.

"Mr. Hatchett." Then he muttered harshly, "*Used* to be in charge anyway," and glared outside in Boggs's direction.

The tent flap opened, and three men, two whites and a black, shuffled into the tent. Jefferson, the black enlisted man, had obviously been one of the men washing vehicles because his fatigues were soapy and soaked. Thiel, a small man with black hair and bushy eyebrows, had OD paint on his hands. It was hard to determine what chore Watson had been involved in, but he was a big blond kid who wore his fatigues skin tight.

I made Sergeant Reynolds relinquish the chair behind Captain Boggs's desk, and I sat in it. Mitch sat on the edge of the desk. The four men we were about to question stood in a line in front of us, their arms crossed behind their backs.

I spoke to them as a group but tried to watch each man individually.

"Last week out on patrol you guys ran into some unfriendlies and got into a brief firefight. Sp/4 Berkley, a member of your patrol, was killed."

"That's not exactly right," Sergeant Reynolds said.

The others stared down at the dirt floor; only Reynolds looked at Mitch and me.

"Would you care to correct me, then, sergeant?" I said.

"Yes, sir. Berkley was not killed in our firefight with the VC per se. Berkley was already dead. Actually, Berkley was the reason we got into the firefight. If he had stayed out of sight like he was supposed to, he might still be here today. May I clarify, Mr. Hatchett?"

The others, except for Thiel, had raised their heads and were now watching Reynolds. "Please do," I told him.

He shifted his weight from one foot to the other.

"Our job that night," he said, "like the many other nights we went

out on those recons, was to set up along a well-traveled trail about
three clicks out. That's three thousand yards, give or take. We were
only to monitor any movement along the trail by the VC. We were
not to engage the enemy. Understand, Mr. Hatchett, this brigade is
set up in part to monitor movement all along the Ho Chi Minh
Trail. But the Ho Chi Minh Trail is not a trail like the Appalachian
Trail is a trail. It's a whole system of roads and trails from Hanoi to
Saigon, and the trail we were monitoring is just one small part of it.
We'd done this quite a few times before, whenever orders came
down from brigade."

Sergeant Reynolds drew out a cigarette, offered the pack to all of
us, and continued. "Berkley was on point, maybe fifty yards ahead
of us. He was to wait for us out of sight at a spot where the trail
forked. Suddenly we heard a burst of gunfire ahead. I tried to raise
Berkley but couldn't, so we crept forward to find out what had
happened to him. About the time we saw him, lying at the fork, we
began taking fire from VCs."

"Heavy fire," Watson added, nudging Reynolds. "What would you
say, sarge, a dozen VC?"

"Probably that many at least. Like us, a small patrol." Reynolds
drew on his cigarette. "We returned fire, of course, and moved in to
get Berkley out of there. I assumed he was dead, leastways he wasn't
moving, but no way was I going to leave him there." He paused and
looked at Jefferson.

"Go on," I said. Thiel caught my attention. He was the only one
of the four soldiers who didn't seem to want to look directly at
Mitch or me or the others and didn't seem anxious to contribute.
Instead he scowled at the dirt floor and busied his hands by picking
dried paint off them.

"I had Jefferson here on the horn calling for mortars to cover us
when we made our way back to Victoria," Reynolds continued. "I
was finally able to make it to where Berkley was and drug him back
out of fire. These guys kept the gooks busy while I was doing that.
Turned out we didn't need mortars."

"So you four and Collins were together when Berkley was ahead
on point? You're fortunate no one else was killed."

"We had plenty of cover. The jungle's pretty thick in there,"
Jefferson explained.

"How far did you have to drag Berkley?"

"Only fifty feet or so, to where the trail bent a bit. About that far, wasn't it, Watson? Then I threw him over my shoulder and carried him back to Victoria while these guys covered our retreat. But the VC weren't following us. I think they were as surprised by the encounter as we were."

"It's very commendable getting Berkley out of there."

"I wasn't going to leave him, Mr. Hatchett. He was in *my* command, and he was a good friend. I wouldn't want to be left out there, alive or dead. He was a great guy."

The others, except Thiel, nodded agreement.

"How long did the firefight last?" I asked. "Thiel? Any idea how long?"

Thiel snapped his head up, surprised. "Ah, I-I-I'm sorry. What?"

"About ten minutes. Maybe twenty," Sergeant Reynolds answered.

"About that," Thiel muttered.

"Seemed like a lifetime," Jefferson added.

"I'll bet it did," I said. What they'd just described was a common firefight, however short it was. I'd heard nothing earth-shattering or unusual in their account, so I shuffled some papers on Captain Boggs's desk, leaned back so I could see the entire group better, and asked the question I wanted answered most. I directed it at Sergeant Reynolds.

"When you finally reached Berkley lying there dead on the trail, you say you dragged him back fifty feet or so." Reynolds watched my lips intently as if he were reading each word as it came out of my mouth. "How did you drag him? I mean, where did you grab him to drag him?"

Without hesitation Reynolds said, "At first I grabbed him under the armpits. But his shoulder was broken and it was flopping in the shattered socket and hard to get ahold of, so I reached down and grabbed him by the shirt. Like this."

Reynolds stepped behind Jefferson, reached over Jefferson's shoulders with both arms, and grabbed handfuls of fatigue material in the area of Jefferson's shirt pockets.

"And that's how you got him out? Holding on to his shirt?"

"Yes, sir," Reynolds said.

"Was his shirt buttoned?"

"I suppose so. I believe so. Yes. Why wouldn't it be?"

"Steel pot?"

"He wore a slop hat." Reynolds appeared puzzled momentarily, then recovered. "Boots, too," he said. "Berkley had his boots on in case that's the next question about how we dress."

Thiel was still looking pretty sour, but the others smiled at Sergeant Reynolds's smart-aleck remark.

I ignored it, but privately I enjoyed it because he had inadvertently given me a little more cover to disguise what we were really after. "Were his boots laced?" I asked.

"Hell, no. They were untied, and he was always tripping over them. Of course his boots were laced. His shirt was buttoned. His hat was on. His —"

"Was he wearing a flak jacket?"

"No. Berkley didn't like them. Too confining, he said. They don't stop bullets anyway, and Berkley always said that while your upper torso might get protected from shrapnel, your groin and face are exposed. He never wore a flak jacket."

"So you grabbed him by his shirt and dragged him back?"

"That's correct, Mr. Hatchett." He ground his cigarette out on the floor with his boot. "Why all the questions about how he was dressed? Is the army becoming fashion-conscious these days?"

With grim, stone-faced expressions, every man including Thiel was watching me, awaiting the answer. Apparently this time none of them saw anything funny in Reynolds's attempt at humor.

I sat forward in the chair and studied them. Finally I said, "It's something we have to do from time to time. This just happens to be one of those times."

I thought it was a great answer — truthful, in a vague sort of way.

After the session, in which everyone basically verified Reynolds's account of the firefight, we followed the four men out of the tent. I kept my eye on Thiel as the group meandered toward the mess hall. I could tell they were talking fiercely among themselves. Once out of earshot they stopped suddenly, and I watched Sergeant Reynolds spin Thiel around, speaking to him sharply, stabbing a finger into Thiel's face as he spoke.

"Shouldn't we have interviewed them all separately?" Mitch asked as we watched the foursome enter the mess tent.

"We could have done it that way, yes. And we still can. I wanted to view them as a group first and see how they interacted. Besides, if something happened out there, you can bet they've got their story straight. These infantry units are close-knit groups. But remind me to call the CID office at base camp sometime soon. I have to make a few arrangements."

Mitch nodded. "Interesting about the shirt, wasn't it?"

"If Berkley was killed by VC in that firefight with his shirt on, that leaves us with those new kind of bullets the VC must have."

"Or," Mitch said, "maybe the VC tackled him, opened his shirt, shot him, then buttoned his shirt again."

Although I chuckled, I added, "You might be closer to the truth than you realize."

Captain Boggs was approaching us from across the company area.

"Where to from here?" Mitch wanted to know.

Before I could answer, Boggs spoke, "You done?"

"Yes, we are," I said. "Thank you."

"Anything I can do to help, let me know."

"There is one thing. Tomorrow morning after your inspection, let's say at 1100 hours, would you bring Thiel up to the command bunker in Sector Blue? I'm going to need him for a few hours."

"Just Thiel? Not the others."

"Just Thiel. And don't say anything to anyone, even to Thiel, about where you're taking him."

"Can do," Captain Boggs said.

"What do you have planned?" Mitch asked.

I donned my baseball cap. "Tomorrow you, me, Thiel, and a detachment of MPs, combat ready, are going out to where Berkley was killed. It seems Thiel might be the weak point in the group and the one we now want to separate from the others. I want him to show us just where on the Ho Chi Minh Trail Sp/4 Berkley was killed. I agree with Willard. I don't think Berkley was killed by the VC. At least not in that firefight."

The Village

The jungle foliage on both sides of the path we followed was so thick hardly any sunlight reached the ground, giving me the sensation we were walking in perpetual twilight.

The path was a well-traveled one and wide enough that we could walk two abreast on it. I'd sent two MPs on ahead as point men even though our chances of stumbling on the enemy in midmorning so close to the brigade firebase were slight. The VC loved the night.

Two MPs brought up the rear, five others were with Mitch and me and Thiel. But all of us were armed with 16s and M-79 grenade launchers just in case.

Earlier, when we met Thiel at the command bunker and I told him that I wanted him to take me to the spot where Berkley was killed, his only response had been a pained, twisted look and a slight nod. Then he mumbled a profanity I didn't quite understand.

We hadn't gone very far down the trail when the MPs on point radioed that they had reached the fork in the path and would wait for us. But when we finally caught up with them, Thiel said it was the wrong fork. "It forks again up ahead," he said. "This path here" — he indicated an equally well-traveled path to the left — "goes into a small village somewhere over there." He motioned with his head in a generally easterly direction.

We moved on, deeper into the jungle, where the moist heat, trapped air, and mildew made it feel and smell like we were pushing through a large sun-steamed terrarium dripping with condensation.

Thirty minutes later, a couple of thousand yards down the path, we congregated at the spot where Berkley died.

"Somewhere right in here is where he was lying," Thiel said, pointing at the confluence of two trails. He studied the earth and kicked at some leaves and debris. "In fact, here's some of his blood."

Sure enough, among some dead leaves I could see large blotches of dried blood that the ants and flies hadn't gotten to yet.

Thiel sat down beside the path, leaned against a tree, put his head between his knees, and rocked his torso slowly, rhythmically.

"Where does this trail lead?" I asked of the left fork.

"The right one goes on and on to I don't know where. Hanoi, maybe," Thiel answered. "The left one intersects with another trail up ahead that eventually also leads to that village I told you about back there. It's that trail we were to monitor. The VC were coming up the right fork when Berkley encountered them."

"How far away is the village?"

"A couple of clicks maybe. You can also get to it by vehicle, but you have to drive almost into Phu Bien and then take a dirt road back to it."

I concentrated on studying the thick broadleaf foliage growing profusely where the firefight had taken place.

Things weren't quite right — something was missing.

An MP called to me and pointed at the ground. There I spied three spent M-16 shell casings scattered off the path. "Aren't many empty casings," I said to Thiel, "for a fifteen-, twenty-minute fire-fight. How many rounds you think you guys got off before dragging Berkley out of here?"

"Hundreds, maybe. A thousand, who knows?" Thiel said, his head still down between his legs. "The VC, or civilians, come along and pick up any spent cartridges, Mr. Hatchett. They can either reload them and use them on us, or they sell them for the brass. That's why you don't see many lying around. They must have over-looked those there." He raised his head and stared across the path at me. "Why am I here with you, Mr. Hatchett?" he asked. "Why are we doing this? The CID doesn't normally do this. Berkley is dead. Berkley was killed. In a firefight. Here. By VC. That's all there is to it."

Again I scanned the heavy growth of trees, vines, and under-growth at the hub of the firefight. In the mountain region of north-western Pennsylvania where I come from, the forest grows thick and dense, although not as thick as the steamy jungle, and I was thinking of that forest back home when I suddenly realized what was missing. I pressed Thiel further.

"So Berkley was lying here, where this blood is. Reynolds reached him while you guys were firing at VC, who were firing at you — what? A thousand rounds fired all told, you said?"

"I don't know," Thiel said. "I don't know. I wasn't counting rounds fired. There were a lot of rounds fired. It could be a thou-sand. Twelve of them, five of us, each firing a couple or three clips; each clip twenty rounds. Maybe more, even."

"And you saw Reynolds dragging Berkley back, is that right? He was dragging him by his shirt? Where were you?"

"Somewhere right in here. I — Mr. Hatchett, I don't know how many firefights you've been in, but you lose all senses during one. Things get confusing. You are scared out of your wits. Your only thought is to lay down as much firepower as you can, as quick as you can. Understand? Your only intention is to get out of there. Alive. That's what I and the others were doing while Reynolds was dragging Berkley."

I figured the time might be ripe to give Thiel something to chew on, something to take back to his buddies, something to make him a little jumpy. I'd seen enough. Or rather, not enough, and that's what bothered me. "You're right," I said. "I've never been in a firefight like this. But there's something that isn't quite right here."

"What's not quite right here?" Thiel's voice rose in impatience and anger and disbelief. "What's not right here, Mr. Hatchett? Berkley was lying right there. Look at his blood. You found some shell casings. What's not right? Are the trees not growing right? That path not right? What's not right?"

I leveled a look at him to let him know I was dead serious about what I was about to tell him. "For a small area of thick jungle where a thousand rounds, maybe more, maybe less, were fired, I find it odd that there's not one tree scarred, not one branch nicked or broken by a bullet, not one leaf stripped. Could you tell me, Thiel, how a thousand rounds could be fired through this thick growth in this small area and not *one* of them hit so much as a twig? What kind of bullets were you and the VC using anyway?"

Thiel stared at me for several moments, mouth agape, face flushed a bit, maybe from the heat. His eyes skipped over the nearby branches. The corners of his mouth twitched nervously. Then he put his head back on his knees. "I don't know," he said. "I don't know."

I turned to Mitch and the MPs. "Let's head back," I said. "Tomorrow afternoon we'll pay a visit to that village."

"I suppose you're going to want me to go with you then, too," Thiel said, rising to his feet, dusting himself off.

"No," I said. "We'll go alone from here on out."

The birthday party that evening in Military Intelligence's company area was in full swing by the time I arrived, after making a call to the CID in base camp to set things in motion there.

Because part of MI's job was to interrogate POWs and it was part of the MPs' job to guard POWs, MI and MP units were often set up right next to each other. The small detachment of intelligence personnel on LZ Victoria included birthday boy Tom Fingers, the commanding officer Mr. Sommers, and three others. These men, as well as Mitch and two MPs, sat in lawn chairs outside MI's command tent drinking beer. Tom Fingers was well into his cups by the time I got there.

There were times in Vietnam when you'd never know a war was going on, and this was one of those times: a bunch of guys off duty, sitting around in the cooling evening under a silver sky, drinking beer, joking, and barbecuing ham steaks.

"Mitch tells me you're interested in Bravo 457," Mr. Sommers said after I'd gotten comfortable in a lawn chair, beer in hand.

"Bravo 457?"

"That's what we call that village you're going to tomorrow. It's got a name, but it's easier to refer to it as Bravo 457."

"You're familiar with it, then?" I said.

Sommers, a recent law school graduate before being drafted into the army, still had a boyish, preppy look to him even in his jungle fatigues and short GI haircut. Like Mitch and me, he wore no rank insignia, and I guessed he was either a lieutenant or, like me, a warrant officer.

He stirred in his lawn chair, crossing a leg. "We had a great informant in Bravo 457. We'd pop in from time to time, talk with the villagers — individually, of course, so that no one else in the village would know who was passing us info about VC or NVA movement through the area. Most of the population — women, old men, and children — aren't very reliable and are uncooperative, but we managed to find one good one there. Well, he used to be reliable, anyway."

"The others are VC sympathizers?"

Sommers scrunched his face.

"Hard to tell. They could be sympathizers; they could be VC. Could be, too, they just don't want to be involved with us or the VC. They like our money, mind you, but all in all I get the impression they want to be left alone. What's your interest in the village, Hatch?"

"I want to look around. I want to see if it's the kind of place a guy could kick back in, you know, relax a bit, maybe take his shirt off."

"I'm not sure I understand that, but I'm thinking, if you don't mind, me, Fingers, and one other, plus our interpreter, will tag along. It's been a while since we've been out there, and I'm getting a little worried about our boy."

"Oh?"

"The last couple of months or so he's been inaccurate in his information. It used to be that we could bank on it. At least, we've dished out a lot of money for information. But lately we'll have reports of VC movement along a trail that leads into the village, yet our informant will tell us there've been no VC through. I'm fearing he may have been turned. We haven't used him in a while."

"Is your other source reliable, you think?" I asked.

"It better be. It's an American infantry unit. They send recons out whenever we request it through brigade."

"You mean units like the 2/11th infantry?"

"I can't tell you that. But that might be close. Do you mind if we go in with you tomorrow?"

"I wouldn't mind at all," I said. "I'd welcome it."

Sommers tipped his beer can my way. "Excellent. If you want information about anything in the village without really asking it, I think you'll find Mr. Fingers has some special talents."

I looked over at Fingers, who was staggering to the beer cooler. Merely standing up seemed to be giving him some difficulty, so it was hard to imagine what his special talents might be.

"We'll drive out tomorrow after lunch," Sommers said.

"I'd prefer to walk if you don't mind. There's a path from the perimeter leading into the village that I want to look at, too."

Sommers gulped down the last of his beer and watched as Fingers came toward him carrying full cans of beer for the rest of us. "Walk, huh? We can do that. We can walk, can't we, Fingers?"

Fingers swayed. "Just barely, sir," he slurred. "Just barely."

The trail to the village offered nothing unusual. It wasn't unlike the trail we'd been on the day before, well traveled and wide, except this one seemed to go downhill more.

It was midafternoon by the time we reached the village. Sommers convinced me that taking a full contingent of MPs with us might be unwise. It was intimidating to the villagers, he said. But fear not, he added, he always had a platoon or two of infantry positioned about a mile down the road toward Phu Bien, just in case we should run into problems. They could be there in a couple of minutes if we needed them.

Only a half dozen ramshackle huts made up the back-jungle village. Most stood in a row, but one hut was built back a bit near the rim of the jungle. The houses were constructed from large pieces of broken and splintered plywood, misshapen tin, thick corrugated cardboard, and whatever else could be salvaged out of American garbage dumps. The air was choked with gray woodsmoke from cookfires, and a strong stench — a thick, musty, pungent odor of animal and human feces, garbage, and unbathed people — burned my nostrils.

About two dozen peasants occupied the village, and they hardly lifted their heads when we emerged from the trail and stepped into the clearing the village occupied.

Of the half dozen huts, the one sitting by itself immediately sparked my curiosity. It looked recently built, yet there was no sign of life around it. Because it was erected from what appeared to be new sheets of plywood, it seemed too new, too well built, as if it didn't belong there.

And of the couple of dozen old men and women stooped over cookfires or standing in the open doorways of their huts, some clutching small children, the frail old woman sobbing with soul-deep, agonizing cries was the hardest to ignore.

She wailed in long, high-pitched sounds to no one as she squatted in the doorway grasping her midsection with one hand, the other hand flailing limply in front of her, her bony fingers clawing air as if she was trying to grab handfuls of something that wasn't there.

When the six of us walked into the village, the crying old woman for some reason picked me as the focus of her attention, or at least it seemed that way. She'd wail mournfully and claw the air, then raise her head, wipe her tearstained face with a dirty sleeve, and watch me for a moment or two before breaking into a renewed burst of sorrow. Then she'd watch me some more. She seemed to be interested in no one but me as Mitch and I moved toward the farthest hut.

Mr. Sommers, the interpreter, and another MI personnel talked with an old man off to the side out of hearing of the others. Fingers more or less meandered around the village grounds looking like he was lost and didn't know what to do about it. I was guessing he was hung over from the night before and still groggy. He'd been pretty quiet on the long walk out, sweating profusely.

Mitch and I stood outside the door of the new hut. The plywood was American, and it *was* almost brand-new, not the kind you'd pull from a dump. The door was closed but not locked, so I pushed it partly open with my foot. Inside I could see a large front room with a dirt floor and a long plywood counter running along one wall. On the opposite side were two chairs and a small table. Two doors led to other rooms built behind the main room. I saw no cooking utensils, no personal objects, no religious statues, no mats for sitting on the floor, no dining area, nothing domestic. I got the impression the hut I was looking into wasn't someone's living quarters but a place of business — a new barroom and whorehouse like the many used in Phu Bien.

When I glanced over my shoulder across the village grounds through the thin, gray wisps of woodsmoke, I was surprised to see Sommers and the interpreter walking towards us, apparently already done with their many interviews. Sommers wiped his hot brow with his sleeve, looking very glum, and stole a look at the old woman, who was still studying me, craning her neck to see what I was doing, and still crying.

When I stepped into the hut, the door didn't open all the way, so I looked to see what might be holding it. Fresh dirt was sprinkled heavily along the floor directly behind it. I pushed harder, scraping the dirt back until the door opened wide.

Inside, I looked behind the counter, where I found a row of washed glasses, an open box of cocktail stirrers, and a container that still had water in it from melted ice, but no booze. Two kerosene lamps were also behind the bar.

I made my way to the two back rooms, but by this time I was pretty sure I knew what I'd find in each room — beds.

Sure enough, each room had two wooden beds built against opposite walls. A thin mattress, a dingy sheet, and a small pillow made up the bedding for each. A curtain fabricated from a blanket hung on a wire so it could be drawn in front of each bed for privacy. A small nightstand held a metal washbasin with a rag and towel for cleaning up, and hooks for hanging clothes were nailed into the walls. It wasn't hard to visualize a jungle fatigue shirt hanging from one of those hooks.

I checked all the rooms for anything to indicate that American soldiers had been there — cigarette butts, discarded clothing, empty food containers, beer cans, American magazines — but I saw nothing. The place was empty except for the bar supplies and the sparse furnishings.

I stepped from the coolness of the hut into the bright sunlight, where I almost knocked down an old man jabbering Vietnamese to MI's interpreter. Sommers and Tom Fingers stood nearby, listening. I was surprised when the interpreter said to me, "He wants to talk to you. He wants to talk with CID."

"He does?" I was amazed the old man knew the difference between Mr. Sommers and his MI group and the CID. But then I remembered that the old woman had also picked me out of the group. I looked over at her. Still squatting, she'd stopped crying and was watching us.

"How does he know who I am?" I asked the interpreter.

He put the question to the old man, who gave a quick reply. The interpreter told me, "He say Mr. Tiger tell him."

"Whooooa, stop right there," Sommers exclaimed suddenly, reaching over and jerking me by the shoulder. He led me with Tom Fingers and Mitch off to the side, out of earshot of the villagers. The interpreter stayed with the old man. The old woman watched our little conference. "You know who Tiger is?" Sommers asked.

I shook my head. "I'm still trying to figure out how the old man knew who *I* was."

"They all know who you are," Fingers said. "And why you're here."

I got the immediate impression there were things going on around me I didn't know about, and I was beginning to feel left out. "How do you know that?"

Sommers explained. "I told you Fingers has some special talents. One of them is that he speaks fluent Vietnamese. His job on these little outings is to meander around the village while we're interviewing villagers. You'd be surprised what folks say to each other when they think someone can't understand them. Not even our interpreter knows that Fingers knows their language. We've picked up a lot of useful information that way."

I was gaining new respect for Tom Fingers. "What did you hear about me?" I asked him.

"That they know you're CID here to look into the death of an American soldier killed in this village."

"Up until now I wasn't sure it did happen here. Did anyone say it actually occurred here? Did anyone see it happen?" Oh, hope against hope.

"No. Just that you knew it did."

I didn't know any such thing, but it was looking more and more promising. "Thiel," I said mostly to myself. "He told the others I was coming out here. He's the only one who could have. And they told — so, who is Mr. Tiger?" I directed this at Sommers.

"Bigtime. Bigtime VC. At least so we've always suspected. Tiger's his nickname. He's a successful Vietnamese businessman, something of a hometown hero in Phu Bien. And if what we know is true, he is very high up in the Vietcong organization. He's the enemy, Hatch. Trust me."

"Do these villagers know Tiger is VC?" I asked.

"Probably not," Sommers said. "To them he's a businessman, a countryman, a hero, a source of income, too, probably. He would not announce to these villagers he was VC any more than he'd tell us. But this is the first I've heard of his being involved in anything out here. Knowing what we know now, though, it fits in."

"What do you mean?"

"Our informant is dead, Hatch. The kid was dragged off by the VC a few nights ago and killed, hacked to death. That's his mother over there crying her heart out, poor soul."

I glanced back at the woman and saw she was gone, probably into her hut.

"Her parents were killed by the French when they were here fighting this same war. Her husband was killed either by Americans or VC during the Tet offensive when the VC tried to overrun Phu Bien. Caught in the cross fire. Just an innocent civilian in the wrong place at the wrong time. And now her son is killed by the VC. Would you care to venture a guess at whose side she might be on?"

"No one's, I would imagine," I said.

"Exactly," Sommers said.

"I've got to find out what this old man knows."

"Be careful. Pretend you know nothing about Tiger. He's just a businessman. We want to keep it that way. And the information is probably going to cost you. That's why he came to you."

"How much?"

"Depends on how hungry he is. If you need money, I have some here." Sommers pulled his wallet out and stuffed a hundred piasters into my hand. "Try not to pay any more than that. That's probably six months' wages for this guy."

At first I was hesitant about paying for information, paying a possible witness for his testimony. MI could get away with that; they could use bought info. I couldn't. On the other hand, if he could give me something concrete — names, dates, or perhaps he was an actual eyewitness — I could go from there. I couldn't pass it up. I'd be further ahead with purchased information I couldn't use than without it. It sure beat tromping around in the jungle looking under leaves for leads.

Turned out the information wasn't all that good. Not totally bad, mind you, but he wouldn't be a star witness in any court-martial, that was for sure.

The old man was smoking something in a pipe that smelled like oily rags burning, and he had his own particular air about him that made me stand back a ways. He folded the money I'd given him, and through the interpreter he said, "The Americans come here at night sometimes."

"How many? And always at night?" I spoke through the interpreter but not to him, preferring to watch the old man.

He held up six fingers to the interpreter and nodded. "Always at night," the interpreter said. "Usually about six of them come in from the jungle down that path we used."

The old man began to jabber in Vietnamese, a longwinded account of something. I could only wait until he was done.

Finally the interpreter said, "He say they come here at night and stay with the prostitutes Mr. Tiger brings for them in his jeep. Mr. Tiger, he leaves. The soldiers are not here every night, but they stay all night to just before dawn. Then Mr. Tiger come back and pick up girls and take them to Phu Bien."

"Ask him what happened the night someone was shot here. When did it happen? Did he see it? Ask him like that, in those words."

It seemed like forever before the interpreter said, "He say last week it happened, but he did not see. He was in his house when shots were fired in Mr. Tiger's house, where the Americans and the Vietnamese prostitutes were. He say maybe five or six shots he heard. Not all at once. Then the soldiers ran out carrying another soldier, running down the path into the jungle."

"Ask him if he would recognize any of the men if he were to see them today. Were they white soldiers or black soldiers?"

A moment later the interpreter said, "He say he does not recognize them because it is always dark and he is always in his house. He does not know."

I pointed at my shoulder and my 6th Division patch sewn there.

"Ask him, did they wear one of these?" There were hundreds of units in the area, and I was hoping to pin it down as close to the 2/11th as I could. But before his answer could be translated, the old man shook his head no, so I knew he'd seen no unit patches either.

"What else can he tell me about what happened that night?"

Vietnamese was exchanged between the interpreter and the peasant. The old man shrugged. Then the interpreter said, "He does not know any more than what he has said."

"Just that he heard several shots last week in the hut and the GIs came running out carrying a body and the GIs come here always at night but not every night, and Mr. Tiger provides the entertainment?"

"That is correct."

A good interpreter not only translates but also is not afraid to use his own insights into the people he is speaking with, so I asked, "Do you believe him?"

"Yes. He is telling the truth, I think."

"Ask him one more thing. Ask when Tiger told him about me, and what did he say?"

The question was put to the old man.

"He say Mr. Tiger drive his jeep from Phu Bien to the village this morning. This man help Mr. Tiger load boxes from the hut to his jeep. He does not know what was in the boxes, but they were very heavy. Mr. Tiger tell him he must get them out because a very tall American is coming today and will be asking questions about what happened here. Mr. Tiger say he does not want to talk with the American CID soldier."

"How many boxes? How big?"

A few moments later, "He say maybe ten and so large enough that they almost did not all fit in the jeep."

"Do the VC ever come here?"

"Hey, Hatch," Sommers interjected sternly. "Watch it. You're in my territory."

"Sorry," I said, "just that one last question."

The MI interpreter glanced at Sommers to see if he should ask the question or not. Sommers nodded to go ahead. "Just that one," Sommers told his interpreter.

"He say," the interpreter said after putting the question to the old man, "he does not think the VC come here." The interpreter looked skyward, adjusted his steel pot on his head, added as an aside, "But he is lying about that, Mr. Hatchett."

Before we left the village, I had MI's interpreter address the entire village, asking if any of the villagers had any information regarding the shooting that took place in their midst the week before. All I got in response were blank, hollow looks and stares. As we left, I glanced back at the old woman. She sat squatting outside her hut again, rocking slowly on her haunches, her arms folded around her bony knees, her scraggly black hair hanging down her face, her dead, unblinking eyes following my every step until we were out of sight.

Sommers, Mitch, and I lagged behind the others on the trail back to Victoria.

"I'd say the trip was fruitful for you," Sommers said.

"Oh yeah. If I believe the old man, I'm now sure something did happen, and I know where it happened. I just don't know why or who in particular did the shooting. My problem is, I've got to be able to place Reynolds and his patrol in that village that night. That's all there is to it. I've got to chip away at the wall of secrecy and complicity they've built around themselves. That isn't going to be easy, but I can use what I already know, and I'm hoping I can use Collins as a kind of battering ram."

"Collins?" Mitch asked. "The one on R&R?"

"I have him on ice right now. When I called the CID yesterday, I told them to pick up Collins the minute he stepped off the chopper back from R&R and to hold him at the MPs' in base camp and let him talk to no one. He's in for a real surprise. He doesn't have the slightest idea we even suspect something went on on that patrol. They'll fly him to Victoria when I'm ready for him. Maybe he'll talk."

"What do you think were in the boxes Tiger stuffed in his jeep?" Mitch asked. "If it were anything of value, why would he leave them in that village in the middle of the jungle?"

"My first thought was so the VC could pick them up; then I realized Tiger probably wouldn't risk the villagers' knowing he has VC connections. So more than likely he was storing them there, out of sight. I'm guessing it's military stuff."

"Why's that?" Mitch asked.

"Remember when we heard Captain Boggs complaining that

they were missing a lot of items, food, starlight scopes, radios, and God only knows what else? I want to check with him later to see how his inventory came out finally."

"Ah, Jesus, whether Tiger's storing it or passing it out to VC, either way the VC eventually will end up with whatever it is," Sommers said. "You're sure it's military materiel?"

"It's a very good chance. If it *is* happening, Reynolds and the boys are in way over their heads and don't even know it. They probably think Tiger is just another man out to make a buck off the black market. They could be selling him military stuff out here in the village, or maybe in Phu Bien. Things bought cheap at the PX in the MACV compound in Phu Bien, too, probably. The only limit over here is your own imagination when it comes to stealing and selling something."

"You think they're getting free use of the girls as payment?" Mitch asked.

"I hope they're getting more than that. Those girls would be nothing more than openers for a guy like Tiger. He'll keep asking for more and more, sucking the men deeper into his scheme. After a while it gets so bad, you can't refuse."

"That jibes with Willard's saying Berkley told him that they were up to no good again and that it was getting worse."

"Right-o. They may have gone from bringing girls onto Victoria to meeting some out here and then on to selling stuff to Tiger. They could have met Tiger sometime while they were running around in Phu Bien. I think that's where those starlight scopes are. The VC have them now and are using them on us if Tiger is a high-level VC. I don't know what else is going to turn up missing in Boggs's inventory, but no one loses *two* starlight scopes. They probably stole them right under the nose of a very inattentive Lieutenant Macy."

"We don't know for sure it was military equipment Tiger got out of there," Mitch said.

"Well, whatever it was, he was not supposed to have it and took the stuff out of there in a hurry. He didn't want me seeing it. If it were just business or personal items, he'd know I'd have no interest in them, nor any authority to take them." We walked in silence along the path. "I've just had another horrible thought, though." What had suddenly occurred to me stopped me dead on the trail.

Sommers and Mitch stopped, too. "What?" Sommers asked.

"Your informant. You said lately he'd become unreliable. You were basing that on what the patrol of the 2/11th reported. Correct?"

Sommers nodded. "We were more or less comparing reports, yes. We were testing his reliability. If he proved out, we could use him elsewhere, pay him more. I suppose we're not much unlike Tiger in that respect."

"Well, try this on for size. There's a very good chance the patrol hasn't been going out to monitor movement. They've been at the village every night they were out. They might have sent one man down the path to keep watch for any VC, but that would be it. Of course, if Tiger is as high up as you say and the patrol was dealing in stolen military goods, Tiger would make sure his little operation wasn't interrupted by a VC patrol wandering in. It's the VC he's buying the stuff for."

Mitch said, "So the patrol is in no real danger, even though they don't know it."

"That's right. Tiger would see to that. But these guys have to write a report when they come in. If they aren't where they're supposed to be, how would they know if there was any movement along that trail? They don't. So they make up something for a report. What I'm saying is, your informant might not have been wrong at all. Probably hadn't been turned. It makes sense because if he did turn to the VC, why'd the VC kill him?"

"I wonder why my informant never told me this was going on. He wouldn't necessarily know who the patrol was or what their job was, and they wouldn't know him, but he should have mentioned these guys staying all night in the village."

"Did you ever ask him?" I said.

Sommers grunted no and continued down the path. "I would never have thought to," he said.

"Could be he didn't want to cross Tiger in what he might have seen simply as just another black-market operation, the kind run all over Vietnam. Could be *he* was getting money from Tiger, too. He wouldn't know Tiger is VC any more than Reynolds does. We're dealing with a lot of unreliables here."

"Whatever," Sommers said. "Now I'll have to go through all the patrol's reports and consider them tainted. Two weeks ago they reported that a company-sized unit of VC passed through the area down that trail. What you're saying is, that could be a boldfaced lie."

"What was your informant's report on that?"

"I don't know. By that time I'd stopped talking with him, figuring he'd been turned."

"I want these guys," I said to Mitch. "I've got a plan that will require a little theatrics from you. Maybe it'll shake something loose and one of those buzzards will start talking."

The Wall

As it turned out, wanting them and getting them were miles apart, theatrics or no theatrics, plan or no plan.

Once back on Victoria, my first step was to revisit Captain Boggs to find out what had turned up missing from the 2/11th's inventory. I found him in the mess hall, clipboard in hand. He was counting something on the floor.

"This is a good one," he said. "I have a requisition form here signed months ago by Lieutenant Macy for a hundred sheets of plywood and picked up at supply by Sergeant Reynolds. It's noted on the form that the plywood was to be used to replace rotting plywood on the floor of the mess tent. Not only do I not see any new plywood on this floor, but that many sheets is enough to cover this entire mess tent three times. That's what caught my attention. I've done carpentry work back in the world. A hundred sheets is thirty-two hundred square feet."

I didn't bother telling him I knew where his plywood was. "What else seems to be missing?" I asked.

He glanced down at his clipboard. "Let's see here: two radios, two starlight scopes, untold cases of Lerps, five jeep tires. I think, but I'm not sure yet, two M-79 grenade launchers plus a case each of tear gas, high explosive, and shotgun rounds for the grenade launchers. The rounds would be hard to trace, but Reynolds said the M-79s were destroyed in a firefight and he thought Lieutenant Macy just forgot to report them destroyed as he should have.

"We're supposed to have an extra medium-sized tent around here, too, but I don't see it. Reynolds said he saw Macy doing something with it one day. We've got a new generator. I don't see that the old one was ever returned, yet it's nowhere around here. And here's another, a good one: our potable-water trailer was stolen. According to Reynolds, an infantry unit that was pulling out sneaked in, hooked up to it, and stole it. The theft supposedly was reported to the MPs."

"I'll check it out," I told Boggs. "Mitch would have a copy of the report." I had a feeling the report would be there. That's not to say the water trailer was actually stolen by another unit, though.

"By the looks of this, and I'm sure there'll be more, I'm lucky I've got a chair to sit in." Boggs slapped the clipboard hard against his leg. "What the hell was Macy doing all this time?"

It hadn't escaped me that Sergeant Reynolds's name seemed to pop up an awful lot. If Reynolds was stealing and then black-marketing the stuff, he was going about it well, mixing it up and always having a good reason for things being missing. When he couldn't come up with one, he blamed Lieutenant Macy, who was now half a world away.

"Did any of those men I talked to in your tent go into Phu Bien after I brought Thiel back yesterday?" I asked. I was hoping to discover who had tipped off Mr. Tiger and sent him scurrying out to the village.

Captain Boggs thought for a moment. "Thiel did. He drove in an hour or so after you brought him back. He said Sergeant Reynolds told him to pick up the laundry in Phu Bien."

"Did you hear Reynolds tell him that?"

"No. I just gave Thiel permission. I was too busy counting up everything we don't have. I have to do it because apparently Reynolds can't count very well. His inventory and mine aren't anywhere near close. Especially when it comes to ammo."

The next day I had them separated and under guard.

Reynolds was put in the provost marshal's office. Watson was in the MPs' commanding officer's tent. Jefferson was being watched in Mitch's hooch. Thiel got the empty POW compound. I was saving MI's command tent for when it was time for Mitch to bring Collins in from the chopper pad. Mitch knew the part he had to play, and he had what he needed with him.

I went from tent to tent hitting each soldier with everything I had: Willard's conversation with Berkley the morning before he was killed; Berkley's jungle fatigue shirt; the lack of any sign of a firefight where they'd said they had one; the old man in the village telling me of GIs being there; the gunshots in the hut and the body being carried out; the missing items from their compound — I listed them one by one; Mr. Tiger.

Even in the face of all that, they didn't budge. They didn't waver from their version of what had happened. Whenever I tried to get into particulars, like Berkley's shirt, they went vague. "Things were real confusing in the firefight." Or, "I wasn't watching." Or simply, "I don't know."

I concentrated on Thiel, hitting him hardest, but he had grown a little more sure of himself and more fortified. I hoped it was a false security.

"Come on, Thiel," I said to him. "I know what happened. Instead of being out on the trail where you were supposed to be, you guys were going to that village and meeting girls that Mr. Tiger brought out to you. You were doing this regularly. But something happened that night. Was there an argument? Was it that Berkley didn't like the increasing amount of stuff you were selling to Tiger? Who shot Berkley in that hut?"

Thiel sat there stone-faced.

"I don't know, Mr. Hatchett. I don't know where you got all that. Berkley was killed out on the trail where I showed you."

"Like hell he was, Thiel. He was shot in the hut, and you guys carried his body to that spot and then staged a fake firefight by firing into the air. You had to have some way to explain his death."

"You're not hanging nothing on me, Mr. Hatchett, simply because you think you've got to have someone," Thiel said. "All you have is suspicions and the word of an old man. I've never been in that village in my life that I remember. How much did you pay the old man? Did any of the other villagers verify it?"

I ducked out of the tent without answering that.

All the others were basically the same.

Jefferson: "The old man is probably VC. You ever think about that, Mr. Hatchett? He'd tell you just about anything. I may have been in that village once or twice, I don't know. I've been through a lot of villages."

Watson: "I don't know about the shirt. I didn't see it. Do you know for sure it wasn't unbuttoned? Maybe he was taking a breather when the VC saw him, and he'd unbuttoned his shirt to cool off."

Reynolds: "You think I stole all that stuff? Hell, the water trailer

should be or better be on a report right in this MP office somewhere. It was stolen by another unit. It happens all the time over
here, one unit stealing off another. The plywood was used for
something else, I think. I can't remember what Lieutenant Macy
did with it. I don't know about the shirt. I can't explain the shirt.
Maybe it was unbuttoned after all. I don't know any Tiger. There
are lots of tigers around. Did you know, Mr. Hatchett, this is the
area Teddy Roosevelt used to come to to hunt tigers? It wasn't
called Vietnam then. But I don't know a man named Tiger."

"I'll tell you where the plywood is," I countered. "It went to build
that hut."

"Prove it," Reynolds said confidently. He knew what I knew: the
plywood was untraceable, no numbers on it.

I ignored his brashness. "And I'll tell you about that shirt. Berkley's shirt was off when he was shot in the hut. He took it off,
undressing for one of the whores, and then something happened
and he was shot. Before you carried him out, you had to put his
shirt back on. But you forgot about the shirt needing bullet holes in
it to match the wounds. You couldn't know Pfc. Willard would pick
the shirt up. That's how it worked."

He stared straight ahead. "I've never been in that village. Never.
Never been any nearer to it than where those recon patrols took
us." A smart-aleck, cocky grin passed over his face; apparently he
sensed my frustration. He laced his fingers behind his head and
leaned back. "I found Berkley lying dead on the trail. Thiel told me
you found his blood there. Shell casings, too. Maybe I was wrong
about his shirt being buttoned. Maybe it *was* open. It gets —"

"I know, I know," I said. "It gets pretty confusing during a firefight."

"Right on, Mr. Hatchett."

I figured it was time to bring in Collins.

I had all the men brought to the PMO tent. I threw open the tent
flaps so they'd get a good look when Mitch pulled in with Collins in
the jeep.

Through the open flaps we watched Mitch lead Collins across the
MP area toward MI's areas. Mitch held a starlight scope, which
actually belonged to the MPs, and he was playing his role well.

Mitch made sure the group in the PMO tent got a good look at
the starlight scope. He waved it at Collins as if he were talking to
him about it.

"Good," I said to the group as they sat in the tent with their eyes glued on Mitch and Collins. "You see we have your friend," I told them. "I'll find out what he has to say. And it looks as if Mitch finally caught up with Tiger. Do you guys recognize what he's carrying?"

None of them spoke. Thiel lowered his head and put his hands over his face; I sensed a crack in the wall. Sergeant Reynolds tried to snicker, wanting to give the impression he was unconcerned, but it wasn't very convincing. Watson and Jefferson continued staring wide-eyed past the tent flap but saying nothing.

I turned to leave the PMO. Even if Mitch's theatrics didn't get to them, I still had the possibility Collins would talk, so I was feeling confident, very confident, when I said, "I'm going to leave you guys in here alone. I'm going to give you one more chance to come clean on this. I'm going to give you a chance while I see what Collins has to say. You guys discuss among yourselves what you want to do." I motioned for the MP in the tent to leave and went to see Collins.

Collins was worse than the others; not quite as cocky as Reynolds but just as firm in his story.

I knew why they were corroborating each other's lies.

This was a group of men, like many infantry units, whose lives often depended on the other guy's being dependable, being there for him in the worst situation a man can find himself in, the very hot, frantic, life-and-death experience of a firefight. Who lived, slept, ate, talked about families and futures together; shared laughs and heartaches with each other. They lived and died together. To lie for one another was nothing.

Collins's version was an echo of what the others had said: Berkley was killed on the trail by VC. He didn't know about a shirt or even anything about Reynolds's dragging Berkley out of there. He was too busy off to the side firing at the VC. Things get pretty confusing, he said. (Oh, how I hated hearing that again and again, however true it was.) He didn't think he'd ever been to the village; knew no one named Tiger; knew nothing about selling anything to anyone. Had no idea, in fact, why Berkley might think one of them wanted him dead. Berkley was kind of a weird farmboy anyway, Collins stated.

While I escorted him to the PMO tent to join the others, I could feel my confidence ebbing. For a brief moment I began to wonder if maybe Berkley *had* been killed by the VC in just the way they said. But then, I believed the old man. I'd seen the spot Berkley was supposedly killed in and had my doubts about that. I had Willard's statement, and I had the shirt. But I wasn't anywhere near as sure of myself as I had been when I'd first brought them to the MP area. At this point I sensed that instead of my chipping away at them they were chipping away at me, at my confidence and determination; the sledge hammer was being weakened by the sheer heft of the wall.

What I lacked was any physical evidence, or even a reliable statement, to verify my suspicions. Without either I couldn't place them in that village, let alone connect them to what happened there.

When Collins entered the tent, he winked at Reynolds. Reynolds gave him a slight nod in response.

"Well, Mr. Hatchett," Reynolds said, "if you're about done with us, I'd like to get back to our area. I've got to start packing. I'm due to go back to base camp tomorrow to begin being processed out of this country."

"None of you are going anywhere," I said sharply. Nothing I'd said all day had the effect that telling them that did. Reynolds frowned.

"What do you mean?" Thiel asked.

"I mean you all are going to be confined to quarters until this investigation is over. No one's going anywhere. This isn't the end of it." I bent down and got right in Reynolds's face. "And I'll put a stop on your orders for Fort Dix, sergeant."

"You can do that?" His lower lip twitched spasmodically.

"Not only can I, I already have." I hadn't actually done it, but I *could* do it and I intended to make it my first order of business once I got to base camp.

"How long will the investigation take?" Thiel asked. "I'm due to be discharged from the army within the month, maybe earlier if I get an early out."

"How long?" I said. "As long as it takes. And sometimes I move real slow. If I were you, I wouldn't be planning any big coming home party just yet."

Thiel swore out loud. "Jesus," he said.

The first winning blow I'd scored all day.

"And if your investigation turns up nothing?" Sergeant Reynolds asked. "Then we can go home?"

"Then you can go home. But not until I'm satisfied, and I warn you, I'm not easily satisfied."

The telephone rang, and an MP picked it up. "He's right here," the MP said and handed me the phone. "One of the MPs guarding the front gate wants to talk with you."

From the other end I heard, "Mr. Hatchett, this is Sp/4 Jones out at the main gate. I have a female Vietnamese civilian who insists on talking with you. She doesn't speak English, so bring an interpreter. Luckily a Special Forces jeep was going through, and one of the Green Berets translated for us. She says she wants to talk about some GI being killed by another GI in a village somewhere. She says she was working in the hut when it happened. She says she works for someone named Tiger."

I could not believe what I was hearing. One of the prostitutes, I thought. That was going to be my next step, to find them and question them. They were the only other ones in the hut when Berkley was killed, and they wouldn't have the allegiance to the patrol that the men had for each other. What a lucky break, I thought. A softhearted whore.

"I'll be right out," I told the MP. "Make her comfortable. Treat her like a lady. Don't try anything with her no matter how good-looking she is." Many of the Vietnamese women were very good-looking, and I figured that a man of Tiger's stature would only employ top-of-the-line girls. Last thing I needed was a sex-starved MP making unwanted advances on what I hoped would be my top-of-the-line witness.

The MP snickered. "You don't have to worry about that, Mr. Hatchett," he said.

I sent an MP to MI to get their interpreter and told the group in the PMO, "Don't go anywhere just yet. It seems one of your girl-friends has something to say."

By the stunned, ashen looks that spread over their faces, I assumed I'd scored another blow. For me, things were beginning to brighten suddenly. But when I got to the main gate, it was my turn to be stunned.

The female Vietnamese waiting for me was not a young, good-looking prostitute. It was the old woman who'd been crying in the village, the mother of Sommers's dead informant.

A Mother's Story

"Tell her I can't pay her. Tell her it isn't that I don't want to, I just can't."

The interpreter spoke to the woman as we drove slowly back to the PMO. I wanted to give her time to tell me what she knew before we stood face to face with the patrol.

"She say she does not want to be paid."

I stole a sidelong glance at the somber old woman in the passenger seat of the jeep.

For warmth against the cool evening she wore a thin shawl draped over her bony shoulders and a faded, thin, print blouse that looked like it hadn't been washed in weeks. She had on typical black silk pajama bottoms and a cone-shaped straw hat. She held onto the hat to keep it from being blown away by the air of the moving jeep rushing back in her face. Her skin had a dark yellow tint to it and was cracked and wrinkled like old, worn, dirty leather.

The interpreter was in the back, leaning over her shoulder.

"Ask her what she saw in the hut. Why was she in the hut?"

"She say," said the interpreter, "sometimes she work for Mr. Tiger. She pour drinks for the prostitutes and the American soldiers sometimes; sometimes she bring them what they ask for. Every morning she clean the hut when they are all gone."

"What happened the night the soldier was shot?"

"She say they argue loud. She does not understand what they argue about. But she thinks they had too much to drink. And she see them smoke some, ah, some pot. How you say? Marijuana?"

"Okay, go on."

"She say the one GI who got killed, he come out of the room where he was with the prostitute, and he argue with another GI and push him hard against the wall. Then the GI who was pushed, he point his rifle at him and he shoot him."

"Would she recognize the man who did the shooting?"

"She say each one shoot the American soldier after he was shot the first time. She would recognize them all. She say also she think the shot GI was dead because she go to him and she grab his hand and she can feel the life leave him then. They push her aside, and each soldier shoot the dead American again."

"What were the others doing during all this?"

"She say they looked very scared, and they argue some more. Maybe, she think, they do not like to shoot the dead man some more. But they do. Then they talk and argue some more. Then someone go get the dead GI's shirt, and they put it on him and carry him out of the village."

"So one man shot him and then the others went up and put a bullet in him? Where'd they shoot him, in what part of his body?"

The interpreter said, "Here." He motioned to his upper torso.

I pulled the jeep to a stop. "Was Mr. Tiger there when the man was killed?"

"She say no. She say Mr. Tiger always there when they arrive at the village, but Mr. Tiger, he always leave. He come back the next day and take the girls to Phu Bien."

"Does she know the girls, their names, where they live?"

"Oh yes. She know the girls."

This Vietnamese woman might make an iffy witness, but if the prostitutes verified her account, that could be testimony weighty enough to place the patrol in the village.

"What did she do after they left?"

The interpreter touched her shoulder, asking the question. "She say she clean up the hut and she go get some dirt and spread the dirt on the large amounts of blood from the GI bleeding on the floor so the flies do not come around."

"Where was the GI lying when he fell bleeding?"

"She say right behind the door."

"And that's where she spread the dirt?"

"Yes, that is correct, Mr. Hatchett. She did not want the flies to drink the blood."

I could have kissed that old lady. She knew where on his body Berkley was shot, and she knew about the dirt spread on the floor. I was beginning to believe her.

"Ask her why she didn't tell me this when we were in the village?" There was still the possibility that she knew the old man had made money with his story and saw an opportunity to make some, too. Maybe she'd hit me up later. There was also the possibility she was telling me her story because she was a VC sympathizer bent on getting some GIs into trouble. Being a VC sympathizer would most certainly call her testimony into question. But Sommers didn't seem to think that was the case with her, and he knew her tragic history better than I.

"She say she did not say anything because she did not want to at first. Then she changed her mind this morning after she saw you in the village. She say she came here because she does not want the others in the village to know she talk with the American CID soldier."

I jammed the jeep in gear and drove on. "Tell her I want her to identify the men who were in the hut that night. The one who first shot the GI and then the others."

She nodded once, agreeing.

Each man's putting a bullet into Berkley certainly explained why the patrol had been lying for each other. They all had a hand in Berkley's death.

"And tell her I'm very sorry about the death of her son."

The interpreter translated as we stepped from the jeep in the MP area. She responded by glaring at me across the jeep, her hollow black eyes unflinching and angry, almost accusing, like she thought I was insincere in my condolences, or worse, she was blaming me, a U.S. soldier, for her son's death. She rattled off a few terse, angry Vietnamese sentences.

The interpreter said, "She say how can you be sorry about his death? The VC kill him and she does not like the VC, but if there was no Americans, there would be no one for the VC to fight. No war. And her son would be alive." The interpreter shrugged as if it made perfect sense to him, too.

So it really made little difference to her whose side I was on. She didn't like us any more than she liked the VC. We were fighting for some cause, however vague it was sometimes to us, but it was not *her* cause. In her mind all of us had a hand on the machete that hacked her son to pieces out in the jungle. We all had a hand in killing her husband in Phu Bien and maybe even her parents.

As we walked to the tent, I was bothered by why she'd sought me out with her story. Why was she getting involved?

I don't believe I've ever seen so many dumbfounded expressions on so many men as there were on the faces of the five from the 2/11th when I escorted the old woman into the PMO tent.

Mouths dropped open as if they had weights tied to their chins. They sat in folding chairs staring at her, their faces awash with disbelief. One of them swore under his breath. They all fidgeted nervously in their seats. Someone said, "Oh, God."

None of them rose, so I said, "Have you men forgotten military training? Stand up when a lady enters a room."

"A lady?" Sergeant Reynolds laughed harshly. He was the only one who didn't rise. "That old hag? I'm not standing up for *her*."

Behind Reynolds stood a black MP who was as big as a mountain. I told him, "Sergeant Reynolds is having difficulty standing up. Would you help him?"

"Gladly," the MP said.

He grabbed Reynolds's shoulder with a huge paw and a vise-like grip and jerked him to his feet in one swift motion.

"Get your hands off me, nigger," Reynolds shouted angrily.

The black MP released his grip when he had Reynolds on his feet. With a slight smile he shrugged the slur off and stepped back. He'd been called that before, I imagined, busting up barroom brawls. It was part of his MP training — to learn you're going to take insults from GIs, racial insults included. It was Jefferson who surprised me. The black infantryman shot a hot, angry look at Reynolds, and I sensed that the mere presence of the old woman was having a crumbling effect already. They were already coming apart. Suddenly they all seemed very, very uneasy; once cocky and sure of themselves, they were now angry, feeling pinched. And she hadn't even begun to point fingers yet.

"Ask her," I said to the interpreter, "if she recognizes any of these men."

The old woman gave them a casual glance and replied.

"She say all of them plus the dead GI come many nights to the village. These men were the ones who were in the hut when the GI was killed. She has seen them all there many times."

"Who shot the GI the first time?"

No one as much as twitched for the longest moment.

Finally, "She say that one get pushed and he shoot the one who push him." The interpreter pointed at Sergeant Reynolds.

"That lying gook!" Reynolds shouted. "She's VC. I've always thought she was a VC."

I looked at the big black MP again. "It seems Sergeant Reynolds is having his usual problems keeping his smart mouth shut. If he speaks out of turn again, cuff him and stuff him with something."

"Will do," the MP smiled.

Back to the interpreter. "And the others?"

He translated her reply. "She say, after Reynolds shoot the GI, this one," he pointed at Watson, "shoot him. Then that one," he indicated Collins, "then that one and that one." He pointed at Jefferson and Thiel in that order. Thiel had his face in his hands. The others, except Reynolds, looked at the ground. Reynolds was glaring at the old woman.

"Any smart remarks now, Sergeant Reynolds?" I asked.

"Oh? I'm allowed to speak now, am I? Well, let me tell you this. Are you going to take the word of that old lady against ours? I'm telling you she's VC. I've always thought that."

"How do you know her, Reynolds? You've already told me you've never been near her village. How could you suspect this woman of being a VC if you've never been there?"

"Shut up, Reynolds," Jefferson said. "He's right. You talk too much. And you definitely say the wrong things sometimes."

"Ask her if these men know Tiger."

The answer: "Of course they know Mr. Tiger. He bring the girls. This one," the interpreter pointed at Reynolds again, "she say he always have some drinks with Tiger, and they talk outside the hut before Mr. Tiger leave the GIs with the prostitutes. Sometimes he put some small things in Mr. Tiger's jeep that they carry with them when they come in from the jungle. Oh yes. They all know who Mr. Tiger is."

"What did he put in the jeep?"

The old woman shrugged as she answered the interpreter.

"She say she cannot see because she is always busy with the GIs and the prostitutes."

"How much did you pay her?" Sergeant Reynolds asked me.

I nodded to the interpreter to ask the question.

The interpreter said to Reynolds, "She say she does not want money. She was not paid. The American CID soldier does not give her any money."

"You're still taking the word of a gook peasant over us," Reynolds said, his anger rising. "She must want something. Ask her why's she doing this."

Now *that* was a question that concerned me. I'd read that a lawyer won't ask a question he doesn't already know the answer to. Right then I couldn't have agreed with that more. What if she replied, "Mr. Tiger tell me to." That would throw her reliability and thus her testimony right out the tent flap. But I thought she was acting on her own. And I was curious myself about why she'd offered to speak when she didn't even like us, when she blamed us, in part, for the death of her son. I told the interpreter to ask her, because I had to know.

There are things that are universal in this world, and facial expressions are one of them. Her face suddenly took on a contented, peaceful look, as if she had been waiting for the question and wanted very much to answer it.

She took a long, deep breath that led me to believe she was organizing her many thoughts. When she spoke, it was so rapid that the interpreter translated as she talked, as if he were she.

"She say, after he was shot, I held the GI's hand, like I told you, and he grip my hand and then I could feel the life leave him in that hut. I did not think much about it then. Only that he is very young. I have lost a husband and my parents. So what is it to me if this GI dies, too, I think.

"She say, then a few days later my son is killed by the VC. She say, now I have no one; no husband, no parents, no son. I am like a single cloud floating in the big sky."

"I wandered lonely as a cloud," I thought. She had never read Wordsworth, I was sure, but the best poetic images are also universal.

"She say, I spend my days crying for my son, and I think a lot about the dead GI and I wonder what the GI's mother will say in America when she learns her son is dead."

"Berkley's mother she's talking about?"

"That is correct," the interpreter said. "She say, I think about the GI's mother, and I think how sad she is going to be. Perhaps the GI's mother is farmer like myself, I think. Is her life hard, too? We are from different countries, and we are great distances apart and we do not know each other, but we are both mothers who have no sons now; hers killed by Americans, mine killed by Vietnamese. We have lost them in war. So for this we are near, too, I think. This is what I'm thinking while I mourn my son."

I interjected, "Tell her Berkley's mother is a farmer." I wasn't sure she was, but I wanted her to keep talking.

He told her, and the woman smiled a little smile.

"She say, I do not know about America. I am told it is very big. Very rich with big farms. I have seen pictures of these. I am a poor woman who has three cattle and some chickens. That is all I have now. But I am like the GI's mother because we are both mothers who have lost our sons. So I cry for my son and I cry for her son and I cry for the GI's mother, too."

Out of the corner of my eye I watched Thiel shake his head hard and then stand up and stare out the tent flap, listening to the old woman.

"I come to you and tell you all this about what I see in the hut and what I think," the interpreter said, "because I want someone to tell the GI's mother her son did not die alone. The GI's mother will want to know this. Tell her I held her son's hand when she could not. I was glad to do this for her because we are both mothers. He did not die alone."

Thiel was shaking his head harder and harder, and when he turned to face us, his eyes were moist.

"All that is pure hogwash, chickens and cows," Reynolds said. "It proves nothing. It's nothing but talk from a VC."

But the woman kept on talking.

The interpreter said, "She say, you should give this to the GI's mother. She will want to have it. She say, after these men ran out of the hut carrying the body, I found it on the floor of the hut near where the GI died and they put on his shirt."

The old woman reached into a tiny pocket in her shawl and held her open palm towards me.

The story she'd just related was an expression of universal motherhood, one mother feeling the need and loss of another, a wide ocean away. What she held in her small palm, however, was just then more vital to me than motherhood. It was the final link, the concrete piece of evidence I had sought that put the patrol in the village. Coupled with her testimony and the prostitutes' testimony when I located them, I now had the patrol cold.

It lay in her hand like a jewel glittering in the tropical sun that poured through the open tent flap: a new Zippo lighter engraved *Robert Berkley 2/11th Infantry 6th Infantry Division.*

"And she found this in that hut that night?"

"That is correct, Mr. Hatchett," the interpreter said.

I held up the lighter so they all could see it and announced, "I have an American GI who will swear at your courts-martial that Berkley was in possession of this lighter only a few hours before he went out on patrol with you guys. How could his lighter end up in that village that night unless you all were there and not out on the Ho Chi Minh Trail where you said you were?"

For the first time since I began interviewing this group they were speechless. All Reynolds could manage was a cold stare. Collins wiped his hands down over his face and pulled at his lower lip. Watson and Jefferson slouched in their chairs and scowled at their feet. Thiel shook his head faster and faster, looking at the lighter. "Ahhhh, man," he said.

And the wall came tumbling down.

The Letter

In the following days, Thiel was the most cooperative. The shooting had happened pretty much the way I'd figured.

Berkley, Thiel said, was becoming increasingly uncomfortable with what Reynolds was selling to Tiger. Berkley didn't mind the plywood, which they loaded into a truck and hauled into Phu Bien to give to Tiger there. He didn't mind the nonarmament items like cases of food. But when they began taking starlight scopes and M-79s and ammo on patrol with them to sell to Tiger in the village, that got to be too much.

And Tiger kept asking for more and bigger items and paying more, and when Reynolds said he thought he could get his hands on a few LAAWs — Light Anti-Armor Weapons, a kind of one-shot, throwaway bazooka used against tanks — Berkley issued his final complaint, which started the argument that got him killed.

Reynolds feared that Berkley would go to their new CO, Captain Boggs, and report everything that had been going on. It was Reynolds's idea that everyone should put a bullet in him so they would all have had a hand in it. Thiel said he had trouble with that, so he shot Berkley in the shoulder. He thought Berkley was already dead by then.

"We would contact Tiger in Phu Bien the moment we knew we'd be going on patrol," Thiel explained. "Tiger would bring the girls out that night."

There was only one big surprise for us, from Thiel.

Sommers was with me; he had a stack of the bogus intelligence reports the patrol had filed. "Here's one here — a whole company of VC passed along that trail, you reported," Sommers said sharply. He was not a happy camper. "I have to assume that that never happened, that none of these reports are accurate."

"Oh, the one on the company of VC is true," Thiel told him.

"You saw a company of VC pass through the village? An entire company? While you were in bed with whores? Come on, Thiel."

Thiel shook his head.

"We didn't see them. What happened was, a kid came to us when we first got into the village that night. I don't know who he was, just a kid who lived there. He was all excited about something, and he didn't speak English very well, but he was babbling about some VC. Sergeant Reynolds took him outside and talked to him, and when Reynolds came back into the hut, he was grinning, saying, 'Well, the kid gave us something we can put on our report for tonight. He told me he'd seen a company of VC going through a couple of nights ago. I paid him a few bucks for the info.'"

Sommers was simmering, his words precise and hot:

"That kid did not speak English. Who translated for Reynolds?"

Thiel thought a moment. "Tiger did."

Sommers spun around and left the tent shouting, "Tiger? You idiots. You got that kid, my informant, killed. Tiger is VC."

I realized then that the woman was right — that in fact there was an American hand on the machete the VC used to hack her son to death.

My two-page letter to Mrs. Berkley was almost complete. I had promised the old woman that I'd write to her, detailing everything the old woman had told us. It was the only thing she'd asked for. I offered to have it translated so she could read it, but she only wanted to get back to her village, back to her life.

I'd also promised the old woman that I'd send Mrs. Berkley the lighter when the trials were all over and the members of the patrol began serving hard time in Leavenworth. For the time being we needed it for evidence.

I was searching for some way to end the letter.

On my desk was a recent issue of *Stars and Stripes;* the newspaper's lead story was a report on the peace negotiations just beginning in Paris. I added to the letter, closing it out:

> In reading about Henry Kissinger and his entourage of diplomats and statesmen and politicians and generals currently beginning to ne-gotiate a peace with a similar group of men from North Vietnam, and how they say it'll probably take a year to reach an honorable agreement

that satisfies both sides, I'm given to wonder about some things. Can any peace be dishonorable? How many more will die while the negotiations plod along? In reviewing the entire incident involving the death of your son, I also wonder what would happen if the widows of soldiers and the mothers of men who have died on both sides sat down and talked peace. I feel they would cut right through the ideological barriers that so often bog peace processes down. Somehow, I think, they'd find an end to all this with haste and without argument.

My deepest sympathies,

> Carl Hatchett
> Warrant Officer
> Criminal Investigation Division
> United States Army

I sealed the letter and stood gazing out my office window, out across the olive drab — very drab — military compound that was headquarters for the Sixth Division's war machine, out toward Pleiku and the parts of that impoverished city I could see, up and across the high blue tropical sky.

Two small clouds were drifting, wandering, floating.

GARY KRIST

An Innocent Bystander

FROM *Playboy*

THE GIRL HAD nothing on her feet. It was the first thing I noticed about her. That and the oval splotches of mud running up one side of her pale leg and onto her short white shorts.

The mud was actually what made me stop. I don't usually pick up hitchhikers, no matter who they are or how unthreatening they look. But the sight of those mud spots was ominous. This girl looked like she was in trouble. As if she'd been running away from something, barefoot, through the mud.

This was a Monday, early October, around twilight, the day after Keszler had given me the boot — "seeking more vigorous representation elsewhere" was how he'd put it. Pompous jerk. I was feeling a little dazed and was driving out to the Island to think things over. Keszler was my biggest client.

Anyway, I'd gotten off the LIE around Nesconset and was taking secondary roads out to the beach house. The weather was warm for October, and there are some beautiful roads back there, where you can pull off and hear the wind in the pines and get the resiny smell of pine sap.

A look of relief broke out on the girl's face when I pulled over.

"So was she actually hitchhiking?"

"What do you mean?"

"Did she have her thumb out, or did you just see her by the road and stop?"

"I'm not sure. I mean, she must have been hitchhiking, right? Why else would I have even thought to stop?"

"You said she looked like she was in trouble. Maybe you just stopped to make sure she was all right."

"No . . . no, she was hitchhiking. Now that I think about it, I can remember seeing her thumb out. She had it out in this defiant way, almost daring me to stop."

"So she *was* hitchhiking."

"Why? Does it make a difference?"

"It might."

"Thanks," she said as she climbed into the car. Her long brown hair swung toward me, and then swung back again as she leaned out to pull the door shut. Now that she was in the car, I could see that she was a little younger than I had first thought — seventeen, eighteen, maybe. She wore an old, oversize work shirt that made her look like a kid.

"You okay?" I asked.

She looked up at me through stringy bangs. "Yeah, are you?" She had an accent, something a little Southern, I thought, but sometimes the locals out on the Island sound Southern to me.

"Where are you going?" I asked.

She hesitated, as if that issue hadn't occurred to her yet. She shifted her legs. They were long for her body. Long and white and spotted with mud. "You going as far as Riverhead?"

"I could go that way," I said. Then I shifted into gear and pulled away. "What happened to your shoes?"

"I threw them at somebody."

"Oh."

We rode for a few minutes in silence. The girl smelled strongly of cigarettes and something else, something like insect repellent. She had her hands folded in her lap and was quietly examining her varnished nails.

"Where in Riverhead do you want to be dropped off?" I asked.

"I'll tell you when we get there."

"But which part of town? So I know which way to go."

She heaved a big sigh and turned away from me, toward the window. "Look, mister," she said, "I just been thrown out of my apartment, okay? And I'm not really sure where I'm going, okay? I have friends in Riverhead, but I'm not sure which ones are home."

I just nodded, a little pissed that this girl was getting impatient with me.

"Sorry," she said after a while.

I nodded again.

Night had set in by this time. I flipped on the headlights, making a white tunnel of the trees ahead of us.

"My name's Maddy," she said then, in a different tone. "Short for Madeleine, my aunt's name." She held out her hand.

"Jack," I said, looking away from the road for a second to shake the offered hand. She was smiling. Nice smile.

"And what do you do, Jack?"

"I'm an agent."

She seemed to think this was a joke. "Like, a secret agent?"

I laughed. "No, no. I represent people. Artists. Writers, mostly."

"You represent them?"

"I negotiate contracts for them. Sell their stuff. Keep them calm."

"You mean writers like Stephen King?" she asked.

"I wish," I said, thinking again about Keszler. "But that's more or less the right idea."

"Shit," she said. "And you do that for a career?"

"Yes, I do. And what do *you* do for a career?"

"Hah," she said, as if my question had been a worthy retort.

Feeling guilty then, I added: "Well, I guess school is pretty hard work, too."

"I wouldn't know," she said. She dragged her hands through her long hair, lifting it and letting it fall, so that it pattered on the vinyl. "God, I hate fighting with people. Even with assholes like my boyfriend." Then she looked at me, hard. I could feel her eyes on me. "I just bet you're sitting there thinking what it would be like to go to bed with me."

"She said that?"

"Her exact words."

"Christ, I'm surprised you didn't drive off the road."

"It took some effort, believe me."

"Incredible! You should have pulled over right then and told her to get out of the car."

"I know."

"It should have served as a warning to you."

"I know."

"So what did you say to her? How do you answer a statement like that?"

"With the truth."

"The real truth?"

"Yes, damn it. The real truth."

"I hate to disappoint you," I said after I'd recovered, "but you're absolutely wrong. For one thing, I have a daughter about your age." I eased my foot on the accelerator and brought our speed back down to fifty. "I don't know what could have brought on a comment like that, I really don't. I'm trying to help you out here."

"Okay, okay, I'm sorry," she said. "It was a stupid thing to say. Let's just forget I said it."

"Because, you know, you don't say things like that. You don't have any idea."

"Okay, okay," she said, and then — to my amazement — she started to cry quietly. She wiped her eyes on the tail of her oversize shirt. "I said let's forget it. I say stupid things sometimes, I know that."

We drove on in silence for a while. I looked at my watch. I was supposed to give McManus a call at 8:00 — it wasn't going to be a fun call, with the thing about Keszler — but I really didn't want to use the car phone. It's virtually impossible not to look like a self-important asshole with a car phone in your hand.

"Okay if I smoke?" Maddy asked after a while. She pulled a crumpled pack of Camels out of the breast pocket of her shirt.

"Sure," I said.

She took one out of the pack, lit it with a white plastic lighter, and inhaled deeply, stylishly. She had a self-consciously careless way with a cigarette, something you see in a lot of kids her age. You wonder if they practice all day in front of mirrors.

"So what's your daughter's name?" Maddy asked finally. "The one who's my age?" We'd already passed through Stoat's Hollow. The pines had given way to farms — dark, empty fields of corn stubble on each side of the road.

"Megan. She's fifteen."

"That's a lot younger than me," she said. "Any other children?"

"No."

"You going to meet up with the family now?'

I hesitated a second. I could have lied, but what I said was, "No, my wife and I have been divorced for eight years. Megan lives with her in Portland. Portland, Oregon."

Maddy nodded. The light of the dashboard threw a green glow over her face. Green smoke seemed to be rising in the dark space of the car. "Everybody's got a sob story these days, I guess."

"Yeah," I said, turning on the air.

Maddy was asleep when we got to the outskirts of Riverhead at 8:30. I pulled into the parking lot of a 7-Eleven near the edge of town. There were some teenagers hanging out next to the Dumpsters at the other end of the lot. Two girls — just younger than Maddy, I guessed — pranced around in ripped jeans and leather jackets, their teased hair floating around them. The boys were grabbing for the lapels of the girls' jackets, laughing and generally acting like goons.

I shook Maddy awake. "We're here," I said.

She jumped when I touched her, and blinked furiously. "What?"

"We're in Riverhead — I need to know where you want to be dropped off. Where do your friends live?"

She didn't answer right away. She rubbed her eyes, then groped for her pack of Camels. She lit one, took a long pull, and exhaled noisily. "Acquaintances, really," she said.

"Do they know you're coming?"

"I didn't get a chance to call." She stared down at the cigarette in her hand. "Look, I was hoping I could maybe stay with you. I mean, now that I know your intentions are honorable and all."

Apparently, her comment about my wanting to sleep with her was some kind of test, and I'd passed. "You can't stay with your parents?" I asked.

She rolled her eyes the way my own daughter does. "Well, if you can find my mom, you should be a detective instead of a secret agent. And my dad's been dead for eight years."

I had to ask then: "Maddy, how old are you?"

"Eighteen," she said. She scratched the edge of her mouth with the pinkie of her cigarette hand. "Look, have you got room in your house? Just for the night? Until I can figure out what to do."

What could I say? Megan's room was empty. She probably wouldn't be needing it until the next summer visit.

"Okay," I said. "Just until you figure out what to do."

*

"Let me make sure of this: She asked *you* if she could stay at your place?"

"Yes."

"You didn't suggest it yourself in any way, verbally or nonverbally?"

"Nonverbally?"

"Use your imagination."

"Jesus, will you stop?"

"You asked for my advice. I'm just asking questions that would be asked. By people who don't know you as well as I do."

"Fine, fine, fine. The answer is no. I didn't say or do anything suggestive in any way."

"Good. Go on."

The house was dark when we arrived. The light timers were out of synch somehow, probably from a power failure during the week, but there was a half-moon that night. I pulled into the drive and parked. As we got out of the car, I could smell the damp salt air and hear the roll of surf from behind the dark bulk of the house.

"I'll go ahead and turn on some lights," I said. "Wait here. And watch your bare feet on the gravel."

I walked quickly up the path, opened the front door, and went inside, snapping on lights. The house had that thick, stale smell to it. I'd been coming to the house like this — at night, after a long drive — all summer and fall, but it still made me a little uncomfortable. I usually put the stereo on right away, or the television.

I turned on the outside floods and went back to the car. Maddy wasn't there. She'd left the passenger door slightly open, so that the overhead light was on and the warning bell was chiming. "Maddy?" I called. I leaned gently against the door until it clicked shut, then went around and opened the trunk for my suitcase. I grabbed it and a bag of corn and tomatoes I'd picked up at a farm stand on the way out. "Maddy?"

I thought she must have gone around back, so I followed the flagstone path along the side of the house and through the overgrown trellis to the beach. The floods from the house threw huge buttresses of white light toward the water. Maddy was standing at the foot of her long shadow, staring straight out, her arms folded. Something clenched in my chest when I saw her. A few months earlier, my own daughter Megan had stood there, just like that, watching the ocean for hours. Something had seemed wrong, and I asked Megan again and again what the problem was. But she said she just liked to look at the water — she liked to look at something that big and oblivious to everything. I thought there was more to it, so I kept asking until she got pissed off. "You will never understand anything anyway!" she shouted at me on her last night, and then marched into the house. This comment worried me. I mentioned it to her mother on the phone, but Claire told me I was paranoid. "She's an adolescent, Jack," she said. "Adolescents brood. It goes with the territory."

"So did she seem depressed?"

"Megan?"

"No, the other girl. Maddy."

"No, not depressed. Pensive, maybe. Thoughtful. But, hell, everybody gets thoughtful staring at the ocean. It's like a fire in a fireplace."

"Was there anyone else on the beach that night? Anyone who might have seen her standing there?"

"No one I could see. The houses are pretty far apart at our end of the beach. And this was a Monday night, a month after Labor Day. Most of the houses on the beach were probably empty."

"You're sure?"

"No, I'm not absolutely sure."

"Do you like the ocean?" I asked, coming up behind her.

She turned and looked at me. Her face seemed unbelievably pale and thin in the glare of the floodlights. "Jesus," she said, shading her eyes, "you must do pretty good as an agent to have a house like this."

"I've had it for a long time. My parents bought it. Back when there was nothing out here but fishermen and abstract expressionists."

The comment was lost on her. She just kept staring at me from the shade of her upraised hand. "You must be forty and something, right? Forty-five?"

"Forty-three," I told her.

She smiled and turned back toward the water. "God, wouldn't

Drew be surprised to see me here? He probably thinks I'm spending the night in somebody's car or something."

"Drew is your boyfriend?" I asked.

"Yeah," she said. "Or at least he was." She reached into her
pocket for another cigarette.

"Hey, are you hungry?" I asked her. "There's not much in the
house, but I stopped for some corn and tomatoes before I picked
you up."

"Do you have eggs? And maybe some cheese?" she asked.

I shrugged. "I think so."

"Well then, listen. I'll make omelettes — my famous cheese-and-
tomato omelettes." The idea seemed to give her energy. "You just sit
back and let me make you some dinner, okay? As my way of thank-
ing you for being such a good guy and putting me up and all?"

"Sounds great," I said. "I have to take a shower anyway. Let's go
inside and I can show you around the kitchen."

We went in. Maddy looked around the house, clearly impressed,
running her hand over the furniture, the vases and ashtrays and
books. I found it a little embarrassing. I don't think of myself as
particularly rich, but to this girl I guess I was. When I led her into
the kitchen, she pulled a couple of copper pans off the hooks and
inspected them like they were artifacts from some lost civilization.

"Show me the eggs and where you keep the canned stuff and
then go away," she said.

I did, and then went upstairs for my shower. By the time I came
back down, dressed in sweatpants and a T-shirt, I could smell on-
ions and cigarette smoke all through the house. The table in the
dining room had been beautifully set, and she'd opened the sliders
to the deck so that the ocean sounds came in on the breeze. There
was a bottle of white wine in the ice bucket, and a Dylan CD in the
stereo. Maddy came out of the kitchen with a platter of steaming
home fries. "I couldn't find any mushrooms," she said, slipping past
me and putting the potatoes down on the table. "We'll just have to
suffer."

"You know, I might be able to find you some shoes," I said. Maddy
was still barefoot. "I think my wife left a box of old sandals up in the
attic."

"Later," she said, slipping back into the kitchen for the eggs.

We both ate quickly, conscious of the clicks and clatters of the silverware and the ridiculous little gongs the wineglasses made when we knocked them against our plates. At one point, I thought I noticed Maddy shivering — it had gotten a little chilly — so I went and got one of my cardigan sweaters. I put it around her shoulders and she just stared at me, as if amazed that anyone would do something like that.

"You were drinking wine. Do you have any idea how much she drank?"

"Well, a lot. I'm not sure exactly how much, but she kept refilling both our glasses."

"How many empty bottles did you find?"

"Hell, I don't —"

"How many?"

"Three."

"You drank three bottles of wine between you?"

"I probably had just one myself. She was drinking more than I was. I mean, when I found her later in the TV room, she had another bottle open."

"Two bottles then. A girl of, what, 120 pounds?"

"Thereabouts."

"Shit. Not good."

We finished dinner. Afterward, I brought down the box of sandals and let her go through it in the TV room while I cleaned up the dishes. She was already pretty far gone, and kept coming into the kitchen, modeling the different pairs of sandals while I loaded the dishwasher. Her feet were a size or two smaller than Claire's, and some of the sandals looked huge on her. She was getting kind of silly, parading around in these oversize shoes, with a lit cigarette hanging unsteadily out of her mouth. When I was about finished, she came in with the worst sandals of the bunch — rainbow-colored, plastic-strapped things. She pranced over to the refrigerator and pulled out another bottle of white.

"Hey," I said. "Maybe we should go easy on that."

"Fuck it, Jack," she said, an edge of real nastiness in her voice. "I've had a bad day, okay?"

The surprise must have registered on my face, because she softened immediately. "Oh come on, Jack," she said. She slinked over to me in the godawful sandals. "Let's be friends again." She put her hands on my ass and leaned against my chest.

"Oh, Christ."
  "I want you to understand that I didn't invite this in any way."
  "Yeah."
  "I made that very clear to her. I repeated . . . I reiterated what I'd told her in the car."
  "She sounds a little crazed, this girl."
  "You don't know the half of it."

I babbled on, but she lifted her head and stood on tiptoes to kiss me. Finally, I put my arms around her and started to kiss her back, but then there was an incredible crash to my right. Broken glass and a big brown rock skittered across the kitchen tiles. Maddy screeched and jumped back. I collected myself and ran to the broken window to look out, but I couldn't see anything but darkness. Then I heard somebody moving through the dining room. He must have run around to the deck and come in through the open sliding doors. He burst into the kitchen — a tall, heavy guy with long brown hair and a goatee, about thirty, in a denim shirt and black pants. He was spitting curses and heading right toward me.

"So this is the boyfriend?"
  "Drew, yeah. She must have called him when I was in the shower. Told him where she was."

Before I knew what was happening, the guy straight-armed me into the refrigerator. "What the fuck is *this?*" he shouted. Maddy was behind him, trying to drag him off me. I started talking, trying to explain, but he just pushed me. Just as I was bouncing off the refrigerator again, he threw a punch. His knuckles caught me on the ear and suddenly I was going down. My head hit the refrigerator handle on the way.
  The next few minutes are a little unclear to me. My left ear was hot and buzzing like an alarm clock, but I could hear them shouting at each other. Pots were hitting the tiles all around me, and then I heard dishes crashing. Maddy was screaming, trying to get the guy to calm down, but it wasn't working.

Finally, they moved out of the kitchen and continued the fight
somewhere else in the house. I tried to get to my feet. My thought
processes started coming back. I could hear them in the living
room. He was banging around, ranting about how he can't trust
her, calling her cunt, whore, everything in the book. She was shouting back at him. I stumbled over to the kitchen telephone, figuring
to call 911, but then I stopped. There was no more sound in the
living room. I could even hear the ocean again. He was gone.

"So wait a minute. I don't understand. Why did she call the boyfriend?"

"She told me she just wanted to rub his nose in it, make him
jealous. 'Hey, guess where I am, asshole' — that kind of thing."

"So this guy drove over and was watching you through the windows? Did she know that he was there? Was that why she came on to
you, for the audience?"

"It's more complicated than that."

I picked my way through the pots and broken glass in the kitchen.
Maddy sat on the living room floor in the corner near the stereo,
her head down and her arms hugging her knees to her chest. She
was crying.

"You okay?" I asked.

She didn't look up. Through the tangles of her hair, I could see a
red contusion on her cheek, where he must have slapped her. "I'm
sorry," she kept saying. "I just wanted to make him jealous. I didn't
think he'd go ballistic."

"It's okay."

She looked up at me. Her eyes were puffy and red, but I think
that was just from crying. "There's no hope for me and him. I keep
thinking, maybe, but there really is no fucking hope."

I looked around the living room. He'd turned over a few chairs,
and there was a framed antique map of Europe that he'd smashed
against an end table. The corner of the table was jutting through
the parchment, right where the Alps would have been. "You think
he'll be back?"

She sniffed a few times and then said, "No. He'll never be back.
Didn't you hear him? He never wants to see my fucking face again!
Me and my fucking big ideas." She began crying again, really weep-
ing.

I crouched beside her and held her shoulders, which were amazingly thin under the rough, heavy cotton work shirt. "*Shhh,*" I whispered to her. "Everything will be okay."

We stayed like that for a few minutes. Finally, I said, "You need some sleep."

I helped her to her feet. She gave me a pathetic little smile and then I took her upstairs to Megan's room, half holding her up, like a hospital intern leading a patient. I pulled back the covers and settled her into bed in her clothes. She went along without a word. "Goodnight," I said. Then I turned out the light and closed the door.

I went downstairs and spent the next hour cleaning up, cursing myself for getting into this situation. I taped a piece of cardboard over the broken kitchen window and swept up all the glass. Then, sometime around midnight, I double-checked all the locks and went upstairs to my own room. I brushed my teeth, looked over my bruised face in the mirror, and went to bed. But I couldn't sleep. The sound of the surf, which usually lulls me, seemed to be keeping me wide-eyed. I lay in the dark room and thought about how this situation would look to anyone on the outside. I thought of what my friends would say if I ever told them about it. "Did you hear, Jack picks up this eighteen-year-old hitchhiker — at least she says she's eighteen — and takes her back to the beach house. . . ." I felt nauseated at myself and what I'd turned into — a forty-three-year-old man, alone, a washout as a husband and as a father, making a fool of himself with a girl half his age, a girl in a vulnerable situation.

After what must have been two hours of lying awake, I got up and cracked the door open. Megan's room down the hall was dark, the door open, but there was a light from downstairs. A flickering light — the television in the living room.

I crept down the stairs. Maddy was lying on the couch, still in the work shirt and muddy shorts, with one of my ex-wife's sandals dangling from a single toe. She held a wine bottle against her chest and stared blankly at the television.

It took me a second to realize what she was watching. An old family video. She must have found it in the cabinet under the VCR.

The tape was of Megan when she was a baby — a little after her first birthday. It had been taken on the beach, right out behind this house. Claire and I had just given her a new red sand pail and shovel, which she seemed delighted with but somewhat confused by. This was when she was just walking. I hadn't looked at the tape in years.

It was an ordinary family video, I guess: beach scenes, dunking baby's feet in the surf, building sand castles. Megan's diaper was sodden with seawater. She sat, digging the shovel into the sand and laughing, totally self-absorbed.

"She looks so happy," Maddy said then from the couch. I hadn't realized she knew I was behind her. "She looks so goddamn fucking happy."

On the screen, Megan lifted a shovelful of sand to her mouth. The camera shook, and a female arm shot into the frame to stop her. Then a cut to a different scene — Megan running toward the camera, then running back to her seat, then starting all over again. Laughing.

I leaned over and pulled the wine bottle out of Maddy's arms. She let it go easily, her eyes never leaving the screen. "You made a mess of it, too, I guess," she said. "Just like everybody else."

I took the bottle out to the kitchen. It was half full, and I poured the rest of it into the sink.

When I came back into the TV room, Maddy had gotten up from the couch and gone outside. She'd left the sliding door open. I shut it but didn't lock it, turned off the television, and then went back up to bed.

"Did she ever come back in?"

"I don't know. Maybe she did. I'm not sure."

"And she was very drunk by this time?"

"Very."

I heard her walking around outside, muttering. Then she parked herself under my open bedroom window and started calling to me in stage whispers. "Come on, Jack," she said. "Come out and play." She threw a couple of pebbles at the window. "I said, come out and play, Jack. Don't be this way. We can take the car and go get some cigarettes someplace. Pleeeease." She laughed — a bitter, sort of mirthless sound. "What difference can it make, Jack? Come on out."

I ignored her. Eventually she must have gotten bored, and I heard her voice trailing away down the beach.

In the morning, she was gone. I got up around eight, went down to the kitchen, and made some coffee. I made a full pot, enough for two. I assumed that she was outside, maybe taking a walk on the beach.

I cleaned up. The living room smelled of cigarettes and day-old wine — she must have spilled some. The sofa pillows were wrinkled and jammed into a corner. I could see the dent from her head in one of them.

By ten-thirty I knew she wasn't coming back. I figured she must have gone out to the main road and hitched a ride into town. Back to the boyfriend, I thought. Give it another shot with old Drew.

I tried to do some work — I had a contract to sign off on by the end of the week — but I couldn't make any progress. The whole mess was too much in my head, so to clear it I decided to take a walk down the beach. It was a windy morning but surprisingly warm. There were a few people out — some of them walking dogs, some jogging, some doing both. It was that weird limbo stage at the shore — halfway between crowded summer and deserted winter.

About a mile or so down the beach, I saw a guy in an overcoat, looking totally ridiculous, walking through the sand in shiny brown shoes. I watched him for a while and realized suddenly that he was heading straight toward me.

"Morning, sir," the guy said, trudging up to me. "I'm Detective-Sergeant Michaels."

I stopped walking. "Good morning."

"Are you looking for someone?"

Every instinct in my body was shouting out the answer to that one. "No. Why? Somebody lost?"

He shrugged. "You might say that. Some kid washed up down the beach a way. Just a couple hours ago."

"Boy or girl?" I asked carefully.

"Girl. Woman. Whatever. Looked about seventeen or so."

I felt nothing right then. I don't understand why, but I felt nothing. "Drunk?"

"Probably." The detective gave a kind of commiserative sigh. He was about my age, maybe a little older. Gray just starting around the temples. "You didn't see anybody on the beach last night, did you, Mr. . . . ."

"Avallone. I've got a house about a mile down that way." I was thinking all kinds of things now. Could the boyfriend have come back and drowned her? "No," I said after an awkward pause, "I didn't see anybody." Then: "It wasn't, well, a murder or anything, was it?"

"No, no, nothing like that." He turned and looked toward the surf for a second. "Anyway, Mr. Avallone, if you hear anything or talk to anybody who might have seen this girl, let us know, okay? Most likely it was suicide. Too cold for a midnight swim, and kids her age, they get into a scrape, this is their solution."

"Seventeen isn't exactly a kid," I said.

The detective laughed. "You sound just like my daughter." He shook my hand and walked back toward the dunes.

"You realize that what you did there was a crime, right? If somebody wanted to nail you, you're nailable right there."

"Okay, so I'm nailable."

"You lied to a cop. In the moral universe, that's no big thing. But a judge could make a big thing of it if he wanted to. Besides, it was stupid. The boyfriend. He knew she was with you. He was bound to tell them, eventually."

"Not necessarily."

"Why not necessarily?"

"Just hold on. I'm coming to that."

I spent the rest of the day recleaning the house, trying to get rid of all traces of the night before. I kept the local news on, on every radio in the house, to see if anything was mentioned about a drowning. Nothing. Then, as I was getting ready to start dinner, I noticed the note on the refrigerator. It was written in pencil on the back of a takeout menu: "What we did was a mistake, like everything else in my life. Maddy."

I carried the note over to the table and sat down.

"But Jack, you didn't —"

"Shut up a minute. Just let me finish the story."

The boyfriend's call came about an hour later. "Listen, asshole," he said. "I don't know if you did it or if she did it to herself. Basically, I don't care. Either way, you got a big problem. But for $20,000, I could forget that whole thing last night. She didn't call me, I didn't go to your place, I didn't see you groping her ass or sticking your tongue down her fucking throat or nothing."

I was too stunned to say anything.

"Do we understand each other?" he asked after a second.

I didn't answer. I was unable to speak.

"I'll give you a minute to think about it," he said. "I can wait."

I drove into the city the next day. He'd said he wanted the $20,000 in cash by noon, but when I told him that would be impossible, since I didn't have an account on the Island, he gave me until five in the afternoon.

It wasn't difficult to put the money together. I cashed a couple of checks against my personal and business accounts and got the sum together by lunchtime. Then I drove out to the mall in Islip where he wanted to meet.

"You paid him. I can't believe you paid the guy."

"I had no choice."

"What do you mean, you had no choice? Some miserable kid does something stupid, it's not your fault. You were a bystander, an innocent bystander!"

"Come on, you're the lawyer. You know what kind of trouble this guy could have made for me. It's how it all looks. The girl committed suicide practically in my house. It's a lot to explain."

"But Jesus Christ, Jack."

"Besides, I've got Megan to think of. And what would Claire say? Would she let Megan come here anymore if this got out?"

"No. Okay, I see your point. It's just, I don't know. I'm a little surprised."

"Surprised that I would pay $20,000 to keep my life from going down the tubes?"

"Well, when you put it that way —"

"And when you get right down to it, $20,000 isn't a hell of a lot of money."

"I guess not. For what it's buying. But from a legal standpoint, if this ever gets out, it's practically an admission of guilt."

"It won't get out."

"You can't know that for sure."

"Believe me, it won't get out."

*

I arrived at the mall a little before five. Drew was already there, in a satin Mets jacket, eating a taco in the food court. He looked up and grinned when he saw me. "Put it on the table," he said.

I took the envelope from my coat pocket and placed it beside his jumbo soda. He put down the taco, wiped his fingers daintily on a napkin, and picked up the envelope. He looked inside quickly and then stuffed it into the pocket of his jacket. "If it's not all there, you'll be hearing from me."

"It's all there." I stood for a few seconds, looking down at him. "You don't feel anything for her, do you."

He smiled, wiping his goatee with the napkin. "Nah," he said. "She was a pain in the butt anyway. Too emotional."

I gave him one last look of contempt and then walked away.

I spent three more days at the beach house, working on the contract, trying to concentrate. I went out every morning to get the paper. I read through the whole thing, but there was no story about a girl drowning herself on the beach. I even took the chance of asking around town. Nobody had heard a thing, though the guy at the wine store told me they don't like to report suicides. Too many copycat adolescents in the world.

By Saturday morning I had finished with the contract and decided to drive back to the city. On the way, I found myself exiting the LIE again. It was morbid, I guess, but I wanted to go back to the place where I'd picked up Maddy on Monday night. I pulled off the road, stopped the engine, and got out. There were high bushes bordering the road, and on the other side of them was a cluster of garden apartments — cheap, poorly built townhouses — which could have been where Maddy lived. I was afraid of meeting up with Drew, so I didn't investigate. After a few minutes, I got back into the car and drove away.

At this point I was hungry, so I drove into town to get some lunch. There was a big, busy-looking diner on the main drag in town, so that's where I stopped. I had to wait a few minutes, but finally the waitress took me to a tiny table near the kitchen and gave me a menu. I decided quickly, ordered, and then settled back to look around. That's when I noticed a familiar-looking guy sitting in a booth across the diner, near the windows. I tried to place him for a few seconds before it hit me: Detective-Sergeant Michaels. The cop on the beach.

I was confused. I wondered if he could be in town investigating

Maddy's death. Or was it just a coincidence? Maybe he lived in this town, where property had to be cheaper, and just worked out in the Hamptons. But then a girl came out of the ladies' room and slipped into the seat across from him. It was Maddy.

"Maddy? The same one?"

"The same one."

I sat there, staring, until the whole story became clear to me. Then I got up and walked over to their booth. As I came up to them, I heard Maddy saying, "Right, Dad. I'm sure he would," or something like that. Michaels — or whatever his name really was — caught sight of me. "Shit," he said under his breath.

I stopped right in front of their booth. Maddy looked up, recognized me, and then looked down into her coffee cup. "Oh, dear," she said in an ironic little singsong.

"So you three do this a lot?" I asked. "Or was I just the first sucker?"

"Listen," the father said, "I don't know what you think you're going to do about this —"

"Relax, Dad," Maddy said. "He won't do anything." She looked up at me again, with a little smile. "Isn't that right, Jack?"

I kept my eyes on Maddy, but I said to her father, "This is the kind of thing you teach your daughter?"

"Hey, loverboy," Maddy said. "You're one to talk about fine, upstanding behavior with young ladies in distress. Besides, at least his daughter talks to him."

I didn't answer. I just kept looking down at Maddy, looking for some sign of regret or guilt — something that would tell me that at least part of what happened that night was real. But there was nothing like that in her eyes.

"So," she said then, "we're okay on this, right, Jack? You don't talk about us to the police, and we don't talk about you to your wife and daughter. Right?"

I couldn't believe an eighteen-year-old girl was saying this.

"Right?" she asked again.

"And what did you say?"

"What do you think I said? What do you think I *should* have said?"

"I think that you should have said, 'Right.'"

"And so I did. I said it and walked out of the diner. And I haven't seen or heard from them since."

"So that's it, then. You don't need any legal advice. Chalk it up to experience. True, you're out twenty grand, but meanwhile your ex-wife and daughter won't find out about any of it."

"Right."

"You didn't do anything wrong. You were the victim here."

"Yes."

"And so you move on. A little wiser, maybe, but none the worse for wear."

"Right. None the worse for wear."

PHILLIP M. MARGOLIN

The Jailhouse Lawyer

FROM *Legal Briefs*

"I'M LYLE RICHMOND and you're listening to Talk Radio. My very special guest tonight is six-foot-five, has a full head of wavy gray hair, steely blue eyes, and the squarest chin this side of Mt. Rushmore. If I also said that he is wearing a Stetson hat, a bolo tie, and Ostrich-leather cowboy boots, I'd bet that most of you in my listening audience would guess that we're going to be speaking to criminal defense attorney Monte Bethune. He's visiting us just one week after winning a stunning acquittal for Iowa Governor Leona Farris, who shot her husband in front of millions of viewers on national television.

"Welcome to the show, Monte."

"Thanks for having me on."

"Did your lucky outfit win the Farris case for you?"

"I wish it was that easy, Lyle. I give all the credit for the governor's acquittal to the jurors, who were able to see through the government's smoke screen and find the truth."

"I'm sure you had a little part in leading them through that screen of smoke, Monte."

"I try, Lyle."

"Our listeners will be pleased to hear that you're in our fair city on a book tour to promote your autobiography, *The Best Defense.* They can meet you tomorrow afternoon at Benson's Books on Comstock and Vine from three o'clock to five."

"That's right."

"How's the book doing?"

"*The Best Defense* is going to debut at number four on the *New York Times* bestseller list, this Sunday."

"Congratulations. And I can tell our listeners that it deserves to be there. This is some terrific book."

"Thanks, Lyle. I wrote it to try and give my readers an idea of what it takes to try high-profile lawsuits."

"You certainly do that. The chapter describing the way you won that forty-million-dollar verdict against Dental Pro had me on the edge of my seat."

"My clients deserved that verdict. It was only by sheer luck that my investigator was able to prove that Dental Pro was using radioactive materials to make their dental implants."

"You were up against some high-priced legal talent in that case."

"It seems that the other side always puts its best lawyers against me."

"Sort of like those showdowns in the Old West where the young gunslingers would call out the fastest gun. You always beat them to the draw, though."

"Not all the time, Lyle. I've lost my share. I even talk about some of those losses in my book."

"The Chicago Strangler case."

"That's right. There was a case where I was definitely outgunned by a bright, young DA."

"That was Everett Till, wasn't it?"

"The current governor of Illinois. Every time we meet, Everett thanks me for putting him in the statehouse."

"Is Till the best you ever went up against?"

"Whew. That's a tough question to answer, Lyle."

"Is that because you've been up against so many hotshots?"

"No. That's not the problem. Everett is definitely the lawyer who tried the best case against me, but he's not the best person I ever faced in court."

"I don't get you, Monte."

"The best person I ever tried a case against wasn't a real lawyer. He was a jailhouse lawyer."

"What's a jailhouse lawyer?"

"A con. Someone who learned his law while serving a jail sentence."

"You mean a crook?"

"Exactly. But this fella was one very smart crook."

"I sense a story here, Monte. One that didn't find its way into *The Best Defense*."

"You've got me there. I guess the problem is that this story is a little embarrassing."

"Spill, Monte. I'm sure all my listeners would love to hear about a convict who could get the best of the best lawyer in the USA."

"Okay, Lyle. I don't mind telling tales on myself, and this case was tried when I was still a little wet behind the ears. Not that I would have seen what was happening even with all my experience."

"Let's hear it, Monte."

"Okay. Now, this happened in 1970. I was two years out of law school and two years into my stint as a deputy district attorney in Portland, Oregon. You're a little young to remember those days. The war in Vietnam dominated everything. Then, there was Black Power. Bobby Kennedy and Martin Luther King had been assassinated, and every day brought more riots and protests. I guess you could say that there was general chaos across the United States, with the exception of the Multnomah County District Court, where I was stuck trying shoplifting cases, drunk drivers, and other boring misdemeanors.

"I was specializing in traffic cases on the morning I was assigned *State of Oregon v. Tommy Lee Jones*. It had been a rough week. After a string of victories, I had lost two tough Driving Under the Influence cases, back to back, and I needed a win. A big smile crossed my face when my supervisor told me that Tommy Lee was handling his case Pro Per. That means by himself, without a lawyer. There's an old maxim I'm sure you've heard that holds that a lawyer who represents himself has a fool for a client. That maxim is doubly true for a jailhouse lawyer. Knocking off a top defense attorney was more satisfying than steamrollering a poor fool who thinks that he's Perry Mason, but a notch was still a notch.

"District Court Judge Arlen Hatcher's courtroom was on the third floor of the Multnomah County Courthouse, an intimidating concrete monster of a building that takes up a whole block in the center of Portland. The older courtrooms are stately, with marble columns and polished wood. Hatcher, a career prosecutor before his judicial appointment, had only come on the bench eight months ago. He was stuck in a newer courtroom that had been squeezed into a space previously occupied by an administrative office. Plastic and imitation wood dominated the decor.

"Two long counsel tables stood before the judge's dais. Tommy Lee was sprawled disrespectfully in a chair in front of the table closest to the jury box. His wild Afro, scraggly goatee, and soiled jail clothes made him look fierce. Any lawyer worth his salt would have made certain that Tommy Lee shaved and came to court in a suit, but Tommy Lee could not afford to hire an attorney and he refused to let the court appoint one.

"'You the pig they sent to pers'cute me?' Tommy Lee snarled when I walked to the other table. His bravado didn't faze me, and I flashed him a patronizing smile.

"'Simmer down, Tommy Lee,' warned one of the two jail guards who were assigned to watch the prisoner.

"If you're wondering why Tommy Lee was so heavily guarded when the charge was only reckless driving, you might be interested in knowing that two months after the traffic citation was issued in Portland, Tommy was rearrested on a fugitive complaint out of Newark, New Jersey, that charged him with murder. Tommy Lee was also handling his extradition battle by himself.

"The bailiff rapped the gavel and Arlen Hatcher stomped in. The judge was tall and lean and walked with a slight limp. His cheeks were sunken, his eyes narrow, and his thin lips curled into a wolfish grin whenever he overruled a defense objection. Judge Hatcher loved to bedevil defense attorneys, and he was always happiest at a sentencing.

"I jumped to my feet when Hatcher took the bench, but Tommy Lee stayed seated. Old Arlen fixed the defendant with his death stare. Tommy Lee didn't blink.

"'Please stand when the judge enters,' the bailiff ordered menacingly. Tommy Lee uncoiled slowly, his eyes still locked on the judge. When he was fully upright, I called the case and the judge told the bailiff to call for a jury. That was when Tommy Lee made what I thought was his fatal mistake.

"'I don't want no jury,' he said.

"'What?!' Hatcher asked incredulously.

"'One pig or six fascist sheep, it don't make no difference.'

"Old Arlen turned scarlet. 'You ever hear of contempt?' he growled. 'One more reference to barnyard animals and you'll be an expert on it . . . Mr. Jones.'

"Now, I'm certain that 'Mr. Jones' was originally 'boy,' but Hatcher quit calling Afro-Americans 'boy' on the record after the Oregon Supreme Court reprimanded him. Actually, Hatcher wasn't any more prejudiced against blacks than he was against any other defendant.

"That was another reason why I thought that Tommy Lee was a fool for defending himself. He needed a lawyer who knew the ropes. Hell, with a client like Tommy Lee, any lawyer in the county would have swallowed nails before letting Arlen Hatcher handle the case.

"'You understand that you have a constitutional right to have your case tried by a jury of your peers?' Hatcher inquired.

"'Whatcho think? I ain't dumb. I also know I have me a right to not be havin' no jury.'

"A gleam appeared in Hatcher's eye, and his lips twitched from the effort of suppressing his glee at having Tommy Lee's fate thrust into his hands. I could almost hear him calculating the maximum sentence he would be able to impose after he found Tommy Lee guilty.

"'Very well, Mr. Jones,' Hatcher said, 'I'll be glad to hear your case. Are you ready to proceed, Mr. Bethune?'

"My only witness was Portland Police Officer Marty Singer, a big happy-go-lucky man, who was painfully honest. Marty always told the truth on the stand. Some deputy district attorneys complained that Marty's honesty had cost them cases, but I preferred him as a witness because jurors always believed him.

"As soon as he was sworn, I established that Marty was working as a traffic patrolman on February 8, 1970. Then I asked him if he had made an arrest that night in downtown Portland for reckless driving.

"'At 9:35 P.M., I was on patrol on Salmon near Third,' Singer said, 'when I saw a vehicle weaving in and out of traffic at a high rate of speed. I put on my lights, but the car continued to drive erratically for a block or so before it pulled over.'

"'What did you do then?'

"'When both cars were parked, I exited my vehicle and approached the driver. The first thing I did was ask him for his license. While he was trying to extract the license, I leaned close to him and smelled the odor of an alcoholic beverage on his breath. This, coupled with his erratic driving, made me suspect that the driver was intoxicated, so I asked him to exit his vehicle.'

"'Did you ask the driver to perform any field sobriety tests?'

"'I did,' Singer replied.

"'What did you ask him to do?'

"'I had the driver walk a straight line, count backward from one hundred, and repeat several words that are difficult for impaired drivers to pronounce.'

"'How did he do?'

"'To my surprise, he passed all the tests. That's why I charged him with reckless driving instead of driving under the influence of intoxicants.'

"'Officer Singer, did you examine the driver's license?' I asked.

"'Yes, sir.'

"'Who was named on it?'

"'Bobby Lee Jones,' Singer answered.

"My heart dropped into the bottom of my brilliantly polished wingtips.

"'Er, you mean Tommy Lee Jones, don't you, Officer?' I asked, in order to give Singer a chance to cover his gaffe.

"Singer looked confused. 'I'm . . . I think it was Bobby Lee,' he said. Then he brightened. 'But, later, he said he was Tommy Lee Jones.'

"'Later?'

"'When I said that I was going to arrest him.'

"'Then the driver said that he was Tommy Lee Jones?'

"'Right. He told me that he had borrowed his brother's license without his permission.'

"I breathed a sigh of relief and pointed at the defendant.

"'Is this the man that you arrested?'

"For the first time since Singer had begun his testimony, Tommy Lee came alive. He sat up straight and stared at Singer as if daring him to make the identification. Singer hesitated.

"'Yes,' he answered shakily, 'I think that's him.'

"If this had been a jury trial, Lyle, I would have been dead after Singer's crappy identification, but old Arlen hadn't heard a word since Tommy Lee called him a pig. Hell, Singer could have testified that the driver was a Caucasian dwarf and it wouldn't have made any difference as far as Tommy Lee's fate was concerned.

"'Did you arrest the driver and take him to jail?'

"'No, sir. He was polite and cooperative, so I gave him a citation, told him his court date, and let him go home.'

"'One last question, Officer,' I said. 'Did something happen before the defendant's court date that caused him to be taken into custody?'

"'Yes. He was picked up on this murder case out of New Jersey.'

"Of course, this was all totally improper, mentioning the murder. A real lawyer would have objected and asked for a mistrial. But all's fair in love and war. If Tommy Lee wanted to represent himself, he'd have to live with the consequences of his decision. To my delight, I could see Judge Hatcher writing the word 'murder' on his pad. He circled the word a few times. Then he gave Tommy Lee another dose of the death stare.

"'No further questions,' I said.

"Now, a good defense lawyer would have made mincemeat out of Singer's ID and would have had a good chance to win the case, but Tommy Lee seemed to be his own worst enemy. First, he put on his fiercest face. Next, he stared at Singer menacingly. Then, he began to insult my witness.

"'Ain't it true that you told the brother you stopped, who ain't me, that you would fix his case for fifty bucks?'

"'That is not true,' Singer answered, as his ears started to glow. Marty went to church regularly and he took the teachings of the Bible to heart. Accusing him of dishonesty was one of the worst things a person could do.

"'How much you say you'd charge him, then?'

"I objected, Hatcher whacked his gavel down hard, and the trial continued with Singer and the judge glaring at Tommy Lee.

"'You say that this so-called arrest was on February 8, 1970?' Tommy Lee asked, his tone heavy with sarcasm.

"Singer nodded.

"'You drunk or shootin' up, like you usually do on that date?'

"Hatcher smashed his gavel down before I could object.

"'One more impertinent question like that,' he warned, 'and I'll hold you in contempt. This is an officer of the law up here. Show him some respect.'

"Tommy Lee leaped to his feet.

"'I got no respect fo' a honkey pig who perjures hisself and say he be arrestin' me when I wasn't there,' Tommy Lee screamed.

"The two guards wrestled Tommy Lee back onto his chair. Singer was seething. Hatcher had begun to drool. I just sat back and enjoyed the show. With each word he spoke, Tommy Lee was digging himself a deeper grave into which I knew I would soon be booting his body.

"'How come you so sure you arrested me?' Tommy Lee challenged when all was calm again.

"'I remember you,' Singer said, a lot firmer in his identification than he had been when I had questioned him.

"'Don't all us niggers look the same to you?' the defendant asked with a sneer.

"Singer was really angry now. 'I have no problem distinguishing one black man from another, Mr. Jones,' he replied firmly.

"'Ain't it really true that the man you stopped was my brother, Bobby Lee, who gave you my name to beat the rap?' Tommy Lee asked, violating a rule that every first-year law student knows. Every time Tommy Lee challenged Singer's identification, he was giving the officer an opportunity to restate his opinion that Tommy Lee was the person that he had arrested.

"Singer looked grim and shook his head. He was adamant now.

"'You are the person I arrested, Mr. Jones.'

"Tommy Lee swung around toward the back of the room and pointed to a black man who was seated there.

"'Ain't it him you stopped?' he challenged.

"Singer studied the man. His hair was neatly clipped and he was clean-shaven. He was dressed in a three-piece business suit, a white silk shirt, and a maroon tie. He was everything that Tommy Lee was not, and it only took Singer a moment to answer the defendant's question.

"'That is not the man I arrested.'

"'You still sticking to your nonsense story that it was me you stopped on February 8, 1970, even after bein' face to face with this man?' Tommy Lee asked incredulously.

"'It was definitely you that I stopped.'

"The verdict was a foregone conclusion. I never saw anyone bury himself so badly in all my life. I rested and Tommy Lee had no witnesses. At least he'd had the common sense to stay off the stand. At the time, I thought that was the only thing he had done correctly. Hatcher took all of half a minute to find Tommy Lee guilty."

"I'm confused, Monte. I thought you said that this Tommy Lee guy was the best you've ever gone up against in court. It sounds to me like you pounded him into hamburger meat."

"That's the way I saw it, too. I remember laughing my way through lunch as I told the other deputies about my victory. But Tommy Lee had the last laugh.

"I only saw him once more after his conviction. It was three weeks later. I was handling Criminal Presiding when the bailiff called Tommy Lee's extradition case. The man the guard led into the courtroom looked the same and was dressed in the same jail clothes, but his attitude was different. He smiled when he saw me and extended his hand.

"'You sure got the best of me, Mr. Bethune,' he said, and I noticed that the thick Negro drawl had disappeared.

"'I was just doing my job, Mr. Jones,' I assured him. 'Nothing personal.'

"'I'm aware of that,' Tommy Lee responded.

"Judge Cody took the bench and I told him that this was the time set for Tommy Lee to contest New Jersey's request that he be extradited to its jurisdiction so he could be tried for murder. Based on my experience with him in our court case, I expected Tommy Lee to come out swinging, but he surprised everyone by waiving extradition and agreeing to return to New Jersey voluntarily.

"'You're certain that's what you want to do?' Judge Cody asked. He was very conscientious about protecting the rights of those who appeared before him.

"'Yes, Your Honor,' Tommy Lee replied politely.

"'All right,' the judge said. And that was the last I ever saw of Tommy Lee.

"But it wasn't the last time I thought about him. See, Lyle, I knew, in my gut, that something was wrong. He was just so different in the two court cases. The way he talked, the way he walked. What had caused Tommy Lee's transformation from a wild-eyed radical to a polite and well-mannered citizen? That question really bothered me, but it wasn't until a little before quitting time, two weeks later, that I figured it out.

"Tommy Lee and the well-dressed black man he said was his brother did look alike. It was the wild Afro and the soiled jail clothes and the radical-black histrionics that had thrown me off. Had Officer Singer really arrested Bobby Lee Jones? Was Tommy Lee taking the rap for his brother? That was the logical explanation. Bobby Lee looked successful. Tommy Lee was a bad actor with a long record of arrests and convictions. That was it, I decided.

Tommy Lee was taking the fall for brotherly love. It made me think better of him. For a moment, I felt a warm glow.

"Then a warning bell began tinkling in my subconscious, and I suddenly felt an attack of nausea. The extradition file was in a cabinet on the other side of the office. I raced to it and my hand shook as I grabbed the manila folder from the drawer. I prayed that I was wrong, but I was certain that I wasn't. As I read the extradition warrant, I could see Tommy Lee pointing at Bobby Lee Jones as he asked Marty Singer, *You still sticking to your nonsense story that it was me you stopped on February 8, 1970, even after bein' face to face with this man?*

"And I recalled Singer's firm and unequivocal response: *It was definitely you that I stopped.*

"You see, Lyle, that murder. The one that took place clear across the country, three thousand miles away, in New Jersey. According to the extradition papers, it was committed on February 8, 1970."

JOYCE CAROL OATES

Secret, Silent

FROM *Boulevard*

HE WAS TELLING ME he couldn't drive me to the interview after all. Saying, "I know I promised, honey. But I don't see how, things being what they are, this can be." And I hear these words but can't at first believe them. For I'm hurt as a child is hurt, slapped with no warning in the face, and I'm hurt as a seventeen-year-old is hurt, in my pride. Wanting to cry *You promised! You can't do this! I thought you loved me.*

It was an evening in April. We were in one of the rooms of the upstairs house as we called it. And we were having this conversation that would alter my life, anyway Dad was having it, informing me on Thursday evening that he couldn't after all drive me three hundred twenty miles across the daunting breadth of New York State for an interview at Albany State University where I'd been awarded something called a Founders' Scholarship for tuition, room and board, provided I completed my application with an interview on campus; which interview had been scheduled, after numerous telephone calls, for Saturday morning at eleven o'clock. To arrive at the university by that time we would have had to leave home no later than four o'clock in the morning. Yet now Dad was telling me he'd have to work on Saturday morning; his foreman at the shop wanted him, for time-and-a-half wages, which couldn't be turned down. *Things being what they are* meaning he needed the money, our family needed the money, he hadn't any choice.

Nor could my mother drive me. "You know I can't be away from Grandma for so many hours."

I told Mom yes, I knew.

"Please look at me! I'm talking to you."

I told Mom yes, I knew she was talking to me.

"I know you're disappointed, but it can't be helped. When you're older you'll understand, things happen to us that can't be helped. Poor Grandma —"

I wasn't listening. At the time I didn't understand how my mother was terrified of her own mother dying, though Grandma was eighty years old and had been ill for years; how despite all circumstances, and some of them grim, there's a profound distinction between being a woman who still has her mother and a woman who does not. What I heard of my mother's plea was *Things happen. Can't be helped. When you're older you'll understand.* That deadly refrain. That litany of defeat. My young heart beat hard in defiance *Oh no I won't, not me!*

"I've figured out a way I can get to Albany, without Daddy driving me. By Greyhound bus."

"So far? Alone?"

"I won't be alone, Mom. There's another girl in my class" — with ease I supplied the name, an acquaintance and not a friend, a name my mother might recognize — "who's going to be interviewed, too. I asked around at school today. Her father can't drive her either."

All that day I'd planned this, these very words. To be spoken without reproach or rancor, simply a statement of fact. *There are other fathers who can't help their daughters at such crucial times. It's an ordinary matter to be remedied in ordinary, practical ways.* I'd called the Greyhound station: there was an overnight bus that left Port Oriskany at 11:10 P.M. that night, made numerous stops along the Thruway, and arrived in Albany at 7:50 A.M. tomorrow. Presumably, passengers slept on the bus.

My mother stared at me. I was so effervescent, so happy, all smiles; so very different from the way I'd been the previous evening, and from my truest, most secret self. I expected her to object to such an adventure, my traveling such a distance, overnight, meeting with strangers in a city where we knew no one, had no relatives, and in fact Mom did object, but weakly, saying she didn't think it was a good idea for young girls to be traveling by themselves, but Dad shrugged and declared it was fine with him — "Hell, the girl's no fool, she can take care of herself." He was relieved, obviously. He needn't feel any guilt now. Fondly he squeezed my shoulder, he called me "sweetheart."

In this way, it was decided.

Dad drove me to the Greyhound station that night. The bus, which looked massive, spouting exhaust in a bluish cloud, was already boarding when we arrived at eleven o'clock. Dad had been drinking after supper and his handsome, ravaged face was flushed but he was nowhere near drunk, only in good spirits; he'd probably be dropping by one of his taverns before returning home. First, he saw his daughter off for her interview, gave me a big hug and a wet kiss on the side of my face, and told me, "Take care, sweetheart! See you tomorrow." There was no sign of my classmate, whoever she was supposed to be, but Dad wasn't suspicious as Mom would have been. He seemed to believe me when I pretended to be pointing out someone on the bus, waving happily to her — "There's Barbara. She's saving me a seat."

Most of the passengers were men traveling by themselves, but there were several women, among them, hurrying late to board, a striking young woman who might have been in her mid-twenties, with crimped auburn hair and thin arched eyebrows and a very red, moist mouth. She called out, "Driver, wait for me *please!*" This was intended as a flirtatious joke, for the bus driver wasn't about to leave just yet; he laughed and assured the young woman she'd gotten there in time, and did she need help with her suitcase?

I was several passengers ahead of this woman, making my way along the bus aisle, but I observed through the windows that, as she hurried past my father out on the pavement, the two of them glanced searchingly at each other. Their gazes held for a long moment as if they were waiting to recall that they knew each other — but, too bad, they didn't. So the young woman in staccato high heels climbed up into the bus, breathless, with an air of entering a space in readiness for her, like a stage; she took for granted that people would be looking at her, women and men both, and was careful to make eye contact with no one. By this time most of the single seats had been taken. I'd found one of the last ones, toward the rear of the bus; I glanced back at the auburn-haired young woman hoping she'd follow me and sit with me, but she didn't notice me, and took a seat with one of the better-dressed men passengers who'd risen gallantly to give her the window seat.

They were three seats ahead of me on the other side of the aisle. I would hear them talking together for the next forty minutes as the Greyhound heaved its way through Port Oriskany streets and out to the Thruway. The man's voice was indistinct but persistent; he did most of the talking; the young woman's responses were few, and punctuated by nervous laughter. I wondered how it was possible to fall so quickly into conversation with a stranger; there was something thrilling in it, risky and dramatic.

I'd brought with me *The Plays of Eugene O'Neill* and was midway in that strange, surreal play *The Hairy Ape,* which was so different from the other O'Neill plays I'd struggled through, and fascinating to me, for I believed I would like to write plays someday; but my attention was drawn repeatedly to the couple several seats ahead, particularly to the auburn-haired woman. Who was she? Why was she traveling alone on an overnight bus to — where? The bus's final destination was New York City. I wanted to think she was headed there. She had the looks and style (I thought) to be an actress or a showgirl of some kind. I'd had an impression of a fine-boned profile, a delicate nose and wavy shoulder-length hair, the sharp gleam of gold earrings. She'd been wearing a dark blue raincoat shot with iridescent threads which she'd removed with some ceremony when she took her seat, folding it and placing it in the overhead rack with her bags. Around her neck she'd knotted a stylish silk scarf, crimson peonies on a cream-colored background. I was curious to know what her companion was saying to her so earnestly, but there was too much noise from the bus's motor; it was like trying to hear my parents' murmurous voices through a wall, mysterious and teasing. I had the idea that the man was offering the young woman a drink from a bottle or flask in a paper bag and that she'd declined more than once. (Alcohol was forbidden on the bus.) My heart pounded with a sudden thrill of excitement. I'd deceived my parents, and they would never know. I would escape their plans for me, whatever those plans were, or were not: my mother had several times said plaintively that it was too bad my scholarship at Albany couldn't be "cashed in" — we could certainly use the money to help pay my grandmother's medical bills.

Most of the other passengers had settled in to sleep by midnight; only a few, like me, had switched on overhead lights to read. The auburn-haired young woman and her companion sat in semi-darkness. I'd begun to lose interest in them when I heard a woman's voice sharply raised — "No *sir.*" A man said, "Eh? What's wrong?" trying to laugh. But already the young woman was out of her seat, determined to leave. "Go to hell, mister." She grabbed her coat and the smaller of her bags from the overhead rack and, incensed, began to make her way toward the rear of the bus. Behind her the man stood, protesting, "Hey, wait, hey c'mon — I was only kidding. Don't go away mad." The bus had begun to slow; up front, the driver must have been watching through his rearview mirror, ready to intervene. The young woman stood beside my seat panting and glaring at me. "D'you mind?" she demanded, and before I could tell her no, of course not, she swung into the seat heavily. "That bastard. That *son-of-a-bitch.*" She ignored the scrutiny of others close about her as, charged with outrage as with static electricity, she ignored me. Her oversized handbag of simulated lizardskin was crowding against my legs and her clumsily bunched coat was pressed against me. I'd moved over toward the window as far as I could. I was flattered she'd come to sit with me, even if she hadn't exactly chosen me, and hardly dared speak to her for fear of being rebuffed. Finally, seeing that the man in the seat up ahead had given up, she stood, folded her coat and placed it in the overhead rack, smoothed the long sexy angora sweater she was wearing down over her hips, and sat down again. Her movements were fussy, showy, self-dramatizing. She said, with a sidelong glance at me and a tight smile, "Thanks! I appreciate it. That bastard mistook me for someone I'm *not.*"

"I'm sorry."

"*I'm* not sorry. These damned buses!"

I was somewhat overwhelmed by her. Close up, she was beautiful. Her smooth creamy skin that seemed poreless, unlike my own; her thick-lashed mascaraed eyes; that glisten of female indignation of a kind I could never express except in mimicry or parody. "I don't know why I expect anything better on a damned *bus,*" she was saying. "It's not exactly first-class travel accommodations on the New York Central Pullman. You'd think by now I'd *know.*" I was tempted to tell her that she hadn't needed to sit with that man, or with any man at all. Instead I said again that I was sorry she was upset, but probably he'd let her alone now. "I'm not *upset,* I'm *disgusted,*" she said quickly. "I can take care of myself, thank you."

But this wasn't a rebuff evidently, for a moment later she asked, "What's that you're reading?" I showed her the opened pages and she frowned at the small print as if near-sighted. "'*Hairy Ape*'? Jesus. Never heard of that, what's it about?" I tried to explain, so far as I knew, which wasn't very far, that it was a play set on an ocean liner and there was a fierce, muscular man named Yank Smith who worked with the furnaces and he was proud of himself as a man who made the ship go until — "He turns into an ape, huh? Sure! There's been a movie made of that. I bet. I've seen it. I've seen *him*. Don't tell *me*," the woman said, laughing. I had to laugh with her. Amid a scent of talcum and warmed flesh there was a mild sourness as of whiskey lifting from her. "My name's Karla with a 'K.' What's your name?" I'd drawn back the heavy book that seemed embarrassing to me now. "I'm Kathryn. With a 'K.'" She said, "I'm going to Albany, what about you?" I said, "I'm going to Albany, too." She said, "I've got important business in Albany, what about you?" I said, "I guess I do, too." She asked where I lived and I told her, and I asked where she lived and she said, stiffly, she was between cities — "But not Albany. That's for damned sure." She added, loud enough for her ex-companion to hear if he was listening, "We should sleep then, best we can, and not let any assholes trouble us." Without waiting for my reply Karla reached up and switched out the overhead lights.

I'd shut the book anyway. I wouldn't have been able to concentrate.

The romance of night travel by bus. When you're alone, and no one. The thrill of such aloneness. The strange headachy insomniac nights of such aloneness. I tried to sleep, my eyes shutting upon a kaleidoscope of broken, bright images. I thought — My head is a doll's head, my eyes are glass eyes that open and shut but not with my volition. Through my eyelashes I saw headlights appearing and disappearing like lone comets on the mostly deserted Thruway. Outside was a steep hilly landscape, dimly visible by clouded moonlight. Living in such a landscape as I'd done since birth you don't need to see it to know it's there. *How happy I am. How scared, and how happy.*

It was 3:10 A.M. when the Greyhound lumbered off the Thruway to stop at an all-night service station and restaurant. Karla, who'd been sleeping, woke and poked me in the arm with unexpected

sisterly solicitude. "You awake? C'mon, we got ten minutes." There
was a parched taste like dried glue at the back of my mouth. It was a
relief to be fully awake and on my feet. Only a few other passengers
climbed out of the bus with us, most remained sleeping. Outside,
the air was a shock, so damp and cold. Though this was the last
week in April, a fine gritty sleet was being blown across the pavement. Beyond the dull-glaring fluorescent lights on their tall poles
illuminating the service station and the restaurant there was nothing, as in a stage set. Neither Karla nor I had troubled to put on our
coats and we ran shivering toward the restaurant. I saw that Karla
was barely my height in her impractical high-heeled ankle-strap
shoes. Her coral-pink angora sweater fitted her slender body snug
at her breasts and hips; to emphasize her small waist, she wore a
tightly cinched shiny black belt; her skirt, not quite reaching her
knees, was some shimmery synthetic fashion, dark crimson. "*Don't*
look at that asshole, he's poison," Karla warned me out of the side
of her mouth, like a tough girl in the movies. The man she'd been
sitting with had gotten to the restaurant entrance before us and was
standing by the door holding it open for us, staring at Karla with
doggy reproachful eyes. I supposed he was drunk, he had that look.
But it wasn't possible for me to ignore him as Karla did. I couldn't
be rude. "Thank you," I murmured as Karla and I slipped inside.

The man's lips moved. His face remained expressionless. I didn't
exactly hear what he murmured after me — *Don't bounce your tits,
honey.*

I didn't acknowledge this. So maybe I hadn't heard. I was grateful
that Karla hadn't.

The restaurant was nearly empty, only a single section was open
for service, and a single counterman in a soiled white uniform.
Karla ordered "decaf" — "And make sure it's decaf, man, not
coffee, okay?" — and a large jelly doughnut covered in powdered
sugar which she insisted I share with her — "I certainly don't in-
tend to eat this thing all by *myself*." Consuming the jelly doughnut
with the counterman and other customers looking on was a performance of some hilarity. I wasn't hungry but managed, with
Karla's encouragement, to swallow a few mouthfuls, which tasted
like mashed dough laced with sweet, vile chemicals. Close by at the
counter, the youngish bus driver in his Greyhound uniform observed us smilingly. And other men observed us. "This night!"
Karla exclaimed. Though speaking to me, she was speaking to be

overheard. Yet she seemed sincere, her smooth forehead creased for the moment. Drinking hot coffee, even decaffeinated, diluted with cream and sugar, seemed to enliven her; her eyes, which were a hazy green-brown, were widened and oddly dilated. "Jesus God, Kathryn! I have crucial business in Albany and already it's 3:20 A.M. Feels like I been awake and going for *days*." Sitting on a stool at the counter, legs crossed, sheer black stockings giving a sexy glisten to her shapely legs. Karla turned in restless half-circles. She fell into a spirited conversation with the bus driver, who seemed to have known her from somewhere, and the counterman, a taffy-skinned young black or Hispanic with deep circles beneath his eyes but an infectious laugh. In the joking and laughter that followed — what was funny exactly, I didn't know — especially with the dour doggy man from the bus, Karla's ex-seatmate, sitting on a stool at the edge of our hilarity — the counterman asked me if I was Karla's kid sister and what were "you girls" doing in the middle of the night in the middle of Nowhere, USA? He made an eloquent gesture with his hand to indicate the bleak, tacky expanse of the restaurant, all formica and plastic surfaces, a space large as a warehouse but semi-darkened now and nearly empty of customers. Near the bright-lit entrance to the restrooms a lone cleaning woman was mopping. What if this is all the world adds up to finally, I thought: a lone woman mopping a grimy floor in the middle of the night in the middle of Nowhere. I felt the horror of this vision but heard myself laugh in Karla's bright way. I said, "We have secret business, don't we, Karla? We can't tell." It was a clumsy, blushing flirtation. I might have been thirteen years old. Karla didn't help me, saying with a frown as if distancing herself from a reckless younger sister, "*I* can't tell. I sure as hell can't see into the future that's black as *ink*."

I remembered a line I'd written in my journal, copied from a library book: the author was Thomas Mann (of whom I'd only just heard, had never read) and this was taken from a letter to his son. *The secret and almost silent adventures in life are the finest.*

"D'you mind?"

Back on the bus Karla climbed luxuriantly into the seat beside the window that had been mine, and curled up to sleep. Of course I didn't mind, and wouldn't have spoken if I had.

The remainder of the night passed in dreamy jolts and blurs. Karla slept like a cat; breathed deeply and evenly, low as a cat's purr;

before long she nudged her head against my shoulder. I was stirred that a stranger should so trust herself with me. On the floor was the lizardskin bag pressing against my legs. I would have liked to look inside. In the women's room back at the restaurant I'd caught a glimpse inside the bag of a jumble of items including a plastic makeup kit, a bottle of red nail polish, the metallic handle of what might have been a knife but was probably a cheap hairbrush. And there was Karla's wallet, thick with snapshots and a wad of bills.

In the stark solitude of the night I could hear the snores and occasional mutterings of strangers. Earlier I'd told Karla where I was going, hoping to impress her, but now I was beginning to feel anxiety about my plan. An interview that would decide my college career (for so I thought at that time) after a night spent like a vagrant on a bus; without even a change of clothes, because I hadn't wanted to carry so much. I planned to use the women's room at the Greyhound station in Albany to "freshen up" — my mother's term; I'd remembered to bring a stick of deodorant, but didn't have a toothbrush. Even if my nerves kept me alert and awake I was certain to be exhausted by eleven o'clock in the morning after virtually no sleep the night before. *This is madness. Why did they let me do this. Did they know — I'd fail. Want me to fail. What a fool. Like the Hairy Ape.* I missed my step on the stairs, cried out as I fell. Someone was poking my shoulder, hard. "Hey, Kathryn. Wake up." It was Karla. I was groggy, confused. Somehow, it was morning: a bleak gray dawn beyond the bus's rain-splotched windows. We'd left the Thruway and were passing through the outskirts of a city I guessed must be Albany. I murmured I was sorry, embarrassed; I hadn't thought I was asleep. "You were grinding your back teeth," Karla said. "Like you were having a bad dream."

At the Greyhound station in downtown Albany I felt another wave of panic. I stood on the pavement not knowing where to go next. Karla too was looking quickly about as if in dread of seeing someone she knew. On the bus she'd powdered her face and fluffed out her hair; despite the rocky night, she seemed alert and enlivened. She was carrying a lightweight polyester suitcase as well as her lizardskin bag. "Say, Kathryn — I've got this place I'm going to, you could come with me, okay? Like if you wanted to wash up or whatever." Though I didn't think this was a practical idea I wasn't sure how to decline. Karla said, as if impulsively, "Y'know what — I'll

make breakfast for us. I could get some things." Still I hesitated.
Karla seemed almost to be pleading with me. She added, with a
nervous giggle, "This early in the morning, I don't like to be alone
with my thoughts. The rest of the day's like a god damn *desert*."
"Thanks," I said awkwardly, edging away, "I guess I can't." Karla
must have stared after me as I hurried away almost colliding with
people, to search out a restroom. I knew I was behaving strangely. I
was desperate to splash cold water onto my eyes which ached as if
I'd been crying (maybe in fact I had been crying) and I badly
needed to use a toilet; my stomach churned with tension. I'd been
overwhelmed by Karla's powerful personality and wanted only to
escape her.

Yet, when I emerged shakily from a toilet stall a few minutes later,
there was Karla in the restroom waiting for me, briskly washing her
hands at a sink and smiling happily at me through the clouded
mirror like a kindly older sister. Had I agreed to go with her after
all? "We'll take a cab, Kathryn. You're looking pale. This job interview or whatever it is — what time is it? Not till eleven? You need to
be *fed*."

Why I went with Karla, whom I didn't know, when it was my adamant wish not to go with her, I could not have said. In the cab I
nervously studied a city map the admissions office had mailed me on
which I'd marked in red ink the locations of the Greyhound station
and the university campus which appeared to be some distance
away. Karla seemed annoyed that I was looking at the map. "*I'll* take
you there. It's only a mile or so from my place. You have plenty of
time." She was speaking brightly and rapidly and tapping at my wrist
with her red-polished nails which were uneven, some of the nails
much longer than others. When I told her worriedly that I couldn't
seem to match the streets we were passing with street names on the
map she laughed, took the map from me, and folded it carelessly
and shoved it into her coat pocket. "There! No need to fret. *I* don't
like to be alone with my thoughts either." This made no sense but I
wasn't in a mood to object. My hands were tingling warmly: I was
thinking of how in the bus station restroom after I'd washed and
dried my hands on a coarse paper towel, Karla had seized both my
hands in hers, her hands that were startlingly soft, and rubbed
Jergen's lotion into them so that now my hands were fresh and
fragrant as Karla's though nowhere near as soft. Fall and winter I'd

played basketball at school or practiced shots whenever I could. I wasn't the most competitive girl player at school but there was something fascinating about sinking the ball through the hoop, dashing toward the basket and shooting, or shooting from the foul line, something deeply satisfying even as it was clearly pointless. But the palms of my hands were callused from gripping the ball. Compared to Karla's hands they hardly seemed like a girl's hands at all.

Why I went with Karla, and why I found myself a half-hour later ringing the doorbell of a house, Karla's place as she called it, while Karla remained in the cab idling at the curb not in front of the shabby brownstone rowhouse but a few doors down; why I was with this woman I didn't know, obeying her without question; I could not have said, for my head was a doll's head rattling-empty and finely cracked beneath the hair. As I slid out of the rear of the cab Karla impulsively looped her silk scarf around my neck. "This will keep you warm, Kathryn!" I smiled at Karla not knowing what the gesture meant — if the scarf was a gift I'd certainly return it, for I couldn't accept such an expensive gift from her, but maybe it wasn't a gift exactly and in any case how could I hurt Karla's feelings?

Yet on the sidewalk I'd hesitated, staring at the brownstone house with its four front windows in which blinds had been yanked to differing levels, a weatherworn rowhouse in a block of similar homes, and Karla leaned out the car door — "Just go ring the doorbell, Kathryn. Just to make sure. Nobody's home, I promise." I asked who might be home and Karla said emphatically, "Nobody! But we need to be certain."

The narrow front yard was grassless and rutted and the front stoop listed to one side yet I found myself bounding up to the door buoyant and daring in my ballerina flats, wanting simply to please Karla, not thinking *Where am I, why am I here? Who is this woman?* The morning was raw and scintillating, patches of bright blue sky overhead and a rising sun so fierce it made my eyes water. Everywhere the pavement was wet and glistening. I rang the doorbell and heard the buzzer inside and it was an extension of the morning's raw scintillating mood. I was nervous but not frightened exactly. In my good-girl shoes and nylon stockings that were beginning to run and my plain blue raincoat and Karla's silk scarf around my neck, the long ends fluttering in the wind, the most beautiful scarf I'd ever worn. A scarf that seemed to confer upon me a new, strange, myste-

rious power, an invulnerability to harm or even distress. Though
conceding that there was — there might be — an element of risk in
what I seemed to be doing. A second time, and a third I rang the
doorbell and there was no sound from inside the house; so narrow
a house I imagined that I could stretch my arms across the entire
façade. In the adjoining brownstone a dog had begun to bark
hysterically. Claws scratching against a windowpane.

Karla hurried up the walk behind me and gave me a quick hug.
"Good girl! You're my heart." It would occur to me later that by this
time, in her state of excitement, Karla had forgotten my name. Her
eyes were widened and despite the morning sunshine oddly dilated; there was a feverish glow to her skin. She seemed to me more
beautiful than ever. She'd had the presence of mind to take from
the cab both our bags and her polyester suitcase and she was brandishing on a strip of red wool yarn a key with which she unlocked
the door and drew me breathlessly inside with her. We were con-
fronted by cold stale air that seemed to rush at us, an underlying
odor of something rotted, mustiness like damp newspaper. "Hello?
Hello? Hello? Hel*lo?*" Karla cried, as a guest might call out stepping
into a house whose front door is open. Except for the dog barking
frantically next door there was silence. Yet the interior looked lived-
in, and recently — a pair of men's boots in the narrow hallway at
the foot of the stairs, a plaid shirt tossed onto a chair, in the living
room a space heater, unplugged. In a glass bowl on a table, floating
on the surface of scummy water, was a black-striped goldfish which
upset Karla so she hid her eyes. Her lips moved almost inaudibly —
"Bas*tard.*"

In her staccato high heels, still carrying her bags, Karla marched
back to the kitchen where a faucet was dripping loudly, jeeringly;
here the odor of rot was stronger. She threw open the refrigerator
door and recoiled with a curse from the stink. I didn't want to look
inside, in that instant I was beginning to feel nauseated; exhaustion
was catching up with me; through a crudely taped-together windowpane above the unspeakably filthy sink I could see into the
small back yard grassless as the front, and littered. *A space the size of a
large grave.* By this time the sun was more fiercely blazing and the
April day would rapidly warm except in the foul-smelling house
where the air was still cold enough for our quickened breaths to
vaporize. Yet even now not thinking, at least not thinking coher-
ently *Why am I here? And where am I?* For Karla gave me no time to

think. Scarcely time to breathe. I glanced worriedly at my wrist-watch, seeing with alarm that it was already past nine o'clock and Karla noticed, pinching my wrist, saying, "I promised I'd get you to wherever, didn't I? Stop obsessing. You're getting on my nerves." Karla led me upstairs, my heart beat with anticipation. *You could be trapped: up these stairs and no other way out.* In a dim-lit bedroom smelling of soiled clothes and mildew and stale cigarette smoke Karla dropped her suitcase onto an unmade bed and opened it and began tossing in items from a bureau drawer, and from a closet, articles of clothing. "C'mon, hon, don't just stand there, *help me,* huh?" So I helped, clumsy and hurried, my hands shaking. The bedroom was small and would have been depressing except for its lilac wallpaper, inexpertly laid on the walls (my father had wallpa-pered much of our house, which my grandmother owned, and I knew well how difficult it was to paper walls even if you know what you're doing), and cream-colored organdy curtains on the back windows. The front-window curtains had been yanked down, it seemed, curtains and curtain-rods on the floor as if they'd been tossed there in a rage; these I kept tripping over. Karla said, whis-tling, "Jesus God! Look here." She was holding a lacy red nightgown against herself; the front had been ripped nearly in two. She stared down at the nightgown smiling a peculiar smile as if the nightgown was her own mutilated self. By this time I was anxious to use the bathroom. My bladder ached, there was a loose hot rumbling in the pit of my belly, a threat of diarrhea like scorn. *You'll miss the inter-view. Fail the interview. To erase this shame you'll have to kill yourself.* Karla decided to laugh at the torn nightgown and ripped it further and threw it to the floor.

From the top shelf of the closet Karla took a small but heavy cardboard box and handed it to me to dump into the suitcase. A cascade of loose snapshots, printed documents, and letters. One of the snapshots fluttered to the floor, I reached for it and glancing up saw a man standing in the bedroom doorway. He was just standing there.

Though I was staring directly at this man and though he was surely aware of me only a few feet away he didn't seem to see me at all. He was watching Karla. And he was smiling.

A good-looking man in his mid-thirties, compact and muscled as a middleweight, not tall, with dirt-colored oily hair curving over his ears and thinning at the crown of his head, and a glittery stubble of beard on his jaws; his eyes were coppery as a stove's coils, heated. This was a man who looked as if, if you made the mistake of touching him, your fingers would burn. Karla came out of the bathroom adjoining the bedroom with an armful of toiletries and when she saw this man she gave a little scream like a kicked cat, and dropped the toiletries, and the man said to me out of the side of his mouth without so much as glancing at me, "Get out of here, you. This is between her and me." Karla cried to me, "Don't leave me!" and I stammered I would not, even as the man pushed past me to grab Karla's arm, and Karla was screaming, shoving at him, he gripped her shoulders in both hands and shook her and she punched and kicked and used her elbows against him as in a clumsy violent dance. I picked up one of the curtain rods from the floor and swung it at Karla's attacker, striking him on the side of the head; he turned to curse me and in desperation I swung the rod back this time striking him on the neck, and he grabbed the rod and tossed it aside, the torn curtains still dragging with it as in a comic cinematic sequence, and as I stood paralyzed he punched me with his right fist, a blow to my jaw that knocked me backward, legs dissolving beneath me, and I fell heavily to the floor. There I lay unable to move. I'd been knocked unconscious, concussed, like a boxer who's been struck a blow he has seen flying at him yet hasn't comprehended, and now he's out though his eyes are open and he's staring blankly, not seeing anything, not even the proverbial black lights that mimic death: and by the time vision and comprehension return you understand that a very long time has passed in your life, if only a few seconds by the clock.

Always afterward recalling *How close to brain-death, extinction. The snap of a finger more and you'd be gone.*

And what would they have done with my body, Karla and the man who was her ex-husband, or husband? I've never wanted to speculate.

But this happened instead: as the man turned to me, Karla drew out of her lizardskin bag a knife, a steel-handled eight-inch steak knife, and in a fury began stabbing at him, and the astonished man backed off saying, "Jesus, Karla! Give that to me!" He was actually laughing, or trying to laugh. As if he thought it might be a joke. And there was something comical about Karla's rage, the awkward way she wielded the knife, as a child might, the handle gripped tight in her fist and her blows overhand like a windmill's blades; so

that the man, quick on his feet, shrewd and strong, had reason to
think he could take the knife from her without being cut even as,
trying to wrest it from her by the blade, he was being cut; blood
ran down both his hands in quick eager bright streams. They were
shouting accusations at each other. Cursing each other. Karla had
the man backed against the edge of the bed, the flashing blade
struck him in the shoulder, in the upper chest, he fell clumsily onto
the bed and yet more clumsily onto the opened suitcase, trying to
shield his head with his arms and pleading for her to stop as blood
spilled like a garish crimson blossom down his chest, darkening his
shirt and unzipped suede jacket. "See how you like it! See how you
like it! I hate you! I'll kill you! Why are you here! You're not supposed to be here! You have no right to be here!" Karla cried. But
seeing then what she'd done, she threw down the bloody knife; in
an instant her fury changed to horror and repentance. "Arnie no
— I didn't mean it. Arnie —" She knelt beside the bed, now desperate, asking was he all right, saying he'd made her do it, she was
sorry, don't die on me, Karla was begging, don't bleed to death,
Karla was sobbing. By this time I'd managed to get to my feet
though reeling with dizziness; I leaned over coughing, and a thin
scalding stream of vomit issued from my mouth. When I could
speak, I told Karla I'd call an ambulance and went to a phone on a
bedside table, began to dial 911 when the wounded man Arnie
told Karla, "Take that fucking thing from her," and Karla stumbled
to me, one of her high-heeled shoes on and the other off, and
snatched the receiver out of my hand fixing me with her widened
blackly dilated eyes. "He's all right! He isn't going to die! We can
take care of him ourselves!"

And so we did.

Karla commanded me to help her and I obeyed. Afterward I would
conclude I'd been in a state of shock. And I would wonder at the
logic of bringing a badly bleeding man into the bathroom as he'd
insisted, as I would wonder at the logic of not calling an ambulance.
I would wonder *Did he live — or did he die? Was I a witness to manslaughter? Was I an accessory?* Stumbling and swaying like drunks,
Karla and I walked the wounded man into the bathroom. Each of
us grasped him around the waist and how heavy he was, how his
terrible weight pulled me down. My head and jaw were pounding
from the blow I'd taken, the left side of my face beginning already

to swell. Karla was saying in a dazed voice, "You'll be all right. Honey, you'll be all right. It's just flesh wounds, I think. *You'll be all right.*" Her face looked coarse, makeup streaked in unflattering rivulets, mascara smeared beneath her eyes like ink; I saw that Karla wasn't a young woman only a few years older than me but well into her thirties and now looking her age. In the dank, ill-smelling bathroom with no window and a single bare light bulb overhead the wounded man sat down heavily on the rim of the bathtub, whimpering and cursing with pain. He was panting, yet couldn't seem to take his injuries seriously, impatient with himself for being weakened and slowed down. I would never know if this man, Arnie, was Karla's ex-husband or still her husband but it seemed they'd been married; there may even have been a child involved, and this child may even have died — from what they said, elliptically, and in fragments, and from what I was able in my distracted state to comprehend, this seemed to be the case. Clearly they were lovers even if they'd wanted to hurt each other badly; clearly Karla was appalled at what she'd done to him, the dozen shallow wounds on his hands, forearms, and neck and the deeper wounds in his chest and shoulder. Karla commanded, "Don't just stand there, help us for God's sake." I fetched towels, pillowcases, even soiled sheets from the bed. Clumsily we made bandages, thick wads of cloth to stanch the bleeding, or to try to stanch it; for blood soaked through the makeshift bandages within seconds, glistening on our hands and splattering onto our legs. Star-bursts of blood collected on the tile floor. The wounded man demanded cold-water compresses which may have helped a little. His impatience with his bleeding wounds reminded me of my father's angry impatience with his own infrequent illnesses and gave me a sense of the man's personality. I would never know more about him. I would never know Karla's last name. Though involved in this terrible episode, like sisters baptized in another's blood, I would never see Karla nor hear of her after that morning.

The wounded Arnie was deathly pale but insisted to Karla for Christ's sake he was all right, she hadn't struck deep with the fucking knife and he'd had worse than this happen to him, he'd been shot for Christ's sake and it hadn't killed him. He gave her a wincing grin, saying, "So you did it, eh? Got guts, eh?" — which made Karla cry harder. She was crouched beside him with her arms around him and her forehead pressed against his. I stood in the

doorway not knowing what to do. Next door, the maddened dog
was barking furiously at us through the plasterboard wall, only a few
feet away. The wounded man at last squinted at me asking Karla
who I was, and Karla said, "Nobody. A friend," and the man asked,
"A friend *who?*" and Karla said, "I don't know! Nobody." Karla
didn't so much as glance at me. The wounded man was panting,
scowling; he stared at me for a long moment before saying, "*You,*
you better leave. Don't make any fucking calls, just *go.*" So I did.

On the bedroom floor amid the wreckage of the curtains I discovered Karla's beautiful silk scarf which I carried away with me. *I
deserve this,* I thought.

As in a nightmare it was 11:25 A.M. when I finally arrived for the
interview.

I'd had to run several blocks after leaving the brownstone to find
a pay phone in a drugstore so that I could call a taxi, and I'd waited
with mounting anxiety for a taxi to arrive, and the ride itself
seemed to take forever, and at the university I had to ask directions
to the admissions office, and once in that building at the top of a
steep hill I had to spend frantic minutes in a women's room in a
state of physical distress; afterward trying to make myself present-
able for meeting the associate dean of admissions who would be
interviewing me: for the front of my raincoat was stained with both
vomit and a stranger's blood, and there was a wide, wet stain on the
skirt of my navy blue wool suit which I cleverly disguised by shifting
the front of the skirt to the side and covering the stain with my
raincoat which I'd carefully folded so that the stain didn't show,
and hung over my arm. It looked quite natural, didn't it, for me to
be carrying my coat over my arm, on a warm April morning? Of
course I had to wash my hands and my face; without removing my
nylon stockings (which were now marred by runs) I managed to
lighten the blood stains on my legs. The left side of my face was
swollen so that I looked as if I had mumps on just that side, and
there was an ugly bruise taking shape but this too I disguised, or
believed I disguised, by looping Karla's long scarf around my neck
and tying it in a bow at my jawline. In the mirror I saw an unnaturally pale girl with stark, shadowed, blood-veined eyes and wind-
blown hair and a look about the mouth that might have been
desperation or triumph. *I'm here. I'm here!*

I'd missed my appointment of course. The dean was interviewing other students. His receptionist advised me to reschedule my interview for the following Saturday but I said that wasn't possible — "I'll wait." Staring at my swollen jaw and rumpled clothes the receptionist tried to discourage me but I said I couldn't come back to Albany another time — "I'm here *now*." I must have spoken sharply, for the woman pursed her lips and said nothing more.

You can't deny me, I've come so far.

Waiting in the dean's outer office as other students my age, glancing at me curiously, came and went. Pacing in the corridor outside. And more than once retreating to a women's restroom to stare at my reflection that seemed to waver in the glass. A ghastly radiance shone in my skin. My eyes resembled Karla's — glittery and dilated. And the silk scarf with the crimson peonies was so beautiful, the most beautiful item of clothing I'd ever worn.

Not until 1:20 P.M. would the associate dean have time to "fit me in." And then I was allowed to know it was something of a special favor. The man's name was Werner — I was careful to address him as "Dr. Werner" — perceiving him as one of a sequence of adults in my adolescent life who must be judiciously courted, placated, seduced. This man was frowning yet kindly, with deep dents and fissures in his middle-aged, claylike face; he'd have been willing to forgive me for being late if only I might have explained myself yet I couldn't seem to explain myself except to say tersely that I'd come from Port Oriskany on the Greyhound bus and had been unavoidably detained. "'Unavoidably' — ? You didn't have an accident, did you, Miss —" he peered through bifocals at documents on his desk and pronounced my tricky ethnic name with elaborate care. *Tell him yes! Arouse the bastard's sympathy.* This was a reckless voice not my own which I ignored. I thanked Dr. Werner politely and told him no, I was fine. "Is this your first visit to Albany?" he asked, as if such a fact might help to explain me, and I murmured yes it was. I believed I was speaking normally despite the stiffness in my jaw and a fiery ache that ran along my gumline as if every tooth there was abscessed. Dr. Werner shuffled through documents in my folder, now and then making notations with a pen. Though I knew there were bookshelves in his office it seemed that my vision was narrowed as if by blinders and I could see only Dr. Werner clearly. I was very tired suddenly and yearned to rest my arms on the edge of his desk and my heavy head upon my arms for only just a moment. I saw the man's fleshy lips move before I heard this question — "Why do you believe you would make a good, dedicated teacher, Kathryn?" But I didn't recall having said I wanted to be a teacher or that this subject was the purpose of our conversation. *Tell the man something. Out of pride, you must not fail.* So I spoke. Falteringly at first and then with more confidence. I saw that Dr. Werner stared at me, my dilated eyes and swollen jaw, but I'd long been an articulate child and though I might stammer under pressure, words rarely failed me; especially adult words of a lofty, abstract nature. I spoke of what my own education had meant to me so far, how it had "saved my life by giving purpose to my life"; I spoke of how my grandparents, Hungarian immigrants, hadn't had the opportunity to be educated beyond grade school and were barely literate in English; I spoke of my parents, growing up during the Depression, who hadn't graduated from high school — "I want to be part of the world beyond that. A world of the intellect and of the spirit." Tears stung my eyes, these words so moved me; even as, pandering them to a stranger as I was, in the hope of winning his approval, I felt deeply ashamed. Dr. Werner was nodding, and frowning. Perhaps he was moved, too. Or embarrassed for me. His wide dark nostrils pinched. *He's sniffing you. Smells blood. Menstrual blood, he'd think. Oh, shame!*

My voice, stricken, trailed off into silence. The ache in my jaw was fierce. Mistaking my hesitation for shyness, and liking shyness in a girl, Dr. Werner was deciding he liked me; he concluded the interview by praising my scholastic record which was spread out before him on his desk like the innards of a dissected creature — and my teachers' "glowing" letters of recommendation — and assured me that I was exactly the kind of dedicated young person the university hoped for as Founders' Scholars. The interview was over: Dr. Werner had heaved himself up from his swivel chair, a shorter and stockier man than I'd believed; he was smiling, showing an expanse of pinkish gum, and congratulated me on the scholarship which was, he hoped I knew, highly competitive, awarded to no more than twenty students out of an entering class of eleven hundred; my final acceptance forms would arrive at my home within a few weeks. I said, stammering, "Dr. Werner, it might not be absolutely true — that I want to be a teacher. That I know what I want to do with my life." Dr. Werner snorted with laughter as if I was joking, or he wished to think I was joking. He repeated that the final acceptance forms would arrive within a few weeks and he hoped I'd have a good return trip home. I said, "Then I am — admitted? I'm *in?*" I felt a stab of dismay. Was my life decided? Had I agreed to this? Dr. Werner said, with just perceptible impatience, "Yes, of course. Our interview is only a formality." He extended his hand for a brisk, firm handshake and sent me on my way.

Hurrying down a flight of vertiginous stairs — so like the stairs in my dream of the previous night! — I realized that there might have been blood on my hand, still; that I hadn't been able to scrub every stain off. I could envision Dr. Werner, his claylike face creased in revulsion, contemplating his own blood-sticky hand.

But I won't come back here. Not here.

Returning to Port Oriskany on the 5:35 P.M. bus I was sitting alone, my head slumped against a window. My face was throbbing with pain but it was pain at a distance, for I'd swallowed a handful of aspirins to numb it. Much of that day would be lost to me in cloudy amnesiac patches like strips of paper torn from a wall. How I would explain the silk scarf to my mother, I didn't yet know and wasn't much worried. I was in a state of exhilaration. A state of certitude. On the mammoth lumbering bus like a prehistoric creature vibrating with energy. I wanted to sleep yet my eyes wouldn't close. Far to the west as if at the end of the Thruway, there was a horizon seething with red like the flames of an open furnace.

The countryside darkens by rapid degrees. I begin to see my face reflected in the steamy window. A face-to-come, the face of my adulthood. And beyond it my parents' faces subtly distorted as if in water. For the first time I realize that my parents are a man, a woman: individuals who'd loved each other before they'd ever loved me. And they do love me, only they can't protect me; nor do they know me. I realize that I will leave home soon. In fact, I've already left.

PETER ROBINSON

In Flanders Fields

FROM *Not Safe After Dark*

I CONSIDERED IT the absolute epitome of irony that, with bombs falling around us, someone went and bludgeoned Mad Maggie to death.

To add insult to injury, she lay undiscovered for several days before Harry Fletcher, the milkman, found her. Because milk was rationed to one or two pints a week, depending on how much the children and expectant mothers needed, he didn't leave it on her doorstep the way he used to do before the war. Even in a close community like ours, a bottle of milk left unguarded on a doorstep wouldn't have lasted five minutes.

These days, Harry walked around with his float, and people came out to buy. It was convenient, as we were some way from the nearest shops, and we could always be sure we were getting fresh milk. However mad Maggie may have been, it wasn't like her to miss her milk ration. Thinking she might have slept in, or perhaps have fallen ill with no one to look after her, Harry knocked on her door and called her name. When he heard no answer, he told me, he made a tentative try at the handle and found that the door was unlocked.

There she lay on her living room floor in a pool of dried blood dotted with flies. Poor Harry lost his breakfast before he could dash outside for air.

Why Harry came straight to me when he found Mad Maggie's body I can't say. We were friends of a kind, I suppose, of much the same age, and we occasionally passed a pleasurable evening together playing dominoes and drinking watery beer in the Prince Albert. Other than that, we didn't have a lot in common: I was a schoolteacher — English and History — and Harry had left school at fourteen; Harry had missed the first war through a heart ailment, whereas I had been gassed at Ypres in 1917; I was a bachelor, and Harry was married with a stepson, Thomas, who had just come back home on convalescent leave after being severely wounded at the Dunkirk evacuation. Thomas also happened to be my godson, which I suppose was the main thing Harry and I had in common.

Perhaps Harry also came to me because I was a Special Constable. I know it sounds impressive, but it isn't really. The services were so mixed up that you'd have the police putting out fires, the Home Guard doing police work, and anyone with two arms carrying the stretchers. A Special Constable was simply a part-time policeman, without any real qualifications for the job except his willingness to take it on. The rest of the time I taught what few pupils remained at Silverhill Grammar School.

As it turned out, I was glad that Harry did call on me, because it gave me a stake in the matter. The regular police were far more concerned with lighting offenses and the black market than they were with their regular duties, and one thing nobody had time to do in the war was investigate the murder of a mad, mysterious, cantankerous old woman.

Nobody except me, that is.

Though my position didn't grant me any special powers, I pride myself on being an intelligent and perceptive sort of fellow, not to mention nosy, and it wasn't the first time I'd done a spot of detective work on the side. But first, let me tell you a little about Mad Maggie . . .

I say *old* woman, but Maggie was probably only in her mid-forties, about the same age as me, when she was killed. Everyone just called her *old;* it seemed to go with *mad.* With a certain kind of woman, it's not so much a matter of years, anyway, but of demeanor, and Maggie's demeanor was old.

Take the clothes she wore, for a start: most women were trying to look like one of the popular film stars like Vivien Leigh or Deanna Durbin, with her bolero dresses, but even for a woman of her age, Maggie wore clothes that could best be described as old-fashioned, even antique: high-buttoned boots, long dresses with high collars, ground-sweeping cloaks and broad-brimmed hats with feathers.

Needless to say, the local kids — at least those whose parents

hadn't packed them off to the countryside already — used to follow her down the street in gangs and chant, "Mad Maggie, Mad
Maggie, she's so mad, her brain's all claggy . . ." Children can be so
cruel. Most of the time she ignored them, or seemed oblivious to
their taunts, but once in a while she wheeled on them, eyes blazing,
and started waving her arms around and yelling curses, usually in
French. The children would squeal with exaggerated horror, then
turn tail and run away.

Maggie never had any visitors; none of us had ever been inside
her house; nobody in the community even knew what her real
name was, where she had come from, or how she had got to be the
way she was. We simply accepted her. There were rumors of course.
Some gossipmongers had it that she was an heiress cut off by her
family because she went mad; others said she had never recovered
from a tragic love affair; still others said she was a rich eccentric and
kept thousands of pounds stuffed in her mattress.

Whoever and whatever Mad Maggie was, she managed to take
care of life's minutiae somehow; she paid her rent, she bought
newspapers, and she handled her ration coupons just like the rest
of us. She also kept herself clean, despite the restriction to only five
inches of bathwater. Perhaps her eccentricity was just an act, then,
calculated to put people off befriending her for some reason? Perhaps she was shy or antisocial? All in all, she was known as Mad
Maggie only because she never talked to anyone except herself,
because of the old clothes she wore, because of her strange out-
bursts in French, and because, as everyone knew, she never went to
the shelters during air-raids, but would either stay indoors alone or
walk the blacked-out streets muttering and arguing with herself,
waving her arms at the skies as if inviting the bombs to come and
get her.

When Harry called that Monday morning, I was lying in bed grap-
pling with one of my frequent bouts of insomnia, waiting for the
birds to sing me back to sleep. I couldn't even tell if it was daylight
or not because of the heavy blackout curtains. I had been dream-
ing, I remembered, and had woken at about half-past four, gasping
for air, from my recurring nightmare about being sucked down into
a quicksand.

I heard Harry banging at my door and calling my name, so I
threw on some clothes and hurried downstairs. I thought at first

that it might be something to do with Tommy, but when I saw his pale face, his wide eyes, and the thin trickle of vomit at the corner of his mouth, I worried that he was having the heart attack he had been expecting daily for over twenty years.

He turned and pointed down the street. "Frank, please!" he said. "You've got to come with me."

I could hear the fear in his voice, so I followed him as quickly as I could to Maggie's house. It was a fine October morning, with a hint of autumn's nip in the air. He had left the door ajar. Slowly, I pushed it open and went inside. My first impression was more surprise at how clean and tidy the place was than shock at the bloody figure on the carpet. In my defense, lest I sound callous, I had fought in the first war and, by some miracle, survived the mustard-gas with only a few blisters and a nasty coughing fit every now and then. But I had seen men blown apart; I had been spattered with the brains of my friends; I had crawled through trenches and not known whether the soft, warm, gelatinous stuff I was putting my hands in was mud or the entrails of my comrades. More recently, I had also helped dig more than one mangled or dismembered body from the ruins, so a little blood, a little death, never bothered me much. Besides, despite the pool of dried blood around her head, Mad Maggie looked relatively peaceful. More peaceful than I had ever seen her in life.

Funny, but it reminded me of that old Dracula film I saw at the Crown, the one with Bela Lugosi. The count's victims always became serene after they had wooden stakes plunged through their hearts. Mad Maggie hadn't been a vampire, and she didn't have a stake through her heart, but a bloodstained posser lay by her side, the concave copper head and wooden handle both covered in blood. A quick glance in the kitchen showed only one puzzling item: an unopened bottle of milk. As far as I knew, Harry's last round had been the morning of the air-raid, last Wednesday. I doubted that Maggie would have been able to get more than her rations; besides, the bottle-top bore the unmistakable mark of the dairy where Harry worked.

Harry waited outside, unwilling to come in and face the scene again. Once I had taken in what had happened, I told him to fetch the police, the real police this time.

They came.

*

And they went.

One was a plainclothes officer, Detective Sergeant Longbottom, a dull-looking bruiser with a pronounced limp, who looked most annoyed at being called from his bed. He asked a few questions, sniffed around a bit, then got the ambulance men to take Maggie away on a stretcher.

One of the questions Sergeant Longbottom asked was the victim's name. I told him that, apart from "Mad Maggie," I had no idea. With a grunt, he rummaged around in the sideboard drawer and found her rent book. I was surprised to discover that she was called Rose Faversham, which I thought was actually quite a pretty name. Prettier than Mad Maggie, anyway. Sergeant Longbottom also asked if we'd had any strangers in the area. Apart from an army unit billeted near the park, where they were carrying out training exercises, and the Gypsy encampment in Silverhill Woods, we hadn't.

"Ah, Gypsies," he said, and wrote something in his little black notebook. "Is anything missing?"

I told him I didn't know, as I had no idea what *might* have been here in the first place. That seemed to confuse him. For all I knew, I went on, the rumor might have been right, and she could have had a mattress stuffed with banknotes. Sergeant Longbottom checked upstairs and came back scratching his head. "Everything *looks* normal," he said, then he poked around a bit more, noting the canteen of sterling silver cutlery, and guessed that Mad Maggie had probably interrupted the thief, who had killed her and fled the scene — probably back to the Gypsy encampment. I was on the point of telling him that I thought the Nazis were supposed to be persecuting Gypsies, not us, but I held my tongue. I knew it would do no good.

Of course, I told him how everyone in the neighborhood knew Mad Maggie paid no attention to air-raids, how she even seemed to enjoy them the way some people love thunderstorms, and how Tom Sellers, the ARP man, had remonstrated with her on many occasions, only to get a dismissive wave and the sight of her ramrod-stiff back walking away down the street. Maggie had also been fined more than once for blackout infringements, until she solved that one by keeping her heavy black curtains closed night *and* day.

I also told Longbottom that, in the blackout, anyone could have come and gone easily without being seen. I think that was what finally did it. He hummed and hawed, muttered "Gypsies" again, made noises about a continuing investigation, then put his little black notebook away, said he had pressing duties to attend to, and left.

We never saw him in our street again.

And there things would have remained had I not become curious. No doubt Mad Maggie would have been fast forgotten and some poor, innocent Gypsy would have been strung up from the gallows. But there was something about the serenity of Mad Maggie's features in death that haunted me. She looked almost saintlike, as if she had sloughed off the skin of despair and madness that she had inhabited for so long and reverted to the loving, compassionate Christian woman she must have once been. She had a real name now, too: *Rose Faversham*. I was also provoked by Detective Sergeant Longbottom's gruff manner and his obvious impatience with the whole matter. No doubt he had more important duties to get back to, such as the increased traffic in blackmarket onion substitutes.

I would like to say that the police searched Maggie's house thoroughly, locked it up fast, and put a guard on the door, but they did nothing of the kind. They did lock the front door behind us, of course, but that was it. I imagined that, as soon as he found out, old Grasper, the landlord, would slither around, rubbing his hands and trying to rent the place out quickly again, for twice as much, before the army requisitioned it as a billet.

One thing I had neglected to tell Detective Sergeant Longbottom, I realized as I watched his car disappear around a pile of rubble at the street corner, was about Fingers Finnegan, our local black marketeer and petty thief. Human nature is boundlessly selfish and greedy, even in wartime, and air-raids provided the perfect cover for burglary and blackmarket deals. The only unofficial people on the streets during air-raids were either mad, like Maggie, or up to no good, like Fingers. We'd had a spate of burglaries when most decent, law-abiding people were in St. Mary's church crypt, or at least in their damp and smelly back-yard Anderson shelters, and Fingers was my chief suspect. He could be elusive when he wanted to be, though, and I hadn't seen him in a number of days.

Not since last Wednesday's air-raid, in fact.

*

After the police had gone, Harry and I adjourned to my house, where, despite the early hour, I poured him a stiff brandy and offered him a Woodbine. I didn't smoke, myself, because of that little bit of gas that had leaked through my mask at Ypres, but I had soon discovered that it was wise to keep cigarettes around when they were becoming scarce. Like some of the rationed items, they became a kind of currency. I also put the kettle on, for I hadn't had my morning tea yet, and I'm never at my best before my morning tea. Perhaps that may be one reason I have never married; most of the women I have met chatter far too much in the morning.

"What a turn up," Harry said, after taking a swig and coughing. "Mad Maggie, murdered. Who'd imagine it?"

"Her killer, I should think," I said.

"Gypsies."

I shook my head. "I doubt it. Oh, there's no doubt they're a shifty lot. I wouldn't trust one of them as far as I could throw him. But killers? A defenseless woman like Maggie? I don't think so. Besides, you saw her house. It hadn't been touched."

"But Sergeant Longbottom said she might have interrupted a burglar."

I sniffed. "Sergeant Longbottom's an idiot. There was no evidence at all that her killer was attempting to burgle the place."

"Maybe she was one of them once — a Gypsy — and they came to take her back?"

I laughed. "I must say, Harry, you certainly don't lack imagination, I'll grant you that. But no, I rather fancy this is a different sort of matter altogether."

Harry frowned. "You're not off on one of your Sherlock Holmes kicks again, are you, Frank? Leave it be. Let the professionals deal with it. It's what they're paid for."

"*Professionals!* Hmph. You saw for yourself how interested our Detective Sergeant Longbottom was. Interested in crawling back in his bed, more like it. No, Harry, I think that's the last we've seen of them. If we want to find out who killed poor Maggie, we'll have to find out for ourselves."

"Why not just let it be, Frank?" Harry pleaded. "We're at war. People are getting killed every minute of the day and night."

I gave him a hard look, and he cringed a little. "Because this is different, Harry. While I can't say I approve of war as a solution to man's problems, at least it's socially sanctioned murder. If the government, in all its wisdom, decides that we're at war with Germany and we should kill as many Germans as we can, then so be it. But nobody sanctioned the killing of Mad Maggie. When an individual kills someone like Maggie, he takes something he has no right to. Something he can't even give back or replace, the way he could a diamond necklace. It's an affront to us all, Harry, an insult to the community. And it's up to us to see that retribution is made." I'll admit I sounded a little pompous, but Harry could be extremely obtuse on occasion, and his using the war as an excuse for so outrageous a deed as Rose Faversham's murder brought out the worst in me.

Harry seemed suitably cowed by my tirade, and when he'd finished his brandy he shuffled off to finish his deliveries. I never did ask him whether there was any milk left on his unattended float.

I had another hour in which to enjoy my morning tea before I had to leave for school, but first I had to complete my ritual and drop by the newsagent's for a paper. While I was there, I asked Mrs. Hope behind the counter when she had last seen Mad Maggie. Last Wednesday, she told me, walking down the street towards her house just before the warning siren went off, muttering to herself. That information, along with the unopened milk and the general state of the body, was enough to confirm for me that Rose had probably been killed under cover of the air-raid.

That morning, I found I could neither concentrate on *Othello*, which I was supposed to be teaching the fifth form, nor could I be bothered to read about the bombing raids, evacuation procedures, and government pronouncements that passed for news in these days of propaganda and censorship.

Instead, I thought about Mad Maggie, or Rose Faversham, as she had now become for me. When I tried to visualize her as she was alive, I realized that had I looked closely enough, had I got beyond the grim expressions and the muttered curses, I might have seen her for the handsome woman she was. *Handsome,* I say, not pretty or beautiful, but I would hazard a guess that twenty years ago she would have turned a head or two. Then I remembered that it was about twenty years ago when she first arrived in the neighborhood, and she had been Mad Maggie right from the start. So perhaps I was inventing a life for her, a life she had never had, but certainly when death brought repose to her features, it possessed her of a beauty I had not noticed before.

When I set off for school, I saw Tommy Markham, Harry's stepson, going for his morning constitutional. Tommy's real dad, Lawrence Markham, had been my best friend. We had grown up together and had both fought in the Third Battle of Ypres, between August and November of 1917. Lawrence had been killed at Passchendaele, about nine miles away from my unit, while I had only been mildly gassed. Tommy was in his mid-twenties now. He never knew his real dad, but worshipped him in a way you can worship only a dead hero. Tommy joined up early and served with the Green Howards as part of the ill-fated British Expeditionary Force in France. He had seemed rather twitchy and sullen since he got back from the hospital last week, but I put that down to shattered nerves. The doctors had told Polly, his mother, something about nervous exhaustion and about being patient with him.

"Morning, Tommy," I greeted him.

He hadn't noticed me at first — his eyes had been glued to the pavement as he walked — but when he looked up, startled, I noticed the almost pellucid paleness of his skin and the dark bruises under his eyes.

"Oh, good morning, Mr. Bascombe," he said. "How are you?"

"I'm fine, but you don't look so good. What is it?"

"My nerves," he said, moving away as he spoke. "The doc said I'd be all right after a bit of rest, though."

"I'm glad to hear it. By the way, did your fath —, sorry, did Harry tell you about Mad Maggie?" I knew Tommy was sensitive about Harry not being his real father.

"He said she was dead, that's all. Says someone clobbered her."

"When did you last see her, Tommy?"

"I don't know."

"Since the raid?"

"That was the day after I got back. No, come to think of it, I don't think I have seen her since then. Terrible business, in'it?"

"Yes, it is."

"Anyway, sorry, must dash. Bye, Mr. Bascombe."

"Bye, Tommy."

I stood frowning and watched him scurry off, almost crabwise, down the street.

*

There was another air-raid that night, and I decided to look for Fingers Finnegan. By then, I had talked to enough people on the street to be certain that no one had seen Rose since the evening of the last raid.

We lived down by the railway, the canal, and the power station, so we were always copping for it. The Luftwaffe could never aim accurately, though, because the power station sent up clouds of appalling smoke as soon as they heard there were enemy planes approaching. If the bombs hit anything of strategic value, it was more by good luck than good management.

The siren would go off, wailing up and down the scale for two minutes, and it soon became a sort of eerie fugue as you heard the sirens from neighboring boroughs join in, one after another. The noise frightened the dogs and cats, and they struck up wailing and howling, too. At first, you could hardly see a thing outside, only hear the droning of the bombers high above and the swishing and whistling sound of the bombs as they fell in the distance. Then came the explosions, the hailstone of incendiaries on roofs like a rain of fire, the flames crackling, blazing through the smoke. Even the sounds seemed muffled, the distant explosions no more than dull, flat thuds, like a heavy book falling on the floor, the crackle of anti-aircraft fire like fat spitting on a griddle. Sometimes you could even hear someone scream or shout out a warning. Once I heard a terrible shrieking that still haunts my nightmares.

But the city had an eldritch beauty during an air-raid. In the distance, through the smoke-haze, the skyline seemed lit by a dozen suns, each a slightly different shade of red, orange, or yellow. Searchlights criss-crossed one another, making intricate cat's cradles in the air, and ack-ack fire arced into the sky like strings of Christmas lights. Soon, the bells of the fire engines also became part of the symphony of sound and color. The smoke from the power station got in my eyes and up my nose, and with my lungs, it brought on a coughing fit that seemed to shake my ribs free of their moorings. I held a handkerchief to my face, and that seemed to help a little.

It wasn't too difficult to get around, despite the blackout and the smoke. There were white stripes painted on the lampposts and along the curbside, and many people had put little dots of luminous paint on their doorbells, so you could tell where you were if you knew the neighborhood well enough.

I walked along Lansdowne Street to the junction with Cardigan Road. Nobody was abroad. The bombs were distant but getting closer, and the smell from a broken sewage pipe was terrible, despite my handkerchief. Once, I fancied I saw a figure steal out of one of the houses, look this way and that, then disappear into the smoky darkness. I ran, calling out after him, but when I got there he had vanished. It was probably Fingers, I told myself. I'd have a devil of a time catching him now I had scared him off. My best chance was to run him down in one of the back-street cafés where he sold his stolen goods the next day.

So instead of pursuing my futile task, and because it was getting more and more difficult to breathe, I decided that my investigation might next benefit best from a good look around Rose's empty house.

It was easy enough to gain access via the kitchen window at the back, which wasn't even latched, and after an undignified and painful fall from the sink to the floor, I managed to regain my equilibrium and set about my business. It occurred to me that if I had such an easy time getting in, then her killer would have had an easy time, too. Rose had been killed with the posser, which would most likely have been placed near the sink or tub in which she did her washing.

Because of the blackout curtains, I didn't have to worry about my torch giving me away; nor did I have to cover it with tissue paper, as I would outside, so I had plenty of light to see by. I stood for a few moments, adjusting to the room. I could hear fire engine bells not too far away.

I found little of interest downstairs. Apart from necessities, such as cutlery, pans, plates, and dishes, Rose seemed to own nothing. There were no framed photographs on the mantelpiece, no paintings on the drab walls. There wasn't even a wireless. A search of the sideboard revealed only the rent-book that Longbottom had already discovered, a National Identity Card, also in the name of Rose Faversham, her Ration Book, various coupons, old bills, and about twenty pounds in banknotes. I did find two bottles of gin, one almost empty, in the lower half of the china cabinet. There were no letters, no address books, nothing of a personal nature. Rose Faversham's nest was clean and tidy, but it was also quite sterile.

Wondering whether it was worth bothering, I finally decided to go upstairs to finish my search. The first of the two bedrooms was completely bare. Most people use a spare room to store things they no longer used but can't bear to throw out just yet; there was nothing like this in Rose's spare bedroom, just some rather austere wallpaper and bare floorboards.

I felt a tremor of apprehension on entering Rose's bedroom. After all, she had lived such a private, self-contained life that any encroachment on her most intimate domain seemed a violation. Nonetheless, I went inside.

Apart from the ruffled bedclothes, which I assumed were the result of Detective Sergeant Longbottom's cursory search, the bedroom was every bit as neat, clean, and empty as the rest of the house. The one humanizing detail was a library book on her bedside table: Samuel Butler's *The Way of All Flesh*. So Rose Faversham had been an educated woman. Butler's savage and ironic attack on Victorian values was hardly common bedtime reading on our street.

I looked under the mattress and under the bed, and found nothing. The dressing-table held those few items deemed essential for a woman's appearance and hygiene, and the chest of drawers revealed only stacks of carefully folded undergarments, corsets and the like, among which I had no desire to go probing. The long dresses hung in the wardrobe beside the high-buttoned blouses.

About to give up and head home to bed, I tried one last place — the top of the wardrobe, where I used to keep my secret diaries when I was a boy — and there I found the shoebox. Even a brief glance inside told me it was the repository of whatever past and personal memories Rose Faversham might have wanted to hang onto. Instead of sitting on the bedspread to read by torch-light, I went back downstairs and slipped out of the house like a thief in the night, which I suppose I was, with Rose's shoebox under my arm. A bomb exploded about half a mile away as I sidled down the street.

I should have gone to one of the shelters, I know, but I was feeling devil-may-care that night, and I certainly didn't want anyone to know I had broken into Rose's house and stolen her only private possessions. Back in my own humble abode, I made sure my curtains were shut tight, poured a large tumbler of brandy — perhaps, apart from nosiness and an inability to suffer fools gladly, my only vice — then turned on the standard lamp beside my armchair and settled down to examine my haul. There was a certain excitement in having pilfered it, as they say, and for a moment I imagined I had an inkling of that illicit thrill Fingers Finnegan must get every time *he* burgles someone's house. Of course, this was different; I hadn't broken into Rose's house for my own benefit, to line my own pockets, but to solve the mystery of her murder.

The first thing the shoebox yielded was a photograph of three smiling young women standing in front of an old van with a cross on its side. I could tell by their uniforms that they were nurses from the first war. On the back, in slightly smudged ink, someone had written "Midge, Rose and Margaret — Flanders, 30th July, 1917. Friends Inseparable Forever!"

I stared hard at the photograph and, though my imagination may have been playing tricks on me, I thought I recognized Rose as the one in the middle. She had perfect dimples at the edges of her smile, and her eyes gazed, pure and clear, directly into the lens. She bore little resemblance to the Rose I had known as Mad Maggie, or indeed to the body of Rose Faversham as I had seen it. But I think it was her.

I put the photograph aside and pulled out the next item. It was a book of poetry: *Severn and Somme* by Ivor Gurney. One of my favorite poets, Gurney was gassed at St. Julien, near Passchendaele, and sent to a war hospital near Edinburgh. I heard he later became mentally disturbed and suicidal, and he died just two or three years ago, after nearly twenty years of suffering. I have always regretted that we never met.

I opened the book. On the title page, someone had written, "To My Darling Rose on her 21st Birthday, 20th March, 1918. Love, Nicholas." So Rose was even younger than I had thought.

I set the book aside for a moment and rubbed my eyes. Sometimes I fancied the residual effects of the gas made them water, though my doctor assured me that it was a foolish notion, as mustard gas wasn't a lachrymator.

I hadn't been in the war as late as March 1918. The injury that sent me to hospital in Manchester, my "Blighty," took place the year before. Blistered and blinded, I had lain in bed there for months, unwilling to get up. The blindness passed, but the scarring remained, both inside and out. In the small hours, when I can't sleep, I relive those early days of August 1917, in Flanders: the driving rain, the mud, the lice, the rats, the deafening explosions. It was madness. We were doomed from the start by incompetent leaders, and as we struggled waist-deep through mud, with shells and bullets flying all around us, we could only watch in hopeless acceptance as our own artillery sank in the mud, and our tanks followed it down.

Judging by the words on the back of the photograph, Rose had been there, too: *Rose,* one of the angels of mercy who tended the wounded and the dying in the trenches of Flanders' fields.

I opened the book. Nicholas, or Rose, had underlined the first few lines of the first poem, "To the Poet Before Battle":

> Now, youth, the hour of thy dread passion comes;
> Thy lovely things must all be laid away;
> And thou, as others, must face the riven day
> Unstirred by rattle of the rolling drums
> Or bugles' strident cry.

Perhaps Nicholas had been a poet, and Gurney's call for courage in the face of impending battle applied to him, too? And if Nicholas had been a poet, was Rose one of the "lovely things" he had to set aside?

Outside, the all-clear sounded and brought me back to earth. I breathed a sigh of relief. Spared again. Still, I had been so absorbed in Rose's treasures that I probably wouldn't have heard a bomb if one fell next door. They say you never hear the one with your name on it.

I set the book down beside the photograph and dug around deeper in the shoebox. I found a medal of some sort — I think for valor in wartime nursing — and a number of official papers and certificates. Unfortunately, there were no personal letters. Even so, I managed to compile a list of names to seek out and one or two official addresses where I might pursue my inquiries into Rose Faversham's past. No time like the present, I thought, going over to my escritoire and taking out pen and paper.

I posted my letters early the following morning, when I went to fetch my newspaper. I had the day off from school, as the pupils were collecting aluminum pots and pans for the Spitfire Fund, so I thought I might slip into "Special Constable" mode and spend an hour or two scouring Fingers Finnegan's usual haunts.

I started at Frinton's, on the High Street, where I also treated myself to two rashers of bacon and an egg. By mid-morning, I had made my way around most of the neighboring cafés, and it was lunchtime when I arrived at Lyon's in the city center. I didn't eat out very often, and twice a day was almost unheard of. Even so, I decided to spend one and three-pence on roast beef and Yorkshire pudding. There was a lot of meat around then because the powers that be were slaughtering most of the farm animals to turn the land over to crops. I almost felt that I was doing my national duty by helping eat some before it went rotten.

As I waited, I noticed Finnegan slip in through the door in his usual manner, licking his lips, head half-bowed, eyes flicking nervously around the room trying to seek out anyone who may have been after him, or to whom he may have owed money. I wasn't in uniform, and I was pretending to be absorbed in my newspaper, so his eyes slid over me. When he decided it was safe, he sat down three tables away from me.

My meal came, and I tucked in with great enthusiasm, managing to keep Finnegan in my peripheral vision. Shortly, another man came in — dark-haired, red-faced — and sat with Finnegan. The two of them put their heads together, all the time Finnegan's eyes flicking here and there, looking for danger signs. I pretended to pay no attention but was annoyed that I couldn't overhear a word. Something exchanged hands under the table, and the other man left: Finnegan fencing his stolen goods again.

I waited, lingering over my tea and rice pudding, and when Finnegan left, I followed him. I hadn't wanted to confront him in the restaurant and cause a scene, so I waited until we came near a ginnel not far from my own street, then I speeded up, grabbed him by the shoulders, and dragged him into it.

Finnegan was not very strong — in fact, he was a scrawny, sickly sort of fellow, which is why he wasn't fit for service — but he was slippery as an eel, and it took all my energy to hang onto him until I got him where I wanted him, with his back to the wall and my fists gripping his lapels. I slammed him against the wall a couple of times to take any remaining wind out of his sails, then when he went limp, it was ready to start.

"Bloody hell, Constable Bascombe!" he said when he'd got his breath back. "I didn't recognize you at first. You didn't have to do that, you know. If there's owt you want to know why don't you just ask me? Let's be civilians about it."

"The word is *civilized*. With you? Come off it, Fingers."

"My name's Michael."

"Listen, Michael, I want some answers and I want them now."

"Answers to what?"

"During last night's air-raid I saw you coming out of a house on Cardigan Road."

"I never."

"Don't lie to me. I know it was you."

"So what? I might've been at my cousin's. He lives on Cardigan Road."

"You were carrying something."

"He gave me a couple of kippers."

"You're lying to me, Fingers, but we'll let that pass for the moment. I'm interested in the raid before that one."

"When was that, then?"

"Last Wednesday."

"How d'you expect me to remember what I was doing that long ago?"

"Because murder can be quite a memorable experience, Fingers."

He turned pale and slithered in my grip. My palms were sweaty. "Murder? Me? You've got to be joking! I've never killed nobody."

I didn't bother pointing out that that meant he must have killed *somebody* — linguistic niceties such as that being as pointless with someone of Finnegan's intelligence as speaking loudly to a foreigner and hoping to be understood — so I pressed on. "Did you break into Rose Faversham's house on Aston Place last Wednesday during the raid?"

"Rose Faversham. Who the bloody hell's she when she's at home? Never heard of her."

"You might have known her as Mad Maggie."

"*Mad Maggie.* Now why would a bloke like me want to break into *her* house? That's assuming he did things like that in the first place, hypnotically, like."

Hypnotically? Did he mean *hypothetically?* I didn't even ask. "To rob her, perhaps?"

"Nah. You reckon a woman who went around looking like she did would have anything worth stealing? Hypnotically, again, of course."

"Of course, Fingers. This entire conversation is *hypnotic*. I understand that."

"Mad Maggie hardly draws attention to herself as a person worth robbing. Not unless you're into antiques."

"And you're not?"

"Wouldn't know a Chippendale from a Gainsborough."

"Know anybody who is?"

"Nah."

"What about the thousands of pounds they say she had hidden in her mattress?"

"And pigs can fly, Constable Bascombe."

"What about silverware?"

"There's a bob or two in a nice canteen of cutlery. Hypnotically, of course."

The one thing that might have been of value to someone other than herself was Rose's silverware, and that had been left alone. Even if Fingers had been surprised by her and killed her, he would hardly have left his sole prize behind when he ran off. On the other hand, with a murder charge hanging over it, the silverware might have turned out to be more of a liability than an asset. I looked at his face, into his eyes, trying to decide whether he was telling the truth. You couldn't tell anything from Finnegan's face, though; it was like a ferret-mask.

"Look," he said, licking his lips, "I might be able to help you."

"Help me?"

"Yeah. But . . . you know . . . not standing here, like this . . ."

I realized I was still holding him by the lapels, and I had hoisted him so high he had to stand on his tiptoes. I relaxed my grip. "What do you have in mind?"

"We could go to the Prince Albert, have a nice quiet drink. They'll still be open."

I thought for a moment. The hard way hadn't got me very far. Maybe a little diplomacy was in order. Though it galled me to be going for a drink with a thieving illiterate like Fingers Finnegan, there were larger things at stake. I swallowed my pride and said, "Why not."

Nobody paid us a second glance, which was all right by me. I bought us both a pint, and we took a quiet table by the empty fireplace.

Fingers brought a packet of Woodbines out of his pocket and lit up. His smoke burned my lungs and caused me a minor coughing fit, but he didn't seem concerned by it.

"What makes you think you can help me?" I asked him when I'd recovered.

"I'll bet you're after Mad Maggie's murderer, aren't you?"

"How do you know that?"

"Word gets around. The *real* police think it was Gypsies, you know. They've got one of them in the cells right now. Found some silver candlesticks in his possession."

"How did they know whether Rose had any silver candlesticks?"

He curled his lip and looked at me as if I were stupid. "They don't, but they don't know that she didn't, do they? All they need's a confession, and he's a brute in the interrogation room is that short-arse bastard."

"Who?"

"Longbottom. It's what we call him. Longbottom. Short-arse. Get it?"

"I'm falling off my chair with laughter. Have you got anything interesting to tell me or haven't you?"

"I might have seen someone, mightn't I?"

"Seen someone? Who? Where?"

He rattled his empty glass on the table. "That'd be telling, wouldn't it?"

I sighed, pushed back the disgust I felt rising like vomit in my craw, and bought him another pint. He was smirking all over his ferret face when I got back.

"Ta very much, Constable Bascombe. You're a true gentleman, you are."

The bugger was *enjoying* this. "Fingers," I said, "you don't know how much your praise means to me. Now, to get back to what you were saying."

"It's Michael. I told you. And none of your Micks or Mikes. My name's Michael."

"Right, Michael. You know, I'm a patient man, but I'm beginning to feel just a wee bit let down here. I'm thinking that perhaps it might not be a bad idea for me to take you to Detective Sergeant Longbottom and see if he can't persuade you to tell him what you know."

Fingers jerked upright. "Hang on a minute. There's no need for anything drastic like that. I'm just having my little bit of fun, that's all. You wouldn't deny a fellow his little bit of fun, would you?"

"Heaven forbid," I muttered. "So now you've had your fun, Fin— er . . . Michael, perhaps we can get back to business?"

"Right . . . well . . . theatrically speaking, of course, I might have been in Aston Place on the night you're talking about."

Theatrically? Let it go, Frank. "Last Wednesday, during the air-raid?"

"Right. Well I might have been, just, you know, being a concerned citizen and all, going round checking up all the women and kids was in the shelters, like."

"And the old people. Don't forget the old people."

"Especially the old people. Anyway, like I said, I just *might* have been passing down Aston Place during the air-raid, seeing that everyone was all right, like, and I *might* just have seen someone coming out of Mad Maggie's house."

"Did you?"

"Well, it was dark, and that bloody smoke from the power station doesn't make things any better. Like a real pea-souper, that is. Anyway, I might just have seen this figure, like, a quick glimpse."

"I understand. Any idea who it was?"

"Not at first I hadn't, but now I've an idea. I just hadn't seen him for a long time."

"Where were you?"

"Coming out of — Can't have been more than two or three houses away. When I saw him he gave me a real fright, so I pressed myself back in the doorway, like, so he couldn't see me."

"But you got a look at him?"

"Not a good one. First thing I noticed, though, is he was wearing a uniform."

"What kind of uniform?"

"I don't know, do I? Soldier's, I suppose."

"Anything else?"

"Well, he moved off sort of sideways, like."

"Crabwise?"

"Come again?"

"Like a crab?"

"If you say so, Constable Bascombe."

Something about all this was beginning to make sense, but I wasn't sure I liked the sense it made. "Did you notice anything else?"

"I saw him go into a house across the street."

"Which one?" I asked, half of me not wanting to know the answer.

"The milkman's," he said.

I didn't want to, but I had to see this through. *Tommy Fletcher.* My own godson. All afternoon I thought about it, and I could see no way out of confronting Harry and Tommy. No matter how much thinking I did, I couldn't come up with an explanation, and if Tommy *had* murdered Rose Faversham, I wanted to know why. He had certainly been acting oddly since he came back from the army hospital, but I had acted rather strangely myself after they released me from the hospital in Manchester in 1918. I knew better than to judge a man by the way he reacts to war.

I consoled myself with the fact that Tommy might not have killed Rose, that she was already dead when he went to see her, but I knew in my heart that didn't make sense. Nobody just dropped in on Mad Maggie to see how she was doing, and the idea of two people going to see her in one night was absurd. No, I knew that the person Fingers had seen coming out of Rose's house had to be her killer, and he swore that person was Tommy Fletcher.

Fingers could have been lying, but that didn't make sense either. For a start, he wasn't that clever. He must also know that I would confront Tommy and that, one way or another, I'd find out the truth. No, if Fingers had killed Mad Maggie and wanted to escape blame, all he had to do was deny that he had been anywhere near her house and let the Gypsy take the fall.

I steeled myself with a quick brandy, then I went around to Harry's house just after eight o'clock. They were all listening to a variety program on the Home Service, and someone was torturing "A Nightingale Sang in Berkeley Square." As usual, Tommy was wearing his army uniform, even though he was on extended leave. He still looked ill, pale and thin. His mother, Polly, a stout, silent woman I had known ever since she was a little girl, offered to make tea and disappeared into the kitchen.

"What brings you out at this time of night, then?" Harry asked. "Want some company down at the Prince Albert?"

I shook my head. "Actually, it's your Tommy I came to see."

A shadow of fear crossed Harry's face. "Tommy? Well, you'd better ask him yourself, then. Best of luck."

Tommy hadn't moved yet, but when I addressed him, he slowly turned to face me. There was a look of great disappointment in his eyes, as if he knew he had had something valuable in his grasp only to have it taken from him at the last minute. Harry turned off the radio.

"Tommy," I said, speaking as gently as I could, "did you go to visit Mad Maggie last Wednesday night, the night of the air-raid?"

Harry was staring at me, disbelief written all over his face. "For God's sake, Frank!" he began, but I waved him down.

"Did you, Tommy? Did you visit Mad Maggie?"

Slowly, Tommy nodded.

"You don't have to say anymore," Harry said, getting to his feet. He turned to me as if I were his betrayer. "I've considered you a good friend for many years, Frank, but you're pushing me too far."

Polly came back in with the teapot and took in the scene at a glance. "What's up? What's going on?"

"Sit down, Polly," I said. "I'm asking your Tommy a few questions, that's all."

Polly sat. Harry remained standing, fists clenched at his sides, then Tommy's voice broke the deadlock. "It's all right, Mum," he said to Polly, "I want to tell him. I want to get it off my chest."

"I don't know what you're talking about, son," she said.

Tommy pointed at Harry. "He does. He's not as daft as he looks."

I looked at Harry, who sat down again and shook his head.

Tommy turned back to me. "Did I go visit Mad Maggie? Yes, I did. Did I kill her? Yes, I did. I got in through the back window. It wasn't locked. I picked up the posser and went through into the living room. She was sitting in the dark. Didn't even have a wireless. She must have heard me, but she didn't move. She looked at me just once before I hit her, and I could swear she knew why I was doing it. She understood and she knew it was right. It was *just*."

As Tommy spoke, he became more animated and his eyes started to glow with life again, as if his prize were once more within his grasp.

"Why did you do it, Tommy?" I asked. "What did she ever do to harm you?"

He looked at Harry. "She killed my dad."

"She what?"

"I told you. She killed my dad. My real dad."

Polly flopped back in her armchair, tea forgotten, and put her hand to her heart. "Tommy, what are you saying?"

"He knew," he said, looking at Harry again. "Or at least he suspected. I told him about the field, about the villagers, the mad-woman."

Harry shook his head. "I *didn't* know," he said. "You never told me it was *her.* All I knew was that you were upset, you were saying crazy things and acting strange. Especially when you came in from the raid that night. I was worried, that's all. If I ever suspected you, that's the only reason, son, I swear it. When I found her body, I thought if there was the remotest possibility. . . . That's why I went for Frank. I told him to lay off it, to let the gypos take the blame. But he wouldn't." Harry pointed his finger at me, red in the face. "If you want to blame anyone, blame him."

"Calm down, Harry," I told him. "You'll give yourself a heart attack."

"It's not a matter of blame," Tommy said. "It's about justice. And justice has been served."

"Better tell me about it, Tommy," I said. The air-raid siren went off, wailing up and down the scale. We all ignored it.

Tommy paused and ran his hand through his closely cropped hair. He looked at me. "You should understand, Mr. Bascombe. You were there. He was your best friend."

I frowned. "Tell me, Tommy."

"Before Dunkirk, a group of us got cut off and we were in this village near Ypres for a few days, before the Germans got too close. We almost didn't make it to the coast in time for the evacuation. The people were frightened about what the Germans might do if they found out we were there, but they were kind to us. I became quite friendly with one old fellow who spoke very good English, and I told him my father had been killed somewhere near here in the first war. Passchendaele. I said I'd never seen his grave. One day, the old man took me out in his horse and cart and showed me some fields. It was late May, and the early poppies were just coming out among the rows of crosses. It looked beautiful. I knew my father was there somewhere." Tommy choked for a moment, looked away, and wiped his eyes.

"Then the old man told me a story," he went on. "He said there was a woman living in the village who used to, you . . . you know . . .

with the British soldiers. But she was in love with a German officer, and she passed on any information she could pick up from the British directly to him. One soldier let something slip about some new trench positions they were preparing for a surprise attack, and before anyone knew what had hit them, the trenches were shelled and the Germans swarmed into them. They killed every British soldier in their path. It came to hand-to-hand combat in the end. Bayonets. And the woman's German lover was one of the last to die."

Tommy paused, glanced at his mother, and went on. "He told me she never recovered. She went mad, and for a while after the armies had moved on she could be heard wailing for her dead German lover in the poppy fields at night. Then nothing more was heard of her. The rumor was that she had gone to England, where they had plenty of other madwomen to keep her company. I thought of Mad Maggie right from the start, of course, and I remembered the way she used to burst into French every now and then. I asked him if he had a photograph, and he said he thought he had an old one. We went back to his house, and he rummaged through his attic and came down with an old album. There she was. The same sort of clothes. That same look about her. Much younger and very beautiful, but it was *her.* It was Mad Maggie. And she had killed my father. He was in one of those trenches."

"What happened next, Tommy?"

"I don't remember much of the next couple of months. The Germans got too close and we had to make a hasty departure. That's when I was wounded. I was lucky to make it to Dunkirk. If it hadn't been for my mates. . . . They carried me most of the way. Anyway, for a while I didn't know where I was. In and out of consciousness. To be honest, half the time I preferred to be out of it. I had dreams, nightmares, visions, and I saw myself coming back and avenging my father's death."

His eyes shone with pride and righteousness as he spoke. Outside, the bombs were starting to sound alarmingly close. "Let's get down to the shelter," Harry suggested.

"No," said Tommy, holding up his hand. "Hear me out now. Wait till I'm done." He turned to me. "You should understand, Mr. Bascombe. She killed my dad. He was your best friend. You should understand. I only did what was right."

I shook my head. "There's no avenging deaths during wartime,

Tommy. It's every man for himself. Some German bullet or bayonet had Larry's name on it, and that was that. Wrong place, wrong time. It could just as easily have been me."

Tommy stared at me in disbelief.

"Besides," I went on, getting a little concerned at the explosions outside, "are you sure it was her, Tommy? It seems an awful coincidence that she should end up living on our street, don't you think?"

"I'm sure. I saw the photograph. I've still got it."

"Can I have a look?"

Tommy opened his top pocket and handed me a creased photograph. There was no doubt about the superficial resemblance between the woman depicted there, leaning against a farmer's fence, wearing high-buttoned boots, smiling and holding her hand to her forehead to keep the sun out of her eyes. But it wasn't the same woman whose photograph I had found in Rose Faversham's shoebox. In fact, it wasn't any of the three — Midge, Rose, or Margaret. There were no dimples, for a start, and the eyes were different. We all have our ways of identifying people, and with me it's always the eyes. Show me someone at six, sixteen, and sixty and I'll know if it's the same person or not by the eyes.

Another bomb landed far too close for comfort, and the whole house shook. Then a split second later came a tremendous explosion. Plaster fell off the ceiling. The lights and radio went off. I could hear the drone of the bombers slowly disappearing to the southeast, on their way home again. We were all shaken, but I pulled myself to my feet first and suggested we go outside to see if anyone needed help.

I didn't really think he'd make a run for it, but I stuck close to Tommy as we all went outside. The smell was awful; the bitter, fiery smell of the explosive and a whiff of gas from a fractured pipe mixed with dust from broken masonry. The sky was lit up like Guy Fawkes night. It was a terrible sight that met our eyes, and the four of us could only stand and stare.

A bomb had taken out about three houses on the other side of the street. The middle one, now nothing but a pile of burning rubble, was Mad Maggie's.

When the answers to my letters started trickling in a couple of weeks after Tommy's arrest, I picked up some more leads, one of which eventually led me to Midge Livesey, now a mother of two boys

— both in the RAF — who was living only thirty miles away, in the country. I telephoned her, and she seemed pleased to hear from someone who had known Rose, though she was saddened by the news of Rose's death, and she suggested I be her guest for the weekend.

Though it was late October, the weather was fine when I got off the train at the tiny station. It was a wonderful feeling to be out in the country again. I had been away for so long I had almost forgotten what the autumn leaves looked like and how many different varieties of birdsong there are. The sweet, acrid scent of burning leaves from someone's garden made a fine change from the stink of the air-raids.

Midge and her husband, Arthur, welcomed me at the door of their cottage and told me they had already prepared the spare room. After I had laid out my things on the bed, I opened the window. Directly outside stood an apple tree, and beyond that I could see the landscape undulating to the north, where the large anvil shapes of peaks and fells were visible in the distance. I took in a deep breath of fresh air — as deep as I could manage with my poor lungs — and for once it didn't make me cough. Perhaps it was time I left the city, I thought. But no, there were police duties to attend to, and I loved my teaching job. After the war, perhaps, I would think about it again, see if I could get a job in a village school.

When I showed Midge the photograph of the three of them over dinner that evening, a sad smile played across her features, and she touched the surface with her fingers, as if it could send out some sort of message to her.

"Yes," she said, "that was Rose. And that was Margaret. Poor Margaret, she died in childbirth ten years ago. The war wasn't all bad for us. We did have some good times. But I think the day that photograph was taken marked the beginning of the end. It was the day before the third Ypres battle started, and we were field nurses. We used to go onto the fields and into the trenches to clean up after the battles." She shook her head and looked at Arthur, who tenderly put his hand on top of hers. "You've never . . . well, I suppose you have." She looked at her husband. "Arthur understands, too. He was wounded at Arras. I worry about my boys. Just remembering, just thinking about it, makes me fear for them terribly. Does that make sense?"

"Yes," I said.

She paused for a moment and poured us all tea. "Anyway, Rose was especially sensitive," she went on. "She wrote poetry and wanted to go to university to study English literature when it was all over. French, too. She spoke French very well and spent a lot of time talking to the poor wounded French soldiers. Often they were with the English, you know, and there was nobody could talk to them. Rose did. She fell in love with a handsome young English lieutenant. Nicholas, his name was." She smiled. "But we were young. We were always falling in love back then."

"What happened to her?" I asked.

"Rose? She broke under the strain. Shell-shock, I suppose you'd call it. You hear a lot about the poor boys, the breakdowns, the self-inflicted wounds, but you never hear much about the women, do you? Where are we in the history books? We might not have been shooting at the Germans and only in minimal danger of getting shot at ourselves — though there were times — but we were *there*. We saw the slaughter firsthand. We were up to our elbows in blood and guts. Some people just couldn't take it, the way some of the boys couldn't take combat. I'll say this, though, I think it was Nicholas's death that finally sent Rose over the edge. It was the following year, 1918, the end of March, near a little village on the Somme called St. Quentin. She found him, you know, on the field. It was pure chance. Half his head had been blown away. She was never the same. She used to mutter to herself in French and go into long silences. Eventually, she tried to commit suicide by taking an overdose of morphine, but a doctor found her in time. She was invalided out in the end."

"Do you know what happened next?"

"I visited her as soon as the war was over. She'd just come out of the hospital and was living with her parents. They were wealthy landowners — very posh, you might say — and they hadn't a clue what to do with her. She was an embarrassment to them. In the end they set up a small fund for her, so she would never have to go without, and left her to her own devices."

After a moment or two's silence, I showed Midge the book of poetry. Again, she fingered it like a blind person looking for meaning. "Oh, yes. Ivor Gurney. She was always reading this." She turned the pages. "This was her favorite." She read us a short poem called

"Bach and the Sentry," in which the poet on sentry duty hears his favorite Bach prelude in his imagination and wonders how he will feel later, when he actually plays the piece again in peacetime. Then she shook her head. "Poor mad Rose. Nobody knew what to do with her. Do tell me what became of her."

I told her what I knew, which wasn't much, though for some reason I held back the part about Tommy and his mistake. I didn't want Midge to know that my godson had mistaken her friend for a traitor. It seemed enough to lay the blame at the feet of a Gypsy thief and hope that Midge wasn't one of those women who followed criminal trials closely in the newspapers.

Nor did I tell her that Rose's house had been destroyed by a bomb almost a week after the murder and that she would almost certainly have been killed anyway. Midge didn't need that kind of cruel irony. She had suffered enough; she had enough bad memories to fuel her nightmares, and enough to worry about in the shape of her two boys.

I simply told her that Rose was a very private person, certainly eccentric in her dress and her mannerisms, and that none of us really knew her very well. She was a part of the community, though, and we all mourned her loss.

So Mad Maggie was another of war's victims, I thought, as I breathed in the scent of the apple tree before getting into bed that night. One of the uncelebrated ones. She came to our community to live out her days in anonymous grief and whatever inner peace she could scrounge for herself, her sole valuable possessions a book of poetry, an old photograph, and a nursing medal.

And so she would have remained, a figure to be mocked by the children and ignored by the adults, had it not been for another damn war, another damaged soul, and the same poppy field in Flanders.

Requiescat in pace, Rose, though I am not a religious man. *Requiescat in pace.*

It should never have happened, but they hanged Tommy Fletcher for the murder of Rose Faversham at Wandsworth Prison on 25th May, 1941, at eight o'clock in the morning.

Everyone said Tommy should have got off for psychiatric reasons, but his barrister had a permanent hangover, and the judge had an irritable bowel. In addition, the *expert* psychiatrist hired to evaluate him didn't know shell-shock from an Oedipus complex.

The only thing we could console ourselves with was that Tommy went to the gallows proud and at peace with himself for having avenged his father's death.

I hadn't the heart to tell him that he was wrong about Mad Maggie, that she wasn't the woman he thought she was.

DAVID B. SILVA

Dry Whiskey

FROM *Cemetery Dance*

WHEN I WAS A BOY, I would look at my father and see everything right with the world. He seemed bigger then. At the end of the day, he would come in from the fields with his shirt slung over his shoulder and the sun at his back, and every muscle in his body would be perfectly defined. I had looked up to him back then, like most boys looked up to their fathers. And I had wanted to grow up to be the same man that he was.

The rub of it is . . . time has a way of changing the order of things.

My father had started drinking nearly twelve years ago, not long after my mother had died of ovarian cancer. At first, though I was only eleven at the time, I thought I had understood: *any*thing to help forget that bone-thin skeleton, that rictus smile that she had become just before her death. It was an image that haunted me for a long time afterward. And it was an image that had never stopped haunting my father.

Now, I was sitting in the truck, staring at the house, wondering how things could change so much in just ten or twelve short years. It was mid-morning. The sun was already high in the sky, and there was a dark shadow enclosing the front porch. I stared a while longer, then climbed out of the truck and closed the door.

By the time I made it to the front steps, my father had come out of the house, dragging himself across the porch like a man who had been ill for a long time now. The screen door bounced off the jamb behind him. He fell into one of the rattan chairs my mother had bought, hawked up a wad of phlegm, and sent it flying over the porch railing. "What're you doing here?" he asked.

"Just thought I'd come by and see how you're doing. That's all."

"Yeah?" He scratched at the stubble on his chin, which had been growing for better than a week by the look of it. It hadn't been all that long ago that the first signs of gray had begun to sneak in. Now, it was almost *all* gray. "Well, I'm doing okay. Anything else?"

"Heard you were in town last night."

"Believe I was."

"Heard you got booted out of the Forty-Niner."

"Did I?"

"That's what Len Dozier says."

My father nodded slightly, as if that sounded close enough to the truth to suit him. Then he buried his face in his hands and let out a slow breath of air that seemed like an effort to control something inside that he found frightening. When he looked up again, I was reminded of the fact that *this* was the morning after. His coloring was ashy, his eyes bloodshot. "I might have," he said. "I don't exactly remember."

"How'd you get home?"

"Drove."

He thought maybe he had taken Buzzard Roost Road, which was the long way home no matter how you figured it. But he really couldn't be certain. He might have gone down Old Forty-Four and across. To be honest, he finally confessed, he couldn't recall much of anything about last night. "Things get a little fuzzy after I stopped at the Forty-Niner."

He stared down at his hands then, silently, with that look of shame that I'd seen cross his face a thousand times before.

"Have you eaten breakfast yet?"

"Uh-uh."

"Then let's get some food in you, okay?" I cooked him up some eggs and bacon and poured him a cup of strong, black coffee. We sat at the table in the kitchen. For a while we talked about the drought that had settled over the state the past four years, wondering how much longer it was going to go on. It hadn't proved to be as bad as the '77–'78 drought yet — *that* one had been the worst in the state's history — but summer was here now and it was going to be a long time before we were likely to see any new storms move through.

After breakfast, I cleared the dishes off the table, and placed them in the sink. "I've gotta be going, Pa."

"You working today?"

"Len Dozier needs a hand repairing his tractor."

"Well, you go on, then."

"Are you gonna be all right?"

"I'll be fine."

He walked me to the front porch, the suspenders hanging loosely around his waist, his gait a bit shorter, a bit slower than it generally was when he had had a belly full of whiskey to move him along. Outside, there were shimmering waves of heat rising off the bed of my father's old pickup, and in the distance, you could see a mirage in the crease between two brown hills. It looked a little like a pond. But there hadn't been a pond there in nearly five years now. Not since before the drought.

My father had let the farm go to hell after my mother had died. It had always been a small farm: four fifty-acre parcels, about two hundred acres altogether. It sat near the base of the foothills, with South Cow Creek flowing lazily along its southern border. He leased out two of the parcels: one for grazing, the other for bee-hives in the winter months when the bees were dormant and there wasn't much call for pollinating. He had his own small herd, too, about twenty head of cattle, and that was pretty much it.

I stopped at the foot of the steps, wanting to be on my way and feeling a little guilty for it.

"You looked yet?" he asked me.

"No, Pa."

"You gonna?"

"Sure." I didn't know when this routine had first started. Like everything else, I suppose it was around the time that my mother had died. Definitely, sometime after he had started drinking. I was used to it by now, and I guess because nothing had ever come of it, it seemed more like a routine than a real concern. But I gave the front end of his truck an honest look anyway.

He drove an old Chevy flatbed with aluminum running boards and an unpainted right front fender. The fender had been re-placed several summers back after he'd clipped a fence post — trying to avoid a jackrabbit, he claimed. The rest of the truck was in fairly decent shape, considering its age.

Something was wrong with the front end, though. I noticed that almost immediately. The bumper, which was secondhand scrap he had brought home from the junkyard and painted off-white, had been smashed up against the front grille. It looked as if someone had taken a sledgehammer to it. And just above the bumper, the lens of the headlight was broken, its mounting ring dangling loosely off to one side. If that weren't enough, there was also a good-size depression in the top of the left fender, where it looked as if the metal had been crimped at a weak spot almost directly over the wheel well.

Last night, on his way home, my father had hit something.

"Jesus."

"What is it?" he asked.

I ran my fingers across the bumper. There was a dark stain that looked as if something had spilled over the top edge and had run down the white paint. It was shaped something like a waterfall, with a mix of thick-and-thin lines flowing unevenly, top to bottom. At first thought, it looked like a kid might have taken a black Magic Marker to it. But when I looked closer, I realized the color was brownish red, and it hadn't been done by any Magic Marker. Because it was a blood stain. "Oh, God."

"What?"

"You did it, Pa. You finally did it." I looked up at him, and he was standing at the edge of the porch with an arm wrapped around the post like it was the only thing holding him up. His face had turned ashen, and for the first time this morning, there was a hint of sobriety behind his eyes. "The bumper's smashed, and there's some blood, Pa. You hit something last night."

I spent most of that afternoon at Len Dozier's place, working on his tractor. We got it up and running sometime around four, so I stopped by the market in Kingston Mills, picked up a couple of steaks, some potatoes, a 64-ouncer of Coke, and headed back to my father's place. When I had left, he had been sitting at the kitchen table, staring vacantly into his half-empty cup of coffee. It was only a matter of time, I figured, before the coffee was replaced by whiskey, and if that had already happened, it was a good bet I was going to find him passed out cold on the living room couch.

But that's not where I found him.

He was sitting on the front porch, next to a pile of plastic bags filled with bottles and cans. I climbed out of the truck with the grocery bag in one arm, and as I closed the door, I watched him toss an empty whiskey bottle into the air. It sailed a good fifteen or twenty feet, landed smack-dab in the middle of a feeding trough with *loomix* stenciled across the side, and then shattered with the harsh sound of a bottle landing in a recycling bin.

"What are you doing, Pa?"

He didn't bother to look up. As I went through the gate, he popped the tab off a can of Budweiser, dumped the contents out through an opening between the porch slats, then crushed the can and tossed it in the direction of another pile only a few feet away. It fell short, making almost no sound at all.

"Pa?"

When he finally did look up, his face was drawn and haggard, and though I had seen him like this before, *this* time was different. This was not a man who had hung one on while I had been gone. It was a man who had looked at himself in the mirror and had been frightened by what he had found.

"Pa, what's the matter?"

He stared at me a moment, something apparently aching silently inside him. "You ever meet Lloyd's kid?"

"Joey Egan?"

He nodded.

"Yeah, a couple of years ago, I think. When I was helping with 4H."

"He died last night," my father said mechanically. He took a bottle of Johnnie Walker Black Label out of the plastic bag next to him, gazed fondly at the label, then unscrewed the top and emptied out the whiskey. "It was a hit and run, off Buzzard Roost Road. He was on his way home after a school dance."

"Are you sure?"

"It was in this morning's paper," he said. Then he sent the empty bottle sailing across the yard, end over end. A spattering of sunlight glittered off the glass just before the neck of the bottle landed against the side of the trough and fell apart before my eyes. I'm not sure I even heard the sound it made. It seemed a thousand miles away just then.

"Maybe it wasn't you," I suggested.

"You're forgetting the blood on the bumper, Will."

"Yeah, but . . . Jesus, don't you remember anything from last night?"

"Not after I left the bar." He pulled another bottle out of the bag, poured the liquid down an opening between the slats, and flung it in the direction of the front gate this time. It landed short, in a soft mound of dirt where my mother had once planted a bed of wild violets and Shasta daisies, even some brown-eyed susans. *Just because we live on a farm,* she had said, *doesn't mean we can't have a little color around the place.* The bottle kicked up a cloud of dust that lazily drifted away on the evening breeze.

I plopped down in a chair next to him. "So what now?"

"You can join me if you want." He handed over a six-pack of beer.

The farm sat at the west end of a valley. It was a little past five now, the last week of May. The shadows from the hills were beginning to lengthen, and I could feel the coolness of evening coming on. I popped the top off the first of the cans, poured out the contents, and began my participation in a ritual that took nearly an hour before it was finished.

We never discussed calling the police. I suppose we should have at least discussed it. But what was the point? It wasn't going to change the fact that there was blood on the front end of my father's pickup. And it wasn't going to bring little Joey Egan back either.

In a strange way, though, what had happened had already started to bring my father back. He had been hiding inside a bottle for a long, long time, but suddenly it looked as if he might at last come out and show himself. If he did, I didn't want to risk losing him again.

We barbecued the steaks on an old grill out back that night. We had planned to eat outside at the picnic table under the dogwoods, but the mayflies were swarming, so we ended up inside at the kitchen table instead. It wasn't until we had finished the meal, and I had poured him a cup of coffee that I noticed his hands were shaking.

"Are you all right?"

He nodded, appearing unaffected. "The booze is wearing off. That's all."

"You sure?" He looked warm, and a little haggard. Though I had seen him looking much worse after an all-night bend.

"I'll be fine."

"You want me to stay tonight?"

"No, you go on home. I'll be all right."

I stacked the dishes in the sink, wiped my hands off on a kitchen towel, then turned around and stared at him. When you're a kid, you never think about your father as being old. I wasn't a kid anymore, of course. But I had thought of him as an old man for a good many years now, and I wondered briefly when it was that *I* had become the father, and he the son. And I wondered how much longer he was going to be with me.

"I'll come by in the morning," I said.

"No need."

"Just to check to see how you're doing."

"If that's what you want."

Joey Egan's funeral was held three days later. He was buried in a family plot in the Black Oak Cemetery on the outskirts of town, next to his mother, who had died of pneumonia the year before. After the services, I drove my father home and stayed with him that night, because I was afraid that he might start drinking again. He hadn't shed a tear since the day my mother had died. But in the truck, on our way out of Black Oak, he had broken down and started a long, painful crying jag.

More than just his drinking, I guess I worried about him doing something crazy that night.

The next morning, my father woke up with a hangover.

He came dragging into the kitchen sometime around nine, his eyes bloodshot, his brain apparently pounding unmercifully at the inside of his skull. He stopped at the sink, shading his eyes against the morning sun, and took a drink of water right out of the faucet. It was the 117th straight day without rain, and while the well hadn't gone dry, it sometimes took a while before anything came out of the spout.

"How's bacon and eggs sound?" I asked.

He shook his head guardedly. "Nothing for me, thanks."

"You gotta eat something." I had already tossed some bacon in the skillet. He hadn't been eating much of anything since the accident, and I had promised myself not to let him get away with it again. But he looked like the man of old this morning, like a man coming out of a stupor: ragged and foul and slightly out of touch with his surroundings. I didn't think he was going to be able to keep his food down even if he tried. "Christ, you didn't go on another drunk last night, did you?"

He looked up at me, his lips dry and chapped, his face expressionless. "You know I didn't. You were here all night, weren't you?"

"Then what the hell's the matter with you?"

"It's a dry drunk," he whispered hoarsely. He wiped his hands across the front of his undershirt, where one strap of his overalls was unfastened and hanging loosely. "It happens sometimes," he said. "When you've been drinking as long as I have."

"All the more reason to get some food in your stomach."

"Maybe." He shut off the faucet and moved to the table, where he sat down a little gingerly, and let out a halfhearted sigh. "I saw Joey Egan last night," he said.

"Joey's dead, Pa."

"He came into my room and stood over my bed. There was a mess of cuts and scratches all over his face. Looked like some fool had taken the business end of a pitchfork to him. And I think his left arm was broken. It looked that way at least."

"It was a dream, Pa."

"No, it wasn't no dream. He knew how your ma died."

"Everyone knows she had cancer. That's no secret."

"But the cancer ain't what killed her, Will."

"What?" We had never talked about my mother's death, but she had been sick for a good many months before she died. For a long time afterward, my father had always said that it was the consumption that got her. I guess it was less painful for him to think of it that way. It took a long time before he was ever able to use the word *cancer.*

"I couldn't stand to watch her suffer," he said.

"What did you do, Pa?" He looked up at me, a man whose rounded shoulders reflected the heavy weight they had been carrying, and suddenly I understood everything. All the nights at the Forty-Niner. The way he had pulled back from me after she had died. The way he had pulled back from everyone. I understood it all. "You killed her, didn't you?"

"I . . . I placed a pillow over her face," he said softly.

"Jesus."

"She was in so much pain . . ."

And then my father broke down and cried for the second time in less than a week. I sat next to him, with my arm draped over his shoulders, feeling helpless. Guilt carried a heavy price, and my father, I suspected, had been paying a hefty markup for a long, long time.

After a while, he caught himself and took in a deep breath. "I'm all right," he said uncertainly. He stared out the kitchen window, off to the distance, where a small twister had kicked up and was swirling the dust across the open field like a child swirling finger paints across a paper canvas. I had never noticed the burden in his face quite the way I noticed it just then. Here was a man who had been killing himself for years with booze, and now he was killing himself without it. I wondered if I had ever really known my father, if anyone had ever really known him.

"Things'll be all right once the booze wears off," I said weakly. "You hear?"

He nodded.

I gave him a pat on the back. "You sure you don't want anything to eat?"

"Later," he said.

I left him around eleven that morning. He was sitting in a chair on the front porch, staring out across the barren terrain, his mind a million miles away. I had gotten myself a six-week stint up in Oregon, hauling trees out of a private co-op that was selectively logging its land, and I reminded him about the job.

"I'll be back in six weeks. Okay, Pa?"

"I ain't going nowhere," he said.

"Six weeks," I repeated. As I drove out the dirt driveway, I caught a glimpse of him in my rearview mirror. There was something standing next to him, something I couldn't quite make out. And the man, himself, was hardly recognizable. A man so completely different from the man of my early childhood that I felt a little rattle of uneasiness run through me. What had happened to him? What had happened to the man who had been as strong as an ox, who had put up the barn by himself one summer, using a block-and-tackle, who had been able to stack a hundred bales of hay in a day and still have the energy to shoot some hoops out back under the last vestiges of twilight? What the hell had happened to that man?

He had grown old, I wanted to tell myself.

He had grown old and alone and empty.

But there was more to it than that.
He had also grown frightened.

I called him twice while I was away in Oregon. Under the circumstances, I guess I should have called more often. But that picture of him in my rearview mirror had been haunting me like a ghost. I kept thinking that I had caught a glimpse of little Joey Egan, standing next to him on the porch. That Joey had been that *something* I couldn't quite recognize, and that he had had one hand on my father's shoulder as if he were trying to hold him down.

The first time I called, the phone rang relentlessly, maybe as many as a dozen times, before my father finally picked it up. "No more," he said sharply. "You hear me? You call me one more time and I swear I'll come out to Black Oak myself and dig up your goddamn remains. You hear me? I'll feed 'em to the damn buzzards and that'll be the end of it."

"Pa, it's me."

There was a sudden, surprised silence on the other end. Then, quietly: "Will?"

"Yes."

"Oh, Christ. Will? That really you? Where are you?"

"I'm in Oregon, Pa. What's going on there? What's all the shouting about?"

"Oregon . . . ," he mumbled, in nearly a whisper. And for a moment, I thought he had gone back to the bottle again. In fact, I was certain that was exactly what he had done.

"You've been on a drunk, haven't you, Pa?"

"What's my boy doing in Oregon?"

"Listen to me. You've been drinking again, haven't you?"

Then the line went dead.

I called him back within seconds, my hands shaking almost uncontrollably as I fumbled with the phone. What the hell was going on? He had sounded like a man on the verge of self-destruction. I couldn't even be certain he had recognized me. Maybe he wasn't drinking again, but if it wasn't the booze I had heard, I hated to think what it might have been.

The phone rang thirty, maybe forty times without an answer. Eventually, I hung up and tried to convince myself that I had probably disturbed his sleep, that I must have caught him in the middle of a bad dream, and that there was nothing to worry about. He had

been tired, was all. The call had wakened him and *that's* why he had
sounded so crazy, because he'd still been half-asleep.

I wasn't able to get hold of him again until nearly three weeks
later. It was the night before I was due to head back to Kingston
Mills. I'm not sure what I expected him to sound like after that first
call. Still a little crazy, I guess. But he didn't sound crazy, and he
didn't sound like a man who would be dead in a few short hours.
He sounded like a man who had finally forgiven himself.

"Is everything all right there?" I asked.

"I'm finally dry," he said serenely.

"What?" I thought I could hear something in the background
that sounded dry and brittle, something that made me think of
autumn leaves and sand through an hourglass. And then he chuckled.

"I think the booze is wearing off," he said. "My head's clearing
up. It's been a long time since I've seen things this clearly."

"Look, Pa, I'm coming home tomorrow. Are you gonna be all
right till then?"

"Fine," he said. "I'm gonna be just fine."

I don't remember what I said in return. But I remember holding
the phone in my hand after he had hung up, and being overwhelmed with a strange jumble of emotions. It had been years since
I had felt close to my father, and suddenly I was terrified that I
might never have a chance to feel close to him again.

Early the next morning, I left Oregon, arriving at the farm
shortly after one o'clock in the afternoon. His pickup was parked
out front, in the same spot it had been parked the day I had
discovered the blood on the bumper. There was a layer of dust a
quarter of an inch thick across the hood, and it was nearly impossible to see through the windshield into the cab. The pickup had sat
there like a dinosaur for nearly two months now. In the back of my
mind, I suppose I knew it would eventually be buried under that
dust like an old desert ghost town. But at the time, I didn't give it
much of a thought.

The front door to the house was unlocked. It had been left
slightly ajar, and just inside there was a strange wind-cut pattern of
sand and dust scattered across the hardwood floor. Kingston Mills
had gone 159 days without rain, and the dust, it seemed, was no
longer content to stay outside.

"Pa?"

In the kitchen, I discovered a pyramid-shaped pile of dirt in the sink, maybe five or six inches high. One of the faucet handles had been broken off. It was lying on the lip of the drain, partially buried by the dirt. I took hold of the other handle, turned it, and watched a slow, steady stream of dirt sift lazily out of the spout.

"Pa?"

I found him, or some general semblance of him, in his bedroom at the back of the house. He was lying in bed, on top of the sheets, his hands folded peacefully across his stomach. He was dressed in the same clothes he had worn nearly every day of his life since my mother had died: an old pair of work boots worn at the heels, a pair of blue-jean overalls with one unfastened strap hanging loosely at his side, and, of course, the long johns he always wore come hell or high water.

Underneath, there was very little left of the man I remembered. Something had happened to him in the few short weeks that I had been gone, something I didn't think I was ever going to be able to understand. Maybe it had something to do with the drought — after all, the well *had* gone dry. Or maybe it had something to do with all those damn bottles he had tossed off the front porch the night he went dry. The booze had kept him going for a good many years. Maybe without it, the well of his soul had gone dry, too. I don't know. All I know is that the man I discovered at the back of the house was all dust and bones.

He looked as if he had been dead a very long time. I had spoken with him last night, but here he was now, less than twenty-four hours later: his skeletal hands peeking out from beneath his shirt-sleeves, his teeth bared in a dreadful, lipless grin, his eyes no more than dark, empty sockets.

Like the flowers my mother had planted out front, after an unquenchable thirst, my father had simply shriveled up and died.

There's a prayer from the Book of Common Prayer that reads: *Earth to earth, ashes to ashes, dust to dust, in sure and certain hope of the resurrection unto eternal life.* I find myself often thinking back to these words.

My father was buried in the Black Oak Cemetery, two rows over from Joey Egan. A bunch of the guys from the Forty-Niner came by the house afterward, drank a little beer, and talked about the good times they'd had together. Mostly, though, they seemed to stare off into the distance, reflecting on things that I suppose I will never be privy to.

Late in the afternoon, Lloyd Egan pulled me aside and told me about a man they had locked up in Sparks, Nevada. They had caught him robbing a small Mom and Pop liquor store and during the interrogation, he had confessed to Joey's hit-and-run. He had leaned across the seat to roll down the passenger window, he had said, and his car had drifted onto the shoulder, and . . . and there was Joey, turning around, his eyes bright and surprised, just as the car made impact. The man had stopped and got out and realized that the boy was dead, and then he had got back into the car and had driven off. It had apparently been haunting him ever since.

Lloyd took a swig of his beer, and gazed off into nothingness, looking like he was on the verge of tears. I put my arm around him, tried to comfort him, and then led him back into the kitchen, where someone was telling a story about the time my father had had a few too many and had gone home and tried to shoe one of the steers.

Several days later, a storm moved in off the Pacific and dropped nearly five inches of much needed rain across the north state. It was the beginning of the end of the drought. But it had come too late for my father.

To this day, I don't know what it was he hit coming home from the bar that night. It could have been a deer or a cow, I suppose. But it wasn't Joey Egan, and I'm grateful for that, grateful beyond description.

I still think back to those times when I was a boy and he would come in from the fields with his shirt slung over his shoulder and every muscle of his body taut and perfectly defined. And like most boys, there are still the times when I wish I could have grown up to be that man.

The shame of it is . . . I don't think I ever really got to know who he was.

L . L . T H R A S H E R

Sacrifice

FROM *Murderous Intent*

IT WAS THE HOTTEST DAY of the year, middle of August, heat and humidity both in the nineties, sun a ball of relentless fire in a hard blue sky. I had just returned to my office after a 10K run that was supposed to raise money for research on heart disease. It seemed appropriate: I felt like cardiac arrest was imminent. My gym shorts and T-shirt were soaked through with sweat. My plan to take a long shower had just been thwarted by a cryptic phone call from the chief of police: "You there? Don't leave." *Click.*

When the door opened, I was untying my running shoes. I left them on, laces dangling. The office already had enough of a locker-room ambiance. My visitor was a well-mannered young lady, though, and didn't even wrinkle her nose.

"You look like Hulk Hogan," she said, after we exchanged hellos and she had taken a seat across the desk from me. "Well, not your *face*," she added.

"Thank you," I said, and I meant it sincerely.

"Your hair's the wrong color, too." There seemed to be a bit of accusation in her tone.

"I could bleach it."

She nodded solemnly. "But your face is wrong. You wouldn't look like him anyway."

"True," I said. My face had been called a lot of things over the years but never *wrong*.

"He said you can help me."

"Hulk Hogan did?"

She gave me a scornful look. "That man at the police station. He *said* he was the chief of police, but I don't know. He didn't *look* like a chief of police. Not like on TV. On TV they wear . . ."

"Suits?"

"Uh-huh. He had on blue jeans."

"Kinda hot for a suit today."

"He looked like a cowboy. And he had freckles. More than me even."

Her freckles were sprinkled like fairy dust across her cheeks and nose. Two dark, skinny braids hung just past her shoulders. Short curly tendrils had escaped and clung damply to her face. She missed being pretty by a nose — but she'd grow into it in a few years and then she'd be a knock-out. A faded kitten graced the front of her limp pink T-shirt. Her denim shorts had frayed hems and her canvas shoes had long since gone from white to dingy gray. She stood up suddenly, reaching into her shorts pocket and extracting two pieces of grape-flavored bubble gum. "Want one?" she asked.

"Thanks." I took the proffered piece, which was warm from being in her pocket. We sat in companionable silence for a moment, chewing on big wads of purple gum. When mine was soft enough to talk around, I said, "What do you need help with?"

She was trying to blow a bubble; her tongue stretched a hole in the gum. "Phooey."

I blew a bubble about the size of a softball, holding it long enough to bask in her admiration before sucking it back in.

"I can't do it." Her chin puckered a little bit.

"How old are you?"

"Seven."

"I think I was eight before I could blow bubbles."

She perked up, the future suddenly looking brighter. After chewing for a while and trying another bubble, she spoke with sudden urgency: "Jennifer's gone."

"I see. It's a missing person case."

"Uh-huh. Can you find her?"

I wanted to say yes. Instead I said, "When did you see her last?" as I flipped a steno book open and poised a pen over it.

"Yesterday. I left her in the backyard. I'm not s'pose to — Mommy told me and told me to take good care of her — but I forgot and then she wasn't there anymore."

"I see. What does she look like?"

She picked up the end of one of her braids, holding it delicately between her thumb and index finger, then drew it across her face, beneath her nose, like a plaited mustache. Apparently the gesture indicated she was engaged in thought. When she let go, the braid swung back into place and she spoke briskly. "Her hair's red. Not red really, it's more like orange but people always say red hair. That's funny, isn't it? It's orange."

"Red hair." I wrote it down. "I guess it's just a figure of speech. What about her eyes?"

"Blue."

"Sounds pretty."

"Oh, she is. She's beautiful. Mommy's real mad 'cause I lost her. She told me and told me I better take good care of her 'cause she cost — I don't know how much — a whole lot."

"Uh-huh. What was she wearing?"

"A blue dress made out of . . . like shiny stuff. With lace and a ribbon right here." She touched the delicate hollow in her throat. "And white shoes but she didn't have any socks on. Her socks got lost."

"How long have you had her?"

"I got her for my birthday."

"When was that?"

"July eight. I'm seven years old. I'll be eight years old on my next birthday."

"Uh-huh. About how big is . . . uh . . ."

"This big." She held her hands about a foot apart. "Her name's . . . well, her real name's Megan Ann, but I call her Jennifer."

I nodded solemnly, as if I followed the logic of that.

"Mommy doesn't . . ."

I waited expectantly.

"She doesn't like me to use that name."

"Megan Ann? It's a pretty name."

She nodded, and for just a second I thought she was going to cry, then she abruptly said, "He said people pay you money." She made it sound as though there just might be a little larceny in my soul.

"The police chief? Well, he's right, I usually get paid, but — do you know what a sliding scale is?"

"There's a slide in the playground."

"This is different. A sliding scale means I charge different people different amounts. It depends on how much they can afford to pay me."

She considered that briefly, then stood up and dug into her shorts pocket. She put some linty coins on my desk. Two quarters, one dime, seven pennies. Sitting down again, she said, "Is that enough?"

"That should do it."

"Are you going to find her?"

"Well, I'll try to. I can't make any promises."

She looked at the coins on the desk, apparently having second thoughts.

"I tell you what — I'll work on a contingency basis. That means you only have to pay me after I find her. If I don't find her, you don't owe me anything."

Her face brightened and she quickly returned the coins to her pocket.

"I need some more information before I can start looking. First, what's your name?"

"Kristin Michelle Baker." She spelled all three names for me, slowly, standing up and leaning over the desk to peer at the steno pad, checking my accuracy.

"What's your address and phone number?"

"Um . . . one one seven South Twenty-first Street. Apartment H. It's right over there." She pointed vaguely eastward. "We don't have a telephone."

"Okay. You had a long walk to the police station."

"It was hot."

Her apartment building was two blocks east of my office and half a block south, an old building that had seen better days, many years ago. Her walk downtown would have taken her straight down Main Street to Seventh, where the police station was. From my office to the center of town, Main Street is lined with businesses and traffic is fairly steady. My building is at the end of the business district, though, and once you cross Nineteenth and head east, you're in a neighborhood that's as close to a slum as you can get in a small town. "Is your mom at work?"

"Um . . . Mommy doesn't work anywhere."

"So she's at home?"

"She's taking a nap."

"I see. Well, Kristin, I'll get started on this right away. Why don't I walk down to Twenty-first Street with you?"

"I know how to go."

"I just thought I'd keep you company. Just to the corner of Twenty-first, okay? I won't go all the way to your building."

I retied my shoes while she considered that. When I stood up, she abruptly — and a bit belatedly, I thought — asked if my name was Mr. Smith. I assured her it was. She nodded, then stood up and walked to the door. I followed her outside and we walked down to the corner, then continued east for two blocks. At the corner of Twenty-first and Main I waved good-bye as she headed south. I could see the front of the apartment building and I waited until she ran across the weedy front yard and disappeared from sight.

During our walk, I had asked a few more questions. Kristin had moved to town at Christmas time. It was just her and her mother. Daddy "went away." She would be in second grade in the fall and liked school, except for the boys, who were, in her words, stupid and yukky. I didn't take offense: To her, boys and men were two entirely different species. She had asked some kids in the neighborhood about the doll — Megan Ann, mysteriously nicknamed Jennifer — but no one admitted knowing anything about it. She wasn't able to tell me the brand name, which pretty much eliminated my plan to replace the missing doll with an identical new one, thereby attaining hero status in Kristin's eyes, not to mention earning sixty-seven cents.

Back at my office, I got rid of the gum and brushed the sour taste from my mouth. I like my bubble gum bubble-gum-flavored. After showering quickly, I dressed in cut-off jeans and a T-shirt, then drove down to the police station where the chief of police was sitting on the steps leading to the main door, a clipboard on one knee. I sat down beside him, saying, "Air conditioning on the fritz again?"

"Yeah, at least I can pretend there's a breeze out here. Kristin Michelle Baker get to your office all right?"

"Yeah, I walked her down to Twenty-first. You keep sending me clients like her, I'll have to file bankruptcy. You know anything about her mother?"

"Nope. Just that she oughta not let a little girl that age wander all over town by herself. Maybe she's not so bad though. I offered

Kristin a ride home and she told me her mama told her not to get in cars with strangers. Still, those blocks past your building aren't the kind of place I'd want Philip the Second hanging around."

"She *lives* there, Phil."

"I know that. It's just . . . somebody oughta be keeping an eye on her. I'm sure her mama doesn't have any idea she walked all the way down here."

"I took the case. Now what am I going to do?"

"Buy her a new doll."

"She couldn't tell me the brand or anything."

"Well . . . talk to her mama."

"I don't know. . . . A strange man wanting to buy her daughter a doll? She'll think I'm a child molester."

"Just explain it to her. She gives you any funny looks, have her give me a call. How'd the run go?"

"I made it all the way without keeling over." I stood up and dusted off the seat of my shorts. "Maybe I will talk to her mother."

On the way over, I spotted Kristin in a yard around the corner from her apartment building, playing with three other little girls. When Kristin's mother opened the door, I regretted my decision to talk to her. Kristin's birth had undoubtedly had an impact on the teen pregnancy statistics. Her mother wasn't more than twenty-two or -three, a short woman with small features that seemed crowded together in the center of her face. Her face was extravagantly made up, her nails blood red, her long dark hair a thick mass of tight, spiraling curls. The cost of the perm alone would have paid for basic phone service for a few months. The front door opened directly onto a sparsely furnished living room.

"Mrs. Baker? My name's —"

"Jeri Lynn," she said, smiling perkily and winding one long spiral of hair around her index ginger. "'Mrs. Baker' sounds so *old*." She leaned against the doorjamb, hip cocked.

"Jeri Lynn. My name's —"

"Is this about the car? Look, I mailed a money order . . . um . . . oh, gee, two days ago?"

"No, I'm a private detective and I —"

"I just forgot about it. I mean, I had the money and everything, but I — a *detective*?" She took a step backward and seemed poised to flee. Her voice was harsh: "You're a cop?"

"No, a private detective. My name's Zachariah —"

"What do you want?" She fidgeted from foot to foot, her fore-head creased.

"I met Kristin today and she told me about losing Megan Ann and I wanted to ask — "

I was talking to a door. A slammed door. I knocked on it. Nothing happened. I knocked again, got the same response. From the rear of the house I heard a shout: *"Kristin Michelle! You get home right this minute!"*

Apartment H was on the south end of the eight-plex. I walked around the corner of the building and stood with my back against the wall, right next to an open window. I heard an electric fan with a rattle in its motor. If I heard a slap or a cry from Kristin, I planned to kick the door in. What I heard was the back door slamming, then Jeri Lynn Baker, speaking in a hoarse voice: "We're going on a trip, Kristin, okay? Throw your clothes in here, just whatever's in your drawers, okay? Hurry, Kristin. We gotta go quick."

"Where are we going, Mommy? I was playing with —"

"Get your clothes."

After that I heard drawers slamming and sobs that weren't com-ing from a seven-year-old. Kristin said, "Mommy, what's wrong?"

"Nothing, honey. Just hurry, okay? That's enough, we don't need everything. Wait right here, okay?"

I heard nothing for a moment, then it sounded like the front door opened and then quietly closed again. A moment later, Jeri Lynn said, "Let's go. *Hurry.* You don't need that. I'll get you an-other one. Let's *go*, Kristin."

"I wanna take him with me, Mommy."

"Oh, for — all right, bring it. Now come *on*."

I ran to the back of the building and then down the length of it and down the other side, ending up at the front corner of Apart-ment A, where some bushes provided a little cover. I crouched behind them and watched Jeri Lynn toss a bulging canvas suitcase into the trunk of a fifteen-year-old tan Toyota. Kristin was standing by the car, one hand fiddling with a braid, the other clasping a teddy bear.

"Get *in*, Kristin." Jeri Lynn opened the passenger door and gave her daughter a little shove. Kristin got in the car and her mother ran around to the driver's side, and a moment later they were heading down the street, the tailpipe clouding the air with blue haze. I ran to my car, an old Camaro that fit right in on this street.

As I drove, I fumbled with the catch on the dashbox, finally getting it open and pulling out my cellular phone. The Toyota had turned east on Main Street. I managed to hit the right buttons on the phone and got through to the police station.

"I need to talk to the chief. He was sitting out front a few minutes ago."

"You know how hot it is in here, Zack? The air condi—"

"Get the chief. It's urgent."

"Ain't it always? Hold on."

The Toyota was two blocks ahead of me. Another few blocks and we'd be out of town and on a county road heading east. If she didn't make any turns, she'd link up with Interstate 84. From there, she could head west toward Portland or she could go southeast and be in Idaho in not much more than an hour if she made good time.

Phil finally came on the line. "What's up?"

I told him. He said, "What is it with you? Everything you do turns into some kind of major disaster. What do you want me to do? There's no law against taking a sudden trip."

"I don't know, Phil. Can't you stop her, check on the welfare of a minor, something like that?"

"You see her mistreat the kid?"

"No, but —"

"You got the license plate?"

I had committed it to memory before Jeri Lynn got in the car. I gave it to him and described the car. He said, "She's going to be in county jurisdiction pretty quick and soon as she hits the Interstate, she's in state trooper territory. I don't know . . . I'll see what I can do. Stick with her. I'll call you back."

When the phone rang again, we were on the Interstate, headed south, about a mile between us. Phil asked where I was, then said, "Okay, a state trooper's going to pull her over on some pretext, but chances are they aren't going to find any reason to hold her. They're just checking to be sure the little girl's okay. I don't know what else I can do. She hasn't done anything wrong. She's got a driver's license and a valid registration."

Ten minutes later a state trooper streaked by in the fast lane. He changed lanes, slowed, and followed Jeri Lynn's car for a mile or so before turning on his light bar. Both cars drifted into the break-down lane and stopped. I drove past them. Jeri Lynn was out of the car, standing by the back bumper. The trooper was pointing at a rear tire, which did look a little underinflated. Jeri Lynn was nodding her head rapidly. I pulled onto the shoulder half a mile down the road and looked behind me. Jeri Lynn was still out of the car. The trooper was leaning inside the driver's window, apparently talking to Kristin. A moment later, he walked back to his car. Jeri Lynn got back in hers, and soon after that, I heard them both drive past. I didn't see them because I was looking the other way in case Jeri Lynn decided to check out the driver of the Camaro parked by the side of the road.

I'd followed the Toyota about five miles farther when the phone rang. Phil said, "The trooper says Kristin seems fine, told him all about her teddy bear and how she's going to be in second grade next year and how her mama's taking her to see some friends in Idaho. He didn't see anything suspicious. Jeri Lynn was a little nervous, but getting pulled over by a cop does that to people."

"Something's wrong."

"Tell me what and if it's against the law, I'll do something about it. You got plenty of gas?"

I did, but a trip to Idaho hadn't been on my agenda. "Yeah, I guess I'll stick with her. She has to stop sometime."

"Just watch how you handle it. You don't have any business hassling her either. Enjoy the drive."

Jeri Lynn exited the Interstate in Baker, stopped at a gas station to have some air put in her rear tire, then pulled into the parking lot of a store across the street. Kristin got out of the car and followed her mother inside. They both looked hot and sweaty. I'd been traveling in air-conditioned comfort, but I bought a couple of sodas from a vending machine at the gas station in case I got thirsty. I was back in the car when Jeri Lynn and Kristin came out of the store, Jeri Lynn carrying a brown grocery bag and a six-pack of Pepsi.

She found the on-ramp to I-84 after a couple wrong turns. We headed southeast at a steady sixty miles per hour and before long we crossed the state line and entered Idaho.

I wondered how much money Jeri Lynn had. She'd pulled the old the-check-is-in-the-mail routine when she thought I was from the finance company, and Kristin said she didn't have a job. Welfare

payments don't stretch too far. If she had a credit card it was probably maxed out, and a daddy who "went away" probably wasn't
paying child support. She wasn't likely to have much cash. Unless
she was dealing drugs, and that's why she was on the run.

She had started to panic when she thought I was a cop, so she
had to be up to something. Since she didn't have any outstanding
warrants, I figured it wasn't the past she was running from, it was
something in the present that she didn't want the cops to find out
about.

The phone rang thirty minutes later. "Where are you?" Phil
asked.

"Approaching Boise."

"I talked to her landlady. She's lived there eight months, doesn't
always pay the rent on time but that's the only problem. Strictly off
the record, I checked out the apartment. She doesn't have much
and none of it's illegal. What'd you say to her exactly?"

"Not much. She kept jumping to conclusions and interrupting
me. First she thought I was there to repo the car, then I told her I'm
a PI and she thought I was a cop and started getting fidgety and I
told her I'm a private detective and tried to explain about the doll
and she slammed the door in my face and five minutes later she was
packed and running."

"Doesn't make any sense. Maybe she was already planning to
leave before you got there."

"No way. She was yelling at Kristin to get her clothes and throw
them in the suitcase and she was crying, too."

"Still doesn't make any sense. You must've said something to set
her off."

"Honest, Phil, *nothing*. She barely let me get a word in edgewise
anyway. I didn't even have a chance to tell her why I was there
before she shut the door. Any chance of finding out if she's got
family in Idaho?"

"I'll give it a try. Talk to you later."

When we reached Boise, she left the Interstate to fill up the tank,
but instead of stopping at the first station, she drove around, checking prices I assumed, since she finally stopped at a no-frills gas
station with prices a few cents lower than the others. I drove past
and pulled into a full-service island at another station. While a kid
in greasy coveralls topped off my tank and checked under the

hood, I kept an eye on Jeri Lynn's car at the station a block away.
Jeri Lynn and Kristin had walked around the side of the building to
the restroom.

When she finally left the station, she headed toward downtown
instead of back to the Interstate. I'd second-guessed wrong and had
to make an illegal U-turn in heavy traffic to follow her. Ten minutes
later we were lost in downtown Boise. Jeri Lynn must have been
confused when she left the gas station. Eventually she found the
street we'd come in on and headed back toward the Interstate.

I was one car behind her when we stopped at a traffic signal near
the gas stations we'd stopped at earlier. The driver of the blue
pickup between us suddenly jerked his wheel hard to the right and
drove into the parking lot of a hardware store. I swore under my
breath. Behind me, the driver of a delivery truck tapped his horn,
wanting me to move forward and fill up the gap left by the pickup.
I saw Jeri Lynn's head tilt up as she checked her rearview mirror. I
bent my head down, hoping she couldn't see me clearly. Behind
me, the delivery truck's horn blasted, loud and long. I sighed and
drove forward. Jeri Lynn was looking into the mirror again. Just as
the light turned green, she turned around in her seat to get a better
look at me. We were close enough for me to see the shock in her
eyes, the fear on her face. The driver behind me laid on his horn
again. Jeri Lynn turned around and drove off.

During the mile-long drive back to the highway on-ramp we
passed dozens of open businesses, several pay phones, a cop direct-
ing traffic around a fender-bender, and a patrol car parked in front
of a donut shop. Help was all around, there for the asking, but Jeri
Lynn wasn't asking. She knew I was behind her, knew I had been
following her for a couple hundred miles, but she wasn't scared
enough to get help. Or maybe she was too scared of what the cops
might find out if she complained about a private eye following her
across the country.

Thirty minutes later, the phone rang. "Where are you?" Phil
asked, his voice fading in and out.

"Idaho."

"You want to narrow it down a little?"

"I would if I could. She left I-84 at Mountain Home. We're on a
two-lane blacktop heading north. I haven't seen a road sign since
we left Route 20 ten or fifteen miles back."

"You're heading up toward the Sawtooth Mountains?"

"Yeah. She knows I'm here, Phil." I told him how Jeri Lynn had spotted me in Boise and chose to drive into the boonies with me on her tail rather than go to the cops.

"Interesting," Phil said. "I haven't come up with any relatives in Idaho. No one seems to know much about her. Look, you must have said something that scared her. Give it some thought. Talk to you later."

I'd already given it plenty of thought but I went over my conversation with Jeri Lynn one more time. She thought I was there about the car, I told her I was a private detective; she got nervous, thinking I was a cop; I cleared that up; she didn't seem particularly reassured; she asked me what I wanted; I started to explain about the doll; she slammed the door. When I heard her shouting for Kristin to come home, I'd assumed she was mad at the little girl for talking to me. But she hadn't seemed mad at Kristin, she was just suddenly in a real big hurry to get away. Why? What did I say that set her off?

I suddenly remembered that I had used the doll's name, thinking it would lend some credibility to my story. Megan Ann. But Kristin called her Jennifer because her mother didn't like the other name. Didn't like it? Was that what Kristin had said? No, her mother didn't like her *using* the name. When I mentioned Megan Ann, I got a door slammed in my face. I thought that over for a few minutes, then I called Phil again. The transmission was weak, his voice faint and echoing so that his words seemed at times to overlap mine.

"Where did she live before? Did you find out?"

"Vacaville, California, but only for a couple months. San Jose before that."

"How about seeing what you can find out from Vacaville."

"Like what specifically? She doesn't have a record and there aren't any warrants out on her."

"Find out how many children she had then."

"How many children?"

"I used the doll's name, Phil. Megan Ann, only Kristin calls her Jennifer because her mother doesn't like her using Megan Ann. What if it was the name that upset her? I said something about knowing Megan Ann was gone."

There was a moment of silence, then Phil said, "I'll call Vacaville."

He didn't call back for almost an hour.

"Where are you now?"

"Still Idaho. We're in the Sawtooth Mountains and she isn't going anywhere in particular. She stays on Highway 75 for a while, then takes a side road that loops around and puts us back on 75 and then she takes another side road and does the same thing again. She's just driving. She'll be out of gas before long."

"Okay. Here's the bad news: The Vacaville cops checked with her landlord there. She had a husband and two kids — two little girls. He didn't know their names. The other one was two or three years younger than Kristin, which means she'd be about four now. I talked to the landlady here again and to some of the neighbors. She never mentioned another kid to any of them. Looks like she misplaced her somewhere. You ready for the rest of the bad news?"

I suddenly felt sick to my stomach. The confirmation of my worst fears tends to do that to me. "Go ahead."

"Vacaville's got a file on an unidentified white female, age somewhere between three and four years, left in a nurse's car in the parking lot of a hospital not too far from where Jeri Lynn lived. The body was found eight months ago. Just before Jeri Lynn showed up in Oregon. Cause of death was a bullet in the face."

I told Phil I'd call him back as soon as I figured out where I was. I put the phone on the seat beside me and wiped my sweaty hand on my shorts, thinking of the fear on Jeri Lynn's face when she spotted me. I must have been her worst nightmare come true, the past come back to haunt her, following her cross country, hot on her trail, breathing down her neck. Well, she deserved it, didn't she? Possibly it was her husband who pulled the trigger, but what kind of mother would keep quiet about it and agree to leave her child's body in a stranger's car in a parking lot? I wondered if Kristin knew what happened to the real Megan Ann. Had she witnessed it? I hoped not.

The road we were on was narrow and winding with long switchbacks. A dense forest of pines climbed the hill to the right of the car; to the left was a steep drop-off. The Toyota was a hundred feet ahead of me, moving slowly, the brake lights constantly flashing as Jeri Lynn negotiated the sharp turns. Except for an occasional car passing by, we had the road to ourselves.

The Toyota's brake lights suddenly lit up and the car stopped abruptly in the traffic lane. The passenger door opened and Kristin got out. Her mother leaned over and jerked the door closed, then hit the gas, the tires spewing up dust and gravel. Kristin turned away, covering her face for a moment against the cloud of dust, then she started plodding toward my car, head bowed, braids swaying by her chin, teddy bear dangling from one hand. When I rolled to a stop beside her, she simply opened the door and got in, not saying anything, just leaning her head back against the seat and closing her eyes. I fastened her seat belt, then drove off after the Toyota.

"What did your mother say?" I asked.

"She said you're going to take me home."

"Okay. Kristin, what happened to Megan Ann?"

". . . Her name's Jennifer."

"I don't mean the doll."

Kristin didn't answer. She chewed thoughtfully on a braid while I drove. I'd sped up a bit and the Toyota was only a couple car lengths ahead of me now. I called Phil again and told him I had Kristin. He asked if I'd spotted a helicopter yet. "The Idaho state police are looking for you. Might take them a while since I could only give them a rough idea where you are. Stick with her, okay?"

When I put the phone down, Kristin said, "She cried all the time. It gave Mommy a sick headache."

"That must've made your mother mad. Megan Ann crying all the time."

"It made her head hurt. Megan Ann wouldn't stop crying. I told her and told her to stop but she wouldn't." She pressed the teddy bear against her face for a moment, hugging it tight.

At the crest of the hill, Jeri Lynn suddenly stuck her left hand out the window and let something drop on the road. A brown purse. Before I could decide whether to stop and pick it up, the Toyota's left turn signal began to blink. There was nothing to the left. I watched, knuckles turning white on the steering wheel. The Toyota's speed suddenly increased, the car moving quickly away from me on the downgrade, which ran straight for half a mile or so before veering off to the right. Jeri Lynn Baker was doing at least eighty when she made her left turn off the side of the mountain. I glanced at Kristin. She was resting her cheek on her teddy bear's head, her face turned away from me.

I braked the Camaro a minute later, pulling as far to the right as I could, tree branches almost brushing the passenger side. "Stay in the car," I said to Kristin. I ran across the street. The drop was steep enough that the upside-down Toyota looked like a discarded toy. As I watched, flames licked across the bottom of the car. I went back to my car and leaned in the window.

Kristin was staring straight ahead, a single tear trailing slowly down her cheek. I didn't know if she'd seen her mother's car go over the edge and I didn't ask. I heard a distant flutter which quickly grew louder, turning into the brisk chopping sound of helicopter blades. The chopper came into sight ahead of us and swooped down into the canyon.

"She said . . . she said you'll take me home, but . . . there's nobody there. Daddy went away and Megan Ann got hurt bad and Mommy took her to the hospital . . ."

"Someone will take care of you, I promise. Wait here a minute, I'll be right back."

I jogged down the road and picked up the purse. Sticking out of it was a cylinder of stiff brown paper, part of the grocery bag. I unrolled it and smoothed it out as I walked back to the car. Jeri Lynn had written the note while she was driving, the words scrawled unevenly across the paper. *I shot my daughter Megan Ann by accident and left her at a hospital in Vacaville in December. Kristin doesn't know anything about it. She wasn't there when it happened.* She had signed her name and written the date beneath it.

The helicopter suddenly rose from the canyon and shot away. As the sound faded, I heard a siren, coming steadily closer. I went back to the car and slid behind the wheel. Kristin was hugging her teddy bear, staring at the sky where the helicopter had been. An Idaho state police car pulled up behind the Camaro. The trooper came to the driver's side window and leaned down. I talked to him briefly, keeping my voice low, and gave him Jeri Lynn's purse and the torn piece of grocery bag. When he headed to his car to use the radio, I turned to Kristin.

"We can find your father. Grownups have to work and pay taxes and things like that. We can find him. Did he . . . Did you get along with him okay?"

She nodded. "But he was mad at Mommy."

"Because of what happened to Megan Ann?"

She nodded again, another tear rolling down her cheek. "He said Mommy had to tell, but she wouldn't, so he went away. Mommy was mad at him. She said it was all his fault 'cause she told him and told him she didn't want that gun in the house."

I turned my head, looking away from Kristin Michelle Baker with her freckles and skinny braids and tear-stained cheeks. Gray smoke drifted lazily upward from the canyon where Jeri Lynn Baker's car was burning. *Driven to her death.* The phrase repeated itself in my mind several times. The smoke formed a slender spiral, the top blowing off to the west and disappearing.

"I was just . . . I told Megan Ann she had to stop crying 'cause Mommy had a sick headache, but she wouldn't stop. I was showing her some stuff, the stuff in Daddy's drawer, so she'd stop crying." I turned to look at her. "Is Mommy coming back?" she asked.

"I don't think so." After a moment, I added, "Sometimes . . . sometimes people have to go away even if they don't want to."

Kristin's chin quivered. "It's okay. Megan Ann got hurt bad and had to go to the hospital. She can't come home yet. Mommy said she has to go take care of her." She sighed and added, "She told me and told me not to play with that gun."

JOHN UPDIKE

Bech Noir

FROM *The New Yorker*

BECH HAD a new sidekick. Her moniker was Robin. Rachel
(Robin) Teagarten. Twenty-six, post-Jewish, frizzy big hair, figure
on the short and solid side. She interfaced for him with an IBM
PS/1 his publisher had talked him into buying. She set up the
defaults, rearranged the icons, programmed the style formats, ac-
cessed the ANSI character sets — Bech was a stickler for foreign
accents. When he answered a letter, she typed it for him from
dictation. When he took a creative leap, she deciphered his handwriting and turned it into digitized code. Neither happened very
often. Bech was of the Ernest Hemingway save-your-juices school.
To fill the time, he and Robin slept together. He was seventy-four,
but they worked with that. Seventy-four plus twenty-six was one
hundred; divided by two that was fifty, the prime of life. The energy
of youth plus the wisdom of age. A team. A duo.

They were in his snug aerie on Crosby Street. He was reading the
Times at breakfast. Caffeineless Folger's, D'Agostino orange juice,
poppy-seed bagel lightly toasted. The crumbs and poppy seeds had
scattered over the newspaper and into his lap but you don't get
something for nothing, not on this hard planet. Bech announced
to Robin, "Hey, Lucas Mishner is dead."

A creamy satisfaction — the finest quality, made extra easy to
spread by the toasty warmth — thickly covered his heart.

"Who's Lucas Mishner?" Robin asked. She was deep in the D
section — Business Day. She was a practical-minded broad with no
experience of culture prior to 1975.

"Once-powerful critic," Bech told her, biting off his phrases.
"Late *Partisan Review* school. Used to condescend to appear in the

Trib Book Review, when the *Trib* was still alive on this side of the Atlantic. Despised my stuff. Called it 'superficially energetic but lacking in the true American fiber, the grit, the wrestle.' That's him talking, not me. The grit, the wrestle. Sanctimonious bastard. When *The Chosen* came out in '63, he wrote, 'Strive and squirm as he will, Bech will never, never be touched by the American sublime.' The simple, smug, know-it-all son of a bitch. You know what his idea of the real stuff was? James Jones. James Jones and James Gould Cozzens."

There Mishner's face was, in the *Times,* twenty years younger, with a fuzzy little rosebud smirk and a pathetic slicked-down comb-over, like limp venetian blinds throwing a shadow across the dome of his head. The thought of him dead filled Bech with creamy ease. He told Robin, "Lived way the hell up in Connecticut. Three wives, no flowers. Hadn't published in years. The rumor in the industry was he was gaga with alcoholic dementia."

"You seem happy."

"Very."

"Why? You say he had stopped being a critic anyway."

"Not in my head. He tried to hurt me. He did hurt me. Vengeance is mine."

"Who said that?"

"The Lord. In the Bible. Wake up, Robin."

"I thought it didn't sound like you," she admitted. "Stop hogging the Arts section."

He passed it over, with a pattering of poppy seeds on the teak breakfast table Robin had installed. For years he and his female guests had eaten at a low glass coffee table farther forward in the loft. The sun slanting in had been pretty, but eating all doubled up had been bad for their internal organs. He liked the cut of Robin's smooth broad jaw across the table. Her healthy big hair, her pushy plump lips, her little flattened nose. "One down," he told her, mysteriously.

A week later, he was in the subway. The Rockefeller Center station on Sixth Avenue, the old IND line. The downtown platform was jammed. All those McGraw-Hill, Exxon, and Time-Life execs were rushing back to their wives in the Heights. Or going down to West Fourth to have some herbal tea and put on drag for the evening. Monogamous transvestite executives were clogging the system.

Bech was in a savage mood. He had been to MOMA, checking out
the new art. It had all seemed pointless, poisonous, violent, inept.
None of it had been Bech's bag. Art had passed him by. Literature
was passing him by. Music he had never gotten exactly with, not
since USO record hops. Those cuddly little WACs from Ohio in
their starched uniforms. That war had been over too soon, before
he got to kill enough Germans.

Down in the subway, three groups of electronic buskers — one
country, one progressive jazz, and one doing Christian hip-hop —
were competing. Overhead, a huge voice kept unintelligibly an-
nouncing cancellations and delays. In the cacophony, Bech spotted
an English critic: Raymond Featherwaite, former Cambridge emi-
nence lured to CUNY by American moola. From his perch in the
CUNY crenellations, using his antique matchlock arquebus, he
had been snottily potting American writers for twenty years, cour-
tesy of the ravingly Anglophile *New York Review of Books.* "Prolix"
and "*voulu*," Featherwaite had called Bech's best-selling comeback
book, *Think Big,* in 1978. When, in 1985, Bech had ventured a
harmless collection of sketches and stories, *Biding Time,* Featherwaite had written, "One's spirits, however initially well-disposed
toward one of America's more carefully tended reputations, begin
severely to sag under the repeated empathetic effort of watching
Mr. Bech, page after page, strain to make something of very little."

The combined decibels of the buskers drowned out, for all but
the most attuned city ears, the approach of the train whose delay
had been so indistinctly bruited. Featherwaite, like all these Eng-
lishpersons who were breeding like wood lice in the rotting log
piles of the New York literary industry, was no slouch at pushing ahead, through the malleable ex-colonials. Though there was
hardly room to place one's shoes on the filthy speckled concrete,
Featherwaite had shoved and wormed his way to the front of the
crowd, right to the edge of the platform. His edgy profile, with
its supercilious overbite and artfully projecting eyebrows, turned
with arrogant expectancy toward the screamingly approaching D
train, as though hailing a servile black London taxi or Victorian
brougham. Featherwaite affected a wispy-banged Nero haircut.
There were rougelike touches of color on his cheekbones. The tidy
English head bit into Bech's vision like a branding iron.

Prolix, he thought. *Voulu.* He had had to look up "*voulu*" in his

French dictionary. It put a sneering curse on Bech's entire oeuvre, for what, as Schopenhauer had asked, isn't willed?

Bech was three bodies back in the crush, tightly immersed in the odors, clothes, accents, breaths, and balked wills of others. Two broad-backed bodies, padded with junk food and fermented malt, intervened between himself and Featherwaite, while others importunately pushed at his own back. As if suddenly shoved from behind, he lowered his shoulder and rammed into the body ahead of his; like dominoes, it and the next tipped the third, the stiff-backed Englishman, off the platform. In the next moment the train with the force of a flash flood poured into the station, drowning all other noise under a shrieking gush of tortured metal. Featherwaite's hand in the last second of his life had shot up and his head jerked back as if in sudden recognition of an old acquaintance. Then he had vanished.

It was an instant's event, without time for the D-train driver to brake or a bystander to scream. Just one head pleasantly less in the compressed, malodorous mob. The man ahead of Bech, a ponderous African-American with bloodshot eyes, wearing a knit cap in the depths of summer, regained his balance and turned indignantly, but Bech, feigning a furious glance behind him, slipped sideways as the crowd arranged itself into funnels beside each door of the now halted train. A woman's raised voice — foreign, shrill — had begun to leak the horrible truth of what she had witnessed, and far away, beyond the turnstiles, a telepathic policeman's whistle was tweeting. But the crowd within the train was surging outward against the crowd trying to enter, and in the thick eddies of disgruntled and compressed humanity nimble, bookish, elderly Bech put more and more space between himself and his unwitting accomplices. He secreted himself a car's length away, hanging from a hand-burnished bar next to an ad publicizing free condoms and clean needles, with a dainty Oxford edition of Donne's poems pressed close to his face, as the whistles of distant authority drew nearer. The train refused to move and was finally emptied of passengers, while the official voice overhead, louder and less intelligible than ever, shouted word of cancellation, of disaster, of evaluation without panic.

Obediently Bech left the stalled train, blood on its wheels, and climbed the metallic stairs sparkling with pulverized glass. His insides shuddered in tune with the shoving, near-panicked mob about him. Gratefully he inhaled the outdoor air and Manhattan anonymity. Avenue of the Americas, a sign said, in stubborn upholding of an obsolete gesture of hemispheric good will. Bech walked south, then over to Seventh Avenue. Scrupulously he halted at each red light and deposited each handed-out leaflet (GIRLS! COLLEGE SEX KITTENS TOPLESS! BOTTOMLESS AFTER 6:30 P.M.!) in the nearest city trash receptacle. He descended into the Times Square station, where the old IRT's innumerable tunnels mingled their misery in a vast subterranean maze of passageways, stairs, signs, and candy stands. He caught an N train that took him to Broadway and Prince. Afternoon had sweetly turned to evening while he had been underground. The galleries were closing, the restaurants were opening. Robin was in the loft, keeping lasagna warm. "I thought MOMA closed at six," she said.

"There was a tieup in the Sixth Avenue subway. Nothing was running. I had to walk down to Times Square. I hated the stuff the museum had up. Violent, attention-getting."

"Maybe there comes a time," she said, "when new art isn't for you, it's for somebody else. I wonder what caused the tieup."

"Nobody knew. Power failure. A shootout uptown. Some maniac," he added, wondering at his own words. His insides felt agitated, purged, scrubbed, yet not yet creamy. Perhaps that needed to wait until the morning *Times*. He feared he could not sleep, out of nervous anticipation, yet he toppled into dreams while Robin still read beneath a burning light, as if he had done a long day's worth of physical labor.

"English Critic, Teacher Dead in West Side Subway Mishap," the headline read. The story was low on the front page and jumped to the obituaries. The obit photo, taken decades ago, glamorized Featherwaite — head facing one way, shoulders another — so he resembled a younger, less impish brother of George Sanders. High brow, thin lips, cocky glass chin. ". . . according to witnesses appeared to fling himself under the subway train as it approached the platform . . . colleagues at CUNY puzzled but agreed he had been under significant stress compiling permissions for his textbook of postmodern narrative strategies . . . former wife, reached in London, allowed the deceased had been subject to mood swings and fits of creative despair . . . the author of several youthful satirical

novels and a single book of poems likened to those of Philip Larkin
. . . born in Scunthorpe, Yorkshire, the third child and only son of a
greengrocer and a part-time piano teacher . . ." and so on.

"Ray Featherwaite is dead," he announced to Robin, trying to
keep a tremble of triumph out of his voice.

"Who was he?"

"A critic. More minor than Mishner. English. Came from Yorkshire, in fact — I had never known that. Went to Cambridge on a
scholarship. I had figured him for inherited wealth; he wanted you
to think so."

"That makes two critics this week," said Robin, preoccupied by
the dense gray pages of stock prices.

"Every third person on this island is some kind of critic," Bech
pointed out. He hoped the conversation would move on.

"How did he die?"

There was no way to hide it; she would be reading this section
eventually. "Jumped under a subway train, oddly. Seems he'd been
feeling low, trying to secure too many copyright permissions or
something. These academics are under a lot of stress, competing
for tenure."

"Oh?" Robin's eyes — bright, glossy, a living volatile brown, like a
slick moist pelt — had left the stock prices. "What subway line?"

"Sixth Avenue, actually."

"Maybe that was the tieup you mentioned."

"Could be. Very likely, in fact."

"Why are your hands trembling? You can hardly hold your bagel." The poppy seeds were pattering on the obituary page.

"Who knows?" he asked her. "I may be coming down with something. I went out like a light last night."

"I'll say," said Robin, returning her eyes to the page.

"Sorry," he said, ease beginning to flow again within him. The
past was sinking, every second, under fresher, obscuring layers of
the recent past. "Did it make you feel neglected? A young woman
needs her sex."

"No," she said, preoccupied by the market's faithful rise. "It made
me feel tender. You seemed so innocent."

Robin, like Spider-man's wife, Mary Jane, worked in a computer
emporium. She didn't so much sell them as share her insights with
customers as they struggled in the crashing waves of innovation and

the lightning-swift undertow of obsolescence. It thrilled Bech to view her in her outlet — Smart Circuits, on Third Avenue near Twenty-seventh Street, a few blocks from Bellevue — standing solid and calm in a gray suit whose lapels swerved to take in her bosom. Amid her array of putty-colored monitors and system-unit housings, she received the petitions of those in thrall to the computer revolution. They were mostly skinny young men with parched hair and sunless complexions. Sometimes Bech would enter the store, like some grizzled human glitch, and take Robin to lunch. Sometimes he would sneak away content with his glimpse of this princess decreeing in her realm. He marveled that at the end of the day she would find her path through the circuitry of the city and come to him. The tenacity of erotic connection anticipated the faithful transistor and the microchip.

Bech had not always been an object of criticism. His first stories and essays, appearing in defunct mass publications like *Liberty* and defunct avant-garde journals like *Displeasure,* roused little comment, and his dispatches, published in *The New Leader,* from Normandy in the wake of the 1944 invasion, and then from the Bulge and Berlin, went little noticed in a print world flooded with war coverage. But, ten years later, his first novel, *Travel Light,* made a small splash, and for the first time he saw, in print, spite directed at himself. Not just spite, but a willful mistaking of his intentions and a cheerfully ham-handed divulgence of all his plot's nicely calculated and hoarded twists. A New York Jew writing about Midwestern bikers infuriated some reviewers — some Jewish, some Midwestern — and the sly asceticism of his next, novella-length novel, *Brother Pig,* annoyed others: "The contemptuous medieval expression for the body which the author has used as a title serves only too well," one reviewer (female) wrote, "to prepare us for the sad orgy of Jewish self-hatred with which Mr. Bech will disappoint and repel his admirers — few, it is true, but in some rarefied circles curiously fervent."

As he aged, adverse phrases from the far past surfaced in his memory with an amazing vividness, word for word — "says utterly nothing with surprising aplomb," "too toothless or shrewd to tackle life's raw meat," "never doffs his velour exercise togs to break a sweat," "the sentimental coarseness of a pornographic valentine," "prose arabesques of phenomenal irrelevancy," "refusal or failure to ironize his reactionary positions," "starry-eyed sexism," "minor, minorer, minor-most" — and clamorously rattled around in his head, rendering him, some days, while his brain tried to be busy with something else, stupid with rage. It was as if these insults, these hurled mud balls, these stains on the robe of his vocation were, now that he was nearing the end, bleeding wounds. That a negative review might be a fallible verdict, delivered in haste, against a deadline, for a few dollars, by a writer with problems and limitations of his or her own, was a reasonable and weaseling supposition he could no longer, in the dignity of his years, entertain. Any adverse review, even a single timid phrase of qualification or reservation within a favorable and even adoring review, stood revealed as the piece of pure enmity it was — an assault, a virtual murder, a purely malicious attempt to unman and destroy him. The army of critics stood revealed as not fellow wordsmiths plying a dingy and dying trade but satanic legions, deserving only annihilation. A furious lava — an acidic indignation begging for the Maalox of creamy, murderous satisfaction — had gradually become Bech's essence, his angelic ichor.

The female reviewer, Deborah Frueh, who had in 1957 maligned *Brother Pig* as a flight of Jewish self-hatred was still alive, huddled in the haven of Seattle, amid New Age crystals and medicinal powders, between Boeing and Mount Rainier. Though she was grit too fine to be found in the coarse sieve of *Who's Who,* he discovered her address in the Poets & Writers' directory, which listed a few critical articles and her fewer books, all children's books with heart-tugging titles like *Jennifer's Lonely Birthday* and *The Day Dad Didn't Come Home* and *A Teddy Bear's Bequest.* These books, Bech saw, were her Achilles' heel.

He wrote her a fan letter, in a slow and childish hand, in black ballpoint, on blue-lined paper. "Dear Deborah Freuh," he wrote, deliberately misspelling, "You are my favrite writer. I have red your books over 'n' over. I would be greatful if you could find time to sign the two enclosed cards for me and my best frend Betsey and return them in the inclosed envelop. That would be really grate of you and many many thanx in advance." He signed it, "Your real fan, Mary Jane Mason."

He wrote it once and then rewrote it, holding the pen in what felt like a little girl's fist. Then he set the letter aside and worked carefully on the envelope. He had bought a cheap box of a hundred at an office-supply store on lower Broadway and destroyed a number before he got the alchemy right. With a paper towel he delicately moistened the dried gum on the envelope flap — not too much, or it curled. Then, gingerly using a glass martini-stirring rod, he placed three or four drops of colorless poison on the moist adhesive.

Prowling the cavernous basement of the renovated old sweat-shop where he lived, Bech had found, in a cobwebbed janitor's closet, along with a quaint hand pump of tin and desiccated rubber, a thick brown-glass jar whose label, in the stiff and guileless typographic style of the nineteen-forties, proclaimed POISON and displayed along its border an array of dead vermin, roaches and rats and centipedes in dictionary-style engraving. In his thieving hand, the jar sloshed, half full. He took it upstairs to his loft and through a magnifying glass identified the effective ingredient as hydrocyanic acid. When the rusty lid was unscrewed, out rushed the penetrating whiff, cited in many a mystery novel, of bitter almonds. Lest the adhesive be betraying bitter when licked, and Deborah Frueh rush to ingest an antidote, he sweetened the doctored spots with some sugar water mixed in an orange-juice glass and applied with an eyedropper.

The edges of glue tended to curl as they dried, a difficulty he mitigated by rolling them the other way before applying the liquids. The afternoon waned; the roar of traffic up on Houston reached its crescendo unnoticed; the windows of the converted factory across Crosby Street entertained unseen the blazing amber of the lowering sun. Bech was wheezily panting in the intensity of his concentration. His nose was running; he kept wiping it with a trembling handkerchief. He had reverted to elementary school, where he and his peers had built tiny metropolises out of cereal boxes and scissored into being red valentines and black profiles of George Washington, even made paper Easter eggs and Christmas trees, under their young and starchy Irish and German instructresses, who without fear of objection swept their little Jewish-American pupils into the Christian calendar.

Bech thought hard about the return address on the envelope, which could become, once its fatal bait was taken, a dangerous clue. The poison, before hitting home, might give Deborah Frueh time to seal the thing, which in the confusion after her death might be mailed. That would be perfect — the clue consigned to a continental mailbag and arrived with the junk mail at an indifferent American household. In the Westchester directory he found a Mason in New Rochelle and fistily inscribed the address beneath the name of his phantom Frueh fan. Folding the envelope, he imagined he heard a faint crackling — microscopic sugar and cyanide crystals? His conscience, dried up by a century of atrocity and atheism, trying to come to life? He slipped the folded envelope with the letter and four (why not be generous?) three-by-five index cards into the envelope painstakingly addressed in the immature, girlish handwriting. He hurried downstairs, his worn heart pounding, to throw Mary Jane Mason's fan letter into the mailbox at Broadway and Prince.

Like the reflected light of a city set to burning, the lurid sunset hung low in the direction of New Jersey. The streets were crammed with the living and the guiltless, heading home in the day's horizontal rays, blinking from the subway's flicker and a long day spent at computer terminals. Bech hesitated a second before relinquishing his letter to the blue, graffiti-sprayed box, there in front of Victoria's Secret. A young black woman with an armful of metered nine-by-twelve envelopes impatiently arrived at his back, to make her more massive, less lethal drop. He stifled his qualm. The governmental box hollowly sounded with the slam of the lid upon the fathomless depths of sorting and delivery to which he consigned his missive. His life had been spent as a votary of the mails. This was but one more submission.

Morning after morning, the *Times* carried no word on the death of Deborah Frueh. Perhaps, just as she wasn't in *Who's Who,* she was too small a fish to be caught in the *Times'* obituary net. But no, they observed at respectful length the deaths of hundreds of people of whom Bech had never heard. Former aldermen, upstate prioresses, New Jersey judges, straight men on defunct TV comedies, founders of Manhattan dog-walking services — all got their space, their chiseled paragraphs, their farewell salute. Noticing the avidity with which he always turned to the back of the Metro section, Robin asked him, "What are you looking for?"

He couldn't tell her. "Familiar names," he said. "People I once knew."

"Henry, it seems morbid. Here, I'm done with Arts and Sports."

"I've read enough about arts and sports," he told this bossy tootsie, "to last me to the grave."

He went to the public library, the Hamilton Fish Park branch on East Houston, and in the children's section found one of Deborah Frueh's books, *Jennifer's Lonely Birthday,* and checked it out. He read it and wrote her another letter, this time in blue ballpoint, on unlined stationery with a little Peter Maxish elf-figure up in one corner, the kind a very young girl might be given for her birthday by an aunt or uncle. "Dear Deborah Frueh," he wrote, "I love your exciting work. I love the way at the end of 'Jennifer's Lonely Birth-day' Jennifer realizes that she has had a pretty good day after all and that in life you can't depend on anybody else to entertain you, you have to entertain your own mind. At the local library I have 'The Day Dad Didn't Come Home' on reserve. I hope it isn't too sad. 'Teddy Bear's Bequest' they never heard of at the library. I know you are a busy woman and must be working on more books but I hope you could send me a photograph of you for the wall of my room or if your too busy to do that please sign this zerox of the one on the cover of 'Jennifer's Lonely Birthday.' I like the way you do your hair, it's like my Aunt Daphne, up behind. Find enclosed a stamped envelope to send it in. Yours hopefully, Judith Green."

Miss Green in Bech's mind was a year or so older than Mary Jane Mason. She misspelled hardly at all, and had self-consciously converted her grammar-school handwriting to a stylish printing, which Bech slaved at for several hours before attaining the proper girlish plumpness in the *o*'s and *m*'s. He tried dotting the *i*'s with little circles and ultimately discarded the device as unpersuasive. He did venture, however, a little happy face, with smile and rudimentary pigtails. He intensified the dose of hydrocyanic acid on the envelope flap, and eased off on the sugar water. When Deborah Frueh took her lick — he pictured it as avid and thorough, not one but several swoops of her vicious, pointed tongue — the bitterness would register too late. The bitch would never know what hit her. A slowed heart, inhibited breathing, dilated pupils, convulsive movements, and complete loss of consciousness follow within seconds. He had done his research.

The postmark was a problem. Mary Jane up there in New Rochelle might well have had a father who, setting off in the morning with a full briefcase, would mail her letter for her in Manhattan, but two in a row and Frueh might smell a rat, especially if she had responded to the last request and was still feeling queasy. Bech took the Hoboken ferry from the World Financial Center, treating himself to a river view of his twinkling, aspiring home town. He looked up Greens in a telephone booth near the terminal. He picked one on Willow Street to be little Judy's family. He deposited his letter in a scabby dockside box and, leaving the missive to move on its own tides toward Seattle, took the ferry back to lower Manhattan. The writer's nerves hummed; his eyes narrowed against the river glare. What did Whitman write of such crossings? "Flood-tide below me! I see you face to face!" And, later on, speaking so urgently from the grave, "Just as you are refresh'd by the gladness of the river and the bright flow, I was refresh'd, Just as you stand and lean on the rail, yet hurry with the swift current, I stood yet was hurried." That "yet was hurried" was brilliant, with all of Whitman's brilliant homeliness.

A week went by. Ten days. The desired death was not reported in the *Times*. Bech wondered if a boy fan might win a better response, a more enthusiastic, heterosexual licking of the return envelope. "Dear Deborah Freuh," Bech typed, using the hideous Script face available on his IBM PS/1. "You are a great writer, the greatest as far as I am concerned in the world. Your book titled 'The Day Dad Didn't Come Home' broke me up, it was so sad and true. I don't want to waste any more of your time reading this so you can get back to writing another super book but it would be sensational if you would sign the enclosed first-day cover for Sarah Orne Jewett, the greatest female American writer until you came along. Even if you have a policy against signing I'd appreciate your returning it in the enclosed self-addressed stamped envelope since I am a collector and spent a week's allowance for it at the hobby shop here in Amityville, Long Island, NY. Sign it on the pencil line I have drawn. I will erase the line when you have signed. I look forward to hearing from you soon. Yours very sincerely, Jason Johnson, Jr."

It was a pleasant change, in the too-even tenor of Bech's days, to ride the Long Island Rail Road out to Amityville and mail Jason Johnson's letter. Just to visit Penn Station again offered a fresh perspective — all that Roman grandeur from his youth, that onetime temple to commuting Fortuna, reduced to these ignoble ceilings and Tartarean passageways. And then, after the elevated views of tar-roofed Queens, the touching suburban stations, like so many knobbed Victorian toys, with their carefully pointed stonework and gleaming rows of parked cars and stretches of suburban park. In Amityville he found a suitable Johnson — on Maple Drive — and mailed his letter and headed back to town, the stations accumulating ever shabbier, more commercial surroundings and the track bed becoming elevated and then, with a black roar, buried, underground, underriver, undercity, until the train stopped at Penn Station again and the passengers spilled out into a gaudy, perilous mess of consumeristic blandishments, deranged beggars, and furtive personal errands.

Four days later, there it was, in four inches of *Times* type, the death of Deborah Frueh. Respected educator was also a noted critic and author of children's books. Had earlier published scholarly articles on the English Metaphysicals and Swinburne and his circle. Taken suddenly ill while at her desk in her home in Hunts Point, near Seattle. Born in Conshohocken, near Philadelphia. Attended Barnard College and Duke University graduate school. Exact cause of death yet to be determined. Had been in troubled health lately — her weight a stubborn problem — colleagues at the University of Washington reported. Survived by a sister, Edith, of Ardmore, Pennsylvania, and a brother, Leonard, of Teaneck, New Jersey.

Another ho-hum exit notice, for every reader but Henry Bech. He knew what a deadly venom the deceased had harbored in her fangs.

"What's happened?" Robin asked from across the table.

"Nothing's happened," he said.

"Then why do you look like that?"

"Like what?"

"Like a man who's been told he's won a million dollars but isn't sure it's worth it, what with all the tax problems."

"What a strange, untrammeled imagination," he said.

"Let me see the page you're reading."

"No. I'm still reading it."

"Henry, are you going to make me stand up and walk around the table?"

He handed her the cream-cheese-stained obituary page. Robin, while the rounded points of her wide jaw thoughtfully clenched and unclenched on the last milky crumbs of her whole-bran flakes, flicked her quick brown eyes up and down the columns of print. Her eyes held points of red like the fur of a fox. Morning sun slanting through the big loft window made an outline of light, of incandescent fuzz, along her jaw. Her eyelashes glittered like a row of dewdrops on a spiderweb strand. "Who's Deborah Frueh?" she asked. "Did you know her?"

"A frightful literary scold," he said. "I never met the lady, I'm not sorry to say."

"Did she ever review you or anything?"

"I believe she did, once or twice."

"Favorably?"

"Not really."

"Really unfavorably?"

"It could be said. Her reservations about my work were un-hedged, as I vaguely recall. You know I don't pay much attention to reviews."

"And that Englishman last month, who fell in front of the subway train — didn't you have some connection with him, too?"

"Darling, I've been publishing for over fifty years. I have slight connections with everybody in the print racket."

"You've not been quite yourself lately," Robin told him. "You've had some kind of a secret. You don't talk to me the breezy way you used to. You're censoring."

"I'm not," he said, hating to lie, standing as he was knee-deep in the sweet clover of Deborah Frueh's extermination. He wondered what raced through that fat harpy's mind in the last second, as the terrible-tasting cyanide nipped down her esophagus and halted the oxidation process within her cells. Not of him, certainly. He was one of multitudes of writers she had put in their places. He was three thousand miles away, the anonymous progenitor of Jason Johnson, Jr.

"Look at you!" Robin cried, on so high a note that her orange-juice glass emitted a surprised shiver. "You're triumphant! Henry, you killed her."

"How would I have done that?"

She was not balked. Her eyes narrowed. "At a distance, some-how," she guessed. "You sent her things. A couple of days, when I came home, there was a funny smell in the room, like something had been burning."

"This is fascinating," Bech said. "If I had your imagination, I'd be Balzac." He went on, to deflect her devastating insights, "Another assiduous critic of mine, Aldie Cannon — he used to be a mainstay of *The New Republic* but now he's on PBS and the Internet — says I can't imagine a thing. And hate women.'"

Robin was still musing, her smooth young mien puzzling at the crimes to which she was an as yet blind partner. She said, "I guess it depends on how you define 'hate.'"

But he loved her. He loved the luxurious silken whiteness of her slightly thickset young body, the soothing cool of her basically factual mind. He could not long maintain this wall between them, this ugly partition in the light-filled loft of their love match. The next day the *Times* ran a little follow-up squib on the same page as the daily book review — basically comic in its tone, for who would want to murder an elderly, overweight book critic and juvenile author — stating that the Seattle police had found suspicious chemical traces in Frueh's autopsied body. Bech confessed to Robin. The truth rose irrepressible in his throat like the acid burn of partial regurgitation. Pushing the large black man who pushed a body that pushed Featherwaite's. Writing Deborah Frueh three fan letters with doped return envelopes. Robin listened while reposing on his brown beanbag chair in a terry-cloth bathrobe. She had taken a shower, so her feet had babyish pink sides beneath the marble-white insteps with their faint blue veins. It was Sunday morning. She said when he was done, "Henry, you can't just go around rubbing out people as if they existed only on paper."

"I can't? That's where they tried to rub me out, on paper. They preyed on my insecurities, to shut off my creative flow. They nearly succeeded. I haven't written nearly as much as I could have."

"Was that their fault?"

"Partly," he estimated. Perhaps he had made a fatal error, spilling his guts to this chesty broad. "Okay. Turn me in. Go to the bulls."

"The bulls?"

"The police — haven't you ever heard that expression? How about 'the fuzz'? Or 'the pigs'?"

"I've never heard them called that, either."

"My God, you're young. What have I ever done to deserve you, Robin? You're so pure, so straight. And now you loathe me."

"No, I don't, actually. I might have thought I would, but in fact I like you more than ever." She never said "love," she was too post-Jewish for that. "I think you've shown a lot of balls, frankly, translating your resentments into action instead of sublimating them into art."

He didn't much like it when young women said "balls" or called a man "an asshole," but today he was thrilled by the cool baldness of it. They were, he and his mistress, in a new realm, a computerized universe devoid of blame or guilt, as morally null as an Intel chip. There were only, in this purified universe, greater or lesser patches of electricity, and violence and sex were greater patches. She stood and opened her robe. She emitted a babyish scent, a whiff of sour milk; otherwise her body was unodiferous, so that Bech's own aromas, the product of seven and a half decades of marination in the ignominy of organic life, stood out like smears on a white vinyl wall. Penetrated, Robin felt like a fresh casing, and her spasms came rapidly, a tripping series of orgasms made almost pitiable by her habit of sucking one of his thumbs deep into her mouth as she came. When that was over, and their pulse rates had leveled off, she looked at him with her fox-fur irises shining expectantly, childishly.

"So who are you going to do next?" she asked. Her pupils, those inkwells as deep as the night sky's zenith, were dilated by excitement.

"Well, Aldie Cannon *is* very annoying," Bech reluctantly allowed. "He's a forty-something smart-aleck, from the West Coast somewhere. Palo Alto, maybe. He has one of these very rapid agile nerdy minds — whatever pops into it must be a thought. He began by being all over *The Nation* and *The New Republic* and then moved into the *Vanity Fair/GQ* orbit, writing about movies, books, TV, music, whatever, an authority on any sort of schlock, and then got more and more on radio and TV — they love that kind of guy, the thirty-second opinion, bing, bam — until now that's basically all he does, that and write some kind of junk on the Internet, his own Web site, I don't know — people send me printouts whenever he says anything about me, I wish they wouldn't."

"What sort of thing does he say?"

Bech shifted his weight off his elbow, which was hurting. Any joint in his body hurt, with a little use. His body wanted to retire but his raging spirit wouldn't let it. "He says I'm the embodiment of everything retrograde in pre-electronic American letters. He says my men are sex-obsessed narcissistic brutes and all my female characters are just anatomically correct dolls."

"Ooh," murmured Robin, as if softly struck by a bit of rough justice.

Bech went on, aggrieved, "He says things like, and I quote, 'Whenever Bech attempts to use his imagination, the fuse blows and sparks fall to the floor. But short circuits aren't the same as magic-realist fireworks.' End quote. On top of being a smart-aleck he's a closet prude. He hated the sex in *Think Big*; he wrote, as I dimly remember, 'These tawdry and impossible wet dreams tell us nothing about how men and women really interact.' Implying that he sure does, the creepy fag. He's never interacted with anything but a candy machine and the constant torrent of cultural crap."

"Henry, his striking you as a creepy fag isn't reason enough to kill him."

"It is for me."

"How would you go about it?"

"How would we go about it maybe is the formula. What do we know about this twerp? He's riddled with insecurities, has all this manicky energy, and is on the Internet."

"You have been mulling this over, haven't you?" Robin's eyes had widened; her lower lip hung slightly open, looking riper and wetter than usual, as she propped herself above him, bare-breasted, livid-nippled, her big hair tumbling in oiled coils. Her straight short nose didn't go with the rest of her face, giving her a slightly flattened expression, like a cat's. "My lover the killer," she breathed.

"My time on Earth is limited." Bech bit off his words. "I have noble work to do. I can't see Cannon licking return envelopes. He probably has an assistant for that. Or tosses them in the wastebasket, the arrogant little shit." He averted his eyes from Robin's bared breasts, their gleaming white weight like that of gourds still ripening, snapping their vines.

She said, "So? Where do I come in, big boy?"

"Computer expertise. You have it, or know those that do. My question of you, baby, is could we break into his computer?"

Robin's smooth face, its taut curves with their faint fuzz, hardened. "If he can get out," she said, "a cracker can get in. The Internet is one big happy family, like it or not."

The Aldie Cannon mini-industry was headquartered in his modest Upper East Side apartment. He lived, with this third wife and two maladjusted small children, not on one of the East Side's genteel, ginkgo-shaded side streets but in a raw new blue-green skyscraper, with balconies like stubby daisy petals, over by the river. His daily Internet feature, "Cannon Fodder," was produced in a child-resistant study on a Compaq PC equipped with Windows 95. His opinionated claptrap was twinkled by modem to a site in San Jose, where it was checked for obscenity and libel and misspellings before going out to the millions of green-skinned cyberspace goons paralyzed at their terminals. E-mail sent to fodder.com went to San Jose, where the less inane and more provocative communications were forwarded to Aldie, for possible use in one of his columns.

Robin, after consulting some goons of her acquaintance, explained to Bech that the ubiquitous program for E-mail, Sendmail, had been written in the Unix ferment of the late nineteen-seventies, when security had been of no concern; it was notoriously full of bugs. For instance, Sendmail performed security checks only on a user's first message; once the user passed, all his subsequent messages went straight through. Another weakness of the program was that a simple |, the "pipe" symbol, turned the part of the message following it into input, which could consist of a variety of Unix commands the computer was obliged to obey. These commands could give an intruder log-in status and, with some more manipulation, a "back door" access that would last until detected and deleted. Entry could be utilized to attach a "Trojan horse" that would flash messages onto the screen, with subliminal brevity if desired.

Bech's wicked idea was to undermine Cannon's confidence and sense of self — fragile, beneath all that polymathic, relentlessly with-it bluster — as the critic sat gazing at his monitor. Robin devised a virus: every time Aldie typed an upper-case "A" or a lower-case "x," a message would flash, too quickly for his conscious mind to register but distinctly enough to penetrate the neuronic complex of brain cells. The program took Robin some days to design; especially finicking were the specs of such brief interruptions, amid the seventy cathoderay refreshments of the screen each second, in letters large enough to make an impression. She labored while Bech slept; half-moon shadows smudged and dented the lovely smoothness of her face. Delicately she strung her binaries together. They could at any moment be destroyed by an automatic "sniffer" program or a human "sysadmin," a systems administrator. Federal laws were being violated; heavy penalties could be incurred. Nevertheless, out of love for Bech and the fascination of a technical challenge, Robin persevered and, by the third morning, succeeded.

Bech began, once the intricate, illicit commands had been lodged, with some hard-core Buddhism. BEING IS PAIN, the subliminal message read; NON-BEING IS NIRVANA. Invisibly these truths rippled into the screen's pixels for a fifteenth of a second — that is, five refreshments of the screen, a single one being, Robin and a consulted neurophysiologist agreed, too brief to register even subliminally. After several days of these equations, Bech asked her to program the more advanced NO MISERY OF MIND IS THERE FOR HIM WHO HATH NO WANTS. It was critical that the idea of death be rendered not just palatable but inviting. NON-BEING IS AN ASPECT OF BEING, and BEING OF NON-BEING: this Bech had adapted from a Taoist poem by Seng Ts'an. From the same source he took TO BANISH REALITY IS TO SINK DEEPER INTO THE REAL. Out of his own inner resources he proposed ACTIVITY IS AVOIDANCE OF VICTORY OVER SELF.

Together he and Robin scanned Cannon's latest effusions, in print or on the computer screen, for signs of mental deterioration and spiritual surrender. Deborah Frueh had taken the bait in the dark, and Bech had been frustrated by his inability to see what was happening — whether she was licking an envelope or not, and what effect the diluted poison was having on her detestable innards. But in the case of Aldie Cannon, his daily outpouring of cleverness surely would betray symptoms. His review of a Sinead O'Connor concert felt apathetic, though he maintained it was her performance, now that she was no longer an anti-papal skinhead, that lacked drive and point. His roundup of recent books dwelling, with complacency or alarm, upon the erosion of the traditional literary canon — cannon fodder indeed, the ideal chance for him to do casual backflips of lightly borne erudition — drifted toward the passionless conclusion that "the presence or absence of a canon amounts to much the same thing; one is all, and none is equally all." This didn't sound like the Aldie Cannon who had opined of Bech's collection *When the Saints,* "Some of these cagey feuilletons sizzle but most fizzle; the author has moved from not having much to say to implying that anyone's having anything to say is a tiresome breach of good taste. Bech is a literary dandy, but one dressed in tatters — a kind of shreds and patches, as Hamlet said of another fraud."

It was good for Bech to remember these elaborate and gleeful dismissals, lest pity bring him to halt the program. Where the celebrant of pop culture would once wax rapturous over Julia Roberts's elastic mouth and avid eyes, Aldie now dwelt upon her ethereal emaciation in *My Best Friend's Wedding*, and the "triumphant emptiness" of her heroine's romantic defeat and the film's delivery of her into the arms of a homosexual. Of Saul Bellow's little novel, he noticed only the "thanatoptic beauty" of its culmination in a cemetery, where the hero's proposal had the chiseled gravity of an elegy or death sentence. The same review praised the book's brevity and confessed — this from Aldie Cannon, Pantagruelian consumer of cultural produce — that some days he just didn't want to read one more book, see one more movie, go to one more art show, look up one more reference, wrap up one more paragraph with one more fork-tongued aperçu. And then, just as the Manhattan scene was kicking into another event-crammed fall season, "Cannon Fodder" now and then skipped a day on the Internet, or was replaced, with a terse explanatory note, by one of the writer's "classic" columns from a bygone year.

Bech had made a pilgrimage to the blue-green skyscraper near the river to make sure a suicide leap was feasible. Its towering mass receded above him like giant railroad tracks — an entire railroad yard of aluminum and glass. The jutting semicircular petals of its balconies formed a scalloped dark edge against the clouds as they hurtled in lock formation across the sere-blue late-summer sky. It always got to the pit of Bech's stomach, the way the tops of skyscrapers appeared to lunge across the sky when you looked up, like the prows of ships certain to crash. The building was fifty-five stories high and had curved sides. Its windows were sealed but the balconies were not caged. Within Bech a siren wailed, calling Aldie out, out of his cozy claustral nest of piped-in, faxed, E-mailed, messengered, videoed cultural fluff and straw — culture, that tawdry, cowardly anti-nature — into the open air, the stinging depths of space, cosmic nature pure and raw.

NON-BEING IS BLISS, Bech told Robin to make the Trojan horse spell, and SELFHOOD IS IMPURITY, and, at ever-faster intervals, the one word JUMP.

JUMP, the twittering little pixels cried, and JUMP YOU TWIT or JUMP YOU HOLLOW MAN or DO THE WORLD A FUCKING FAVOR AND JUMP.

"I can't believe this is you," Robin told him. "This killer."

"I have been grievously provoked," he said.

"Just by reviews? Henry, nobody takes them seriously."

"I thought I did not, but now I see that I have. I have suffered a lifetime's provocation. My mission has changed; I wanted to add to the world's beauty, but now I merely wish to rid it of ugliness."

"Poor Aldie Cannon. Don't you think he means well? Some of his columns I find quite entertaining."

"He may mean well but he commits atrocities. His facetious half-baked columns are crimes against art and against mankind. He has crass taste — no taste, in fact. He has a mouth to talk but no ears with which to listen." Liking in his own ear the rhythm of his tough talk, Bech got tougher. "Listen, sister," he said to Robin. "You want out? Out you can have any time. Walk down two flights. The subway's a block over, on Broadway. I'll give you the buck fifty. My treat."

She appeared to think it over. She said what women always say, to stall. "Henry, I love you."

"Why the hell would that be?"

"You're cute," Robin told him. "Especially these days. You seem more, you know, together. Before, you were some sort of a sponge, just sitting there, waiting for stuff to soak in. Now you've, like they say on the talk shows, taken charge of your life."

He pulled her into his arms with a roughness that darkened the fox-fur glints in her eyes. A quick murk of fear and desire clouded her features. His shaggy head cast a shadow on her silver face as he bowed his neck to kiss her. She made her lips as soft as she could, as soft as the primeval ooze. "And you like that, huh?" he grunted. "My becoming bad."

"It lets me be bad." Her voice had gotten small and hurried, as if she might faint. "I love you because I can be a bad girl with you and you love it. You eat it up. Yum, you say."

"Bad is relative," he told her, from the sage height of his antiquity. "For my purposes, you're a good girl. So it excites you, huh? Trying to bring this off."

Robin admitted, "It's kind of a rush." She added, with a touch of petulance as if to remind him how girlish she was, "It's my project. I want to stick with it."

"Now you're talking. Here, I woke up with an inspiration. Flash the twerp this." It was another scrap of Buddhist death-acceptance: LET THE ONE WITH ITS MYSTERY BLOT OUT ALL MEMORY OF COMPLICATIONS. JUMP.

"It seems pretty abstract."

"He'll buy it. I mean, his subconscious will buy it. He thinks of himself as an intellectual. He majored in philosophy at Berkeley, I read in that stuff you downloaded from the Internet."

She went to the terminal and pattered through the dance of computer control. "It went through, but I wonder," she said.

"Wonder what?"

"Wonder how much longer before they find us and wipe us out. There are more and more highly sophisticated security programs; crackers are costing industry billions."

"The seed is sown," Bech said, still somewhat in Buddhist mode. "Let's go to bed. I'll let you suck my thumb, if you beg nicely. You bad bitch," he added, to see if her eyes would darken again. They did.

But the sniffers were out there, racing at the speed of light through the transistors, scouring the binary code for alien configurations and rogue algorithms. It was Robin, now, who each morning rushed, in her terry-cloth bathrobe, on her pink-sided bare feet, down the two flights to the loft lobby and brought up the *Times* and scanned its obituary page. The very day after her Trojan horse, detected and killed, failed to respond, there it was: "Aldous Cannon, 43, Critic, Commentator." Jumped from the balcony of his apartment on the forty-eighth floor. No pedestrians hurt, but an automobile parked on York Avenue severely damaged. Wife, distraught, said the writer and radio personality, whose Web site on the Internet was one of the most visited for literary purposes by college students, had seemed preoccupied lately, and confessed to sensations of futility. Had always hoped to free up time to write a big novel. In a separate story in Section B, a wry collegial tribute from Christopher Lehmann-Haupt.

Bech and Robin should have felt jubilant. They had planted a flickering wedge of doubt beneath the threshold of consciousness and brought down a media-savvy smart-ass. But, it became clear after their initial, mutually congratulatory embrace, there above the breakfast-table confusion, the sweating carton of orange juice and the slowly toasting bagels, that they felt stunned, let down and ashamed. They avoided the sight and touch of each other for the rest of the day, though it was a Saturday. They had planned to go up and cruise the Met and then try to get an outdoor table at the Stanhope, in the deliciously crisp September air. But the thought of art in any form sickened them: sweet icing on dung, thin ice over the abyss. Robin went shopping for black jeans at Barneys and then up in the train to visit her parents in Garrison, while Bech in a stupor like that of a snake digesting a poisonous toad sat watching two Midwestern college football teams batter at each other in a screaming, chanting stadium far west of the Hudson, where life was sunstruck and clean.

Robin spent the night with her parents. She returned so late on Sunday she must have hoped her lover would be asleep. But he was up, waiting for her, reading Donne. The day's lonely meal had generated a painful gas in his stomach. His mouth tasted chemically of nothingness. Robin's key timidly scratched at the lock and she entered; he met her near the threshold and they softly bumped heads in a show of contrition. They had together known sin. Like playmates who had mischievously destroyed a toy, they slowly repaired their relationship. As Aldie Cannon's wanton but not unusual (John Berryman, Jerzy Kosinski) self-erasure slipped deeper down into the stack of used newspapers, and the obligatory notes of memorial tribute tinnily, fadingly sounded in the PEN and Authors Guild newsletters, the duo on Crosby Street recovered their dynamism. Literary villains of Gotham, beware!

Contributors' Notes

Born in Buffalo, **Lawrence Block** has lived in New York City most of his adult life — although, like Keller, he gets around a lot. His fifty-plus books range from the urban *noir* of Matthew Scudder to the urbane effervescence of Bernie Rhodenbarr, and include four volumes of short stories. A Mystery Writers of America Grand Master, Block has won a slew of awards, including four Edgars.

■ After I'd introduced Keller in "Answers to Soldier," I never thought I'd write further about him. A couple of years later I wrote two more stories about him and realized I was writing a novel on the installment plan. "Keller's Last Refuge" was the ninth of ten such installments, and its source may be found in his initial appearance. Keller's father was a soldier, after all, and how could the wistful hit man, the urban lonely guy of assassins, fail to heed his country's call?

Gary A. Braunbeck was born in the Year of the Rat and has been apologizing for it ever since. He grew up in Newark, Ohio, the inspiration for his Cedar Hill stories, and wrote his first short story at the age of seven. He has published nearly 150 short stories. His first book, *Things Left Behind*, had unanimously excellent reviews.

■ "Safe" took fifteen years to get onto paper, because it hit close to home. I had worked with a janitorial company that cleaned up the aftermath of a murder-suicide. The boss had to find volunteers, not only because it involved the washing away of blood and other sad human remains, but because the man who'd done the killing had taken three other people with him — two of them children.

I wound up cleaning the children's room and will never forget the chill silence nor the overwhelming grief I felt for them as I washed away the last traces of their existence.

Thomas H. Cook was born and reared in Fort Payne, Alabama. He holds graduate degrees from Hunter College and Columbia University, where he was a President's Fellow. He is a four-time nominee for the Edgar Allan Poe Award. His novel *The Chatham School Affair* won the Edgar for Best Novel in 1996. He lives in New York City and on Cape Cod. He is husband to Susan and father to Justine.

▪ "Fatherhood" is my first mystery short story and my first of any kind I have written in over twenty years. But it was a chance to write with the kind of concision that only the short story form provides, to deliver a tale's deepest irony or most unexpected twist with maximum impact. The reader may truly be held in the fist of the story until the writer, not the reader, lets go. For the writer there is no more demanding literary form; for the reader, no more concentrated literary experience.

Jeffery Deaver is an internationally best-selling author of thirteen suspense novels. He's been nominated for three Edgar Awards and is a two-time recipient of the Ellery Queen Reader's Award for Best Short Story of the Year. *A Maiden's Grave* was an HBO movie starring James Garner and Marlee Matlin, and *The Bone Collector,* from Universal, starred Denzel Washington. His latest books are *The Coffin Dancer* and *The Devil's Teardrop.* He lives in Virginia and California.

▪ I rarely put messages into my work For me the point of a story is to surprise, thrill, and entertain, not to enlighten or instruct; there are writers more talented than I who can make brilliant political, personal, and social observations. Last year, though, I was asked to write a story to commemorate a fiftieth anniversary and some of the implications of reaching that milestone. "Wrong Place, Wrong Time" looks at the timeless question of age versus youth. What better way to examine heady philosophical issues than in a story filled with murder, kidnapping, gunplay, and deceit?

Brendan DuBois is a lifelong resident of New Hampshire, where he received his B.A. in English from the University of New Hampshire. He has been writing fiction for nearly fifteen years and lives with his wife, Mona. He is the author of the Lewis Cole mystery series — *Dead Sand, Black Tide,* and *Shattered Shell* — and his fourth novel, *Resurrection Day,* was published in June. He has had nearly forty stories published in *Playboy, Ellery Queen's Mystery Magazine,* and others. In 1995 he received the Shamus Award from the Private Eye Writers of America for Best Short Story and has three nominations for Edgars for his short fiction.

▪ In "Netmail," a computer expert tries to blackmail a man with older, more "hands-on" skills. The computer expert is sure in his expertise and his arrogance that he will emerge the victor. After all, hasn't his generation proven the superiority of computers, the truth that those with computer skills will live and thrive in the years to come? But my older character is not ready to give up. He has ideas of his own. Some of them quite explosive.

Loren D. Estleman has been called "the absolute best in the hard-boiled business" (*Philadelphia Inquirer*). Since his first novel, in 1976, Estleman has published forty-two books, including the Amos Walker mysteries. He has been nominated for the Pulitzer Prize, the National Book Award, and the Edgar Award. He won fourteen national writing awards, including three Shamuses from the Private Eye Writers of America.

▪ I conceived of Amos Walker as a hero-for-hire, quite independent of the practical business of private detecting in the nine-to-five world. In "Redneck" (first published as "Double Whammy"), Walker delivers the results he was hired for but falls short of his ideal.

Gregory Fallis has been a counselor in the psychiatric/security unit of a prison for women, a private investigator specializing in criminal defense work, and a criminology professor. He is the author of one novel and three nonfiction works, all of which deal with crime and detection. He lives on Manhattan's Upper West Side, where he earns a meager living as a writer.

▪ I've always managed to cobble out a living doing things that intrigued me. It wasn't always pleasant, but it seemed better than regular employment. It wasn't until I started writing that I realized I'd spent my life gathering material.

"And Maybe the Horse Will Learn to Sing" is loosely based on actual cases. It's what real PI work is about . . . crisis, confusion, and the hope that somehow things will turn out right.

Tom Franklin grew up in Dickinson, Alabama, and received his M.F.A. from the University of Arkansas in 1997. His work has appeared in the *Nebraska Review, Quarterly West, Smoke,* and elsewhere. His first collection, *Poachers,* was published in June; his novel, *Hell at the Breech,* will appear in 2000. He is married to the poet Beth Ann Fennelly.

▪ I rewrote "Poachers" several times, trying to make it work. Among other problems, I couldn't figure out how to kill the third brother. Then one day my wife (fiancée then) said, "Why does the last brother have to die? You don't need to murder everybody, you know. Maybe the game warden just hurts him."

"Or blinds him," I said.

That evening, celebrating at a restaurant with a deck overlooking Lake Tahoe, I was wondering aloud what would happen if you dripped snake venom in someone's eyes when the couple at the next table exchanged a look, paid quickly, and hurried away.

Victor Gischler received his M.A. in English from the University of West Florida. While he still resides in Florida with his wife, Jackie, he's currently serving a two- to three-year stretch in Hattiesburg, Mississippi, where he's attempting to earn his Ph.D. at the University of Southern Mississippi.

▪ "Hitting Rufus" was a breakthrough for me. I've knocked around the last few years, trying to find a voice and a genre with which I feel comfortable. These elements clicked finally, and I've gained confidence in my writing. "Headless Rollo," forthcoming in *Plots with Guns,* is another Charlie the Hook story. I'm halfway through a novel with Charlie as the hit man turned hard-boiled hero. I've also written hard-boiled poetry. So far, nobody wants it.

Ed Gorman's most recent suspense novel is *The Day the Music Died,* which the *Wall Street Journal* said "wonderfully evokes the sorrows and pleasures of a certain Midwestern past." Gorman has won the Shamus and been nominated for an Edgar and a Golden Dagger. The author of several crime novels and five collections of short stories, he is editorial director of *Mystery Scene* magazine.

▪ I've always been fascinated by (and terrified of) how quickly one's life can change. One mistake, one accident, and a life can be altered forever. I'm equally fascinated by the sense of the shadow world I knew back in my drinking days — petty crooks, grifters, ex-cons, thieves of every description, and all those fallen middle-class alcoholics like myself who seemed to be trapped in a David Goodis novel. I've expanded "Out There in the Darkness" into a novel called *The Poker Club.* It will be published next year.

Joseph Hansen has published thirty-five books, the best known being the Dave Brandstetter mysteries. In 1982, he began writing stories for *Ellery Queen's* and *Alfred Hitchcock.* Not all are about Hack Bohannon, the ex-deputy sheriff who runs a stable on the central California coast, but most are. For much of his writing life he lived in Los Angeles, but when Jane, his wife of fifty years, died in 1994, he moved to Laguna Beach.

▪ In 1991, I think it was, federal agents surrounded the cabin of a survivalist in northern Idaho to attempt to arrest him. The story made headlines. The man's fourteen-year-old son was killed. But what haunted me was the absolutist, contrarian mind-set of the survivalist and the people among whom he lived. Down the years, I'd wonder how I could get them into a story. Bohannon's sidekick, rodeo veteran George Stubbs, died, giving me an excuse to send Bohannon to Idaho to take his old friend's body home for burial. Bohannon would stumble into an encampment of these outsiders, and how he saved himself would account for the plot.

David K. Harford was born and raised in the northwestern Allegheny Mountains of Pennsylvania, where he lives today. From 1968 to 1969 he served as a military police investigator for the 4th MP Company, 4th Infantry Division, in Vietnam. "A Death on the Ho Chi Minh Trail," the third in the Carl Hatchett series, draws from those days.

▪ I've been a freelance writer for over twenty-five years — published so many magazine articles, I've lost count. Poetry, too. When I concentrated on my first love, the mystery short story, I realized there were no mysteries coming out of the Vietnam War years. Carl Hatchett was born then.

The trick to writing good military-related stories is to use jargon familiar to military people and at the same time slide in explanations for nonmilitary readers so they don't feel lost or left out.

Gary Krist is the author of two *New York Times* Notable Books — the novel *Bad Chemistry* and the short-story collection *Bone by Bone* — as well as another collection, *The Garden State.* His second novel, *Chaos Theory,* will be published in 1999. He lives with his wife and daughter in Chevy Chase, Maryland, and can be reached at www.garykrist.com.

▪ I've always been interested in the way we tell tales to get what we want — tales that are sometimes misleading, sometimes blatantly deceptive, but hardly ever true. Two such tales are told in "An Innocent Bystander," and although one is more clearly a manipulative fiction, each has its own ulterior motive.

During a twenty-five-year career as a criminal defense attorney, **Phillip M. Margolin** appeared before the U.S. Supreme Court, represented approximately thirty people charged with homicide, including a dozen who faced the death penalty. His novels frequently appear on the *New York Times* bestseller list. *Heartstone,* his first novel, was nominated for an Edgar, and his second, *The Last Innocent Man,* was an HBO movie.

▪ Early in my career, I was appointed to represent a defendant who was being held on serious charges. I made it clear to him that there was no way that any judge would release him on bail. He promptly fired me and represented himself. The next day I ran into him in the courthouse lobby. He told me that he had persuaded the judge to release him. "The Jailhouse Lawyer" is my tribute to these lawyer wanna-bes who, every so often, prove to be a lot sharper than we law school graduates.

Born and raised in upstate New York, **Joyce Carol Oates** now lives in Princeton, New Jersey, where she is a professor of humanities at Princeton University and co-edits the *Ontario Review* with her husband, Raymond Smith. She is a member of the American Academy of Arts and Letters.

Under the pseudonym Rosamond Smith, she has published six mystery-suspense novels.

▪ There's a hybrid of genres to which I'm drawn that might be called "memoirist-fiction." These stories evoke considerable emotion in me as I compose them. I seem to return to a past life, often adolescence, in a kind of waking dream; I see again places I've lived. I embark upon adventures I'd once had, or almost had; as in a dream, I'm led into experiences I can't control, yet which possess a dream-logic. "Secret, Silent" grew out of a strange episode when I traveled by Greyhound bus to be interviewed (by a rather odd male administrator) for college. The seductive young woman may belong to another time. The domestic situation is analogous to my own, though somewhat altered. The distress over some problem with one's clothing is familiar to anyone who has been an adolescent girl, as is the sense of dreamlike strangeness in being alone in an unfamiliar setting through a night. The ending is emotionally autobiographical.

Peter Robinson was born in Castleford, Yorkshire. His first novel, *Gallows View* (1987), introduced Detective Chief Inspector Alan Banks of the North Yorkshire Police, who has since appeared in nine more books and three short stories. *Past Reason Hated* and *Innocent Graves* both won the Crime Writers of Canada's Arthur Ellis Award for Best Novel. *Wednesday's Child* was nominated for an Edgar. He lives in Toronto.

▪ I did a lot of research on the Second World War for *In a Dry Season*, especially research into conditions at home. One story made mention of the murder of an eccentric old woman in the village of Scarcroft, near Leeds. Old Miss Barker used to dress in nineteenth-century fashions, such as feather hats and buttoned boots, and was found beaten to death in her cottage; there was no apparent motive and her killer was never found. That started me on the story. The rest, of course, is pure invention. I was particularly interested in the contrast between a domestic murder and the wholesale, state-sanctioned slaughter of war.

David B. Silva lives in rural northern California. He is the author of more than one hundred short stories and the winner of the 1991 Stoker Award for superior achievement in the short story. *The Disappeared* is the most recent of his four novels.

▪ "Dry Whiskey" is about my favorite subject: families. I am continually amazed at the complexity of family relationships. The people we know who have the greatest influence on how we turn out as adults, we often don't understand at all. Will and his father never chose to be thrown together. It was their lot and they struggled to do the best they could with it. But like most families, their relationship was an evolution, with rules and roles changing with time. The words that went unspoken between them were far more telling than the words we read.

L. L. Thrasher is the author the Zachariah Smith series (*Cat's-Paw, Inc.* and *Dogsbody, Inc.*) and the Lizbet Lange series (*Charlie's Bones* and the forthcoming *Charlie's Web*). "Sacrifice" is her first published short story, and it was nominated for the 1999 Edgar Allan Poe Award. She lives in Oregon with her husband and their two teenagers.

- I started writing "Sacrifice" with just a glimmer of an idea: a little girl asks a PI to look for her missing doll. I liked the interaction between them, the contrast between innocence and experience. I had expected to write about the PI's search for the doll, which would have some connection with a crime. I was on the second page when the little girl suddenly explained that the doll has two names, and the rest of the story became clear to me. This wasn't a story about a missing doll; it was about a tragedy. It isn't a story of innocence lost; it's a tale of innocence maintained, of the core innocence of childhood that is untouched by even the most dreadful of experiences.

John Updike, born in Shillington, Pennsylvania, in 1932, graduated from Harvard College in 1954. After working for *The New Yorker,* he moved to the North Shore of Massachusetts and has been a freelance writer ever since. He is the author of eighteen novels, ten or so collections of short stories, six collections of poetry, and five books of essays and criticism.

- Henry Bech appeared in a short story called "The Bulgarian Poetess" in 1964. Like me, he is a writer, but in other respects he lives a life I envy but have not lived. While looking through the two Library of America volumes of crime novels from the thirties, forties, and fifties, I got the idea of Bech as a *noir* hero. Murdering critics is something most writers, I suspect, have wanted to do, and once Henry got going, there was no stopping him. As a boy and young man, I read a great deal of mystery fiction. As an adult, I have always been leery of violence and character assassination, but I found that once you get going there is an intoxicating pleasure to it. Evildoers, beware!

Other Distinguished Mystery Stories of 1998

HERRMANN, JOHN
  Mother's Helper. *Murderous Intent,* Spring
HESS, JOAN
  Caveat Emptor. *Murder for Revenge,* ed. Otto Penzler (Delacorte)
HILL, JOE
  The Collaborators. *Implosion,* no. 8
HOWARD, CLARK
  The Halfway Woman. *Ellery Queen's Mystery Magazine,* February

IVRY, BOB
  It Scares You Is Why You Do It. *Esquire,* February

JORDAN, PAT
  Frenchie. *Playboy,* August

KELMAN, JUDITH
  Erradicum Homo Horribilus. *Murder for Revenge,* ed. Otto Penzler (Delacorte)
KNIGHT, ARTHUR WINFIELD
  Easy as Pie. *Private Eyes,* ed. Mickey Spillane and Max Allan Collins (Signet)

LEWITT, SHARIANN
  The Secret Marriage of Sherlock Holmes. *The Confidential Casebook of Sherlock
    Holmes,* ed. Marvin Kaye (St. Martin's)
LINDLEY, STEVE
  Halfway Dog. *Alfred Hitchcock Mystery Magazine,* April

MAGUIRE, D. A.
  The Jet Stone. *Alfred Hitchcock Mystery Magazine,* December
MILLER, REX
  Sideways. *Private Eyes,* ed. Mickey Spillane and Max Allan Collins (Signet)
MORRELL, DAVID
  Front Man. *Murder for Revenge,* ed. Otto Penzler (Delacorte)

RICHTER, STACEY
  The First Men. *Michigan Quarterly Review*

SCOTT, JUSTIN
  A Shooting over in Jersey. *Murder on the Run* (Berkeley)
SOLOMITA, STEPHEN
  The Favor. *Hardboiled,* July
STRAUB, PETER
  Isn't It Romantic? *Murder on the Run* (Berkeley)
STRIEBER, WHITLEY
  Desperate Dan. *Murder on the Run* (Berkeley)

TORRES, RICHARD
  End of the Line. *New Mystery,* vol. 6, no. 1